Ralph Gibson

Richard Price is the author of seven novels, including *Clockers, Freedomland, Lush Life,* and *Samaritan.* He has received an Academy Award in literature from the American Academy of Arts and Letters, and shared a 2007 Edgar Award as a cowriter of HBO's series *The Wire.*

Also by Richard Price

Lush Life

The Wanderers

Bloodbrothers

Ladies' Man

Clockers

Freedomland

Samaritan

The Breaks

Richard Price

Picador

Farrar, Straus and Giroux

New York

THE BREAKS. Copyright © 1983 by Richard Price. All rights reserved. Printed in the United States of America. For information, address Picador, 175 Fifth Avenue, New York, N.Y. 10010.

www.picadorusa.com

Picador® is a U.S. registered trademark and is used by Farrar, Straus and Giroux under license from Pan Books Limited.

For information on Picador Reading Group Guides, please contact Picador. E-mail: readinggroupguides@picadorusa.com

The author gratefully acknowledges permission to reprint lines from the following: "Everybody Needs Somebody to Love" by Solomon Burke and Gerry Wexler, copyright © Keetch, Caesar & Dino Music, Inc., 1964; used by permission. "That's Life" by Kelly Gordon and Kay Thompson, copyright © Bibo Music Publishers, 1964; c/o The Welk Music Group, Santa Monica, California; international copyright secured, all rights reserved; used by permission. "It Was a Very Good Year" by Ervin Drake, copyright © Dolfi Music, Inc., 1961, 1965; all rights controlled by Chapelle & Co., Inc. (Intersong Music, Publisher).

Designed by Anna Gorovoy

Library of Congress Cataloging-in-Publication Data

Price, Richard, 1949–
    The breaks / Richard Price. — 1st Picador ed.
        p. cm.
    ISBN 978-0-312-56651-7
    1. College graduates—Fiction.   2. Young men—Fiction.   3. Working class—Fiction.   4. Triangles (Interpersonal relations)—Fiction.   5. Self-actualization (Psychology)—Fiction.   I. Title.
    PS3566.R544B7 2011
    813'.54—dc22

                                                                        2011013107

First published in the United States by Simon and Schuster

First Picador Edition: July 2011

10   9   8   7   6   5   4   3   2   1

For my father, Milton Price
For my aunt, Elaine Beck
For my editor and friend, Herman Gollob
and with all my love for Judy Hudson.

Acknowledgments

I would like to thank the following organizations for their support:
Yaddo Colony
MacDowell Colony
National Endowment for the Arts
New York State Creative Artists in Public Service

PROLOGUE

THERE WE WERE, scattered around the Arts Quad, the proud men and women of Simon Straight College, Class of '71: a thousand gowns casually smoking joints and playing Frisbee with their mortarboards as the parents shook hands under the trees.

In the 93° heat my own gown felt like a horse blanket but I'd have sooner set myself on fire than lowered the zipper that was gnawing my Adam's apple. After three generations of teamsters, cabbies and mailmen, the Kellers had finally scored for a college graduate. I was the happy ending to our private little American Everyman play. I had worked construction every summer, was in hock up to my ass with student loans, and with all that my father still wound up paying through the nose, but that was the way it was. Four years earlier, we had sat down with my three acceptance letters and decided that if we were going to do it up, we would do it up right. I could have gone to Fordham University on a half-scholarship or C.C.N.Y. for free, but from where we were coming, a Simon Straight car sticker was priceless.

My father was standing within earshot of me, talking to Larry Arthur's old man under the shadow of the runny bright-green copper Founder's statue. Mr. Arthur was the only guy my father recognized. They had met my junior year over parents' weekend at the fraternity house. They weren't what I would call soulmates, but George Arthur was hard to forget; he was six foot nine.

"Yeah, well, Peter got on the waiting list for Columbia Law School but, ah, we figure, *he* figures and I kinda agree, that instead of goin' to some ambulance-chaser factory on short notice, he's gonna move back in with us, get a good one-year job, save his money, get a nice bank account going and reapply next year. This way he'll be a year more mature, experienced, because they like that, kids who've been out in the world, he can pay his own tuition and ah, like that. . . ." My father tapped his cigarette on the toe of the Founder's shoe, slipped the butt into the corner of his mouth, and hiked up the skirt of his jacket by slipping his hands into his front pants pocket. He tilted his head to the side as he talked because Mr. Arthur had a good ten inches on him.

"And I'll tell you, I myself am pretty impressed with Pete's maturity. I think it's unusual these days with all this shit goin' on"—he murmur-slurred the word shit—"for a kid to be that sensible . . . you know? In addition, ah, of course, his stepmother would love to have him around another year . . ."

Mr. Arthur chuckled politely, his eyes briefly darting from my father to some other parents.

"Look, I'll be perfectly frank with you, Mr. Arthur." He squinted in candidness and touched his own chest with his fingertips, his unlit cigarette bouncing between his lips. "We're very very proud of Peter"—he held his hand out to Mr. Arthur's chest—"as I'm sure you are of Larry, but, ah, I am not an educated man. I've been working in the Post Office for twenty years." He grimaced. Arthur was a patent attorney. "In fact, Pete's the first kid in our family, all my cousins' kids, everybody, the first one to go to college. And when he got in *this* place—you know, what do they call it? The Harvard of Upstate New York?—we were fit to bust, so even if he goes no further, you know what I mean? We'll see what happens . . . but for now, I admire that kid's sensibleness . . . I really do."

Mr. Arthur squinted in acknowledgement. He had a silvery, slightly sloppy William Buckley crop. My father had a jet black pompadour fronting for an almost totally bald crown.

Both my father and Mr. Arthur were dressed in their tribal costumes; Old George in kelly-green slacks and a loud patchwork summer-weight sports jacket, my father in a blue and white double-knit suit and white Flagg Brothers loafers.

"Yo Pete." Two gowns weaved across the grass toward me.

I spit on my fingertips and ran them down my cheeks so they'd look like tearslicks. "This is the proudest day of my life, Larry," I deadpanned.

"Yeah, me too. Bam-Bam, tell him what happened."

"You know that check I got from the phone company?"

"What check?"

"The return on our deposit from September. It bounced. The Alexander A. Graham Bell Telephone Company. Their fucking check, to *me*, bounced . . . heads up!" he shouted and I ducked as a mortarboard went screaming by like Oddjob's steel derby. Mortarboard Frisbee was catching on. The entire quad was zipping with low-flying caps, the tassels erect with momentum.

"Stay down . . ." Bam-Bam snagged one backhand as I remained in my squat. Bam-Bam, my man, a fat handsome wop, first generation Scarsdale.

"So this is the proudest day in your life, Pete?" Larry was already grinning, halfway to a laugh, waiting for show time.

Okay. Here we go. "Absolutely Lar . . . I mean, I know it's different where you're coming from, Dobie Gillisburg, but, ah, in my part of Yonkers it's still the Depression, you know what I mean?"

He laughed without opening his mouth so it sounded like a violent snore. Bam-Bam stood slightly behind him and winked at me.

"I'm serious, man, it's rough. My fucking father delivered ice to fifth-floor walk-ups in Hell's Kitchen to get me through here."

"Ice." He chuckled.

"Yeah, Lar, *ice.*" I shook my head sadly. "You know, and his bad leg is one thing, man, but ah, I don't know if you ever noticed this but he's got artificial arms, my father."

The pud actually looked over to where my old man was talking to his.

"You crack me up," he said tentatively.

"Well, *now* he's got artificial arms, I mean *real* artificial arms, but up until two years ago he couldn't even afford them, man, he had . . . *pliers* bolted into his shoulder sockets. Do you have any *idea* what it must feel like to lug a cake of ice up five flights of stairs with fucking *pliers* for arms?" I hunched up as if to make my shoulder caps kiss across my chest. "Do you know what *hell* that plays with your upper back?"

He cracked up like the out-of-towner he was. Actually, even Bam-Bam started laughing.

A cool breeze wafted across the Quad. It felt wonderful, hopeful . . . "I love you guys," I suddenly blurted, surprising myself, and to cover my embarrassment I grabbed them both in headlocks and we clinched in a clumsy huddle of affection.

Over their bowed heads I saw my stepmother, Vy, standing by herself, smiling, lost, holding her purse in front of her pleated skirt with both hands. Vy. As usual, her hair was lifted, teased and frozen into an iridescent rust helmet. She'd been going to a beauty parlor every other day since I'd known her, but instead of making her look hard, it accentuated her breakableness. She had a fragile, tentative face; shining eyes under eyebrows dyed to match her hair and permanently arched in some kind of wet expectation, nose all flared nostrils under a sharp narrow bridge, lips parted and slightly tremulous over buck teeth. She was only five feet tall and a living testament to the expression "Terror makes you slender," since she weighed in at ninety-eight pounds. My real mother had tipped the scales at two hundred and fifty, soaking wet. Vy never touched or held an object; she gripped. She never turned to a voice; she whipped around. Everything about her promised a nervous breakdown, and in the five years that she'd been married to my father I always felt at least half bad about never "extending myself," but that was that.

"My fucking buddies," I said as we all simultaneously harrumphed and stepped back from each other.

That day, because he was a good audience, Larry was my buddy. I couldn't stand him as a roommate freshman year in the dorms, couldn't stand him as a fraternity brother for two years after that, and I couldn't stand him as a Senior Independent, but it was Graduation Day.

The three of us had been in Pi Omega, a Jewish house. Bam-Bam got in because New York Italians were honorary Jews and Larry got in as one of the token midwesterners. Jewish fraternities had a hard-on for WASPs. They couldn't tell the difference between a good guy and a jerk, everybody being temporarily blinded by all that blond hair. If Larry had been two milligrams more together he would have probably gotten rushed by one of the American houses, where everybody brought their lacrosse sticks down to breakfast.

"So, Mister Pete." Bam-Bam smiled. "I'll save you a carrel at the law school."

I felt my heart descend and all I could manage was a wink. I loved Bam-Bam like a brother, but it killed me that he'd gotten into Columbia and the best I could do was waiting list. I had graduated with honors in English, dean's list half the time, and it was all Bam-Bam could do to scrape up a B average as a government major. But his father was a big shot with the Teamsters and Bam-Bam was smart enough to make a lot of noise on his application about wanting to be a labor lawyer. That recommendation from George Meany his father managed to score for him probably didn't hurt either. Bam-Bam was no dope. He'd probably make a great lawyer.

As for me, I had nobody to blame for my waiting list status but myself. The night before the law boards I'd picked up a townie in a local beer palace and crawled into the examination room at seven A.M. the next morning with my eyeballs hanging out of my head. I had been accepted at my "safety" school, St. John's, but nobody went to their safety. I had to reapply the next year. I had to wait it out.

"Pete," Larry whispered, "check it out." He bent down and raised the hem of his gown to his knees. He was wearing pants legs only up to his shins. Apparently he was nude from the kneecaps up.

"You're an asshole, Larry." There was nothing in my voice or expression that even hinted at amusement.

He dropped his hem and straightened up, a freaky grin plastered across his face. "We can't all be comedians, Pete . . ."

"That's for sure." I looked away.

"We can't *all* be as funny as you, Pete."

"That's for sure." I was desperately trying to hold on to the good head that had me hugging everybody minutes before.

"Hey! Hey! C'mon guys, let's sing the school anthem." Bam-Bam the labor mediator.

"No, man. I mean it. The guy makes Bill Cosby look dull." Larry was just warming up.

"Oh Si-mon Straight, oh Sii-monn Straight . . ." Bam-Bam blared off key.

"Hey, I'm serious, Pete . . . it's a gift you have, a rare gift."

"Hey, Larry, c'mon, sing along." Bam-Bam gripped Larry's forearm. "Oh Si-mon Straight . . . c'mon Larry, I don't know the rest of the words."

Larry shook him off. "I mean it, Pete. I don't even know why you're bothering with law school. I mean right now you're probably good enough to work bungalow colonies in the Catskills . . . don't you think?"

I jammed my hands under my armpits. "Larry, you're not my friend," I said still looking away.

"You're not *my* friend," he responded with spunk.

"No, no, you don't understand. I *hate* you," I whispered tenderly. "I hate *you!*"

It sounded like we were proposing to each other.

"Larry, are you gonna sing with me, or what . . ." Bam-Bam threatened.

Larry gurgled in anger and stalked off.

I took a deep breath that released itself in shuddering gradations. Bam-Bam came up behind me, put his hands on my collarbones and squeezed. "It feels like you got rocks under your skin, chum."

Bam-Bam was the only guy in the world who could touch me affectionately without my shooting through the roof.

"Are you gonna let that stroontz get to you?" he whispered like a manager working on his fighter between rounds. It suddenly struck me how much I was going to miss him. My anger started to fade, but I felt a strong dose of the Horrors coming on. A year at home. No job, no law school.

Home. The last four years would be wiped out and I'd be sixteen all over again. I envisioned myself doing stand-up comedy in some ratty casino in Kerhonkson, New York, twenty yards from a handball court. Maybe I should do it. Help.

"Tom-mee!" From thirty feet away Bam-Bam's mother bawled out his name in her cigarette rasp as if she was yelling from a fifth-floor window. She stood there holding a camera under her arm like a football helmet; a tough dark wiry lady wearing a silk blouse, an outrageous slit maxi skirt and high heels. She had permanent smoky rings under her eyes.

"Relax, you putz." Bam-Bam gave my collarbones a final painful squeeze and walked across the grass to his family.

Mrs. Bambara caught me staring absently at her slit skirt and she tilted her chin in my direction. "Whatta *you* lookin' at, hot stuff . . ."

I laughed, blushing, and waved her away.

"You got a nice roommate, Tommy. He's tryin' to look up my dress."

"Cut the crap, Ma."

I stood there watching Bam-Bam get into a pose for his mother with his little brother, Bam-Bam II, and his father, Big Bam-Bam. The three of them stacked up, the kid on his knees, Bam-Bam in a shortstop crouch over his head and Big Bam-Bam behind him, standing erect, chest puffed out in pride, fists on hips. Without moving his body or his smile, Bam-Bam murmur-yelled for me to join the picture. I made like I didn't hear.

Mrs. Bambara was probably the only camera bug who could squeeze off a shot with a cigarette butt hanging from her lips. I was nuts about her. So was Bam-Bam.

She barked, "Freeze!" and I heard the whining whirr of a photo rolling out of a Polaroid. The three Bam-Bams crowded around her and started yelling at the picture to develop faster.

I felt a tap on the shoulder, and as I turned somebody grabbed my cheeks and kissed me on the lips, forcing a stream of marijuana smoke down my throat. I immediately coughed it out, teary-eyed, waving the cloud away from my face.

"That was a graduation present, Pete . . ."

"Thanks, Nance." My cough had a honk in it. I hated grass.

Miss Kiss was Nancy Stemko, an on-again off-again girlfriend. She wasn't anything to write home about except for beautiful wavy carrot-colored hair that lay dramatically against the black severity of her graduation gown. We were in the off-again stage, and it seemed that it might last awhile, since she was engaged and heading for the University of Missouri School of Journalism. Everyone's gone to the moon.

"Your folks here?" She dropped the roach on the grass and ground it out with a high-heeled sandal.

Each time I tried to answer I wound up doubled over in a coughing spasm.

"That's okay, Pete. I'll talk to you later." She walked off toward her parents.

I could still feel her hands on my cheeks. I hadn't gotten laid since Easter.

I moved toward my father, who was still bending Mr. Arthur's ear with more Up from Ellis Island bullshit. I listened to him run down how his mother's oldest sister bought it in the Triangle Shirtwaist fire of 1911. If the Kellers had to design a family crest it would be crossed AFL-CIO and CSEA union cards on a field of time clocks.

"So what's, ah, what's Lenny's plans?"

"Larry," Arthur gently corrected.

"*Larry.*" My father was feeling good. I could hear him play jingle bells with the change in his pockets as he rocked back and forth on his heels.

"Well, Lar will be staying with myself and his mother this summer . . . we live outside of Saint Paul."

"Saint *Paul!*" My father raised his eyebrows.

". . . and ah, come September, I think he's heading out west to California."

"Cali*for*nia!" He raised his eyebrows again. He was waiting for Mr. Arthur to continue, but Arthur just smiled.

"Does he have a job out there? Or is he goin' for the girls?" he heh-heh'ed.

"Well . . ." Mr. Arthur gave another mild chuckle. ". . . neither actually . . . I guess he squeezed his way into Stanford Medical School."

"That's great," my old man said weakly, the jingle bells losing their beat, then picking up again double time. "That's great."

I got hit on the arm with the point of a flung mortarboard, then whipped it back so hard that the guy opted for ducking. Those things can really fucking travel.

Part One

WAITING LIST

THAT EVENING I WAS BACK IN SQUARE ONE, the high rise apartment in Yonkers, back in my child-ass bedroom. I wandered through the house with my hands out, palms down like I was blind or a medium. The wallpaper in the foyer was smothered with my life: among other things, a Greenwich Village sidewalk artist's miniature silhouette done when I was seven; my pompadoured bar mitzvah studio shot, chin over right shoulder; high school graduation shot, chin over left shoulder; and the latest, my hot-off-the-presses college diploma already polyurethaned and mounted on wood. The living room was plastered with a mixture of Picasso prints, House O'Art prints of aged rabbis and of women praying over sabbath candles, and pictures of houses and animals my whacked-out stepgrandmother had made from various types of uncooked macaronis and other pastas in her recreational therapy sessions at The Home. On top of the big color TV, an orange facsimile Olmec head squatted next to a hinged stand-up double-leaf photo frame, one side displaying cut-out snapshot heads of me from infancy to college in chronological order, the other side my father, infancy to Army. The photo exhibit was put up by Vy after the wedding.

I remember them going through The Box on one of their dates. The Box had been in our family longer than myself. It was a cardboard Fleischmann's Whiskey carton in which we had tossed every photo ever taken of the Kellers and the Rabins. Seventy-five years of faces, from a sepia portrait of my maternal great-grandfather Schlomo or Blomo Rabin taken by some Rumanian Mathew Brady, to an Instamatic of me and Bam-Bam at Daytona Beach our junior year.

That date. I remember the three of us in the living room, them on the couch, me, a sulking spread-legged high school junior sprawled out on the easy chair. My father had The Box on his lap and he kept passing photos to Vy, who received each one with trembling fingers and a tiny oh! Her bony ass was perched on an impossible half inch of couch as if to sit back would have been a shattering faux pas. My father would say, "Yeah, an' this one," Vy would go, "Oh!" and I'd hiss through my nostrils. After I had left the room to go to bed, I came back in later unexpectedly just as Vy had put a tentative hand over my father's knuckles. I stood there until she caught me staring, until she whipped that hand back into her lap and blushed an arterial red.

I'm not going to waste time denying resentment of some lady taking over my mother's slot, but there's more to it than that. Vy was just wrong. She was too heartbreaking and still. She tried too hard with me. Every day with her was like a first date for the three of us. She trembled, she yearned, she was childless. I couldn't imagine her going through childbirth and living. My mother was so big and yowly that apocrypha has it I had popped out of her like a piece of toast. My mother had been a walking tragedy too, but grand-opera style. She was a Hatpin Mary at the wrestling matches. She took me to monster movies and the Roller Derby. She ate entire roast chickens in the middle of the night. She made the walls vibrate. She cried watching game shows. We were both histrionic hambones: as a two-year-old I got hysterical at the noise of the stand-up vacuum one day, and she tossed it out our ground-floor window in the Bronx, screaming, *"Bad* vacuum!" The scream, the crash and the waste of money had doubled my hysteria, but it was the thought that counted.

We were quite a team. We were always bringing up each other's rear. Countless times between the ages of three and nine I'd spend all Saturday afternoon with her at some triple monster movie matinee, both of us loaded down with enough fruit, sandwiches and liquids to gorge out the Third Army. She'd be the only patron over fifteen and the only human over one hundred and fifty pounds. If that wasn't enough, she considered herself a deputized matron, always yelling at kids to shut up or to ditch their butts as Gorgo or Godzilla melted down some skyscraper and roared out "Mama!" in dinosaur talk. The kids would always goof on her and I'd sit there in terror of walking out of the movie at twilight, fantasizing about me and her back to back under the marquee, taking on an entire audience of savage eleven-year-olds. That last stand never happened, but invariably by the time we got home my entire body would feel like a fist.

As a kid I was a little rageball; I *liked* to fight with other kids; I even enjoyed the fights I lost, but if I was mixing it up in front of our building I had to fight quietly because my mother had radar ears and thirty seconds after picking up my battlecry she'd come lumbering out to the stoop in her housedress to yank the other kid's arm halfway out of its socket. It made no difference to her if I was winning or losing. Sometimes she'd yank the kid out from *under* me, squawking at him to leave me alone, snatching defeat out of the jaws of victory. I even remember one particular fight where in the midst of mutual headlocks I asked the other kid to stop grunting so loud.

The thing was, no matter what number she pulled, I was never scared *of* her, always *for* her. I could see right through to the nut of her loneliness. I was smarter than she was, even as a little kid, and it killed me, just ripped me up.

Her name was Mimi Keller née Rabin, and she died when I was in fifth grade. She had an embolism watching daytime TV. My father came home from work, found her in her favorite chair, the tube on, assumed she was asleep, washed his hands, came in, changed the channels and watched a half-hour show, "Beat the Clock," he claimed, before he sensed something was wrong. Fortunately, I was staying at a friend's house and he didn't reach me until the next day. I remember his being so hysterical I thought he was laughing, and it took a while for the news to sink in, but when it did, I went off like a siren for three days. The weird thing was I never cried, just bellowed and howled in a dry-eyed rage. They didn't let me go to the funeral, and I stomped around a neighbor's house like a vengeful dwarf. I was incensed that the tears wouldn't come, and I remember standing in that neighbor's living room roaring at myself in the mirror, a furious red-eyed ten-year-old, mouth open wide enough to stuff with a softball. And speaking of stuffing, whereas some kids in their despair and terror might stop eating, I began to wolf down and shovel in everything in sight. I ate so much, I puked up half my meals—in protest, in tribute. Laryngitis finally shut me up.

When I was a senior in high school, I saw a short clip of an old "Beat the Clock" show and I was finally struck by the irony of the title. I tried it out on my father but he didn't get it, and I didn't push it.

Five weeks after the funeral my father and I moved out of the Bronx into our Yonkers apartment. The three of us had been on a waiting list for two and a half years, and the vacancy notice came in four days after her death.

Our block in the Bronx, a row of a dozen fortress-like five-story

deco apartment houses near Yankee Stadium, had been turning
P.R. faster than you could say Roberto Clemente. Synagogues were
converting into iglesias, groceries into bodegas, candy stores into
botanicas and half the fruit and vegetables in the stands looked as if
it came from a truck farm on Mars. It was the type of neighborhood
which had housed dentists and judges in the thirties and early forties, cabdrivers and plumbers in the late forties and early fifties and
by the time we wanted out, it was all factory labor, welfare, old
Jews and families like us; people with their bags packed and no
money to move. In 1957, our super, Moses, an old black with cotton-
white hair like God in *Green Pastures*, was shot in the ass in the
boiler room. The next super, a young Dominican named Angel, was
arrested for burglarizing six apartments in the building, and the
guy after him, José, never left his basement digs. Somewheres in
between Angel and José, my father was mugged by two kids in
front of the building at seven in the morning. They wanted the fake
fur collar of his corduroy coat and as one of them held a blade to his
belly the other cut free the synthetic rat hair around his neck. They
were so small that my father was ordered to squat so the little prick
could reach the collar. I walked around with a rock in my hand for
six months after that.

The building he and I moved to in Yonkers was called The
Rhonda. It was one of three modern high-rises constructed around
a huge grass circle ringed by a dozen bench and street lamp en-
sembles. The two other high-rises were called The Ellen and The
Sherry, and the complex itself was known as The Leslies. Leslie
was the builder's wife and each building was named after a daughter. We had moved from stoop and dumbwaiter-land to a home with
a gargling wishing well, blue pinlights, and veined mirrors in the
lobby. The Leslies were built originally as luxury apartments, but
the builder overestimated their desirability and in order to salvage
his ass had to drop rents and open it up to the Kellers of the world.
All our neighbors were fellow refugees from the boroughs, and I
always sensed a subtle aura of gratitude around the mailboxes, ele-
vators and laundry room, the main areas of involuntary congrega-
tion. People seemed to wink at each other a lot.

I loved Yonkers. Almost immediately the Bronx was reduced in
my mind to a hazy collage of fist fights, monster movies and my

mother's painfully slow side-to-side gait on the street. I loved the apartment, my new school and my new friends. I loved the tacky "modernness" of our lobby, my Hebrew school, the Chinese restaurant up the street. But more than anything, if I had to sum up the exhilaration of the move, it would be in the words of my father, our first day living in The Rhonda. He and I were standing alone in the middle of that huge grass circle facing the three high-rises. Twenty yards behind our backs was a four-lane highway jammed with White Plains–bound commuter traffic. To our left, a few hundred yards up the road was a Miracle Mile; two dozen neon crappo carpet clearance and pancake joints. It was six o'clock and as I looked up toward the commercial stretch, all the neon had lit the underbelly of that purple twilight, toasting it a champagne gold. It was beautiful, pure Zane Grey—except for all the cars and the high-rises. But my father, the first day in his life living outside the Bronx, just stood there, not looking at anything, sucking up huge lungfuls of air, eyelids fluttering, nostrils quivering. Suddenly he put both his palms on the top of my head and let loose with a hoarse fervent whisper "Ahh . . . the *coun*try!"

It was the Wild West, Future World and Disneyland for me. In fact, my only source of anxiety, other than working out the loss of my mother, was watching TV with my father. I'd never realized, until it was just me and him, how nothing he was, how little he settled for. The silence in our living room at nights made me sweat. With my mother around, I never really paid much attention to him, but witnessing his deep lumphood was terrifying to me, and in that first year together I developed a strong fretful love for him. The beam of worrisome protectiveness I had showered on my mother for nine years or so, was now aimed at my father. To me he was as helpless as a sheep and I was the sheepdog.

As I said, I got right into a new pack of friends and on weekend nights we'd run up and down the Miracle Mile, go to Adventurers Inn, Carvel's, Pizza World, and then we'd crash on one of the benches around the grass circle to discuss girls, which ones had hair yet, what's better, a Lotus or a Maserati and what's on the Twilight Zone. We had our bench, the Kids' Bench, and two benches down was the Fathers' Bench, where all the fathers hung out. They'd be sitting there, hunched over, elbows on kneecaps, murmuring, and every once in a while they would burst out in one of those "Oh oh Jeez!"-type belly laughs, at which point the Kids' Bench would go berserk because we knew that type of laugh meant that they were talking about cunt. We'd just fucking explode. "WE HEARD THAT!" "YOU NATHTY MAN!" "BIG ERNIE! I'M GONNA TELL YAW WIFE!" and the fathers would just wave us off, tell us to go play in traffic or something and then we'd get all blurty, haw-hawing just this side of sexual hysteria.

My father wouldn't hang out on the Fathers' Bench as much as the other men, and at first I decided it was because he was too tired from working so hard in the Post Office, but that was horseshit; they *all* worked hard. And it wasn't because he was grieving for my mother; it was just him, his nature, he was *always* like that. But it would drive me wild, because those guys *liked* him; he was a nice guy, my father.

The men would have a poker game on Friday nights and sometimes he'd play, but more often he'd just go to the movies instead and I would fucking flip. I'd be yelling at him the next day, "How come you didn't play! How come you didn't play!" And he'd just give me this shitty shrug. . . . And they were *good* guys, they weren't clannish, everybody made the same money, it was him, it was him. Sometimes I'd be sitting on the Kids' Bench and I'd look over and I wouldn't see my father on the Fathers' Bench with the others and I'd go upstairs and drag him down saying, "Big *Hump* wants you!" or "Big *Larry* wants you!" And then when he was down I'd have half an eye on his action on the other bench and half an eye on my own, just making sure he was talking or laughing or whatever. It was very draining.

In the fall, on Saturday or Sunday mornings all the kids would play a massive game of touch football, choose up sides, and sometimes the fathers would be full up on their bench, if they got down that early, and watch the game. And when *that* happened, the games would turn into blood baths, because we'd be hopped up, leaping, flying, diving, you name it, all with one eye on the Fathers' Bench. Very dangerous.

I remember one particular Saturday morning game more than any other, because it seemed as though the entire complex shooting match of our relationship got played out in about ten minutes flat in front of an audience of two dozen fathers and sons.

It was on a glittery cold November morning. Me and my friends were out on the grass field choosing up sides, the fathers were on their bench, when suddenly, "WEE CHAL-LENGE!" The fathers all rose and came stomping onto the field. It took us a second to catch on to what was happening, but when we did we went berserk. The fathers were gonna play us! Hot damn! But they were very self-conscious. I could see it in how they came marching onto the field; bumping into each other, laughing too easy, jingling the change in their pockets. They were wearing Hush Puppies, shiny slacks. They were definitely not from camping trips and psychology; just some Life-of-Riley heads, big stiffs on a goof bender that morning, and plus, they were in horrible shape: pot bellies, cigarettes, jowls—I don't think any of them had really thrown a football or broken into a dead run for at least ten years. Nonetheless, the whole thing was very exciting, we were all yelling the rules at them, "TEN MIZZIPPI, NO TACKLING, FOUR DOWNS," circling them and yapping like agitated pups. They stood in a tight clump as if lassoed, casually hacking up the grass with their heels and drawling back at us, "Yeah, yeah, yeah."

I was standing there looking at one father, Big Irv, who didn't have any sons. Irv had three daughters and even though he was a mechanic for the police department I had always thought that there was something pink and gray and soft about him. He had a gentle wavy pompadour like Rudy Vallee and wore white Ban-Lon socks. I was just looking at him and wondering if he felt bad about not having any sons, when my eye fell on another Sad Case, Big Ernie. Ern had been a war hero with the Gliders but he didn't have any kids at *all.*

He was going to play, but he was standing on the sidelines with his hands in his car coat. So there I was, feeling sorry for Big *Er*nie, feeling sorry for Big *Irv*, when suddenly I realized *my* goddamn father wasn't there, *again*, and I wigged. I yelled for everybody to hold it, I gotta get my father, and one of my friends started whining, "Ca*man* already!" and I almost jumped on his face. I said, "You just *wait!*" I turned to the men and said, "Why don't you guys have a cigarette?" And I was shocked because six of them actually took out their packs. I started running up the stairs in a sweaty panic; what if he's not dressed, fucking *Irv*'s playing, he got three daughters, fucking *Er*nie's playing, he don't even *have* kids; and I burst in yelling "Dad! You gotta come down!"

My father was sitting there at the dinette table in his slacks and his bathrobe, sipping coffee and it caught me up short, because that's *all* he was doing, sipping coffee—no newspapers, no TV, not even a radio on. I felt a jolt of enraged misery and I started tugging on his sleeve. "Hurry! It's an emergency! All the guys are waiting for you!" I ran over to the window and they actually *were* waiting.

He said, "What, what's goin' on?"

And I repeated, "Daddy, it's an emergency. I swear to God on the Holy Bible . . . don't wear those pants . . ."

I dragged him downstairs, pushed him toward the fathers' team, all the fathers going "*Lou*-eee! *Lou*-eee!" and he put on a little hustle-jog, clapping his hands and bouncing his shoulders, which made me give out with a blurty chortle-squawk of excitement, and now, now, we were ready.

The kids were going to kick off. We had not stopped barking since "We Challenge!" So we're lining up and shouting all these combat kick-ass directives across the line, "RED DOG THIRTY-FIVE DIVE ON FIVE BLITZ GANG TACKLE CLOTHESLINE . . ." We didn't even know what any of that shit meant. It sounded like we were hallucinating. It was just a stupid kickoff, you ran down, tagged the guy with the ball and that was that. Meanwhile, the fathers were in a huddle. Now, no one ever got in a huddle to receive, so, what's going on? The huddle broke, the fathers spread out, we kicked off, boom . . . they pulled a number on us. Instead of running interference, blocking us out like you're supposed to do, the fathers ran downfield, hopping and bellowing, acting like total lunatics, flapping their arms and going "OOK! OOK! OOK!" so by midfield three-quarters of the kids were curled up on the grass in totally disoriented hysterics and laughing fits. The other quarter just wandered around in a shellshocked daze looking every whichaway but downfield like they refused to believe what they saw. There was only one kid who was totally undeterred, this heavyweight Catholic kid, Patrick Kelly. He made a beeline for the father with the ball, but the father, Big Hump, just picked up Kelly and ran with him under the other arm. I mean, we were only ten, eleven, tops. Meanwhile, Kelly, upside down, was screaming, "You're tagged! You're tagged! I don't care! You're tagged!"

Myself, when I saw my old man come hopping downfield, his thumbs in his ears, cross-eyed, making those stupid chimpanzee noises, I started laughing so hard I just sank to my knees. I was so happy I was braying like a fucking mule. But then something frightening happened. I *really* couldn't stop laughing and I started losing my breath. My stomach began to cramp, and I felt a frightening tightness across my chest. I was hysterical. Tears splashed down my cheeks and I was gasping and sobbing. There was a crowd around me and my father was on his knees patting me on the back like he was trying to burp me. I felt totally ashamed, as if I had been caught talking in my sleep. I pulled out of it fast, pulled away from him and got up fussing over grass stains on my kneecaps. He said, "Maybe you should sit out a few downs." I completely flipped and in front of everybody I just mimicked him to himself; "Maybe you should sit *out* a few downs," in a nasty, faggy whine, like a vicious little shit, and I instantly felt horrified. My father didn't get mad. He looked confused, as did everybody else. It seemed to me that everybody took one step back from us.

I went right back in. The game was over on the next play anyhow, because one of the fathers twisted his ankle, but I'll never forget that kickoff, never forget it. And even now, whenever I see some older guy sitting alone in a Chock Full O' Nuts or in a movie theater I get totally crazed. I can't help it. I lose it completely. I don't know whether to kick his ass or take him home.

———

I never really believed it was mourning that kept my father indoors; it was depression, apathy, that ability he had to eat a whole meal in silence, without even a newspaper in front of his nose.

And I don't think it was just *any* woman I would have opposed, it was Vy. Five years after my mother's death, when my father finally started dating, I was crazy about the first girlfriend, a tall schlubby blond divorcée named Inez. In fact, my father finally started going out because I had had it with him curled down in front of the TV every night.

When I was fifteen I sent away for a membership application to Single Again, a mixer club for divorced or widowed adults. It took a month of harassing for him to fill it out and promise to go to an upcoming dance in a catering hall on the Bronx side of the Whitestone Bridge. Then I dragged him to Korvette's and made him buy a new sports jacket. When I kicked him out of the house the night of the bash he said, "Don't worry Mom, I'll be home on time." Very cute. But unlike any mom I ever heard of, I hoped he wouldn't come home until dawn. I had fantasies of a victory breakfast with a lot of double entendres, winking, and elbow nudges. He got home at eleven P.M.

He didn't meet Inez until three months later at a coffee-and-cake social put on by the Tenants Caucus in the basement of our building. That lasted three dates until she moved out of her efficiency apartment to live in San Diego with her daughter. Six months after that, Vy came to our door one Sunday morning, freaked out because there was a praying mantis on her windowsill. She had moved into Inez's vacant digs, and apparently Inez had left a note for the new tenant, anticipating a single woman I guess, to the effect that if there was ever an emergency to call on Lou Keller in 8G. My father did his Sir Walter Raleigh routine, flicking away the mantis with a rolled-up magazine, and the rest is history. Maybe he was just hot for the apartment.

The day he approached me to ask for my "permission" to marry Vy, a setup if I ever saw one, I rifled through her wallet, which she had left in our dinette. I wanted to find something to show me who the hell she was beyond the tremulous politeness, the pyramid of Lark stubs in the living room. What I came across, besides her teller's ID from the bank where she worked, was a black-and-white photo of her deceased husband, Martin Korn, and a mimeoed copy of the salt-free diet that the doctor had prescribed to forestall the heart attack that killed him anyhow. Martin Korn had been a supervisor in an all-night cafeteria, and the photo was of him on the job, standing behind the steam table; a grim static lump with a big bald head, dead eyes and a moustache. Even though the picture was black and white I could sense that his short-sleeved white shirt had a slight yellow tinge under the arms and around the collar. I envisioned him as a man who *liked* boiled food, as much as he probably could have been said to have "liked" anything. Carrying around that salt-free diet sheet three years after his death was classic Vy quiet heartbreak.

And maybe that was the biggest thing I had against Vy. I think what she saw in my father was another Martin Korn and I think she was right. Because I can't deny that my father was ten times happier with Vy than he was with my mother; in fact they were inseparable. When my mother was alive she went to bed alone because he was on the night shift at the Post Office. Saturdays were me and her at the movies. Sundays me and her at wrestling matches or Roller Derby. I never even knew where my father went on his days off.

When Vy and my father got married in the local synagogue, I was the best man. In a fit of melodrama the day before the wedding, I went alone to visit my mother's grave. I stood staring at the glazed granite and imagined I was in a movie. There would be a harmonica solo in the background and I would have to deliver a short folksy humble address, but I couldn't think of anything to say. Two rows away from me a girl my age was putting plastic flowers on her grandfather's grave. I sauntered over and tried to pick her up. Halfway through my "Do you come here often?" she started sobbing. I wanted to invite her as my date to the wedding, but I punked out.

Later that day I went to the bank, pulled out my two hundred dollars and in a pique of violently excessive generosity bought them a honeymoon at Brown's Hotel in the Catskills. Whenever I was murderously enraged at someone I always flooded them with gifts. It was a real mindfuck.

My mother had outweighed my father by a hundred pounds, and once a friend of mine in second grade said that when they stood side by side they looked like the number "10." I was closer to each of them than they were to each other, but I turned out more like Mom, a flake, a class clown, a fighter/loner, than like my father, or so I hoped, and if what really made my old man happy was goddamn Vy with her salt-free reliquary, where the hell did that leave me?

———

Usually when I came home on a school vacation I would feel like some character in a Russian play rediscovering the old precious mansion of my lost youth; every stick of furniture, everything in the closets seemed wondrously new and nostalgic at the same time. That lasted on the average three hours. Then Couch Paralysis would nail my ass until it was time to go back to campus. But that graduation night, as I sat with my hands in my lap on the green tassel-hemmed sofa under the marble-veined mirror, staring at a small framed barn made out of linguini, I realized I *had* no campus to go back to, and I began to lose my Cherry Orchard glow immediately.

I could hear the newscaster drone from their bedroom TV down the hall, and I turned on the living room TV to drown it out. Just as Johnny Carson ballooned into focus, I saw Vy standing like a bouffanted apparition on the carpet line between the foyer and the living room.

"Hi," I murmured and sat up a bit.

Vy stood there in her nightgown and her bathrobe, hesitated, her thin lips working, her eyes as usual wet with nervousness. In a burst of decision she propelled herself across the room and perched next to me on the couch.

"Peter . . . I just wanted to say mazel tov for today. You made your father so proud I can't tell you." She couldn't decide what to do first, put the hundred-dollar bill in my hand or kiss me, and she wound up kissing the side of my nose while sticking the money between my knees. "This is from me, doll. Go out and have a good time."

I immediately felt like a punk, and I grabbed her in one of my semi-annual hugs.

Behind her back Sammy Davis Jr. was pointing to Mac Davis and giving the long-jawed glass-eye to Carson. "Johnny, this cat, this cat . . . he won't tell you this about himself because he's a truly humble dude, but I gotta let the cat out of the bag . . ."

As soon as we broke the clinch, Vy rose to retreat to the bedroom.

"Vy?" I said softly.

She wheeled at the carpet-break.

"Can I bum a cigarette?" How big of me.

"Of course you can." She dug into the deep pocket of her bathrobe and pulled out a pack of Larks sheathed in a vinyl case. She handed me four and a disposable lighter.

"Vy?" Put out a little bit, bung-hole.

"Yeah, doll." She stood over me nervously fingering the cigarette case.

"Thank you."

"Peter, I'm proud of you too."

I expected her to bolt, but she stood there wanting to talk. I started getting nervous.

"Well, I'm proud of *you*," I said and blushed at the inanity of the comment. "Maybe I'll come downtown to the bank next week and we can have lunch."

"Oh, I'd *love* that, honey." She looked as if she was about to cry. She took off for the bedroom and as I stared at a frantic comic in an orange jumpsuit I began to get teary myself. I swore I'd make that lunch.

The comic's name was Herman Contardo, and his schtick centered around what it was like growing up half-Italian, half-Jewish.

"Are you kidding me? My parents would fight, it would sound like this: Ay! Oy! Ay! Oy! Ay! Oy!"

He was giving me a headache. Recruited by the Mafia to do their books. Getting nervous at his bar mitzvah and breaking out into "Volare" halfway through his *haftarah*. Everybody's a comedian.

When he finally collapsed into a chair on the side of the throne, Carson asked him how old he was.

"I'll be eighteen next week, Johnny."

Damn. I flashed on Larry goading me to become a comic. I couldn't be a comic. A class clown does not a comic make. It was easy enough to wipe out a group of friends from the comfort of a familiar couch or under a street light on a spacy night, another thing to get up there on a stage, to do auditions, to disregard the diploma. I'd fold like a jackknife. Realism. Law School. Don't be a dropout.

I studied the bill. A hundred bucks. My father had given me a typewriter. Bam-Bam got the whole summer in Italy with relatives. But then again Bam-Bam had been accepted to Columbia Law.

Maybe I should have bitten the bullet and gone to St. John's, but every time I thought about that place I remembered Howard Handball and I balked. I picked St. John's as a safety because when I was in high school I had played handball one day at a beach club with two teen-aged friends and a fortyish putz named Howard. Howard was tanky and uncoordinated, but he had heart, which made him play even worse. It was a brutal August afternoon, and he was nude except for sheer diving trunks and heavy black sneakers. His hairy balls kept slipping out every time he stretched for a shot. Halfway through the match the three of us were swallowing guffaws, afraid to make eye contact. Our first blatantly faulty adult. Howard was a lawyer. Howard went to St. John's Law School.

Ever since I had heard the expression "Hanging Judge" on "Gunsmoke" when I was six, I had it in my head to be a lawyer. In first grade our teacher once made every kid stand up and say what they wanted to be in case they grew up. All the boys said cowboy-soldier-policeman-fireman like what else is new, and all the girls said model-nurse-blah-blah. But I declared, "*Law*yer!" and blew the old biddy out of her socks.

Ever since then I was the Lawyer, the Judge. I had my ace, my specialty. As much as I goofed on myself being the last chapter, the happy ending in the Keller saga of Only in America, no matter how many sociology and psychology courses I might have aced in the previous four years, I'd be lying if I didn't admit that I'd bought the Brooklyn Bridge on that sentiment. I owed too many people even though most of them were either dead or entombed in Florida condos.

There had been too many weddings and bar mitzvahs with too many uncles and aunts squinting up at me or slapping me on the back and saying "So! Mr. College Man!" or "When I divorce your uncle are you gonna help me take him to the cleaners?" followed by: "Ettie, cut it out. Pete's gonna be a corpo*r*ation lawyer, right, kid?"

Right.

I *was* the first Keller to make it to college, and I wanted to be successful, I wanted a house in the burbs complete with pipe rack and stand-up globe in the den; for me, for them, for me.

One thing, though, that the class clown and the Hanging Judge had in common was that commitment, that conviction in me to stand out, to be different. Even at the age of six or seven I always felt a cutting edge behind my obstreperousness, my clown act. I *had* to score yoks. I *had* to paint my face like an Indian whenever I got a crack at the Art Corner in Free Play. I *had* to fling wet elbow macaroni at the girls and scream "worms!" All my antics had teeth; no laughing matter. And I was sure it involved my mother, me pursuing her outsized-ness, her loneliness. And I hoped it didn't have too much to do with Keller père, the man whose claim to fame was eating a seven-course meal without raising his eyes from the next forkful, that Reincarnation of Martin Korn. The big problem at this point in my life was that pursuing the Hanging Judge brand of uniqueness wasn't so unique anymore. Everybody and his cousin were going to law school. And judging by the kinky-haired jump-suited sociopath cavorting on the tube, being a comic seemed a fairly pathetic dream to follow, too.

Ed McMahon let out with one of his patented guffaws, and I snapped off the box.

———

That graduation summer was the worst. For starters, I had nobody to play with. I'd spent the last four years three hundred and twenty miles away from home, and I'd come out of Straight with two buddies, Bam-Bam, who was hoisting toenail vino with a dozen uncles in Calabria two days after graduation, and Larry, who was in St. Paul, Minnesota, where he belonged.

As for my Yonkers associates, half were burned out on drugs or early marriage, and the rest were still shooting hoops behind the high school. Anyway, it had been all over between me and the stay-at-homes as far back as the Thanksgiving break my freshman year when I returned to The Rhonda, said my howdies, zipped around the apartment, touching everything, and then bee-lined down to the basketball courts looking like Doonesbury in a six-foot scarf and a maroon stadium coat. I had "Simon Straight" printed on everything but my underwear, Frantz Fanon's *The Wretched of the Earth* in my hip pocket and two square inches of chin lint, all I could grow in three months, dangling under my preening smirk.

I can't believe I really expected to be joyously mobbed by all those guys going to various local community colleges or working full-time. What I got was a thirty-second break in the game; six guys coolly nodding "How ya doin'," standing there in dungarees and high Cons and giving me the once-over like I just stepped off the stagecoach from Back East.

Somebody enunciated very slowly, very distinctly; "Si-mon Straight," and a plague of sniggering broke through the court. Before I knew it everybody was back into the game, and I was standing alone, grinning in mortification and fury.

Theoretically, coming out of four years with two friends didn't upset me. You change scenery, you start from scratch. Besides, how many hard and fast 3:00 A.M. buddies did *any*body have at *any* point in their lives? I always felt that not only were people basically solo, but that a lot of them took pride in their own secretiveness, in how little anybody knew their hearts. The assholes. So *theoretically* I didn't feel bad about my situation but in reality, there were days and nights in that ensuing postgraduation summer where I would have killed for a half-hour of horselaughs. Still, I had other things on my mind. For starters, the Hanging Judge had to land a gig that would awe the next year's admissions board at Columbia.

Easier said than done. The want ads in the *Times* required experience I didn't have, and I was forced to go the route of employment agencies, which meant blow-drying my hair every morning, wandering around hot-June Manhattan unemployed in jacket and tie, little pink introduction cards in my hand, the waiting, the interviews, the lying, the humiliation . . . The only real offer I received was from an agency itself; after six bum leads, one guy who was sending me out said that the job market was for shit, but *they* had an opening and offered me a shot at being a commissioned employment counselor.

Every once in a while someone would send me for an interview near the Grand Central Post Office where my father worked. He pulled nine to five in the philatelist cage and I would stand in line with the stamp collectors, all male and none of them what you would call handsome, and wait to surprise him. He was always glad to see me, always called over his co-workers for me to shake hands with through the bars. All the stamp collectors on line called my father Lou, although he never held stuff on the side for anybody, no favorites. In school I had always referred to my father as a Federal Philatelist's Agent, never a mailman. He once brought home for me six brand-new plate blocks from the European Freedom Fighters series, but I couldn't get into it.

––––––

A few weeks after graduation I got a job off the street working in the garment district unloading forklifts for La Belle, a woman's blouse outfit. I didn't take it out of desperation. I took it because I was beginning to feel physically shitty about myself, a little doughy, and I thought I could use the exercise. My heavyweight executive job was on the way, but meanwhile it would be nice not to have to hit up my old man every day for pocket money. Big mistake. All I remember about that one week was food and heat. The work was stunningly dull and like everybody else I lived for the little quilted silver food truck that came around at noon and three. I didn't have anything to say to any of the other workers and at lunchtime I usually found myself alone, propped up against the building, my ass on the Seventh Avenue sidewalk. I would sit spreadlegged with exhaustion in sweaty baggy dungarees, my T-shirt like a damp towel, forearms slicked with dust and oil, just sitting there, squinting into the concrete and traffic mirage heat, scarfing down a strawberry Yoo Hoo and a sandwich cooked in its own plastic wrapper while looking up at dressed-to-kill secretaries in high heels, lipstick and sheathed thighs, clipping by me with their commercial diplomas, their double-digit IQs, not even looking down at me, not even seeing me. And I didn't even care. All I could deal with was the bloated sweetness in my belly and the fact that the humidity allowed me to fingerpaint on my own skin. That was the job I had in mind for myself because I was getting out of shape.

I quit the day one of Vy's friends, a garment-district bookkeeper, came walking by as I was squatting on the sidewalk eating a Ring Ding on my afternoon break. Flushed with embarrassment, I shot to my feet, spearing my shoulder on the bottom of a ground-floor window grate. She didn't even notice me and continued walking uptown.

The entire month of June was siesta hot. The weather combined with my home-again emotional jet lag to give me a psychosomatic case of tired blood. After spending the mornings staggering around for a job, or shaking hands with my father, I had to fight off the desire to go back up to Yonkers and take a nap. If I was too beat to track down leads in the afternoons I'd duck into movies or museums. I knew that in my mental state, naps could kill.

At nights, the three of us would sit in the living room, watch "Cannon," "The Mod Squad," ABC's Monday Tuesday Wednesday Thursday Friday Night at the Movies, the news, Johnny Carson and crash.

I didn't watch too much television in college, but when I did it was with a loud crowd around the dorm lounge, the fraternity lounge or in my senior year garden apartment with Bam-Bam and some dates or neighbors. Whatever we watched in those four years was secondary to the wisecracks, the eating and the grass.

TV nights with my father and Vy were silent affairs. At first I tried to drum up some group hysteria, frantically insulting Cannon's fatness, or Chester's limp on the "Gunsmoke" reruns, but the best I could score were some polite chuckles from my father. Vy wouldn't know a funny line if it bit her on the ass. I had never seen her laugh in my life.

One night toward the end of June on "N.Y.P.D." we saw a cop come across his partner lying in a pool of blood with what looked like a cannonball wound in his gut. The cop bent down and said, "Are you okay?" and I exploded with a half-dozen responses in ten seconds. My father missed the wounded cop's answer because of my floor show and wincing in irritation asked Vy what the guy had said. Vy quoted it back verbatim, and "An Evening with Pete Keller" closed out of town forever.

The next morning, I woke up and realized I had two choices: either get on the stick and land some kind of job that would make me feel like a human being, or wind up as the subject of an article in the American Journal for the Study of Mass Murderers.

I covered the kitchen table with the Want-Ad sections of every newspaper I could find and started making calls. I answered one ad for someone who desired to break into the magazine world, but after a twenty-minute veiled conversation with a woman who described herself as "Personnel Master," I figured out that the position was for a Boy Friday in the office of a small erratically published dominatrix journal.

The second call went better. There was an ad in the *Village Voice* requesting verbally aggressive people. I got a Mrs. Himmel on the line and found out I had reached a phone-soliciting outfit called American Communicators. Mrs. Himmel sounded cool and regal with a slight trace of the Danube in her voice. She seemed relaxed and intelligent, so I took a chance and told her I had a college degree. She cooed with approval and that spurred me on to reveal that I had graduated from the Harvard of Upstate New York, honors in English, how's *that* for verbal. It was my first interview where the extent of my education didn't do me in, and laying out my resumé for Mrs. Himmel made me feel like Clark Kent slowly unbuttoning his white shirt.

I don't know if it was her leisurely curiosity or just my hunger for a real conversation but it turned out to be the best talk I'd had since college. I wanted to give her my life story; the tears, the fears, the laughs. I totally forgot it was a job interview and I wound up running down every accomplishment since kindergarten except for winning the triple crown in punchball for the 1957 season.

She requested my presence for an orientation meeting the next day and I hung up so excited that I walked around the house for a half-hour absently clapping my hands.

American Communicators turned out to be a rat's maze of eighty-five phone cubicles in an office building on Lexington Avenue. The outfit was run by Mrs. Himmel and her husband, refugee psychoanalysts from Germany via Denmark. When I found out she was a shrink I felt slightly manipulated, but not too badly.

The Himmels hired out their setup to any organization that needed a phone campaign to sell products, raise funds or take polls, their clients ranging from the state government to a soft-core porno magazine.

Mr. Himmel was a beard and a pipe, a heavyset fortyish Freudian-looking gent who said nothing and strolled out of the plant two minutes after casing over the six new employees, myself and five women, that his wife had hired over the phone.

Mrs. Himmel, whom I had planned to marry, was something else. From the neck down she was a slender, stylishly dressed woman of about forty, but she had a pouchy powder-white face topped with a frosted hairdo the color of polished copper.

She worked out of an elevated glass booth equipped with a switchboard and overlooking the maze. The six of us had to stand at the booth's open door, as she sat, headphones on, frowning in concentration, connecting and disconnecting wiretaps to the various phone lines below. She moved smoothly and mechanically, like an efficient daydreaming operator, but at one point she suddenly paused, lifted her hand to the right earphone, hunched her shoulders and listened more intently.

"Adrian?" she purred. "I'm so glad your mother is feeling better. You may leave now . . . we'll mail you your check for this week."

Out on the floor, a pony-tailed woman rose from her cubicle, face red, and left the room without looking up at the booth. Apparently Adrian had just been nailed making a personal call. Mrs. Himmel went back to her switchboard, plugging away for a few minutes, then stopped again.

"Julio? . . . I recall the Power Plower comes with a money-back guarantee, don't you? . . . You think that might have affected the gentleman's decision? That's okay. That's okay. Make your next call."

Five minutes later, when she finally put aside the headphones and slowly rose to greet us with a bemused dissecting gaze, we were all "oriented." The woman standing next to me, swollen with pregnancy, muttered "Fuck *this* noise . . ." and headed for the door. It was a long walk and she broke into three distinct trots before she made it to the elevator banks. Everybody else in the group looked reduced to quivering blobs of acquiescence but strangely enough I wasn't intimidated. I found the Himmel Behavior Modification strategy despicable but ingenious.

———

I had always told everybody my father was chosen to be a Federal Philatelist's Agent because he knew how to relate to people, you'd be amazed at the variety of types and temperaments that a Philatelist's Agent has to deal with, blah blah. So at first, despite Mrs. Himmel's act, I was geared up about the work because I could say it required the same skills. But that horseshit lasted about three days and by the end of my first week I was into the Camel Walk; a forward stagger on the balls of my feet as if I was about to collapse in the Gobi. I would punch in at 8:04, one minute shy of a half-hour's pay dock, and do my walk down the twelve rows of brightly painted pegboard-lined cubicles, a sea of murmurs, dialings, clickings, rising in a muted muffle over that labyrinth of hi-gloss circus-colored soundproofing. Mrs. Himmel was always in her elevated glass-enclosed booth, headphones on, wiretapping away to her soul's delight. I was sure she was constantly wet behind that console.

Sometimes, I would stop in mid-shuffle, until she glanced down at me and then, acting as if I didn't know I was being watched, resume my stagger to the cubicle.

Of all eighty-five people in that room she was the only person I had instantaneous eye-lock connection with. Although we hadn't exchanged a civil word since the phone talk, I felt as if we'd known each other for centuries, and I had an instinctual sense of exactly how far I could go with her. She was a shit to me, but she allowed me to snap back and sulk out like a bad sonny boy. If anybody else gave her lip, they would get the ax.

Once some guy got canned for walking in fifteen minutes late from coffee. I appeared five minutes after him and all I got was a long-suffering smirk.

I must have reminded her of somebody.

She liked me.

My station was 8E. Every morning I would plant myself, elbows on the formica desk slab, cover my mouth with my hands and stare at the black wall-phone mounted a foot in front of my face on the glazed sky-blue pegboard. The booth to the right was British Racing Stripe Green; to the left Emergency Yellow; to my back, St. Joseph's Aspirin Orange, all so glossed and shellacked I could comb my hair in the sheen. Every day I would come in and squat like a shrub until my phone rang twice fast. I would never pick up, just raise my head without turning around in an "okay, okay" gesture to Mrs. Himmel who I knew was daggering my spine from ten yards away.

I didn't really pay attention to any of my co-solicitors. I was numbed out and pissed off and I never really physically saw anybody anyhow unless they stood up. Besides, since it was a suck-ass job, the turnover was phenomenal. Between the "I quits" and the "you're fireds" people just weren't around that long.

But that began to change one morning, a number of Mondays into the job, when I overheard something in 8D that made me hang up my phone in mid-spiel. At first I couldn't make out what was being said because of the soundproofing, but by the urgent murmuring, the erratic rising and falling and the sighing I knew 8D wasn't working off the call stack.

I inched my chair back past our partition and copped a listen: "Stop *talk*ing like that! So you'll get another slave . . . No . . . No . . .

he's *not* the only African in New York . . . and what kind of pill are you planning to take? . . . how many? . . . uh-huh . . . uh-huh . . . so does this mean you won't be around for my birthday party? Uh-huh . . . uh-huh . . . yeah . . . Don-*nalld*, Don-*nalld*, I'm *not* making fun of you . . . who's going to talk *me* out of suicide if you kill yourself? What time is your session? . . . What do you *meeen* you feel too crazy to have a session? . . ." He cackled in delight then suddenly turned around to see if it looked as if Himmel was eavesdropping. He caught me sitting slightly behind him obviously listening, staring back at him goggle-eyed. He gave me a quick wink and a beaming conspiratorial smile then returned to his conversation. "I re*peat*, Donald, who's going to talk me out of . . . who? Emory? *Em*ory!! Are you serious? . . . I've totally alienated Emory. Besides, he's too busy freaking out about cellulite . . . no, bubby, I've alienated everybody but you, and if you die my ass is truly in a sling. . . . I'm serious, Emory thinks he has cellulite . . . I know that . . . remember last year? When he thought he had a yeast infection? . . . Donald? Is that a laugh I hear? . . . uh-huh . . . Donald, can we start this conversation again? *Hi* Donald . . ." He turned back to me and smiled in weary triumph. "This is James. I was just calling to see how you were. . . . ah-hah . . . ah-hah . . . is that so?"

I sat there grinning at the melon slice of flesh that showed between the back of his beltless dungarees and the sweatshirt that had crept up his spine. There was a copy of *Variety* on his desk slab.

I immediately fell in love. Not homosexual love, but in love with his homosexuality, his Auntie Mame rap, his copy of *Variety*. I was a real turkey and a boing-boing tourist around that stuff and the novelty of it all knocked me out. As I looked down the row of cubicles I noticed sticking out of hip pockets like popsicle rockets two more copies of *Variety*, a blue-titled *Show Business* and a *Backstage*. I got up to go to the bathroom and slowly zig-zagged through the aisles, listening to people for the first time. There was an amazing thrum of trained modulated voices. I passed four women my age sitting in a row; long-necked, long-fingered, long-spined like a brace of swans. By each chair lay an oversized shoulder bag. The zippers were open on two and I saw jumbles of slick body stockings, wool leggings, a plastic bag of sunflower seeds, a roll-on deodorant.

Every day after that I found an excuse to troll the aisles. I took notice of people punching in or out. Everybody, male and female, seemed to carry some kind of oversized bag with a change of uniform or costume in it. Everybody seemed to project from the diaphragm. I found out that one chubby bespectacled schlubbette, a girl who carried a purse instead of a shoulder bag and who I was sure was a no-talent, had produced, directed and animated a three-minute cartoon on the letter "N" for "Sesame Street."

The story was that I found myself surrounded by the most gifted collection of minimum-wage earners in the city.

There was a telethon-sized time chart along one wall, and most people consulted date books before signing up for the next week's schedule, trying to work around classes, rehearsals, auditions. The phones were in operation seven days a week from 8 A.M. to 10 P.M., plenty of space to customize wage time against the hours necessary to put in for future greatness.

It took me a few days to get a sense of all this and when I did I experienced an ecstatic anxiety the likes of which I hadn't felt since losing my virginity.

I wanted in. I wanted to play.

The person I focused on was my neighbor in 8D, the suicide counselor. His name was James Madison. Two or three years older than me, he had a high forehead that was so shiny pink and blemish-free that it looked boiled. That forehead, combined with phosphorescently white teeth and a short fastidious lacquered-looking jet black Jerry Lewis crop gave him a spanky-squeaky aura and made him seem like the type that would go into shock at the sight of a soiled ashtray, but in fact he was a stone slob. McDonald's cartons grew under his chair, he nigger-lipped his cigarettes, and tight T-shirts and jeans betrayed the blubbery physique of an old madam. No matter, he was my new hero. All I wanted was for him to wink at me again the way he did that day and make me feel like a regular.

After that fateful eavesdropping, I always made a point of saying hello every time our eyes met, and giving him a wry smile. He was definitely thrown by me. He might even have feared for his life.

Sometimes when I went out for coffee I'd pick up one for him, too. Unasked. He would thank me but his face would be pinched and his voice would be tentative and we'd have a short strained conversation that went nowhere. Once I asked him what he did and he told me he was a gay ventriloquist. Pushing my luck, I asked him what his dummy's name was. When he said "Dolly," I said, "Oh, I get it . . . James and Dolley Madison," and he drawled, "No . . . James and Dalai Lama." The same thing happened to me with everybody else too. It was like I had totally forgotten how to have a conversation. All I knew from was prestigious colleges, Dean's Lists, Yonkers and that vague future vision of a palace in the burbs complete with pipe rack and stand-up globe in the den. My priorities, my reflexes, were so different from everybody's around me that any time I tried to get over I always wound up feeling like a big dopey bear galumphing into a clearing to play with the deer. I kept asking people what college they'd gone to. If they were originally from Wisconsin or Pennsylvania I'd want to talk "home state" for hours, prattling on about Fighting Bob La Follette or the Amish. If they were gay I'd want to talk about gay rights.

I felt a hankering finger-twitching yearning around the cubicles that was so strong it was clogging me up. Even Himmel was part of it. As a kid, my class-clown nickname had been Speedo. I wanted to be called Speedo again. Like all the dancers, the ventriloquists, the actors, I wanted to bask in my own unique brand of ace-hood.

To hell with The Hanging Judge. People at American Communicators didn't know the difference between law boards and floor boards and I started to feel my own gray sense of duty about the year's game plan.

So far, the way I'd been going about beefing up my resume wouldn't get me into a study-at-home private investigator's course. I had always been good at getting what I wanted from institutions, "job market" be damned, so I knew my self-sabotage ran deeper than just atmospheric intoxication with A.C.

Speedo. I hadn't thought about my standing daydream of being a comic since Larry called me out on Graduation Day. Actually it wasn't even a daydream, it was more like a little extra oomph I carried around with me. But now I mulled it over constantly. It felt audacious, outrageous. How do you "do it?" How do you get your balls up? How do you get up there and wipe your ass with that American flag of the Leslie Houses, the college diploma?

Nobody at A.C. was actually trying to ice me. People were basically friendly but I just couldn't relax. I couldn't be myself. And to be around them but not *of* them was giving me a ferocious case of the Who Am I's. I was one of the few New York natives in that room, but I punched in and out every day feeling like Jethro Clampett, and what started out as an exciting revelation about A.C. soured into a nightmare of frustration. If I heard of someone getting a toe hold on his dream all I could feel was panic. A guy six phones down from me who performed in a life-sized Punch and Judy show with his girlfriend quit one day because they had received a traveling grant from the government to tour Eastern Europe. That same day an elegantly slender Watusi-woman passed out slate-gray performance announcements for a dance concert her three-person company was putting on in a church in Hell's Kitchen, and by that noon I had developed a horrible habit of fanning my knees like grasshopper joints.

I would go home every night overloaded with a stop-don't stop-stop career panic. One night I got into a wildly gesticulating argument with my parents about interracial marriage. It was a time-tested sure-fire irritant. I told them I was in love with an African dancer at work, and they hopped around the living room as if the TV was on fire. I came on like Frederick Douglass, and the debate ended when I accidentally back-handed a plaster camel off the credenza into smithereens on the floor. They retreated to their bedroom to watch the black-and-white TV, and I wound up alone slouched down hollow-eyed, clutching the armrest of the couch like a whacked-out king in the last act of a tragedy, chain-smoking, watching Johnny Carson in color, my knees going like generators.

I started telling people at work I had my own place in Brooklyn.

Maybe I should have quit the job, but the more jammed I felt, the more obsessed I became about holding my own. Sometimes I would spend all day trying to think of something to say to James Madison or anybody that would show them what a whip I could be. I was Speedo, as fast as a fuck. I could always crack people up if the time and place were right, but now it seemed like the only person cracking up was me. I was convinced, in my isolation and confusion, that everybody at A.C., in addition to being talented and driven, was also tight with each other; that they all hung out together, all belonged to the New York, New York—When You Wish Upon a Star Club, and anytime one of them was fired, or quit, or more than one left work together for the day, I'd find myself straining in my seat wanting to blurt out "Where you *going?* What are you *doing?* Where you *headed?* What's *happening?*"

————

Things finally, finally, started loosening up for me the day my next door neighbor in 8F, an acting student named Terry Steinmark, got nailed calling his answering service and was canned on the spot. It was only 8:15 and as he packed up he was still yawning and scraping crud from the corner of his eyes.

At nine o'clock James Madison's phone got hit with the two-ring signal and when he turned around Mrs. Himmel was beckoning him with a curled finger. He went up to the glass and was back at his station in 45 seconds carrying a cassette, an armload of tapes, a new call stack and a new script sheet.

All of us at A.C. were divided by rows into two campaigns: one was hawking Power Plower, a body-building device, and the other was a fund-raising drive for Public Television. Our row was on Power Plower, but Madison had just been switched to the Public TV campaign. Himmel didn't say why, but my theory was that with James's faggy voice he probably wasn't having too much success selling muscle-building equipment to America. He was totally pissed at being switched. It had sounded like he was having a ball, rapping and goofing and flirting with all these out-there guys who had mailed in coupons from the backs of comics and muscle magazines, and now he was going to be stuck talking to sober comfortable enlightened liberals. Not only that, but the rap that had to be used on the Public Television campaign was totally humiliating and insulting to both ends of the conversation.

Each solicitor on that program was equipped with a cassette machine that was jacked into the phone, and when they got their mark on the line they had to say, "Hi, Mrs. Yahooty? This is (your name) calling for . . . (whatever the Public TV station is in the area of the country you are working) . . . and I have a friend here who would like to talk to you about station XYZ. Do you have a second?" At which point they plugged in their "friend," a thirty-second taped appeal for a donation from Julia Child or Helen

Hayes or James Earl Jones, depending on the demographic break-down of the area under attack. What drove everybody crazy was that line "and I have a friend here," as though Helen Hayes was sitting in their lap. And under no circumstance was anybody al-lowed to deviate from the prepared script, so in every other row people were gritting their teeth and plugging in their cassettes feeling like total assholes.

James Madison made a dozen calls using the Julia Child cassette. I could faintly hear her loopy tea-time voice coming through the soundproofing. It was starting to drive me berserk but not as much as it was getting to him because two calls later, he reached behind him and tapped two pals in row seven, which was back-to-back with us, raising his eyebrows in an invitation for them to listen in on his next call. They furtively put their chairs in reverse so they were within earshot. Even though I wasn't invited I leaned left and forced an in-crowd casual smirk on my face.

"Hello, is this Mrs. Gretchen Lacy of Mobile, Alabama? Hi, my name is James Madison and I'm calling you for Channel 12 WBNF Television. Are you familiar with the station? . . . Yes? . . . Good. Well, Mrs. Lacy, I have a friend here who'd like to talk to you about Station BNF. Do you have a second for her? Okay-ay . . ." but in-stead of plugging in the tape he did a perfect impersonation of Julia Child with all her high-pitched ditsy-dotty old aunty inflections: "Haloo, my name is Julia Child. Usually when we talk, I'm *whack*-ing apart veggies for a *bwee*-ya-base but today, I'd like to discuss something else . . ." He had it down cold.

The two guys went wild. I was too self-conscious of my status to laugh, but it was a total scream. He spent the next hour imper-sonating Julia Child, Alistair Cooke and Dick Cavett, and by eleven o'clock at least half the room had managed to make it past his sta-tion for the James Madison show.

A half-hour before lunch a tall happy-looking square-shouldered girl with an armload of cassettes and tape paraphernalia sidled her way down our row toward Terry Steinmark's vacated booth. She ruffled James Madison's hair as she passed behind him and when he looked up she gave a short mischievous wave.

"Randye!" he squawked in delight.

She had a long horizontal shoulder bag made out of some kind of patchwork brocade so I guessed she was a dancer, but unlike the swans she was big-boned and slightly hunky. She wore dungarees and a T-shirt emblazoned with a colorful tourist's map of Cape Cod across the tits. The T-shirt was child-sized and her belly button showed.

"Public TV," she chortled, "whackin' apart a bweeyabase . . ." She leaned back past the partition and tapped me on the back. "What the hell is bweeyabase, anyhow?" It was one of the rare times that anybody spoke to me first and I must have sounded like Porky Pig attempting to get it together around "that's all folks" as I scrambled for a witty answer while restraining myself from jumping in her lap. Her two front teeth were both chipped at the meeting point between them, and her eyes were permanently pulled down at the outside corners so that she looked like she was about to say "awww" or something wistful. Mrs. Himmel hit her phone with the rings and she ducked back to work before I could spit anything out. Thirty seconds later she grabbed my arm. "I can't believe it!" she laughed, "I'm calling Billings! I grew *up* there!"

James Madison was starting to get bored doing his impersonations but he did at least one more that morning for Randye, reaching across my back to get her attention. The fucker never once directly invited me to listen in.

————

At the lunch break, Randye stood up at her station, placed the flat of her palms on the small of her back, arched her spine and rocked from side to side. She touched her toes with the backs of her wrists. She had long strong thighs, a high ass bulging with muscles and small tits for her frame. She clasped her hands over her head and pulled her arms as high as they would go. She didn't have an ounce of fat on her but she had a rib cage as big and wide as a beer keg. That and her goofy smile made me think of the expression "gal."

Both James Madison and Randye hung in at their desks eating bag lunches. I wanted to go out and get something but I wanted to talk more, so I took a pass on lunch.

"How's Dolly?" Randye scarfed down a fistful of vitamins before pulling out a wedge of cheese blackheaded with caraway seeds.

"Dolly's in the hospital." James Madison sighed.

"Wha-at?" She looked alarmed.

"She's got Dutch elm disease."

"She's got . . ." Randye started before she grimaced at being taken.

I raced in my head for a tree disease that could one-up Dutch elm. Blanko.

"James, do you want some coffee?" I offered. They had both pulled out their chairs to cross their legs and sat facing each other across the back of my station. I turned my chair around to make a cozy threesome, my kneecaps fanning.

"No thanks." He gave me that queasy questioning look.

"Would *you* like some?" I asked Randye.

"Uh-uh. Aren't you eating?" She sounded concerned.

"Nah, my stomach hurts." I winced, making a pass at my gut, embarrassed in front of James Madison, but pleased at the attention.

"You should take vitamins. . . . *James!* I can't believe it! I'm calling Billings."

"How nice. . . . You traveled two thousand miles so you could support yourself by calling home." He raised an eyebrow.

"It's so neat. . . . Herron's from Billings too." She tapped me on the leg. "Herron's in our company. There's only five of us and three are from Montana . . . by co*incidence*!"

I nodded and tick-tocked my head in attempted fascination.

"Where're you calling, James?" she asked.

"Mo-bee-ull." He hammed a drawl. "Yesterday I was calling some sea island off Georgia."

One of the woman dancers came over and tapped Randye on the shoulder. "Oh! I almost forgot!" Randye jumped up. "I have to go get some tickets for something," she laughed. "I'll see you later" more to James than to me, and suddenly it was just the two of us.

"Sea islands," James muttered to his sandwich, shaking his head sadly.

I was afraid he would walk off or turn to one of the other solicitors before I could engage him in a one-on-one conversation, so I shot out the first thing that came into my head.

"It's really amazing how many gay people work here." I said it with a serious reflective lip-biting frown on my face.

He straightened up in his chair. Two of the male solicitors in row seven who overheard me turned around.

"Well . . ." James shrugged. "That's because most gay people really enjoy talking on telephones." He said, it straight-faced and I nodded in enlightenment but the two guys in row seven snickered and I immediately burned red with instant wise-up. James Madison slightly tilted his head while staring at me straight in the eyes as if to telepathically agree with me that I was nothing but a total ass-hole, but my shame was so deep, my defeat so profound, that I just stared right back at him with a helpless crinkled anger, an exasper-ation, a look that said, "I'm *trying*, you motherfucker!"

I cut my lunch short and went back to making calls, my voice dull with despair.

Five minutes later, James Madison tapped my arm. I looked up.

"Meet me in the john." He rose and left the room.

I walked into the multistalled men's room. James Madison stood leaning back against the hot-air dryer, his arms across his chest. I almost gagged on the overpoweringly sweet smell of cherry-scented urinal cakes. I sat on a sink, not looking at him.

"What do you want from me, Peter?" He said it without anger, but also without gentleness. "What do you want?"

I stared at his shoes; orange construction boots, pale yellow at the scuffs.

"I want to be like you . . ." I shrugged with confusion at my own answer.

He squinted at me, his face going through a different expression for every way that that could have been interpreted.

Suddenly I jumped, stammering out, "I don't mean like that," holding my hand out like a stop sign. Fuck. That sounded even worse.

"Like what?"

"You know," I pleaded.

More silence.

"Are you some kind of fag hag?" he inquired politely.

I thought you had to be a woman to be a fag hag. "No, I'm not," I said soberly. "It has nothing to do with that . . . I just think you're a very fucking weird person, you constantly blow my mind, and I like you a lot."

He chewed that one over for a moment, shrugged somewhat disparagingly and began to walk out of the bathroom, his arms still crossed over his chest. Although he didn't say anything to me I could tell he was fighting down a smile. An hour later, he leaned across the partition between us and muttered, "*I'm* fucking weird. . . ."

———

The next morning I sat staring at my phone while James Madison made six calls.

Six not-homes. Six implacably perky "Hi! This is James Madison, calling for WBNF-TV? Is . . . he's not, huh?"'s. All across the room there was that same theatrical "Hi!" from all the booths.

My phone rang twice and I almost shot my knees through the desk slab. I took the first pink slip off the stack of fifty: Watertown, N.Y. The day before I had Queens. Three more goddamn digits to dial. I overheard James Madison imitate Roberta Peters, dropped the phone on my shoulder and started dialing. The receiver had had a gray foam shoulder-cradle a month ago, but I'd developed the habit of picking at the pad until by that week nothing remained except the plastic curved shell which cut into my skin by the end of the day.

"Hi!" The game show host chipperness in my voice always amazed me, given my head. "This is Pete Keller calling for Power Plower, is . . ." I glanced down at the slip. "Tommy . . ." I hesitated. It looked like Tommy Mglxgpyk. Why couldn't they get transcribers who had mastered the alphabet? "Tommy home?"

"Hole on." A young girl shouted back into the house, "Tommeee! Tele-phone! . . . I don't know!" she bitched. "Some guy!" Then back to me, "Who's calling?"

"Pete Keller for Flower Power . . . Power Plower!"

"I don't know!" she shouted back into the house. "Just come get it! I gotta go!" Then came the noise I had come to hate in the last seven weeks more than fascism. The abrupt crack and bang of the dropped receiver followed by the pendulum-paced knock of the receiver swinging on its cord repeatedly smacking into the wall or washing machine. Listening to the rhythmic bangs was like being slowly slapped in the face over and over.

"Yeah?"

"Hey Tommy?"

"Yeah?"

"Hey, this is Peter Keller from Power Plower?"

"From who?"

"From Power Plower."

"Whatta you talkin' about?"

That always happened on that product. Only morons read those magazines.

"Well, Tom . . . my friends at *Pecs and Lats Magazine* got a card from you saying you were interested in hearing more about Power Plower, the complete iso-tensile body-builder in a bar? And they asked me to personally call to give you a little more info on the Power Plower."

"Oh . . . that's that thing . . ."

"That's right, Tom. The Power Plower is based on a system of isometric tension that is guaranteed to make you into the monster of your dreams. Each Power Plower is made of Vulcan forged steel and comes in a portable carrying case complete with instructions for proper use."

"Aw*right!*"

As much as I hated the work it always gave me a rush to score a sale.

"Look, if you want I can mail you out a Power Plower within minutes of this phone conversation, Tom, and if you don't see results all over your body in six months you just mail it back to me and I'll *double* back your money . . . where do you live, Tom?"

"Watertown."

"You can have it at your door in five days. Five days, Tom. I got one right in my hands with your address on it. All I got to do is run down to the post office. You want it?"

"Yeah."

You got it, you putz.

I automatically pulled out an order card, setting it next to the pink call slip.

"Okay, Tom, now the Power Plower is forty-nine ninety-five, and you can pay for it one of two ways. Either just drop us off a check for the whole thing and get the mess over with quick, or if you prefer, you can pay in seven installments of eight dollars each, which between you and me comes out to fifty-six bucks."

"I'll pay for the whole thing in one."

"Smart guy, Tom." I checked "sale" on the pink slip. "Okay now, how do you spell your last name?"

"I thought you had one all made out to me."

"Just doublechecking . . . you know how the mail is."

"I don't know."

"Well, believe me, the mail can get pretty snafued if you know what I mean, now how do you spell your last name?"

"I said I don't know."

"You don't know."

"No." He sniffed absently.

"You don't know." I was smiling. "Um . . . hey . . . that's cool . . . that's okay there, Tom, I understand . . . ah . . . listen, one last question before I mail it out . . . how old are you?"

"Eight."

I threw down my pen in disgust. The kid must have a gland problem. He sounded eighteen.

"Eight, Tom?" I crossed out the "sale" check.

"Yeah."

"Okay, now . . . I don't personally care, Tom, but the law states that you gotta be sixteen years of age to buy a Power Plower over the phone like this, otherwise I need your dad's permission." Forget it. "Is your dad home?"

"Naw, he's workin'."

I checked "call back" on the slip and scribbled "ask for father" after that.

"What time do you expect him back, Tom?"

"Seven?"

"We'll call back then, okay?"

"Yeah." The kid hung up.

Before making the next call, I slowly turned my head to check out Mrs. Himmel who was heads down, wiretapping away. I whispered into the mouthpiece, "Eat it, you slut." No reaction. A little Russian Roulette to spice up the day.

"Hi! This is Pete Keller for Power Plower. Is Jim Timothy home?"

"Jim's dead," an elderly woman answered. "Who is this?"

"Bob Smith for Power Plower," I mumbled, stunned.

"Jim's dead!" She started crying. "What do you want?"

"Nothing. I'm sorry." I hung up, sucking air through my teeth.

James Madison yawned and slid his chair back past the partition so he was behind me. "How ya doin'?" He yawned again, stretching his arms high and arching his back.

I only turned my head. "I just called a stiff."

"Gawd!" He touched his chest with his fingertips and winced like he just opened his lunch box to discover Mom packed him a shit sandwich that day.

I fought down an impulse to edit my dialogue. We were pals now, I was pretty sure.

"How's Julia doing?"

"Julia's dead . . . I'm bored with Julia. I'm thinking of doing celebrity voices immediately and then switching to a tape of *me* making the appeal. You know, like saying, 'Hi, this is Alistair Cooke. Is this Mrs. Ching of Mobile? I have a friend here who'd like to talk to you if you've got a second . . .' and then switching to my own voice. 'Hello, this is James Madison.' " He shrugged.

Randye came in, breathless, late, her arms filled with cassettes again. "Hi yo," she laughed. She stood over her station, stacking and sorting. "How's it going, Peter?" I was pleased and startled that she knew my name.

"I just called a stiff." I grimaced, looking like What Is Death What Is Life.

"Aw . . ." she groaned, tilting her head and narrowing her eyes again. She absently reached out and ran a sympathetic hand through my hair. Her fingernails were bitten down to the limit and her fingertips billowed over the nail line in tender pink puffed arcs.

An hour later after blowing fifteen calls in a row I tapped her on the shoulder. "Randye . . . Randye, do you wanna hook up, go get a movie or some coffee with me?" As I asked her I realized I was grimacing and shaking my head "no."

"Let's have lunch!" she said with sprightly neutrality, Annette to Frankie.

Good enough. Yah hah.

I picked up the phone again, checked out Himmel. "Gonga say you suck big python cock," in a Hollywood Bwana tone.

For the next two hours I fantasized about Randye taking me back to her apartment. I envisioned a tiny studio with a huge brass bed in the Village, cats, a candy dish filled with cocaine—watch them cats. I sold four Power Plowers, including one to a woman. One guy I called didn't want one and then turned around and tried to sell me a car.

Lunch was rough. We went down to a coffee shop in the lobby of the building and as soon as we were seated I got into a riff with the waitress because she freaked at Randye's bringing in a Glad bag of vegetable spears and ordering only tea.

Randye was wearing a souvenir T-shirt of San Francisco that also had a map on it and for a half hour my eyes kept dropping to the small intestine-like twistings of Lombard Street, "The Crookedest Street in the World."

"So James tells me you live in Brooklyn. I've never been to Brooklyn. I'm just a little ol' cowgirl." She guffawed.

I stared at her. Brooklyn. That's right, I lived in Brooklyn.

"It's nice." I shrugged. "What do you mean cowgirl?"

"Aw, I grew up in Montana."

"With the pitchforks and the boots and the dungarees and the guys working for your father's ranch, Lem and Clem and Slim and they saw you flower from a little heifer to a full-grown cow-woman?"

She waited me out. "Nope . . . my father's a gynecologist . . . but I was a champion rider in the junior rodeo!" She nodded encouragingly. She was fucking around with a cucumber sliver and it sprang out of her fingers and flipped across the room.

"But I liked dancing, and I left, and I came here and I'm in a new company, five of us, we're all rejects from other companies, but we're good and we got a grant and I think we're gonna get an even bigger grant than we got now and then I can quit this and take more classes and dance dance dance all the time!"

"Why don't you just get money from your father? The guy's a doctor." Champion rider.

"I don't care. He'd give me money if I wanted. So'd my boyfriend . . ."

Shit.

"He don't like me working, he also don't like me dancing or living by myself . . . I don't think he likes me . . . he's crazy. You should meet him; you know what he does all day? He goes to wine auctions. He's crazy. He bought a two-thousand-dollar bottle of wine last week. That's nuts."

"He's a vintner?" I asked listlessly.

"What's that? I'm dumb." She laughed.

I wasn't sure if a vintner was a wine grower or a liquor store owner, but I meant the owner.

"Oh, naw. He just buys the stuff. He's got a wine cellar in his brownstone."

"So what's he do?"

"I don't know." She shrugged. "He won't tell me. He's crazy. He's got a machine gun in his house . . ."

"Say what?"

Suddenly she became doubly desirable. I wanted to save her and I felt totally intimidated. By her.

"Doesn't that freak you out?" I had ordered a BLT which I hadn't touched yet. Somehow the toast was not just cold but wet.

She pshawed. "He's got guns all over the house. Under cushions, everywhere. The thing is I'm ten times a better shot than him, I'll bet. I don't want to talk about him. I'm pissed off about him but you'd like him. Everybody does. He's okay," she said wearily. "You should see us dance, though . . ."

"You and him?"

"Him! Haw! No, I mean the company. We don't have a name yet. We're thinking of The Great Plains Dance Company because everybody's from the West. You should come see us, you'd love it, we're doing a college tour next month in New Jersey. I'm the smallest person in the company, can you imagine? Bob? In the company? He used to play football for the University of Kansas . . ." She tucked her fists under her armpits and flapped her elbows. I guess that meant something with football.

"You *have* to have played football to catch *me!* . . . You don't eat enough." She nodded at my sweaty sandwich. "I have to lose weight too, but I'm in good shape. Oh! You can come to our rehearsal tomorrow! It's great! You'll love it. It's crazy. Now I work here eight hours a day and rehearse eight hours. I'm going to drop dead. Maybe I should let my boyfriend support me. No! My father. Aw fuck 'em both. But you have to come to the rehearsal tomorrow because frankly, between you and me, you have to get out of the house more."

My gut sank. I felt like a child.

She gave me a half-smile and eyed me craftily. "Right?" she encouraged in a sing song.

"Everybody would really like you. I'll give you the address and everything later. It's a lot of fun . . . everybody gets drunk as shit after. That's why I was so late today. I think you should come. You're funny."

When we got back to the phones I was totally buzzed. I wasn't even thinking about romance. In fact I was surprised at myself for getting turned on to Randye. Despite the fact that I had been surrounded by all that Dancer Ass for almost two months, I didn't see them as flesh and eyes. They existed to me more as symbols, as examples of the singular determination I couldn't get together for myself, and I was too preoccupied, too tense to slip into a lust or romance head. It didn't alarm me; I understood what was going on.

As far as Randye went, I realized I didn't crave her as much as I did the image of me hanging out with that crew of hulky dancers, all of us pirouetting drunkenly into the Manhattan night. I felt pissed at my father, at my bedroom. It was a good invigorating rage, like sucking in mountain air. Ahh . . . the *coun*try, indeed.

James Madison tapped me on the shoulder, one hand over his mouthpiece. "I got it now. . . . Hellauw? Missis Betsy Mims?" He gave me that soul-satisfying wink. "This is Alistair Cooke. Yewshally when you hear me I'm prattling on about the py-*ra*-mids but today I've got a friend here hew'd like to talk to you about something maw urgent" . . . and then in his own voice, "Hi, Mrs. Mims? This is James Madison . . . hello? hello?" He hung up shrugging.

He tried it again and scored for a twenty-five dollar donation.

"Okay, listen up." I made a call with him tilting into my booth.

". . . and if you send us a statement notarized by a doctor that there wasn't at least a six-inch increase all over your body after using Power Plower for three months, we will *double* your money back. You know Steve, I myself started using Power Plower last year, about fifteen minutes a day? Last month I had to go out and buy a whole new wardrobe because none of my clothes fit anymore . . . I even had to buy longer ties . . . and if I'm lyin' I'm dyin'

and my mama's home cryin' . . . that's right . . . tha-at's right . . . and
Steve? I'm gonna tell you something I don't tell many people because I don't like to sound like I'm bragging, but ever since I myself
started using Power Plower about six months ago?" I dropped my
voice. ". . . I can whip the shit out of anybody I know." *That* nauseated me with anxiety, but ka*chang!* it was a sale.

Madison snorted, half-shrugging as if it killed him not to be the
only comic in our row, and he came back with a Jacques Cousteau
appeal for funds. It sounded more like Maurice Chevalier. In any
event, it was a hang-up.

I came back with a Power Plower pitch that included some story
about how I destroyed someone who was hitting on my girl. "So I
says, listen up you jive hump, if I ever see your fucking face . . ."
Ka*chang!* another sale.

Madison countered with a balls-up move. He imitated Chico
Marx, who had been dead many years. No sale.

Suddenly his phone rang twice and we both jumped like kids
caught by God with fuckbooks. Mrs. Himmel was giving him the
crooked doom finger and as he left his desk I sprouted a hatband of
sweat.

He was back at his station in thirty seconds, a pink trembly grin
on his face, his eyebrows in a high frozen arch. "Hmph, the old cunt
caught me," he said out loud to himself.

As he gathered his personal effects, his eyes fluttered in smiley
anger. "Well, one last call." He sat down abruptly, dropped the phone
on his shoulder, and dialed the top number on his stack. "*Hi*, Mister
Jimmy Ray Jackson of Mobile, Alabama? This is James Madison
calling for WBNF the TV station? Do you know it? Fantastic. Well,
Mr. Jackson, I have a friend here who'd like to talk to you about
BNL, BNF, do you have thirty seconds? . . . Terrific." He paused,
scooping up breath. "Hello, I'm James Earl Jones and I'm calling you
on be-*hawf* of your area's public television station . . ." His imitation
was flawless; nasal, masculinely cavernous and dignified. ". . . and so
you see that your public station can-*nawt* continue to survive without
your support, so please, please become a patron of the station . . .
because if you don't we'll send three big niggers around to break your
face . . . thank you." He slammed the phone down and gathered his
shit. "Fuck . . . you!" he hallooed to the glass booth through cupped

hands, then marched down the aisle to the elevator banks. Himmel didn't even look up. I said, "Hey wait!" Other people whistled and applauded, but nobody really gave a shit. It was too common an occurrence. It was a big game with everybody. Besides, they'd all probably see him later at Lincoln Center or the theater or wherever the hell everybody went afterwards.

James Madison marched proud, his chin high like a principled nobleman heading for the guillotine. I slapped my thigh in despair. Randye was in the john. Himmel was already back to wiretapping.

When Randye returned I leaned into her booth and grabbed her arm. "She fired Madison."

"How come?" She slurped from a can of V-8.

"He was doing those calls."

"James . . ." she murmured fondly.

I went back to making straight-script Power Plower calls. A half-hour later, a wraith-like male with oversized tortoise-framed glasses settled into James's chair. He had a soft fuzzy voice like Jiminy Cricket. Suddenly Randye screamed into her phone and half the place turned to her booth, some people standing and peering down their noses to see over the partitions.

Oblivious to the attention she squealed bright-eyed, staring at her pegboard.

"Tracey! I can't believe it! I'm calling from New York. I'm in this place *selling* shit? And your name came up in the stack! Yeah, New York! . . . yup! Still dancin'! I can't believe this! How's Spencer?"

When people got wind of what the hooplah was, they retreated to their booths, some smiling.

When she finally got off the phone, forgetting to ask her friend for a pledge, she touched my arm, "Ain't that a kick in the head?"

Suddenly her line was hit with two rings, and wheeling around she saw Himmel doing her blank-eyed crookfinger routine.

Randye stood hunched over in outrage outside the glass booth. "But that *wasn't* a personal call! Her number was in the stack!"

Himmel pretended that Randye had already hit the streets.

Randye furiously stuffed her shit in her shoulder bag, took her stack of tapes and tossed them on the floor. Her mouth was a tight line and her eyes were glistening with teary outrage. I didn't know what to do. I couldn't think of anything to say. In her anger she was ignoring me. Great Plains Dance Company. Remember, Great Plains Dance Company. She swung her bag over her shoulder and marched out to the elevator bank, her wet eyes straight ahead. She stepped on two of the tossed-off tapes, the plastic cracking nastily under her sneakers. I felt that a sympathetic walk-out on my part would be forced, redundant and bad drama. She didn't even fucking look at me. Great Plains Dance Company. No wait. That was tentative. They didn't have a name yet. They didn't have a goddamn name yet. Sayo-fucking-nara.

Fifteen minutes later, a bald man, deep into his thirties, with a firm animated face, took Randye's booth. I imagined him a Savoyard or some other kind of pleasing hambone. His voice was so loud it was as if the soundproof partition had vanished. I felt immortal and doomed. I would be there forever, my co-workers coming and going like mayflies, all dancing, all singing.

By 4:30, both of the chairs in the adjoining cubicles were creaking and making wooden sputters against the floor as their antsy tenants moved back and forth. My mouthpiece began to have a black plastic bad-breath funkiness that made me swoon. I lost a close sale. The next call was going to a monastery.

"Your mom blows dead Japs under the bridge," I crooned into the receiver, then started dialing. Brother Terence. Brother Deltoids.

A hand on my shoulder. I turned and gasped. Mrs. Himmel stood over me. Tall, peering down, bloodhound-faced, rouge-tinted hanging cheek-flesh under frosted copper hair, eyes somehow blue, yet conveying a dead lights-out-no-one-home-in-the-mercy-department effect. Her hand lay like the flat of a samurai blade on my shoulder.

She didn't say anything, just serenely stared at my forehead, as if she were contemplating what a lovely ashtray the top half of my skull would make. She moved her hand from my shoulder up to my hair, lazily curling her fingers through my locks. My shirt was plastered to my ribs with sweat. I think I might have started getting turned on. After thirty seconds she evenly whispered, "Get out."

As I semi-proudly stomped out on rubbery legs to a few lackadaisical byes and *auf Wiedersehens*, I was suddenly hit with the knee-buckling realization that I was in the midst of my first September since 1954 where I was not in school.

I was amazed at how quickly the sight-and-sound explosion of torrid midday midtown worked on me, making A.C. fade. Walking around, killing time, trying to get my bearings before I headed back up to Yonkers, I felt the honking and the heat weaken my grip on that world up there. I couldn't focus, I couldn't marshal memory, I couldn't exactly remember what Randye or James Madison looked like. Everybody in the street seemed to be walking in the opposite direction or waiting in lines and I felt like shouting Hold it! Hold it! I didn't leave Manhattan until a stuttering Englishman, young, blond and bewildered-looking, came up to me and asked me if I would go fishing with him. I said, "Not now, thanks," and boarded a north-bound bus.

"I walked on that telephone job today."

My father and I were sitting on opposite sides of the green couch watching one of those "You're a piece of shit, Charlie Brown" animated TV specials.

Both of us made self-consciously masculine growls of boredom at the show but we didn't change channels.

"Did you hear me? I quit that job."

"Tch, naa," he groaned mildly. "You jerk."

"I don't know, Pop. I can't imagine any law school's gonna be too snowed by this work year I'm havin'." There was something stagey in my voice. I didn't really feel any great loss for myself. My regret had more to do with disappointing him, hurting him by not being this effective, sensible, pre-law school student adult after all. I think I was experimenting with ways to break it to him that Columbia was out, although I had no idea of what was in.

I sat there, eyeing him, waiting for a reaction.

"I feel ashamed of myself." I winced halfheartedly.

"Well . . ." He raised his eyebrows and shrugged, eyes still on the television. "These things take time, nobody said they didn't."

He shook his cigarette pack to shoot up a few butts past the silver foil and extended them to me.

"Listen . . . ah . . . how would you like to work in the Post Of-fice?" He held a match under my cigarette.

"Come again?" I looked up squinting.

"I said how would you like to work in the ol' P.O.? I think I can swing something with this pal to get you a shot as a mail handler—you know, only temporary, it would be lousy hours, four to midnight with mandatory overtime, but what the hell, you get a ten percent pay differential after ten o'clock, you can save some dough, you know . . . I know this guy . . . you just take the exam and ah . . ." He winked. ". . . we'll fix you up."

The right side of my face started freezing up on me. I saw in the veined mirror alongside my head that I was half smiling. When he said "We'll fix you up," I imagined the "We" as a team of masked surgeons. My eyes glossed over and I had to blink them back into focus.

My father was sitting with his leg crossed over his thigh, not looking at me, just slowly smoking and thinking something at the coffee table.

"That's not gonna do too much to impress Columbia." My tongue felt like wet wool.

He shrugged. "Well, look, you gotta be practical . . . it's a rough situation out there now with jobs . . . so you worry about Columbia later."

Charlie Brown tore ass downfield to kick a football held by Lucy. She pulled it away at the last second and he landed on his head. Just smack the bitch, Charlie Brown.

———

Things continued to sink.

Three weeks later I was a postal worker, assigned to the huge G.P.O. on Eighth Avenue and Thirty-Third Street. I worked in a gloomy light-green railroad station-sized room under dream-like grimy overheads. I sat on a slanted high stool in front of a conveyor belt and a big sorting grid like the mail box plan of an apartment building. Gray plastic bus boxes stuffed with city mail would come down the belt for us to sort into zip codes. There was a row of twenty of us working on our slanted stools. We couldn't talk and we had to keep one foot on the lowest rung of the stool at all times. We had to punch out to take a leak, and once you got to the bathroom the merciless fluorescents made your reflection look as though you had blueberry chips imbedded in your face. It was like working on the wrong side of the Berlin Wall.

Sometimes when I spaced out, I would look up from my fistful of mail, up toward a corner of the celestial ceiling of the amphitheater and into the windows of Postal Heaven, a narrow room that was wedged into a corner under the ceiling like a press box over a stadium. The room seemed to be some kind of observation post but the guys I would see loping back and forth up there, the Postal Gods, never seemed to look down at us in the pit.

My first paycheck, covering a two-week period, was for four hundred and seven dollars. That was the first time in my life I had taken home over two hundred dollars a week. For a thank-you present I went out and bought my father a forty-dollar full-color coffee table book on World War II.

Even though my shift was supposed to pack it in by twelve we were rarely allowed to leave before two A.M., so more or less I was part of the midnight shift, and the midnight shift was manned by midnight people; bull dykes, transvestites with five o'clock shadow, shy young pasty-faced Clark Kent heads with patchy mustaches and dreams of Jack the Ripperhood, a half-dozen straight tough Puerto Rican chicks who were into having fist fights with each other on the coffee breaks, and a sprinkling of older guys with seniority whose notion of having it made was doing next to nothing and getting paid for it.

It was the flip side of A.C. People had dreams of going to refrigerator-repair school, private-investigator school, getting on the day shift. The place was a lotus land, all desire, all anxiety, strictly nickel and dime, and to save myself from the seductive mediocrity surrounding me I re-embraced my original law school game plan; stand-up globe, pipe racks and all.

At first I wouldn't talk to anybody, half out of snobbery and half out of some contract with myself to be solo and in pain as long as I held the gig, as if cracking a smile or getting into a conversation would taint my aspirations. But I would listen to people, eavesdrop. Every night I would go into the vending machine room on my breaks and sit one Formica table away from four guys my age, three

P.R.s and a disco Ginny, and I'd suck coffee while they acted out favorite movies and talked irons in the fire. Every once in a while I'd go out on Ninth Avenue and watch the Ricans duke it out, but mostly I'd satellite that foursome in the Bird of Paradise room, going yes no yes no to myself like a fourteen-year-old at his first dance.

It took a stroke book for me to break the ice. One night I had found a coverless *Oui* magazine on my usual chair, and after listlessly thumbing through the greasy nudes I came across something that made me squawk loud enough for everybody in the room to jump.

"It's got a scratch-and-sniff centerfold," I apologized.

Heads jerked back in chorus.

"Yeah, I ain't kidding!"

The next thing I knew I was hunched over their table and all five of us were staring at an oil-drenched spread-legged waify blonde, her eyes shut against the sun, her thick French lips forming a dreamy meaty O. She was nude except for a cockeyed baseball cap and bright yellow knee socks and there was a peel-off tab over her twat. Nobody lifted a finger to remove it. "She's nice," one of them said mildly. We all started thumbing through the magazine. I pulled up a chair, ready to lay them low with a devastating riff on every picture, every cartoon, but the mood was one of studiousness, four sets of sober beetlebrows poring over the pages as if it was the Talmud. When in Rome, and all that. So I held my tongue as long as I could, trying to come off self-possessed and absorbed, as if I had never seen a picture of a tit before, or as if the five of us were so tight that words were extraneous, but in fact I couldn't focus on one nude, one body part, one pubic hair or eyeball.

After ten minutes of silence I couldn't stand it anymore and I just exploded.

"Aw, man . . ." They looked up at me, a ring of neutral but polite expressions. "Do you guys remember the first time you scoped out a stroke book?" I reared back and squinted at them. "I was living in Yonkers? And there was this dude named Jay Jay? He had this fucking tuxedo store, Bold Men Tuxedos? It was fucking boss. The window had all these out*rage*ous vines, nice colors, one time I went in there? I was about nine. I wanted to buy some links for my old man, you know, for Father's Day? Jay Jay had this fucking stack of *Play-*

*boy*s, man, yea high." I held my hand palm down, as if it was resting on the head of a five-year-old. "The dude was wrappin' up the links and I'm like this . . ." I cocked my head, narrowed my eyes and made as if I was furtively flipping through the edge of the imaginary stack. ". . . I can't see shit and I was too fuckin' scared to open 'em up . . . so the dude sees me peekin' but he don't say shit or nothin', but when I'm out the door? You know, like heading home? He goes 'Yo kid . . .'" I tilted my head as if beckoning someone over to sell them a bad watch. "So I go back to the store? and Jay Jay's starin' over my head, he's just lookin' out at the traffic, and he says, 'Gimme ya book' and he takes my fuckin' loose-leaf and he slips a *Playboy* in the math section and he says, 'You gonna let your mother find this?' I was in fuckin' shock . . . I walk all the way home, turn around and walk awwl the way back to Jay Jay's, duck my fuckin' nine-year-ol' head in his door, drop my goddamn voice and say, 'Thanks, man.' "

The back-to-work buzzer rang and the table broke without comment. I felt about as low as I could get.

As we walked back to the stools one of the Puerto Ricans tapped my arm.

"You go to college, right?"

"I graduated."

"*Gra*duated?" He reared back. "Where'd you go?"

"Ah, Simon Straight," I mumbled, to make it sound like it wasn't all it was cracked up to be.

"You went *there?*" he said wide-eyed, and despite myself I felt proud.

"Shit!" He shook his head. "That's a*maz*ing, man . . . you know? Because my fucking sister goes to Bronx Community and she speaks better English than you."

For the next two hours I glowed with molten concentration, never taking my eyes off my endless mail call, not even punching out for a whiz or a cigarette on the pot. I felt like an ant.

When we all clocked out at two A.M. the Puerto Rican guy came up to me again.

"Did you really go to that school?"

"Yeah."

"Because my sister really *does* talk better than you . . . what you major in?"

"English." I laughed.

"God-*damn!*" He shook his head sadly and grabbed my elbow, gently, urging me to walk and talk with him as we made our way to the street. "What's your name?"

There was something scoutmasterly and paternal in his tone, but I didn't find it totally unpleasant.

We went over to a Treaty Stone bar where some of the night shift caught one for the road if they got off before last call. The place had a glass brick front and red-and-blue neon piping between the mirrors. My man's name was Nelson Maldonado.

"So what are you doing in the P.O. if you went there, you gonna work your way up to Postmaster General?"

"Naw, my father works at Grand Central . . . he's a philatelist's agent."

"A what?" Nelson ducked his head low, as if to peer up my nostrils.

"He sells stamps." I blushed. "He got me this gig . . . I'm going to law school."

"That's good, that's good." He nodded. "Be a corporation lawyer, man, they make the most money."

We sat and drank. I felt relaxed. The Merry Mailman.

"So you grew up in Yonkers, hah? Westchester." He winked and clicked his tongue. "High . . . on the . . . *hog!*" He raised his hand for a slap.

"Whoa, whoa." No slap coming. I put up both hands in front of my chest. "No fuckin' way . . . it's like a housing project, are you kidding me?"

"As you were, men," he said to himself, lowering his hand to his drink.

"No way . . . in fact, I was in the Bronx until I was ten."

"Yeah? I don't know the Bronx too well. I'm from Brooklyn."

"Oh yeah . . . oh yeah . . . I'm not talking Riverdale either . . . We're talkin' tenement town . . . it was all *your* people . . ." I tilted my chin at him. "That *bad* element."

"You know Jackie Gleason? He's from my neighborhood, man."

"That's great, does he come back and visit often?"

"Right." He smirked, no jerk.

"You know, my mother died watching 'The Honeymooners'?"

"Are you *ser*ious?" He hunched forward in astonishment, his short hair making him look like a snake.

Sometimes the semi-joke of "Beat the Clock" didn't seem that funny to me, not that "Honeymooners" was that much better, but I mainly switched titles to make the conversation dovetail. If he had said Bud Collyer was from his neighborhood I would have been perfectly happy to give him the truth.

"Do you think about that now, you know, when you watch that show? You know, do you think of her?"

I shrugged. I was moved by the way Nelson said "her." Very gently, very respectfully. I felt a strong rush of friendship.

We went back into silence, both sitting face-to-face, sidesaddle on the bar stools. I noticed that he had one foot on the lowest rung, Post Office style, and I felt like crying.

When I looked up at him I saw that he was staring down at my shoes. I realized that I had my leg propped just like him and that he was thinking the same sad thought about me. Fucking, fucking job. He gave me a small smile, then frowned at his knuckles. "You know, sometimes I get this picture in my head of everybody in there working in those paper hospital gowns."

The image was so nauseating, so correct, that I just turned to the bar and dropped my head on my arms like a burned-out lush. Corporation lawyer. Hospital gowns.

I felt Nelson's shoe on the back of my heel gently knock my foot loose from the bottom rung of the bar stool.

"Hey . . ." He flicked my arm with his fingers. "That's not us, man . . . you wanna hear what *I* got goin'?"

"No." I sat up, though.

"I got an application in at the Police Academy . . . I'm gonna be a fucking cop, man. You know why? Because I wanna work with suicides . . . jumpers . . . you know, the guy that goes out on the ledge and raps to jumpers? I'd be good at that because I understand people. People think I'm nuts because bein' a cop is so dangerous. That's bullshit man, more firemen die. My *brother's* nuts, he's gonna be a fireman, but dig, after twenty years I can quit at half-pay, he can quit at half-pay being a fireman and then me an' him can go into business together. You know what we gonna do? We're gonna open a dating service with computers and everything. You come in to us for a date you don't just get a name and an address and wind up with some fucking mule with syph and pointy teeth. You come in, sit down, we'll show you videotaped interviews with the chicks. Same for the chicks, they come in they see tapes too, so they don't wind up with some guy with cysts on his face, or glasses . . . or some *big* fuckin' coconut. Look, I'll take on everybody who comes to us because I believe beauty seeks its own level . . . what you find attractive I'd probably vomit on . . ."

I started to laugh. What a shmegeg.

He put out a placating hand. "Or the other way around . . . anyway that's twenty years from now. I gotta be a cop first . . . they said I'm gonna hear this week . . . because *this* fucking place sucks *any* way you cut it, right?" He cocked his hand behind his ear, waiting for me and we smacked palms sidearm, letting the grip sway in the space between us. Made my night.

Me and Nelson developed a Silent Tightness, a Limited Best Friendship. We never got together again one-on-one, never had another drink after work, and I'm not sure why, because every time I saw him I felt that tingling of possibilities that you feel around an intense new friend. And I knew he was feeling it too, because every time we looked at each other we both quickly turned away, fighting down knowing smiles. I didn't know what the problem was. It wasn't racial and it wasn't fear of sexual attraction to a guy, because that never entered my head except in the most abstract way like it does with anybody with half a brain. To tell the truth, I think I just felt too beat down and depressed to pursue anything that was going to demand any intensity out of me. Nonetheless, even though we only hung out as part of a loose group, we still helped each other out on a daily basis to ego-survive the Post Office, him by letting me know he understood me, and me by letting him know that I *understood* that he understood me; that neither of us were total shmucks, per se.

One day Nelson didn't show. At the coffee break one of the Puerto Ricans said Nelson wouldn't be coming back; his appointment to the Police Academy had come through.

———

On Halloween night, my father went to a postal union meeting and I found myself alone with Vy. I didn't feel like watching TV, and as she sat in the living room going through a carton of Larks and guarding the bag of little Snickers bars for the munchkins that rang our bell, I wandered around the apartment looking for trouble. When I was a kid I went on the mandatory search for rubbers through my father's dresser, scoring a half-empty box of Ramses, and for a six-month stretch I let go of the Hanging Judge project to declare myself a future Egyptologist.

A few years after my mother's death I checked that drawer again and found an unopened box of Natural Lambs and two *Playboy*s. I periodically checked the box after that to see if the seal was cracked. It never was, although the magazines kept changing, and depending on my mood, it alternatively relieved and disturbed me.

That night I wound up at the dresser again but found no rubbers and no *Playboy*s. I raided Vy's drawers and discovered a diaphragm case. I lifted out the diaphragm and read the size off the rim. I was amazed to find she took a whopping 85. Maybe she wore it as a night-cap. Next to the case under a tidy cone of padded bras was a paper-back of Henry Miller's *Sexus*. I had the same damn edition in my bookcase. On the inside of the cover she had written "Property of Vivian Keller." That simple inscription knocked me out more than the diaphragm. I had never seen her name written in her own hand before; never thought of her as taking the name Keller. I put every-thing back, went into the living room, and sat down on the couch.

"Hey Vy?"

She automatically reached for her cigarette case and presented it to me.

"Nah. Hey, listen . . . do you remember when I came back from school we were supposed to have lunch? We never did that. Is to-morrow good?"

Trick or Treaters rang our bell, and I shot up, grabbing the Snickers bag and feeling like a chastened Scrooge heady with the joy of giving.

The next day I didn't wake up until eleven o'clock. On my days off I always tried to be out of the house by ten to fight off the Gregor Samsas and the flabbyness of the hour hit me like a hangover.

All the way down on the subway to Forty-Second Street I was moaning a whyoh-whyoh-why mantra. I needed a lunch with Vy like I needed more television in my life. I got off at Times Square

and walked two blocks west before I grudgingly admitted to myself
that I was headed in the wrong direction. I worked my way back
through a gauntlet of bad guys hissing out their inventory of mood
regulators under the shade of movie marquees. When I was a senior
in high school I bought a joint on the street that turned out to be
freeze-dried bacon bits; a fast two-dollar education.

I killed some time window-shopping a display of deflated love
dolls, the heads resting squarely on their folded bodies. They were of
both sexes. The male model looked like Mark Spitz complete with
singles-bar mustache; the female sported a dowdy blond Dutch milk-
maid flip. All the dolls had dead pop eyes and lips molded in a generous O like startled goldfish.

Somebody came behind me and offered acid, grass, ludes and
coke. I moved down two storefronts and checked out a display of
at least a hundred foreign brands of cigarettes. Someone else behind my back started barking, "Coke! Coke! Coke!" like a chained
dog.

Coke. I only did coke twice in college. Each time I wound up
happily babbling, "I don't *feel* anything, do *you?*" Maybe if I did
some before meeting Vy, lunch would be survivable. I didn't consider myself street smart, but I hadn't just staggered out of Penn
Station for the St. Patrick's Day Parade either. I'd heard enough
about scoring coke on the street to expect 90 percent baby laxative,
but it still could be worth shitting my brains out to make it through
the next ninety minutes. I decided to chance it and immediately
experienced a psychosomatic coke trill. I live for danger. I passed
on a half-dozen dealers who were either too loud or too freaky-
looking. One grim Carib wearing a backwoods Cuffney cap
snapped out, *"Coke!"* and it sounded to me like *"Kill!"*

I was just about to punk out when I noticed a café au lait spade
leaning calmly against the window of a souvlaki palace. He wore
razor-creased cuffed chinos and a crisp white T-shirt, the chest emblazoned with an iron-on full-color head of Marcus Garvey. He had
a full square flat-topped Afro, clipped and groomed with topiary
precision. I couldn't tell if he was a dealer, but when he caught me
studying him he started crooning: "Ludes, grass, coke, boys, girls,
automatic weapons, Sabin vaccine, Broadway twofers, my cherry

sister, *your* cherry sister." As he ran it down, his voice became progressively musing and ironic.

A three-digit IQ. I didn't know whether to do business with him or just hook up and catch a Truffaut film.

"That Marcus Garvey?"

"Now you *know* it's Garvey, right?" He twisted his lips into a wry beleaguered smirk.

"You know you guys all look the same to us Cape Codders. How's the toot?" Coming from my mouth, the word "toot" sounded so embarrassingly Mod Squad I had to stifle an apology.

Despite the quippy tone, my kneecaps were running like motorized pumps.

"The *toot?*" He squinted incredulously. "Where you from, Boston University?"

"Give me a break. I'm here for a convention. So how is it?"

"How's the *toot?* It's right out of a diplomatic pouch. The shit's got wings . . . do you believe me?"

"No? Yes?" I shrugged like a white guy.

"No." Someone walked between us and tried to sell him grass. My man waited him out like he was so much sound pollution, a passing truck with a busted muffler.

". . . but it ain't cut with Ajax and it ain't cut with speed. Ten for a party favor. Fifty for the family size."

Ajax.

I followed him into the outer lobby of an office building, both of us gazing out at the street and doing the transaction without moving anything but one lower arm, our hands blindly thumb wrestling, exchanging paper down by our thighs.

When we strolled back outside I asked him if he went to B.U. He answered with a weary drawn out "Puh-leeze" and walked away.

I headed east. Vy's bank was on Second Avenue. Between Sixth and Fifth I ducked into a hectic deli, but I was too paranoid to head right for the bathroom, so I bellied up to the take-out counter and bought a Chinese cookie. It was as big as a forty-five record, with a hard chocolate splat in the center. I sat down at a shaky table and made a big show of scarfing down every crumb.

The coke was folded up in a quarter of a page from *Newsweek;*

the thin streak of powder cutting across a photo of some African little Napoleon addressing his color guard.

I did it up with my fingertips, and when I walked out I probably looked like I had been in there twirling pizza dough.

It started off nice. I strode toward the East Side with a chest like a weight lifter and my head bursting with golden options. Vy was a super teller. In fifteen years she'd never made a counting error. I admired that but I never said so. She loved Billie Holiday. I had always wanted to get into Lady Day. I passed a record store and decided to buy her an album, but the minute I stepped inside something in me collapsed. The fluorescent overheads, combined with the inane mountains of no-talent albums in the discount bins shoved me out the door backwards.

As I walked toward Madison I heard myself involuntarily mutter, "Down, down, down."

By Lexington I started feeling impatient and hyper. Everything seemed too slow to be believed: red lights, stunned pedestrians, the time it took to get to the next red light.

When I finally reached the bank I felt like crying. Every object, every human seemed maddeningly static. My stomach was screaming, "I *hate* cookies!" and I felt like someone was shaking me by the scruff of the neck. I was trembling and kept shooting out my knees like I was about to do the limbo rock. That cocksucker must have slipped me enough speed to wake up a corpse.

Vy was working a lunch-time line of businessmen. I watched her count out a stack of bills, the money whipping between her hands as fast as newspapers shooting out of a printing press. When she saw me standing across the carpeted room by the desk area she gave me a quick smile, turned to her boss, chucking a thumb in my direction, and then held up two fingers to me before taking on the next customer. I sat down on a Naugahyde couch ten yards from a bank executive who thank God ignored me, and I rifled through an unbearable stack of magazines. Even the cartoons seemed too busy for ingestion.

After what seemed like two hours of waiting, Vy finally emerged on the civilian side of the counter. Walking briskly, we headed for a Greek luncheonette. I had to restrain myself from breaking out in a trot. Every twenty yards I asked her how far we had to go.

The luncheonette was called Two Guys from Corfu.

One wall was covered with the obligatory serene Grecian sea-port mural, heavy on the azure, but outside of that, there was nothing about the room conducive to chewing and digestion. The place was totally in synch with my state, and right up Vy's normal metabolic alley.

Under a nonstop sound track of clattering dishes and pidgin English barks to the grill, waiters in short-sleeved shirts zipped around balancing plates straight up to the biceps like they were racing a stopwatch in a game-show stunt. It seemed as if every customer was chain-smoking. The minute we sat down I started reeling like a weighted punching toy, my eyeballs bugging. Vy picked up on me in seconds and instinctively responded to my crazed vibrations with her own. Between us we made the table rattle like a freight train.

"I only got forty-five minutes for lunch." She winced at her watch.

"No problem." I touched my head to the table.

The menu looked unconquerable, everything seemed too heavy. There was no fucking way I could eat.

"I'm so glad you're here." Vy gave me a pained look and lit a Lark.

"Do me a favor, order me a Greek salad, okay? I gotta go to the bathroom."

I bolted from the table, almost colliding with a loaded-down waiter, and locked myself in the john. I sat on the pot, my face in my hands, and had a jet-propelled attack of diarrhea.

When I returned to the table, the food was already there, and I was confronted by an enormous oblong plate hosting a mountain of pale lettuce, whiskered strips of anchovy and meteor-sized chunks of feta cheese. At least the check was down too.

"They ran out of olives." She looked distraught.

"That's okay."

"You could send it back."

"It's okay." I started clicking my tongue against the roof of my mouth.

"They'll take it back."

"I can't *bear* olives!"

"You can have my lunch if you want." She had some kind of creamed meat sandwich.

"It's perfect, I swear."

Vy grabbed the hairy forearm of a passing waiter. "Nick . . . this is my stepson."

He gave me a tight bow. "Nice lady," tilting his head to her like he had water in his ear. A jewel of perspiration quivered on the top of his nose.

"Nick, he ordered Greek salad. There's no black olives? Jimmy said they ran out. I never heard of that . . ." She shrugged in confusion.

He hissed sadly. "Delivery strike."

"But this is my stepson!"

I buried my hands in my face again.

"I *kill* them for you." He raised his chin and ran a thumb across his throat.

"You don't have any in the basement or anything?"

"Vy . . ." I couldn't stop the clicking.

Nick vanished.

"I don't understand, they're so good in here."

Before I could answer, Nick reappeared, laying down a monkey dish with extra anchovies. "On me because I *love* you. *Crazy* about you."

Vy flushed with soulful relief, her eyes more moist than usual.

I stared at the food as though it was an exam I hadn't prepared for. Vy gingerly touched the rim of her plate.

"You liked Billie Holiday, right?" I picked up a piece of lettuce with my fingers and put it down again.

"Billie Holiday? Oh . . . I used to wear a flower behind my ear like her for years." She touched her earlobe with trembling fingers. It struck me that she wasn't just being a typical Jewish mother with the olives. She was genuinely out of her mind.

"What kind of flower? Vy, I can't eat. I'm sorry." I touched my temples and widened my eyes to get more air around the rims.

"I can't either." She dropped her arms on either side of her plate. Relieved, I did the same. There was a spastic eloquence in our hands. Our twitches seemed so synchronized that if we could have gotten the rest of our bodies into the act we could have won a jitterbug contest.

"Did you fall in love with my father right away?"

"He's the kindest man in the world, your father."

What else, what else. How's life. How's tricks. How's how's how's . . .

"Vy, I'm on drugs right now." My face crinkled. I felt embarrassed.

She got very still, not even blinking.

"It's okay. You can shake if you want." I laughed. As soon as I confessed I felt calmer.

"Are you addicted?" Still unblinking, she started chewing her thumbnail.

"No no no." I let my laugh get hearty. "I just did something stupid. I bought cocaine in Times Square. It had a lot of stimulants in it, but it's okay, it's like taking too many diet pills. Everybody in college does it, you can't get your diploma unless you've done it. It's okay. Don't tell my father. I feel better already. Tell me about Billie Holiday. I almost bought you a record, don't worry about it." I almost felt happy. I even touched an anchovy.

Vy reached across the table and put a hand on my forehead. She was wearing a chain bracelet and a gold Statue of Liberty tickled my nose.

"Vy, you don't get fever. You just get jumpy."

"What did you do in the bathroom?"

"I had diarrhea, it's nothing." I never saw Vy so calm.

"Do you want me to take you to the hospital?"

"Oh no, no." I pshawed and leaned back in my seat crackerbarrel style. "'God Bless the Child Who's Got His Own.' That's Billie Holiday, right? Let's just talk . . ."

"What do you feel . . . what's going on inside you?"

My first impulse was to say, "I feel like you." Maybe I didn't get burned after all. For ten dollars I was learning what it was like to have to live in Vy's body.

"Just jumpy, jumpy. Maybe I should have a beer, a drink. That works against it. What do they have here, Ouzo? Retsina?"

Vy plopped her purse in her lap and started burrowing around. At first I thought she was digging for money, still bent on taking me to a hospital, but she came up with two amber prescription bottles.

"Here." She took a pill from each. "This is a Valium, this is a Compazine for your bowels. Take them while I'm sitting here."

She slid her water across the table, disregarding my own glass, and absently nodded approval, her front teeth glistening between her slightly parted lips, as I downed the trancs.

"Let me call the bank and I'll take you home."

"It's totally unnecessary, *to*-tally . . ."

"Then here . . ." She nose-dived into the purse again and came up with a twenty-dollar bill. "Take a cab. Promise me, and don't have a drink . . . you could make trouble for yourself."

I picked up the check and shoved it in her face. "No, let *me* pay, I insist . . ." If she had laughed, my chaos would have been complete.

"Let me see just one more time." She put her hand on my forehead again, the Statue of Liberty resting on the bridge of my nose like a soothing amulet.

———

For the next week at some point in each evening Vy would corner me and whisper, "How are you feeling?" or "Did you have any flashbacks?" her eyes metronoming across my face for the truth. She would never crack a smile, never admit by word or expression that it was really a courtship, an excuse for intimacy. One night she was feeling so comfortable with me she said, "That was so stupid. I'm so mad at you I can't tell you." I loved it.

After the drug crisis ran its course, we were both at a loss for another topic and began to fade from each other for a week or so until she got it into her head to be my pimp. She would come home with flyers announcing singles weekends, or clip ads for dating services and leave them on my desk, but I wouldn't have any of it. I found that route both embarrassing and beneath me; I was no Marty. Besides, the Post Office was pounding me into the ground, and I had no sex drive. I didn't want to do the Hi there's. Also, I worked a lot of nights, weekends too; it was hard to score at breakfast. But all that aside, my deepest resistance came from the creepy realization that Vy's campaign was just like the project I had been on when I was a teen-ager—getting my father to break bread with a woman. I was becoming my old man—a celibate numb-nuts, working in the Post Office and staring at the tube night after night. I had lost my cutting edge, the adrenaline outrage I felt at A.C., and I couldn't drum up the necessary fury to blast out of the muck. I felt like someone freezing to death; I knew what was happening, but I felt so sleepy—let me just lie here for a few centuries. Rebuffing Vy's offers for a good time was the only form of protest I seemed capable of; I was afraid that in my present state, if I were to go to one of Vy's fun fests I'd probably pick up some girl, score a hand job, and get married.

———

I woke up one day in November, had brunch and watched some afternoon TV, my usual ritual before heading off to the Post Office, when it dawned on me that I had not missed one day of work since starting out in the late summer. I undressed and got back in bed, imagining Randye and James standing side by side near my desk like the ghost team in *Topper*, witnessing my crummy stasis, clucking their tongues and emitting a tandem "Awwww."

The next day, after punching in and starting to work my grid, the crew foreman, pointing up to Postal Heaven, told me I had to see a Mr. Franco in Personnel. I vaulted up the stairs thinking that maybe somebody found my resumé and I was being transferred to a desk job.

Opening the door to Postal Heaven, the first thing I saw was a giddy shot through the opposite wall window of the pit below, looking like a grimy ant farm. The room I found myself in consisted of a row of government-issue dark green dented metal desks and swivel chairs, a middle-aged lifer working inside each ensemble. All the lifers seemed to have this uniform of oversized white short-sleeved shirts, crepe-soled shoes and some kind of chinos or trousers, belted up two inches below the breastbone like who cares anymore. They were unruffleable and quiet, moving around as if they were silently humming to themselves some not-on-the-program tune. I asked some bespectacled lump for Franco. He jerked a thumb to the desk way back against the wall, the only one without a window view of downstairs, the only one that had a chair set up for interviews. And there he was: a rat with bifocals staring up his nose at me, his hands clasped against his lips, elbows on his bare forest-green metal desktop. He had dyed black hair, parted and flattened like Fearless Fosdick, a little whippet of a dyed mustache and a sharp triangle of a nose.

He stared unwaveringly at me as I made my way down the lane

of desks to my waiting seat. Behind him taped to the green wall
was a calendar open to November with a photo of the Capitol Dome
with close up out-of-focus cherry blossoms in the foreground. As I
sat down he said, "Where were you yesterday." His voice was as flat
as a talking computer.

"I was out. I had a throat cold . . ."

He slammed the desk with the flat of his palm and started shout-
ing at me: "YOU MOTHERFUCKING LITTLE LIAR YOU THINK
YOU CAN COME IN HERE LIE YOUR WAY INTO A FEDERAL
JOB AND PISS ON ALL OUR REGULATIONS JUST BECAUSE
YOU WENT TO COLLEGE YOU GET THE FUCK DOWN
THERE AND DON'T EVER LET ME SEE YOU UP HERE
AGAIN."

I was grinning in shock. He was screaming at me in an absolute
monotone. Not only that, but after the slammed palm and short outburst he did not move one muscle anywhere in his head or body.
The other desk zombies just went about their business, not so much
as missing a stroke or raising an eyebrow.

As I slowly rose from my seat, swirls of perspiration matting my
shirt to my stomach, I saw, extending from his shoulder blade, what
I at first took for the white ridged grip of a dagger. It was one of the
rear handles on his wheelchair. As I rubberlegged my way past the
other desks I caught an aerial glimpse of my vacant slant stool. I
turned to scope out Franco before I left the room; he had resumed
his original position, hands clasped to his mouth, elbows on his
spotless objectless desk top, but now his eyes seemed unfocused,
sunk into his head as if he had picked up on the interior loony tune
that was the rage of the room.

Downstairs, whipping through busbox after busbox, I now understood why the absentee rate was so low, although I had a marginal
thought that Franco's tactics might not be legal. I wondered if my father ever had to go and see him. I envisioned Franco chewing my old
man out, me bursting in and flinging him, wheelchair and all, through
the window into a stack of busboxes and slant stools far below.

————

On my next vacation, six days later, the phone woke me up.

"Pete . . ."

"Yes! Hello! . . . who's this?" I cleared the crud from my eyes as the digital on my bedside flapped to 11:11.

"It's Tommy."

"Tommy . . ." Tommy? "Bam-Bam!!"

"How you doin', guy?"

"Where *are* you? You're back! How was Italy? Oh, great! you're back!"

"It was good."

"How long you been back? I can't believe it, are you home?"

"I'm down here now."

"Here, where . . ."

"The school . . ."

"Columbia?" I thought he meant here, Yonkers, here, my house.

"I'm really doin' it, Pete."

"How come you didn't call before?"

"Oh man, they've been busting my nates, killing me to death."

"Are you having a hard time?" My voice got gentle.

"Actually, I'm doing pretty good."

I felt disappointed.

"You know, but it's like fucking *work*, Jim . . . my brain's flayed . . ."

"So how long you been back?"

"Three months more or less. When we getting together?"

"Name it and claim it." I felt low. Three fucking months. Pick up a goddamned phone, my friend.

"What's tomorrow like?"

"Tomorrow's good . . . you want to meet up by you in Scarsdale?"

"Well, I got a place by the school. I only go home every other week or so for dinner. . . . Why don't you come down to Columbia? I'll be bookin' all day. I'll show you the law school. It's a trip."

"Sure."

"Three o'clock good?"

"Yup."

"You know how to get here?"

"I'll find it."

"We're on . . . I'll meet you in front of the law school. It's on Amsterdam and 116th."

"No problem."

"So how's everything with you, good?"

"Yup." I was pissed.

"Okay, I got to split . . . three o'clock."

"Yup."

After hanging up I jumped out of bed, took a brisk shower, ate a brisk breakfast and moved through the rest of the day with brisk aimlessness.

Going down to Columbia, I took the wrong subway and wound up in Harlem, my mood alternating between anger at his three-month wait and bafflement at my own blanking out on him for the same time period.

I had never seen the Columbia campus and was surprised at its meagerness. Simon Straight had been like a National Park; Columbia couldn't even make it as a Simon Straight parking lot.

I walked across the central red brick esplanade, scowling at the buildings. The main quad was bookcased in between two huge granite fortresses that were as boring as a Sunday afternoon in February; 1950s migraine bleary. Every student looked like a science-fair finalist. A horn-rimmed middle-aged woman wearing a sari under her coat stopped me to ask where Dodge Hall was. I actually knew; I had passed it coming in through the iron gates, but I just shrugged and kept walking. I felt like a shit, though, and it took all the fight out of me. It wasn't Bam-Bam. It wasn't the architecture. I was walking through Columbia University, home of Peter Keller's rejection letter, and I found myself surrounded by thousands of people who had been accepted, who were not working the Post Office, who were superior human beings.

I spotted Bam-Bam before he saw me. It was a cold December day, the sidewalk scabbed with patches of dirty ice, but he was coat-less, dancing in place to keep warm. He wore cuffed chinos, loafers, a pin-striped shirt with the starched cuffs neatly folded up to the forearms, and a soft navy blue sleeveless pullover. His hair was cut short, out of his face for the first time since high school. I was used to his dressing like a greaser Sammy Davis Jr., everything skin-tight and shiny, but now he looked like a catalogue model for a menswear chain with branches in Cambridge and Georgetown. Trouble.

I took a deep breath. "Yo, College!"

"Pete!"

We hugged and slapped backs.

He'd lost a lot of weight, too.

"Shit, man, you look like you just stepped out of *Love Story*."

"The new me." He took my arm and walked me into the building.

"The new you . . ."

With his hand on my arm I felt as though I was being escorted back to my hospital bed. He steered me into a student lounge, one wall a solid bank of thrumming vending machines. There were a few blasted-looking vinyl couches, some plastic aqua and salmon bowling-alley chairs and white "mod" coffee tables scattered about under nightmare fluorescents. It looked just like the "R&R" room at the P.O. There were a dozen law students about, and I didn't like the looks of any of them. The women seemed dowdy and out of it; totally straight, heavy smokers with too-short bell bottoms and loafers; bangs with barrettes. The men seemed anxious and unplayful, acne pits glowing with radiation under the overheads. James Madison would drop dead here. Randye would laugh the room into the sick bay. I felt a combination of intimidation and righteous contempt. I fuck law school where it breathes. These people were walking bad breath. These people were going places.

"So . . ." Bam-Bam leaned back on a couch and smiled at me. I was sitting in a light blue plastic hand. "I tell you, babycakes, you don't know what work *is* . . ." He absently scraped a thumbnail across his brow.

I would have felt better if he had said *we* didn't know what work is. He had been the laziest fuck in the history of Straight College.

He put both his legs up on the couch and leaned his head back against the armrest. Maybe I should have brought him a nice cold compress.

"I tell you, Pete, I been thinking about you . . ."

"Yeah?"

"Maybe you should have gone to St. John's after all. . . . It's not that bad a school . . . three borough DAs are St. John's graduates." He threw an arm over his eyes.

"Yeah? Maybe I should have gotten myself a recommendation from George Meany . . ."

"I knew the guy, Pete . . ." He lifted his head a few inches.

I felt bad. It was a low blow. "You want a creamsicle, B.B.?" I stood up digging into the front pocket of my dungarees.

"I said knew him, Pete."

"Right, right, forget it."

Now I had to buy myself a creamsicle.

———

"So how's work?" He sat up a little bit, his arms propped on the armrests, making his chest jut. He looked dazed, uninterested in his own question. No doubt law school was a grind, but I found his Dying Gaul act obnoxious. I drew strength from my own disdain.

"Work is work . . . you know, it's like the real world." I couldn't bring myself to admit I worked in the P.O. I peeled the paper off my pop and dropped it on the coffee table between us.

"I might not even go back to school for a while . . . I get more of a sense of substance around me at work than I ever did here." I took in the lounge of "here" with a wave of the creamsicle.

"That's good, that's good." Bam-Bam was nodding off again, his eyes closed under the mask of his hairy forearm. At least he didn't shave his body.

"Yeah . . . I didn't even tell you what I'm doing." What. "I'm writing copy . . . travel copy for an agency, a travel agency." I was awed by my own bullshit. I knew I was crimson-faced, my extremities tingled with potential mortification.

"Copy? What's the outfit?" He sounded bored still, but I had a gut sick intuition that he was on to me. Even though I was lying, I was pissed that he wasn't more impressed.

"The outfit? U.S. Travel Air . . . Company." And to cover the absurdity of the name I ran down my best copy. "I don't know if you've seen this ad . . . it's two people on a beach shot in the distance over a foreground close-up of a conch shell that looks like a giant hairless cunt . . . and the tag is . . . 'MARTINIQUE, ellipse, ellipse, ellipse, UNIQUE. . . .' And there's another one . . . the same conch shell with a woman's tan feet on either side of it, and in the sand you can see the shadow of her breasts cast by the sun. It's obvious she's topless . . . we got a model with nipples like radio dials. . . ." I started getting turned on. Maybe I *should* go into advertising.

"And what's the tag?" Bam-Bam was smiling in his sleep.

"The tag?" No problem. "'If it's romance you *seek* . . .'" I sounded like Rod Serling. "'Come to Marti*nique*,' . . . and 'seek' is spelled S-E-E-Q-U-E to visually rhyme with Martinique. I know it doesn't sound like much of a gig, but you'd be surprised at the bucks they gamble on these ads. They're probably gonna send me to the Seychelles in the spring . . . I'm getting good on these beach bits . . . U.S. Travel Air . . ." That didn't sound so bad. "Sounds like a front."

"I'm sure it is." Bam-Bam sat up and smacked his gums like an old fart trying to get out of bed in the morning. I was surprised he didn't scratch his ribs. "Coffee . . ." He struggled to his feet. "I'm getting addicted, you want some?"

"I'm high on life."

He trudged off to the vending machines. I couldn't tell if his weariness was exhaustion with his work or with my bullshit. Why'd he agree when I said it sounded like a front? Then I realized that that was exactly what my ad company was . . . a government agency front. The mailman who came in from the cold.

Bam-Bam hunched over his plastic cup inhaling the steam. I had to get out of there. Suddenly in that moment, staring at the tip of Bam-Bam's nose a half inch away from being scalded, him crouched down like an asthmatic over a vapor pot, I knew I'd never go to law school. It was too alien, too hostile, too phony Bam-Bam, phony me. Too unconquerable, painful. Too many vending machines. I was nowhere to be found in that room.

"Tommy . . ." A tall thin flat-faced Chinese woman with those awful ankle-high bell bottoms moseyed over and absently snaked her fingers through the back of his hair. Without looking up from his caffeine meditation, he curled a hand around the back of her thigh.

"Hey babe . . . Pete? This is Elaine . . ." Eyes to me, then up to her. "Petey's my best buddy from last year. I told you about him." We nodded to each other with total smiling indifference. She was pretty in the sense that no Oriental woman ever seemed ugly to me. She and Bam-Bam had the same blue-black sheen and texture to their hair.

"Tommy, I left the key in the laundry room. I'm locked out."

Bam-Bam dug into his collegiate pants pocket and gave her a key ring, which had a Chinese character soldered onto the rim.

She walked out of the lounge without saying goodbye. Fine with me. She might have been taller than he was.

"So you guys living together?" I tried to affect Bam-Bam's weariness.

He closed his eyes and bobbed his head in gentle admission. I was amazed at how little I gave a shit.

"Getting married?"

He shrugged with that same creamy smile.

"Where she from, Hong Kong?"

"The province of Youngstown, Ohio . . . her father's a newspaper editor."

"You know, I once went out with a black chick . . ."

"So!" He sat up and looked awake for the first time.

"What do you mean, so?"

"So you once went out with a black chick, *so?*"

"Yeah, Deirdre Weeks from Straight, did you know her? She was our year." I felt like a fool. It was a stupid thing for me to say; oh yeah, speaking of chinks, I once ran with a nigger. I was wrong, but I resented his pedantic instructional phony *"so?"* He knew what I was talking about, he knew I blew it and he knew that *I* knew I blew it. I found his staged outrage more obnoxious than *my* fart of a comment.

"Okay, Bam-Bam, I'm sorry, forget it, okay?" The defeated disgust in my voice made him pull back.

We sat and stared at a triple coffee-ring stain which linked together like the Ballantine Beer logo. When things got painful Bam-Bam always got a tight little smile on his face, his eyes downcast. It was as much a mask of anger as it was awkwardness. I just wanted the fuck out. It was over. Me, him, law school, the bell-bottoms, Joe College, out, out, I wanted out.

We sat there for a good long five minutes contemplating the coffee rings.

"What . . ." I looked up into Bam-Bam's averted smile. I had no farewell speech. Maybe he did.

He shrugged. "Nothin'."

We would be walking out on each other under false pretenses. I didn't want it to happen, but I thought of Seeque Martinique, and I was up on my feet. "Yeah, so, you probably should get back to the libe, right? I got to split too, awright?" I made no effort at skin contact. "See you, Bam-Bam."

Without losing his smile he softly sang, "See you around," loading up the melody with as much irony, as much you-know-that-I-know as the words would bear.

School's out.

———

The next morning over breakfast my father told me that Bam-Bam called.

"Last night?" I felt tense. Once I left the school I had no desire to "work things out."

"No, no. It was like two nights ago. I forgot to tell you. He wants you to come down and visit him at Columbia."

"I spoke to him. I was down there yesterday."

"Oh yeah? How's he doing? He's a good kid, that Tommy." My father smiled at his toast.

"He's okay . . . I think we're going to lie low around each other for a while. Law school's gone to his head a little."

"Was he giving you a hard time about working for the Post Office?"

"Nah." I pouted.

"Because when I talked to him about it he seemed very sympathetic. I mean he understood what the job thing is like."

"You *told* him I was working there?"

"Yeah." He shrugged and my body shriveled with humiliation. I looked like I was shivering. Martinique, unique.

———

The next day at work while arguing with "Tommy" in my head, I leaned too far back on my stool, lost my balance, and wound up drop-kicking the entire busbox of mail high into the air to prevent myself from landing on my skull.

I started drinking; not too much, though, because it turned out to be a deceptively expensive habit. I'd go into the Treaty Stone near the Post Office, have two shots or so and get choked up and teary, thinking about that long-ago football game where I had humiliated my father or imagining different possible scenarios between him and

Franco. Rapt with remorse, I'd stagger into a Rexall or an appliance store to buy him and Vy a seventy-five-dollar Mr. Coffee machine or a fifty-dollar teakwood carving of a rabbi's head. The most expensive thing I'd ever bought them was a one-hundred-and-seventeen-dollar phone answering machine, but they, I, we, never got around to installing the proper wall jack so it stayed in its box.

———

For the three weeks before Christmas, everybody at the P.O. was working mandatory twelve-hour shifts. I had the option of going in on December 25th for double wages, but I was honestly exhausted. I didn't really need the money unless I planned to get my own apartment, but I was still going through the charade of saving up for law school. I had three thousand dollars in the bank.

Christmas night I was sitting in the living room watching *Miracle on 34th Street* with Vy and my father.

"I hear they're making a black version of this now." I took a cigarette from Vy's case.

"Really?" My father pouted with interest.

"Yeah, *Miracle on 116th Street.*"

"You're kiddin'!"

No matter what was happening in my life, I always felt happy on Christmas—a school break reflex.

"Oh yeah . . . Godfrey Cambridge is gonna play Santa Claus, and the Jackson Five are playing Natalie Wood."

"No shit." He didn't laugh. He seemed nervous. Glancing at Vy, exchanging significant eyebrow language he got up and went to the closet. Maybe they bought me a present.

He broke into a cardboard box under the coats and came back into the living room gripping our old electric menorah. It was white plastic with eight orange flame-shaped bulbs.

"You know what tonight is, my son?" He seemed so tense his chest was slightly heaving.

"Oh, Chanukah, right?" I picked up on his mood and started jiggling my foot. "I haven't seen *that* for a few years."

"Buddy boy, you want to do me a favor? Let's light the lights."

"Sure . . ." That would be nice.

"You remember the prayers?" He knelt and plugged it in, lighting five flames. He placed the menorah on the windowsill and loosened the lit bulbs until they went out.

"The prayers? Nah. Just light 'em."

He took a slim paper prayerbook off the top of the television and absently thumbed through the pages. The front cover announced the book as a gift from Schapiro's, "the wine so thick you can cut it with a knife."

"They have them in phonetics, I'm pretty sure." Vy shot me a hopeful glance. A setup.

"Just light 'em . . . wha'd you do, buy Israel Bonds today?" I laughed uneasily, fighting down anger.

"It would be so nice," Vy pleaded.

My father whipped out two black yarmulkas from his rear pocket. Because my mother had died, I'd been the only one of my friends allowed to wear a black yarmulka *before* his bar mitzvah.

I felt like lead. "I don't want to do it."

"What do we ask you?" He put his on and adjusted it to a rakish tilt.

"What?" I didn't understand the question.

"Nothing!" He extended mine to me on the couch.

I got it. "No . . ." I started getting scared. What would be the big deal?

"No?"

"No . . ." I had never refused him anything ever.

Vy bit her lip.

My father moved in a tight circle of frustration.

"Look . . ."

"No . . . no way . . . no . . ."

He stopped dancing in place. "Ahh . . . shit." He waved me off and stalked out of the room, his face twisted with agitation and impotence.

I felt horrible, but nothing doing. I stared at the television with double vision. Vy ticked her head in misery.

He came stomping back in. "You know, you're acting like a twelve-year-old."

Boom. I jumped up. "No! No! You *want* me to act like a twelve-year-old! Whatta you gonna do, give me a present after? You gonna give me a dollar? *Fuck* it!" An out-of-body experience. God would

write me in the Book of Death come Yom Kippur. Fine with me. My
father's hands dropped to his side. Vy jumped up and grasped his arm.

"It's *shame*ful!" she gasped at me.

No more "I'm so mad at you." She was pissed for real. I wanted to
say, "What about that lunch with the cocaine?" The two of them
glared at me like I had wet leprosy. Okay, okay, the sides were drawn.

"Fine! It's you and her! You and him! I'm on the *moon!* I'm not
here! I'm away!" I didn't even know what I was saying. "You *want*
me to be twelve! You *want* me here! I'm *dy*ing here! I'm on the
moon!" I wheeled and stared at myself in the veined mirror. My
face was red and sweaty. No help there.

When I turned back to them, my father was staring at the carpet, the lower part of his face pouchy and sour as if he were chewing aspirin.

"Peter . . ." Vy's voice was softer. "We love you, but we're not
any happier with this situation than you."

Rocked again. I never thought of that—how *they* felt.

"We . . . there's that *we.* . . . You and him. What's *we,* a . . . a
corporation? An ad*miss*ions board? *We!!"*

My father suddenly burst into tears, his mouth an ugly wound,
head jerking with each sob. I was terrified and started bawling myself. Vy broke down too, clutching my father's arm with tremorous
fingers.

The three of us wailed away like Greek mourners.

I held my forehead, my eyes straining out of the sockets. I was
going nuts. I wanted them dead, and I was so horrified at that sentiment, the pureness of it, that I rushed over to them blubbering apologies and "I'll do it"s. I took my yarmulka from his limp fingertips
and dropped it on my head. To keep my hands from their throats, I
grabbed them in a bear hug, squeezing them together as hard as I
could, crunching them until my arms shook, until Vy's shoulder was
halfway through my father's chest.

"Kids today, hah?" I managed to slip between sobs, "Kids today, right?"

———

That incident completely broke my back. I said the prayers, reading
the Hebrew, not the phonetic breakdown, for eight nights running,

screwing in a flame-contoured bulb each night then breaking out into profuse apologies for my attempted parricide. I apologized so much they became embarrassed. They wanted to forget about it, but I couldn't stop. I went out and bought Vy a rare Billie Holiday album for twenty dollars. My father got a lavish book on the Holy Land.

Whenever I thought back on that fight, my father crying, I felt such a mixture of horror and pleasure that my body would involuntarily twitch as if I had just downed a shot of whiskey. I couldn't tell if I'd gone too far or not far enough, and the confusion had me so badly frightened I started playing it manically close to the vest.

I stopped bitching about the Post Office. What had been getting me through my shifts was a silent chant, "It's only temporary," but I didn't need that mantra anymore. I just did my job. I halted the in-house guerrilla warfare. I stopped sulking. I started a fitness regimen. Every day I woke up at ten in the empty apartment, did an hour of calisthenics, had a cigarette, made brunch, listened to a record or watched an hour or so of afternoon TV, had another cigarette, headed into Manhattan, did my work quietly and conscientiously, got back to the sleeping house at one-thirty, or if we had compulsory overtime, two-thirty, three-thirty, sat, had a smoke, half a milk-glass of Scotch and sacked out until ten the next day.

In February I took the law boards again. It was way too late to apply to the majority of schools, and I had no intention of doing so anyhow. Taking the exam was just part of my "I'll be good" charade. I was totally out of my skull by then. Everything I did was either by insensate reflex or with the crafty paranoia of a retired double agent. But whatever the script called for, I moved through my days with the outward serenity of a priest. Vy and my father seemed happy, at any rate.

The boards were given in a lecture hall in the City University Graduate Center on Forty-second Street. I did no preparation and zipped through the booklet with awesome concentration and steadiness, although I had no idea if I would wind up scoring a rock bottom 400 or a perfect 800.

When I got the test results in the mail three weeks later I was amused to see I scored a 748, which was somewhere in the ninety-fourth percentile and 130 points higher than my senior year score.

In late March I allowed Vy to set me up with the daughter of one of her bank-teller cronies, and I sailed through that date with that same serenely radiant 748 mentality. She lived in an ex-elegant apartment house in Washington Heights, a neighborhood that was undergoing the same throes of transformation as my old Bronx block, devolving from dentists to adolescent warlords. She was in her senior year at City College, clever and good-looking. We went to a local movie house, one of those 1930s palaces that was decomposing with the neighborhood. I sat through two flicks without trying to jump down her blouse, my I-have-the-strength-of-ten-because-my-heart-is-pure act driving her crazy. At one point, her frustration drove her to lean her head against my shoulder, but I never felt so pleasantly detached, so free of sexual anxiety in my life. Priests had it knocked, I was sure of it. Harems must be theirs for the asking. I left it at the door to her apartment with a peck on the cheek and some I'll call you's.

Two weeks after that, again with Vy's urging, I went down to a dating service. They were situated in the same building as American Communicators, and I almost balked, half out of fear of running into someone I knew, mainly Mrs. Himmel, and half out of fear of picking up some of the agitation energy I had left in the building. I was also worried that maybe Raymond had leap-frogged the police academy in his life-plan and was running the outfit. I checked the directory in the lobby for Mary Heartline Video Visions, and saw that A.C. was no longer listed. The security guard told me they went out of business, and I took the news with a slightly panicky sense of loss.

The way Mary Heartline worked was for fifty dollars you were videotaped answering Dating-Game-type questions and then shown videotapes of women who fell into your age and education requirements. Later on, if any of your choices chose you at a subsequent screening, everybody got laid.

I paid a receptionist, filled out a multiple-choice questionnaire and got sent into an office to be videotaped.

My interviewer looked like a cross between a young Mary Martin and a young Nanette Fabray—a trim buoyant untouchable pixie in an arctic blue pants suit and a bright silk scarf knotted like an ascot. From the moment I sat down all I wanted to do was put it in her ass.

As she "hmmed" through my completed questionnaire I took stock of the room. An enormous blow-up of Groucho, another of W. C. Fields mounted onto cardboard backs covered the near wall, a mariachi band forged out of soldered nails danced across her desk, and a color photo of her smiling under a five-foot-wide sombrero and wearing the same pants suit stood in a fake tortoise-shell frame on the windowsill between two coffee mugs holding toothpick-propped avocado pits which hadn't begun to produce shoots yet. A video camera was bolted into the edge of her desk and aimed at an empty director's chair in front of a lavender backdrop which covered the entire wall opposite Groucho.

"So!" She clapped her hands. "Simon Straight, huh? I just interviewed a Straight man this morning. Maybe you know him, Barry . . ."

"I don't want to know." I held up a hand.

"Fine." She dipped her head and shrugged. "Have you ever been videotaped before?"

"Well, yeah, once, but that was on the David Susskind show and I demanded they only shoot me in shadow."

She laughed, I winked. I was in my Father Keller headset. I'd flow through the taping like ice water down a gently sloping mountain.

"Was that in Mexico?" I tilted my chin at the photo on the sill.

"Yucatán. Have you ever been there?"

"Nah." I noticed that a stuffed furry monkey was dangling from one of the armrests of my chair, its eyes two red felt circles which, although containing no eyeballs, managed to communicate that the monkey was cross-eyed.

"That's Harpo."

She set me up in front of the backdrop, threw me some stock quips so I would relax, turned on the camera and got right into the good stuff.

"What's your life goal, Pete? Or should I call you Peter?"

"Peter." I made a church steeple with my fingers. "I'd like to own a catering hall . . . weddings, bar mitzvahs, you know . . . and

I'd like to have a large family and settle down . . . you have some tape in your hair." I fingered my temple.

She blushed and pulled out a tiny square of Scotch tape from the side of her head.

"Shall we do that over?"

"I can edit. . . . And where would you like to live with this large family?"

"Near the catering hall . . . I like to walk to work. Suburbs, I guess.' Great Neck, Kings Point. I need green, lawns, lots of green lawns."

"Fine." She made a note.

"City's an insane asylum."

"Okay, next question."

"It's all animals now. You take your life in your hands going out for a paper."

"I know. What's your fantasy location for a date . . . sky's the limit."

"In bed."

"C'mon, Peter." She frowned at me like I was a randy oldster in a geriatrics ward.

"Okay, okay . . . in bed in a window display in Bloomingdale's."

She startled me by exploding with a short guffaw, and I fell in love. She sat there, elbow propped on the desk, her face resting on the back of her hand, her head jerking with suppressed snorts. She had turned away from me, and I stared at the short licks of ash hair that covered her neck. "Ayy . . ." she turned off the camera. ". . . you gotta give me a break."

"Just edit."

"Film's expensive, my friend." She was still smiling, weary-looking but enjoying the show.

"I'll be good. I'll be good. Just roll 'em. I'll take it from that question."

She clicked the switch.

"Fantasy location . . . on a beach in Martinique . . . just me, her, and a pitcher of Harvey Wallbangers."

She winked, no dope.

"And what would your ideal date be, on the inside?"

"Tight." What a setup. "Tight, meaning self-possessed, her own man, you know."

She looked to heaven and bit her lip. I stared at her crotch. I was having a ball.

"You're a funny guy. Is a sense of humor important to you?"

"Mine or hers?"

"Hers."

"Well, yeah . . . I like a woman who can laugh, who plays life for the mad pinball game it is, who sees every day as an adventure, who's as comfortable on the job as on the back of a horse at a dude ranch." She shook her fist at me.

"Do you have any sports interests?"

"Ballooning, squash, rock climbing, laser chess."

"What kind of music do you like?" Her voice was getting blurty with suppressed laughter again.

"Oh, classical, you know, 'Flight of the Bumblebee,' any old fifties rock and roll where at least two guys in the group are now driving school buses or dead from drugs, some sitar, some madrigal stuff, but not to excess."

"Is education important to you?"

"I like a girl who can read as well as write, because I *am* a bit of a culture vulture, but I'm no snob."

I was thawing out, feeling more like my old self than I had in almost a year.

"Okay, last question. How would you describe yourself in just *one word*." She looked as if she couldn't wait for my response to that one.

I took my time, waiting to come up with a show-stopper. I wanted to sit and answer her gossipy questions all day. I felt depressed that I was on my last question. I stared at the lens, not wanting to give up the word, not wanting to go home, not wanting to slip into my slick madness.

The camera held me like a gun. "One word."

"Drowning." My voice was as level as a dead man's EEG. In the sudden quiet I became aware of the gravelly whine of the camera.

We locked eyes.

"Drowning." I shrugged. "Oscar time, hah?" I nodded toward the machine without looking away from her.

She made no move to turn it off, and we sat contemplating each other.

"How many guys come in here and wind up asking you out?"

"Every fucking one," she answered in a grim monotone.

Suddenly the door swung open and she calmly almost somnambulistically clicked off the camera.

"How are ya!" The interloper had a face like one of those male love dolls; fluffy layered hair, thick groomed mustache.

"Kate? Sorry to interrupt. I need those tapes."

"Jim took them home." She was still staring at me.

He glanced down at the front page of my questionnaire. "Did you get a chance to tell Pete about the San Juan junket? We only have three places left."

———

Four days later I got an envelope from Mary Heartline. Enclosed was my uncashed check and the calling card of a psychotherapist with a scribbled note under his address: "You're too smart not to . . . Kate."

Overestimated again. I remembered that phone conversation of James Madison's that I had overheard, where he had wound up cackling in gleeful dismay, "What do you *meeen* you're too crazy to have a session!?"

———

In the beginning of April I took one last shot at a social life. Vy had clipped an announcement of a mixer and put it on my desk. I wound up at a Hebrew Center on the Queens side of the Throgs Neck Bridge. The evening was sponsored by an organization called "Upbeat" that staged soirées in various halls in Brooklyn and Queens; guys jacket and tie, gals no jeans.

At the door I had to pay a fifteen-dollar membership fee, was hand-stamped and given a newsletter that told me about discount weekends at hotels, cruises, and had photos of honeymooning couples (Steve, a law student at Adelphi, and Valerie, an elementary ed major at Queensborough) who had first met at some Upbeat mixer. If I married someone I met at an Upbeat function and let them use our picture in the newsletter we'd be given a twenty-five-dollar gift certificate good at any Korvettes.

I tried. I really did. But it was a stone bust, because I went alone and once I finished dancing, if there wasn't a conversation happening all I could do was step back a few paces and stand At Ease. The bar was a collapsible dais table covered with a heavily starched and repaired red tablecloth. The tonic was flat. There was an army of fruit peels and maraschinos lined up in Tupperware containers. The bald surly bartender was wearing a monkey jacket that exactly matched the tablecloth. My goddamn plastic drink glass was cracked and dribbled vodka on my pants.

The band was "Hard Knox," five guys in their early twenties wearing Indian ponchos and bell-bottom dungarees. They all had blow-dried shoulder-length hair and three of them sported droopy Zapata mustaches. I could tell they were ex-greasers from the skin-tightness of their bells and the gravelly double-entendre banter that flew back and forth up there between songs. The lead singer strutted across the stage with a swaggering fake limp, as undeniably a Bronx trademark as a dueling scar on a Kraut.

They looked as if they were having a great time and I felt envious and embarrassed. I wanted to be one of the Hard Knox, not a below-deck Bozo, but in fact I was neither.

They played all the mandatory covers; Joe Cocker's "A Little Help from my Friends," and endless "Eleanor Rigby" à la Vanilla Fudge, and Santana's "Evil Ways." Halfway through the Classics IV "Stormy," while I staggered around in circles with a girl who could have been the heroine from *The Glass Menagerie*, I realized I knew the bass guitarist. We had beaten up each other for months in front of my apartment house when we were both in fourth grade. Alan Rosenbaum. And the lead singer was Carmine Milano, the drummer Jimmy Scalisi.

I felt so creeped out I broke from the catatonic clinch with my dance partner and split. As I stood in the middle of the parking lot and squinted around for my car, someone tapped me on the shoulder, and I wheeled to face the sad-looking girl I had just wordlessly dumped.

She shrugged apologetically. "Do you want to go somewhere and talk?"

I sat behind the steering wheel of my car, arms flung out over the top of the seat back as she frantically yanked on my prick, which drooped over her fist like an old flower. She started getting freaked and jerked harder, moaning "C'mon!" like we were in a speedboat with a storm coming and she couldn't get the outboard to turn over.

"Jesus Christ! Don't *yell* at it!" I wrapped my hand around hers and started pumping until we were both splattered.

We cleaned up in silence and bolted from the car through our respective doors like fraternity jerks doing a Chinese fire drill.

―――――

The next morning I awoke from a dream in which I was swimming in a tiny fish bowl. The water was so soupy with algae and droppings that I kept bumping into the plastic diver. I didn't know if I was a human or a fish. I kept trying to snort like a panicked horse. A voice announced, "Now you know why goldfish look so pop-eyed."

I jumped out of bed and stood in the middle of the bedroom in my underwear, my mouth twisted in futility and shock. When I got my bearings, I sat down at the desk, running a shaky hand across my lips. The alarm-radio clicked on. "He-hey! It's a bee-hee-yootiful April seventh out there, sixty degrees, count 'em, six-oh, so dig out that sun-reflector, go up on the roof and make yourself pretty!"

I opened the windows to get a taste of that sixty-degree wine. My favorite day of the year was always that one benign freak of weather, usually in February, where everybody wound up staggering around open-coated, giddy with nostalgia and optimism. But that year's winter had been tenacious and gray, and as the perfumed promise breezed into my bedroom I found myself murmuring "April."

Suddenly I was assaulted with a nagging sense of Big Trouble. At first I thought it was simply nightmare residue, which would have been fair enough, given the obviousness of the metaphor, but it felt more specific, as though I had forgotten something, a wallet, an oven burner, an exam. The minute I thought "oven" I smelled Filthy Fire, burning rubber or an overheated appliance. I checked the outlets behind my bed, then wandered around the house checking plugs. In the kitchen I lifted the top panel of the stove and checked the pilot light. Nothing. I sat in the living room, blinded by sunlight, and tried to shake that burning smell. Somewhere I had read that to experience a scent hallucination like that was an early sign of a brain tumor. After a half-hour, I went around the house again and pulled all the plugs—lamps, blenders, clocks. I even blew out the pilot light, which might have been more dangerous than to have left it on. I sat back down feeling embarrassed at my actions and turned on the television, which I wouldn't have unplugged if my life was at stake.

Joe Franklin clasped his hands over his crossed knee and grinned at some ancient songwriter. " 'Spring Fever' . . . did you write that on a day like today?"

I knew what the Big Trouble was. Spring. April. Law schools were in the process of mailing out acceptances and rejections, and even though it was a dead issue with me, I felt socked with its finality. I had kept up the charade, never announced my decision to my father, maybe half believed I'd get around to applying, but that was now officially irretrievably finished. My brain tumor evaporated.

I went back into the kitchen and relit the pilot. I replugged the lamps, and the kitchen appliances.

There was something fishy going on here. In all these months that I'd been performing my insane charade, not once had Vy and my father brought up the matter of law school. And when I took the law boards again, I kept it to myself because I knew that if my father and Vy found out, it would blow the whistle on all three of us.

It was getting late. Fuck work. I watched a few hours of afternoon reruns and left before either of them would come home.

I knew I was avoiding them, knew I was delaying a showdown, but I just didn't have the stamina to see it through just right then.

I drove down to midtown and caught a number of movies I was less than dying to see.

I got back to Yonkers a few hours before dawn. Before I packed it in I was surprised to see that the kitchen wall clock only read twelve-fifteen. Then I noticed the dangling cord. I'd forgotten to replug the motherfucking clocks.

The next noon I woke up to the sounds of my old man puttering around in the kitchen. It was his day off. Columbia. My stomach roller-coastered. I had to go to work too. I had to face Franco again for missing the day before. I had to face my father and cash in everybody's chips. I was scared to death, and lay in bed over an hour.

I stood in the kitchen doorway and watched my father eat lunch in his irrepressible style. He peered down at the sandwich in his hand after every bite. His eyebrows arched and he just *looked* at the sandwich while he chewed, as if something was written on it. I felt an instinctual body-wracking desire to protect him.

He saw me standing there and perked up. "Well, good morning America!" pointing to an empty dinette chair across from him. "You hungry?"

"Dad . . ." I pinched the bridge of my nose and waited for him to finish eating. He briefly sucked the fleshy part of his thumb, then wiped his hands on his pants legs. He stared at me, raising his eyebrows expectantly.

"What's up?"

"You're not going to believe this," I sighed, absently tapping the side of my finger on the edge of the table. "I forgot to reapply to Columbia . . . it's too late." I shrugged, staring at my finger. "I'm sorry . . . maybe I can . . . maybe I can get them . . . I'm sorry."

A reflective hiss leaked out of an upturned corner of his mouth. He raised his eyebrows and compressed his lips while absently wiping his hands on his pants again, his head turned to the wall. "Awright . . . look . . . odds are you wouldn'ta gotten in again anyhow. I mean, you didn't do nothin' so special this year that they would change their minds. . . ." He stretched to his feet. I saw my eye socket and cheekbone in his belt buckle.

"Nothing so special?" My voice was dull. "I took the goddamn boards again."

He stopped under the door frame. "Yeah?" Too mild.

"*Yeah* . . . you know what I scored? Seven forty-eight . . . That's *Yale*, my man, that's *Harvard*."

"No shit." He put his hands in his front pockets and leaned against the wall.

"No *shit*." I still couldn't raise my eyes to his face.

"So why didn't you send out some applications?"

"Why didn't you ask me about it in December?"

He lurched upright and slowly rubbed a shoe against the back of his pants leg. "Why? Because, I'll tell you the truth, I didn't think you really wanted to go anymore. You're a big boy, Pete. I don't have to hold your hand."

"Hold my *hand!*" Shock beads of sweat erupted on my stomach. "I was doing it for *you!*"

"Me?" He reared back and pressed his fingertips to the center of his chest. "Don't do it for *me*, my son. I don't want to wind up murdered in my sleep some night. Not for *me*. You do it for *you* . . . not me."

I covered my mouth with my hand and stared hot-eyed at his empty plate.

"Do I make sense?"

"Yeah," I snapped.

"I don't want to be dead in my bed."

"Good point."

He stood there for a while, finally patting me on the shoulder, the last pat lingering like a limp caress. "It's awright, buddy . . . we'll get 'em next year."

At three o'clock I got on the Jerome Avenue subway line and started the haul down to the Post Office. I usually took my car, but I didn't feel like driving. I wanted to keep my hands on my kneecaps. By River Avenue and 161st Street, the Yankee Stadium stop, I was smelling fire again.

The car rocked and moaned into Manhattan. Everybody's lolling face looked flayed, grim and deep-set, slaggy like unfinished clay busts. I started thinking about getting screamed at by Franco, whether in fact, his methods *were* illegal and abusive of postal workers' human rights. I got into a fantasy of myself spearheading a movement of postal workers to expose Franco and a system that sanctioned and profited from his psychopathy. I imagined being interviewed by a *Village Voice* muckraker, holding forth on how the postal system systematically reinforced a spirit-crushing, aspiration-crushing parent-child environment that resulted in creating and sustaining people with permanent curvature of the soul and a terminal case of self-revulsion—all in the name of efficiency. The Hanging Judge strikes again.

By Columbus Circle I wasn't thinking about anything. At Times Square I realized that if I stayed on the job three more months I could take the exam for assistant mail-handling foreman. At Penn Station, my stop, I was eating breakfast in a truckstop diner as dawn was breaking over the Kansas plains. I was wearing good fucking steel-toed boots that laced halfway up my calf.

Just past Fourteenth Street, a young black guy with no legs was wheelchaired through the car-connecting doors by another young black guy. They both had these glaring reproachful hollow-cheeked burning stares. The guy in the wheelchair had a cardboard sign around his neck that said, WHEN I DIE I'M GOING TO HEAVEN BECAUSE I ALREADY BEEN TO . . . Below the two dots was a map of Vietnam drawn in Venus paradise pencil colors. Both of them wore beat-up flak jackets and those militant back-to-Africa knit skullcaps. The guy in the wheelchair had a dirty pink blanket over feed-bag-shaped leather stump-protectors where his kneecaps would have been. He held a waxed paper cup that was already heavy with change.

The riders twisted their raped faces into their papers. Just what the doctor ordered: wheelchairs, angry niggers, forgotten Vietnam veterans . . . have a nice day.

They began to work the car. The pusher would slide the wheelchair in front of a passenger, then take his hands off the handles and straighten up completely. The guy with no legs would shake his cup under the passenger's nose. Neither of them would budge until the cripple got his coin. Then the wheelchair would get pushed maybe six inches. The guy would let go of the handles, straighten up and the cup would be shoved into the next face. People in the car pretended they didn't see those guys working their way up the line. Everybody was staring at their papers or at the running reflections on the windows, but hands were furtively calculating change in jacket pockets. I had my quarter ready. Everybody gave. My mother used to say, "I cried because I had no shoes until I saw the man who had no legs." I wondered if I was man enough to be in combat. It was hard to speculate. I heard two guys at work say Franco won the Silver Star in Sicily in World War II. I wasn't going to let these cocksuckers intimidate me. You'd be in a flying rage too if you'd lost your legs.

When they were only four riders down from me, the car-connecting door at the other end slid open with a rush of magnified train racket and a T.A. cop stood there, nightstick held at both ends. The three of them froze in a momentary stare-down. They all looked surprised.

Suddenly the guy behind the wheelchair turned around and tore ass through the cars. I was shocked that he would abandon his friend; they were both militants.

The cop still didn't move. Then the guy in the wheelchair gripped the armrests, the cup in his teeth, raised his torso a foot out of the chair, and suddenly shot these completely healthy long legs straight out from the false bottom of the chair. He grabbed his cup out of his mouth and hobble-ran after his partner. The leather stumps strapped to his kneecaps slowed him down. He must have been six foot two. The startled cop didn't make a move until the second guy was into the next car, then took off after them.

I started breaking out in a dry laugh, elbowing some humorless lower steerage bastard to my left to get in on the joke. "GO!" I shouted through cupped hands, hunching over into the aisle. "GO!" Suddenly I was standing in the middle of the colorless car. "GO! GO! GO!" laughing and pumping my fist like I was in a stadium. "GO!" I felt my chin slowly tilt upwards until I was staring at the running fluorescent fixtures; my skull filled with slow-motion images of the guy's legs shooting out from under him and over. "GO!"

Next thing I knew a man and a woman were murmuring "Y'awright? Y'awright?" I was lying on the incredibly dirty floor, the rail clatter doing a sound massage on my back.

I got off the train at Franklin Street, switched to an uptown platform and headed home.

When I got in at six, the place was deserted. There was an engraved invitation on the kitchen cutting board:

> YOU ARE CORDIALLY INVITED TO
> A TESTIMONIAL DINNER
> FOR NATE SAPERSTEIN
> ISLE OF CAPRI ROOM
> PARADISE CATERERS
> 1621 BURNSIDE AVE
> THE BRONX

It was signed "Abe Fein—Social Committee Chairman, Brothers of Zion Lodge #62."

My father was vice president of the lodge. Every six months they had a testimonial dinner for one senior lodge member or another in order to raise money for the college scholarship fund. I myself had been a Sophie Isaacs Memorial Scholarship recipient four years running although it was only 150 bucks a year.

I watched TV for an hour in the living room, went into the kitchen, reread the invitation and called Paradise Caterers from the engraved phone number. Dead in his bed.

"Good evening, Paradise . . ." The guy who answered the phone sounded as if he had a pencil propped to take my lunch order.

"Yeah, good evening. I think you should know that there's a bomb, a pipe bomb in one of your rooms, I'm not saying which one. It's set to go off in forty-three minutes . . ."

"Get off my goddamn phone, you asshole." He hung up on me.

I felt relieved and childish.

They got home two hours later. I was watching TV again.

"Oh ho, boy!" They both were smiling with excitement as they rustled off their coats in the living room.

"What's up?" I lit a cigarette.

"You wouldn't believe what happened tonight, buddy." The clatter and skid of the coat hangers made me wince. My father, still smiling, took off his glasses and cleaned them on his handkerchief as he stood spreadlegged to the side of me. "Guess what we had for dessert?"

"A *bomb* scare," Vy shot out over her shoulder on her way to the bathroom.

The cheery way they were smiling at me made me feel in my swoony dream state that they both knew and approved of the fact that I was the Mystery Caller and that it was Great Fun.

"I'm eatin' I'm eatin' I'm eatin' and I see these two cops come into the room with the manager. I think somebody's double-parked but I turn to Vy and I was gonna say ain't that peculiar, they'd send two cops in for that? and sure enough the manager takes the microphone off the dais there and says um . . . I'm sorry but something came up and we have to vacate the building. We got some crank calling up, but we have to play safe . . . and stupid me . . . when the guy said crank, I thought like an obscene phone call. Somebody musta called up and made a bomb threat . . . I thought we're gonna lose Vy altogether." He laughed. "But surprisingly enough, nobody panicked, people got up, left . . ."

"Of course it helped that everybody was half snockered." Vy came back in, reaching up inside her skirt to pull down her slip.

I smiled interestedly, feeling like as long as I acted amused it would be okay. I slowed down my fanning kneecaps.

"There was this big police department van outside . . . sure enough it's the Bomb Squad."

"That sidewalk was funny . . . in the middle of this crappy neighborhood there's maybe two hundred people standing around in suits and tuxedos . . . cause you know it wasn't just *our* dinner that got screwed up. There was a shvartze wedding next door and something else too . . . some anniversary party."

"Remember that guy?" Vy tilted her head and smirked.

"What guy? . . . Oh! One of the shvartzes. Man, he musta been drinkin'. I don't know *what* he musta been drinkin' . . . he was . . ." My old man cracked up. "He was dressed real sharp, ruffled shirt, nice red dinner jacket . . . he started coming on to Helen on the sidewalk."

"Helen Hoffman?" My eyebrows arched with polite curiosity.

"*Nah!* He wasn't *that* drunk!"

"Hey!" Vy playfully punched him in the arm.

"Helen, Joey's wife."

"You shoulda seen Helen's face . . . you know she's always complaining that Joey never takes her out . . ."

"So what happened . . . was there a fight?"

"Yeah . . . you know between who? This colored guy's wife came over, and gave him such a *zetz* with her pocketbook . . ."

"Everybody was laughin', us *and* the shvartzes." Vy moved in front of the TV. "Maybe we should get the news on . . ." She began spinning the dials.

"Yeah, maybe that place blew up after all." My father shrugged, staring at the Channel Five anchorman whose chin was the exact width of his temples.

———

I temporarily scared myself sober with that moronic stunt, but I wasn't nearly as frightened by it as I'd been by that fright we'd had over the Chanukah lights.

A few weeks later I was playing some albums and I came across a Doors cut called "The End." It was a long creepy theatrical number about a kid whacking out his parents while they slept. In some ways I felt like a six-year-old imbecile fashioning a sheet into a cape and jumping out his window after watching "Superman," but that night I gave in and placed a second call to a movie house in Hartsdale where they had gone to see a Bob Hope flick.

The way I saw it, what it boiled down to was involving myself in an extravagantly dangerous gamble. I wanted to get caught by my father. I wanted him to accuse me so I could confess. I wanted him so pissed off he'd kick me out of the house. I was still feeling stuck in the muck too deep to get out on my own and I needed help. He owed me some help. I just hoped he caught on before I got nailed, because I in no way wanted to wind up in jail or a hospital.

When I got the movie manager on the line he was very polite and understanding, and I felt insulted by his calm professionalism. To save myself from appearing like a lone whacko I declared the bomb a gift from the Mamaroneck chapter of the Che Guevara fan club and signed off with "Viva Che!"

An hour later they came in laughing with astonishment that this should happen to them twice. Vy was a little shaken up. "I dunno, maybe someone's after *us!*"

"What do *you* think, Pop?" I felt like a shrink coaxing out some self-realization.

He just scowled and waved off the suggestion.

I played around with the idea of slashing his tires or putting sugar in his gas tank, but that felt too much like hand-to-hand combat; it was too physical and even though the phone calls were more dangerous I couldn't really and truly imagine getting caught. In elementary school, my friends and I had made prank calls all the time.

A month later, more or less, the first anniversary of my graduation, I placed a third call to the Moon Garden Chinese Restaurant, where they had gone for dinner, two blocks away from the house. I gave myself a Southern accent and dedicated the bomb to the Committee to Free Bear Bryant.

They came in a half-hour later, absolutely silent, gray-faced with shock.

A week after that, I got nailed, ninety minutes after my fourth call, thirty minutes after my father carried my hysterical stepmother into the apartment from Ricky's Clam House on Central Avenue.

We were both trying to calm her down when the doorbell rang. I knew the jig was up. The two detectives were both fat and fortyish. They looked bigger than the whole apartment. The one guy who did the talking had a kind puffy uncle-type face. He looked so kind and big and informal that my first reaction to him was that he was an insane-asylum doctor or some kind of institute head coming to get me, but in fact, he was a cop.

"Ah, Mr. Keller . . ." He stood in the foyer, hands in pockets, staring at his shoe tip. "We recorded the last call off the trace." He briefly caught my eye over my father's shoulder. "In fact, whoever made the calls, didn't call *to* here, as we anticipated, they called *from* here. We picked up the call to the restaurant from your line . . ." He looked at me again, tight-lipped, as if he was going to say Shame On You. The other fat detective was reading my laminated diploma on the wall.

"What trace?" I challenged my father.

"These guys put a wiretap on our phone after last week in case the guy called here." My old man was so freaked, it hadn't dawned on him yet that the cop was telling him that *I* did it, that they had caught *me* by accident. Vy emerged, drying out from the blubbers. "Lou, what's goin' on?" Her twisty lips quivered with sobs and she walked in slow motion.

"You mean to tell me our phone was *tapped* all week?" I barked at my father. "I'm making all sorts of calls to all sorts of people, *private* calls and they're listening to everything I say from my own bedroom and you didn't even *tell* me? God!" I angrily grabbed my jacket off the striped mini-couch in the foyer, nodded "Let's go" to the cops and headed toward the door with them.

"What happened?" Vy was getting hysterical again. "Where's he going?"

I gave the cops a quick hurry-up wave with a snap of my wrist down low by my thigh. They sashayed toward me at the door, hands in their pockets.

"Lou?" a shrieky question from my stepmother.

I just hoped to God that we wouldn't have to wait too long for the elevator.

———

The detectives drove me over to the Westchester County Jail, one guy in the back seat with me, the other driving. I wasn't scared. I was embarrassed. On the ride to White Plains I kept expecting them to berate me, or at least peer at me with disgust, but all they did was talk to each other about how deceptively expensive the State University colleges were. The guy next to me had a son enrolled at Binghamton, and in a desire to get them to either start yelling at me or at least ask me why I did it, I piped up, "Binghamton's a great school. What's he majoring in?"

He chewed it over long enough for me to think he wasn't going to answer. "Music Composition."

I couldn't tell if it embarrassed him or that he just wanted me to shut up. I shut up, feeling as though I was stuck in a car pool with two middle-aged office managers who had to tolerate my presence for the sake of economy, instead of an unmarked police car heading for an arraignment.

———

At the jail I was frisked, had the insides of my shoes examined, got fingerprinted, had my mug shot and my valuables and belt placed in a manila envelope. I kept expecting someone to come down on me for what I did, but the whole thing was as impersonal as collecting unemployment. Nobody even looked me in the eye, and I hid behind the officialness of it all.

It was too late for an arraignment, and I was held in a detaining cell overnight. The room was no worse than a freshman dorm, a hell of a lot cleaner, and I even had a roommate who was a major improvement over Larry Arthur. His name was Iowa Davis, or so he said, and he had been busted for selling blotter acid in the county courthouse lobby where he had gone to defend himself against a parking ticket. Iowa was nineteen, had hair down to his ass and was tripping.

I told him I'd been arrested for shouting "Fire!" in a crowded movie theater, but he didn't get it.

At lights out, he hissed me over to his cot while dropping his pants. I had totally forgotten all those prison documentaries on public television. My asshole puckered shut and retreated up into my stomach.

As I sat there buzzing with terror, frantically searching for a disarming unantagonizing way to say No, he removed a flattened pellet of opium that had been taped to his nuts.

"Ten dollars, my man. You'll sleep like a baby." He carefully removed a pubic hair stuck to the gummy black pill. "Eight dollars." He shrugged.

The next cell over, some wise guy started wailing, "I don't wanna die!" in perfect imitation of the death row con in *The Last Mile*.

Some of the overnight guests started shouting for him to shut up, but I heard a few cops crack up in laughter.

From the moment I was arrested my mood had ranged from protectively phony flippancy to petulant irritation at my father for not picking up on what was going down earlier, for allowing that goddamn wiretap to be set up. But when Iowa dropped his pants, everything went, all my posturing. I was going to jail. Fuck, I was *in* jail, and from what I understood I had the choice of getting gang-raped or picking a "protector" who would ream me up to my tonsils and then make me do his laundry. Pilfered spoons sharpened into knives, throats slit in the shower. Muslims getting up at dawn for their study group then going out and killing white boys at Free Play. Fucking television.

I sat on the edge of my cot and watched Iowa sleep. After a few hours I woke him up by hissing his name from across the cell. I didn't want to shake him in case he was one of those guys who instinctively whipped out a knife when abruptly woken up. I heard of a Vietnam vet who'd killed his wife that way.

"Yeah, what?" He didn't move from his fetal curl.

"Do you think they'll send me to jail?"

"For yelling Fire?"

Shit. "Yeah. I did some other stuff. I phoned in phony bomb threats."

"Oh yeah?" He seemed impressed.

"So you think they'll send me to jail?"

"Jail?" he grunted, as if thinking it over. I sat drying my palms on my kneecaps, waiting for that hallucinating asshole to pass sentence. He slipped back into sleep, and I sat up all night.

In the morning I was handcuffed and bussed over to the White Plains courthouse for my arraignment. Handcuffs. What the hell did they expect me to do, break free, grab a phone and make another bomb threat?

When we got to the building there was some trouble by the side entrance where I was supposed to enter, and the two black cops who were my escorts were told to send me in through the main entrance.

The minute we got inside the lobby I stared around wildly and started babbling, "Oh! This is an incredible place! Was it built with WPA funds? That mural looks like a Diego Rivera! Ah! Bauhaus!" Jabbering away trying to convince my cops that I was a good little boy, a *bright* little boy.

The courtroom was empty except for a three-man set piece; the judge on high with an elbow resting on either side of his water pitcher, and two lawyers standing below, flanking him.

One lawyer was mine, a fortyish overweight guy in a corduroy jacket; the other was an assistant D.A. The judge wore bifocals, sewing glasses, and it made him look like a stern aunt. They were all talking and laughing and I felt like an intruder.

As the D.A. read off the detective's report, they stared at me as if I had just farted in an elevator.

From the minute I entered the room I literally felt like throwing myself on the mercy of the court. As the report droned on it was all I could do to keep myself from bursting out with "Am I goin' to jail?" like a six-year-old asking a doctor if he's getting a needle.

For that fourth call, which was tapped, they had me down claiming the bomb was placed by the Committee to Free the Indianapolis 500, but no one thought that was very funny.

The judge leaned his head on the heel of his palm and pushed back his glasses. "You're quite a card, Mr. Keller."

"I'm . . . I was under a lot of emotional stress. I'm really sorry, Your Honor." Saying "Your Honor" like that brought on a brief wave of giddiness which I kept to myself.

"I'll bet you are . . ."

"I am, I really am. That wasn't me."

"Well, it certainly wasn't me . . ." He touched his chest. "Was it either of you?"

The lawyers laughed, and I felt a flush of hope.

"If I release you on your own recognizance, Mr. Keller, will you be making any more calls?"

"I'll sew on mittens, I mean it." I raised my hand as if I were being sworn in, my legs going like jackhammers.

He released me without bail and set an appearance date for three weeks later, instructing me to get a lawyer.

The cops stepped forward, and I probably should have shut up and left immediately, but I felt so grateful I had to talk.

"Listen, I just want to thank you. I can't believe I did that. I mean, when I said that wasn't me I didn't mean I didn't do it. I meant that wasn't *me*. Last year I got into St. John's law school, and I was on the waiting list at Columbia, and I took the law boards last February again and I got a 748. I really want to go to law school. I mean, I don't know if I can go *now*, but maybe I can do paralegal work. I don't know. I must have been out of my mind . . ." I yammered on, and no one made any move to shut me up.

They just squinted at me with a half-curious, half-distasteful look as though they were all thinking "I'm glad that's not *my* fuckin' kid." And I could sense it, too, but I couldn't shut up. I felt myself slipping into a shamelessly childish transparency, my dignity somewhere down by my knees, but I could have cared less. I plowed on about how I didn't know what had come over me, how ashamed I was of myself and I started getting this sensation, like a low-grade flu, that I could feel where all my bones were met. I knew they were looking at me as if I was some neurotic bug, but I just couldn't stow it.

Finally the judge had enough and cut me off. "See you in three weeks, Mr. Keller."

One of the cops put a hand on my arm, and I turned to the empty pews, but three steps later I wheeled around. "Oh, Your Honor? I was just wondering, would you have any idea which town around here has the Washington Irving house? I think it's Tarrytown. I'm not sure. I rarely get up here and I've never been to that . . . the Washington Irving house."

When we got outside, my father was pacing in front of the jail bus. When he saw me he froze, face taut with fear.

"I can go home!" I gave him thumbs up and he reared back and clapped his hands once over his head in relief.

I had to go back to the jail to pick up my valuables, and he drove alongside the bus the entire way.

———

"So anyways, I need a lawyer."

"We got you one," my father murmured behind his hand.

He and Vy sat on the couch watching me pace in front of the TV. I had been home for an hour acting nonstop buoyant, pacing, drumming out riffs about Iowa Davis, the court scene. My father never took his hand from his mouth. Vy kept her hands in her lap, not even going for a cigarette. They made me feel as if I was waving a gun around the room.

"Who's the lawyer?"

"Marty Klein from the lodge."

"Oh great. Was he at that testimonial dinner I emptied?"

"I didn't ask."

I finally plopped down in the easy chair.

"Aren't you gonna ask me why I did it?"

The three of us sat breathless waiting for my explanation.

"You don't want to know?"

My father's fingers chattered nervously along his jaw line.

I opened my mouth to run it down, but before I could get out the first word, I felt a sneak preview of the exhausted state I'd be in after my tenth rephrased explanation. No matter how I'd say it, I'd wind up sounding like I was headed for a diet of mush and Thorazine.

"It's complicated." I hooded my eyes with a hand. "I don't really understand it myself."

Not surprisingly, they seemed to accept that explanation.

"Would you like me to move out?"

"You're my *son*, Peter." He closed his eyes in pain.

"You're not answering the question."

"Whatever you do, Peter, this is your home."

I felt defeated. Not by his evasiveness, but by the realization that in spite of everything I still needed him to say the word.

"This is your *sanc*tuary."

I took that with a smile that dropped into an incredulous gape.

"Peter . . ." Vy's voice came out in a nervous croak. "I told your father about the cocaine. Do you think that . . ."

"Yeah . . . it was a cocaine flashback."

"Are you in trouble with drugs?" There was fervent terror in his voice.

"Look, the only time I have a drug problem is when I can't get any drugs." I screwed up my face to ridicule the question.

He closed his eyes in blessed relief. What we have here is a failure to communicate.

"So are you going to punish me?" Even though I said it as playfully as I could muster, I started getting tense myself.

My father kept his eyes closed.

"You want to spank me?"

"Peter, cut it out."

"Aren't you even *an*gry at me?" I felt as if I was begging. No answer.

"How about you?" I turned to Vy, and she jerked back almost through the wall. Shit. They weren't mad; they were scared. They might also have been worried, but they were scared to death of me. What the hell did I expect?

"Maybe you should send me to my room. Yeah, send me to my room."

I got up, went to my room, closed the door and fell face down on the bed, dropping into a blank sleep.

———

Marty Klein's office was over a restaurant in the Fordham Road shopping district of the Bronx. As I walked into the fake wood-paneled reception room, a young black kid sporting tight cornrows got smacked across the face by his mother, an unbelievably obese short woman with large burning eyes set in a head that looked connected to her shoulders by a towel of fat. The kid took the blow with sullen resignation, barely rearing back, then sauntered to the door with his heaving mom in tow. Marty Klein and his secretary watched the whole scene with impassive immobility; Klein leaning against the door frame of his rear office with his hands in his pockets, the secretary slouching forward across her desk with her cheek pressed into her palm.

As they made their way down the steep stairs Klein looked up at me and shook his head in weary resignation. "Purse snatcher. The devil made him do it. Who are you?"

"Phone bomber."

"Oh right, Lou Keller's kid. C'mon in."

I sat in front of his desk as he stood and stacked papers.

"Phone bomber . . . the devil made you do it too?"

He was about five foot four, in his early thirties with thin hair, a thick mustache and large round tortoise shells. As he cleared away the clutter I saw he had a bald spot like a tonsure. His office had that same fake wood paneling as the reception area. Over a low shelf filled with an intimidating brace of law books hung his diploma from St. John's.

"Actually, the kid didn't say the devil made him do it. That's Mom's idea. This is the fourth time for me with these two. Everytime they come here she pops him on the jaw. They're right out of one of those early sixties urban realism movies . . . 'Mah baby's a *good* boy' . . . whap!" He smacked his fist into an open palm, then finally sat down and removed his sports jacket. Sighing, he reached for a fresh yellow pad and took a ballpoint from an empty marmalade jar. "So, phone bomber, you ever been in trouble before?"

As I ran down my story he laboriously filled out ten sheets of handwriting, occasionally shaking his bald spot in either amusement or contempt. When I finished, he raised his head from his writer's hunch and blinked at me as if I'd just woken him up. "Why'd you do all this?"

"Can we plead temporary insanity?"

He dropped his pen, blew air out of puffed cheeks and leaned back in his chair, his hands clasped behind his head.

"Look, Keller, you got a pain in your stomach, you go to a doctor. He asks you what's wrong, what do you say, 'I have an inflamed spleen? I have peritonitis?' *No.* You say you have a fucking pain in your stomach and you point to it. *He* says if you got an inflamed spleen. You don't do *his* job, and you don't do *mine*. I ask you why you did it, you give me data, you give me information . . . don't talk shop with me . . . am I getting through to you?"

Even though I couldn't afford to fuck with him, I did a slow pan around his piss-ass office to register my own contempt. "You don't like me very much, do you?"

"What am I, a professional companion? You don't pay me to like you. You pay me to defend you. And you're gonna need some god-damn defending. They got you on aggravated harassment, disturbing the peace and false reporting of an incident. You should have snatched a purse."

"Do you think I'll go to jail?" I felt a mild case of the whirlies coming on.

He picked up on my fear and calmed down. "Well, that depends on a lot of things. . . ."

"Do you think I'll go to jail?" I tried to control the warble in my throat.

He hissed through his teeth and tapped his eraser tip on his notes. "No . . . I don't think so . . . you're a straight kid, no record, college, my guess is you'll get an ACOD, an adjournment on contemplation of dismissal, which means in effect you're on probation for six months, after which, if you keep your nose clean, they seal up the records, and it's like it never happened."

"Ahh . . ." I almost oozed out of my chair.

He studied me with a small reflective smile. "You worried about getting raped in prison?"

I nodded dumbly.

"So would I. We're probably *both* fruitcakes. My secretary thinks I am because I never try to throw some dick her way. The day I graduated law school my fortune cookie says, 'The wise wine merchant never samples his own product.' Translated into Fordham Road-ese that means 'Don't shit where you eat.' So she tells everybody I'm a fag because I'm a wise wine merchant. I despise her and her ilk, all her ilk, every last ilk . . . anyway, I can't guarantee you an ACOD, but . . . ah . . . last year I had this other kid, The Rock Dropper. He got caught dropping rocks from an overpass onto cars on the Bronx River Parkway. The kid was a brainiac, Bronx Science, N.Y.U. ACOD . . ." He gave me a wide tight smile of triumph.

"You know, I took the law boards in February . . ." trying to beef up my own brainiac status. I didn't want to tell him I got into St. John's because I was afraid of insulting him.

"Oh yeah? What was your score?"

"Seven forty-eight."

"Seven forty-eight? When I took them, you know what I scored?"

"What . . ."

"Five seventy-seven, and that's with cheating, but you know something funny about this desk?"

"What?"

"Look on what side the 748 is sitting and what side the 577 is sitting."

"You *asked* me my score. I'm not trying to antagonize you." I felt as much a prisoner of his rhythms as my father and Vy did of mine.

"I drive a Cadillac, what do you drive? Ah, never mind. I'm going off the deep end." He wiggled his hand in the air. "Awright, look, I want you to tell me, without any legal language, any analysis, any color commentary . . . why did you do the phone calls? Go."

He bent over a clean sheet, pen poised.

"No."

"Go."

"I don't feel it anymore."

"Go."

"I was in a bad mood."

"Go."

"I swear to you . . . I *don't know.*"

He looked at me and nodded his head in acceptance.

"And I'm not crazy."

He shrugged. "Okay, now, I'm going to want you to do something. When the Rock Dropper got his ACOD he was also court-ordered to seek counseling, which despite my 577, I anticipated. And what I had him do between his arraignment and the sentencing was to start seeing a shrink on his own, to show the court he was seriously trying to come to grips with himself. . . . And . . . I want you to do the same." He dug out his wallet and started flipping through credit cards. "Here you go . . ." He handed me a bone-colored business card. "Every boy should have a shrink. I'd see her myself if I weren't perfectly normal. Leah Catcher . . . like *Catcher in the Rye* . . . she probably likes sensitive, pained types like you. I want you to call her as soon as you leave the office, which is in two seconds. I got a subway slug manufacturer coming in. 'Bye . . ."

The shrink seemed like a great idea. Someone to ask me more questions. It would be fun.

At the door I turned back and pressed my luck. "Yeah, listen, I'm almost afraid to ask this . . . were you at that testimonial I cleared out?" I was wincing.

"Yup." He closed his eyes and gave me that wide compressed lips smile. "Don't worry about it. It was a fucking boring dinner."

In the week between Klein and Catcher I just hung around the house. I never formally quit the Post Office, assuming that once I'd been arrested I was as good as fired, since it was a federal job. Basically I had nothing to do except wait for my shrink appointment, which I looked forward to more and more each day. I was intent on going in there and blowing her away with my perceptiveness, but I had no idea what to say. The only thing I knew for sure was that I had to get out. I had to leave this apartment that was no longer mine, and start my own life.

If I got that ACOD I was gone.

There was only one thing I had to fix before I could leave. Ever since I returned from my arraignment, the apartment had become The House of Fear, and if I left without cracking the tension I knew I would never come back. That might have been one last desperate justification for hanging in, but I didn't think so. I was feeling too sober and chastened to dismiss it. Long-winded explanations and ardent apologies wouldn't cut it; my father and Vy were too tight for that approach. So I decided that if I could just get them to laugh, or push them to the point of exasperation where they could break out of their terror long enough to tell me to shut up already for chrissakes, I would feel enough of my bill had been paid for me to clear out with a good head.

The living room was my arena, and night after night I engaged in long endless bouts of talking back to the television, drowning out ten minutes of Showtime at a clip in the hopes of at least a snigger or a small "shoosh," but they remained as well behaved as hostages, cocking their heads to listen attentively to my blather like RCA Victor dogs confronted by their master's voice.

In my desperation I became tasteless, barking out sexual advice to Granny on the "Beverly Hillbillies" and Aunt Bea on the "Andy Griffith Show."

Once when the phone rang, I jumped up, screened the call and leaned into the living room, the receiver pressed against my chest; "It's a bomb threat. Do you want me to take a message or are you here?"

Nada.

———

Doctor Catcher's office was a penthouse in Riverdale, a section of the Bronx so piss-elegant and green that residents always responded "Riverdale," never "the Bronx" when asked where they lived. Catcher wasn't there, and I was met at the door by a six-foot-tall, gray-Afroed, mannishly handsome black woman in a deep maroon caftan, My first reaction was to leap into her arms and squawk "Mama!"

"Dr. Catcher? Hi, I'm Peter Keller."

"Leah's a little behind schedule, Peter, come in." Her voice was as rich as an opera singer's. I looked down and saw that my left foot was on the wrong side of my right.

"Would you like some tea?"

I followed her into a deep and wide kitchen with immaculate white surfaces. Various types of pastas curlicued inside tall cork-stoppered glass cylinders and a spice rack as big as a bookcase was mounted on a wall covered with blue and white Dutch tiles.

"I'm Karen, was that herbal or Lipton's?" She paddled across the floor barefoot.

"Tea is good," I mumbled, enthralled. "Lipton's . . . tiny little tea leaves."

"That's Tetley." She chuckled like a good sport.

The first sip burned off half my taste buds.

"Leah teaches today down at Hunter and sometimes she gets stuck in traffic."

"Me too." I looked out the kitchen window and saw the raw blood-brown Palisades on the Jersey side of the Hudson River. "Riverdale," I mumbled.

"You can wait for her in the office." She led the way down a narrow hallway into a small room and closed the door on me.

The office seemed to have been built with a child's bedroom in mind, tight and rectangular. Pre-Columbian pottery rested on handsome Burmese teak cabinets; aborigine boomerangs and South Sea war clubs hung on the linen-covered walls. Two manly tufted leather recliners trimmed with brass studs faced each other across a woven sea-grass rug. I paced between the recliners, trying to figure out which was mine, until I spied a stack of spiral notebooks on the side of the chair nearest the door. I went to the wall and ran a finger along the razor-sharp edge of an ancient thong-sewn battle ax. I didn't notice the hairline of blood that angled across my middle finger until I sat down and pushed my chair back to the point where my feet were level with my head. The room had me helpless and off balance. I knew I would be incapable of lying to Dr. Catcher. Also, there was no doubt in my mind that she was older than Karen, and that she was white. I sat there alone for what seemed like a half-hour, eyeing the pottery, the weapons, the vacant leather chair. I started fantasizing about Catcher coming in stark naked, covered with whitish tribal mud, pendulous breasts swinging free. Even though I was sure she was a lesbian I would have bet my savings account that she had grown children, daughters probably, with Ph.D.'s or M.D.'s, who were at that moment happily inoculating swollen-bellied babies in some jungle hell.

The door swung open just as I began to relax and I embarrassed myself by kicking up my feet in an effort to get the recliner up to the erect position.

"Sorry I'm late."

"No, it's me!" The chair finally pulled itself together. In tune with the room, Dr. Catcher was a dead ringer for Margaret Mead; pushing sixty, sporting a gray pageboy bob and black-rimmed round no-nonsense glasses. She wore loose wide wale corduroy pants, a denim work shirt, and carried a thick walking stick fashioned out of a knobby black wood.

"The damn buses run on rubber bands, I swear." She maneuvered herself in front of her recliner then dropped down heavily, making the whole thing jerk back into second gear, the footrest tilting upwards. As she struggled upright to prop the walking stick against the wall, I noticed that one of her legs was supported by a brace. "So Peter, what brings you here?" She took a black cigarillo from her breast pocket, held it in midair and smiled at me. Her lips were thick but precisely defined. She held her grin and her unlit cigarillo as I desperately scrambled for a way to tell her that I knew she was a lesbian but it was okay. Fortunately nothing came to mind and feeling the pressure of her motionless expectant posture I had no choice but to get right into it.

I ran down the whole year from graduation to Marty Klein. I left out my hallucinated Burning Smells in fear of her demanding that I submit myself to a brain scan.

She held the unlit cigarillo a foot from her face for the entire forty-minute tale. Her grin also stayed put, shrinking and expanding with different incidents. She jarred me by laughing at four points in my narrative: the cocaine lunch with Vy; the Chanukah fight; my father's flip response to my not going to law school; and my first bomb call. Her eyes never left my face, they seemed part of her grin, narrowed with Zenlike attentiveness but holding an easy humor.

She grunted mildly when I came to the end, and snapped her cigarillo in half.

"Not exactly a blue-ribbon year for you. . . . What do you make of it?"

"I was angry?" I sounded as if I was apologizing for coming in unprepared.

She raised her eyebrows and gave me a tight smile.

"I mean, what do *you* think?" I tilted my chin at her.

She shrugged and clasped her hands across her belly.

"I really don't know what to say right now. . . ."

I noticed that the door was covered with dark brown cork board for soundproofing and I was hit with a fear that everything I had spewed out in the last hour reeked of a reasonable madness.

"I have to get to know all the principals better."

"Did Klein talk to you about me?" Now she could add paranoia to the prognosis.

"No." She shrugged again. I felt she was humoring me.

"You're not . . . whatever I say to you . . . oh shit . . ." I started sweating. "You don't declare people insane, do you?"

"I ran out of declaration blanks." She gave me a wide smile. "Are you in danger with the draft?"

"Oh God, no." I laughed with nervous relief.

"Let me just get one thing straight . . . so you plan to live there until you can . . . how'd you say it? Break the tension?"

"Well yeah, I mean, I should, right?" Wrong. She was really good.

"How long do you think that would take, a week? A month? Six months?"

"Three weeks?" I pulled that out of my ass. "What are you saying, I should go now?"

"I'm not saying, I'm just asking."

Yeah, sure.

"What, don't you think I should stay?"

She looked at her wristwatch. "Well, let's talk some more about this next time."

I left the office feeling fine. She really was great.

———

That evening I did my last show. I was planning to take the night off but I got into it by reflex. The three of us were watching a twenty-year-old movie about the trials and tribulations of interns working in an urban hospital. The picture was corny and facile, featuring your standard kind-but-gruff Head Doctor, your angry young black intern, your stunningly beautiful female intern and all the other Dr. Kildare heads. The main point of interest seemed to be in spotting all the actors who, in the two decades since the movie was made, had skyrocketed to B-level stardom.

Vy started it, not me.

"I'm dying, look how *young* he is!" She pressed her palm to her cheek.

"Who's that, Tony Curtis?" My father pushed his glasses up his nose.

"He's a *baby. Look* at him!"

"Oh yeah, and that's the 'Combat' guy, Morrow, Vic Morrow."

"Is that Vince Edwards? Ah! *Another* baby . . ."

My turn. "Oh and look!" I pointed to a ninety-year-old man staggering around in a hospital gown. "Can you believe that's Walter Brennan? He looks like a *tyke!*"

They stared at me in confusion.

I nodded toward the token black intern. "Can you believe that's Paul Robeson? Must have still been in *diapers*."

"That's Paul Robeson?" She goddamn well knew that it wasn't Robeson. I felt insulted and alienated by her cautiousness.

I pointed toward Connie Francis playing a nurse. "I don't think I've ever seen Shelley Winters look so good." Please call me on it. Please call me on it. Please call me on it.

"Oh, that's Shelley Winters? I didn't recog . . ."

"Cuh-*mon!*" I wailed in exasperation, making them both ass-hop on the couch. "That's *not* Shelley Winters! Who is it!" I held them at gunpoint with my eyes.

Vy squinted at the screen. My father hissed almost impercepti-bly and studied his hands. There was something in the set of his face, his refusal to study Connie Francis, that promised an explo-sion in the end. But instead of feeling hopeful, I was stopped in my tracks by a baby-sized epiphany: maybe what I had been interpret-ing all along as fear was simply their crude and misdirected attempt at kindness, what I had been calling lack of spine was really Hercu-lean patience. It was a tossup what would make me feel worse, their kindness or their fear.

"Annette Funicello?" Vy ventured.

"The one and only." I smiled at them and calmly went back to watching the flick in polite silence, intent on meeting their possible kindness with my own. Something to discuss with Catcher, just in case she could solve all my problems twenty minutes into the up-coming session and we had some time to kill.

———

I had been looking forward to that second session all week, but from the minute I found myself back in the recliner everything went wrong.

"What I'd like to do, Peter, is get some more information on your parents, get more of a sense of who they are, what it was like for you growing up in Brooklyn."

"The Bronx."

"The Bronx . . . we can pretty much start anywhere, but why don't you give me some early memory of the three of you . . . just for starters . . ."

"What . . . like if I ever walked in on my father screwing my mother wolf-style?"

Her grin shrank but held its shape, projecting a weary patience. She must have seen ten thousand precocious bozos like me since the day she hung up the war clubs. She made a big show of glancing at her wristwatch and peaking her eyebrows as if to say, "Look, shmuck, it's your money and my time, so get on with it."

Fair enough. "Look Dr. Catcher," I leaned forward until my elbows were dug into my thighs. "I'm sorry about the wise comment, but I have to tell you, the only reason I'm here is because I don't want to go to jail and Klein thought it was important that I do this. I'm not kidding myself or you or anybody, I probably need more therapy than God, but ah, I heard somebody once say something like 'I'm too crazy to see a shrink right now' . . . do you know what I mean?" I was wincing, remembering Klein warning me to let people do their jobs.

"You mean you want to come in here once or twice before the arraignment, and we can just sit around, relax, read some magazines . . ."

"No! No! We can talk, I *wanna* talk . . ." I was sounding more and more absurd and obnoxious with every descent into elaboration. "Ah shit . . . just tell me what to do . . . ask me anything . . ." Even that sounded horrible.

"Look, Peter, maybe I should've said this last time, in fact I'm sorry I didn't now, but let me reassure you that no matter what goes on between us, I will do everything in my power to keep you out of jail."

My head sank into my shoulders and I smiled with chagrined gratefulness.

"Not so much because I'm morally opposed to the penal system, but because unless they put you in some minimum-security golf club, I doubt very much you'll be able to survive in there."

I tried very hard to stiffen with bruised masculinity but it was all I could do not to decompose in a blubbery freak-out.

"Do you think I'll go to jail?"

"I doubt it. . . . I hope not."

"You got the Rock Dropper off, right?"

"The who?" Her brow wrinkled and her smile became cautious.

I noticed for the first time the face of her watch; it was a large black diver's model, one of those multidialed, multigauged jobs where you could time how long it took for you to kill a shark. If *she* were going to jail, *she'd* survive.

"I should tell you something else, Peter. I'm an analyst, which means I don't usually do short-term work. I don't do crisis counseling unless something comes up in the course of therapy, but if you feel that you want to work on something strategic right now, I can hold off."

"I gotta get out of here," I blurted. "Not here—that house. I got to get away. I get that ACOD, I got to go."

"What about cracking the tension?" I couldn't tell if she was being sarcastic.

"It's cracked, I gotta go."

We spent the rest of the session packing my bags. I had never thought about where I'd move. I had close to five thousand in the bank at that point, enough to go anywhere, settle in and take my time getting work. Yonkers was out. Catcher suggested Manhattan but I didn't feel ready for that. I had no desire to go to some other major city except possibly Boston, but after batting that around for a few minutes I couldn't feel any excitement. She asked me if there was any place at any time where I had felt particularly happy or functional and before she had the whole question out I said "Buchanon," my body seconding and thirding the motion with sparks of adrenaline.

She didn't do headstands of empathic elation, but she saw me light up and got me talking about the Straight years. In my excitement I made it sound like a cross between the best of Max Shulman and *This Side of Paradise*. She seemed focused on whether I'd go up there not knowing anybody anymore and wind up feeling isolated, but I pointed out that if I moved to Los Angeles or Boston or even Manhattan I'd have the same problem. At least if I headed upstate I would be in familiar surroundings. We discussed the dangers of going back to a place in an effort to try to retreat into the past. She said that college students were no longer my peers and that if I headed out to a new city at least I'd be surrounded by people in the same boat as I was. I wound up bargaining her down to going up there temporarily, until I got my sea legs. I told her that I had no intention of trying to revert to Freddie the Freshman again, that I could take graduate classes and, above all, that I dreaded the notion of becoming one of those fixtures who hang around a college town for a decade after their graduation. I didn't want to become a hippy carpenter with a B.A. in English and I didn't want to become a regular at the bar where I had first thrown up when I was eighteen. I don't know if I believed any of what I was saying, but my excitement had me spewing out a blue-streak of mature perceptiveness. Impressed by my own ad-libbed sensibility, I strolled out of the office whistling "Fight, Straight, Fight."

———

I got the ACOD. Armed with a two-page confidential statement from Catcher, Klein, elbows on the judge's bench, got into a ten-minute over-the-clothesline chitchat with the judge and the Assistant D.A. while I sat between my father and Vy in the empty courtroom. At one point Klein pointed to something in Catcher's report and the three of them started laughing. By the time Klein returned to our table, my nuts were aching from my worrying them like a two-bead rosary.

Before passing sentence the judge chewed me out with a five-minute lecture, not a word of which I heard, although my head was bobbing like a plastic cat in the back window of a car.

There was a hairy moment once we left the courthouse: my father had gotten a parking ticket. Plucking it free from the wipers, he said, "I guess we're *both* in trouble with the law, huh?" And without any shaped thoughts in my mind I found myself walking from the rear passenger door, around the back of the car to where he was standing by the left front wheel and bumping him with my shoulder. It was a light bump, like the tap you get when walking through a crowd moving in opposite directions, and after making contact I just completed the circuit, walking around the front grill and winding up back at the rear door. I don't think he even noticed what I did, but for the entire ride home I almost drove myself crazy trying to figure out if that nudge was a substitute for a hug or a haymaker.

With the heat off, my resolve to move out began to falter. The mood around the living room the night of the arraignment seemed more relaxed, and I held off telling anybody I was leaving. I felt myself in the throes of comfyness and premature nostalgia for the apartment. I was convinced that I was right in interpreting their walking-on-eggshells routine as bungled kindness rather than fear.

We watched *The Manchurian Candidate* and retreated to our bedrooms. I hadn't made one wisecrack all evening. In bed I started reminiscing about Buchanon: party weekends at the fraternity, getting high with Bam-Bam and two pick-ups and winding up in a nude four-way pile-up in our kitchen. I tried to drum up memories of classes, of intellectual discovery, but all that came to mind were visions of sexually chaotic wonder; my crunched fingers scrabbling for the hair line under girdles; watching a drunk pledge lose his virginity to a Townie whore in front of the whole brotherhood during Mercy Week.

I knew I was psyching myself up with Forward into the Past games, but it was working. I was filled with determination again and around midnight I got up and headed for the other bedroom to tell them that I was leaving.

Usually they left their door ajar when they racked out, but that night it was closed. I paused before knocking in case they were screwing, but all I heard was brief murmurs of conversation. Light illuminated my toes from under the crack.

"Hey folks?" I simultaneously rapped lightly and turned the knob. The door was locked.

"Yeah. Peter?" I heard my father's voice from the bed. There was no noise to imply anyone was getting up to let me in and I stared at the unyielding doorknob with a wet buzz of shock. They had never locked the door before and the only reason it would be locked then, or ever, would be to keep me out. To keep me from whacking them out in their sleep.

"Peter, is that you?" from very far away, faint with tension.

"Forget it, never mind." My voice had a light high tremor. I stood frozen, hoping against hope for some sound of sex. For five minutes there was breathless silence on both sides of the door. They must have known I was still standing there so I made a noisy show of padding away and closing my bedroom door. Then I crept back and gently pressed my ear against the wood. My vigil was finally rewarded with the lazy flap of a turned page.

———

The next day I waited for the house to empty, got up, packed two bags and left a note.

Part Two

LINOLEUMS-
VILLE

IT WAS ELEVEN A.M. AND HOT. From two apartments over I heard a perky upstate DJ banter with a breathy giggling teenager phoning in a song request, followed by the kaleidoscopic squawk of someone fiddling with the station tuner and finally stopping for hundreds of bagpipes doing "Amazing Grace." I was sitting fully dressed on the corner of my made bed, staring at a framed hanging the previous tenant had left on the otherwise bare bedroom wall: a poster for a photo exhibit called "Blockade Era Berlin 1946–1949." It was centered by a black and white shot of a war-ravaged Tiergarten totally decimated except for two structures: a distant colonnade, whose solitary fluted height accentuated the devastation; and an ornate statue of a medieval hunter standing beside his horse, triumphantly holding up a fox by the scruff of its neck over four baying flipped-out hounds. The hunter, with his spread legs and proud puffed-out belly and chest, was headless, and the pedestal of the sculpture, which I guessed to be about six feet high, was pockmarked with bullet holes. Since moving in the day before, I had gotten into the habit of studying the spray pattern of the bullet holes, trying to figure out what would have been the optimum position to assume against the pedestal to have survived World War II without a scratch.

The image of that statue had been bouncing around in my head like a pop tune since the landlady had first shown me the apartment nearly twenty-four hours earlier.

It had taken me six hours to make the drive from Yonkers to Buchanon but only two hours to land an address; college town real estate was always an easy knock in the summer months. The place was a furnished one-bedroom on the top floor of a three-story fire trap, but it had a creaky porch overlooking a highway cloverleaf—what my mother would have called "a moving view."

By six in the evening that first day I was completely moved in. After tossing the last ball of socks into the top dresser drawer with an unstoppable hook shot, I wandered around the apartment absently touching things, then went out, bought some sheets and blankets, picked up a few Big Macs, came back and crashed for twelve hours.

———

As the last bagpipe expired on "Amazing Grace," I got up to pull down the manila window shades. My shoes made a sticky ripping sound against the floor, which was covered with linoleum. That was another reason why I rented the place; I hadn't seen serious linoleum since our old apartment in the Bronx, and I found it comforting. Not only did I have linoleum, but the design it bore was a photo-realistic print of rug strands, a wall-to-wall picture of a brown rug. In the living room was a wall-to-wall picture of a lawn—thousands of grass blades, complete with the fleeting shadows of a flock of birds.

I walked into the kitchen to make some coffee and was startled to see six bulging shopping bags waiting to be unpacked, three on the old homey white paint-glossed kitchen table and three on the tomato-red Formica over the unbalanced clunky wooden silverware drawers. Earlier that morning I had gone across the highway to one of the discount caverns and stocked up on kitchen and bathroom necessaries. I couldn't even remember what I had bought or how much the whole show had come to.

Sticking out of one bag was a mustard-colored rubber prong— one of the base supports of a color-coordinated dish drainer and drip mat. The business end of a garlic press peeked out at me from the top of another bag.

There was a seventh bag on the floor. I pulled out a long stapled rack of corn-on-the-cob skewers. The cardboard back was decorated with a picture of some smiling goat-bearded hill-jack, barefoot, bib-overalled, cone-hatted, eating corn and winking at the consumer. I think I'd had corn on the cob once since I was twelve. And then I noticed the kitchen linoleum. When I moved in I'd thought it was just various ugly shades of green with occasional white splotches, but as I stared at it just then it revealed itself to be an amazing printed square of ocean complete with lapping waves and scary whitecaps so that if you really concentrated and stared hard you could develop a nice little vertigo.

The phone rang. I didn't even know I had one. It was the phone company asking me to come down and give a deposit to keep the line open.

I sat on the living room floor tapping a fingernail absently against the spine of the receiver, picked it up and let it rest on my shoulder as I dialed.

"Yo." My father picked up.

"Hi . . ." I murmured sheepishly. "It's the Mad Bomber . . ."

He hesitated. "Yeah, well, don't you worry about it, buddy."

We had a short conversation about my new place, both of us skirting the issue of my abrupt departure, zeroing in on inane obsessional details ranging from the health of my ten-year-old car to the importance of washing new pots, pans and silverware before you use them for the first time—especially Teflon-coated stuff. He didn't ask for my phone number.

When I got off the line, I debated calling Catcher—amazingly, the court hadn't mandated I see a shrink—but I wasn't sure what to say and I opted for writing her a thank-you letter.

———

I slowly cruised through town heading toward the campus. I lived in the townie student section, dubbed Linoleumsville, with its two-story asphalt shingle apartment houses, its repair shops, the grimy windows filled with vacuum cleaner parts and filthy gardenia plants, its cowboy bars, nigger bars, movie marquees advertising meat prices, little Mom-and-Pop grocery stores with their pressed tin ceilings and Corn Flakes pyramids.

As I shot up the ramp to the Exterior Street Bridge, Linoleumsville was a clapboard sea of bleached mints, chipped ochres and dirty chlorine blues all dominated by the absurdly beautiful gold dome and slashed cross of a Byzantine church.

I made my way into Downtown, a mixture of reddish-brown Victorian office buildings, most of them gutted and restored into mini-malls, a few salad bar restaurants, a darling diner, two monstrously huge department stores, a ski shop and a brand new ultra-modern windowless mega-piazza of monolithic state buildings. From there it was over another bridge into Professionalsville, the green section with its spaced-out manorial private homes all clipped, groomed and sparkling for a Preserve Our Precious Heritage paint commercial. This was where the big fish in the little pond lived. I drove at ten miles an hour down the quiet broad sprinklered streets. It was a brutal August day. Everything seemed steamy green and deserted. I coasted past a hot little chickie, a gymnastic-thighed sweet sixteen dawdling in flip-flops and cut-offs. An off-season professor came jogging up behind her. He was wearing gym shorts emblazoned with the school name. His sweat-slick chest was covered with furry gray corkscrews. He was tanly bald with tufts of frizz puffed out over each ear like a clown. He wore rimless octagonal glasses and a sweat band. He looked firm and serious and as he passed her he stared straight ahead as though she were invisible. He stopped two blocks later, sat and did some spread-legged cooldowns on the edge of someone's lawn. As the girl passed him by, he scoped out her High School Ass with an intensity that could have impregnated.

I drove over another bridge and headed toward campus, a brick, concrete and glass eruption gouged into the side of a mountain. I made my way up the campus driveway past huge tear-shaped islands of manicured grass, painfully hot and dull to look at, tended by bare-chested grimacing groundskeepers.

I parked behind Hopper Hall, the English building, walked around to the front, and sat on the side of a fountain along the main esplanade. It was two weeks before registration, one week since the summer session had ended, and the place was devastatingly isolated. From where I was sitting, I could see, in an uninterrupted vista, four perfectly aligned fountains. The only sounds were the twittering of the birds and the wavering nasal droning of a distant fogging machine. I felt this wasn't a real campus but one of those idealized architect's models on someone's display table. And I wasn't human, just a token figure stuck on the side of one of the fountains to give it human perspective.

A small wiry silver-spectacled Indo-Arabic graduate student emerged from Hopper. He wore an oversized lime-green short-sleeved shirt with a pen flap. He squinted hello, scowled at the sun and entered the Computer Sciences building.

Two minutes later out of the same door emerged a tall Ichabod Crane kink-haired undergraduate with a knapsack on his back, khaki shorts and a ten-speed bike with an impossibly high seat. Also grimacing at the brightness, he hoisted himself up on one pedal and as the bike slowly began to roll he absently threw his leg over the seat. Then a fat kid wearing a yarmulka came thunderously jogging by. Then a girl, blond, trim, small-breasted with Izod blouse and pressed shorts—everything so neat and in place that she was almost invisible. Then nothing. Fifteen minutes of nobody. I started singing to myself. First in a whisper, then speaking tone then shouting:

"*KICKS* JUS' KEEP GETTIN' *HAR*-DER TO *FIND*, AND ALL YOUR *KICKS* JUST AIN'T GIV-IN' *YOU* PEACE OF MIND . . ."

I let myself fall backwards into the fountain. It was only six inches deep and had a decorative layer of pebbles. I sat back up on the ledge, streaming water.

"CAUSE YOU DON'T NEED *KICKS* DA DUM DUM DUM . . ." I belted out, frowningly checking my skinned elbow.

"TO *FACE* THE WORLD EACH DAY . . ."

A milky-pale top-heavy blond girl in wrinkly white painter's pants and a maroon Danskin walked by, hands in pockets, trailed by a large happy mutt. She smiled at me when she saw I was drenched, but it was nothing personal.

"What's the story, morning glory!" I grinned, what the hell.

She didn't answer, just smiled again and walked into the building with the dog.

The sun dried me out in five minutes. I started getting a headache from the heat. I drove over to the bar-laundromat-record-store strip adjacent to campus and hit Steve's, the only bar where I came closest to considering myself a regular, which meant dropping in once a month. I thought it would be good for me to start making the rounds, but afternoon bars in a heat wave are sloppy, sticky affairs and I felt disgusted and useless from the minute I walked in.

The tables were empty and there were only three dredge-heads on the stools, one of whom had been sitting there since my freshman year. The air was dank with beer and humidity. I ordered a Utica Club and watched ten minutes of "Bonanza" on the elevated TV. Behind me the long wall held a cartoon mural of the 1940 Simon Straight Arrows, the only team to make it to the Rose Bowl. When I had first laid eyes on the massive group caricature five years earlier it had filled me with a boola-boola reverence, but now as I stared at its reversed image in the bar mirror all I could think of was how many of those guys were probably dead. I finished my beer and that was the end of Round One.

Round Two was better; I went by the phone company and paid my deposit. While filling out forms, I felt my spacy bone-raw malaise start to lift a little. I had moved into my first post-college apartment and I was in the process of taking care of the small details of a new life.

I went over to Con Ed and straightened out my utility arrangements, that feeling of tentative pleasure revving up to a strong glow of intense satisfaction. The whole Suzie Homemaker routine was turning into the most fun I'd had since the first half of my video interview with Mary Heartline.

Running out of billing chores, I made it back to the mall, bought some stationery and ordered a few thousand gummed return-address stickers:

> Peter Keller
> 20 Harry R. Haney Drive, Apt. 7
> Buchanon, New York 14838

On a definite roll now, I drove around searching for the bank with the most idiosyncratic name and opened up checking and savings accounts at Southern Tier Maritime and Agricultural.

The bank officer showed me a sample book of check styles and I was torn between the Polynesia series, featuring orange and yellow drawings of sunsets and pearl divers splashing across the amount and signature lines, and the America the Strong series, which had Minutemen and G.I. Joes charging toward the date blanks. I took one of each—what the fuck, I was putting thirty-five hundred dollars in savings and a thousand in checking. I added my phone number to the address information that would be printed on top. Papa's got a brand new area code.

From the bank I decided to make it out to the suburbs and scout out my old fraternity house. I didn't imagine anybody would be there, definitely not anybody that I would know—the last crop of pledges when I had still been active were going to be juniors—but I had a fantasy of coming on like living history, holding court with a few new brothers and regaling them with Tales of Yesteryear.

As I coasted down the steaming serene streets I felt myself inflate with a desire for conversation, horselaughs, handshakes. I also felt a rising panic that the house would be shut down for the summer. I made myself drive at a crawl as I passed the other fraternities, sororities and house plans, all infinitely more attractive-looking than the dump that I was headed for.

The Pi Omega house was a low-slung two-story white cement monstrosity, fifty yards long and graced with two prefab colonnades in front of the main entrance. It was situated on a quiet crossroads and made a foursome with three other venerable structures: the AGPi house, a white boys' frat, buff stucco cross-hatched with wood beams like a Bavarian ski lodge; the SRO sorority, an unadorned three-story brick peeking demurely from behind tall hedges; and what the guys in our house had dubbed as the Church of Christ the Anti-Semite, a Lutheran split-level futuristic nightmare with a steel cross and redwood exterior.

I pulled up in front of the house and let the engine run. The place looked deserted and I started to sink with disappointment.

The parking lot was empty. The summer heat had split and ruptured the asphalt as if someone had lost control of a pile driver. Despite the mausoleum quiet I took heart when I noticed that there were millions of flies buzzing around the garbage pit that my pledge class had dug as our group project.

I pulled into the lot and walked across to the tacky colonnades, simultaneously straining my brain for a way to break in and wondering if tiptoeing around the empty house would be a violation of my ACOD.

The door was ajar and I stepped inside. Instantly I was socked with a dizzyingly nostalgic odor that could best be described as a combination of industrial detergent and overcooked vegetables. The house was silent and I moved tentatively through the foyer yodeling out shy Hellos every few feet.

I turned into the living room, an enormous dump so big that it comfortably held six separate faced-off squares of furniture. My sophomore year some appalled alumni gave us a few grand for home improvements and the Decorating Committee, six legally blind idiots, went out and bought twelve sectionals and twelve chairs all in the same brown and white washable plaid. The house voted to keep the turquoise wall-to-wall living room carpet.

I stood dead center in the hot and filthy room, slightly drunk with a mixture of trespass and memory, gazing spacily at a battalion of dust motes drifting down across powerful beams of sunlight that came blasting through the undraped windows.

The silence was abruptly broken by the clattering sound of someone tripping down the metal-trimmed stairs from the second-floor dorm rooms.

"Can I help you?"

I turned to face a bearded kid perched a half dozen steps up from the landing. He looked scared.

"Oh yeah, no. I'm, I was a brother here two years ago. I just came by to check it out. I knocked."

"What's your Gamma number?"

The National organization of PiO assigned each campus chapter a Greek letter. Straight's was Gamma, and each brother was given a Gamma number at his swearing-in. What the fuck was my Gamma number?

"Gamma four ninety-nine," I winged it. "Peter Keller." I felt like a jerk but I didn't want the kid to freak on me. I wished there had been a secret hand flap or bird call I could reassure him with. Four ninety-nine did the trick though, and he trudged down to the landing.

"Mark Schiff, Gamma six twenty-eight." He strode across the carpet to shake hands.

The kid looked absurd. He couldn't have been more than nineteen but he was sporting a full Amish beard with a clean-shaven upper lip. That face shrubbery would have looked good on Captain Ahab, but on Schiff it looked like a Halloween purchase from Woolworth's. I sensed a small whiff of my old defensive contempt breaking through the years but even that felt sweetened by nostalgia.

"I'm just watching the house, it's closed. You wanna come downstairs?"

He turned and headed for the floor below. He had an amazingly fat ass. It looked as if he was wearing Pampers under his dungarees. He was also short.

As I followed him down I tried to figure out why I hated him so much. I think it boiled down to my refusing to believe he was a brother. I felt outraged, not so much by his jerky beard or his wagon-train ass, as by his youth. I knew Catcher had warned me that college students were no longer my peers but if this kid shaved, he could do Ivory Snow commercials. He made me feel past it; way way past it.

The bottom floor was half below ground level, divided into the dining room and what I guess could be called the playroom, since it boasted a big color TV and a pool table. Actually I think we called it the Chapter Room but if the other new brothers looked like Schiff, playroom would be more appropriate.

Schiff got involved in an aimless game of solitary pool using a tipless cue stick. The cue ball kept clicking off at unscheduled angles and after a few minutes he gave up and started to roll the balls by hand, trying to bank them into the pockets. Those cue sticks had always been without tips and hearing that naked ineffectual click again stirred up another sensory memory, the feeling of cruddy spacy boredom on a class-free afternoon, the crumbum paralysis of self-revulsion that kept you at that food-stained felt until the dinner gong.

The plaster walls were lined with huge framed chronologically ordered composites of the brotherhood, from 1956 to the present. I found the four in which I appeared, my portrait rising closer to the top as I went from freshman to junior. In a halfhearted attempt to drum up some memory-lane talk I was about to call over Schiff when I noticed that in the picture taken when I was nineteen I had also sported a beard. It was only a goatee because I couldn't grow hair along the sides of my face, but I knew that if I could have, I would have. It would have looked better than Schiff's, though.

Bam-Bam's cocky greaseball smile filled me with sadness and anger. I still loved the asshole, but that was that.

In the house composite taken my freshman year I scanned the top row of senior portraits and checked out the three faces that I had idolized five years earlier; Jerry Marx, a fat slob, a hotel-management major who made his way through college by playing poker and running his uncle's kosher Catskills hotel in the summers; Stuey Krauss who, despite his number-one ranking in the electrical engineering school, drove an XKE and got laid more than the whole house combined; and David Furman, a handsome Philadelphian who was so

shy and pulled into himself that nobody had ever called him anything but David—not even Dave. I had always felt attracted to him
for his tragic but dignified bearing, and for the fact that he was a
body builder who earned money as a male model for art classes.
Those three guys were permanently ensconced in my pantheon of
superheroes and even though I was fully aware that time marches
on and today's pledges were tomorrow's gods for the next generation, as I stood there glaring at that six-year-old composite I refused
to accept the ongoingness of things, the fact that today's Mark
Schiff could be tomorrow's Jerry Marx, that Schiff's future nostalgia would have any validity compared to my own.

"You were the Hellmaster, right?" Schiff strolled over, shaking
two cubes of cuetip chalk.

"Nope."

"But you were something, right? I know I heard your name . . .
oh wait!" He snapped his fingers and sprayed me with crumbs.
"Sorry . . . you were the funny guy, right?"

"Right." I felt half pleased, half dismissed.

"That's really wild, you know? Because a lot of the brothers
consider *me* the funny man now. You want to come up to my room
and get high? I'm starting to talk back to the television. So what do
you do now, go to law school? Everybody's going to law school."
He headed up the stairs, his ass swaying from side to side.

"Actually I was in jail. I spent all year phoning in bomb threats
to movies and restaurants."

"Funny guy," he lilted.

Funny guy. As a Pi Omega, I had finally graduated from Class
Clown to Insult Comic, cracking everybody up with dead-on imita-
tions of the brothers. It got so bad that whenever I sat down in the
dining room everybody would be staring at me with these stupid expectant grins waiting for me to blast off with an impression of Mon-
sieur Gramont, our alcoholic Haitian cook, or the "Steinies," three
juniors, Stein, Steinberg, and Steinman, who were inseparable. I was
never vicious though; in fact, a lot of the guys would ask me to "do
them," and sometimes I would wind up feeling more like a visiting
caricature artist than a brother—which was not great.

———

I had completely forgotten how claustrophobic the bedrooms were. Schiff's place was like the back of a cave, the walls painted midnight blue and his bunk fashioned out of medievally thick wood, each piece looking as though it had been taken from a dismantled ox cart. Two narrow wire-legged Formica desks were jammed together under the window and littered with letters from home—Cedarhurst, by the postmarks—and with dope paraphernalia, including a glass hookah as big as a Pyrex coffee maker. Even the air was boxed in, a sweetish cloud of strawberry incense and old joints.

"This is the one great thing about taking on the house in the summer, man, having my own room. Which one was yours? They're all locked."

"I was right across the hall."

"Shmekele's room."

"Who?"

"Shmekele." He loaded up the water pipe. "His name's Kenny Tuckerman, but he's a *shmekele* so that's what we call him. Here you go." He passed me the pipe. "I use wine instead of water . . ."

It was weak dope, which was just as well. "How come you got that beard?" I started smacking my lips and humming to myself.

"Why? Because I got a fat ass. I got tired of everybody making fun of my ass so I grew the beard to distract them. You know, like fighter planes used to draw bull's-eyes on harmless parts of the fuselage to draw the fire? Now they call me Moses, but that's a fuck of a lot better than Panda Butt, don't you think?"

"Yup." The kid was okay. There was a long row of nineteenth-century novels on the windowsill, a bright yellow USED sticker glued to the spine of each book.

"I got a theory about comedy . . . it comes out of deformity . . . deformed people . . . did you ever see a good-looking comic? It's all us . . . you know Jackie Gleason?"

"I heard of him." Who's us.

"You know I read somewhere that he once lost so much weight he was skinny but he put it right back on because he didn't feel funny anymore . . . my ass is forever but I'm afraid to lose my virginity because it might have the same effect . . . I did a paper on it for Psych; 'Interrelations between Comedy and Physical Deformity' but I got a C because the Prof was almost three hundred pounds."

"No sense of humor." I started getting bored.

"Yeah, my motto is 'fuck ya if you can't take a joke.' I got this really old Nichols and May album, you want to hear it?"

"I'll pass, thanks." I couldn't believe I once lived in a room that size. Bam-Bam had even hung a fishnet on the side of the bunk bed.

"Are you tired? You can lay out on my bed if you want. I never jerk off on the sheets."

"Nah, I think I'll head out, thanks."

"I was gonna see *Fantasia* in town tonight. Walt Disney was a head, it's real obvious if you go stoned. You wanna come? It's playing with a bunch of old Betty Boop cartoons. You ever see them?"

"About fifty times . . . I think I'll just crash." I got up and sauntered toward the door and air.

He followed me out offering up alternative movies for the evening.

"So where do you live now, The Apple?"

"I live up here." I thought of my Polynesian checks.

"Are you married?"

"Divorced." We stood at the base of the stairs.

"Shit, man, if my parents got divorced I'd flip out."

I felt jarred by the connection and sat on an impulse to say, "I'm not your father."

"Well look, Gamma six twenty-eight, I'll see you around, all right?"

"Yeah, okay, hey listen, you know we got an opening for Den Mother, you know House Adviser? If you want I could recommend you. You could eat here free."

"I'll chew it over." I headed for the door.

"Yeah, hey come by tomorrow. I'm gonna get some tips for the cue sticks . . . We could play some eight ball."

"I'll chew it over . . ."

————

The next day I woke up to the realization that I had pretty much run out of rounds to make and a few hours later I found myself completely freaked, sitting on the side of that desolate campus fountain again. The heat drove me indoors and I wound up wandering through Hopper Hall, starting out at sub-ground level where a lot of the English faculty had their offices. I did it pretty much by reflex, having graduated with English honors.

The hallway was cool and shadowy. Strips of computerized grade reports from last spring hung thumbtacked from cork pads on locked office doors. I meandered down the abandoned corridor, reading off familiar professors' names, checking out the few new ones. Most of the professors decorated their doors with either some droll university-life–oriented New Yorker cartoon, a movie still of Bogie, a shot of a jogger, or a flyer announcing a conference which was relevant to their field.

Outside of the flyers everything I saw up there I remembered from over a year ago.

I wandered back up to street level and cased out the English Department bulletin board. Maybe I'd take classes in September. A photograph across the hall caught my eye. Taking a closer look, I involuntarily clapped my hands. It was a shot of a grossly overweight man standing on a deck next to a huge marlin suspended upside down from a dock scale. The fat man, his chin uptilted to the photographer, was smoking a cigar and wearing a fiendish pair of Hawaiian-print swimming trunks. He had one outstretched hand possessively yet casually flat against the big fish. The scale over the marlin registered 425 pounds. Someone had red-inked a stand-up scale under and behind the fat man. That one read 426 pounds. In the lower left corner of the shot was a fishing boat, *The Thin Man* painted in a rainbow arc across the transom. Over the photo was a name tag in a metal slot, PROF. JACK PETTY. Over that was a veneered wood sign, CHAIRMAN'S OFFICE, DEPT. OF ENGLISH, USE OTHER DOOR.

"They made him chairman," I said out loud in that unnatural tone that people use to talk to themselves when they want to be overheard.

"Fat Jack," I barked. "Awright!"

Two years before, Fat Jack had been my idol. I was a Petty's Punk, one of the few handpicked undergraduate Fat Jack worshippers who were chosen to aid him in the teaching of his mammoth lecture course, "The Twentieth Century Popular Novel." On Mondays and Wednesdays Jack would lecture and on Fridays the 250 students went to the mini-seminar of their choice: Raymond Chandler, Harold Robbins, Louis L'Amour, James Cain (mine), Ian Fleming, Mickey

Spillane or Jack's own Dashiell Hammett section. We'd examine the books from psycho-socio-historico-politico perspectives. A real horseshit gut.

As Petty's Punks we didn't get paid; we got extra credit and once a month Jack would throw a dinner for us and our dates in his big house in Professionalsville, which meant booze, Jack on the trumpet, dancing and at least two pass-outs.

Fat Jack.

I ran out to my car giddy with the idea of seeing him again, my head speed-scenarioing past scenes, future scenes. We were almost neighbors, peers as it were, now that I was out of school. Hey Fat Jack! Jack! You old devil! Hey el Professor! Yo! Petty! I drove across the bridge and back down by the sprinklered lawns. Amazingly, the little nubile pubite was still patrolling the pavement. I wanted to tell her I had no more time for that nonsense. I turned up Byron Street and stopped in front of a long two-story brick house with ludicrous Southern Plantation columns.

Jack's nine-year-old, Tucker, was sitting on the front step. Kids freaked me out. I never knew how to talk to them.

Is your Dad in? Is Jack in? Is your Pop in? Is Daddy in? Is Professor Petty in?

I trudged self-consciously casually up the gravel path. "How ya doin'?" I put on an upstate folksy accent.

Tucker just squinted at me.

"Is your Jack around?"

"My father doesn't live here anymore. My parents are having a trial separation. He lives in the Coach House Apartments behind the Plunkett Mall . . ."

I backed down the path, nodding my thanks. Tucker dug at the gravel with his finger. "You should call before you come over."

————

I went home and got Jack's new number. Separated. He'd probably be a total wild man now. Even though I had been a guest in his house at least half a dozen times I had only a hazy recollection of his wife. I don't think she liked our debauchery very much and she rarely came out of the kitchen. Whereas Jack was an eater and an appreciater, she seemed to be more of a server and a cleaner. The only time I remember her breaking bread with everybody was at a late-spring barbecue in their back yard. She seemed nice; she smiled a lot at any rate. But what I remembered more distinctly was Jack's behavior in her presence—strained and subdued—his unhappy moody face making his bad-ass barbecue chef's hat and apron look twice as ridiculous.

"Hello?"

"Hey Jack!" I almost screamed into the phone.

"Yeah?"

"It's Peter Keller!"

"Oh hi, Pete."

Oh hi, Pete.

"Jack, how you doin', man? I'm back in town. Did I wake you up?" I started to waver, smiling ferociously into the phone.

"No, no . . ." Then silence.

"So you're a bachelor, huh?"

"Yup . . . I guess."

"Hey listen, man, whatta you doin' for dinner tonight?" I started pacing and hopping to keep my uptempo going.

"Uh . . . I dunno, Pete . . . I'm feelin' . . ."

"C'mon, man, let's grab a few steaks . . . my treat." I winked.

"Look, I'm feelin' kind of . . ."

"Jack, please." Something snapped and the words came out in a husky urgent plea. I caught myself immediately and stood up straight, but I wouldn't take it back.

Jack sighed. "Awright, kid, why don't you come over here about seven . . . I got stuff here."

"Beautiful."

———

The Coach House development was a six-month-old grayish-beige garden complex with a severe staggered New Mexican cliff-dweller look. Even though the buildings were either two or three stories high, there were no outside walkways or balconies for the top floors, just individual spiral stairways dropping to the ground like fire poles.

"Jack!" I jumped on the shadowy hulk in the doorway. I couldn't see his face but I knew the slope of those shoulders and the smell of that cigar.

"Howyadoin', howyadoin'." He patted my back absently and ushered me inside. I hated being patted.

"Here it is . . ."

I stared at the barren living room: shiny but cheaply finished wood floors, spotless walls, an old black Barcalounger and matching ottoman, a thin ratty spongy couch on wire legs, a twelve-inch portable TV on a steamer trunk and a row of books balanced on the radiator.

"I haven't had time to fix it up . . ."

In front of the couch was a TV tray on folding legs holding a candy-pink plastic serving plate with sixteen slices of cold cuts: four white American, four baloney, four luncheon meat and four yellow American, all arranged in staggered rows. There was a jar of mustard and an open stack of Wonder Bread, a canned root beer and a butter knife.

"Dig in, kid." Jack gestured toward the couch.

"Wait a minute, how about you?"

"Nah, I'm not hungry. You want a drink?"

I followed him into the kitchen; too many new wood cabinets, a baked-bean–crusted pot on the electric range, and a card table in the corner. Jack poured himself two inches of Scotch in a McDonald's glass and opened the refrigerator. I turned my head away. I didn't want to see what was inside.

The couch was constructed so that when you sat back your ass was lower than your knees. I had to perch myself on the edge; even then the stack table was up to my chest and I had to reach up for my food.

Jack sat across from me, collapsed into the Barcalounger, his stained Hush Puppies crossed on the ottoman. He watched me eat, his head resting on the extended thumb of his cigar hand. He weighed almost four hundred pounds, but he looked drawn. His turkey pouch lay unjiggling under his chin, his eyebrows looked hoary and white, his eyes and mouth were pulled wearily down at the corners and he stared dully from my plate, to over my shoulder at the wall. He was driving me crazy. I wanted that gravelly machine-gun laugh, some bawdy homemade ditty.

"So you're a single man, hah?" I wiped my lip with the back of my hand.

He shrugged, stuck the dead cigar in his mouth and smoothed back his straight hair with both hands. The turkey pouch quivered slightly.

"Yeah, I think it's for good this time. I think it's for good . . . we've been separated before but . . ." He pulled out the cigar, spat absently on himself and brushed his shirt with his fingertips.

"She couldn't take your doggin' around?" I was treading on thin ice, but I'd rather he got pissed at me than die on me.

"I'm the one who asked for a divorce." He tilted his head to his other hand.

"Was *she* foolin' around?"

He closed his eyes and ever so slightly shook his head. "We just had a bad Independence Day weekend. I woke up that Monday morning with a headache that wouldn't quit and I said that's it for me."

"Wow . . ."

"I just want a divorce. I'll give her everything except *The Thin Man* and the bike . . . she says she'll give me a divorce only if I see a shrink so I've seen three shrinks. Each one thinks getting divorced is no big deal, but they want to stop me eating and smoking before I kill myself. This last guy even said how can you justify wanting a new lease on life when you shovel in enough food for a family and smoke seventy-five cigars a week? So I go see these guys, I call Nancy to tell her what the guy said, she tells me to stop seeing him or she won't give me a divorce, then she calls me back two hours later to give me the phone number of a new guy. I go see the new guy, he tells me the same thing, let's put the marriage issue on hold, how come you're so fat? Tomorrow I see a fourth guy." He shrugged. "I think she's trying to get me committed . . . trying to get someone who'll put me in the bin . . . I dunno, she's a good woman." He gave out with a staccato belly laugh, relit his stub and spit again. I sat up straight with hope.

"You know, she thinks it's so and so that made me leave or so and so or so and so . . . not true . . . not true . . . it's none a them, it's all a them . . . an' Christ, Petey, I *love* broads. I always have, I always will. I get together with the next one, she's gonna have to learn to live with it too . . ."

"Yeah, right." I nodded grimly like I had the same problem. Go Jack go.

"You know, it was always easy for me . . . I'm a father figure or something. . . ." A little color started coming into his face.

"But take that weekend, the Fourth of July . . . I'm watching the ball game in the den, she comes in, she says 'You have to talk to Erland, he's masturbating in his room and it smells of semen . . .'" He raised and collapsed his hand in exasperation, winced, paused, turned his head away as if counting to ten, and turned back to me. "Of *course* he's whacking off in his room, what the hell do you *expect* from a fourteen-year-old, what the hell am I supposed to say to him?"

I shrugged in agreement.

"She says 'I don't care *what* you say to him. The room smells of sex . . .' So I go up to the kid's room and I say, 'Jesus Christ, Erland, if you're gonna beat off buy a bottle of Airwick or something before you get us *both* in trouble.' Okay . . . so that's settled . . . the next day it's Jackie, the eighteen-year-old, the big one . . . she saw a woman's footprints up against the inside of the windshield in the kid's car, he's been screwing his girlfriend in the front seat. She wants to take his car away." Jack glared at me, his cigar held daintily at cheek level, his chin firm. "I . . . will . . . not! Then go talk to him . . . Okay, so here I go again, the Airwick man, two in two days. I go out to the kid by his car. I say Jesus Christ, Jackie, if you're gonna screw a girl in your car use the defroster, use the windshield wiper . . . and I see he's laughin' at me and I get real mad, not at him, I don't blame him, so I says, fer chrissakes use yer goddamn room! And you know what?"

"That's exactly what he did." I felt happy.

Jack nodded yes.

"And his mother catches him in there that night and he says to his mother that Dad said it was okay. All *hell* breaks loose and she wants to punish all the guys in the house, she wants Erland and Jackie to sign up at Misericordia to do volunteer Meals on Wheels every Saturday and Sunday and I said 'Oh no! Oh no!'" Jack waved his cigar hand straight out in front of his face. "Oh no! You gotta be fuckin' kiddin'!" He laughed. "And then she says she wants *me* to do it too! You *gotta* be fuckin' kiddin'." Jack bolted forward in his chair, arms plopping down on the armrests, bursting out in a full-blooded two-ton woodpecker laugh. "Meals on Wheels!" He was laughing so hard he started speaking in falsetto. "Can you fuckin' imagine? The poor kid's been beating off all day and as punishment he's gotta serve food to sick people. And *me* no less! I gotta do it too! You know? I mean it's me all along . . . it's not the boys. Look, we're laughin' now, but at the time I blew my fuckin' top, kid." He drifted off into light chuckles, staring into his smoke. "You know what the problem was, Pete? She wasn't my type . . . she's a sweet woman for the right guy but she wasn't my type." We were both smiling. He looked twice as healthy as he did when I walked in. "Ah, look, kid, I'm forty-four years old . . . and it wasn't gonna improve . . . I had nothing to lose. I'll give her everything but my motorcycle and *The Thin Man*. I'm not fooling anybody. I'm a three-hundred-and-sixty-six-pound middle-aged man and I'm telling you it wasn't worth the security. You want some more root beer?"

I shook my head no. Someone sneezed in the next apartment. The walls were so thin I could hear the clicking sounds wet nostrils make when rubbed with a handkerchief.

"You know, Peter?" Jack beamed at the ceiling. "I think everything I just said to you is a big bunch of bullshit. I could handle her." He shrugged. "The kids could handle her. I could've stayed in that house and screwed around to my heart's content. It wasn't any of that . . . I think what it was was that I was scared to death of no more curves in the road. I could see straight down to the toll booth. I have to keep shaking things up. I have to." He stuck the dead-again cigar in his mouth and held out both hands palms up, one pointing to the books skylining the radiator, one to my cold cuts. "So now I'm here, some fun, hah?" He snickered and for a moment his face sank again, his skin sagged and his fingers hung limp from his curled wrist. "So, what brings you back to town?" he said in a thin monotone, his eyes over my shoulder.

I saw him start to go down again but before I could say anything he popped up. "Aw Christ, it's good to talk to you, Petey. I haven't talked to anybody all summer. I'm sorry about my mood, kid, it's just a rough time. I'm not myself, that's why I wasn't so hot on getting together. You want some more root beer? Just bear with me, I'll be back on top. It was just a hell of a summer, you know?"

"I'm with you all the way, Fat Jack . . ."

"So how the hell you been? *Where* the hell you been? You look worse than me . . . gimme one a those." He lurched upright, snagged two slices of luncheon meat and inhaled them out of sight before his ass crashed back into the Barcalounger.

"Well, I'll tell you Jack, if you ever run out of road curves . . ." I let it hang.

"You having a rough time with law school?"

"*What* law school? I didn't get in."

"Aw, I thought you were on your vacation."

"Not only am I not in law school, I'm on six-month probation."

Jack pulled his chin back. "What kind of probation? I thought you graduated."

"*Legal* probation, captain. I got arrested last month for false reporting of an incident, disturbing the peace and aggravated harassment . . ."

"Did you get into a bar fight or something?"

I was flattered by the question. I ran down the entire year, all the jobs, the lonelyhearts club scene, my father, the television. . . . The only problem was that every time I tried to relate an incident, what a job felt like, what a date felt like, what watching TV felt like, it always came out funnier than I wanted. I'd be cracking up halfway through my own recitation. And when I got to the part where the detectives came to say they found me out on the wiretap I stood up and acted out all the parts, my stepmother's hysteria, the dicks' laid-back Broderick Crawford style, my own huffy exit.

"God! I can't even talk in private on my own phone!" I hunched over in front of Jack, my face stretched and seamed in squinty astonishment, "Can you be-*leeeve* my fucking balls!!!"

Jack winced. "Ssh, easy kid, these walls are like tissue."

"Wow." I pulled back, shaking my head at my own saga. My face was beet red. The second Jack sshed me I realized I had been shouting since he'd asked me if I got into a bar fight. I sat back down on the lip of the insane couch. Jack was still wincing. He had been wincing since I began. I looked up at him leaning his head against his palm, his cigar stub looking as if it was sticking out of his ear. He stared at me, bit his lip, and sadly shook his head. "So then what happened?"

I ran down the rest of my update in a rapid dull monotone, leaving out any incident or detail that might be misconstrued as comic.

I took it right up to my disastrous pilgrimage to the fraternity. When I finished I realized that I hadn't written Catcher that thank-you note yet.

Jack took in part two of my story with weary hisses, commiser-ating tick-tock movements of his head and, at the worst parts, eyes closed in pain.

"And you know, this is kinda rough too, right now . . . it's lonely, this is a creepy time to be up here. It's limbo zone right now with no school and I still got that physically shitty feeling about myself, that insect thing from when those guys were looking at me . . ." I rolled my neck. "I think I'm gonna take up running or weight lifting . . . try to work out or something. I already stopped smoking . . . but anyways . . . I dunno, I'm climbin' the fuckin' walls still, I guess." I shrugged and laughed. My head hurt.

"Aw Christ, Pete." Jack's palm gave his right eye an oriental slant as he continued to stare at me. "It's good to see you kid . . . I'm sorry you had such a rough year."

"Yeah, well, Brave New Worlds and all . . ."

"So what are you gonna do for dough?"

"I got about four thousand, a little more; I can hang in for a while. I'll get some job in town . . . I worked in Kresge's last year. I can probably do that, or hit the malls or something."

"Well shit, do you wanna teach?"

"Are you kidding?" I sat up straight.

"No?"

"Yes! Where?"

"I can throw you a section of Freshman Comp and take you on as an adjunct. It's not much, maybe twenty-five hundred for the term."

My heart was banging away on the inside of my face. I let my hands dangle down the front of the couch. I slowly nodded my head, my mouth open. "You're serious, right?"

"Sure."

"How could you do that though? How can you hire me now?"

"Hey, I'm the chairman." He casually waved. "I can do anything I want . . . besides, they like me better after last term. I only went twenty thousand over budget. The term before I was over by thirty so I saved them ten thousand." He laughed.

I stifled half a dozen Oh wows and Oh Gods. "Do I get an office?"

"Yeah, we'll fix you up with an office . . ."

"You're the fuckin' *best*, Petty. How the hell did you get to be chairman?"

"Well, Harris died the summer you graduated and the only three eligible guys not too obviously senile were Fonseca, Turley and myself. Fonseca I don't have to tell you about, Turley wasn't interested and that leaves me." He held his cigar aloft and raised an eyebrow. "So I'm the chairman . . . I'm very good too . . ."

"Do I have to be there at registration?"

"Nah . . . it might be a good idea to hang around your office for the students though."

"My office . . ." I murmured. "Jack, I fucking love you."

"Yeah, well . . ." He smiled. I sat there filled with a brandy warmth. I stared at Jack's thick forearms. I wanted a steak.

Neither of us spoke for a few minutes. I noticed that for balance, the right rear leg of his Barcalounger was sunk into a paperback, *The Gospel According to Peanuts*. It must have been Tucker's, packed by mistake. He had another kid too, Donald, who was sixteen. Jackie, Donald, Erland, Tucker.

"Hey Jack? . . . If you were my father, what would you have done with me after I got caught?"

He didn't answer right away. "I dunno. If you called up a restaurant where I was eating and I had to leave my meal?"

I started chortling.

Jack sat up straight, his face red, eyes intense and bulging, his pouch going wild. "I'd break your fucking ass!"

He started barking, leaned across the room and slapped my kneecap. "Oh God." He collapsed back in the Barcalounger. "I feel good now . . . I feel good. Jesus . . . did I ever tell you about my father? He was really something else . . . played semi-pro baseball, ran a charter boat out of the Keys, cut a record, man, he did everything. *God* I loved his ass." Jack chewed his lip and shook his head in glassy reverie. "He wanted me to play football. I got an athletic scholarship to the University of Florida . . . but anyway my father . . . yeah, my old man was famous for his steel stomach. He'd eat anything for money—glass, pebbles, shoes—the guy was a one-man Saturday

Night. You know how he died? He ate a poison-ivy sandwich for a ten-dollar bet. He had a thirty-two-inch waist, my father. He died from eating a sandwich."

Jack finally tossed away the cigar butt and gave a soft laugh. "Real good guy though. Listen, let me kick you out, I gotta see a shrink at eight tomorrow."

He struggled to his feet.

"Wash your dishes before you go, okay? I hate washing dishes."

———

When I got back to my place I was startled to discover one last pregnant shopping bag in the kitchen. I started pulling things out like an amnesiac opening self-bought birthday presents. Besides the garlic press and the corn skewers I discovered that I had bought three family packs of generic toilet paper—twenty-four rolls in all—and three bags of brightly colored sponges—forty-two in all. For the life of me I could not remember a single purchase and the selections I'd made were scaring me to death, but then I pulled out a corkscrew, which was sort of optimistic, and next I came to a smaller bag, the paper twisted around the neck of a bottle. I ripped open the bag and held triumphantly aloft, label at eye level, a nineteen-dollar bottle of champagne.

———

The day after I saw Jack I went to the administration building to find out what office I'd been assigned, and of course there was no record of my being hired.

Jack was nowhere to be found. I grew totally frantic. At his wife's house I found out from his oldest kid, Jackie, that he'd gone to fish off Key West and was living on *The Thin Man* for the next week. I called the Coast Guard and asked them to contact him somewhere out in the Atlantic, trying to communicate to them that the matter was life and death but not really, don't freak him out, just tell him to call Peter.

He phoned me from a bar that night, fairly pissed when he heard I only wanted to remind him that he should tell the administration about me. I put on my vulnerable crazy-kid routine and he softened up enough to tell me his secretary was arranging it and yes, I was definitely hired, no backsies.

The next day I tried to persuade the custodian to unlock Hopper B-33. He refused because I couldn't prove it was mine. Besides, I looked like a student.

I was so wired I couldn't concentrate. I got into watching clocks and calendars. I went out and bought a book on the art of teaching Freshman English, but I couldn't read anything more complicated than a cartoon with a caption, even comic books seemed too busy for me. I began to feel even more keenly the solitude of the town; my lingering emotional hangover from the last year's events intensified. I remembered what I'd said to Jack about maybe running or going to a gym to sweat that malaise out of my bones. The phys. ed. center was closed so I scouted gyms around town.

There was a smoked glass health spa in between a Lum's and an Arby's on the town's Miracle Mile—a low-flung flagstone facade with a sharply slanted roof, two fountains and an eternal flame on the lawn. But I didn't like Nautilus machines. I'd taken Nautilus as a gym elective my junior year and had felt as though I was trying out for the Mercury space program. Besides, the spa was four hundred a pop, no partial memberships.

On the outskirts of Linoleumsville I found another place called Zybysko's Health Institute. It was on the second floor of a two-story puke-green shingle building over an Electrolux dealership. As I trudged up the narrow stairs to the pointing-finger sign on the second landing I heard haunted-house clanks and groans. The hall smelled like hot feet.

There were three rooms off the corridor: one was a Guys 'n' Dolls Unisex Barber Shop, the other two were the campus of the Institute. I stood in the doorway of one room with my jaw on the floor watching a dozen Institute associates stomp around like dinosaurs in T-shirts in front of floor-to-ceiling mirrors. A traffic jam of narrow padded benches—some flat, some slanted—almost concealed the nubby industrial gray carpet and the room was littered with iron. No Nautilus, not even Universals, just dumbbells and barbells.

The only touch of decoration in the place was the centerfolds of bronzed human ripple factories from *Strength and Health* magazines Scotch-taped over the mirrors, some of them straight out of the 1950s, stiff and fake Grecian.

None of the Institute members bothered to check me out. They were union-card types, a real bunch of Ottos, lurching around in baggy gym shorts and high black Keds. They sported pompadours and didn't give a shit about fitness, sleekness, or conditioning. It seemed they loved to lift up heavy things and put them down again.

The weirdest thing about the place was that no one there seemed to be under thirty. I guess the younger townies used the university or the Community College gyms, or maybe they preferred ball sports.

Only one guy in the room wore street clothes. He was reeling around on a locked right leg. His right arm hung dead at his side. Despite the heat he wore a stretched-out turtleneck. Noticing me in the doorway, he reared back, kicking up his bum leg like a pitcher, and picked his way across the room. I couldn't tell if he was a lifter too because his clothes were too baggy.

"Help you, son?"

"Is this where the Chinese Cooking class meets? My daughter spilled Krazy Glue on my wok but I can double up with somebody else if it comes down to it."

He stared at me straight-faced. "No . . . there's no classes here."

"I'm only kidding." I gave out a hearty chuckle. "Do you have any memberships available?"

"For a class?"

"No, for the gym. I was only kidding about the class."

"'Cause we don't have any classes here . . ." He walked into the corridor, curling a finger over his shoulder for me to follow. I walked stumblingly slow behind his rolling limp. His desk was alongside a wall rack supporting a brace of upended barbells. The room also had chinning bars, slantboards for sit-ups and a strange chain link contraption with a barbell and a slant bench set up for bench presses.

I wrote out a check on his desk.

"Stand up." He tilted his chin at me and gave me the once-over, leaning to his side and squinting as if to get a better view.

"You go to college?"

"I'm a professor."

"How many classes you teach?"

"One."

"Good. I want you here every day . . . have your mail sent here . . ." I was disappointed he didn't comment on how young I was to be a teacher.

He opened a desk drawer and pulled out two mimeographed lists. The first was my lifting routine: Monday, Wednesday and Friday it would be crunches, hanging knee-ups and twists, fifty each for my gut, then ten different routines—presses, pullovers, dips, chins and laterals—for my chest, back and shoulders; Tuesday, Thursday and Saturday the same stomach itinerary followed by ten assorted routines of curls, lifts, lunges, raises, extensions and hack squats for my arms and legs. The other list was "Roy's Bulk-up Diet," a four-meal-a-day program including two separate cooked meat dishes, three different cereals or desserts with sweet cream, two puddings, a quart of milk, grape jelly, muffins, sandwiches and a malted. I figured I'd be shoveling in food nonstop for eight hours then lifting weights for another eight, which would leave me eight for sleeping.

I looked up and saw over Roy's head a Dax-framed picture of him ripping a phone book in half while smiling at the photographer. His arms had been huge. I stared at the folds in his turtleneck trying to use my X-ray vision to see what he looked like now. He studied me studying him. "I can still do that . . ." He lifted my check, raised a pair of feminine glasses to his eyes and read my name ". . . Pete."

A huge sweaty lifter, a refrigerator with a head, came in, sat on the desk and thumbed through a weird sepia-tone magazine called *Man of Bronze.*

"Roy, did *Health and Strength* come in?"

"Why don't you guys buy your own fucking magazines?"

The lifter shrugged and got up, leaving a huge horseshoe of sweat on the desk.

"I'm still a strong bastard . . . a grenade went off in my hand." He tapped his dead arm.

"Were you in the service?"

"No, I was a fucking male nurse at Misericordia and we ran out of Ex-Lax . . . wha'dya think?" He smiled.

Zybysko's Health Institute saved me from going insane for the next two weeks. I was in better shape than I thought; none of the crunches, the knee-ups, the elevated sit-ups made me cramp. I kept the weights light, twenty-pound dumbbells and no more than fifty pounds on the barbells. Sore felt good, meant something was happening. My favorite routine was the decline barbell press. There was only one bench and barbell set-up in the whole gym, and since the routine was crucial for just about everybody, there was always a crowd of guys hanging around the apparatus, some smoking cigarettes, waiting for their set. It was like the office water cooler, the sociable routine.

The first few days I felt too self-conscious to take a turn with everybody around, so I just watched.

It was a simple set-up. A short forty-five degree slant board was positioned with the lowered end under a barbell that rested on two metal supports. The lifter hooked his kneecaps over the padded high end and let his body roll down the length of the bench, his blood-gorged head resting on the padded lower end, two feet lower than his knees. The barbell was directly over his collarbone. He would reach up, lift the bar off its support and proceed to do his set while another lifter, standing behind him, would hover over the action, his hands near the bar in case the first lifter got tired or lost his grip and preferred not to have his larynx crushed. I watched these three particular guys who worked out together, same time same station, every day. They would rotate, one on the bench, one spotting the bar and the third stomping around, heaving like a bellows, chinning and curling everything in sight to psych himself up for his turn. They went around the horn like that until they each did five sets of decline presses.

If there was no one else waiting, they would pull out the bench, reverse it so their heads were higher, their feet flat on the ground in a sumo squat, and do inclines. They all weighed at least two hundred pounds and had pecs with deep-cut definition like armor plating.

One guy was bald with auburn muttonchops and freckles; one was crew cut with a receding hairline, a long dog nose and big teeth; and the third had a full biblical beard, a huge stomach and prescription sunglasses.

At the end of the first week I made my move. As they were setting up, stacking plates onto the ends of the bar, I sucked it in and asked if I could join the party. They once-overed me and said sure.

Everybody hesitated for a second and I extended my hand to the guy closest to me.

"Pete Keller."

"Red Messing."

We all shook hands, lurching forward with extended mitts and down-sloping heads, murmuring names. They let me go first since I was the lightest and probably the weakest. I hooked my knees over the edge, curled down the board and smacked the back of my head on the barbell. The guy with the muttonchops, Red, touched the back of my neck and guided me under the bar. He was spotting for me. Upside down, seeing the three of them—all older than me, bigger than me, with those absurd balloon heads—made me chortle with nervousness. They had seventy-five pounds on for me and I made it through my first set with no sweat and they all murmured approval. When I sat up, feeling like a miniature Godzilla, they put on another hundred pounds of plates and went at it, hunching over and barking encouragement. When it was my turn again, they removed the extra plates, and I did the presses a little more confidently. By the fourth set, fifteen minutes later, my arms were on fire, my elbows locking with relief at the peak of each lift, and my face felt like a clenched fist. When they started growling and bawling at me, "Get it, Pete! One more! C'mon, *one* more! Go, Pete!" my first reaction was, How nice that they should care . . . do not make them mad, and I found myself arching my back off the board and doing two more quick presses, then a trembly torturous third, Red whispering hotly in my ear, his palms under the bar, the other two guys shouting from the sidelines, their faces pinched in empathy, their voices squeezing out "C'maaan" as the bar slowly inched up to the supports where I curled back my wrists and dropped it in place with a crash. When I raised myself up smacking my forehead this time, air-headed and giddy, grabbing onto the kneecap end for support, they all cheered and clapped and I felt as if I'd just popped out of the womb.

I began to live for that hour on the bench with those guys. I started going to a diner with them every day to bulk up on malteds and roast beef after the workout. I was walking pigeon-toed and bowlegged like them. I bought myself a little blue gym bag like theirs. I was into the way they would walk to the diner, their heads sunk into their huge sloping shoulders, carrying that dainty little gym bag at the end of two curled fingertips. It was the gym bag that made them larger than life and cartoon-hero powerful. It added perspective.

The beard was an ex-jailbird majoring in hypnotism at the Community College, Red was a short-order cook at the college, and the crew cut was a gas station owner and a member of the Klan whose gym bag was emblazoned with a bumper sticker, "Out of work and hungry? Eat a conservationist."

By the second week I was a regular. After doing all my bicep routines I liked to lean out the window facing Exterior Street, looking bored and tensing my arms. I was more into advertising my membership than my muscles, but I think I could actually feel a little tightness that wasn't there before, a few foreign-feeling outcrops over my ribs and in the backs of my upper arms. I began lurching around frowning at my triceps like everybody else.

———

Even though my life seemed to be coming together, one of the things that was still fucking me up was my father. He never called me, and the few times I phoned him he sounded slightly formal and under the gun.

When I told him that I had been hired to teach he said "Really?" his voice filled with a lukewarm amazement as if I had just pitched a four-hitter.

One night, about a week and a half after I started at the gym, I got him on the line and early on in the conversation I told him about the gym, my new meathead pals, the different exercises and so on, and about ten minutes later he said, "So, are you getting any exercise up there?"

I snapped at him, "I just got finished *telling* . . ."

And he said, "Oh oh oh oh yeah yeah yeah sorry sorry . . ."

In that moment I realized he was still afraid of me, afraid to anger me. I felt myself drift out in space like an astronaut with a snapped lifeline, slowly spinning, getting smaller and smaller.

———

Labor Day weekend, the gym and the rest of the world were closed, including all the twenty-four hour diners. It was too hot to watch

TV, I had seen all the movies in town and I wound up in the Grey-hound station drinking coffee and writing a poem on my napkin about all the bus-heads, the incredible Greyhound subculture of loners and poor families in this country, armies of sideburns and small suitcases, big belt buckles and obscure tattoos. And nobody ever talks, except on the bus-station pay phones where, squinting, they read names from small scraps of paper to operators.

When I finished the poem I folded up the napkin, put it in my wallet and walked out into the Terminalsville section of town. I'd done some writing as a student, mostly poetry, and I'd been pretty good, good as in "clever," but I never took it seriously. A few teach-ers had encouraged me, Jack for one, but after knocking off a piece of "creative" writing, I usually felt slightly embarrassed and a bit like a rip-off artist.

The day after Labor Day, students began arriving, and like a long beard in the desert I was joyous for the company. I walked around the freshman dorms watching cars pull up and unload, lots of big boats, Electras and New Yorkers, a few Caddies. I keyed in on one father, burbed out in shades and a neck chai, wearing cream-colored slacks and white patent-leather loafers. He was unloading his kid's speakers and amp while the mother smoked cigarettes and issued verbal memos, one hand clutching the collar of a wired-up eight-year-old. The father, hunched over a turntable, paused and squinted open-mouthed at the awesome vista of mountains and towers while his son, slightly dressed up as if visiting grandparents and straining under the load of a carton of records, duck-walked into the dorm.

Over in Linoleumsville the hip non-frat upper classmen were moving back into their houses and boarding rooms. One guy wear-ing construction boots, khaki shorts and a mildly politicized T-shirt pulled out a milk crate of New Directions and *Livre de Poche* pa-perbacks from the sliding side door of a ratty van and, smiling ironically, lugged it past three tasty senior girls in cheap halters, rubber thongs and Aunt Jemima kerchiefs sitting and smoking on the broad gray paint-glossed stoop of their ramshackle house.

I was so grateful for all this company that I walked up and down Exterior Street, up and down the dorm lanes, absently clapping my hands.

Registration started the next day in the gymnasium and I was finally allowed in my office: a gunmetal gray desk, a swivel chair sliding around on a transparent plastic square floor protector, floor-to-ceiling steel bookshelves with adjustable notched shelves and a four-by-four cork board. My window overlooked a little courtyard where the secretaries liked to have lunch. After rolling around on my casters for fifteen minutes, I went home and got my Berlin blockade-era poster to put up on the office wall. Then I found an antique store and bought a weird bulbous gem-studded bronze lamp for my desk. I also picked up an ashtray in the shape of a miniature rubber tire—a souvenir of the U.S. tire exhibit of the 1939 World's Fair. For my book shelves, all I had was my black and silver 1930s Rockwell Kent–illustrated edition of *Moby Dick*, a novel I had been trying to finish since junior high school.

I went up to the English office and made a big deal of rummaging around the supply closet, taking a stapler, a box of pointless pencils, some school stationery and a roll-call book.

I flirted and joked with the secretary, a quiet friendly lady named Fiona, whom I vaguely remembered from my senior year. She was the one who really ran the English Department, acting as informal ombudsman, Xerox queen, psychological nurse and faculty wife-at-large. She had a way of giving me the impression I was the only one in the department she could curse in front of; when someone else came into the office she cut off our conversation with a "hold on" raise of the eyebrows and spoke to the intruder with an entirely different, official voice, while I lingered and doodled, feeling like part of the in crowd.

At noon, stapler and pencils lined up on my desk, my one book in alphabetical order, my alliance with the secretary established, I sat and waited for customers.

After a half-hour of jumping up any time a student passed my doorway I started contemplating pulling them in from outside like a rug salesman in an Arab bazaar.

When I finally left the room to wander down the hallway, I headed for the first slanted rectangle of light in my path, which was emanating, unfortunately for me, from the open doorway of Dr. Aaron, who was known as a legendary fetus, a notorious bore. As I passed his threshold, I made the mistake of raising my head and getting stopped in my tracks by the extremity of his decorating statement. Aaron, the department's Folklore man, was in addition to all his other magnetic traits a total Book Loon, and his office was a dizzy cave of floor-to-ceiling tomes, with half again as many stacked and scattered about like tree stumps across the floor. Behind the desk, which supported two tall spires of volumes curving in surrealistic impossibility on either side of the blotter, sat El Professor—paunchy and middle-aged. With his thick shaggy gray-streaked hair, goatee and heavy black glasses, he looked like a learned buffalo.

He rocked in his swivel chair, oblivious to my shadow, stroking his chin hairs and reading a thin black paperback of *Njals Saga.*

"Hello?" I gave his door a rap.

"Sorry." He didn't look up. "We're sold out."

"Excuse me?"

"All the sections are closed."

I found that hard to believe.

"Oh no." I stepped inside. "I'm on the faculty." I liked the sound of it.

He finally raised his head, shoebrush eyebrows arching over the thick frames of his glasses.

I picked my way around the book stumps and made it toward the desk. "I'm Peter Keller. I'm teaching Comp. I thought I'd introduce myself."

"Oh!" He struggled to his feet and shook my hand. He was wearing comfortably bunchy gray slacks and a cheap thin much-washed black turtleneck that showed off his kettledrum gut. "Have a seat." He offered me a chair piled high with more books. "Just throw them anywhere."

The man was definitely dug in for the duration. Besides the school-issue steel shelves, he had three other bookcases, old scarred walnut giants, two with cut glass-paneled doors. The ambiance appealed to the triple Monster Movie Matinee fiend in me.

"Yeah, I have a section of Comp. I graduated from here a year ago. I don't think I ever had a class with you, though."

He nodded and played with his goatee. His eyes could have been looking anywhere behind the headlight camouflage of those goggles.

"I once tried to get into your *Nibelungenlied* seminar but I wasn't

fast enough. That thing must have closed out in minutes." Haw. He
leaked a small smile but remained silent.

I didn't know what else to say. I knew he hated Tolkien, but I
couldn't get into that rap.

"You seem very nervous," he mused.

I was both startled and pleased by the intimacy of the comment.

"I'm *very* nervous." I whirled my head in emphasis. "Has any
teacher ever vomited in their first class?" The question was false. I
hadn't even started thinking about lesson plans yet but I wanted
him to ask me more personal stuff.

"Not that I know of . . ." he shrugged.

That seemed to end that. I felt as if I was on a disastrous blind
date. "I know a lot of athletes vomit before a big game"—Jesus
Christ—"but they're usually okay after that . . ." I trailed off, looking down at my hands, and envisioning Tolkien in a Green Bay
Packer uniform kneeling before a toilet. I noticed that all the books
in the stack closest to my feet were in German.

"Well . . ." He shifted in his chair, which emitted a flock of
squeaks, "in Caligula's time, the Romans would put a rotten fish in
a silver bowl out in the sun. After a day or two the fish would decompose into a liquid they called *garum*. So if a Roman felt stuffed
full at an orgy he'd just drink some *garum*, vomit, go back in and
keep eating."

"That's wild."

"Do you know the English derivative of *garum?*" he followed
through, his voice turning sly.

I frowned at the ceiling and thought hard about how much four
years of tuition had come to.

"Give up?" He folded his arms across his chest.

I shrugged and took a stab. "Gore?"

"Right!" His teeth gleamed through his beard. Despite the lu-
nacy of the conversation I felt ecstatic with triumph.

A sad fat ripple-chinned girl knocked on the open door.

"Sorry, we're sold out," he sang.

"I know," she said wearily. "I'm registered already." I got up and
arched my back which protested with a loud alarming pop. "I should
get back to my office."

"Do you know the English adaptation of the Latin *coynt?*" he blurted nervously, his grin turning greasy with anxiety.

Coynt was the ancient source of "cunt." I was shocked that he threw that at me in front of a coed and I tried to save his ass by pretending that I didn't hear him. You nathty man. I was torn between disgust and a pathetic kind of tenderness.

"Well, drop in any time." He shot up to shake my hand, bumping one of his precariously balanced spires, which began to reel in a slow-motion prelude to disaster. Before I could move, Aaron plunked his chin on top of the pile and hung his arms down the sides to brace the entire stack. "Drop in any time."

"Will do . . . maybe we can go out for some seafood." He didn't get it.

I jogged back to my office and sat behind my desk, mulling over a vision of Aaron as a klutzy satyr, lusting after dumpy shy coeds. If he hadn't come out with that *coynt* line so abruptly, so recklessly, I don't think I would have been so amazed. Behind the clumsy ugly bad timing must have been true panic and dismay. And maybe his asking me about my nervousness was just another unharnessed outburst and he had been grateful for the detour into vomiting through the ages.

It struck me that if I had gone through that brief scene a few years earlier when I was still a student I probably would have felt nothing at all for the man. I would have left his office relishing his tripping on his dick purely for its anecdote value. I felt proud of myself. We're growing like a tumor here.

I spent the rest of the day alternating between guarding my desk for thirty-minute spells, and trolling the halls to drop in on my fellow faculty.

On my sixth hallway patrol, a photo pinned to an office cork board stopped me in my tracks; it was an eight-by-ten glossy of Joel Grey's leering painted face from *Cabaret*. It must have been posted within the hour because there was no way I would have missed it on my previous rounds.

I covered the brass-framed name slot with my palm and tried to guess the prof's identity. I was sure it was somebody I knew because the photo triggered a pulse of connection, a flash of hazy imagery. *Cabaret.* Nazis. Germany. 1920s. Who. Who. Crown. It had to be

Crown. I peeled my palm from the door as cautiously as if I had trapped a fly, and when I saw that I had nailed it, I gave a little leap of triumph. Bill Crown was one of the best teachers I'd had in sixteen years of school. His field was Modern Drama, and the Brecht seminar I'd taken with him my junior year belonged in the Education Hall of Fame. I rapped on his door, not really expecting him to be in, and when he droned "enter" I squawked as if spooked.

"Hi!" I gave him a wide wave and an ear-to-ear smile. Scanning a mimeo sheet, he had his feet crossed up on his desk and was leaning so far back in his swivel chair that I felt I should be checking his teeth for cavities. He looked at me as if I was an unplugged television. I felt hurt that he didn't recognize me.

"I'm Peter Keller. I was in your Brecht seminar a couple of years ago." Bruised ego made my voice tentative.

"I know," he lilted coolly, shrugging his shoulders and returning his attention to the mimeo.

I felt myself flush with paranoid confusion. As far as I could remember I had never fucked his wife or his daughter. I had never talked behind his back. I was completely crazy about the guy so fuck *you*, Jack.

I stood there feeling like a total sap. He ran his eyes down the page and absently scratched his nose as if I were already gone. Just for spite I asked him if I could sit down. That got me another minuscule shrug of indifference.

At a loss for an appropriate response, I decided to play it his way, taking a seat, clasping my hands across my gut, stretching out my legs and taking stock of my surroundings with what I hoped was an expression of bored imperiousness. Even though the bookcases were filled to capacity and two huge theater posters dominated the walls, I was overwhelmed by a sense of barren but tasteful spaciousness that made me feel as if I were in a great hall. His books were arranged in order of descending height heedless of subject or author, a display of anal precision that I found totally impractical, and the two posters were in mint condition, wrinkle-free and protected by unbordered glass. Crown himself seemed like part of the statement, an eerily handsome man with facial features so precisely defined that he almost looked effeminate. In his mid-forties he could easily pass for thirty with his unblemished pale gold skin and a sleek physique as trim as an alley cat. He was draped in expensive threads, every-thing starched, razor creased and as wrinkle-free as his posters. Something was bugging me about the posters.

One was in German, announcing a production of *Waiting for Godot* at the University of Heidelberg: white lettering and a shad-owy photo, as stark as a negative, of Beckett's roosterlike big-beaked and pop-eyed profile. The other was a real collector's item: Odets' *Waiting for Lefty*—original cast, vintage 1930; black lettering on a blood-red background; under the cast list a vigorous union meeting, the proles drawn in with brawny curves à la Thomas Hart Benton.

I glared at those posters, feeling so frustrated by my inability to make the memory connection that I totally dropped my blasé act, hunched forward and started furiously scratching the side of my face.

To distract myself, I began staring at the bookshelves at the far end of the office to see how many titles I could read off the spines. Halfway through the second shelf I spotted the familiar black Grove Press paperback of *The Threepenny Opera*. Suddenly everything clicked into place. It wasn't the posters, it was the plays. Three years earlier, in a bar after class, Crown had used those two plays to make a drunken self-loathing joke, a minor aside in a two-hour boozy nightmare involving him and ten of his students that had been so disorientingly freaky and ugly it deserved to be a sup-pressed memory.

Crown had flipped out our entire seminar one day when in the middle of a lecture on *The Threepenny Opera* he tossed the play text in the general direction of his desk and broke out into a Kurt Weill medley, getting into it body and soul, prowling between the chairs like a walking sex crime while singing "Mack the Knife" in an un-nerving croon, then transforming himself into Polly Peachum's old man and belting out the joys of a life of poverty and mayhem.

After class we dragged him to a bar and barraged him with ques-tions about his non-academic past, to which he responded with sul-len grunts and by throwing back vodka shots like a Russian. It wasn't until he was totally drunk that he told us the sad story of his acting career; steakhouse piano bars, singing meat commercials on the radio, Macheath at the New Haven rep while going for a Mas-ter's in theater at Yale and then three years in New York and Boston, the highlight of which was playing the understudy to the screaming fag in the road company production of *The Boys in the Band.*

When a girl bombed on rum and cokes started sobbing, he patted her hand and said, "It wasn't so bad, actually I turned *down* two parts . . . they wanted me for Lefty in *Waiting for Lefty* and for Godot in *Waiting for Godot.*" The posters weren't up in his office at that time.

Just as we were about to take him home some other drunk shmuck started haranguing him about how he wasn't a burnout, he only *thought* he was a burnout and how he shouldn't *be* here, man, he should be on *stage.* Crown responded by whipping off his toupee, flinging it into the kid's face and walking out, leaving us to stare at his hair, which lay on the table like a run-over woodchuck.

We had all been so traumatized that by the next class, when Crown showed up with a second toupee, everybody was suffering from selective amnesia. In fact, I couldn't remember even one replay conversation about that incident, casual or serious, for the duration of the term.

Even now, sitting in his office three years later, the impulse to deny memory was so strong, I couldn't bring myself to raise my eyes to his hairline. But at least I had a context for his cold shoulder— I was a witness. I felt frustrated because there was no way for me to tell him I loved him, that what had happened back then didn't make a difference.

"So, to what do I owe the honor of this visit?" Crown grudgingly mumbled, his nose still buried in the mimeo.

"I'm staff now. Petty hired me as an adjunct."

As I expected, he freaked.

Dropping his arctic front and snapping to attention, he glared at me with startled dismay. "Really . . ." He took his feet off the desk.

"Really." I tried to make myself sound apologetic.

He made a big play of scowling at his watch and two seconds before he opened his mouth to usher me out of the office I was standing and heading for the door.

"Well, I gotta go. I just dropped by to say howdy . . ."

He made no move to see me out.

———

While sitting at my desk mulling over Crown's case I overheard an argument between Tony Fonseca and some sputtering older male voice that I couldn't place. Fonseca had been my own Freshman Comp teacher and my first impulse was to bolt out into the hallway and reintroduce myself, but something told me to sit tight.

"But this is *my* office!"

"Oh yeah?" Fonseca drawled. "You want it? You go over to Boxely Hall, get a hold of those fucking painters, tell them to get all that shit, the ladders, the buckets, the rollers, the canvas, everything, you tell them to get it the hell out of room 220 so I can move in the way I was supposed to, and this bad boy's yours. Meanwhile this is my last known address . . . so . . . I'm here."

"But this is *my* office!" I heard the rattle of papers. "It's in the directory! I have *stu*dents coming! Where am I supposed to meet them?"

"I told you what you should do, Mossi." His voice sounded mock-helpless.

Mossi. The Elizabethan Man. Haw. Students used to drive him bats by calling Edmund Spenser's filibuster "The Dairy Queen." Mossi was a purple-faced prick who was born to torture and be tortured in return.

"But my students are coming *now!*"

"That's *your* problem, my friend . . . why don't you meet them outside under the spreading chestnut tree? I'll let you put up a note." Fonseca, on the other hand, was simply born to torture.

Mossi made some chokey sounds of impotent outrage, finally pulling it together to utter a warning. "I'm going to Dr. Petty!" It sounded like the threat of a six-year-old.

"Do that." I heard Fonseca close his door, presumably in Mossi's face.

Mossi stormed off down the hallway. In the brief instant that he was framed by my threshold, he resembled a wizened figurehead from an ancient battleship prow: head thrust forward, teeth clenched, gray crew cut nicely complementing his purple complexion. I felt sorry for his class; he'd probably spring a midterm on them in the first meeting.

Back when I had been a freshman I enjoyed Fonseca as a teacher because he was the king of irreverence, a bright, quick get-down wise-ass, but I had never chummed up to him because his act, an urban ditty-bop routine, was too much like my own adopted persona, and I always wound up feeling he was making fun of me.

As a seventeen-year-old Bronx-Yonkers provincial, I felt intimidated by the international range of backgrounds—Hong Kong, Texas, England, Episcopalian prep schools, long-haired freshmen who had Harley Davidsons, others who played sports I had never even heard of like Rugby—and in order to keep my head above water I came on strong with a streety Bowery-Boys identity, exaggerating the slumminess of the tenements and playing down the boojy trappings of our apartment.

Fonseca's was the only class where I found myself completely devoid of shtick—it takes one to know one, I guess. But a lot of the other guys who were less self-conscious or self-aware bought his bit to the hilt and followed him around the school like baby ducks. He was sort of the failed-writer-in-residence, and he wound up putting all his creative energy into cultivating an Angry Young Man Pied Piper charisma.

Most of his followers were guys who "almost" grew up inside the five boroughs and came on like Avenue A conga-drum players in his presence, putting "dis" and "dem" or Latino inflections in their speech even though they had seven-hundred-plus college boards and were mainly middle-class Jews. They walked like him with an affected rolling limp, eyebrows arched with irony, and they made nonstop wisecracks about burbed-out or boojy students even though the majority of them came from Tennisville. There was a lot of offhand talk about bad niggers and hip spics, a laid-back racism, half contempt, half awe, all affected. And lots of talk about Jewish chicks. Everybody else said, "this Jap." Fonseca's guys said, "this Jewish chick." I used to watch him rolling down the hall in his brown leather car coat followed by these guys all tossing up side-mouthed tidbits to the emperor for his delectation.

Fonseca looked like a forty-year-old punk; a swarthy chesty bruiser never to be seen without his dark brown hip-high leather car coat, winter or summer.

The fact that most of the faculty saw right through him and held him in contempt just played into the scenario; his student entourage was second only to Fat Jack's.

After Mossi vanished, I still felt tempted to knock on Fonseca's door, but I ultimately took a pass on it because I was still feeling buzzed by my interlude with Crown. One trip to Palookaville a day was enough.

At a quarter to five, Jack waltzed into my office. He was wearing a short-sleeved shirt plastered with calypso singers, his dead cigar screwed into his teeth, his skin blackened with sun.

"Ready to roll, kid?"

"You look great, Jack."

"I had a great time, I caught a fucking giant squid."

"I'm not getting any customers here."

"You're all filled up. It's automatic—they just divide the whole freshman class into all the Comp sections—you'll have plenty, don't worry."

"So here we go, hah?" I grabbed my stapler and my box of pencils. "I'm ready for Freddy, Jim . . ."

Jack laughed. As he turned for the door his whirling calypso singers made me feel as if I had a carousel in my office.

"Oh, listen . . ." He tapped his ring against my door frame. "I moved out of that place."

"You moved back in with your wife?"

He smiled at me sheepishly, almost apologetically. "I'll talk to you about it sometime . . ."

I had no idea how to teach Comp. The text I bought was deadly dull and I couldn't do most of the exercises myself. I realized that I didn't know shit about grammar or sentence construction except in an intuitive automatic way. I could write a sentence, an essay, a thesis, but I didn't know how to condense, abstract and examine the building blocks. What's more, I didn't want to. It was migraine dull.

The next morning I wandered into the English office with this wild hair up my ass that I was going to be booed out of the classroom to cries of "Fraud!" ten minutes into the first session.

"You look glum . . ." Fiona was sucking off the mist from her cup of thermos coffee. She had one of those six-million-dollar IBM typewriters as big as a computer humming away in front of her.

"Man, I don't know how to teach Comp . . ." Man.

She shrugged. "Don't worry about it . . . just do whatever you want."

"Yeah, but I don't know about grammar . . ."

"Who does . . . look, usually what everybody does is just teach what they like. Brown's got his class reading Fitzgerald. Carpenter's got them divided into debate teams. Fonseca's got them writing stories; Miller's got them writing poems . . ."

"I like that . . . stories . . . can I do that? Can I have them write stories?"

"Sure . . ." She shrugged. "Look, everybody hates it, everybody's gotta teach it . . . so have fun . . . they'll learn more from you if you're enjoying yourself . . ."

"How about Jack, how does he teach it? He's got them reading *Fanny Hill* and Mickey Spillane?"

"Huh . . . Jack hates it more than anybody. He got out of teaching it this year."

"Because he's chairman?"

"No, because he hired you to take his section."

I felt tickled by the slight con job.

————

The first class was a disaster. I had twenty-four kids around a three-table "U" in a nice sunny classroom. I made them introduce themselves and state their hometowns. There were eight Long Islanders, four upstaters, eight Westchesters, a Chicago, an Atlanta, two Jersey Oranges and a Madras India.

It was nine A.M. on a Monday morning so for most it was the first college class in their lives. I looked out at them and said in all earnestness, "You have no idea how weird it is to be on my side of the desk." They all laughed. They probably would have laughed if I said, "Take out your notebooks," but being that I was shitting pickles myself, I thought that what would make me a big hit was to deliver the straight poop nonstop, and without further ado I launched into a protracted Professor Bottom Line harangue about the school.

For the life of me I don't know what made me think that they would appreciate me, their first professor, telling them that half the faculty was senile, that eighty-five percent of what they would learn in the next four years they would forget, that they shouldn't let their parents' expectations dictate their choices—look who's talking—and that if they were smart enough to get accepted here they were smart enough to do well but that they had to decide whether the whole thing was worth it. The few laughs I got in the beginning quietly died about ten minutes into the spiel, so I tried harder to be behind-the-scenes irreverent. But the harder I tried, the more silent they became, until half the students had gone from ramrod straight to sprawling across the table, their cheeks sunk into their palms. I was sinking into panic, convinced I was boring them to death, when the kid from Atlanta shot up, tears in her eyes, and said, "Then what the *hell* did I come *up* here for!" scooped up her books and stalked out of the room with a sonic-boom slam of the door. The others were perfectly still, maintaining their variety of slouched positions, some in shock, some in agreement. Vibrating like a tuning fork, I mumbled or maybe shouted at them to write five hundred words describing a place they'd never been to, and walked out the door.

I went right out to my car and drove to Zybysko's Monday-Wednesday-Friday High Noon Decline Bench Press Club. As I stood around in my T-shirt shouting blind encouragement to Red, my whole body was throbbing like I had the flu. The Mad Bomber takes on the world of education and blows away two dozen eighteen-year-olds with a half-hour glib bullshit rap. But no matter what I did, I was unable to shake the image of that despair-blasted class; that teary right-on-the-money exit . . . and when I slid down the bench and grasped the knurled grips I couldn't even get it up to disengage the bar from the supports.

Jimmy the Klansman was spotting, the other two loomed upside down waiting for me to let it rip. My hands ached as if I had arthritis. Suddenly I realized that I should be tracking down every kid in that class to apologize, starting with Atlanta, not hanging upside down with some lunatic-fringe racist's crotch between my eyes. I twisted up to a sitting position, muttered something about stomachs and tore out of there.

I had forgotten to take registration, there was no class list yet, I didn't remember anybody's name, so I sat in my office with the door open hoping some of them would come by to chew me out. I sat there in that gray metal room all afternoon in a panicky cloud of guilt. I cruised the halls and the student union, looking for kids to apologize to. I went up to Fiona to tell her everything, as though she had this power to exonerate or punish me, but she was busy with students. I dreamed about the girl from Atlanta two nights running.

On Wednesday morning I got to class at eight forty-five. Every student ambling into the classroom over the next twenty minutes was a living pardon. The ones who nodded hello I would have got down on my knees to. As they settled in, I saw to my whacked-out astonishment that they had actually brought in the assignment I'd given. Nobody was glaring at me, a few were talking amiably to each other, birds twittered outside the window.

". . . Listen . . . before we start I'd like to apologize to you for all that gibberish I was spouting last class. I was very nervous, it was my first class too and I was coming off a real wingding of a summer and I had no right to be so offhand with that stuff. I guess I'm as scared of being here as you are, and I blew, so . . ."

The class was silent.

I couldn't shut up. Resolving everything seemed only two more explanations away. About ten minutes into my sob story I realized that they were bored to death, so I tore myself away from the confessional and forced myself to take attendance. I'd lost four students to Monday's speech, including Atlanta.

As much as I wanted to keep on blubbering, I had to bite the bullet and launch the class.

"OK, look, the thing about apologizing is that it can become addictive . . . once you get into it you start to *enjoy* apologizing and right now I feel like I can get an apology roll going for that last class that would carry us into the middle of next semester . . . so let me cut it short and say that today is day one, class one, and this is what we're gonna do every class. I'll give you a sketch assignment. We'll butcher up a few in here out loud and I'll demolish the rest in the luxurious privacy of my den at home." I had them go around the horn and read their stories out loud. I was feeling so crummy that I lavished praise on every flat 500-word monotone.

Halfway through the class, three students burst in, flushed, winded and murmuring apologies, something about a flat tire or a dean.

I sank in my chair with relief. Three more precincts heard from. It looked like we'd lost Atlanta but that was all. My mood began to soar as the round robin continued, each story sounding better than the last, until the final two about a haunted house in New Jersey and an Irish bar in Boston seemed respectively like pure Poe and an outtake from *Dubliners.*

"OK . . . that was great, really great . . . anyway if you need to talk to me outside of class, my office is Hopper B-33. I'll be there every afternoon on class days, otherwise I'm at Zybysko's Health Institute on Exterior Street or staggering around the Plunkett Mall looking for the perfect salad bar, any questions? No? Good, for Friday I want you to go down to the Greyhound station, observe people, and write up a description of an interaction and I promise from now on the only advice I'll ever give you about stuff not pertaining to this class is things like don't sit on strange toilets without lining the seat with paper first. Class dismissed."

I burst out of there exploding with happiness. I bench-pressed ninety pounds that afternoon and fired such ardent verbal pepper at Red that everybody in the gym twisted turret-necks toward the sound of my voice.

The class was a gas. I was winging assignments at them three a week, not because I was into being a taskmaster but because I loved it. I painstakingly corrected every story, and I was totally straight with them about their work, which was no great shakes. They were all bright but they didn't have too much to say. The writing was clever but lightweight, all dressed up with no place to go. I kept my office hours, but few came by. It was okay, the class was rolling.

I couldn't teach for shit but I was entertaining and funny and I knew more than they and I usually told at least one long personal anecdote or horseshit tale per class. It wasn't exactly what I'd call a "dream" job, but compared to the dreck I had been doing before, I felt like the Secretary-General of the U.N.

At night I sometimes hung out at the Rathskeller, in the basement of the student union, drinking beer out of gigantic wax cups and playing Fooseball with whatever students of mine that I ran into, but I felt creepy socializing with them; it put a strain on everybody. I spent a few evenings with other teachers in that first month of school but nothing that broke the sound barrier.

Strangely enough, the most depressing evening for me was the night I had dinner with the guy closest to my age on the English faculty, David Howard. Howard was twenty-six, with a brand new Ph.D. from Princeton in semiotics. He had a wife in the veterinary medicine school and a six-month-old son. The Howards were good decent people, curious, alert and ready to laugh at the slightest suggestion of a wisecrack. But, despite their vigorous charm, the outing was profoundly disastrous to my psyche. They weren't smarmy or overly doting parents, but they couldn't hide their stunned amazement, their reverential fascination, with their infant son's every motor function, his every response to the world. Here was the kid, flowering before our very eyes, and if the empathic intensity of his parents had been any greater they'd have been wearing Pampers. They made nuclear families and child-rearing miraculous and beatific experiences, but all this felt far removed from the realities and needs of my own life, whatever they might be.

The next day, in a bid to have at least one social evening where I'd come out feeling good about myself, I stormed into Fat Jack's office and demanded that he invite me over for dinner as soon as possible. Like the solid citizen that he was, he called it for that same night.

I was supposed to come back to his office at six but when I returned he was deep in a conversation with Tony Fonseca, and I stood out in the empty reception room without announcing my presence. Fonseca was sitting on Jack's desk, wearing his brown leather car coat over a white T-shirt and frowning down at his jiggling knee. He looked agitated. Jack was leaning back in his recliner, his brow wrinkled, a hand over his mouth. They talked in low confidential murmurs, neither voice carrying with any clarity out to the reception room. Even though I couldn't hear anything that was being said, there was something both exclusively intimate and unreachably adult in their tones that made me feel jealous and isolated. I couldn't imagine Jack relating to me in that way and I felt like stiffing him for dinner.

At one point Fonseca's voice rose. "What am I, a fucking high priest? What do they want from me?" and Jack responded with a helpless shrug and a weak flap of his hand.

When Fonseca finally lurched to his feet, absently tucking in his T-shirt, I instinctively moved to the far window of the outer room, so when he rolled out past me into the hallway he never even noticed I was there.

All the way to Jack's house I sulked as hard as I could, but Jack was the type of guy who gave people so much emotional elbow room before calling out the therapy hounds that I would have had to hold my breath and chew up the carpet before he would have asked me if I was upset.

The big house in Professionalsville was furnished in department-store-window moderne; brand new antique chairs, raw cotton matching sectionals, and machine-made laminated wood stand-up globe lamps and tables. It was the type of layout you admire for its cleanliness. Jack's wife, Nancy, was a smug plug of a woman, short and dumpy, sporting an inoffensive pixie haircut and a creamy smile of triumph at Jack's return.

After three drinks I was too high to maintain my pout, but it was replaced by a growing irritation at both Pettys. It was nearly impossible for Jack to hide his feelings, and all through the evening he acted apologetic, not toward his wife, but toward me. With every sheepish droopy look he threw in my direction, I got the sense that he felt he had disappointed me by moving back in. I wouldn't have cared if his attitude said "that was that and this is this," but his self-consciousness bugged me as much as his wife's quiet gloat.

After the liquor loosened me up all I wanted to do was demand that he play me back word-for-word his conversation with Fonseca. Not that I gave a damn about Fonseca's problems but I wanted to crack that code of exclusivity, that adult murmur that had made me feel as if once again I had been handed the children's menu.

I never brought it up though, because Nancy was always in the room with us. I knew she read Jack's mood toward me and she wouldn't let the two of us out of her sight. I didn't even feel safe enough around her to dump on any of the faculty, because I had a feeling that if she thought I was too threatening to her happy home she'd tell everybody in the department what I'd said about them.

By the time we sat down to a dinner of meat loaf and roasted potatoes I was totally engaged in a silent war with her, and Jack had been reduced to a prize.

"Hey Jack, you remember that time here when you crushed your trumpet?" I was looking straight at Nancy, who raised an eyebrow and served him up another slice of meat loaf.

"My trumpet?" He winced as if he was hearing the bad news for the first time.

"Yeah, that party . . . don't you remember? You got bombed, took the trumpet into the bathtub and passed out on top of it after playing 'Tijuana Taxi.' It took four guys to roll you over . . ." I laughed, starting to get lost in the genuine pleasure of the memory. "That thing looked hammered, man. It looked like a medallion."

Jack whimpered in discomfort and screwed up his face in an if-you-say-so expression.

"Jack?" Nancy smiled. "Maybe you could play us something after dinner . . ."

No matter what raucous memory I brought up, Jack responded squeamishly, as if someone had shoved a pinky up his ass, and by the time I was ready to leave I felt like handing over my sword to his wife.

Jack walked me out to my car, a hand on my shoulder as if he had a twisted ankle.

I was in a full-tilt boil but when I turned to him and saw his face writhing in apology I hugged as much of him as I could get my hands around. "I fuckin' love you, Petty . . ." He hugged me back, rocking me as if he were about to break out in a lullaby.

When we broke, he smiled for the first time that night and ruffled my hair, almost throwing me to the sidewalk. "It took *six* of you stringbeans to roll me over . . . four of you couldn't even comb my hair."

———

I really *did* hang out at the Plunkett Mall. I liked dawdling around under the dome and the Muzak and I went there at least two nights a week the way someone would go to a street fair. Basically I lived for my class and Zybysko's. Life could have been a little more lush, but compared to how things had been going previously, the month of September was stone la-de-da.

But by the first week in October I began to feel like something was Burning again. It all started the night I went to see a monster movie on campus. It was the East Coast premiere of *The Stalker*. The flick was debuting at the school because the young director,

Rom Braverman, was an alumnus—in fact had graduated in my class, although I never knew him. The flick was pretty scary; it was shot in black and white with all unknowns and a weird discordant soundtrack that consisted of a squealing sax, a drum, and what appeared to be the sound of glass thrown down an echo-chamber-equipped mine shaft. The Stalker was a faceless slasher terrorizing an apartment building and the screams were fairly easy to come by, lots of Boo!-type shots of suddenly thrust-open doors, people walking down corridors with many left and right turns to them. But there was something in the mood, the starkness, the very cheapness of the film that made it memorable.

When the lights went up Horace Dooley, the ascot-wearing permanently drunk head of the Film Department, got up in front of the screen and announced that Rom Braverman himself was here tonight and would give a talk upstairs in one of the lounges. A murmury wave of delightful surprise shot through the auditorium, my voice not contributing, and most people headed upstairs.

There was a huge fireplace in the room, and Rom sat in an easy chair with its back to the inferno, blocking the blazing hearth so that his hunched-over frame, elbows on the armrests, fingers meshed in a cat's cradle, was bordered by tongues of flame. I'm sure he did it for a Prince-of-Darkness effect, because from the back of the room where I had to stand it looked as though the chair was on fire and he was rapping to us from his living room in Hell.

Dooley stood by Braverman's throne and prattled on about how Rom had made the picture in four weeks on a budget of two hundred thousand dollars and how even though it wasn't due to open in New York for another three days, the picture had already grossed two and a half million on the West Coast and got great reviews out there and would meet the same reception in the East and how a rave was scheduled in next week's *Time Magazine* and a profile of Braverman was being done for the Arts and Leisure section of the Sunday *New York Times* and what a wunderkind, wunderkind, wunderkind, and I remember Rom as a skinny freshman and he hasn't put on much weight since, hah hah. And through all this Braverman sat in that vulture hunch, smirking and occasionally jerking his shoulders in bemusement. He had the absolute balls to show up for this rap session in a black T-shirt, dungarees, a five-day growth of beard and a gold Cartier wristwatch, as though he was trying to deny that his outrageous success had got to him.

One thing Dooley said in his intro was dead on; Braverman sure was a gaunt little fuck. He was about my height but minus my physique. His dark eyes were slightly sunken and ringed, his hair jet black shaggy. His mouth was tight and ironic. When he began fielding questions he spoke with an animated self-assuredness that I found jarring and distasteful.

Every time he opened his mouth people tittered. He was affectedly candid and full of jive-ass anecdotes about Hollywood heavyweights, how they were all assholes and "the real ghouls" except one executive at United Artists who was "good people."

When someone asked him how he raised the two hundred thousand, he sighed. "Let me tell you something, it's a good thing *Stalker* hit, otherwise we might be having this talk on the bottom of the East River, know what I mean?"

"No, what do you mean?" asked an open-mouthed frizz-haired kid sitting crosslegged in a Grateful Dead T-shirt at the foot of Braverman's fiery throne.

"What do I mean . . ." Rom sighed. "I mean after going to many sources, all legal, and being shown many doors because I was untested and only twenty-two, I finally went to two gentlemen, a Mister Cheech and a Mister Chooch . . ." He paused, raising a wry eyebrow. ". . . two fellows who are very fond of sipping espresso in the back of a certain downtown social club."

Everybody fell hypnotically silent. He was full of shit.

"What did you leave for collateral?" the same kid asked more quietly.

"*What* collateral," he said wearily, pinching his thumbs and his index fingers together and gently shaking his hands in front of his chest like a hambone Italian actor. "My collateral was my addiction to breathing."

"What kind of interest did you have to pay?"

"The vig? Seventy-five percent plus my fourteen-year-old sister."

Everybody laughed nervously, awed as if they were sitting in front of the hero of Pork Chop Hill, someone who has killed and has been shot at. He was full of shit. The "vig." He didn't get any money from the Mafia, or if he did he was a bigger asshole than I thought, blabbing about it in front of seventy-five kids. What the fuck would *I* go to the Mafia for? What did *I* want to do so strongly that I would risk my life for the freedom to do it up right? He was totally full of shit. I started my wild kneecap fan dance again as if I was at A.C., as if I had a seatbelt strapped tight across my chest.

"Mr. Braverman?"

"Rom . . ."

"Rom. Do you like all this attention? The interviews?"

"Yeah! But, hey look, you got to realize it's all external, you know? I still have the same problems I've always had relating to people. I still have to wake up and walk around with me every day. What do you think I do, jump out of bed, look in the mirror and go, 'Hey! It's Rom Braverman!' What can I do? Sign an autograph for myself?"

Laugh. Laugh.

Suddenly Braverman leapt up, grabbed a spiral notebook from a girl, ripped out two pages, whipped a ball point from his front pants pocket and furiously began scribbling his signature over and over. He tore off pieces of paper and began handing them out to the crowd, kids waving their hands and crying out "Me! Me! Me!" He pulled it off without cracking a smile, barking out "Autographs! Fresh autographs!" like a hot-dog vendor in a stadium. The whole show took less than two minutes and when he threw himself back in the chair still unsmiling, he let the raucous applause caress him like a trade wind.

I felt intimidated by the grim speed with which he went through the stages of his act. More than anything else he said or did, that speed combined with the immobility of his expression gave me the strongest glimmer into the confidence and determination that he must have possessed to make that movie.

Skinny or not, I was suddenly convinced he'd be a bad person to fuck with.

When the room got quiet again, weak ripples and mutters still breaking out in spots, Rom hunched forward. "Hey, is Johnny's still open?"

"Yeah!" some guys shouted, their eyes wet and dancing.

" 'Cause I'm *dyin'* for a triple suicide sub." He held his chest and winced. "I ain't had one since graduation . . . anybody who wants to . . . let's go over there." He stood up and waved thank you. People applauded. A gaggle of kids followed him out, and as the remainder of the crowd dispersed, sighing and cooing, I stared at Horace Dooley, who was beaming and glowing at Braverman's swiftly retreating T-shirt. I wondered if Dooley was really as proud of this motherfucker as he appeared, or if he was sick with envy, like me.

I went home in bad shape. My only consolation was that although Braverman and I were in the same class, born the same year, he was eight months older.

But the next day I read in the school paper that a senior hockey player on the school team had just signed with the Chicago Black Hawks. When I got the local town rag and *The New York Times* I scoured stories, squibs and photos to check out the ages of the people deemed worthy of ink; rock stars, rapists, congressmen, highway accident victims, actresses. I went to the library and pulled old issues of *People* magazine to find out the ages of the two or three enfants terribles on the Up and Coming page. Some of them got to me, some of them didn't. I didn't really care about those seventeen-year-old Science Fair maniacs who had worked out a cure for dying, I figured they were driven, abnormal, and unhappy prodigies; besides, that wasn't my field. But those whose accomplishments were more superficial and glamorous gave me the anxiety sweats; the twenty-one-year-old marketing genius millionaires, the nineteen-year-old award-winning poets or ballet swans. I found myself thinking about Randye and James and that whole brigade again, wondering if they were still doing A.C.-type gigs or were getting Emmys and Tonys and touring Holland with mime troupes by now. I got crabby in class, breaking balls and coming on impatient about the lack of Nobel Prize-caliber fiction. I started feeling a sand-clock panic about what *I* had up *my* sleeve, what *my* star stuff was made of.

To make matters worse, a few days later Crown strolled into my office, no knocking, no may I come in, no hellos, and took the seat across the desk from me. I had sworn to myself that I would do my best to stay out of his sight for as long as I'd be teaching in order to minimize his agony, and to see him sitting there, smiling to himself and running his fingers across the gem-studded base of my kitschy lamp, paralyzed me. For the first time ever, though, I found myself scrutinizing his wig. Usually I could spot a rug on a back-row baritone in a fifty-man choir, but Crown's hairpiece was totally undetectable from two feet away.

"It's a toupee, okay. . . ." He smiled, still studying the lamp and I squawked as if I'd just been caught beating my meat.

"No!" I barked and stared wildly around the room.

"It *better* be no." Crown chuckled and leaned back in his chair, hands behind his head. "It's five hundred dollars' worth of yak hair. So was the one I left in that bar."

I gave him a squeamish smile.

"Ah, listen . . . I just had some news, I thought you might be interested."

"Really?"

"I just took an emergency leave effective next week."

"What's an emergency leave?"

"Give me the leave, or I quit. That's an emergency leave. See, it gives me a year and a half, now. I, ah, I have a sabbatical coming up in January, it's a full year . . . I was going to take a visiting professorship at Skidmore but . . . I'm not . . ."

I moved my lips, repeating his words verbatim to myself in a spacy effort to connect and converse. "What are you gonna do instead?"

"Casting calls."

"Casting calls . . . you're gonna audition actors?"

"Nope. I'm going to audition myself. I'm going to New York and make the rounds . . . give it another shot . . ."

"You're gonna be in a play?"

"If I can land something. I just wanted to tell you because . . . you know . . ." He grimaced, tick-tocked his head and made fluttering gestures with his hands.

Yeah I knew. I felt a glow of joy for him.

"Yeah, but wait a second. What if you don't get something for a while? Or, ah, you get in something that's gonna be longer than the sabbatical? What are you gonna do with school?" I felt totally alert.

The corners of his mouth dropped into a playful pout and he shrugged devilishly.

"Fuckin' A . . ." I muttered, nodding in admiration.

"Yeah, I thought you'd like to know."

"You better take down those posters . . ."

"You want them?" He held out a hand to me.

"No," I startled myself with the speed of my answer. I felt more numbed than touched by his offer. "I just bought six posters." I stammered. "They're at the framers . . . thank you anyhow." My chest turned icy. "Thank you, really." I was afraid to elaborate. Crown shot me a queer look, but then his face relaxed into a tired understanding smile.

He slowly rose to his feet.

"Man, if your acting is half your goddamn teaching . . ." I blurted, filled with panic. My legs were trembling.

He smiled dreamily at my empty bookshelves and patted his toupee.

"*Do* it, Crown!" I almost growled.

Taken aback by my intensity, he shifted his gaze to my bulging unblinking eyes, studying me with a calm but worried frown.

Embarrassed, I stared at my ashtray, waiting for him to leave, but suddenly in a gesture that shocked me almost to tears, he leaned over my desk and tenderly cupped my face, my chin in the pit of his dry palm, my cheekbones in the light brace of his thumb and fingertips. I didn't pull away, but neither did I raise my eyes until he was out of my office.

Later that same day, I whipped through a stack of assignments, working with the same dull blind anger that got me through busbox after busbox back in the Post Office.

The stories ranged in tone from self-consciously wooden to a smugly grandiose world-weariness, and feeling infuriated by the uniform lack of belly, I responded with a series of end comments that were nothing more than flippantly vicious one-liners.

I didn't sober up until one of my students stopped by the office to hand in a rewrite of her submission because she knew her story was lousy.

After she left I searched through, the carnage to find her earlier draft and I was horrified to see that I had drawn big red X's across every page and had scribbled over her heading, "Would you please be so kind as to take the goddamn wax out of your ears in class and listen to what I say?"

I wound up scissoring off my comments on every story and re-reading the entire batch, but even in my chastened state, they still stank.

The worst student in the class was a black kid, James Tucker, who insisted on writing mock-baroque tales of knights and fair maidens, everybody harking and hailing, thee-ing and thou-ing until the cows came home. In the classroom he was rigid and studious, a maniacal note-taker, but no matter what I said or suggested, his work never varied from tenth-rate Prince Valiant panel captions.

All I knew about him was that he came from Newark, New Jersey, never smiled, was a dead ringer for Martin Luther King down to the mustache, and that if he didn't improve, he'd be staring at an F come Christmas.

In a bid to straighten him out I had him come to my office and give me some clues as to what was going on in his head.

I was surprised to find out that James was twenty-two and an ex-Marine who had pulled a tour of duty in Vietnam.

I asked him to write a story or a scene about Nam and he gave me a flat No. It took a half-hour of cajoling to get him to change his mind. I had to promise him that no one would see it but me, that I wouldn't Xerox it and keep a copy, and that I wouldn't write comments on it.

A week later he handed me a ten-page nightmare about the torture and interrogation of a fifteen-year-old VietCong who had thrown a grenade into a whorehouse. The narrative was still clunky and wooden, but the dialogue was air-tight and ear-perfect, completely devoid of thees and thous; that is, the dialogue that I could read—half of the interrogator's lines and all the fifteen-year-old's lines were in Vietnamese.

The class after that, he went back to wizards and dragons, and feeling somewhat over my head, I didn't try to stop him. I even tried to turn him on to Tolkien and C. S. Lewis.

———

After Crown left campus I started thinking about being an actor. I couldn't sing or dance—just the thought of it embarrassed me. I had a hard time imagining myself letting go, putting on a rubber face in front of people and belting forth with "Zip-a-dee-doo-dahhzip-a-dee-ay! My o my what a won-der-ful day!" bouncing around like a shameless boing-boing. But I knew I could do straight-faced heavy dramatic stuff—if the character was urban American. At least the idea of that type of role seemed relatively easy, unembarrassing. I was a good mimic at any rate. It didn't seem as though it would be so hard.

There was an acting class in the Theater Arts Department that I decided to sit in on. The teacher was Jim Doobie, a bald guy in his thirties with a waxed handlebar mustache and a welterweight frame. I went to his office to ask for permission to sit in and at first he balked, but when I said I was good friends with Bill Crown he relented.

The class was in the Ernest Tushkin Playhouse on campus. Students were broken up into two-person work teams. They had to get up on stage and present their assignment while the other students slouched in the first few rows and observed. It seemed safe enough, but the first thing Doobie did in class almost had me scrambling for the exits. He had everybody, me included, stand in a circle on stage and led us through loosening up exercises. It was like a California touch-me–touch-myself sensory awareness session. The very thing I was terrified of.

We had to shake out our arms, rotate our necks—which wasn't *that* bad—but then we had to shake out our mouths, which I found totally mortifying. This involved all these vocal calisthenics— lolling out our tongues like lascivious cretins and crooning out "Flaph-flaph-flaph," then rotating our jaws, crinkling our faces and going "Meee-yawrr, meee-yawrr, mee-yawrr," as Doobie patrolled the circle, his nose in our faces to make sure we were doing it with gusto. As Doobie got closer to me during the Flaphs, my voice got tinier and tinier and I started trembling and sure enough, when he stood in front of me he grabbed my chin and shouted "C'mon, Keller, stick it out!" and eyeball to eyeball, tongue to tongue we shouted "Flaph! Flaph! Flaph!" at each other until he was satisfied and I was standing there on Jell-O legs.

When we were finally allowed to retreat to the seats, I kept going and headed for the rear door of the auditorium. I had to start out with Stanley Kowalski, not flaph.

I had no sex life. I bought the respectable stroke books, the ones that were padded with investigative journalism and liberal editorials, jerked off every morning before getting out of bed, but I made no moves to find myself a girlfriend or a fast fuck. I think I was still in a body cast from the summer and I threw everything I had into teaching and lifting weights.

My celibacy neither turned me on nor freaked me out. I had a context for it, I felt I still needed to play close to the vest with my emotions and I knew that in time I'd come around. The closest I came to sex play was to maintain a harmless non-verbal flirtation with a girl in the class named April Wenzel.

She always sat facing me at the far end of the short central table. The autumn had turned out to be a long Indian summer and April usually wore thin white ribbed men's sleeveless undershirts, white short shorts and white jazz shoes. She had cupcake bosoms, Halloween orange hair and her slanty-eyed face was splashed with freckles. By the second week of classes we got into playing eye-contact games, just straight out eye contact, no winking or body language. I was heavy into fantasized scenarios. In one class while I ran down the difference between showing and telling to the kid from India who had just read his story about Thuggees on the road to Bombay, she blew me on a dune under a full moon. But in a later class while one kid was reading a sad tale about Jews in Czarist Russia, and I was harmlessly daydreaming about fucking April on an altar, I caught her eye and, instead of just meeting my gaze like every other time, she firmed up her mouth and slowly nodded Yes at me. My heart zipped around my rib cage and I looked down at my fascinating side-by-side fingernails. The next thing I knew everybody was staring at me, waiting for my take on the rabbi's revenge on the Cossack. I turned the discussion over to the students and I lost it again, staring at April's slowly swishing freckled knees.

At the end of the class I told them to write me a day in the precriminal life of either Son of Sam, Richard Speck or George Metesky, and I was out of that room and over to the gym before you could say "Don't shit where you eat."

I got some hot papers out of that assignment. One, unfortunately, was April's. She wrote a scene of "the morning after" Son of Sam's honeymoon; the two newlyweds sitting and silently eating breakfast in their honeymoon cottage. No eye contact, no smiles, not even newspapers. Son of Sam's bride clears off the table and retreats to the bedroom, closing the door behind her. Son of Sam rises, still in his bathrobe, walks out of the honeymoon cottage, goes into the little garden and slowly starts ripping out all the flowers.

It was a little heavy but sharp for an eighteen-year-old.

Another of the good ones also focused on Son of Sam. It was entitled "Doctor Death or Problem Six," and it was written by this kid Charles LoCicero. LoCicero had thirteen-year-old Son of Sam pacing and lurching around his bedroom, his walls plastered with cutouts and pinups of wrestlers, the largest being a glossy center-fold of a three-hundred-pound monster in a black mask named Doctor Death. Sam is chewing up the rug with his pacing. The air is choking with the smell of his mother's beef stew from the kitchen. Sam is speed-rapping to himself, "Here's to *you* Mis-sus Robinson, here's to *you* Mis-sus Robinson and . . . to . . . *you* Mis-sus Robin-son . . ." He stops in front of Doctor Death, crosses his arms over his chest like a mummy and gives a stiff brisk bow from the hips up and continues pacing. "Co coo ca *choo*, Mrs. Robin-son . . ." He goes over to the window and says to the gray streets, "Hi Cathy? This is David Berkowitz . . . did you work out problem six?" then whirls around back into the center of the room, wincing and shaking out his arms like a swimmer, then back to the window. "Hi, Cathy? This is Davy Berkowitz . . . did you work out problem five?"

LoCicero was one of my invisible silent students, a short bull-necked kid from Long Island who was a shot putter on the freshman track team. Every class he would sit there slouched down, knees spread, stone-faced, dismantling and reassembling his pen. I never knew if he was bored or shy.

Usually I let the students read their work out loud on a volunteer basis but I was so pleased with these scenes that I broke protocol and read them out loud myself. I didn't say who the authors were, and two sentences into Charles's he raised an eyebrow up from his disemboweled Parker Pen, hoisted himself up from his almost prone slouch, put the pen pieces in his shirt pocket, hunched forward on his desk and frowned down at his clasped hands.

The class went berserk. It was the best piece written to date. And when I said "That's Charlie LoCicero's," he ducked his head down in brief acknowledgement and continued to stare at his hammy knuckles.

April's piece didn't go over as well since it was a little more subdued and I wound up having to explain the piece's qualities. I rushed through it pretty quick because I didn't want to linger on her case, told them to write me a story involving a gun, and dismissed the class.

I was back in my office at two that afternoon, reading the school paper and absently touching my pecs.

At ten of five, just as I was closing shop, in walked trouble. "Are you leaving?" April stood on tiptoe in her skinny-minny whites at the door as if she was trying to keep her balance at the lip of a pool.

"No, hey, come in." I sat down smiling, my chest anvil-chorusing.

"No, I was just looking for Professor Aaron's office . . . do you know where it is?" She sat down. She didn't shave her armpits and little flames of orange curled there like creeping heartbreak.

"I was really impressed with that sketch." I rolled my chair up until my solar plexus was flush against my desk. I couldn't take my eyes from the arch of her armpit. "What's your major?"

"You liked that?" She wrinkled her nose in self-effacement.

"So how's school treating you?" I rolled my chair back.

"Do you like theater?" She squinted at me speculatively.

"I love it. I'm a . . . in . . . I love it." I thought it would be pretentious of me to say I'm thinking of pursuing it.

"Well, I'm in this theater company." She shrugged deprecatingly. ". . . in my hometown? It's called the Roscoe Players. You probably never heard of it."

"I've heard of Roscoe . . ." I started doing figure eights with my chair on the plastic floor protector.

"Well, I'm in this play we're doing. Roscoe's only an hour from here and we're doing *Picnic* by William Inge. Do you know it? It's about this drifter who comes into a small town and drives all the women crazy, you know, stirs everybody up . . . it's all right . . . I'm playing one of the leads, this girl Madge . . . my father's in the play too . . . he's also the director . . . Anyway, we open Friday night. It's been a drag since school started because I've been taking the Greyhound back and forth to Roscoe for rehearsals . . ." She smiled. "I almost died when you told us to write a bus station sketch . . . I had to go to the Greyhound station that afternoon anyhow . . . I wrote it on the bus . . . I bet I was the first one to finish it. But anyway, we're opening in a week, on Friday, and I just wanted to know if you wanted to come and see the play . . ."

The idea intrigued me since I was planning on copping an Oscar myself now.

"Sure, what night's it running?"

"Well . . ." She stuck a finger in my ashtray-tire and whirled it around. ". . . I was thinking it would be great if you could come out Friday night because then maybe you could drive me back to campus after the play otherwise . . ." She stopped. ". . . is that creepy for me to ask?"

"No! No! That's cool. Friday's fine." I shrugged. My heart jumped as one of the casters slipped over the rim of the plastic floor pad and my chair dropped half an inch on the starboard side. "That's fine."

"Great, so I'll give you a ticket in class next Friday, okay? I can't go out there with you because I got early rehearsals and all . . ." she said drearily, "but we can come back together."

"Yeah, don't worry."

I didn't know what else to say. The interview was obviously over but she made no move to leave. It was after five o'clock now and the only sound from outside my office was the rhythmic creaking of someone's swivel chair a few rooms down the hall. We sat in the thumping stillness and made that eye contact again. I dropped my gaze to the ashtray. A vein in my temple was going like neon, my head dull with overload. She splayed her palm flat on my desk, arching back her fingers as if examining her nails. Her face was deadpan, staring down at her hand. I rolled my chair belly up to the desk again, also staring at her hand, the down line of her shoulders. She had goose pimples along the arch of her armpit.

I slowly laid my hand down next to hers, my pinky barely grazing her thumb. The creaking down the hall stopped and the room became perfectly silent. Suddenly April broke the trance with a sound from the back of her throat that was somewhere between a soft grunt and a whimper. It was a sex sound and I started shaking.

My shoulders jerked toward her, then I jumped up, sending my chair skidding back off the plastic square into the wall.

"What am I, nuts?" I was shouting. I walked to the window. "Friday's a bad day for me. No way." When I turned back, I was alone.

———

That night instead of cruising the mall, or going to the movies, or playing pinball in the Rathskeller, I slowly floated down the Miracle Mile towards Chee Lok. I had heard about the place ever since my sophomore year, but no one I ever knew—no one from the school—had ever gone there. Chee Lok was a Chinese singles bar for Townies. During the day it was just a Chinese restaurant on the side of the highway sharing a parking lot with a sprawling mock rustic motel, but three nights a week the management brought in local bands and opened up a forty-foot-long bar, and the motel rented rooms by the hour.

I turned off the highway in front of a big blindingly fluorescent square sign: CHEE LOK, in bamboo characters. The parking lot was full, mainly with big waxy American cars, and I had to park in back facing the three-tiered motel and the placid phosphorescent pool. The vestibule of Chee Lok had overlapping wooden shingles that belonged on the exterior of a house. A stand-up black felt announcement board heralding Rotary meetings and a J.C. luncheon was framed with an Early American–style molding. To the left of the vestibule was the restaurant, with red flocked wallpaper, red vinyl booths and huge, bulbous dragon-decorated Japanese paper lanterns. The room glowed pink. All the waitresses were white.

To the right of the vestibule was a big dark room with a round dance floor, a small stage and a long bar with a fake grass canopy; they were striving for "Polynesian Hut" but the result looked more like a drink concession at Disneyland. The bar area was packed with upstate types; women with helmet-shaped hairdos and safari jackets, men in solid-color shirts and plaid pants, or dark shirts and light pants, flat parted hair and long thin sideburns.

The band started up, three not-young men in long Christmas Red sleeveless tunics; drums, guitar and trumpet.

They started in on "Evil Ways" and the floor filled with taut-jawed couples, the guys moving back and forth like they were trying to push hip-high things behind them. The only Chink in either room was one of three furiously busy bartenders.

I never got farther than the vestibule. No more "Upbeats." I took it home.

———

I dreamed I was walking with April in a forest. She was naked. I was fully dressed. She disappeared and I was crouching alone in a clearing. Strange rare forest creatures started emerging from the brush and trees around me. Winged animals, not exactly birds, in unbelievable color combinations; mauve and purple, russet and white, deep blue and butter yellow. Even though I expected them to bolt on seeing me, I found out that I had the power to pet them without making them afraid. Some came right up and nuzzled me with their furry or feathery heads. I never wanted to leave the forest.

I woke at midnight with a sexual craving so ferocious that I couldn't even masturbate; I just slowly rolled over and over under my blanket like a chicken on a spit.

I got up, dressed, went down to my car and headed for Chee Lok. But instead of turning into the parking lot, as soon as I saw the glowing sign I floored the accelerator. I flew by so fast that all I saw out of the corner of my eye was the gleaming blur of the fluorescence bouncing off the fat steel haunches of an army of parked cars. A mile up the road I pulled a U-turn and headed home.

I had been doing good and I almost blew it in a bad way. No more of that nonsense. All I wanted to do was run a tight class, pump iron, and wait for January.

I stood shirtless in the dark in front of my full-length closet mirror. There was enough moonlight coming in to gleam off and highlight the beginnings of my new ridges and cuts. I tensed everything I had as if I was doing a pose-down. My slightly enlarged shoulder caps glowed like baby skulls, the cuts got deeper, the ridges sharper. My nipples twitched in my tight pecs. I knotted my fists to make the veins rise in my arms. I held it.

———

Seven o'clock the next night I pulled into the Plunkett Mall parking lot across from a burgundy Morgan slant-parked across three spaces. The first thing that always hit me stepping into the Mall was the echoey clip-clop of women's shoes, the sound bouncing between the Monsanto tiled ground and the vaulted benevolent dome. Everything had a hollow distant dream-tone like sounds and voices heard while half asleep on a hot beach. As I walked down a shop lane trimmed in tiny frosted mirror bulbs, "A Hard Day's Night" wafted through the Muzak system. Three trees stretched toward the roof, each in its own redwood tub of pebble-covered earth. Two pretty Irish-looking Townies walked by, pigeon-toed, one in clogs, one in thongs, both with jutting buns and fist-sized busts.

A tight high-cheekboned mid-lifer, attractive and business-skirted, clipped by with an attaché case, her oversized sunglasses nesting in her short feathery layered hair.

Two old women, identical twins, shared a box of caramel corn. They wore shapeless cardigans, their teased hair floating over their lipless faces, their plaid elastic-waisted slacks flood-high, baring too much sock and ridge-soled shoe.

Lurchy high-school guys in down-brimmed golf caps and store-bought football jerseys stood like busted robots watching a girl with purple eyes and an ass like an inverted heart walk by holding hands with her blond boyfriend, who wore a mix 'n' match ensemble of dashiki and Topsiders. A lot of people had Frankenstein posture, a fused spine tilted slightly forward from the hips. I stopped over at the Reader's Island, a wood-shingled kiosk, and bought a copy of *Variety*. Once again I found myself thinking about the phone solicitors at A.C. and that fuckhead Braverman.

There were no shops, there were seventy-two Houses, Homes, Pubs, Sheds, Attics, Corners.

I hung a right at one of the sequoia trees and walked past a cutesy greeting card and notions place, everything in sight with a cat on it. Next door was Casa Pottery; floors, walls and stock all mohave-textured, in clay-gray, rust or mustard.

In front of the open-faced plaid-carpeted Home Organ Center a glossy-eyed bronze-suited salesman spacily played an electric organ with two fingers, belting out a combination snare drum and maraca bar mitzvah samba beat that was too real to be believed.

An eight-year-old with "Here Comes Trouble" on his T-shirt got backhanded by his old man, who was simultaneously pushing a stroller. The kid was smacked so hard his feet left the ground. He didn't cry, just frowned warily and moved away with prim exacting sneaker steps. The organ salesman shifted to the sound of kettle-drums, absently rolling his neck and stretching his eyebrows.

Chaucer's Pub had its name up in gothic characters, the big black C in a brightly colored plastic mosaic square like the first letter in a text scribed by monks.

I took a small wedge of Danish Tilset offered from a butcher block by the free-sample lady in front of a mammoth cheese store, HICKORY HILL spelled out overhead in illuminated plastic logs.

The name of the game that Saturday evening was, Do Not Go Back to Chee Lok.

From up ahead I heard hollow splashing and the echoey shouts of kids. I was approaching the central piazza where four twenty-foot-high swashing fountains shot up from a coin-littered goldfish pond.

As I got closer, the height of the jets began to shrink, dropping in shuddering graduations. When I got to the clearing they were completely shut down. A maintenance man, keys jangling, walked past me wiping his hands on a handkerchief. Some crewcut heads began rolling in jukebox-sized speakers on dollies in front of the fountains. They looped ropes through weighted metal stands to cordon off the area around the equipment. Two others carried in a coffin-shaped electric piano. A little concert. I walked back to Chaucer's Pub and I had a light dinner, reading down the list of top-grossing movies in *Variety* while I ate. There was a purple bruise-colored rose in a thin-necked glass on my table and as I sipped my coffee I stared goggle-eyed at the endless possibilities of its petals. I had to put the rose down out of sight on the seat of the chair facing me.

Chaucer's had its own Muzak so I didn't hear the band start up, but when I came out they were in full swing, the lead singer belting out "Me and Bobby McGee."

I couldn't see them because there was a curve of spectators semi-circling the group. I couldn't tell why the crowd didn't stand closer or why they formed that semi-circle, but when I got up to the action I saw that the standees were all parents, arms across their chests, pocketbooks dangling and they were bordering a settlement of their kids, mainly pre-pube girls who were sitting crosslegged in front of the band.

The goal-post banner behind the group announced them as "The

Waves." Underneath that was written, "The Official U.S. Navy Rock and Roll Recruiting Band." They were all dressed in crisp creased dark blue pants, starched white short-sleeve shirts and big black patent-leather cop shoes. They all looked in shape. On the side of the fountain a recruiting officer was sitting at a stack table.

The lead singer, a clean-cut spade with a short crop, started singing, "Help Me Make It Through the Night," squinching up his face with feeling, his elbow cocked higher than the hand mike. Crooning and trailing cord, he slowly picked his way through the clump-garden of twelve-year-olds, all of them tilting away from his legs, until he came to a fat girl with long hair. Still singing he crouched on the balls of his feet, the mike between his lips and her arterial red face.

"I said *help* me, baby . . ." he spoke, pausing, then sang, "Help me make it throoo the niiight."

Her body trembled with furiously embarrassed giggles as if she were sitting on a six-pack of batteries, and twenty minutes later I was belly-up at Chee Lok tossing back Mai Tais like I was washing down aspirin.

The Chee Lok crowd looked grim. The band on the stage was Chinese, Terry and the Pirates, three guys and the Dragon Lady on bass, who wore a black one-shoulder Spandex top and skintight dungarees tucked into spiked knee-high boots. Her long bluish-black hair was partially in corn rows. They were all young and funky, a little too bad for the place, making everybody dance to James Brown's "Signed, Sealed and Delivered." No matter how nappy the music got the only kind of dancing people did was some variation of the cha-cha.

The man on my left was at least sixty, the man on my right, dead.

"AAAOW! You know signed . . . sealed and de-liverred, is a pack-age containin' mah heart . . . to open ee-it . . . re-*moo*ve the wrap-per, yeah . . . but . . . P*leeese*! . . ." The Dragon Lady leapt forward and belted out the tag. "Don't tear it a-part."

The band cracked up, oblivious to the forty or so dancers jerking around as if they were trying to scrape cowshit off their Neolites.

"Thank you . . . we'll be back in twenty minutes." They broke into their break theme, that old Charlie Chan Chinatown sound of

shimmering cymbals and chinky-chonky notes that always reminded me of wind-up dolls mechanically bowing and moving
around on tiny pittering feet.

I was standing near the end of the long bar. To my left, the counter
made a right angle and extended about six or seven feet to the mirrored wall. At the end of that short arm stood a mid-twenties-looking
Helga in a loose mint-green Hawaiian blouse. Her skin was very
white. She had pale freckles, slanty glinting eyes and a square upturned nose. Her mouth was wide and her front teeth, which were as
big and white as Chiclets, were settled into the meat of her lower lip
as if she was lost in thought. Her hair was long and sandy, parted
tight in the middle and divided into two swirling ram's horns of braid
pinned over her ears like Wagnerian earmuffs. There was a hint of
grim hopefulness in the cast of her eyes and mouth, as though she
was a lousy judge of men but refused to give up. She didn't have a
drink, just stared off, leaning against the wall, one elbow on the bar,
spacily twirling a tiny fuchsia Mai Tai toothpick umbrella between
her fingers.

I casually sauntered out a few feet so I could check out the rest.
She had her mint-green shirt bloused into a tight pleated pair of
khaki pants, which showed off her generous but solid butt, and she
wore a heavy wooden pair of brown brass-studded clogs. I thought
of the Victorians getting hot over "well turned ankles."

Some Toyota salesman came over to ask her to dance, but she
smiled apologetically, dimples appearing like bullet holes, and he
walked away. I ordered another Mai Tai. I didn't know what the fuck
she was doing at Chee Lok. I assumed she was with someone. I
hoped she was with someone, but ten minutes went by and no boyfriends appeared. I looked down at my hands and was embarrassed
to see that I was imitating her, twirling my little cocktail parasol between my fingers too. Looking up we caught each other's eyes; she
smiled, the dimples sinking in, and I looked down again, dropping
my umbrella. This could be fucking trouble. In the past, anytime I'd
go to a dance or a bar, my eyes would wander, I'd say, "Nice one
nice one hey that's nice oooh that one too," but I wouldn't even
bother to yearn or talk to them, an unthinking reflex to prevent myself from wasting time or turning into a moon-ass. But every once
in a while something would click, an eye-zap that said: Switch

realms of expectations my man, I'm people too. I got needs too and they might just be you. And then all I could do was suck up the big, biggest lungful of air and try to hook her into whatever assets I had which in this moment of my life was hard pecs and a New York accent and I was feeling too fucking miserable for words and I needed something to save me right then, like a nice big boyfriend showing up to take her home, because this one was trouble, this one could hurt like a drop kick in the ribs and please God somebody tell me I don't have to find out what her story was.

When I looked up again she was gone from the corner. I didn't feel relieved. I felt fucking lonely.

I motioned to the Chink bartender for another and was startled to see her standing on the other side of me.

My surprise was obvious and I looked away blushing.

She hunched forward, forearms on the bar, still playing with her little parasol and said, "Why don't you try, do you come here often?" She spoke softly to her hands, not looking at me, gently bobbing her head in self-agreement.

Two minutes into conversation I knew I was in physical love because that was the way it always happened to me. It was eyes and face and voice and praying to God that the brains and personalities clicked later on and you didn't wind up ripping out each other's lungs when the bubble popped.

After a while we moved into the deserted restaurant section; there was no fucking way I was going to ask her to cha-cha with me. We sat facing each other, hungry-eyed and bursting with promise under the pink glow of Chee Lok's paper dragons. Conversation seemed to sparkle although I couldn't absorb anything she said. All that registered with me was facial change-ups and the shifting tones of her voice.

She had a habit of saying something low, then eyes downcast she would tighten her lips and nod in agreement with herself. She would say something deadpan, then her forehead would crumple, the corners of her mouth would droop and her eyes would get very deep and intelligently mirthy. And when, after a half-hour of this sublime champagne, she asked me if I'd like to come back to her place, shooting me a good-humored look of mock-coyness, I thought that my heart would explode.

I left my car there and she drove us in her beat-up Pinto. I sat in my ripped bucket seat transfixed with her rough handling of the gearshift, her brass-studded clogs on the pedals, her smiling eyes reflecting the highway lights.

Her name was Kimberly; Kim. She worked in the Geology office at the school, but she wrote stories. She was twenty-eight and she was driving me back to her house. At one point she took her hand off the stick and caressed my thumb like it was Michelangelo marble and I made her pull into an abandoned A&W root-beer stand and we embraced, stretching across the deep reclining bucket seats, her cool fingertips on my neck, her milky smell in my nose, my fucking head thomping over and over . . . This wants *me*. This wants *me*. And then ten minutes later as we awkwardly broke the clinch and she roared back onto the Miracle Mile—*how come*. I always got an attack of the How Comes any time a real sweet face showed me any affection. I couldn't believe it was coming from any sane part of themselves and I'd spend all my time writhing and brooding, waiting for them to come to their senses, which usually, thanks to my act, was in no time at all. It was almost as if I couldn't bear being in love, being so off-balance and powerless. Submitting to a new romance with someone who absolutely knocked me out was pure grief and I always had a bad time. I just hated scenes where I felt so out of control. I hated writhing.

Kim lived on a street of boarding houses in a second smaller Linoleumsville section of town closer to Professionalsville. I followed her up the steps of a converted mansion decaled "The Grand Manor" in gold-leaf stencil on the glass of the front door.

The mansion had been divided into two separate boarding houses right down the center of the squat bulbous ornate Victorian arch, the original front entrance, which enveloped two newer recessed aluminum doors.

Inside, the foyer was as cheery as a black wreath. The walls were a dim banana-yellow stucco uselessly decorated with heavily varnished wainscoting. A cheap chandelier hung like doom, sporting glass tear drops and white plastic candle holders with fake wax drippings beneath flame-shaped light bulbs, half of them out, the other half buzzing like bugs and giving off less illumination than a disposable cigarette lighter. The only thing missing was a few big-nostriled dusty moose heads on the wall. The building still had some of the original ornate oaken touches; each banister rail was carved into the shape of a giant snake, the heads jutting out onto the landings. I followed Kim up four snakes. It was only about ten o'clock and we climbed up a spiral sound-and-smell gauntlet of phones, babies, music and griddle sizzles. The top half of each apartment door was a big wood-framed glass window which the tenants covered with anything from neat discount-house curtains to thumbtacked cheap Indian prints, to limp squares of chenille. One tenant had Scotch-taped his window with computer printout. I could see the silvery action of TV sets through the hangings.

Kim lived on the top floor. The glass of her apartment door was covered with a black and white print of *Guernica*. A little embossed sticker over the doorknob read "20."

Her apartment was bigger than the claustrophobia of the hall-ways would suggest, but it had that same dreary banana-yellow stucco and wood slat trim, dark and oily, which made the place look as if the shades were always drawn or grandparents lived there.

She was Collegetown poor. The living room had a shabby rug, a clunky stand-up lamp, two beat-up exploded-looking upholstered chairs and a sproingy nubby-materialed couch. We hugged under a reprint poster for *The Blue Angel*, my fingers on the flute of her spine, saving the good parts for later. She was big and firm, solid. My mind started to wander during the embrace and that scared me.

"Do you want a drink or some coffee?" she almost whispered, kicking off her clogs and walking into the kitchen with that slightly forward lurch of the Mall People.

"No, thank you." I found myself whispering too.

Her kitchen was pretty big with heavy wooden glass-fronted cabinets and an old-fashioned shallow double sink. Under the cabi-nets in an alcove was a lineup of kiddie cereals with industrial strength sweeteners. An unwashed mix 'n' match whacky stack of multicolored cheap plastic cereal bowls and plates was piled in the sink.

Scotch-taped to a wall were three large crayon-on-oaktag draw-ings sporting wobbly landscapes and one dimensional pie-faced people. One of the pictures was inscribed with a childish hand;

"Mommy is dear. Mommy is grand. She is the best to beat the band. From Anthony Jr."

I didn't read any others. "Are you a schoolteacher?"

"Uh-uh." She foraged around her freezer for ice outcroppings.

Then I noticed the child debris, the toys, the parked plastic vehicles, the little plastic dinosaurs.

"Hey, I didn't know you had a kid!" I said brightly, my cheeks beaming.

"Yeah, well, I didn't tell you." She walked slowly to me, staring down at her three-inch hit of Scotch, which she was mixing with a finger.

"Hey! I *love* kids!"

"Who asked you?" She stood in front of me, still staring down at her drink.

"Is he here?" I sounded so perky and chipper I should have gone back to American Communicators. Of course he was here. We were still almost whispering. I envisioned this poor fucking kid coming into Mommy's bedroom for hugs as I was sticking my yutz in her Dark Place and him being struck deaf, dumb and blind like Tommy. I had forgotten that children still existed.

"How come you didn't tell me? What, you thought it would freak me out?"

"Uh-huh."

"Hey, c'mon, get serious! I'm crazy about kids. I'm no hit and run artist . . ." What a great fucking guy I was.

She softly rolled her forehead against the points of my collarbone, still staring down between us. I twisted my head a little and noticed, with annoyance, that her eyes were not closed with gratefulness. She was staring absently at her flexing and unflexing toes.

Her bedroom was the smallest room in the apartment. She had a queen-sized mattress on the floor. The sheets were light green printed with white branches, the two pillows were sheathed in vivid blue Walt Disney pillowcases; Dopey and Grumpy smiled and scowled at me from their respective sides of the bed. That might be distracting. A one-piece molded plastic three-dollar mushroom-shaped lamp rested on top of a metal wire milk crate standing on its end and filled with paperbacks. Brueghel's medieval revelers kicked up on one wall, Grünewald's cadaverous lovers held hands along another. We embraced for the third time. "I love those guys," referring to the posters.

I moved to kiss her and she embraced me, her whole body shaking as though she was standing on a nerve. But just as I felt my eyeballs start to roll up in my head, she lightly stepped back.

"I think I want to take a shower, okay?"

"I'm not going anywhere."

When she left the room, I sat down on the edge of the bed, my knees up to my chin, and skimmed the titles of her books: a collection of Flannery O'Connor, *One Hundred Years of Solitude*, Strunk and White's *The Elements of Style*, and three books on surviving various things.

On the wall side of the bed I noticed a rectangular brass handle screwed into the stucco about a foot and a half above the mattress. It was too low to hang anything on. Maybe it was there from an earlier arrangement of furniture.

As soon as I heard the hiss of the shower I thought about her wet and naked. Them full hips. I lay back on the bed imagining the water beading under her nipples. What kind of nipples? Big ones. Fat ones. Hard ones.

I got up to go into the bathroom and step into the shower with her, but once outside the room I got lost in the unfamiliar dark apartment; the farther I walked in any direction the more distant the sound of the shower became. I opened one door and heard breathing. My eyes adjusted to the skimpy illumination of a Popeye night light plugged into a low outlet. A black-haired kid, maybe eight, lay coverless on his bed, shaking off the last wet horse-snorts of a bad dream. He was sprawled on his belly, chin dug into his shoulder. His pajamas, blue scissors rampant on a field of white, were accordion pleated with sweat, the tops hitched up to his rib cage, the bottoms almost to his kneecaps. Maybe he was having a nightmare about the banister snakes coming to get him.

Standing there looking down at him, I felt in love with tragedy, with victims.

When she came back in she was wearing a gray satiny Joan Crawford-Mildred Pierce-type dressing gown with puffed shoulders and a knotted sash.

We embraced again in the center of the room. I could feel the fresh dampness of her skin through the heavy gown. A faint hot-shower mist rose from her shoulders to my face.

There was something voluptuously fertile about her and I felt myself sinking with nervous awe into her solidness. I was surprised that I didn't have a hard-on. She went slightly limp in my arms, but when I tried to slip my hand under the knot of her sash between the folds to hold flesh, she foiled me by twisting her hip and crossing her leg. I stiffened.

"Could we just cuddle tonight without doing stuff? It's been a long time and I don't feel on top of it just now," she whispered.

"Sshure," I sshed. "Sshure." She hugged me hard in gratitude. I was furious. "No . . . no, we can't. . . . And I'm not leaving either." I didn't know what the legal complications would be, but I was serious as cancer.

She was silent for a few seconds, then nodded in understanding. I kissed her head and she started to slide down my front, fingers trailing my torso until she was on her knees, her lips on my belt buckle. I was stunned by how easy that was. With a great effort on my part I put my hands under her arms and lifted her to her feet again.

"Let's just get in bed, okay?"

She nodded, tight-lipped, looking wretchedly unhappy.

———

We lay in the darkness, her head on my chest. Her nipples were pale and heavy, her hips flared sharply. Now that I had declared No Exit, all I could do was come on like Mister Snuggy Bear, spooning and murmuring the way she had requested to begin with.

After a few meaty minutes we lay on our sides facing each other. She looked a little happier, but sex just wasn't in the air. She hadn't even glanced at my cock yet, or felt around to see if I had one. That was all right. Just to lie there in the dark, talking nonsense with her, my hands on my own damn flanks, had me feeling a combination of heartache and release so sweet and weird that I started humming.

"Do you want to hear something?" She touched my chin.

"Sure." I had an overpowering desire to physically swallow her in one cartoon gulp. My fingers itched with sign language.

"I want to tell you about my last lover." Trouble in Paradise. I knew it. I knew it. She kissed my trachea. "Six months ago I was living in Florida. I was going to this community college part-time and working as a secretary in this insurance company . . ."

"In Miami?" Teach class, pump iron, teach class, pump iron.

She thought for a moment. "No . . . Jacksonville . . . near Jacksonville."

Oh good, let's play games, let's weird out the pickup.

"Is this real, or this made up?"

"Ssh . . . let me tell you." She proceeded in a hushed monotone, as if she were talking to herself or trying to memorize a long speech under her breath. Her eyes were focused on my throat and her eyebrows rose and fell, taking up the dramatic slack of her voice. "I was working and going to school and they came to me at work, at my desk, and asked if I knew Toy Taylor. They both had suits and those haircuts, so at first I thought they were the police being that Toy was in jail. I said yes, I know Toy, but I haven't seen him in a year." I didn't know what the fuck she was talking about. The near-beatific swoon that almost had me floating off the bed minutes before completely vanished, and I found myself in a mute depression.

"They told me that Toy was going to the electric chair the next week and that there was a new conjugal visitation rights law passed and that prisoners were now allowed to have conjugal visits from girlfriends if they weren't married and Toy requested that he spend his last night with me.

" 'Why me?' I said. 'I haven't seen him since six months before he killed those men, we never even wrote to each other.'

"This one man shrugged. He sat down on the corner of my desk and he looked into my eyes and he said, 'Whether you do it or not means nothing to me, but I think it's only fair to warn you that if you do it there's going to be a lot of publicity. No condemned man was ever allowed a conjugal visit the night before his execution, at least not with the approval of the state, and there's going to be lots of stories and lots of pictures the next day because the warden wants it that way.' Then he leaned closer, squinting like he wanted to see if I had something in my eye, and he said, 'Personally, I wouldn't do it,' and I had to laugh imagining him sleeping with Toy.

"Well, I didn't know what to do. I went home and discussed it with my girlfriend Mary Kay who I considered a lot smarter than me. Mary Kay said if I did it I'd go down in sexual history like Salome or Belle Starr or Catherine the Great and what it boiled down to was me asking myself if I wanted to go down in sexual history. I found this funny since I was a virgin until I was twenty-four. I had done only two bad things involving sex that I could recall.

"Once I deep scratched a boyfriend's back when he was on top of me after he gave me a talk about free love, take *that* to your next free love; and one time I was dating an older man who used to come over my house, snort cocaine with a rolled-up twenty and leave the bill there on the table alongside the chopping razor when he left in the morning like he forgot it. I never knew if he was doing it on purpose, but one time after we had a fight the rolled up bill on the table was a five, so, did I want to go down in sexual history?

"The next day at work my boss got me one of those cute little rubbery desk statues that said under it 'World's Greatest Secretary,' and that night I called those men and said I'd do it.

"I went out and bought a new overnight bag, but I didn't know what to put in it. Should I bring toothpaste? Deodorant? I didn't think I should bring any morning-after things. Poor Toy. All I brought was perfume and a nightgown.

"I took the train. I was surprised there wasn't someone there to meet me at the station and I had to take a taxi up the hill to the prison.

"The next morning at the gate there were reporters and some local people. They started snapping pictures and asking me questions. Did he hurt you? Do you think you're pregnant? What's in the bag? The guards were looking at me like they wanted to know too. By the time I got home poor Toy was dead. My face was in the papers. The obscene phone calls didn't bother me, because my parents were dead. That night I let Mary Kay put her fingers inside me. She put her head between my legs. I quit my job. Everybody knew my face. I could have had any man I wanted. They would circle me at bars but none of them could get it up later on. They were afraid to put it inside me, afraid that I would spread my legs and electric sparks would shoot out. I was the Angel of Death. And you know what? I didn't mind it in the least.

"The funny thing is, me and Toy didn't even do it. He was so miserable all I did that night was hold him. I didn't even get out of my street clothes. . . ."

She nodded that shy tight-lipped affirmation, her eyes still zeroed in on my throat. The whole thing sounded like a recitation, like a story that she'd written and memorized.

I didn't know how she wanted me to respond. I had the heart-sickening thought that she'd told me all this to get rid of me.

"What the hell am I supposed to say?" I felt like crying with disappointment. Angel of Death, my ass.

"You don't have to say anything." She said a light shruggy sing-song and absently pressed a hard finger into various spots on my chest as if she was feeling for a secret panel. "You don't have to say anything."

Okay, she's scared, she's doing a number on me. *I'm* scared, I have no patience. Bullshit, I'm not scared, I'm fucking crushed. I'm angry, and I'm no cunthound animal.

"I mean, how'm I supposed to react, Kim?"

"You don't have to react." If someone could be described as speaking "blindly," that's how she was talking. Embarrassed, cornered. She got into her finger poking a little harder.

"What do you mean, I don't *have* to react . . . I'm lying in bed with you and you're telling me this fucking saga about banging killers—what am I supposed to do?" I realized I was almost shouting because I was in total pain from her finger pokes, which were getting close to puncture force. Her face was knuckled in agitation and a strange kind of confusion.

"That was a story you wrote? Yes or no."

"Yes *and* no," she said like a kid stuck in a defiance rut.

That was it. I sat up to get dressed and she quickly laid a hand on my elbow.

"It's a story . . . it's a story. Can't I tell a story?"

"I have no *time* for this bullshit, Kim. I'm over eighteen." I lay back down and she started in with the finger jabs again.

"Is that a fact?" she said dully.

I hissed in pain from the last poke. "Yeah, that's a fact, and stop fucking *stab*bing me already!"

"Is that a fact," she repeated, but there was a sobby catch in her voice that time and suddenly without looking down she grabbed my cock.

———

She lay under me, her knees almost together, one hand on my back, the other palm down on the mattress below her hip. I was inside her but my legs were saddling her thighs. I arched my back and moved gently, rotating, rolling, sprinting, trying different strokes. Her breath was steady on my raised chest.

"Wait." She twisted and I fell out. She grabbed the Dopey pillow and slipped it under her ass. "Do it hard."

I did it hard, holding on to the carrying straps on the side of the mattress for traction. After ten minutes of concentrated silence, she came, breathing hard through her nose against my shoulder. I came right after, like someone hoisting himself up to a ledge after making sure the person he was carrying got up there first. I lay on top of her, my hand on her forehead like I was checking fever. When I rolled off she started crying, curling against my chest.

"It's hard . . ." She shrugged, sniffling. "It's still hard."

I woke up at dawn, the sky syrupy with the gray promise of rain. Kim slept with her back to me, her left hand dangling from the brass handle, the weight of her arm supported by her jackknifed wrist. I got up to go to the bathroom, aching with the ghostly blues that I knew I'd wind up feeling ever since I first saw her in the bar.

I passed the kid's bedroom again and softly opened the door.

His blanket was on the floor. He lay on his back, arms raised over his head, legs spread and bent at the knees. His eyebrows were arched and his mouth was slightly open as if he was in the midst of a scream. His pajama tops and bottoms were still hitched knee and belly high and the overall image was that of a person frozen in mid-plummet from a great height.

On the back of the bathroom door suspended from two bent nails hung a cheap aluminum-framed full-length mirror. I stood there, staring at myself. It seemed that ever since I'd started lifting weights I'd been spending a lot of time in front of mirrors, but this was different; I was trying to find what Kim saw in me.

There was no way I could call myself handsome. I'd had permanent bags under my eyes since I was three, an inheritance from the Rabins. And my nose, although not exactly a potato, lacked a certain symmetry; it just sort of sat there like a nose. I had nice hair, though, light brown with blond highlights, thick and wavy. I never combed it, just brushed it back with my fingers and it always lay right. When I was a junior I'd let it grow down to my shoulders, but even now, when it was just slightly longer than what would be considered clean-cut, I still had people coming up behind me and calling me "ma'am" because of the long curls. Women always ran their fingers through my locks when we were in bed. Except Kim. I hated my eyes because they were slightly off center and I remember occasionally being called cross-eyed by some of my more compassionate elementary school friends, but sometimes women interpreted my uneven stare as a sign of intense desire. I used to have incredibly long eyelashes when I was younger but they seemed to have shrunk. Too bad for me.

I told people who asked that I was five foot eleven, but that was true only if I was wearing heels. I was five nine and seven-eighths. I was too skinny, never weighed more than one forty-five in my life, but the weights were doing the trick and my body was starting to fit me like a handmade Italian suit; no flab, no belly, nothing that wasn't supposed to be there.

By the time I crawled back into bed I decided that Kim could have done a lot worse.

I awoke at ten to church bells. I was the only one in the bed. The details of the Brueghel print were lost in the sheen of day glare. It was still gray outside. The apartment was silent. I walked around in my shorts, terrified of losing her and slightly afraid of running into the kid.

A big note on butterfly- and mushroom-bordered paper was taped to the lid of the toilet.

"I had to take my son to his doctor's appointment in Richfield. I left breakfast for you in the fridge. Please call me tonight. I miss you already. A of D. (Angel Baby) xxx P.S. It was only a story (you knew that). P.P.S. Your name is Pie."

I found a ring of apple and orange slices on a green plastic plate in the refrigerator. The centerpiece was a hard-boiled egg. She hadn't covered the plate and the apple slices were slightly sworled with rusty brown.

I threw out the fruit so she'd think I'd eaten it and went back into the bedroom. I went through her dresser drawers. Small-cupped bras and satiny cream-colored panties with lace filigree waistbands. A plaid blank-paged diary with a dramatic and useless lock. On the floor of her curtained closet was a pair of old sandals, the shapes and idiosyncracies of her toes crushed and molded into the soles. I started shaking just the way she had the night before.

I was really, truly, dumbly, mallet-whacked in love.

I opened a shoe box next to the sandals and found about three hundred dollars in small bills. A cardboard accordion file behind the shoe box held a dozen envelopes of canceled checks and bank statements chronologically ordered from two Januaries earlier to the past December; her balances ranged from forty-three dollars to six hundred, including a few bouncers here and there, nothing more than twenty bucks worth, though. I spotted a subtraction error that was the cause for one of them . . . I knew she wouldn't have done it on purpose.

There was another accordion file filled with exam booklets and essays. I was surprised to discover that she had been a student at Straight. I couldn't remember if she had told me that or not. I also discovered that her last name was Carmichael—that one I'm sure she told me but it didn't sink in. I wondered if she remembered *my* last name—probably not. She had been a good student, nothing was graded lower than B+. She had written an essay for Aaron's folklore class entitled "Grendel as Gregor Samsa: a study in early English alienation." Aaron had fallen for it and given her an A+, the shmuck. It was exciting to me that she had been a ballsy student; it humanized her, took her out of the vanilla zone of townie blankness.

I came across a big fat stack of essays she had written for Fonseca's creative writing class ten years ago. That knocked me out. We'd actually taken a class with the same guy. We were getting closer and closer every minute. I skimmed Fonseca's comments. On the first submission he'd written "Who are you trying to kid??" The story was entitled "The Darker the Berry" and it seemed to be first person from the point of view of a black whore in Harlem.

After that one though she took off. All Fonseca's comments were raves. On one he'd written "You slay me." Another said simply "4 stars . . . Daily News." Another had a weird intimate twist to it: "Great, as usual," and a little further down, "that was fucked-up of me—I'm sorry."

I had been reading all this stuff while squatting on my haunches balancing myself on the balls of my feet. After a while my kneecaps started to blaze and I reluctantly stood up and began to get dressed.

I experimented with five or six notes I could leave her in response to the mushroom paper but I trashed them all because I couldn't get the right tone. Also, I was afraid the kid would find it first.

Putting on my coat in the hallway I absently gazed at myself in a mirror and was startled to see that I was scowling. I realized that something had been bugging me since I left the closet but I couldn't nail it. I felt fretful and spacy, as if I had forgotten something, or had forgotten what it was I had forgotten. I didn't want to leave the house until I had it straightened out. Something with the kid. No. I checked to see if I had my underwear on. I thought of Kim. I kept wanting to call her Kimberly Fonseca. Maybe I was jealous of his rave comments. But I kept seeing "Kimberly Fonseca" in my mind.

I went back to the closet, hunkered down again and found the essay and story file. Kim Carmichael. Maybe I had absently taken some money from her shoe box. . . . All there . . . three twenty-five. It was driving me crazy. I checked her bank receipt file again and there it was. Kimberly Fonseca. Fuck me. Oh God. I felt a dull buzz, a stoned beam of fear.

You slay me. Who do you think you're kidding. That was fucked-up of me. I'm sorry. Four stars.

I stood up and backed out into the living room as if Fonseca was going to jump out of a corner. Okay. Okay. She'd been his student. They got married. They separated. They divorced. They separated. They're on the verge of getting back together again. He's coming over now with a bouquet of roses. He's very big. Very physical. He's nuts. Crazed. You did it again, you bunghole. You fell in love. And he's going to eat your face off. You're fucking his wife with his kid in the next room. Oh cut it out, you silly thing. For all I know it could just be a coincidence. Maybe she had married someone *else* named Fonseca. Yeah, right. I'm sure there were thousands of guys in Buchanon, New York, named Fonseca. Shit. It had to be him, the kid's name on the drawings was Anthony Jr. My teacher. The teacher. He could take her away from me. He's the teacher. He was big. And how exactly ex was ex? The kid. Visitation rights. Watch yourself. Don't be there Sunday mornings. He was big—running to gut but brawny too, and his Nathan Detroit act made him seem twice as tough as all that. What if Kim was using me to get him jealous? I saw myself in a heap at the foot of the snake banisters as the two of them stood at the top of the landing and hugged and kissed forgiveness and never-agains.

Suddenly I felt cold. I didn't care anymore. It didn't mean any-thing. It was a night. A good night. Not even, really. We'd had a lot of trouble about sex. I didn't sleep that well, anyhow. I was in the midst of somebody else's movie and I couldn't be bothered. Whities. Blondies.

She was a Townie. Townies do that all the time. Townies believe Country and Western lyrics. They like to punch people. They give you a blow job then send around their drunk boyfriends to slash your tires. How could I love a Townie? I was a city boy and no matter how pretty or whatever she might be, I could never see myself at peace or in comfort with a Townie girl. I would always be lonely with her, and she with me.

My parents had a summer house in upstate New York, and as a kid I'd play in the woods behind our property with the locals. One day this blue-eyed crew-cut named Eugene Bohannon, Jr. stuck his hand down the back of his pants, winced at me, and pulled out a small pointy dry turd. He shit in his hand. Townies reminded me of Eisenhower. Their houses smelled like diaper stew. Her eyes were too light. I needed subways and immigration. Bubbas. She had no feelings. But then I thought of her alone in Chee Lok. And the note. And the cheap plate with fruit slices for me. Her wrist curled around the brass handle as she slept. What the aura of whatever her cross was did to her mouth; that tightlipped smile and eyes. Her naked hips were the palest white with light blue tributaries. I envisioned myself slowly dipping my head to her hip, gently breaking skin with my teeth, and her stubby toes spreading in surprise. Kimberly. Kim.

I was berserk about the woman and Tony Fonseca seemed bigger than Kong.

I tried to decalibrate my anxiety as I drove home but all I could think about was further reasons why this one time I was right to worry. Fonseca's ever-present car coat was leather—the guy was into leather. His hands looked like meat hooks—big scarred jobs; the scars probably from punching out cunthounds, or guys who simply said hello to Kimberly, the light of his life. He slammed his door in Mossi's face. He cursed a lot. I couldn't remember if I ever knew he was married. By the time I got back to my apartment Kim had *become* Tony Fonseca in my obsessions and I roamed around the stillness of my place, totally lost in thought, absently touching my furniture. I wanted to call someone for advice and comfort.

I fished out my own collection of essays and stories from freshman year, found the stuff I had written for Fonseca and pored over his comments. All his reactions seemed hostile and sarcastic, pissed off, as if he had been anticipating the number I'd pull on him five years later.

On my first submission, a shockingly racist attempt at satire, he wrote, "I can't tell if you're pulling my leg or not. I hope you are. For *your* sake."

On my second effort, a bush-league parody of greed on game shows, he wrote "Before we enter the classroom, we check our Mad Magazines at the door—you write like a white guy playing basketball in Harlem."

On the third, where I had tried to straighten up and write with fondness about a piece of family apocrypha concerning my father, he had written "very sweet." I had no idea if "very sweet" was positive or negative. It felt mocking, and in an effort to crack his meaning, I reread the story:

> During World War II, my father, serving as a mail clerk in the US Army, was walking down an Austrian street, spaced out, minding his own business, when suddenly he found himself being strafed by a Messerschmitt flying so low and so right at him that he made eye contact with the pilot. He just stood there, knees bent, feet splayed, as if he was pantomiming taking a dump while the plane ripped over his head, two columns of bullets singing and

hopping on the cobblestones on either side of him. Ten minutes after the plane vanished he was still standing there as if he was daydreaming. He shrugged and touched his chest . . . "Whatta ya want
from *me?*" When he got back to the mail room which he ran, he
became aware of a throbbing pain in his right hand. Much to his
surprise, his hand was so tightly balled his knuckles were quivering. When he slowly opened his fist, which stung like hell because
it involved withdrawing three fingernails dug into his flesh, there
was a casing lying in his palm. He vaguely remembered picking it
up right after the plane vanished. The bullet had been red hot, and
he'd burned his skin and eventually left a cylindrical scar across
the top of his palm from pinky to index finger. There were also
three short slit-like scars across the heel of his palm where the fingernails had dug in. That was the only action my father saw in four
years.

My father would tell the story of the bullet now and then, to me, or
in front of company. I would love the way he said his one line, "So
whatta ya want from *me?*" I would stand in front of company myself
when I was a kid and imitate my father telling his tale. I had it down
cold. I could do the up-shrugged shoulders, the raised eyebrows, the
smirky dismay, the exposed palms of either side of my hips. I loved
my father when he did that . . .

I felt ashamed of myself for writing such a transparent portrait of
a father and son wimp-team. I also felt pissed at Fonseca; his "very
sweet" suddenly seemed like a put-down of my family. I started
getting incensed, hard-assed, filled with a Whad-you-say-about-my-
mother? outrage. I took off my shirt, tensed my chest muscles and
tried to scare the shit out of my mirror.

Jack it up. Jack it up. I stomped and scowled around the apartment
like a Hell's Angel on hold. I called myself every limp-dick name I
could think of. Dropping a coffee mug on the kitchen floor, I told it
to go fuck itself. The phone rang. A male voice asked for Carol, and
before slamming down the receiver I told the guy she was still out
from Saturday night and it was time he started wising up.

It took an hour of this embarrassing bullshit to bring me to the
edge of physical and emotional collapse.

In a last desperate attempt to fend off the deep despair that had been waiting for me to finish my asshole dance, I picked up the receiver and called Audie Murphy. I needed him.

"Dad?" I sat on the floor in a pow-wow position.

"Hiya, buddy."

"Dad, how ya doin'?"

"Ah, awright."

"What's goin on?" The fatigue in my voice made me sound casual.

"Ah, Vy's mother died Thursday," he said, like his check to Con Ed had bounced.

"Whaat! Is she okay?" I came alive with a mixture of sympathy and anger.

"Well, we buried her on Friday . . ."

Shit!

"How come you didn't call me!"

"Ah, she was so sick for so long . . ." I could feel him shrugging over the line.

"What the hell does *that* have to do with anything?" I tried to control myself. "How's Vy?"

"Well, what can you say, it's her mother . . ."

"What's *that* mean? Is she hysterical, is she crying, is she telling jokes . . . ?"

Don't fucking bring me down. I felt myself descend into that profound exhaustion again. Kim. I would lose her. I would lose her as sure as I would lose my mind dealing with this fucking family of mine. Suddenly last night, all of it began to dissolve like fragments of a dream.

"Well Vy's sitting *shiva*, we got a few of her friends coming over . . ."

"I'm coming home," I said in a glazed monotone. I was losing my father. I would lose Kim. My jaw began to tremble.

"Nah kid, you don't have to bother . . . Vy appreciates it but . . ."

Funerals. Families. My heart felt like a sprung booby trap. I started to cry.

My father listened to me sob.

I listened to him hiss and sigh.

It was like a conversation between two obscene phone callers. Come on you fucking mailman, deliver the letter.

"Come home, Peter," he said finally, sounding touched and rattled.
"Thank you." I meant it.

"I swear kid, if I knew Vy's mother meant that much to you . . ."
I felt astonishment like a physical high.

"You are a stupid man," I said calmly and hung up.

"You are a stupid man," I repeated to my apartment.

I closed my eyes, bowed my head and tried as hard as I could to remember last night; Kim, Chee Lok, the kid, the bed, Kim. I thrust my hand into my pants and grabbed my crotch. My pubic hair was gummy and damp, balls slick with sex, dick sore. Evidence. Son of a bitch. I snorted and shook my head in chagrined relief. I didn't know whom I felt like more, Lazarus or the Asshole of the Year.

I wasn't insane, just nuts.

Go wash your face, you putz. Crybaby.

Driving to the airport, I tried to convince myself that I was going home to spite them rather than to defend my stake. I kept grabbing my damp crotch to remind myself there were other games in town.

Think Kim. Kim was important. Kim was important. My class was important. Jack was important. Zybyskos was important. Now take all those people and slide them in between you and them. See how that works, Kim was important. Kim was what counts. That girl you just met in a Chink singles-bar, took home and fucked was what's important. You call her from their house tonight. You call everybody and tell them how you met this great girl sixteen hours ago and that even if it doesn't work out you know what love is now and will never settle for less. And if Fonseca didn't like it, fuck him where he breathes.

It worked. It worked so well that I worked myself up into a total froth about Kim. I was in love again without distraction. I got a glimmer of how rich life can be without the neurotic scrambling for yeahbuts . . . Fifteen minutes into the drive I began to see the sky and greenery through the giddy clarity of love shock. I thought the D.J. on the car radio had a wonderful firm voice, had made an excellent career choice. I wished I had a phone in the car. I wanted to reach out and touch someone near and dear just like in an ad for the phone company. I was in the type of powerful mood where I could have endorsed any product with such heartfelt warmth that truck drivers would be stopping on the sides of highways to buy tampons.

But on the last leg of the ride, as I was creeping up a one-lane road that ended at the airport, I got stuck behind a half-dead pickup truck, and I sank into another panic; Kim had asked me to call her today and I didn't know her phone number, and if it wasn't listed, there was no way I could get in touch. The only thing to do was go back to her place and leave a note in her mailbox—no, she wouldn't check it until tomorrow. No mail on Sunday. I'd have to leave it on her door, but if I did that I would miss the plane and lose my family. Until I became the father I was the son. Another scow chugged behind me and I continued to climb the hill. Everything fell apart. I had opted for going to the airport and I felt that everything, everyone I acquired in the last month amounted to shit. I felt furious at April Wenzel for coming on to me and making me lose my self-control. I had been right to hold off on romance. My brain was all over the goddamn place now.

———

The local airport was designed in that dreary 1950s "the future is now" municipal style, complete with two glass display cases, one showing some miniaturized factory model, the other samples of some local bauxite-type byproduct of industry. On the glazed walls there were stupid black and white framed photos of outdated planes flying through clouds, an aerial photo of the airport, a sign saying FLYING DEVILS MEET IN THE WIND TUNNEL LOUNGE, TUES. NIGHTS.

In the fluorescent stillness of the waiting room I looked up Kimberly Carmichael in the phone book. Not listed, of course. Then Kimberly Fonseca. No dice. There was an A. Fonseca though. I stared at his number fearlessly. But no goddamn Kim. Doomed. Wait. It was just a temporary set-back. Call her in the Geology office first thing Monday morning. But she said call me tonight. Please call me tonight. That's okay. Get her tomorrow. Christ, you had a funeral in New York. What's she want? Stop with the melodramatic choices— airport or note. You'll catch her tomorrow. Lighten up on yourself and go back to mooning. And that's exactly what I did. I sat there in the Wind Tunnel lounge and worked on it. I flashed on her sliding down my body, her awesome tremblyness, her averted glance, caressing my thumb in the car, eyes shining with highway signs. The mushroom note. The stack of plastic cereal bowls. The filigree trim on her panties. The thumping magic. There was never any woman like her. Please God, don't let me lose her. That's it. Pump it up. I worked myself into another happily miserable froth. Like miraculous stigmata, the poke marks she'd drilled into my chest started throbbing again. I felt like writing moany poetry. My teeth ached, my eyes burned. I could feel where all my joints met. I felt raped, bruised. A dog. It was similar to the old flu bones but it was a Love Jones, and I felt so wretchedly happy I knew I could survive ten funerals, invited or not.

My plane was put into a holding pattern for two hours over La Guardia. The rain was coming down in a steely Sunday-afternoon curtain. Cars slished along the highway in front of the apartment house. Looking up from the cab I could see that our kitchen chandelier was lit.

Vy sat in her stockinged feet on a wooden crate. My father was tieless, wearing his black mohair suit and a black too-small yarmulka puckered and pinched on the top of his head. The big marble-veined mirrors were covered with black cloth. Three of Vy's friends sat around the living room eating sponge cake. On top of the television was a bottle of Fleischmann's Whiskey and a half-dozen shot glasses.

I had come home with an attitude, but the minute I walked in the door I saw my father jerk back. He said, "Ah . . . he's here!" and Vy jerked around, cried out, "Oh, look at Peter!" and I immediately started babbling apologies and explanations for not making the funeral. Vy wasn't crying but her eyes looked as if they were rimmed with a pink jellied glaze, like a white mouse. Her hair was teased and frosted a rusty bronze as usual, and she was hunched over the crate in a thin black dress. I was amazed at how fleshless her hips were. She really was a small frail woman.

"I'm sorry, Vy . . ."

"Oh, look at you!" She smiled, reached up from her crate and immediately went to squeeze my new arms. I was wearing a tight thin turtleneck. I had my funeral clothes in my gym bag.

I kissed her on the temple. The macaroni pictures were down.

"Look at him . . . college professor." Vy held onto my bicep and turned to her three visitors, packed thigh to thigh on the love seat. There was a lumpy Russian-peasant-looking couple; second cousins or something, and Vy's garment district bookkeeper girlfriend who had passed me on Seventh Avenue when I was eating on the sidewalk. "Look at him," Vy patted my chest like she was folding me into a suitcase. "So, Mommy," she beamed up at me, her eyes glistening, "now we both don't got mothers."

"That's not true Vy, I got a mother." I looked at my father when I said it. He was leaning against the wall, hands in pants pockets and he nodded Good Boy at me. The three on the couch said "Awww" in chorus and Vy reached up, curled her hands around my neck and brought my cheek down to her lips.

"Don't shit me, honey," she whispered without malice. I never heard Vy say "shit" before and I was so startled I laughed.

———

An hour later as my father saw Vy's friends to the elevator I sat on the coffee table so I was on eye level with her.

"Look at you," she sighed, motioning for me to pour her a shot of the Fleischmann's.

"Listen, Vy, I'll tell you something that I did when my mother died that helped me." I leaned forward, my elbows on my knees. "This is gonna sound silly, but any time I thought about her, or thought about being alone, I just started singing this song that was very popular with kids then. . . . It wasn't like a real song . . . it was a TV show theme song, but it was so contemporary and so 'now,' that it cut into the unrealness . . ."

"Just look at you," she smirked.

"Just sing anything you want . . . a show tune . . . something you like on the radio . . . anything that'll keep you here . . . Billie Holiday!" She didn't answer. She smiled sadly, eyeing my torso and arms, ignoring my face.

I blushed. I felt as though I'd just delivered lines in a musical. Any second we were going to burst into "Put on a Happy Face."

"Look, it was just an idea . . ."

She patted my hand. "Look at you." She reared back. "Where'd you get the muscles from?"

I shrugged and poured myself a shot.

"So what did you sing?" she asked gamely.

"What? . . . Some kid song."

"What?" There was something wry and teasing in her voice.

"It's stupid . . ."

"What!" She was going to make me sing. Good for her.

"Fee-lix the cat, the wonderful wonderful cat, Da-da-da-da-da-da . . ." I shrugged. "I forget the rest . . . it was a stupid idea."

When my father came back in, he winked Thank You to me.

"So what time's your plane, buddy?"

"My plane? I was gonna take one out tomorrow . . ." I felt myself getting tight. "I was gonna stay over, if that's okay with you."

"Sure, sure." He said it casually, but he had his hand out in placation.

"It's raining . . . it's *dan*gerous to fly," I said, sounding bruised.

"Hey . . ." He touched his chest. "Stay as long as you want . . . you *live* here."

I stepped inside my old bedroom and realized I'd lost it. Lost my Kim ache, and I whirled around patting myself as if for a wallet. But I worked it back, I willed it back, and to smack it in I picked up the phone to dial Jack and tell him the love news, but he wasn't home.

I tried to call seven people to tell them the news. I even tried to call April.

I wouldn't tell anybody in the house, though. I stayed up half the night doing clock arithmetic with flight times, class times, in-between times, to be able to dash over to Geology. When I left at six A.M. they both stood in the doorway and said, "Goodbye."

I caught a seven-thirty A.M. plane back upstate and was only ten minutes late to class.

———

I drove over to Geology, smoothed back my hair in the shine of a glazed corridor tile and whirled into the doorway envisioning a stiff-backed Kim staring hypnotically into a huge salmon-pink IBM typewriter. No Kim, just some other tune, in a pale green safari suit with a cinched waist, short shock bangs alternately sticking up or slicked down as if she had taken a television into the bathtub with her that morning. She had a hickey on her throat. The name on her desk was Mary Kay Cicero.

"Is Kimberly around?"

"Kim Fonseca?" She gave me the once-over. News must travel fast.

"Fonseca?" I repeated dumbly.

"She's off today."

"Do you know where she is?"

Mary Kay shrugged.

"Tell her Peter stopped by, okay?"

"Will do."

I should have left but I shuffled in place wanting to ask some questions. The best friend of the woman in Kim's story was named Mary Kay.

The phone rang on her desk.

"Joligy," she droned. ". . . Oh *hi*, Tony . . ." she stretched and yawned.

In a total panic I lunged across the desk. "Is that Tony Fonseca?"

Popeyed, she slowly shook her head No and I lurched out of the room completely crazed about Fonseca again. Forgetting my car, I jogged back to Hopper and made it to Jack's office.

———

"Hey, Pete . . ." Jack sat at his desk carefully underlining sentences in a thick fine-printed hardbound book. He was wearing Fiona's bifocal harlequin glasses on his huge hanging face. The glasses had a broken silver beaded chain dangling from one joint. He looked like a big fat Margaret Rutherford.

As I moved closer I saw that he was going through the *Physician's Desk Reference*. Jack was one of those passionate hypochondriacs so devoted to their obsessions that they knew as much about organic danger signs as a first-year med student.

"Jack, I got woman problems."

"You're not boffing one a your kids, are you?" He marked his place with an envelope and whomped the *PDR* shut.

"Fuck no. I'm in love."

"Well, that's great, pal . . ."

"Yeah. I met this terrific woman Saturday night named Kimberly. She works in the Geology Department." I watched his face.

"Kim Fonseca?" He removed his glasses.

"Yeah," I drawled carefully. "She's Fonseca's Fonseca, right?"

He raised his eyebrows and rubbed his mouth. "Well, she was . . ."

"How 'was' is was?" I didn't move my head. My eyes were narrowing.

He shrugged. "They're pretty finished."

"So it's okay, right?"

"I guess." He did not look happy.

"And *he's* okay?"

"I guess."

"Then say congratulations."

He just smiled.

"I'm serious, Jack. I'm walking around with this thing in my head that I'm setting myself up here . . . that they're in the middle of something and I'm just some seventh-inning stretch, or I'm some lyric in a cowboy song that's about to get punched out and I don't want to be a bit player here and I have no idea what I'm talking about so I'm asking you to tell me, to the best of your knowledge, as Fonseca's chairman, that everything I just said is total nonsense and I should stop worrying and enjoy myself. How about it?"

Jack spit tobacco on his shirt, which I took for a good sign. He brushed his chest and leaned back in his collapso-chair which squeaked and snittered in shock.

"You're a good kid, Peter." He squinted out the window. "Go easy. . . . She had a rough time with him, I think."

"Go easy, he says." I stood up, bubbling with relief. "So I'm crazy, right?" I tilted my chin at the hypochondriac's bible. He followed my gaze and reopened the book. "Do you know there have been three documented cases of men experiencing hysterical pregnancy?" Taking the change of subject as a token of reassurance, I clapped my hands and split.

———

As I walked down the street to Kim's creepy boarding house, a kid, who I thought might be Anthony Junior, came zooming down the hilly sidewalk doing about ninety miles an hour standing on the seat of his red and yellow Big Wheels. I tried to envision him in pajamas. He was hunched over, clutching the handlebars, the footless pedals circling furiously free. He had a bizarre adult expression on his face; very stern, his head cocked to the side, a disapproving frown and raised eyebrows. As he flew past me he admonished the air in front of him, "Now what did I tell you about standing up on your Big Wheels? What did I tell you? Do I have to say it again? Do I?" He hurtled down the street toward the traffic, dropped into his seat about ten feet from the curb and brought himself to a half-inch from doom. He immediately jumped off and began running it up the hill again.

His face was grotesque; not unhandsome, but a man's face wrapped around a child's skull, his eyes projecting an intelligence so disproportionate to his age that the prospect of hugging him was chilling.

I stood in front of the house, collecting my shit before I went upstairs. I was nervous because I hadn't called her, it was dinnertime and I was planning a surprise entrance like a big dramahead. What if Fonseca Senior was up there? Jack had given me a lot of "I guesses." Maybe he really *was* guessing. Maybe he was talking out of his ass. I sat on the front stoop. A fat girl in a white hygienist's pants suit came out. A lean integrity-faced graduate student went in, the back of his gray sweat suit rorschached with perspiration from jogging. Probably the guy with the computer window. I watched the gremlin fly up and down the hill on his Big Wheels with his nonstop reproachful patter.

Finally I trudged up the stairs rife with cooking smells and television talk, my palm sliding dryly up the varnished spines of the snakes.

The door had a ringer that twisted like a nose. I focused on the wild-eyed horse in the *Guernica* print plastered on her window. My insides were ballooning and deflating at a comic speed as I heard her clipped steps.

"Hi, baby!" I smiled. Shit. No flowers, no wine.

She sighed, her face collapsing in pleasure, and came at me with hovering arms. "You never called me," she said with soprano relief.

Her weight was totally wrapped around me, her loose breasts pressed flat against my chest, my nose in her hair. I think I said "Ahhh."

———

I watched Kim cook. She had a swimmer's manta-ray curve to her back, a strong swooping taper from her broad flat shoulders to her thin waist, flaring out again at the hips like the base of a vase. That her nimble bony fingers could move with such deft distracted confidence to convert raw food-stuffs into such an abominable meal seemed like a put-on.

The three of us sat around the table eating vile chili and drinking Pepsi. Captain Big Wheels was hers, unfortunately. Rearing children seemed astounding to me. I was amazed that she'd had it, raised it and kept it alive, even though cavewomen did the same. He didn't like me. I didn't like him. I didn't think he liked her too much either. Every time she addressed him he would make a bugeyed gargoyle face, which for him was not difficult, and raise his knife, his entire body jerking forward as if to lunge across the table and strike her. When he did this she would avert her eyes, embarrassed and apologetic.

"How ya doin' in school, Anthony?" I used the same simple raised-voice technique that Vy had used to talk to her late senile mother.

I had been thinking of an opening line for ten minutes and the suddenness and volume of my question startled both of them. He didn't answer, just drank his Pepsi, both hands around the plastic orange bathroom glass.

"Fine, whoever you are!" he said in an equally loud, perfectly mocking tone of voice some minutes later.

"Anthony!" Kim warned.

He bulged his eyes at her and raised his fist, his head sinking into his shoulders. Kim looked like a whipped dog. I wasn't that up on child psychology, but I didn't see what was wrong with reaching across the table and smacking the little fuck.

"Anthony," she tried again softly, "I told you, his name is Peter." She accentuated the "Pe." I hated when people pronounced my name like that. It made me feel that they knew something about me that I didn't.

I waited for his next little explosion, but he changed tactics, and just sighed theatrically while delicately picking the chopped meat out of his chili with his fingers, his head resting on his propped-up palm.

It was a much more effective strategy for him to use than the tantrum ploy. Given Anthony's disturbingly intelligent adult face, his jaded heavy-lidded smirk was nothing less than a withering masterpiece of intimidation.

Kim and I talked with tense politeness about my flights to New York and back. Anthony watched us with that sleepy superior smirk, making me feel like a simpleton.

After ten minutes we stopped talking. It was too strained. I never should have come up unannounced. Maybe everything would have been cool between them if I hadn't been there. I didn't know how deep the current ran but right now they hated each other, I hated the kid, and I was losing my buzz for Mommy too. He was making her look bad. On the other hand, what was I expecting, Dondi? The more I thought about it the more thoughtless I felt about popping up for dinner. Well, she should have said I'll see you after dinner. Well, asshole, you should have called, and not put her on the spot.

It suddenly struck me that this little monster, this Little Anthony, could tell his father on me. I entertained the sensual notion of getting him alone and quietly, calmly, terrorizing him into a lifelong silence about me and his mother. I felt dull with anger; totally under his thumb.

I took a slightly crumpled bread bag off the table, took out the four remaining slices of rye, and continued eating for a few minutes. Suddenly I thrust a finger at his chili.

"Yechh! Look!"

They both jumped back.

"What!" he said.

"You were just about to eat this!" I said with alarm and pantomimed removing some invisible small object off the top of his red gruel.

"You know what this would have done to you?" I intoned like a reproachful doctor, spacing my thumb and forefinger as if I were holding a bullet.

He recoiled in confusion, then looked at his mother for confirmation that I was nuts.

"Do you know how heavy this is? It's like eating iron . . . here." I made to hand it to him. He looked at my face. "Just take it."

He shrugged and made the same configuration of his fingers.

"Now throw it in the air." I took on a bossy serious tone that would brook no bullshit. He made a quick flick of his wrist to humor me.

Staring at the ceiling, I slowly rotated in my seat as if I were positioning myself under a fly ball, brought up the empty bag, my thumb and middle finger pinching the top, then suddenly snapped my fingers, simultaneously jerking the bag down. It looked and sounded as if something heavy just dropped inside.

It was absolutely the only parlor trick I knew, and fairly lame at that. Kim laughed encouragingly. Anthony just returned to his chili, his face resting on his palm. But instead of laying us low with another blasé stare, he looked truly sad.

"Do you want to try it?" I perked.

He didn't even answer me. Everybody at the table looked on the verge of tears. I began to rise and said at crouch point, "Listen, if you people don't mind, I'm going to the bathroom and kill myself."

"Good," he muttered.

Kim didn't even bother to 'Anthony' him.

I sat on the toilet lid. I thought of seeing Anthony go through his contortions in bed that first night, his running babblelogue on the Big Wheels. He was definitely coming from Pain-land, but I couldn't help it. I just wanted him to retreat back into his father's testicles.

When I emerged from the john not knowing exactly what to do, I passed Anthony in his bedroom. The door was ajar and he was holding the paper bag, his arm inverted, elbow crooked and high as though he was attempting ground-level lasso tricks.

He distractedly pantomimed tossing something ceiling-wards, his eyes on the bag, then stood there grimacing as he unsuccessfully tried to snap his fingers.

Feeling a glow of gratefulness, I burst into his room, scaring the shit out of him, and took the bag out of his hand. He backed off as if I was going to belt him. I sat on the edge of his bed. "C'mere." I impatiently beckoned him forward. He stood his ground. "Can you snap your fingers?" I asked briskly, while demonstrating ten snaps a second.

He shmooshed two fingers while eyeing me. I reached out, grabbed his arm and pulled him to me.

"Make the thing with your fingers."

He put two fingertips together.

"Squeeze them."

I watched his thumbnail turn white.

"Harder."

He grimaced.

"Now, snap!"

No snap, a thud.

"Try it again." I took his hand in mine, avoiding looking at his face. "Move your thumb down . . . squeeze . . . now, snap!"

A nice clean pop.

"Do it again." We sat around snapping fingers for a few minutes.

"Ugh." He let his tongue hang out in exhaustion.

"Okay, gimme the bag. Now just make like you're going to snap again but . . ." I positioned the lip of the bag between his fingers. He snapped and the bag crackled.

"Awright!" I clapped my hands. "Way to go! Now throw something up."

He gave a quick bland toss, stared at the bag and snapped his fingers.

"C'mon, Anthony, get into it!"

His name sounded false on my tongue.

I grabbed the bag away, pantomimed flinging something high up, staggered around his room, bag at the ready, my mouth open, eyes bulging; tripped over his rug, scrambled to my feet, caught the object with a snap and fell on my ass again. It killed him but he laughed.

"You gotta get into it, Little Anthony." I gave him the bag. He made a huge contorted throw, took a lousy pratfall, sat up and held the bag triumphant. "You forgot to snap your fingers, shmuck."

We got it down cold. We improvised a game of catch with two bags. I chest-passed a huge boulder across the room, and he caught it with a snap in the bag, then fell backwards from the weight. Both of us were very big on the falling down part.

I rarely looked him in the eye. I barked out my communications. I was dead serious, no-nonsense brisk, and extremely physical. That kept him completely off guard and he adopted my mood of concentration. I was enjoying myself but if that shit had failed I'd have thrown him out the window.

"C'mon, let's go show your mother." I started walking out of the bedroom.

"No, we can't now . . ."

"Why not?"

"Because this . . ." He pantomimed typing, punching his index fingers up and down like sewing-machine needles, his pinkies extended.

From the rear of the apartment I heard a sound like rain on a tin roof.

"What's she typing?"

"Stories."

"Oh yeah?" I felt uncomfortable; a slight tinge of anxiety about the future.

"Yeah." Anthony sat on the edge of his bed, breathing heavily, studying me. "Why'd you call me Little Anthony?"

"Did I call you that?" I smiled, then thought of Big Anthony, stopped smiling.

"I don't like that."

"Anthony, where ah . . ." Watch it. "When's the last time you saw your Dad . . . dy?" Eeesh.

"My father?" He cocked his head, eyebrows rising. "My father's dead."

"Oh yeah?" I said brightly, confused but hopeful.

"He was killed by Mexicans."

"Mexicans?" Street crime?

"At the Alamo."

My heart sank. "No really, Anthony."

"What time is it?" He stretched forward to check the digital clock on his desk. "He'll be here in a half-hour."

When he saw my face go white he cackled "Hee hee hee . . . don't worry, I'm only kidding."

"You're a little fucking shit," I blurted, relieved.

"Hee hee hee." He looked adorably vicious, tickled with himself.

"Cut it out, you little pecker . . ." I was smiling, almost laughing along with him. "When do you see him? I'm serious."

"On Christmas and on my birthday."

"When's your birthday?"

"Tomorrow."

"When's your birthday, shitface?"

"In July . . . do you know him?"

"Who?"

"My father!" He smirked at my innocent act.

"Nope . . ."

"He was a wrestler before I was born. He taught me the flying drop kick and the Boston Crab. Can you do the Boston Crab?"

"Nope."

"You want me to teach it to you?"

"Sure."

"Lie down on the floor on your stomach."

I did as I was told. Anthony stood straddling me, facing my feet, his shoes on either side of my hips.

"Pick up your legs."

I lifted my heels backwards and he tucked my feet under his armpits, locking his arms in the crook of my knee joints, raising my thighs off the floor. It felt slightly painful and I thought about abruptly straightening out my legs and sending him head first into the wall.

"You ready?" He turned his head back to me.

"Yup."

He clasped his hands across his chest so I couldn't release my feet and then simply fell backwards until he was sitting on my ass. I felt screaming rockets of pain shoot up the front of my thighs and collide at the base of my spine. Howling into my fist, I shot my legs out, flipping him on his head.

Upside down, his hands still clasped across his chest, my feet still pressed into his armpits, he started to giggle. I twisted around, unable to turn over, and stared at his blood-gorged gleeful face.

"Anthony," I said sadly, "what can I possibly do to make you cry?"

We fucked around with the bag trick for another half hour. I didn't know what else to do with him so I left him to his own devices and went into the living room. I sat on the couch and thumbed through a *Ranger Rick* magazine. The room was coldly lit by a high open-topped stand-up lamp. I sat there for forty-five minutes. It was painful listening to the distant staccato soundtrack, the abrupt starts and stops, the prolonged bursts of clackings. It made me feel flinchy and indecent, as if I were eavesdropping on someone sitting on a toilet.

When she finally came out, my hands hung between my spread thighs. I glared at her. She shrugged and smiled apologetically at me, the straight bottoms of her big front teeth peeking between her lips.

"Stolen moments," she murmured. "I have to get him to bed."

"Do you want me to go?" I sulked.

"No . . . it's okay." She entered his bedroom and half closed the door.

It's okay. It's okay? I felt rattled. With her trembly hungry semi-timid act, I expected her to do a backwards somersault of an apology when it was obvious that I was pissed, not "It's okay." I thought about her two nights before, staring at her toes when I expected her eyes to be closed in gratitude for my magnitude. It's okay.

She had a rough time putting him out. He was fairly wired and started snapping out at her again. She took it like a sponge, so I wandered around the house and found her writing room, which was a screened-in back porch. On a collapsible card table there was a flat portable typewriter, a skinny folding Tensor lamp and a topless Del Monte string-bean can containing two Bic pens and a white ink-erasing pencil with a bright red duster on the end. There was a neat stack of three 9×12 manila envelopes all stamped up and ready to go, addressed to the fiction editors of a men's magazine, a women's magazine and a quarterly. The envelopes were sealed. I felt a flash of anxious anger. Well, me too. I was going places too. In January. Somewheres.

I hightailed it back into the hallway. Through the open door of Anthony's bedroom I saw Kim sitting on the side of his bed, hunched over his chest. She was speaking in different voices. Anthony squinted up at her, pulling down his upper lip like a chimp and picking his nose.

"And so the Minotaur said to Sunboy, 'Go ahead, try to leave the maze' and Sunboy realized that the maze would follow him and surround him wherever he went."

"It was a portable maze," Anthony declared.

"That's right, like a barrel with suspenders . . . so Sunboy realized that there was only one way out. . . ."

"Fight the Minotaur?"

"Fight the Minotaur." Kim nodded.

"When's Christmas?" he bitched.

"A while yet."

"I wanna see Daddy."

"You can wait, I'm sure."

———

She came back out into the living room where I was waiting, collapsed onto the sofa, her head landing in my lap.

"I guess I got on well with him," I said, fishing.

"Yeah," she said mildly.

She closed her eyes, her nose in my belly. I touched her back; it was a brace of knots. Her lips were drawn back in a thin peaceful smile though, her upper lip slightly protruding over her front teeth. She took my hand and kissed it.

Suddenly she raised herself on an elbow, wrapped an arm around my neck and kissed me full and soft on the lips.

"I was so happy when I opened the door and it was you."

"Look at you." I winced. "Look at that face . . . what are you so happy about with me?"

She rolled into my stomach again and hugged my ribs.

"I can't believe I met you at Chee Lok . . . that place is the most disgusting joint in the world. What the hell were you doing there?"

She shrugged. "What were *you* doing there?"

"No, I'm serious."

"I was just waiting for my friend Theresa. She's got a crush on the owner and I promised her I'd go."

"I didn't see you with any girl . . ."

"She never showed up. Her kid got sick."

"I didn't know you were married to Tony Fonseca," I said mildly, as if I'd just found out she was a Democrat. She didn't answer.

"How did you meet him? Was he your teacher?"

"I don't want to talk about that now," she murmured into my belly.

I turned her head up to my face. "I would like to."

"Can't we just hug for a while?" She tried to turn her face back into me, but I wouldn't let her.

"Tell me about Tony and you . . . I'll tell you anything you want about me, but let's start with that."

She didn't answer.

"How long ago did you get divorced?"

"We're separated, not divorced."

"How long?"

"A year ago."

I did some fast math. Anthony was eight; Kim was twenty-seven; Fonseca, pushing forty. Eight from twenty-seven was nineteen, from roughly forty, was roughly thirty-two.

"How'd you meet, were you a student of his?"

"Uh-huh."

"Did he knock you up?"

"Uh-huh."

"Did you drop out of school and marry him?"

"Uh-huh."

"Why did you go out with him to begin with? What was he, a father figure?"

"I dunno," she singsonged.

"Would you have married him if he hadn't knocked you up?"

"I dunno," again the singsong.

"What was the big deal about him?"

She didn't answer.

"You know, I was a student of his too, you know?"

"Oh yeah?" she said dully.

"I teach writing there too, you know?"

"I know." She shrugged. "You told me."

"So what am I, Fonseca Two?"

"Get serious."

"*You* get serious . . . do you see him now at all?"

She hesitated one second too long before she said no.

I die. I die.

"Is this some fucking game with you two? Am I gonna be head over heels with you and get thrown over when you decide to get back together again? Cause I'm not very fucking stable, Kimberly. Things are going good, but my wings are still wet, and I think you're gonna be a big number for me if things go right, so tell me now before we really get rolling. Are you going to see each other again?"

"I don't even know you," she shrugged into my stomach.

I felt prickles of panic rise on my arms. "Are you going to get together again?"

"Not if I can help it."

"Do you love him?"

"No."

"Did you ever?"

"Yes."

"Do you love me? Don't answer that . . ."

She was already formulating an answer on her lips and even though I cut her off I tried to lipread if it was a "nuh" or a "yuh" sound shaping up.

"Am I the first guy you ever slept with since him?"

"Yes."

"Shit . . . that's bad. That's bad for me."

She sat up again, an elbow digging into my thigh.

"Are you going to leave me?" eyes frowning at my chin, voice heavy with muffled doom.

I didn't know if she was goofing on me. Nonetheless, I ate it up.

"Get real, Kim," my voice wry and comforting.

She put her arms around my neck, trembling away, and spoke low and rapidly, her lips almost brushing mine, "I missed you so much I cried when you didn't call. I was so happy you had to go to a funeral. I was so happy when you showed up at my door tonight . . ."

. "I really banged up the kid by showing up for dinner, hah?" Despite the punitiveness of the question I asked it with a joyous speediness.

"He's okay," she whispered.

"Does he see Tony a lot?"

"His birthday, Christmas."

Check. Check.

"So we're an item, right?"

She laughed and shrugged.

"Say yes."

"Yes."

"Say, 'Peter, we're an item, you and me.' "

"You and I."

"Say it."

"We're an item, you and I."

"You forgot my name."

"Pie."

"It's Peter." I smiled.

"It's Pie."

"I fucking love you, Kimberly. I know it's absurd and premature . . . just don't get turned off to me saying that now." My eyes were wet.

She hugged my neck, her lips pressed in my ear. She didn't say I love you back. Fuck it. I'll get her.

"One last question . . . are we going to embrace ten times in the middle of every room tonight before we get in bed?"

We got to our feet. With an arm around her shoulder, my head low, I slowly walked her toward the bedroom.

"Okay, this is the bubble stage of the relationship now. Everything we do will be perfect, then we'll have riffs and that'll be the true test."

———

"How come that brass handle is there?" I jutted my chin to the wall as I unbuttoned my shirt.

She looked down at herself as she unhooked her bra. She had a big dipper arrangement of beauty marks on her solar plexus. She shrugged, raising her eyebrows.

"Did you put it up there?"

"It's stupid." She avoided looking at me.

"*What's* stupid? Is it a good luck charm or something?" I flashed on bondage. Maybe she was into getting handcuffed and tied to the brass. I flashed on her sliding down to my belt buckle on command. I didn't know if I could handle that. "C'mon, tell me."

She sighed. "This is really gonna sound stupid, but when I lived with my husband we had real wood paneling in our bedroom, with deep wide grooves between the slats, and I used to have bad insomnia and the only way I could get to sleep was if I stuck my fingers in the grooves, for some reason. When I moved out and got this place I still had insomnia and I couldn't afford to put in wood paneling so I went down to the hardware store and bought that grip and put it into the wall. It's a lot cheaper than wood paneling, and it's easier to hold on to. . . ."

"My husband" sounded formal and distant.

She jumped into bed and curled on her side.

"So what you typing in there, a story?"

"Uh-huh."

"About Toy and the Angel of Death?"

"Maybe." She blushed and ran a finger along the brass handle.

"You know, I was thinking about that, that story. I don't know if that's true, that no guy could fuck you . . . her, after. If that chick was the Angel of Death, guys would be around the block takin' numbers. . . . Maybe not." I shrugged.

"You think so?" She screwed up her face in dismay.

"A girl who fucked a famous killer?" I slipped off my shorts and crawled in. "Depends. As far as myself, I'd question her taste in men. Also, I couldn't imagine what she'd see in me, but other guys? Christ, they'd be on her like white on rice . . . I dunno, maybe me too. Why don't you let me read some of your stuff?"

"Let me just tell you stories." There was a casual pleading in her voice.

I knew enough not to try to be creative with sex. She slipped a pillow under her ass. I straddled the outsides of her thighs with my legs and commenced fucking. She would let out with an occasional breathy "hmpf" as if someone were hitting her with a series of interesting facts. That, compiled with my own propensity for holding my breath when I had sex and the fact that the mattress had no squeaky boxsprings beneath it, made for intercourse so silent that we could have screwed behind enemy lines. At one point I stopped abruptly and there was no aftershock of solo movement on her part. She was just lying there letting me have my way. Almost half-heartedly I took it up again, then stopped again.

"Look, I think I know what the problem is," I whispered, then yanked the pillow out from under her. "We've been fucking with Grumpy. We should be using Dopey."

"Stop." She clucked her tongue, but let me slip in the other pillow.

"OK . . . this is gonna be a straight run to orgasm . . ."

"Pie . . ."

"No, I'm sorry, you're right. I should . . . I should . . ."

"Don't make fun of me."

"I'm only teasing you, Kimberly. Don't worry about it . . ." I sounded more fed up than I meant to. I liked "Pie"; it sounded chewy.

We stared at each other with glassy blankness. I started to slide down the mattress to put my head between her legs when suddenly she flipped over on her stomach. One side of her face was pressed into the sheets facing the wall and her hands lay flat, arms bent like cactus branches.

"Do it like this," she murmured, slightly tensing her ass. I sat on my knees between the spread backs of her thighs and gently ran my thumb between her buttocks lightly touching the small puffy button of her asshole and then down to her still dry twat. My cock was like stone. I ran my thumb gently up to her asshole again and let it linger.

"Where?" I whispered awkwardly.

She didn't answer.

I dripped saliva into my palm, swashed it around the head and eased myself partially into her ass.

"Does that hurt?" I spoke low, as if voice register had something to do with it.

She didn't answer. Just lay there, her eyes shut. I slowly moved deeper inside her, lay flat, my belly in the small of her back, and cupped her throat, my thumb caressing her lips, forcing her head to arch up off the bed. I slipped my fingers in her mouth as I moved in all the way and started rolling and plunging in slow earnestness.

Just as I was about to shoot she whispered, "Come out." She rolled over on her back and slipped me inside. "Do it hard." We went back to straight hard charging and when she came, five minutes later, she bit into the thin skin of my collarbone, so that I had to arch my back to pull away from her teeth.

Before she rolled away from me, slipping her hand in the handle like it was a subway strap, she murmured, "Tony used to say I fucked like a man."

———

The next few weeks were real sweethearts. I just about moved in with Kim and the kid, totally getting off on our little nuclear family. She would never spend the night in my place, though. She'd say it was because of babysitting expenses. She balked when I offered her a duplicate key to my place but she showed me where the secret emergency key was hidden for hers.

Despite how quickly we became a team I found out that there was something intimidatingly secretive about Kim. Although I was always welcome in her apartment, it was very clear that it was *her* apartment. She'd never let me read her work—she wouldn't even tell me in which magazines I could find the few stories of hers that had been published. And when I'd try to talk to her about Fonseca and her eight years of marriage, the dialogue would be something like:

"Tell me about Tony; never mind, I don't wanna know."

"Good, I don't want to tell you."

"Why don't you want to tell me?"

"I thought you said you didn't want to know?"

"That's not the point. Why don't . . . *what* don't you want me to know? Never mind, I don't wanna know."

"Good, I don't want to tell you."

"Why not?" and so on.

One time when we were sitting in my car outside of Anthony's school, waiting to pick him up so that we could all go to the Plunkett Mall, I started asking her about Fonseca's visitation rights, why he only got to see Anthony twice a year. She shrugged and tried to stonewall me again, but I kept at it.

"Really, I thought fathers saw their kids a few times a month at least."

"Well, he doesn't." She stared straight ahead.

"Well, how come? Was there a legal agreement?"

"I'm getting a headache."

"I have Bufferin in the glove compartment. . . . Was that what the court decided? Twice a year?"

"It's none of your business." She lowered the sun visor, although the day was cloudy.

"Does Anthony *want* to see him more?"

"Anthony . . ." She whipped her head to me, ready to snap, when suddenly across the street a fight broke out among a bunch of kids who appeared to be about ten. From where we were sitting all we could make out was a pile of flailing extremities; it looked as if everybody was ganging up on one kid.

Kim yelled, "Anthony!" exploded out of the car, ran across the street and started flinging kids off the heap, barking "Get off him, goddammit!" The discarded kids stood around staring at her in awe and fear. By the time I ran up to help, she had worked her way down to the bottom and when the nose-bloodied crying victim, who was decidedly not Anthony, sat up, she backed away in shock.

I found out that I was dead wrong to think of her as a Townie; she'd grown up in suburban Albany, her father was involved in an evangelistic television show racket, working as a composer and lyricist for some Oral Roberts-type goon named Reverend Howie. He wrote songs for Jerry Humphrey, Reverend Howie's main singer on "Calling all Souls."

Even though this Reverend Howie had built two hospitals, one in South Korea the other in Chad, he was a total ghoul, milking his mainly poor followers for five- and ten-dollar prayer cloths, organizing a cripple's parade, and hiring retired athletes at double their last year's pro salary to stump for him. Sometimes his followers, if they had no money, would mail in gold teeth, and Kim told me that he always wore a medallion that was made from a bunch of these teeth melted down and resmithed to his specifications.

And Kim's old man had been on Howie's team for twenty years. He was even a member of the Reverend Howie "Soul Cabinet," as "Secretary of Inspiration."

In any event, Kim's parents had some long money; enough to send her to private schools all her life and enough to pay for sufficient riding lessons so that by the time she was eleven she was in an equestrian show at Madison Square Garden. She didn't get any money from them now, though; they hardly spoke to her.

I told her everything about myself, my parents, Vy, Bronx, Yonkers, and last but not least, my long years at home. When I ran down the part about the phone calls, the arrest, seeing Dr. Catcher, she seemed compassionate and non-judgmental. She didn't hug me and croon "my poor baby," nor did she get weirded out, making more or less of it than it was.

She came to my class one day. She wanted to see me teach, and when she first suggested it I said, "No, don't, okay, come."

Sitting there in the back on the side so that she wasn't facing me, she seemed as big as a statue; a real writer, my girlfriend; not looking older than anybody in the room except for the knowing eyes. She was serious too. No winking, no smiles. She didn't want me to introduce her.

At first my students stared at her but she played it so down and neutral that everybody lost interest except April, who spent the whole class checking Kim out, eyes going from her to me, frowning, not very happy at all.

Fueled by stage fright, I put on a sound and light show that day like I was bucking for the Intensity Hall of Fame. I was all gestures and soliloquies, my voice ranging from a cackle to a boom. I pleaded and I broke balls, soothed and pep-talked. I was the Gipper, Vince Lombardi, To Sir With Love, Lenny Bruce and Will Rogers. One of the readers that day was James Tucker, but instead of hitting us with another Sominex capsule of fairies and Snow Queens, he read a short piece about four black kids in Newark finding out that the funding for their summer jobs had been cut and debating what to do with themselves. One kid wanted to enlist in the army so he could go off to Germany and score blond pussy. Next stop Vietnam.

I felt proud of him.

James shot me the smallest secret smile when he finished reading.

After the class, we picked up some sandwiches in town and went out to a stand of woods beyond the campus to have a picnic.

"Tell me I wasn't good today." I sat on the grass bobbling my sandwich, too charged up to eat.

"You were great, Pie," she smiled and cocked an eyebrow. Serenely impressed.

"Fuckin' A skippy, I was."

"I mean it. They loved you."

"Climb every mountain . . ." My jaw was trembling with triumph.

"That black kid thought you were the best. He loves you."

"*He's* the best . . . has been writing bad Hobbit all term. That thing he read was a breakthrough. You don't know."

"Did you fuck that little redhead?" She smirked.

"No way." I reared back, relieved that I hadn't.

"She's got the hots for you."

"Tough noogies . . . she's very good too."

"I'll bet."

"I'm serious."

"So am I. She's got high drama written all over her."

I let it go at that.

"So I'm good, right?"

"Are you teaching next term?"

"Nah, I'm out."

"I bet they'd give you another class next term."

"Nah." I blushed.

"You should ask. You could be such a great teacher . . . you could go back to school and get a degree." She was sitting with her legs crossed. She reached over and rubbed the back of my hand. "You could be awesome."

For a moment I imagined myself a Great Educator shooting out sparks of inspiration in some hallowed hall, Oxbridge steeple chimes in the background, striding across a grassy campus, birds tweeting, students trotting to keep up. Coming home to Kimberly and sherry and morocco-bound books. So much for rock and roll. So much for jazz. So much for the curved road. No way, José.

"I don't know, Kim."

She made a bitter face at her sandwich. "So what do you want to do?" She sounded sad.

"I don't know . . . I was thinking of heading back to New York."

"Why?" she said too fast. This was bad.

"I don't know. I want to try something else. Something open-ended."

"Like what?" Again too fast.

I shrugged. "I don't know, something with the arts."

"Like what?"

"Relax, okay?"

She shut up and scowled at her fingernails. Goddammit.

"Maybe like, I dunno, acting classes, or try my comedy, working on a film crew, theater crew . . ." I was winging it.

"They have a theater department up here."

It wasn't even worth an answer.

"I dunno . . . something . . . something *special*, you know?"

"Teaching's not special?"

"No." It was my turn to answer too fast. "I mean yeah, it was . . .

it is . . . but something . . . Look. Do you know Crown? The drama guy?"

"I heard he flipped out."

"He didn't flip out." I was pissed.

"That's what *I* heard," she pouted, not looking at me.

"You heard fucking wrong."

We both sat in sullen silence for long minutes. I never really thought about the fact that come January I'd be leaving her too. Shit. I wanted to propose that she and the kid come with me, but I was too afraid she'd flip. Or at least give me a flat no.

"I dunno . . . maybe I will teach . . . get a doctorate . . . I'm bright."

"You're *very* bright," she said in a gloomy monotone.

More silence. I knew I could never talk to her about game plans, and it saddened me, made me feel heavy with despair.

"Yeah, maybe I'll teach."

By that night, we silently agreed to drop it. It was too mighty a subject to deal with right then, and things went back to Euphoria Street. Any time I started thinking about January, I also thought about taking Kim with me. I was sure I could talk her into it. As a writer, her career was portable. I knew when the time came I could swing it. And I left it at that and went back to working on Happy.

It seemed everybody around me was working on Happy too. April got engaged, then broke it off, all in two weeks.

James Tucker continued writing Newark to Nam stories; good stuff too. David Howard's wife got pregnant again. Fat Jack got himself an apartment, although he lived with his family at least half the week.

Crown sent me a postcard from New York saying that he'd landed a small part as a lieutenant in an off-Broadway production of *Pavlo Hummel*. My father and Vy sent me a long letter thanking me for coming home and apologizing for not telling me about the funeral. The letter was in Vy's handwriting, though. And I read in the *Times* that Rom Braverman had been caught at Heathrow coming into England for a film festival with a quarter ounce of cocaine in his suitcase. Things were going so well, I could hardly stand it.

But I never lost my fear of Fonseca. The more deeply involved I became with Kim, the more I feared something or someone taking her away from me—like an ex-husband that she refused to talk about, God knows why.

He was constantly on my mind, and in the absence of historical data I filled in all the blanks from my obsessive disaster-head file of scenarios; he was Conan the Cocksman and their life together had been a porno swashbuckler—nine years of cannibal passion. She'd drop me in a minute for him.

On campus I avoided bumping into him at all costs. In the first week of classes he had his office moved to another building so I was free to roam my own hallway, but I passed on all English faculty meetings, all parties, and when going up to Fat Jack's office I ducked my head in first to see if Fonseca was around. I did the same when I went to the building where my classes were held, scouting out the corridors like a combat veteran coming to a deserted village. I didn't know if the guy was even aware of my existence, let alone my relationship with Kim, but it seemed I was doing everything in my power to make him into the Boogeyman. I guess I could have milked Jack for more hard information but if I'd found out that even a small fraction of my fantasies were true, I *really* would have gone off the deep end. At least this way, when things got too bad, I could always write it off as unsubstantiated paranoia.

But I was constantly ashamed of myself for the swoony obsessive cowardice of it all. I kept promising myself that I'd cut it out, that I'd walk the halls a free man, go to any campus function I wanted to, stop acting like such a neurotic pussy . . . and at the end of October I finally made my move. Jack gave a party for the English faculty at his home one night and I forced myself to show up.

As soon as I entered the big living room I spotted Fonseca standing in a corner flanked by two students. I said, "Oh wow" out loud. I felt fascinated, as if I had walked into one of my own nightmares. I stood in the doorway, glassy-eyed, filled with such a breathless mixture of terror and a weird kind of tenderness that I wanted to sit down on the floor before I fell on my face. Between myself in the arch and him by the window was a murmury chortly harrumphing crowd of twenty-five profs chomping niblets and drinking wine. Fonseca was fucking huge, three times bigger than I remembered. Dressed in a rust velour pullover, bell-bottom dungarees and his trademark brown leather car coat, he stood slightly vulture-hunched, spread-legged, one hand in his front pants pocket, the other pumping pretzel nuggets into his five-o'clock-shadowed face. His black hair was shag cut into an urban Prince Valiant under which one eye was shut, the opposite eyebrow raised in amused disdain. He had a long straight nose and his thin lips were slightly twisted. His whole face was an invitation to exchange smirks. If it ever came down to it, he looked as though he could break me in half. Nonetheless, I had to resist moving closer to him. This was "my husband." This was the man with the wood paneling with the deep grooves. He knew Kim's quivering embrace, he knew how that felt. I should have left but I couldn't. I was overcome with a bizarre impulse to make sure he was happy, and if he wasn't, to *make* him happy, to take care of him. I felt my instinct for survival had suddenly developed some kind of rapture-of-the-deep-disorientation, my gyro had just toppled and I was in a lot of trouble.

His two escorts were dressed in dungarees rolled up at the cuffs, high white sneakers and hooded sweatshirts. They imitated his posture, although they looked nervous and out of place, forced smiles of tension on their faces.

I never realized Fat Jack was so tall. He cruised through the room, chin and cigar uptilted at F.D.R. angle, towering over everybody like a male nurse in an old-age home. He patted backs, laughed at everything, deployed his sons for beer and Triscuits and in general moved through the crowd like a cross between a politician and a ballerina. No wonder they made him chairman; he was five of anybody else there, no pun intended.

A visiting lecturer, a medievalist named David Goodenough, was being introduced to a group of faculty wives. Goodenough was short and slight with a long combed-back mane of prematurely gray-streaked hair and a matching goatee. He wore sunstruck concentric glasses. He stood stiffly next to his wife, a sweet-faced Hasidically dumpy woman with ankles so thick it looked as if her feet were connected directly midcalf. Goodenough would shake hands, bow like a kraut, then spring upright, his hand palm up across his chest, pointing to his wife like a magician presenting his rabbit.

I moved deeper into the room, bumping into David Howard and

a few others whom I knew to chat with, but I was feeling too focused
on Fonseca to get involved in any but the lightest of Hi, good, and
you?-type conversations. People talking to me kept turning around
to see what I was staring at over their shoulders. I grabbed a clear
plastic glass of white wine and a handful of Cheez Doodles from a
Tupperware bowl on a Liberty ship door made into a coffee table.

Someone brought over an athletically thin short-haired woman
to meet Fonseca. She wore a pressed slightly faded black jumpsuit
with a hot-pink webbed belt.

"Tony Fonseca? This is Elizabeth Nancy. She'll be teaching
poetry next term."

Fonseca shook hands, dipping his head, screwing his closed eye
tighter, raising his opposite eyebrow higher. As soon as she started to
turn, he wheeled to Riff and Raff and passed some comment behind
a drawn hand, cracking them up, then immediately turned back to
the party with a look of mock sobriety. I saw that Elizabeth Nancy
caught part of his act and by the fleeting look on *her* face had found
it despicable.

"How ya doin', Tony." Jack came up alongside Fonseca and
slipped a hand around the back of his neck.

Fonseca's face broke out from under the smirks and he smiled
like a kid.

"This man . . . this man . . ." Fonseca said to his students in
mock earnestness, his head bobbing solemnly. "This man . . . is the
man!"

The two kids chuckled self-consciously. The eyebrow smirk
returned to Fonseca's face. He jerked a thumb at his charges.
"These guys are headed for the big leagues, Jack. No Triple A
clubs, these guys are gonna go right from here . . ." he tilted his head
and pulled his hand back to his armpit, paused, ". . . to the majors."
He shot the hand out toward Jack's pompadour.

"Great." Jack smiled, barely looking at them. "Why don't you
guys get some beers?"

David Howard's wife came up behind me as I was deep into
an open-mouthed trance of observation, studying Fonseca's every
move and mannerism.

"Do you want to feel it?" she asked, and I whipped around so fast, blushing and stammering, that she stepped back from me, her hand absently finger-pronged against her chest.

"What? . . . oh hi!" I smiled. "What? Do I want what? I'm sorry, I'm sick . . . a little."

"Are you okay?" She stepped forward.

"Yeah, I'm sick. I am, I'm going home soon. What did you say?"

"No, I just asked you if you want to feel it." She pressed her splayed palm against her belly. "I swear it's crazy. I'm only two months, but it's kicking already."

"Oh, the baby! Yeah, sure . . ." I absently pressed a hand against her perfectly flat stomach and turned my head back to Fonseca.

———

"Big Jack." I lightly wrapped my arm around Petty's gut like a child hiding in an apron as he passed my way.

"He-hey, Petey, good to see ya . . . good to see ya." He absently patted my face with a dry palm. "How's your class going?"

"Great, man, great. I'm doing good with Kim too." I forced myself to keep my eyes on Jack's face. "We really love each other, we really do."

———

Fonseca stood in the doorway, both hands in the rear pockets of his denims, sweeping back his brown leather coat.

"Where you guys gonna be later?"

"Nowhere, we got homework." One of his charges dug the heel of his sneaker into the gravel. They looked relieved to be outdoors.

"Homework!" Fonseca jerked back wincing, then slowly returned to the living room, hunched, grim-faced, pacing, eyebrow high, looking for trouble.

I stood behind two grayheads who were talking about Joyce's pornographic letters to his wife. "Anthony"—one of the guys touched Fonseca's forearm as he was trolling by, hands clasped behind his back. The man's name was Goodge and he was the Shaw man. "Anthony, you might be interested in this . . ."

"I doubt it." Fonseca cut him off with a straight face, turned his back on them and marched directly at me.

I was totally calm as he grabbed my arm, standing directly in front of me, stiff-spined, choking on snorty suppressed giggles, his chin pulled into his neck. "Are they lookin'? Are they lookin'?" he urgently murmured like a lousy ventriloquist.

I stared at the few tendrils of chest hair that crept up toward his thick throat. I had willed him over to me, as sure as if I had had a homing device.

"Are they lookin'? *Tell* me!" He giggled.

I had to duck to his side to see. Goodge and the other professor were yakking away.

"Nah." I felt a film of heartsickness glaze over me.

"Sheesh." He shook his head sadly. "I hate those boring fucks . . . they never talk about people, they never talk about personal things like how's it going, how's the wife, you still on the wagon . . . everything is this charmy chuckly anecdotal shit about dead writers . . ."

My nose came up to his trachea.

Suddenly his face became a mask of startled O's, his chin retreated and he took on a different voice like a stuffy elderly Negro.

"An ah, when ah, Van Buren discovered that Harrison took up a slogan, Tippecanoe and ah Tyler too, well ah Van Buren decided to call himself Owwld Kinderhook 'cause he ah grew up in Kinderhook, New *Yawk*, see? and he figured he ah could get down wit' the people *too*, see? So he signed all his bills 'O.K.' for Old *Kin*derhook, see? And that's how we got the expression *OK* . . . see? . . ." He relaxed into himself again, gave me the eyebrow. "You know what I mean?"

An old duffer entered the room; it was Herkimer, the Shakespeare man. He had a beautiful head of flossy white hair. His lectures had been unbearable, but every third class or so he would just read to us from the tragedies in a voice so stirring and passionate that I had re-upped for two more classes with him.

Some of the faculty turned and hailed him in the archway. Fonseca leaned down to me, his eyes on Herkimer. "That's ow-wld Kinderhook!" he said like Gabby Hayes. "And heere's ow-w-wld Jack Petty!" he said louder as Jack approached us, ushering Doctor Cyclops and his bowling pin wife before him, his hands on their shoulders.

"Tony? Peter? I want you to meet Dave Goodenough. . . ." Goodenough gave us his clicking bow and palmed off, "My wife . . . Alana Goodenough."

I nodded hello.

Fonseca kissed her hand and gave his own head-tilting bow to Goodenough, palming a hand toward me, "My mistress, Ffrancesca Du-vallll . . . and she's goodenough for me . . ." he added in a burst of Groucho sidemouth. A hearty chuckle all around.

When Jack ushered them back across the room, he shot me one last glance over his shoulder.

"Jesus Christ, knock down three of her and you win something off the top shelf . . . owwld Kindercunt." Fonseca drifted, bored with his own word play. "But he's the fucking best . . . big Jack. That's the guy you throw yourself on the grenade for . . . c'mon, let's blow . . ." He tapped me on the chest and lurched through the room.

He walked halfway across the floor, stopped, turned to me and gave an impatient beckoning wave. I had to follow him. Also, somewhere I had the idea that I could just tell him about me and Kim and get it over with. Maybe we could even have a laugh, small-world-ain't-it-style. But it was more than that. It was inevitable that we should leave together. It was right. No, it wasn't right. I just willed it.

The minute we stepped outside his whole show changed. He became sullen and self-contained. His yak-a-minute bottom-line act vanished and I felt I was in trouble. I was walking slightly behind him in the deep gravel out to the street. He was squinting, distracted, on the verge of muttering. It was as though I wasn't there, or was just a caddy for his thoughts.

"Listen," he addressed his boots, "I don't wanna pop your bubble or anything, but if you're thinking about being an English major, everybody's a real dick here . . . what are you, a sophomore?" He said it like a bored tour guide who had memorized his rap. I had the distinct impression it was his standard recruiting line for new flunkies.

"No." I forced a high amused tone. "I teach."

"You teach!" He sounded alarmed. His eyes went from his boots to his side, half looking back to me. I had to pick up the pace. "How old are you?" he demanded.

"Twenty-three."

"Twenty-three . . ." he muttered and turned left on the sidewalk. I had no idea where he was headed. I walked directly behind him now, single file. I felt he'd lost interest in me. At one point he stopped dead in his tracks to watch some racing squirrels and I almost walked nose first into his neck.

He stopped again by his car, unlocked the passenger door, swung it open for me, grimacing at the inert street and sauntered around to the driver's side.

I sat silent, somewhat trancy, in the shotgun bucket seat of his parked Mustang. I had decided that he knew about me and Kim and I was calmly waiting for him to lower the boom. Not physical violence but a really well-worded scary warning. He sat slouched down, his elbow on the armrest, chewing a knuckle and brooding out the window. Every once in a while he would turn his fist to read his watch off his wrist veins, then go back to chewing his knuckle.

I felt that I couldn't talk and wasn't allowed to anyhow.

We sat for twenty minutes in complete stillness. Then a convertible came rolling by, radio blaring "Big Girls Don't Cry," which was one of my favorite songs as a kid. I shook my head as though I was coming out of a daze. What the hell was I doing? He didn't know about me and Kim.

"I'm splitting." I grabbed the door handle.

"What do you teach?" he murmured.

"Comp. I'm part-time." I shrugged. "I used to go here. I was in your class six years ago . . . you don't remember, probably. My name was Peter Keller?"

He didn't answer. I sat squirming for another two minutes, then lunged at the door handle again.

"You wrote that story about your father with the bullet, right?"

I sat back again, my arms dangling down my inner thighs. "Yeah." I fought down a stupid flattered grin.

"You look different." He checked his throat in the rear view mirror.

"I had a beard back then."

He consulted his watch one more time, then started up the engine. "What did I give you, a B?"

"I don't remember."

"I gave you a B."

He drove downtown, past the stores, past the megapiazza of windowless state buildings, cruising easy, silently down into Linoleumsville. At first I thought he knew where I lived and was driving me home, but he turned off Exterior Street before my place and parked in a deserted lot behind an Irish bar. He sat there for less than a minute before he started up the engine again.

"Aw, fuck this depression."

He headed back downtown and pulled into a metered spot in the state building area across from a Victorian building converted into a mini-mall consisting of a French restaurant, a hair stylist and a bar I never heard of called Stanley and Livingstone's, which was downstairs below street level. He headed for the bar. On the street level glass door there was a cartoon logo decal of two black goateed and Afroed explorers with knobby knees and oversized pith helmets, clasping hands soul-brother style like standing arm wrestlers. They each held martini glasses in their free hands.

"Listen, I'll see you around," I called down the steps, but my voice was engulfed in a heavy funky thumping sound track coming from the open downstairs door: "Ah said all the ladies who want Mercedes . . . ah said say Ahhh. Ah said all the men who wanna do it again . . . ah said say Ahhh." All I could see was half of Fonseca's extended brown leather arm holding the door ajar for me at the foot of the stairs.

The place was so dark I heard it more than saw it. From the heh-heh basso sound track of laughter and Sweet Trash coming through the PA I could tell we were in some kind of soul palace. As my eyes adjusted I could see the bar was full up with Large Brothers, some Sisters, and a few white, mainly blond, townie women.

Fonseca strolled from the door to the bar with a cocky Who's-bad-here? limp. One of the brothers—short, barrel-chested, bandy legged, with green eyes and a peaked red crop and goatee—tilted his head out from the bar and monotoned, "Hey, it's Professor 151."

A few of his friends slowly turned, smiled, then went back to their social lives.

Fonseca cackled, letting his tongue hang out, and picked up his gait, his hand high for a slap, as if the man had called him Professor Big Dong.

I leaned against the bar behind Fonseca's broad back and ordered a gin and tonic from the white bartender. To my right was the waiter's stand. The waiters stood between two brass rails filling up their cork trays with lots of Piña Colada– and Rum Punch–type drinks in long thin frosted fruit garnished glasses. They were young skinny blond white boys with that upstate combo of flattened parted stringy sideburned hairdos, muraled shirts and pastel pants. My eyes adjusted to the tinted dimness. The place consisted of a horseshoe bar and a large room with a small dance floor and tables four deep to the wall. Everything was done up in Funky Conrad, a jungle boogie elegance like an ooga-booga bone-through-the-nose cannibal in top hat and tails. The sit-down room was separated from the bar by a stand of burlap-barked fake palm trees. The walls and ceilings of both rooms were covered with rattan. The only light came from short fat candles in red glass bowls, red bulbs in ornate brass stanchions, and from an eight-foot-long gold-barred cage set deeply into the wall farthest from the bar. The cage was filled with lifesized ceramic tigers and panthers. Small bulbs were strategically placed behind their hulking fanged forms to throw them in silhouette.

Behind the almost circular bar was a four-tiered hill of liquor bottles on top of which sat a sulking gorilla. The tables were bamboo, the chairs large fan-backed Victorian wicker Huey Newton specials. Littered across the room were half a dozen ceramic lions reposing on the wine-red rug. From the ceilings hung brass Victorian bird cages inside which perched stuffed black crows. Alternating with the cages were chain-suspended plexiglas goldfish bowls and lush fake potted ferns.

Fonseca smacked me with his arm. "And this is my associate Peter Keller . . . this man here is the Ace of Spades." He nodded at the heavy-lidded red-Afroed guy. "Whoosh Johnson."

"The *King* of Spades." Whoosh scratched his nose, looking out to the dance floor.

"Whatever. . . ." Fonseca shrugged.

Staring up at Fonseca, Whoosh pulled a five out of his skinny corduroys and dropped it on the bar. "Jimmy?"

The bartender laid out three shot glasses in front of Fonseca. Whoosh, half smiling, reached behind him and absently tapped the shoulder of a large Negro tree dressed in a blue suit and silver-rimmed oblong glasses. The big dude nudged a few others and as the bartender poured out three shots of Bacardi 151, Fonseca was being observed by a murmury smirking gallery.

He rolled and flourished his hands around the first shot glass, delicately raised it to his extended lips, snapped back his head and hissed, eyes shut in afterbite.

"Atsa one."

He whipped back all three, grimacing as if his gums were disintegrating. When he was finished he turned to the smirking group and spoke distinctly.

"What . . . it . . . *is!*"

They laughed, mildly shaking their heads, snorting sadly. The guy with the silver glasses muttered "fool." Whoosh, a bemused grin on his slow-moving face, dropped another dollar on the bar. "Jimmy"— his gaze never left Fonseca—"give my man here some *sel*tzer-water."

Fonseca turned to me. His eyes had a red film. "I always do that shit when I come in here . . . it blows them away . . . you ever do 151?" He was sweating but he was stone sober.

"No man, I never did." I was suddenly socked with an overwhelming desire to protect him from them, from his own obtuseness. I wanted him to wise up. I felt as if I had known him for years.

Three white chicks came up to the bar and folded into Whoosh and his friends. The girls were somewhat skanky, with lank hair and rotten posture. One wore a midriff blouse that revealed a doughy midsection. Another had a drab belted dress and horn-rims.

Fonseca regarded them with a raised eyebrow. "Niggers are amazing . . . they got that twisted perspective around white chicks. I've seen these motherfuckers with women I wouldn't fuck with *your* dick . . . these big Bantu bastards'll go after anything blond . . . these skanks never had it so good."

Around the curve of the bar sat a tensely smiling white student, sitting by himself, nursing a screwdriver. He was out of place in a T-shirt, and the red barlight filled his glasses with blood.

"First time I come in here, you know, I sized up the whole scene . . . upstate brothers and white chicks . . . a little piece of soul heaven. I'm at the bar. I'm watchin', I'm watchin'. I see Whoosh's the leader. He's got that big guy with glasses totally under his thumb . . . Davey. Totally under his thumb . . . the other guys, everybody. Hey Whoosh, what's happening, hey Whoosh what it is, Whoosh Whoosh Whoosh, like I said, he's the Ace of Spades here. I dunno what he does outside. I think he day-manages that auto-lock garage behind the courthouse. He's the security guard in the Mammoth Mart, who knows . . . but they're smart in here, see? The owners know what'll get these guys in here."

I wondered if he'd ever fucked Kim in the ass. He must have.

Fonseca jerked his thumb back to the sit-down room. "So they put up all this shit, little white boys as waiters . . . every guy in here thinks he's the Emperor Jones. Big crowd to be had too. There's ten thousand brothers in town and all the other spade bars are real Frankie 'n' Johnnie *hell*-holes . . . so anyway, I was telling you . . . I sussed out Whoosh was the chief my first time in here. I sidle up to him and he orders himself his regular. I see the bartender does up a 151 and Coke. I always had big balls so I says, 'Shee-it . . . and *Coke*' like it should have a twist of pussy hair in it instead of lemon, and I order me three straight-up shots of 151. Ever since then, I had them Mau Maus eatin' outta my palm . . . you heard what they called me. Professor 151 . . . and fuckin' Whoosh even blows for the shots." He belched and his eyes turned a deeper shade of red. "Hey!" He turned to Whoosh and them. "Whoosh, where's TTR at? I want him to meet TTR."

"T . . ." Whoosh called over a tall chubby guy wearing a short denim jacket with matching faded jeans. He had a high forehead and his 'fro and mustacheless beard were mirror images of each other. "T . . . the Professor wants a word with you."

"He-hey it's Doctor 151." He gave a soul shake. Fonseca half turned to me. "You know what this guy's name is? Third Term for Roosevelt Brown. He was born on the day Roosevelt got elected to a third term."

"Un*pre*cedented third term."

"Whatever . . . can you believe that?"

I nodded. I didn't know if I was supposed to laugh.

"I was up this bad boy's crib . . . do you believe he's got a zebra-skin couch?"

TTR went back to his conversation. Fonseca slugged down the club soda, his Adam's apple undulating in ropey contractions. "Zebra

couch . . ." He shook his head sadly. "Shit . . . can you imagine
Mossi in here? Or Aaron?" He laughed at the pathetic thought.

But why on earth would Aaron or Mossi *want* to come in here?

I was snapping out of it again and I wanted to split. He was a
fucking clown.

"Yo Professor," the giant with the glasses bassed down. "How
all's Kim'bly doin'?"

"Kim?" Fonseca straightened up. "Me an' Kim are tightern a
crab's ass." His smile had a clay cast to it . . . too many teeth. To hear
him speak her name made my heart clang like a church bell. What
did he *mean* they were tight? And who were *these* fucking guys?

"You tell her David said hello . . . you takin' care of her?" His
voice had a patronizing adult-to-child singsong ominousness.

"Yeah, sure . . . Hey, I don't wanna dialogue, I wanna dance!"

As I exhaled an endless slow breath that made the ice cubes in
my drink clink, Fonseca moved off, slightly staggering and bowed
down, toward two black chicks at a small table just the other side of
the fake coconut trees. One girl, big-hipped, in glasses and a scoop-
backed floral dress, got up on the dance floor with him. Whoosh
and David cracked up.

I looked to the white student again. His eyes were going from
Whoosh to Fonseca and he was grinning.

Who the fuck *were* these guys? Suddenly Fonseca seemed in-
significant.

I leaned across his space and tapped Whoosh. "Who's Kimberly?"

Whoosh nudged Davey. "Who's Kim'bly." They slapped palms.
My insides turned into a lava lamp. I was ready to fight for Kim,
Fonseca and myself.

"Who's Kimberly?" I repeated flatly.

"Kim'bly was the Professor's lady . . . they all got divorced last
year." He giggled. "Professor don't know that we know, you know?
And he still pretends that they tight 'cause he's afraid that if some
nigger here find out she's free he's gonna ask her *out*, see? Cause she
useta hang *out* here, see? She knows David here since *grade* school.
David went out with her bes' friend from *home*, you understan'? So
we just have some fun with the man, see? Any time we want him to

dance, David just say, 'Hey Professor, how's Kim'bly?' and he's off."
Whoosh nodded to the dance floor where Fonseca, stone-faced and
unhappy, jerked around with his partner. Neither of them looked at
each other. The entire dance floor was filled with black and mixed
couples, the women mostly overdressed in cheap dresses, the guys
tree-trunk-thighed or too tall in a variety of outfits from three-piece
suits with medallions hanging over ties to Panama hats and those
muraled shirts. Everybody did some kind of tight deadpan lurch
and dip, not taking up too much space. Fonseca wasn't bad. He put
his hands in his belt loops and did a tight 360° turn. David laughed.
"See, we just teasing the man."

———

Fonseca drove slowly through town, back in his self-occupied
sulk. It was ten-thirty. I felt like shit myself. I knew those guys
weren't sticking it to Kim, it just wasn't in the tone of their words.
I was feeling like shit because I knew I couldn't tell Fonseca about
me and her yet. He was too easily freaked. I felt bad for him and
his grandiose denseness. I'd totally lost my fear. All I could see
was his foolishness, his loneliness. I felt a floody feeling, a little
bit like love. That warm weepiness that people experience around
retards. I wondered if there was a technical term for love of victims.

"You ready to call it a night, or you want to go someplace else?"
That was me speaking. He shrugged, mildly surprised at my offer
and drove to the parking lot behind the Irish bar where we'd parked
earlier. There were a few cars there now. We went inside.

"Fitzie and Fordham!" he cheered to a white-haired bartender
leaning against his stock and a fat kid in a Fordham University jersey
and an apron.

Fitzie was small and serious-looking. He winked, "Professor . . ."
The kid, about eighteen, didn't even nod hello.

Fonseca grabbed a stool and pointed a finger at Fitzie. "Webster
Avenue?"

"Seventeen thirty-three, apartment 3A," Fitzie answered evenly.

"Awright!" Fonseca swiped at his arm.

I didn't know what the hell they were talking about.

We ordered drinks and Fitzie vanished down cellar steps behind the bar.

"Fitzie and Fordham," he muttered. "See, I like to come here after Livingstone's because it's so fucking boring I can cool out."

Four fat fortyish guys sat on stools five feet down from us. Two young guys, tall and narrow-eyed, who seemed to be friends of Fitzie's son, played air hockey, lunging across the big table in the center of the large room. The clacking of the puck filled the air. The overheads were too bright and the walls and pressed tin ceiling were painted a horrible light breath-mint green.

Various pieces of sports equipment hung from the ceiling on long nylon fishing lines; boxing gloves, a catcher's mitt, an Irish curling stick and directly in front of my face a white football helmet, looking like a skull with a faceguard, its crown covered with a fur of dust. It glowed a very pale green from the reflection of the overheads on the walls. The equipment was too spread out and just dangled there, adding to the cavernous iciness and unhomeyness of the place.

Fonseca smiled at his drink. "Fitzie and Fordham."

Jammed with shit I couldn't say, I awkwardly slapped his back. I wanted to tell him not to let Whoosh and those motherfuckers get to him, but I couldn't. Number one, he would deny that they were getting to him and two, what would I say? Don't let them bug you about Kim, nobody's fucking her but me?

Suddenly he snapped his fingers. "Yeah, I heard your name. You teach Comp. One of my kids mentioned you . . . Yeah . . . how old are you anyhow?" Fonseca looked pained, and in that moment I realized that the only way to make this guy happy was to shoot him through the head.

I got choked up. I couldn't answer him for a long moment, then I blurted out everything that had happened to me since graduation, except meeting Kim. I spoke urgently and dramatically. When I finished, Fonseca was studying my eyes, smiling and looking deep into my eyes.

"You think I'm an asshole, don't you?" he said calmly.

I didn't answer because I didn't know what he was referring to. Maybe this was it. So be it.

"You think I acted like a big asshole in that place coming on like the blue-eyed brother and letting Whoosh get me drunk and all them laughing and shit. You're telling me this third-rate sob story now because you feel sorry for me, right?"

"Right." In my own way I wanted to keep everything honest.

"I'm not fucking stupid. I know those guys are laughing at me. I like it there, though . . . they're not boring academic bastards and they're not deadbeats like at this shithole. Those three 151 shots I do are my cover charge. They're my admission ticket. I always knew that. I always understood that. Let me in the club and you can feel you got it over a professor. I play a high-class white boy waiter with my act, but it's a fucking act, and just because I can play the fool don't underestimate my intelligence." He ducked his head and peered at me as if he were looking over the tops of bifocals.

I felt a little bit better about him and I smiled a penitent "I got you" smile.

"Don't underestimate my intelligence," he said to his drink. "Control . . . it's all about control . . . everybody's gotta think they're on top of everybody else . . . well, shit." He looked to me, then glanced briefly up at the curling stick, the football helmet, then down to his drink again. "It's better than *this* fuckin' place."

The four fat guys broke out in a group laugh.

Fonseca was working on vodka and tonics. I was sipping gin, not getting too high. The clacks from the air hockey game were fast and steady, making me think that those guys spent many hours hunched over that table. They never cried out or laughed.

"You ever read my stuff?" He frowned at his nails, his face almost on the bar.

"I read that story about the lady with the headache, where the delivery boy from the drugstore forgot the aspirin so he just puts his hands on the lady's tit and says, 'This is better' and they wind up getting married at the end."

He snickered down at his nails, as if the story was new to him. "Courtship," he murmured fondly. "That was a true story. That's how my parents met—my father just about raped my old lady when he was a delivery boy. 'This-a joos-ta good!' " Fonseca slapped his own tit. "That was a true story . . ." He held up his empty glass until Fordham sauntered over.

"You ever read 'Fatso'? That was the best story I wrote . . . God, what a fucking year that was . . . I published seven stories . . . got my gig here . . . that was maybe ten years ago. I had an editor at a publishing house calling me every six months for a novel. The guy loved the stuff. He wanted me to write a novel but I just couldn't get started. I knocked up a girl and got married instead. I guess things were going a little too well, so I got myself a wife and child. I couldn't concentrate. It was bad . . . bad years . . . but . . ." He smirked. ". . . Well, that's all past. I got out of it last year . . . so I'm a little bit back on the track."

I broke out of my trance again. Enough with the Mary Heart-line. If I was ever to tell him about me and Kim it had to be now. I got a panicky feeling that every second that passed in conversation was just increasing the headfuck to the point where if I didn't blow the whistle I'd have to break off with Kim or kill him. I sat there, running over gay and sprightly opening lines while waiting for a break.

"I tried calling that guy, that editor, last year. The bastard died . . . he's dead . . . I'm *try*ing though. I'm writing every day. I've started four different novels . . . I got them in boxes in my office. I have ideas every day but I feel banged up a lot . . . I can't concentrate. I write twenty pages at once, sit down, then I stare at it . . . and it just doesn't *hang* right. I mean, if I keep reading it, rereading it, eventually I can convince myself it's okay but . . ." He sighed.

Go. "Tony? . . ." I was so nervous I couldn't catch my breath and he plowed on.

"I dunno, I look back on that early stuff. I read those stories over and over, looking for clues . . . where was I at when I wrote that? What did I know then that I don't know now? I didn't know *shit* then . . . I know a *hun*dred times more now. So what's the problem? You know? And it gets so fucking bad, sometimes I can't even read anymore—other people's stuff—I can't read guys who were coming up with me and are doing good now. I gotta *teach* 'em, but I can't *read* 'em . . . it drives me crazy—why them? I can only read dead people. Can you believe that? I can't even *read* anymore. I can't walk into a bookstore. The thing is . . . the thing is, I'm good. I'm still good. I can dip into any one of those boxes, start reading from anywhere and I can't put it down. But I just don't know what I want to *say* right now . . . I hear a voice in my head all the time like that

TV ad—'Hey *Tony* . . . what's the story?'" He threw back the vodka and raised his glass. The kid bartender hesitated before he poured another round. "Shit, I *hate* rum . . . rum's for vacations."

"Hey, Tony?"

"I'm still good though, man. I'm still good."

I didn't say Hey Tony loud enough. Maybe I only whispered it. I grit my teeth and tried to get my breathing down. The air hockey clacks were making me flinch.

"You know, sometimes I get a little buzz on and I'm in a strange city and I can stare at a goddamn beer glass and I can write a goddamn story about that glass. I can *look* at the sucker and I can write a word portrait that'd *kill* you. I have that gift . . . I have that gift. I mean . . ." He raised his almost drained drink. "Just look at that . . . there's a story here. There's a story in everything. I mean, just *look* at this place . . ." He sighed deeply, then cupped his hands around his mouth. "Hey Tony! What's the story?"

The four on the stools jerked their chins over their shoulders, then slowly returned to their conversation.

"You know, Tony?" Louder. "*Tony?* I gotta tell you something that's a real kick in the head . . ." I finally got my breathing under control, but suddenly one of the air hockey players yelled "Wo!" I almost jumped up on the bar and he was off again.

"It's coming together, though, it's coming together . . . I had an incredible dream I want to work on as a premise for something. I dreamt I knocked off a blood bank with two other guys . . ." He laughed. "We steal jars and jars of blood from a blood bank, gallons of blood. We get in a car, and the cops are chasing us down the main drag and we crack up, the driver loses control, and we smack into a pole or something and all the jars of blood break. No one's hurt, but everybody's drenched in blood and blood is gushing out of the car and the whole street is washed in blood—nobody's ever seen so much blood—and people start flipping out and the cops can't even bring themselves to go near the car . . . and . . . I dunno, I just want to work with that image, that blood thing. I dunno, maybe it would be better on film, a screenplay. It would be an incredible visual . . ." He trailed off, closing his eyes. He looked as if he was going to cry. "Ffuck!" He dropped his head in the crotch of his splayed fingers.

He gripped his temples and the color in his fingernails retreated down to his cuticles.

The foursome talking a few stools over stopped and turned, peering over their shoulders again. The young bartender made a cut-off motion to them. With Fonseca silent I could hear them loud and clear:

"Now I had heard from Jeff that when Andy moved down to Cincinnati his wife got lost on the bus tryin' to find *down*town and wound up in the *colored* section. She was looking for a *rec*ord store and she figured that, well, these people have record stores just like anybody else, so she goes into one place . . . the *Soul* Shack, or some damn thing, and she says, 'Yawl got "Unsent Letter"?' You know, she's got that North Florida accent . . . well, not only did they not have 'Unsent Letter' but the fellow who waited on her left the store before *she* did, waited out*side* in an alley, and grabbed her pocket-book!" The four guys laughed. The air hockey boys stopped playing to listen.

"Now, they got the police, but there was a different guy in the record store when they showed up and of course he said he never saw that other guy before . . . an' here this fella from what I understand he tried to drag her into that alley and all. She had the front of her dress ripped up. Well . . . when Andy *heard* about all this you know what he said?" He leaned forward, eyebrows raised in delight. "Andy said, 'God*damn*, I *told* the woman to join that record club!'"

The four of them broke out in laughter so chesty I thought their hearts might break. The bartender and the guys playing air hockey were laughing too. "Yeah, I told her to join that damn record club . . ." The storyteller sighed, wiping his eyes.

Fonseca slowly raised his head from his hand. His expression was that impersonal smirk he'd worn at the party. He shook his head at me and muttered, "Fuckin' shmucks." Everybody heard him.

"Did you say something?" The storyteller frowned in our direction. He was a fat bastard with an oily black werewolf peak extending down from a receding hairline. All four of them looked too fat and past it but the chunky young bartender had fungo bat forearms and he was slowly wiping a dry glass, which was a bad sign. And the two guys who had resumed playing air hockey were looking at each other now, not the faster-than-a-speeding-bullet air puck, which was a good way to get your fingers smashed.

Fonseca was smiling at me.

"Did you say something?" the storyteller repeated.

Fonseca turned on his chair like Clint Eastwood and squinted. "You look put out, pud."

"Did you say something?" The storyteller was getting totally red-faced.

"Do you want to hit me?" Fonseca inquired.

"I want to know what you said . . . you sonofabitch."

"Do you want to hit me?" Fonseca uptilted his chin, his fingers splayed in invitation beneath a terrifying expanse of jaw and shadowy throat.

"Sonofabitch . . ." The storyteller was backing off.

Fonseca stood up and moved toward him.

"Do you want to hit me?" His fingers stayed frozen under his chin, which was still tilted as if he was about to razor-shave his throat. The two guys at the air hockey table started walking to the bar. I stood up, ready to take his back, fight to the death—but that could have been *me* on that stool and I really wanted those two guys to jump on Fonseca and kill him. Fonseca stood over the storyteller. The guy was completely embarrassed and cowed, nervously trying to make a casual show of lighting an Old Gold. His friends were glaring at the floor, but the two air hockey guys stood behind Fonseca, waiting for a sign from Fordham to jump his ass.

Footsteps thumped up from the cellar and the old bartender emerged with a case of Matt's Premium in his arms.

"I would prefer you to say goodnight, Professor." Fitzie's words were firm and fatherly.

Fonseca's jaw was inches from the storyteller's face but he was distracted. The old bartender didn't repeat himself, just unpacked his beer.

Fonseca smiled and slowly closed his splayed fingers, still shooting up to his chin.

"Webster Avenue?"

"Seventeen thirty-three, apartment 3A," Fitzie said, as if for the millionth time.

Fonseca cackled and the tension broke. The air hockey guys
back-stepped to their game and the four fat guys breathed easy.
Fonseca leaned over the bar and grabbed Fitzie in a bear hug, slapping his back and growling amiably.

Fitzie stared at me stone-faced, his chin on Fonseca's shoulder,
his cheek upsmeared by Fonseca's ear.

"This old Irish bastard used to mix it up with my uncles under
the Third Avenue El, can you believe that? His family used to live
right next door to my Uncle Sonny. On the same floor. Now me and
him are both stuck up here in Siberia." Fonseca's face was beaming
with happiness and good sportsmanship as he turned to me, arm
still around the bartender's neck.

"Good night, Professor . . ." Fitzie was still staring at me with
cool reproach like I was another one. I shrugged defensively.

"Yeah. Good night Fitzie . . . goodnight gents. I was only kiddin' around . . ." He leaned into the four guys. "No hard feelings,
right?" The storyteller stared at his knees, the Old Gold glued to his
lip. "You're an ace raconteur, sir . . . sir? Really."

Fonseca ushered me out, waving and farewelling like it was
Christmas. "Ayyy-yay." He smiled out in the night air, one hand on
my neck. He went over to one of the few cars in the rear parking lot,
a two-year-old station wagon, and pissed into the open passenger's
window, arching his back for height. "Like I said . . . it's better than
this fucking place, you know what I mean?"

I stood there staring at his short fat dick knowing I would never
tell him about me and Kim and that I'd really blown it that night by
hooking up with him.

He zipped up his pants and started walking out to the street, his
hand back on my neck. I started hunching up. "Listen, I only live a
few blocks from here Tony, I'm gonna walk, okay?"

We stood facing each other. He looked down at me, that eyebrow raised in wry judgment. Suddenly I was three feet up in the
air and he had me in a painful bear hug, his brawny arms in a ring
around the small of my back.

"Whatta ya *do*in'? Whatta ya *do*in'?" I squealed in embarrassment and fear. He was stone sober. He was going to kill me. "C'mon,
man!" I winced, my hands on his shoulders. He was laughing, his

face squinty with strain. He dropped me to my feet and I staggered backwards down the street.

"You're fuckin' aces, kid!" he shouted at me. "You got a good heart, and you seen a lotta pain . . . you're *aces!*" He turned away and started walking down the street, away from me, away from the bar and away from his car.

———

There was a note pinned to my cork board when I checked into my office the next morning: "Can you come by me? I have to talk to you—Tony F."

I had a class in fifteen minutes, but I didn't want to go an hour guessing what he wanted.

Fonseca's office door was open but there was no one there. His steel shelves were lined with the obvious. Besides the endless bland college short fiction anthologies were the standard twentieth-century mandatories—Hemingway, Faulkner, Fitzgerald, Wolfe, Woolf, Forster, Joyce, Kafka, Mann—the whole gang. I ran my hand over the bright bindings. The image of Fonseca reading *A Passage to India* or *The Web and the Rock* was comforting, reassuring me that there was someone home other than the ghetto bully. I took a seat and waited. On his desk was a row of more contemporary fiction, all volumes sprouting bookmarks.

Across from me on the lowest level of steel shelf were four open Sphinx typing-paper boxes filled with paper. I waited a few minutes and with no Fonseca in sight I crouched down to look at them.

"There's the man . . ." He stood in the doorway as I squatted on the floor like an Asian peasant. I stood up popping both knees. I'd only caught the first few lines in the first box. "My father never brushed his teeth. He said brushing got rid of all the good stuff. He was foreman of a crew that built highways."

"You looking at my magnum opuses? Take two, they're small." He grabbed both my elbows as he sidled behind me to the power side of his steel desk. "Siddown for a minute." He leaned back in his swivel chair, his jacket falling open to reveal a T-shirt advertising an oyster house in New Orleans.

"Listen, I wanted to talk to you for a second, about last night . . .

I felt kind of shitty after you left. I think I was kind of playing the fool a little too much . . . not with Whoosh and them, but at Fitzie's when I was laying all my shit on you about my work and all and gettin' into that stupid riff with them old cockers . . . that's not me and I don't want to give you the wrong impression . . ."

And then it happened again. I felt overwhelmed with that warm desire to forgive him and make him feel good. "Hey . . ." I held out my hand. "I'm the guy with the third-rate sob story, remember?"

"Nah, that's bullshit . . . I never should have said that to you . . ."

"Don't worry about it. Really, awright?" I glanced down at the Sphinx boxes. "I liked the two lines I read," I offered.

"Yeah?" he snorted. He jerked up out of his swivel chair and brought all four boxes up to his desk. One side was cut away on each box, revealing the different thicknesses of manuscript. He carefully lined up the cut-away sides so they all faced him, covered the boxes with their tops, and pulled two pencils out of his top drawer.

"Watch this." He held the pencils like xylophone tongs and played the boxes. The different thicknesses gave off different tones. He was so good at it I immediately recognized Gershwin's "Summertime." He played it the whole way through and when he finished, standing there, holding both pencils loosely in one hand, he gave me a half-defiant, half-gut-sick smirk as if he'd just been caught with both hands thrust to the elbows up the asshole of despair.

————

"You know you've been making quite a hit with Anthony." Kim was straddling me in one of her dinette chairs, her arms around my neck, her legs draped over my hips. I comfortably ran my palms up and down her marble-smooth thighs under her hitched red-checked skirt. Her face was inches from my nose. My spit-moistened joint had totally vanished inside her.

"I can't get him to stop playing that bag trick." She gently rolled her ass bones across my groin and scratched her forehead.

"Well, that was my whole show."

We were talking as though we were on separate chairs.

"Can I ask you a favor?" She cocked her head, waiting for me to say Sure. "Anthony's got no school Thursday, the kids are off, and I have to work. Could you, do you think you could watch him?" She screwed up her face as if it were obviously a hopeless request.

"Sure." I shrugged, flattered with her trust.

"He *really* likes you."

"Yeah, no problem."

Kim lowered her head to watch our grinding gears. She had unwound her braids and her long sandy hair hung like a shimmery curtain between us.

I slid my hands from her thighs to around her strong ass and pulled her up my body, cool and rocking over my trapped balls.

"So what've you been up to since Monday night?" She kissed me. We were still at that stage where what the other had for lunch was both fascinating and enlightening.

"How the hell can you ask me that now?" I said with coy petulance, but my mouth suddenly filled with a gritty tension.

"Sorry." She dropped her head again, the hair curtain falling as she got back into watching us.

What have I been up to.

"In fact, some interesting stuff went down since I saw you. You'll never guess who I ran into . . ." My voice cracked like an adolescent's. "Big Tony."

She stopped rocking, but still kept her head down.

"I saw him at a faculty mixer at the chairman's house. He looked the same. I even wound up barhopping with him. We went to this soul palace called Stanley and Livingstone's, then we went to a gin mill called Fitzie's . . ." I was addressing the top of her skull. She didn't respond. "He's insane. And I'll tell you the truth, I'm afraid of him. I think I was gonna tell him about you and me so I could get rid of having that hang over my head and really concentrate on us, but I couldn't bring myself to do it. He almost started a fight in the Irish joint. Better them than me, you know? It's weird—he drinks, mixes his booze, acts drunk as shit, but he's cold sober the whole time. I find that frightening."

I babbled on about Fonseca in an innocent chatty tone like some whacked-out auntie going on about someone in the family. Suddenly my hands, which I thought were on her ass, began sliding along her thighs as she began to ease away from me. Before I could say anything else, she stood up so abruptly my cock popped, standing dazed and drafty out of my fly. For a second I thought maybe in my anxiety, talking about Fonseca, I'd absently started ramming it home too hard.

Not looking at me, she swept her hair behind her ears, walked over to the sink, grabbed a sponge and started damp-wiping crumbs off the dinette table as I sat there with my drooping genital bouquet hanging over my spread boots.

She made her way back from the table to the sink with the folded-up sponge. Her hands looked carrot-raw. She turned on the faucet and ran her bare hand along the edge of the sink to wash down any food shreds.

"Kim, you're freaking me out."

She quick-tapped the cereal boxes in line, dried her hands on her skirt and turned out the kitchen light, leaving me sitting in the darkness like furniture.

———

"Kim, what's the deal?"

Her body was lit by a rectangular slash of hallway light coming into the bedroom over my shoulder. She was curled on her side facing the wall, hands crossed under her chin. She wasn't crying. I got in bed next to her and rolled her on her back.

"What's the deal?" I dropped the register of my voice to give it a firm Papa Bear tone.

"You gonna get into this big tortured scene with me now?" I sounded meaner and more offhand than I felt. "It's like a melodrama here. . . ."

"Shut up." She cut me off, her eyes fluttery and glittering. "I have this friend, Theresa? You know how I met her? When I left Tony I didn't even remember how to *talk* to people let alone have any friends. One day I was walking in the Plunkett Mall and in that fountain area they were giving Latin Hustle lessons. I saw Theresa in line with all these old ladies. She was about my age and looked about as miserable as me, so I got in line next to her and learned the Latin Hustle so I could start talking . . . in front of all those jerks watching us dance, I picked her up to be my friend. I even joined her bowling league. Do you like bowling? I sure hope not. So you stay away from him, okay? It's him or me."

I said "no problem" about five hundred times until she rolled into my side, grabbing me across the chest, her face pressed into my armpit so that my hand wound up dangling like a questionmark over my head.

———

"So you went to the S and L?"

She had to repeat the question.

I had fallen asleep. A half-hour had passed with my arm in that awkward curl. I looked down at Kim. She hadn't been sleeping. Her face seemed alert and distracted at the same time.

"Stanley and Livingstone's, you went there?"

"Yeah."

"S and L," she murmured in a preoccupied memory-lane tone.

"Who's David?" I tried to keep the cop out of my voice.

"David's still there?"

I could feel her cheeks stretch into a smile against my ribs.

"Yeah, who is he?"

She shrugged and moved her face down to rest on my stomach. "He's an old pal." She said it as if she was talking about Mister Rogers instead of the nose guard for the Minnesota Vikings. Be cool.

"You know, that's where I met Tony."

"What?" With her head turned away from me like that I couldn't hear too well.

"S and L. That's where we met. I was in his class but that's where we *really* met. We were the only two white regulars in the place." Until she said white I thought she was talking about David. I stared at her head. I regarded it as a UXB, an unexploded bomb lying on my belly.

"Kim?"

She made a noise approximating 'Yeah.'

"What'd you like about him?"

She grunted like a hibernating bear.

"What'd you like about him?"

"Tramp." I could feel her breath wafting through my pubic hair.

"What?"

"Tramp . . . he played me Tramp."

"Tramp?"

"*Tramp!* . . . did you ever hear that album?"

"Tramp! Otis and Carla with the playing cards on the cover?"

"Yeah . . . when he took me home he played me Tramp. Everybody else was into Strawberry Alarm Clock. I know it sounds stupid but . . ."

"No . . . it doesn't." It didn't. I was the only kid on my block listening to Motown and James Brown, angrily ignoring the Beatles. If I had found a girl when I was fifteen who had a record collection like mine, God knows what else we would have had in common. Shit. If I had found *any* girl when I was fifteen. A deaf one. One with cauliflower ears . . .

". . . and hands."

"What?"

"Tramp and hands."

I scrambled in my head for an album or a group named Hands. "Willy and the Hand Jive?"

"He had the biggest hands, Tony. They weren't really, they weren't even really that much bigger than mine, but when he put them on you it was like they covered the world. He would put his hand on my forehead or the small of my back . . ."

Fonseca's hands weren't that much bigger than mine. I saw Kim and Fonseca together naked, absently measuring splayed palms, Kim sweaty, eyes narrowed. Gentle wisecracks. A slick of her blondish hair plastered over her collarbone.

"*Hands,*" I spat. "What do you mean, like a backrub? Like he'd give you a backrub? What the hell are you talking about? What the fuck did he do with hands? You got a dick, a tongue and a finger."

Kim lay dead on my belly facing my feet. We both lay there in a long boiling silence. I could feel a trickle of sweat speed around the outside shell of her ear in the matted hair of my gut.

"You're fucking me over, Kim. You're *lying* to me . . . you're still running with this guy. I *know* you are. This is not for me . . ."

"I am not."

"Swear on Anthony's stomach that you haven't seen him since you two split."

"Pie . . ." she pleaded.

"See, that's the bullshit . . ."

She grabbed my knees as I started to sit up, and before I could get my shoulder blades off the bed she had turned around and was crawling up my body.

"Twice, twice I saw him, twice, but it was horrible—no more no more." She was sucking my chest, crawling up to my chin, smothering my face in kisses and licks, arching her back, her belly pressing into mine, her nipples brushing my eyes. "No more no more I got you now I got you . . ."

She reached behind her, her breasts rising with the effort and slipped me in. Hands. In my freaked-out state I shot immediately, turned us over and started fucking her as hard as I could, reaching high up against her body so that my hard-on was pressing bone. I just slammed away in a total panic, my head filled with fantasies of ravishment. When I finally came a second time Kim was gasping and humming and I turned on my side without saying goodnight. I wasn't really acting sulky or sullen. Those words have connotations of willfulness or premeditation. I was feeling too way out of control for that. Besides, as Kim drifted off to a deep-breathing sleep, I was still as hard as a belaying pin.

Three hours later I popped awake from a nightmare that just wouldn't quit. I was hitting Fonseca in the face. Not exactly in the face, more like the gullet and the throat. Just slugging away at the stubbly scratchy boneless flesh. He was just looking at me. I couldn't see his expression, because I was afraid to meet his eyes, but I could *feel* that he was looking at me with hurt and confusion. I couldn't stop hitting him. I didn't think I was doing any physical damage. I hated the bristly feeling sliding across my knuckles. I was getting nauseated but I couldn't stop. I couldn't look in his eyes. He wasn't fighting back and it was driving me wild with misery.

I sat at the head of my horseshoe as the last few kids came straggling in. I was in a numb stun. I couldn't get Fonseca's hands out of my mind.

"I don't think I can make it today at three." April looked down at me and shrugged like a cruel girlfriend. Fuck her. The conference was for her benefit. I'd rather go to the gym, anyhow. Ever since I'd passed on her play she'd acted the bruised tart in class, making loud flirtatious comments to the boys while furtively checking me out to see if I was gnashing my teeth. My sickness was that I enjoyed that bullshit. I think she even fucked some kid from the class after I saw them together in the Rathskeller. Well, maybe that was *my* fantasy.

I went back to freaking about Fonseca's hands as the first piece was read, a twenty-pager about a guy waking up in a windowless, doorless room, being fed food pellets from a slot and being philosophically interrogated by a robot-precise monotone voice which emanated from a speaker in the ceiling. It was the fifth Kafka Box story of the term. Maybe I wasn't a very good teacher, otherwise they would be too terrified to hand in stories like that.

About halfway through the class I decided to try to pimp off April on Fonseca. It seemed like such a giddily insane notion that I couldn't even think about the morality involved, but if I could get the two of them to dance, Fonseca might be out of the picture for good, his magic hands tied up with someone else's strangest places. Who knew? They might be genuinely happy with each other; *good* for each other, sharing and caring, helping each other climb to new heights of consciousness and emotional harmony. Maybe pimping was too harsh a word, "matchmaking" was more benign; it even had a *Fiddler on the Roof* tone to it.

At the end of class, I got April to agree to meet me in the cafeteria at twelve-thirty for our conference.

A few minutes later I sprinted across campus to Fonseca's office in Boxely Hall. I walked in on him standing on his desk. A giggling coed was seated, facing his Sphinx boxes. On seeing me, Fonseca sank into a crouch, shaded his eyes and pointed in my direction as if I were land. The coed was almost in hysterics. He straightened up, his head brushing the acousticized ceiling panels. "What am I doing, sweetheart?" He hitched up his belt as he looked down at the kid and nodded toward me.

"Professor Fonseca's showing me how to heighten reality in a story." She choked on a suppressed snort.

"Ha-ha, that's good. Tony, you want to have lunch with me?"

I got to the cafeteria with Fonseca twenty minutes before I was supposed to have my conference with April. We ate and talked about the different color combinations that New York City buses had been painted over the years. When April showed up, we were ready for coffee. Even though I knew that April was taking Modern Lit with him, I did introductions. Fonseca barely mumbled hello. I got up to get three coffees. When I returned April was thumbing through a notebook and Tony was leaning back in his tilted chair, hands in pockets and squinting at the dish-piled conveyor belt that ran along the entire wall. As I went through the motions of a critical discussion with April, Tony looked bored. But just at the point where the conference had deteriorated to head nods, compressed lips, Okays and Thanks, he suddenly slid his chair back, hunched over and dropped his face in his magical hands.

"What's the matter?" I furrowed my brow like four out of five doctors.

"I got to get out of here . . . this is *killing* me . . . this is killing *me*, man . . ." Tony pushed hard against his lowered forehead with the heel of his palm.

April crossed her bare knees and lit a cigarette. A paper plate with scrambled-eggs debris was still lying on the table from breakfast.

"Do you *re*alize, Keller"—he squinted and pointed at my chest—"that there are whole communities of hillbillies in Cincinnati? There's all these hilljacks from Kentucky who've gone urban to get away from the mines . . . en*tire* urban hillbilly communities . . . I can write their song for them. I live with them six months, I can tell their story for them . . . there are seven surviving Shakers in Maine." He reared back and glared at me. "Are you kidding me?" He addressed all his comments to my face, totally ignored April. "There's this one street corner in New York . . . nothing but Haitian expatriates . . . a hundred miles from here." Without looking, he pointed at the dish conveyor along the far wall. ". . . a hundred miles from here you got the largest Syrian Christian community in America . . . do you understand me? I wake up some mornings and I just say . . . go . . . get inside and get down with them . . . but this shit is killin' *me* here, I promise you that . . . I wanna get on the road with a Mexican baseball team . . . do you know what I mean?"

He sat and seemed to pace in his seat. He ran his hand over his face as if he hadn't slept in years. April ripped a strip of silver foil from her cigarette pack and folded it into a fat triangle like an American flag at a military funeral.

Go Tony Go.

"You know, and I don't have to be on some brokendown bus in Oaxaca either . . ." He sat up straight and alert, his fingertips in front of his chest. He extended a hand and tapped my arm. "I go to an airport . . . I go to a, a, a, *horse*show . . . and there's all these young ladies. And they all have this fantastic secret . . . this power and amazement to them . . . every one. Okay . . . I'm waiting for a plane . . . Boston to Hyannis. I see some unattractive plump young lady talking to some old bluehair. The kid is all prim and attentive, playing that old Mama Yama like she has been trained to . . . or she's playing instant airport granddaughter to some old Papa Yapa . . . and she's overweight and she's unhappy and she's rich family and she'll always be a good little girl until she's hospitalized and I say *spread* 'em!" He fanned those hands out on the table. "Spread them and show them their own violets . . . their own flowers . . . their own power . . . invade their baths and showers . . . their toilettes . . . show them to themselves . . . pull them out of themselves . . . save their lives with your lights. I can *do* that . . . I can draw the bloom . . . but I can't do that here . . ."

"Sure you can," I said encouragingly.

He hunched over the table again and narrowed his eyes at me. "You see now, this little girl is sitting here and she's shocked . . ." He pointed to April. "She's saying to herself, 'God, he's *weird* for a Professor' . . . see, all she ever hears me talk about is *move*-ments and *ren*-aissances like I'm supposed to be some wind-up lecture programmed *ro*-bot . . . like I'm not supposed to have human feelings."

He was speaking to me in a theatrically loud aside. I didn't know how to react. I didn't know if I was supposed to be nodding in agreement, so I just smiled neutrally.

"She don't even think I have a first name."

"I do *so* . . ." April snapped, fighting down a smile.

"Oh yeah?" He sat up startled, looking at her for the first time. "What is it? . . . Pro*fes*sor?"

"It's *Tony*," she said like So *there*.

"How the hell does she know my name is Tony?" he asked me.

I shrugged. My chest was pooming like high waves crashing down on rocks. I was bulging with power.

"How do you know my name is Tony?"

"I read your stories."

"She read my stories." He looked at me in mock amazement.

April smiled down at her silver foil. Tony reached across the table and slid a thin magazine off April's book pile. It was *Nighthawk*, the student literary rag. Fonseca listlessly flipped through the buff-colored pages. The cover was a sepia-tone photo of an empty rocking chair looking out an attic window.

"You got anything in there?" he challenged her.

"I got a stupid poem," she said. "It's on page twelve, don't read it."

He didn't.

"Do you know how I started writing?" He narrowed his eyes and smirked, nodding in fond memory. "When I was fifteen years old, my old man came home from work, he worked as an aspirin salesman. Some pharmacist that was his client had a kid at City College, the kid got a short story published in the school magazine and his father brought a copy of the magazine into the drugstore to show everybody, all his customers. When my father came in to take his aspirin order, the guy showed it to him . . . 'My *kid* wrote this!' . . . my old man was so impressed he borrowed the magazine from the guy and brought it home and showed it to me. He said that this guy's kid was a pre-med major and when he wrote that story for his English teacher, the teacher's comment was, 'It's a shame this hand will be writing prescriptions instead of literature.' And I could never forget how impressed and moved my father was at some other guy's kid and how fucking insane it made me. And I just started writing then and there. I remember how my father smoothed back the pages of the magazine so carefully and respectfully . . ." Fonseca opened *Nighthawk* and slowly started rubbing his thick fingers along the valley of the spine, his eyes on April. ". . . and I just started writing . . ."

I hmph'ed in appreciation, totally focused on those fingers, those hands.

He continued his rubbing rhythm. "I remember the cover was black and red, black and red, but I can't remember the name of the magazine." He locked eyes with April. He smiled and she laughed, embarrassed, her cheeks turning a pale rose.

"Well, *I* don't know what it was called!" Her voice was deliriously high.

I tried to keep my own voice nice and casual, although if I had

tried to do a yawn I think my whole body would have spasmed.
"Listen, Tony . . . I got to get back to the office . . . I'll see you two
later."

April didn't say farewell. Tony said, "Be good," and leaned back,
raising an eyebrow at April, who lit another cigarette.

"You're not even gonna read my poem? *God*, you're mean . . ."

By the time I got to the gym, I convinced myself that even
"matchmaker" was too heavy a label for what I set up. I preferred to
think of it as "playing Cupid."

By the next day I decided that I hadn't done a goddamn thing.
All that happened was three people had lunch. In fact, it was rude
and contemptuous of Fonseca to hit on one of my students in front
of me like that.

Sitting in my office, I looked through the latest *People* magazine.
In the Up and Coming section there was a photo and squib about a
twenty-year-old poet named Scipio Stevens, a guy with blond rib-
length hair and a self-assured squint. The bottom half of his photo
was sworled with cigarette smoke. He was originally from Brooklyn
but was now living in the poet's quarters in the Sylvia Beach bookstore in Paris. He just had a book of poems nominated for some European prize although he didn't entertain any hopes of actually
winning. He was about to embark on a college tour of the States to
read his poetry although he "hated travel with a passion." Tell me
about it.

"Hey . . ." Fonseca veered into my office and I jumped, jerking
my shoulders up to my earlobes. "What are you doin' for lunch?"

"I got students . . ." I lied. I noticed he had a gift-wrapped box, a
narrow rectangular affair that he kept smacking against his thigh.

"What time?"

"In an hour or so?"

"Good . . . come out with me . . . I wanna show you something."

"I can't go."

"Yeah, you can."

"Nah, I can't, Tony."

"C'mon."

"I got work."

"C'maan."

"I got . . ."

"C'maaaan . . ." He reached across the desk and grabbed me under the armpit.

I wafted straight up, powerless, totally afraid that he was going to tickle me.

It was amazing how endlessly, hopelessly off-balance and self-conscious I felt in his presence. I think I would have felt that way even if I'd never even met Kim.

We stood outside in front of Hopper by the fountain. "Here . . . I picked this up."

I opened the box and pulled out a pair of black heavily opaque futuristic wrap-around shades. "I got that for you . . . put 'em on."

As I slipped them around my temples he pulled out an identical pair for himself. "Look at me . . . there you go. Now we look like we don't give a shit. These kids'll love it . . . we have no heroes . . ." He grabbed my elbow and made me walk. "No more heroes, no more John Wayne, no more John Wayne . . ." He stopped and wheeled me to him. "Look at me."

He steered me down the esplanade, his hand on my elbow. It felt as if his fingers stretched from my bicep to my forearm. I kept my head down as if I was being escorted to an indictment through a gauntlet of photographers. Every blonde looked like Kim.

"She's nice, that girl April . . . a very bright girl . . . very nice."

He ushered me to his car.

I wouldn't get in. He wanted to know why. I couldn't think of anything that would sound legitimate, so after an awkward ten seconds I got in and he drove us downtown. He stopped in front of a deli and pulled out a five from his wallet. "Here, get me a roast beef and sweet pepper. Get yourself whatever . . . I'd go in, but I hate that scumbag in there."

"She's very nice . . . very nice . . ." He nodded firm-lipped as we cruised along the highway. His voice was slightly formal and uncomfortable-sounding. I was starting to get nervous again. He drove five miles into a state parking lot. There were no cars, no people. "C'mon, let's walk." He got up out of the car, sniffed deeply and hocked a lunger into the gravel.

"Where we going?" I sat tight. I had visions of Ziploc body bags lying on coroners' tables, statements to the local press from a medical examiner representing some county that ninety percent of the people in the state had never heard of.

"C'mon, let's have lunch."

He started walking away from the car. I sat tight. When he was thirty feet off, he turned and stared at me with a perplexed frown which made me feel that he was genuinely at a loss as to why I wasn't budging. I felt stupid. I made a big deal of slamming the door, hocking up a lunger myself and then trotting up to him while casually batting my lunch bag between my palms. I shot ahead and sat on a bench but he kept right on walking, motioning for me to follow, his hands in his front pockets, his lunch locked between elbow and ribs. I started getting jumpy because he wasn't talking, and I walked slightly behind. We went about half a mile until we came to what looked like a set from a heavy-handed art film. It was an abandoned zoo, acres of cages, bars, grills, ponds, all empty as if there had been an abrupt mass evacuation, DO NOT FEED THE ANIMALS signs, descriptions of long-gone beasts, a rubber tire still hanging in the gorilla cage, large boulders in the bear cage, dried peanut husks in the elephant cage. The only animal life was a few local sparrows who managed to get inside the deserted aviary through a tear in the mesh.

"Incredible, right? Did you know this was here?" Fonseca shot me a toothy grin.

"Uh-uh."

"Blows your mind, right?"

He adjusted his sunglasses, unwrapped his sandwich and hook-shot the wax paper into a cage that according to the sign had housed antelope. "They closed down the zoo about four years ago . . . the Board of Health said it was the worst maintained zoo in the state. They still don't have the funds to take down the cages. I love this place . . . I come out here every now and then . . ." We walked in front of the gorilla cages. Fonseca clamped the rest of his sandwich in his teeth. Using both hands he hauled himself up, and swung his legs over the top of the bars. He landed hard on his feet, the impact making him bite through his sandwich, dropping the rest on the cement. "Shit." He kicked it away. He wandered through the cage, his hands behind his back, then grabbed the hanging rope and sat on top of the swinging tire. He just looked past me as he swayed over the ground in his leather coat and his shades, his ankles locked for balance. He smiled at me on the outside, his eyebrows rising over the plastic. "You wanna throw me some peanuts?"

"No, a banana." I thought he needed a shave. I leaned my face against the bars; my cheeks were pinched by the flaking paint.

"Hey!" He dropped off the tire and shot a finger at me. "You ever see Smokey?"

"The Bear?"

Fonseca spread his legs as wide as they would go, his ass almost grazing the ground, and started rhythmically pumping his shoulders, his knuckles in the dirt, doing a modified Jerk. "Lum de lum de ah ayyy . . . lum de lum de ahh ayy . . ." In time to his own horn section, legs spread, head down, he covered his ears, then his eyes, then his mouth, one hand at a time, snapping his torso back and forth on every gesture, then finishing it up with a funky slow strut around the cage, stretching his ribs and pounding his chest.

"DO-O MIC-KEY'S *MON*-KEY, CHIL-DREN, DO-O MIC-KEY'S *MON*-KEY, CHIL-DREN."

He was an incredible dancer. He had every stage move down cold. When he finished he leapt back onto the tire. "He was bitch, man. Freedomland 1964."

I'd bet anything he had danced for Kim like that—just fucking around—and she'd loved it.

"When I was a kid my old lady used to say I belonged in a cage." He cleared his throat.

"They all said that," I answered absently. "Cages, barns, brought up in barns . . ."

I thought about my father working in a cage. He got *promoted* to a cage.

I heard my father say, "Hiya, buddy." Eating sandwiches alone in absolute quiet. Him down that street strafed by the German plane. How much more the Nazis must have thought of those two guys in the Messerschmitt than the Americans thought of my old man.

Fonseca had read that story. He remembered it too.

"My father's not talking to me, pretty much," I heard myself say. Fonseca didn't respond.

"My father's not talking to me."

"'Cause of the bomb threats?" He sounded flat and not interested, his eyebrows rising and falling above the frames of his sunglasses.

"I guess so." I shrugged.

"Sheesh," he finally snorted. "Did you ever take a swing at your old man?"

The notion was so repulsive I couldn't even visualize it. "Once."

"It's the most horribly satisfying feeling in the world . . . when I was sixteen I came home drunk, it was Christmas Eve and I mean, I come in furniture-crashing eyeballs-rolled-up, sleep-in-your-own-puke drunk . . . crashing around. . . . The next morning I come downstairs, my parents are sitting there, my younger brother, they're just sitting there in their bathrobes waiting for me, arms folded, a total freeze frame, stone dirty looks. 'What? What I do? . . .' And then I see the fucking Christmas tree. It's lying on its side, all the ornaments were crushed, *glass* all over the carpet, even a couple of the presents were stepped on, squashed . . . whoops! I figured the best defense is an offense so I started yelling at my father that he shouldn't've gotten that cheap tree stand—the screws, they came right out and now *look* at this mess! My father doesn't even bother to answer me. I was one of those high school drinking problems you see on News Specials. I was the only kid in my high school in the enriched program, you know, the Braniac elite corps? The only kid to get suspended three times for drunkenness . . . so they're sick of me, totally fed up. Anyway my father's standing there, not even answering me, he's got a suitcase on the floor by him which I didn't even notice, and he's real calm, which is the worst for him, and he tilts his ear down to the suitcase, still giving me that deadeye and he says, 'I want you to take this suitcase, take it upstairs, put your clothes in it, and get the hell out of our house. I don't care *where* you go, what you do, who you kill, who kills you, I want you out of this house now.'

"Now, I never went up against my father directly. I would do shit like get drunk or fuck up in ways that would jerk him around *in*directly, but I never defied him face to face, mainly because he was my father, but also because he would have beat the shit out of me everytime out of the box. My old man was Hands Brinker and he was no one to dance with. But he was a civilized man . . . he only hit me when he had to . . . whatever the hell *that* means. But anyway, the last time he laid into me I was maybe just fifteen, but it was enough . . . my memory was excellent . . . and here he was telling me to hit the road at sixteen. I mean, get fucking *real!* I was still drunk a little. I really didn't feel like starting a new life just that second . . . I mean, it was Christmas. I was standing in my shorts on the stairs. I looked at my brother, who was like eight, nine, no mercy there, I mean he's a fucking orthodontist now anyway, no mercy there . . . it was probably *his* presents I stepped on. My mother, she never liked me from the git go, so the whole thing was a golden opportunity for her to have a sewing room. So it's me versus him, no extra people dragging on his bathrobe begging him to reconsider. But the thing is, I don't wanna go, I don't wanna butt heads, but I don't wanna go, and from where I'm standing up on the stairs it looked like the whole thing could be resolved if someone just took the goddamn tree and stood it upright again, a two-second production at best, a ten-second sweep-up job of broken ornaments, dock my allowance for the squashed toys and it's Noel, Noel, like nothing happened. So I go down the steps for the tree and my father, seeing I'm bypassing the suitcase, does one of these check slides, moving from where he was to in between me and the tree, so he's blocking my way, and he points to the suitcase. I said to him, 'Look, let me just pick up the tree.' He says, 'Pick up the suitcase.' I open my mouth again, and he says, 'Pick up the suit-case.' And we're standing there, eye to eye, same height, which was a new one on me—I had thought he was taller—and I said, get this, 'What's the matter with you, don't you have any *Yule*-tide spirit?' Not Christmas spirit, *Yule*tide. I sounded like a fucking Hallmark card. Anyway, he hauls off . . . Whap! An open-handed crack on the jaw. You know what? It didn't hurt. I say, 'Let me pick up the tree, Pop,' very casual to show him I wasn't hurt . . . Whap! again. I say, 'Don't hit me anymore.' *Whap!* and before I knew it I slapped him back. It was a real girlish slap because I checked my swing, and on hitting him I had two separate reactions—one, yikes, I just hit my father; and two, what a lousy non-athletic slap, he's probably ashamed of me. So I hit him again, I swear to Christ on the Bible, to show him I had good follow-through. Next thing I know, we're swinging away like Zale-Graziano, and my mother and my soon-to-be-an-orthodontist brother are going berserk, but I'm going wild twice as much as they are. I am knocking the shit out of him. I realize he can't fight for love or money, and I'm standing there . . . I won't hit his face, I keep punching his arms and shoulders. I don't know what it was, I must've really grown since the last time he hit me or something, but I'm whaling the crap out of him now. Anyway, he does pop me one stinger on the jaw, and I must have lost my temper or something, because next thing I know he's on his knees and he looks like he got birds going around his head and my mother's standing there with her hand over her mouth like she's stifling a yawn, except for the eyes which tell the whole story and I say, 'Just let me pick up the tree, Pop, it'll be okay.' So I casually saunter over to the tree; I think I might even have been singing, 'This ain't happenin', oh this ainn't . . . this ainn't haaapening la de la oh this ain't, this aiinn't happening, to meee . . .' and just as I'm about to bend down I feel something, like a twig or a stick bounce off the back of my head, I turn around and on the floor is a rubber-tipped arrow, one of my brother's toys. I figure Dickhead is getting in on the act, so I look up but it's not Dickhead, it's my father, and he's on his knees and his hair is all clumpy, sticking out on the sides like a clown, and he's muttering to himself and futzing around with the little toy bow, fitting in another arrow. He aims it at me with my Mom and my brother standing behind him like he was defending them from me and he's aiming that little piss-ass Cochise bow and arrow at me and he's screaming for me to get out and at first I just wanted to laugh, I thought he must be hamming it up, maybe *he's* drunk. But he looked so agitated and crazed—I'd just beat him up man, his kid just *whip*ped his ass, and he was stone beside himself. So I just raised my hands, 'Don't shoot, Pop, I'm goin'' and I took the suitcase and in ten minutes I was packed and on the street and I stayed at this guy Barry Kaplan's house for a week and I just sat in his room and every day I just drank and wrote poetry about how he was the best father in the world and how much I loved him, I think I was terrified about being able to take over the universe . . ."

Fonseca dreamily swayed on his tire, staring up at the sun through his black shades. "Yeah . . . yeah."

I felt totally transported by the story. I was standing there frowning, my jaw on the ground.

"So are you two guys talking to each other?"

"Me an' my old man? Oh yeah, oh yeah, we're tighter'n a gnat's nuts, we're pals." He nodded, still looking skyward. "We're pals."

"Aw good," I said from the heart, feeling that brandy warmth in my belly, a strange gratefulness.

"He's old now, they live down in Miami Beach. It's like the Bronx with palm trees. They love it, but I hate visiting them; they've got all these friends with beautiful caramel tans and cancer. Die young, stay pretty, that's *my* motto."

"James Dean," I mumbled redundantly.

"So how's Kim doing?" he asked casually, his head slowly lowering from its throat-tanning position to level with my face.

His eyes were blacked out by the shades but he was giving me a tight-lipped grin.

"Good, good." I pouted and nodded with exaggerated casual animation. I was so shocked, I played it like Hey-I-knew-you-knew-it-wasn't-hardly-worth-mentioning. "Good, she's good." I nodded, waiting for my body to send up some kind of signal as to what it felt.

"Yeah? That's good." He kept the grin trained on me.

"I was, ah, I was gonna tell me . . . I mean *you* . . ." My breath was giving out on me.

"Yeah?" He swayed on the tire.

I casually patted the bars and fought to keep my voice register. "Who, ah, how did you know? You know . . ."

"April told me . . . where do you think you are, Metropolis? This is a fucking college town, Jim."

"April told me . . . *you!*" I let out a long yawn-like full-mouthed exhalation to slow myself down.

The grin widened. He was enjoying my freaking out and that pissed me off, slightly helped me to hold it together.

"So, ah, yeah, we're, ah we see each other, I didn't even *know* actually . . ."

"Peter, you know why I'm in this cage?"

I started reciting to myself all the titles on his bookshelf. *A Passage to India, Metamorphosis, The Magic Mountain.*

"You know why I'm in this cage, Peter? Because I didn't want you to feel in physical danger when I told you I knew. You think I *like* being in this cage? You think this is my home away from home or something? I know you're scared of me so I had to think of a place where you wouldn't feel cornered by me, you know what I'm saying? I put myself in here so you should feel safe when I told you the news. I mean, if I wanted to beat the shit out of you it would take me a good thirty seconds to climb out of here . . . you could be halfway to China in thirty seconds. But what I'm sayin' is I don't care. It's over, me and Kim, and it's cool, you don't have to answer to me about her. And I think we can be friends. I put myself in this cage as an act of friendship, do you understand me? I wanted you to feel safe. Do you get what I'm saying, Peter?"

"I would have felt safe in the cafeteria. We didn't have to come all the way out here." I felt part insulted, part afraid and the two neutralized each other and made me calmer.

"Nnah, Peter, we used the cafeteria yesterday . . . that was for setting me up with April. I'm tellin' you, kid, this is as much a pain in the ass for me as it is for you . . ." He slipped off the tire and paced the cage. "Okay, I'm comin' out, so if you still don't trust me you should take off now . . ."

I wouldn't have run if it meant my life. As he climbed up the bars he kept up what was supposed to be a soothing patter of how Kim was a free agent and how he could understand my hesitancy telling him and how it was an awkward situation all around. When his shoe leather clapped the ground and he sighed and groaned about how stiff he was, then bent over to brush dirt from his thighs, I stood tensed and silent, my feet planted, my body slightly tilted forward.

When he straightened up he took off his sunglasses and squinted at me. His eyes traveled down my body and he abruptly laughed.

For a horrible moment I thought my fly was open and I was afraid to look down.

"You wanna hit me, Pete?" He busied himself with cleaning his lenses, his chin nailed to his chest.

To my horror, I realized my hands were knotted in fists. I blushed and thrust them into my pockets.

"Listen Pete, I'm serious. I think we could be friends, two city boys, we teach the same stuff, we like the same people, Big Jack . . ."

"Kim?" I blurted.

He shrugged. "Nah . . . no more . . . I swear on my child's eyes, that's over . . . and I would value your friendship, man." He said it quietly and without sunglasses. "I'm a total fucking mess, but I would value your friendship . . . we could have laughs . . ." He extended his hand. "And for your pimp-ass information, I didn't fuck April." He gave me that raised eyebrow smirk, but his lips were fighting down a stupid smile.

I had a weird overpowering desire to say to him that if he was on the level he should give me a hug.

"C'mon, man, I'm not asking you for a fucking date, I'm asking you to be my pal."

I was going to be gone by January. With any luck I could talk Kim into going with me. Fonseca knew about me and her, so that terror was over with. Suddenly I felt such a rush of euphoric relief that I grabbed his hand and shook it with such ardency it was like the grip that sealed the New Deal.

Fonseca walked me through the rows of cages. "Hey, listen, I will never mention Kim to you again, but one thing—I don't think you should tell her we're hanging out. She'll probably freak on you."

No shit.

"You really didn't get it on with April?" I forced my face into a wry sly grin. I didn't really care if he did or not. I asked it because it sounded intimate and chummy.

"No, I didn't," he said without the slightest trace of irony.

"You see your kid a lot?" My teeth were casually chattering.

"Never." He nodded at his shoes. "I'd just fuck him up. I'm a shit father. I mean, I'll get drunk and start talking about this great kid I got, how much I love him, but I'm full of shit, the kid's better off without me . . . I know it sounds horrible but that's the poop on that."

We walked past the kiddie section of the zoo. All the empty cages were low so the animals could be petted. There were still some petrified goat droppings lying around like grapeshot.

"I want to ask you something . . . do you like rock 'n' roll?" Fonseca put his hand on my elbow again.

"Yeah, sure . . ." We wandered past what must have been a camel or donkey ride; a faint essence of ancient four-legged beast-shit hovered in the air like a dream of Morocco.

"Do you *know* rock 'n' roll?"

"What do you mean, like those maniacs in the oldies shops that can tell you the pressing history of the Phlegmtones' 1953 version of 'Unchained Melody' or something?"

I was starting to feel like myself a little. Starting to loosen up—or maybe it was just high-strung blurtiness. Oh freedom.

"The '53 cut was Al Hibbler, the '64 version Vito and the Salutation, '67 was the Righteous Brothers. There were other cuts, of course, but those were the main ones to get heavy air-play . . ." he intoned without smiling. "Did you ever hear of Nicky and the Naks?"

Nicky and the Naks. What the fuck. But before I knew it I was off and running, "*Sure!* In 1956 they did 'Corn Starch Bath' on the Herpes label; 1957, the theme from *Fiddler on Your Face;* then Rocco Babootz left to form his own group and Nicky and the remaining Naks went over to Fellatio Records and cut two back-to-back monsters in '59, 'Where's My Tie?' and 'Ode to Archie Moore.' But in 1960 tragedy struck when an entire five-story fire escape fell off a tenement building in Corona and crushed the Naks, who were sitting on the stoop singing a cappella. Nicky survived because at the time he was doing a coffee and airplane-glue run."

I felt totally out of control. I wiped my lips.

Fonseca was walking beside me, his head twisted to the side. He was semi-smiling, grimacing in slow-fuse impatient anger.

"Are you finished, or do I have to listen to the whole show?"

"I'm finished."

"So did you hear of them or not?" He was getting angrier, so I reeled it in and calmed down. I could tell this was going to be a real eye-to-eye give and take relationship. November from January was two months.

"Yeah, I vaguely heard of them. I don't know what they did, though." I pinched my face as if straining my memory banks.

Fonseca's face untightened. His expression got formal, his tone informative: "Well, they weren't really what you would call monsters, but they had a few hits and two good albums in the late fifties. I knew Nicky in elementary school. We were in the same class together in P.S. 51. Anyway, it was over for them in a year or two. Nicky was a junkie and fucked up; he tried to make a comeback as a hippie and that was very sad, but ah, it seems he's re-forming a new Naks. I guess he's my age now, thirty-seven, eight, and he latched onto the oldies revival-circuit but ah, anyway, he's playing this weekend in a supper club in Long Island City and I was thinking of going in and seeing him because we were in the same class in elementary school. I don't know if he remembers me, probably not, but I was thinking . . . he would make a great character in a novel. I mean, think of it, a guy approaching forty trying to make a rock and roll comeback after—I mean, he was on top of the world at twenty-two, a fucking has-been at twenty-four. I heard he was all strung out on dope for a while living in a housing project and driving a fucking forklift, and now he's puttin' on the tux again, now he's got a second chance, it's a great fucking story. I could do it too, man, this could be my break, babycakes, I know the streets, the neighborhoods, I could really write a great fucking book . . . so I think I'm gonna go into New York this weekend, catch his show and rap with him. He was a *bad* motherfucker too . . . he really could sing, he really *was* the essence of stoop singing, your smartass bullshit aside, but *good* . . . I mean, let's not get carried away, it was simpy shit, the songs in those days, but ah, he was very pure in his own way, so what I'm trying to say is, I want you to come into the city with me this weekend because this promises to be a little on the freaky side for me, and I'm gonna need some company. I haven't been back to New York in two hundred years . . ."

"Aw, Tony." I was shaking my head in the negative and wincing, but at the same time I felt another rush.

"Aw c'mon," he pleaded. "I need you, man. I need someone I can talk to. I don't wanna fuck it up. I need an arm, I need an arm."

"Aw, Tony." I felt my resistance buckle.

"I don't wanna fuck up, Peter." He looked genuinely scared and I almost caved in. I didn't want him to fuck up either.

"I can't," I shrugged. No way.

He stopped short, his face crumpling in exasperation. "Slow down . . ." He put a hand on my shoulder. "Talk to me . . . listen to me . . . just tell me something. What do you want to do? Tell me what . . . do *you* . . . want . . . to *do*. You know what I mean? I mean who the fuck do you think you are?"

"Fuck you!" It came out as a soprano squawk.

"Nah, nah." He waved me off. "I'm not dressing you down, Peter. I mean literally, who the fuck do you think you are? Who's Pete Keller? Tell me. I'm interested. I'm serious. You wanna teach here? You want *ten*ure?"

Even though there was no trace of irony in his tone the answer was obvious to the both of us. "Exactly." He compressed his lips, no light of triumph in his eyes. "I didn't think so. So tell me. I'm here. I love yah, you little Jewboy, talk dirty to me. . . ." He squatted down into a hunkering position, bouncing on his haunches. I felt that I had to talk fast before his kneecaps popped, but before I could say anything, he looked up at me and started in again.

"I saw you with that *People* magazine on the desk. The Up and Coming page there, that guy, what's it? Scipio Smith?"

"Stevens . . ." I muttered. I was wondering if I still had that postcard from Crown. It had his address on it. Fonseca stood up.

"Stevens . . . exactly, right? Up and Coming. It makes you sick, right? How the fuck do you think it makes *me* feel, blood? I'm thirty-eight . . . I'm gonna be thirty-nine. How's *that* for Up and Coming? I'm *here*, in this town. What, *I* don't count? *I* don't dream? *I* don't have gifts? What . . . you think I play hide the salami with some kid, it makes my se*me*ster? I don't *ache?*"

"I thought we were talking about me."

"We *are*, brother man," he drawled.

I remembered Crown's address.

"Sure," I said, more to myself.

"Aw*right!*" He gave a horsey little skip, spun around and squeezed my arm. "Oh man, oh man, we'll bomb around all weekend. I got a room for us in a hotel in the Village, it'll be wild . . . we'll get the hell out of Mall-land and down with the *real* people!"

"Sure . . ."

"Aw*right!*" He extended his palm for a pound. I tapped it listlessly.

"Why not."

"It's there, my man, whatever it be, it be there . . ."

Somewhere I was so puddle-headed with relief and gratefulness for his not killing me that even without thinking of Crown I would have agreed to go. Not only that, but he was acting afraid of *me,* afraid of my rejection, and that slayed me altogether. I felt sick trying to figure out all the trouble I was setting myself up for with Kim and God knows what else, but it was only a weekend. I could visit Crown. Maybe bump into Randye or James Madison. I could visit the offices of *People* magazine. Yeah, I'd be Fonseca's arm.

"Sure, why not?" I said out loud to myself.

"This is gonna be great—just the two of us, Donald Quixote and Sancho Panza." He squeezed my arm and picked up the pace.

I readjusted my sunglasses. I didn't like being Sancho Panza. Suddenly I felt cool and on top of it. I wasn't Sancho Panza.

"I'm feelin' good now . . ." He winked and made a clicking noise like a camera. "You know? And I'm still thinking about that screenplay idea I had with the blood bank . . . I know this guy."

Still in Kiddieland, we came up to a log fort which was about eight feet high and square. It had windows and knotted climbing ropes hanging from flagpoles extended from the turrets. The whole thing looked like a Christmas dream toy for a millionaire's son.

Fonseca grabbed one of the knotted ropes and just using his hands, pulled himself up to the roof.

"I mean, we are talking irons in the *fire!*" He waved and sank out of sight. I grabbed the rope and hauled myself up, using the logs as steps. On the roof there was no sign of Fonseca, just three dull gray sliding-pond-type chutes that disappeared somewhere inside the fort. I picked one and started belly-sliding down. What the hell was I doing? Ten feet into the chute I stopped moving. It was child-sized and I was slightly stuck. I was in total musty darkness and in my terror I almost called out his name, imagining myself buried forever inside the belly of an abandoned toy fort in an abandoned zoo. For a second I flashed on it all being a setup, an elaborate death trap, but then I was overwhelmed by a terrible fear of Fonseca's sliding down the chute to attack me from behind and in a total bogeyman panic I started wriggling forward on my elbows until I plopped out into the dirt from a square opening about a foot above ground level. I lay on a bed of leaves, my head against the lowest log, and wiped the sweat from my face.

"Hey." I heard him but I didn't see him. "Hey." I looked up. Fonseca's head and shoulders were wedged in a high chute exit, his arms pinned to his sides. He still had his sunglasses on. "Knock this fucking log out here." He jutted his chin helplessly at a loose board below his jammed chest. "I can't believe it . . . I'm fucking stuck."

—

Fonseca insisted on a Victory drink and drove into town to one of those red brick Victorian office buildings that had been converted into a mini-mall.

He swung through a balcony lane of shops, absently snapping his fingers and popping his fist against the flat of his palm. I followed behind, sunk into obsessions and justifications for myself, lies for Kim. The two-story mall evoked some kind of vegetarian Finland; rows of storefronts slightly classier and more exclusive than the Plunkett; a medley of pricey down parkas, carrot juice, bean-sprout sandwiches and oversized rope sculptures. The store names all seemed to have double-K's and double-N's. Lots of Hauses. Lots of Master Charge. He took me downstairs to "Alpenhaus," a restaurant-bar done up in a ski lodge motif; antique snowshoes crossed on the walls, turn-of-the-century sepia prints of bearded skiers, black and white shots of World War II ski commandos; photos of famous ski mountains, the runs colored in like major blood vessels. The waitresses wore Gretel outfits complete with white paper tri-cornered hats and heart-bordered aprons, and the two bartenders were full-bearded, wearing heavy argyle sweaters. The wood-paneled walls themselves gleamed as if someone had just given them a coat of dry-air ski wax.

Since it was close to three o'clock, the room was nearly deserted. We sat on high-backed chrome and leather bar stools, Fonseca twirling in full circles until one of the bartenders came over.

"Yaw . . . I'll hev a Teguila Soonrise hold der schlag, by yiminy, and you Ollie, you'll hev . . ."

"Cut it out. Give me an Irish coffee."

Suddenly from a far corner booth behind us, there erupted a heroic guffaw echoed by a lighter feminine ripple.

Without turning around, Fonseca lowered his head, swooping down toward my elbow. "Hey Ollie? I tink dets de Fot Man, don' choo? Yaw, I tink dets him."

Shit. Fat Jack. I didn't want to be seen with Fonseca.

The bartender brought the drinks, Fonseca's looking like a glass full of pink blood. Fonseca dropped a five, pulled out his straw, tossed it on the bar and got up, hooking my arm for me to follow.

Jack was sitting across from a fortyish tall woman, dressed in a skirt-suit. She had dirty blond hair and there was a fine spray of acne pits across the cheeks of her otherwise handsome face.

Fonseca clicked his heels and bowed.

"He-hey! Tony." Jack slid over to make room. "What's up?" When Fonseca sat down, Jack put his arm across the top of the booth, his hand clutching Fonseca's shoulder.

"Veres Ol-ly?" Fonseca leaned into the aisle to peer at me dawdling, trying to stay out of sight. Jack's face pulled down into a worrying grimace, as I had expected.

I sat next to Jack's date.

"This is Katherine Mooney. She teaches over in Anthropology." Jack lit a cigar, peering at me over the flame. On the table were crumb-littered dessert plates and half-full cups of coffee.

"This is Pete Keller and this is Tony Fonseca."

Fonseca ducked his head, winked and briskly rubbed his hands.

"Katherine's just got tenure, guys," he blew out a cloud that made it hard to see his face.

"Awp!" Fonseca squawked. "Tenure!" He winked at me then twisted around to the bar. "Liebchen! Cham-panyuh, bitte . . ."

"No, no, please . . . I'm drunk already. Jack . . ." She cocked her head. "I gotta go."

"Okay . . . I'll stay here a bit with the guys."

I got up to let her out. She reached across the table and squeezed Jack's hand.

"So what you guys up to?" Jack reared back to get away from his own pollution.

"Whatta *you* up to?" Fonseca smirked and winked at me again.

"Aw . . . we're old friends."

Fonseca lowered his head and leaned across the table to me singing in a whispery bass, "Jumpin' Jack Flash, it's a gasgasgas . . ."

I forced myself to snort in amusement. Now I wanted to be alone with Jack.

"So are you writing anything?" Jack asked Fonseca.

"I'm integrating." Fonseca smiled nervously.

"So it's going good, Tony?" There was a jarring trace of irony in Jack's voice that verged on cruelty.

"Non-stop, Orson."

"Yeah, Pete? For you too?"

"Stop-start," I said faintly.

Fonseca abruptly exploded with a roundhouse cackle. "Ho-ly shit . . . Jack, you know what I was remembering the other day? You remember that place Sonny Liston?"

"What? Oh yeah, yeah." Jack looked as if he wanted to be alone with me, too.

"Pete . . ." Fonseca leaned toward me again. "About five years ago? One summer I went to an artists' colony in the Catskills called the Leston Tunny Institute, remember Jack? It's like a farm converted into an artists' colony and I went there to get away and work, right?" He covered my fist with his hand. "The place was a friggin' *zoo* man, I swear it." He started sniggering. "I swear it . . . They had ten fucking gooney birds, painters, writers, everybody's a case up there you know, the little old lady poets in the crocheted berets wandering around graveyards with spiral notebooks . . ."

Jack looked far away. Not happy.

"Oh Christ . . . they had . . . they . . ." Fonseca broke up in hiccuppy chortles, his forehead on the table, his broad leather-bound back jerking in time to the hysteria.

I started laughing myself.

"This guy, he was a painter . . . he was a fag spade about nine fucking feet tall, twenty pounds . . . what was his name . . . with goggle glasses. I don't know, Afro-Sheen Anderson or something. He couldn't paint, right? He couldn't. So he's fucking frustrated, right?" Fonseca started bleating again, stopped, cleared his throat. "He couldn't paint? So he takes . . . takes . . ." He dropped his head on the table, cooing and moaning. "He takes his f-fuckin' paint brush and . . . ah-ah, he, h-he . . . goosh!" He slammed the side of his fist into his eye and fell back against the booth. "*Goosh!*" He did it again. "R-right in his fuckin' eye with the end of his paint brush." Fonseca's cheeks were wet with tears. "He poked out his fuckin' eye!" Fonseca started howling, twisting around so his knees were free from the table and doubled over as if he was sick. "With his fuckin' paint brush, right? And I'm tryna fuckin' write, right? 'Yahh!

Yee-ah! My eye! My eye!' I'm in there . . . 'I saw the best minds of my
generation,' and all of a sudden 'Yeee-ah!' and I'm going 'Shaddup,
you f-fuckin' f-faggot, I'm tryna write!' 'My eye! My eye!' 'Your *ass*,
you cocksucker!' He's ov-ver in the cowshed. 'Yeee-yah!' I'm in the
chicken coop . . . they gave me a fuckin' chicken coop to write in.
'My eye!' 'Shaddup, you black bastard!' The fuckin' guy lost his eye.
How was I supposed to write? The guy lost his eye. 'My eye! . . .'"
He trailed off. "Right, fat man?"

Jack nodded slowly.

"How was I supposed to work? I got people poking their eyes out.
This other guy, he was like the Poet Laureate of Tunisia or something, the ladies in the graveyard. I'm supposed to *write* here?" His
shoulders kissed his ears.

"What was the poet of Tunisia like?"

"He was a fucking geek," he said. "He used to get up in the middle
of the night and wash his clothes in the swimming pool." Fonseca
hunched his shoulders, gave me a helpless look and broke down
again. "Oh my dear lord . . . Sonny Liston, kiss my piston. What a
fucking 'up' place, right, Jack?"

"It was bad," he said mildly.

"You might say that." Fonseca clapped a hand on the nape of
Jack's neck and beamed fondly at him. He smiled like that for a long
time nodding his head and flexing his fingers on Jack's neck.

Jack, holding his cigar aloft, gave him back a neutral smile. Fonseca started rocking slightly, narrowed his eyes. "This is my lifesaver,
this guy, Pete," his eyes still on Jack. "My life preserver."

Jack shrugged, his eyebrows jumping in awkwardness. He
concentrated on flicking a short growth of ash off his cigar onto the
coffee saucer.

Fonseca finally sighed and withdrew his grip.

"I gotta blow . . . you ready?" He tilted his chin at me.

"I'm gonna stay here for a while, Tony."

"C'mon. I'll give you a ride."

"It's okay, I wanna shop around."

"My-y Mama tol' *me!* . . ." Fonseca about-faced the table "You
bet-ta shopa-*roun!*" And he headed out.

Jack and I sat in silence. I was afraid to look at him, afraid he'd
be mad at me.

"That's a true story?"

"Yup, guy lost his eye." He sighed.

"Were you up there too?"

"Just to get Tony."

"What do you mean, to 'get' him?"

"Well . . . Tony likes to tell partial stories."

"What, *he* poked the guy's eye out?" I was half joking.

"Nope . . . but that graveyard he was talking about with the lady poet?"

"Yeah?" Rape. Ghosts.

"Tony couldn't work up there, right? So he'd get drunk and he'd see that poor old lady go out every day to write in the graveyard. Well, one day he's really in his cups and he comes running out of his studio into the graveyard and starts chasing her all over the place. Scared her half to death. Chased her out. She comes back and gets the director. They go out and Tony's passed out. He'd started knocking over tombstones. It was one of those old cemeteries and he'd knocked over about five stones and then blacked out. The lady wanted to call the cops but the director didn't want any police, so he calls up Kim and tells her to come down and get him right away before there's trouble. Kim doesn't want to deal with it—she's had it with him—so she calls me and I go down and get him. It's very sad. Very sad story."

"Are they still involved with each other?" I looked up finally. My hands were shaking.

"Who?"

"He and Kim."

"No," Jack said calmly.

"I shouldn't be hanging out with him, right?"

"I can't tell you what to do, Pete." He shook his head.

"I mean, because of me and Kim . . ."

"What can I say?"

"You could tell me if I'm in trouble if I do."

He sighed. "If you really want my opinion, no, I don't think you should mess with him. And I'm not even talking about anything with Kim . . . just in general. Tony is Tony an-nd you have to know what you're doing around him, or . . ."

"Or what?" I was shivering as if it was freezing in there.

"Or nothing. He can be very charming, but, he's . . . I don't trust him. I know him ten years or more."

"Tell me about him and Kim."

"What?"

"Anything . . . everything." I had to fight down the impulse to bolt.

"It's not my place, Pete," he said with pained delicacy.

"I'm going to New York with him this weekend."

"Why?"

"I'm gonna help him out . . . it's nothing."

Jack cocked his head, regarding me with a wincing look. "Help him with what?"

"Life . . ."

"What . . ." Jack cut himself off but he looked angry and turned away as if to say It's your funeral.

I felt trapped and in trouble.

"You know, of all the people, Tony is the only guy I can get to the nut of it with."

"What do you mean?" Jack said mildly.

"Tony is the only guy who understands things." I was thinking of that little outburst in the kiddie park about going to New York. About Scipio Smith-Stevens. As soon as I said the words though, it seemed slight and jive. It also sounded like a slap at Jack.

"*What* things?" Jack was on the verge of exasperated laughter.

"I mean he understands what I want," I mumbled, starting to sweat. "I can't talk to Kim about it." That one I said more to myself.

"What *do* you want? I don't understand, still. Talk to me." Everybody wants me to talk to them, talk to them.

"About the future," I said weakly. "He knows from hunger. I understand him too."

Jack didn't seem impressed. "You worried about your future? About what happens next? You want to teach here next term? You're hired." He shrugged. "You want to come into the graduate English program? You're in. I didn't know you were worried, Pete . . . you should talk to me more."

"I don't *wanna* teach!" I whined like a child. "Didn't you ever *not* want to teach?"

"Oh sure, when I was a kid I wanted to be an Olympic diver, but

every time I jumped in the pool, the locker room got flooded." He
laughed.

"I'm serious, Jack."

"What makes you think I wanted to teach? I wanted to play jazz
trumpet. I even had my own group but we stank."

"Ex*act*ly." I nodded, grateful.

He calmed down, smiling at me in sympathetic understanding,
and I felt better.

"So what's gonna happen in New York this weekend?"

"I don't know. I just want to scout around . . . see what's up . . .
see what's around."

"But why do you have to go in with Fonseca? *I'll* go in with you
if you want company . . ."

"*When?*" I felt excited.

"Maybe when the term's over. I have the MLA convention there
in January . . . come in with me."

"I have to go," I said almost begging and got up to leave.

"Watch yourself," he said, not turning to me.

———

I raced right over to Kim's house to not tell her about me and Fonseca and the coming weekend.

She wasn't home from work yet and both Anthony and I sat
there watching cartoons, waiting for Mommy.

Kim finally walked in at five, when she was supposed to, embracing a big brown bag that emitted the tantalizing reek of Chinese take-out.

Anthony gave her a half-wave from his hunchback crouch in
front of the box and as I anxiously unpacked the lo- and chow-mein
cartons, the duck sauce foils—from Chee Lok, no less—Kim went
down the stairs again to get the mail.

She reentered the apartment three minutes later as slow and preoccupied as a sleepwalker. There was a half-drunk smirk on her face
and I envisioned a fast fuck on the stairs, Kim's back being repeatedly bulled against the banana stucco walls, her ankles locked behind
the super's back.

"Fuck-a-doo," she said mildly.

Anthony turned briefly to his mother, but he got sucked back into cartoons.

She handed me a ripped-open envelope. It was addressed to Ronald Hard c/o K. Fonseca. The letter was half torn from a hasty opening of the envelope:

Dear Mr. Hard,

As we are presently trying to upgrade the sophistication level of our fiction at *Man-O-Man Magazine*, I am happy to inform you that we wish to publish "I Was a Whore at Disney World." Of course, there would have to be some revisions, both for considerations of magazine space and possible libel actions by the Disney people, but if you are willing to subject your story to cutting, pruning, and proper noun plastic surgery, please let me know ASAP and a check for five hundred dollars will be coming forthwith.

Looking forward to a fruitful and productive relationship.

Ben Racer
Fiction Editor
Man-O-Man Magazine

P.S. Some off-the-cuff editorial ideas: I'm leery about her sex with the grandfather. Couldn't she stay in that jungle house with his grandson instead?

Also, is there some way to make them white? This has no bearing on my own personal beliefs, but quite candidly, interracial sex might antagonize some of our readers. If there's no realistic way to make the Jamaicans white (beach bums?) maybe we can make the girl black. In any event, I'm looking forward to working with you on this project.—B.R.

P.P.S. I'm impressed with the ease with which you write from the point of view of a woman, but I

guess, as Flaubert said when asked how he managed
to get inside Madame Bovary's head like that, "Je
suis Madame Bovary!"

———

"In . . . the . . . *club!*" Kim laughed, flipping the letter up in the
air and catching it by clapping her hands.

———

"Pie? Are you angry at me?" she asked in a small tentative voice.

"No!" I shot up, eyes blazing. Boom. This was it. My gut was
bulging from MSG even though I had only eaten six spoons of green
and beige something covered in a sweet gelatinous sauce.

"I don't know." She winced. "You were acting kind of funny at
dinner."

We were both sitting on the couch and she dug her toes under
my thighs to placate me.

My head dropped forward in nervous exhaustion. I felt I deserved execution. "I'm just . . . it was a hard day."

"You're not feeling funny about my story?" She almost flinched
as she said it. I didn't understand the question, which she must have
read in my face because she added, "You know, jealous?"

"Oh no! No!" I gushed. I wasn't either. "I swear Kim, no." I just
felt a little tense about leaving town with her ex-husband was all.

"Oh good." She collapsed into herself with relief.

"Oh, no way, sweetie." I arched my brows in sincerity. Once
again someone I was afraid of was coming off twice as frightened
of me. And once again my reaction to that was a rush of love. I
would have done almost anything for her.

Kim was smiling, almost glowing, now that that particular terror was allayed. One down.

"Let me read you this thing in its original version before Bend
Over starts butchering it up." She had the manuscript in her lap. "You
can say whatever the fuck you want. I'm feeling very good."

"Fine." I nodded mildly.

"Maaa," Anthony bellowed from bed. "If you say the ef-word
I'm going to say it too!"

"Anthony, you say fuck all the time anyhow, so get off my case,"
Kim shouted back, preoccupied with the papers.

"God fuck Ah-merri-caa, la-and that I fuuck . . ." Anthony sang humorlessly.

"Anthony, go to sleep."

"Jingle fu-uck, jingle fu-uck, jingle all the fu-uck . . ."

"Anthony . . ."

"Fuck this house, oh Lord we pray-y, make it fuck both night and day-y . . ."

Kim looked up at me on the far end of the couch and stifled a laugh.

"That one was pretty good," I whispered.

"When a fucky meets a fucky, fuckin' throo the ry-ye . . ." he blared.

Kim dropped the manuscript in mock disgust, got up and briskly padded toward Anthony's room, her steps small and rapid, her head cocked, like a ticked-off librarian. She said, "Fuck-fuck-fuck-fuck-fuck-fuck-fuck," as if she was imitating the clucking of an angry chicken.

I followed her to his room, feeling awkward and unsure of my place. I stood in the doorway. Kim was on her knees on the floor, Anthony in the same position on his bed and they were eye to eye nose to nose shouting rapid-fire fuck-fuck-fucks at each other. Kim's face was twisted in a comic Kabuki scowl but Anthony was dead-ahead serious. Suddenly she shifted from fuck-fuck-fucks to shit-shit-shits and Anthony's eyes popped, unsure if it was giving in to her to start saying "shit" also. He spluttered, "Flit-fluck, I mean shit . . ." and made the mortal mistake of giggling. Kim laughed in triumph and threw him down on his back and I could see that it was killing him to be laughing instead of angry. I knew that kid boycott feeling so well myself, but he couldn't help it and for a split second I loved both of them so much that I had to resist doing a three-way pile-on like some Kodak commercial. I left my post at the doorway and went back into the living room, sat on the couch and tried to figure out why, why, I'd promised Fonseca I'd go to New York with him, but that was bullshit because I knew why and it had almost nothing to do with holding his hand. Rom Braverman was why. Scipio Stevens was why. January was why.

———

"So here we go . . ." Kim exhaled and rattled the papers. "I was a whore at Disney World, which as you might or might not know is in Orlando, Florida . . ."

Kim embarked on one of her patented Bad Girl stories, this one concerning a hooker who worked as a dance-hall girl in a re-creation of a Dodge City saloon. She'd proposition male tourists and meet them later in a van parked in the Grumpy parking lot. The guy who drove the caterpillar shuttle through the vast fields of cars was Barry, her pimp.

Coming back from a Jamaican vacation, Barry orders her down to Montego Bay as a thank-you present to a busboy who saved his life when he got cramps while swimming. The busboy doesn't like white women, so he gives her to his grandfather, an octogenarian who lives in the interior. She stays with the grandfather, his wife and their kids and grandchildren in a tin-roofed shack. She was supposed to make it back to Disney World in a few days but decides to stay as the old guy's mistress/child.

Barry shows up at the jungle house to retrieve her and the grandfather whacks off Barry's hand with a machete and sends him on his way.

It was a cool mean story, pretty good, but even though I had been dying to hear some of her stuff, when she finished I felt irritated and impatient. I felt she was in this postured fantasy rut and it made me angry, although I knew enough to keep it to myself. And even more than that, I felt, since I was a few days away from cheating on her with this New York adventure, the last thing I wanted now was for her to share anything with me. To trust me. Not only wouldn't I tell her about the upcoming trip but I had to keep Jack's teaching offer to myself. I didn't want to get started on that one again. Fonseca would understand. Kim wouldn't. Or couldn't. Or wouldn't.

———

"Are you going to help me celebrate?" Kim lay curled up naked on her side. We were on top of the quilts. She tickled my stomach.

"Yeah, sure."

"I want you to take me to Payne House. I made reservations. My treat . . ."

I got hard when she said "my treat." I was going to be a kept man.

Payne House was an overpriced Revolutionary-era inn about sixty miles away. The place had four rooms for rent upstairs, all tiny with water-stained nineteenth-century prints on the walls, huge four-poster beds and a view of the river. I was only there once before, my junior year when I had a football-weekend date, someone's cousin from Simmons College. We spent two days and nights in a ten-by-twelve-foot room with a six-by-eight-foot bed. I got seven hand-jobs. That was the old me, though.

"Great! When?"

"This weekend?"

I felt ice cubes form in my bowels. "I can't," I monotoned. "I have to go in and see my parents." I couldn't even look her in the eye. In that moment I truly believed in God for the first time since I was twelve, because only God could have perfectly timed everything like that.

"To New York?"

"Yeah." I felt myself slipping into a shock of religious awe.

"Can't you go the weekend after?" Her voice was purple with disappointment.

"Nah, I can't, I can't," I mumbled.

"I thought they're not talking to you." Her voice had the slightest hint of accusation, and I flipped.

"Hey! This might be a breakthrough, okay?" I sat there scowling, peeling lint off the quilt.

Kim sat poker-faced, her knuckles up against her lips.

For ten minutes I was in a full boil, furious about how little she cared if I ever worked things out with my parents or not until I got a hold of myself and realized what a lying asshole I was becoming.

"How about next weekend?" I offered, as gently as I could.

"Then I have to go to see *my* parents." Kim sulked.

More silence. I lunged across her ribs for the telephone, lay on her belly so that we formed a cross and I made a reservation at Payne House for the Monday and Tuesday after New York.

"There you go." I lay back, aggressively pleased with myself.

It seemed okay with Kim. She resumed tickling my belly.

"Anthony thinks you're great . . . he can't wait to hang out with you tomorrow."

I noticed for the first time three small reddish-brown beauty marks on the outside of her thigh.

"Tomorrow?"

"Yeah. You said you'd cover him for me, remember?"

"Oh right. Yeah, well, he's a great kid . . ." I played a mental game of connect-the-dots with her beauty marks.

"I think you'd make a terrific daddy . . ."

I instantly recoiled at the word. I wished she'd said father instead. Daddy was strictly from trailer parks and door number three, and I immediately felt trapped. She looked at me with one eyebrow raised in appraisal. "A kid could get a lot from you."

"Hey, give me a break. I'm twenty-three." I laughed. It came out as if I was enunciating the words "ha ha." I regretted it immediately. Kim's face dropped into a hurt hardness; her lips just about vanished and her eyes retreated to the patch of quilt between us. I felt like shit. Until that moment I had never really thought about the fact that Kim was six years older than me. It came out as if I was dancing and prancing outside the cage of her age, doing somersaults and thumbing my nose.

"Nah, seriously . . ." I blurted, "I'm a little scared of kids. I mean, shit, it's easy to be with a kid for a few hours and be the greatest thing since canned beans . . . all you have to do is keep them off balance, you know? Be irreverent and jar them from whatever notions of propriety they have about adults. But it's strictly short-term fun, because that stuff is wearing, keeping them off balance like that, and I don't know shit from Shinola about what to do after. I'm strictly a Saturday morning man . . . it's not even good for the kid because it's all based on palming Ping-Pong balls . . . I'd freak if he got bored or depressed on me." I said all this as fast as an auctioneer.

"I wasn't asking you to adopt my fucking kid. I was paying you a goddamn compliment."

I started six different speed raps and wound up mumbling, "I'm sorry."

Next came silence, my fingers twitching with inarticulate apologies and trying to stay in the frying pan. Now that I knew there was a God I prayed to him to protect me until the weekend was over. "I have to get over getting freaked around kids. I mean, I don't know who I see when I look at a kid. Is it me? Does that make me my old man?" I ran my hands along her flank and I didn't feel flesh. I felt familiarity, the beginnings of familiarity, and it scared me. I dipped my head down and kissed her hip. Goosebumps sprouted under my palm on her thigh and I felt better.

"I mean, I think about my father and me, what he thinks about me, do I make it for him. Do I make it *happen* for him. Is he, *was* he, trapped in his life and how much was that trap composed of me . . ." I felt that if I kept up this reflective drivel long enough she'd get too bored to be effectively angry.

"Me too." Kim shrugged. "I can't believe I have to go up there."

"Where?"

"Home . . . we don't even like each other, me and my parents." She sounded scared.

"So don't go." I shrugged.

"I have to . . . I want to, I dunno, it's my family." And in a sudden burst of gratefulness for the change in subject, I threw my hat in the ring.

"Let me come up with you," I said in a bad-boy tone of voice, as if I was about to beat the shit out of someone in her name. Kim paused, her eyes moving speculatively across my face.

"You really want to?"

"Yeah." I shrugged, putting on an old Bronx accent. I was coming on theatrically hearty, still tense about lying to her about New York, grateful for the opportunity to be a good guy in any way, shape or form.

"Okay." She smiled shyly and lay her head flat on my chest again. My hero.

I lay there staring at the ceiling. I could smell her hair, the scent wafting up to my nostrils. A tawny smell of coconuts. The heat was hissing and anvil-chorusing up the radiators. "So your father would fucking die if he saw that story in *Man-O-Man*, right? Or *any* of them, right?"

She didn't answer, didn't even move her head. She might have been asleep. Suddenly I wanted to level with her. I envied the relief in her face when she got up the balls to ask me if I was jealous.

"Yeah, well, that's good, that's good . . . you're doin' it, you're getting it done. I'm having dreams now, a lot of dreams with me in them. It's good, you're on the move, and I'm gonna start soon too."

"What do you mean? . . ." Her voice got heavy, braced for trouble.

Ease it in there, Pete.

"Well, you know January is a few months, you know and a . . . I can't bullshit you Kim, I don't wanna teach." I apologized. "I can't fake it, there's gotta be something else out there, something with my name on it, you know? This can't be it because here it's not going to happen. I'm starting to fucking hum the Muzak up here . . ." Then I quickly added "I don't mean *here*, meaning here with you and the kid, I mean here, Buchanon."

I felt totally incapable of spitting it out. I lay there, my fingers sifting through her hair. She was facing my feet.

"Right, so you're going to leave here and go take an acting class to be a comic, right? Is that what you said back then?" Her voice was pure sulfur.

"Hey wait, Kim, you *know* you want to be a writer, you *are* a writer, but I *don't know* what I wanna do, right? And I'm not gonna find out in some fucking Collegetown . . . there's no options here. I don't know if I'm gonna take acting classes, maybe I will, I dunno. It could be a good move—maybe I'll be one of those waiters with his resumé in the inside pocket. I don't care. But think about it for a minute . . . what the fuck am I doing *teach*ing—and I'm not putting it down as a noble profession or anything—but *me* . . . what, given all this, am *I* doing *teach*ing? I need to be *learn*ing, I need to be bouncing off things, coming up against things . . . am I making sense? I think I am."

She didn't answer. I couldn't read her silence, and in a sudden burst of desperate euphoria I shot the moon.

"Listen, check this out. Come January, I was thinking, you know, just fantasizing about the three of us moving someplace out of here, you know, like Dubuque or Peoria, or, you know, New York."

"Maybe you can get an extension on your teaching position." Her voice came out in puffs wafting through my pubic hair. She still lay motionless, her face turned toward my feet, her ear glued to my chest.

"You're not listening to me."

"Maybe you can go for a doctorate here."

"Kim, you're not listening to me."

She turned her head a full hundred eighty degrees to me without moving her body.

"Maybe you can join the fucking circus, Pie."

"Anthony, Peter is going to hang out with you today, okay, honey?"

I stood against the sink, not wanting to sit with the kid while he was eating breakfast. With Kim bustling around in clopping heels and laying down a late-to-work perfume track, I would have felt too much like the second child.

"I don't know what he's going to be *here* for. I'm just gonna watch television all day . . . did you sleep here again?" He wheeled to me.

"Of course."

"Don't you have your own house anymore?"

"No, it was an igloo but it got too hot and it melted." Isn't that funny and distracting?

"I'm just going to watch television all day," he said to his cereal.

"Okay, honey." Kim bent down over him to give him a fast peck. He jerked his head back and his hand flew up between his cheek and her lips.

"Anthony, kiss me . . ."

"Kiss my ass," he said calmly.

Kim straightened up and briskly clipped by, not looking at me but furtively squeezing my hand. "I'll be home at five . . . goodbye, Anthony," she singsonged, his last chance to be a loving son.

Anthony waved without turning around.

———

He sat hunched a foot in front of their portable TV for two hours. I was in one of the war-ravaged easy chairs ten feet behind him, a paper bag hanging from each hand, idly snapping the lips of the rims as if catching slow ceiling drips.

By the time I took one bag and crumpled it up to throw at his head, I actually expected it to be half filled with water.

I caught him square in the back of his neck. He didn't jump or twitch, just turned slowly to me as if expecting it.

"I'm bored," I said.

"Then go back to your igloo." He turned to the TV.

I waited five minutes, then threw the other bag at him. It bounced off his bean. He didn't even bother to turn around.

I decided to get up, go over and start throwing him around the room. The physical shit seemed to work when he got in these moods.

When I got down next to him he was crying.

"What's the matter!" I hadn't even laid a hand on him yet.

"I want my mother." His big black eyes were wet and blazing, glaring directly ahead at the TV. His perfect thirty-five-year-old miniature nose and lips and forehead lines were cemented in a resolve not to bawl.

"What do you want your mother for? Just because she left you alone all day with a stranger . . . God, you act like you're eight years old!"

"I *am* eight years old!" He finally looked at me, slightly leaking.

"Well look, it's already ten o'clock, how about some lunch. You want me to make you lunch?"

"No."

"I make it special."

"Tough."

"Okay, you're missing a treat. It's called Peter's Special Lunch for Little Shits."

"What's in it?"

"It's a surprise."

I got up and went into the kitchen. Fuckadoo. I had never prepared a meal for a kid before. Peanut butter and jelly. White bread. Four day old chili Saran-wrapped in a red cereal bowl. A half dredged tub of Happy brand heavenly hash ice cream. Condiments.

I came into the living room with a covered sandwich plate.

"Here you go." I took off the cover to display a nice thick ketchup and ice cream on white bread sandwich.

"Do you want to split this with me or do you want the whole thing for yourself?"

"Eat it." He almost laughed.

Ice cream and bread isn't so bad. It's not that dissimilar to ice cream and pound cake. The ketchup didn't really complement anything, but I only put enough on for show.

"Eat another one!"

"If I make another one *you* have to eat it."

"Okay." He shrugged.

I made a half-sandwich with only a slight smear of ketchup.

When I brought it in, he smirked at me and blurted triumphantly, "I'm not gonna eat it. I just wanted to see if you were stupid enough to make another one."

"Have you ever been called a problem child?"

"I have the second-highest IQ in my class."

"Would you please—please—play ball with me outside?" I smiled.

"I hate ball."

"Please?"

"No."

"*Please*, Anthony?"

"I don't need a babysitter!" he shouted.

"*Please?*"

"Leave me alone!"

"I'll give you a dollar."

He stood up with his terrible adult face wrenched in adult-looking anguish, his fists together in supplicating rage; "I swear on my child's eyes, if you don't cut it out, I'll go crazy . . ." He said it slowly and distinctly. My insides got cold. It was Fonseca's line.

Anthony picked up the sandwich, opened the bread and smeared the ketchup over the TV screen. "Happy now?" He walked out of the living room.

He was standing in his bedroom in the corner, face to the wall as in an old-time school punishment.

I sat on his bed and watched him.

After five minutes I was totally convinced that he would be perfectly willing to stand there all day until his mother came home.

"You know, Anthony, I really like you." It was both a lie and an understatement. "I really want to have fun today. It's my day off too."

He shrugged with childish exaggeration.

There was a constellation of bright plastic dinosaurs on the floor.

I had been a dinosaur freak too, when I was eight.

I picked up a yellow triceratops.

"What's this dinosaur with the horns on his helmet?" I said to his back. "A stegosaurus?"

"It's a triceratops and you know it," he said without turning around. "Stop trying to trick me."

"You tricked *me* with the ice cream sandwich."

He shrugged.

"Where'd you buy all these?"

"They were a present."

"From Kim?" I winced. Say your mom, you idiot.

"From David."

"Who's David?"

"My doctor."

"What kind of doctor?" As if I didn't know.

"Psycho doctor."

"I used to see a psycho doctor too."

"You need one," he muttered, and shifted his weight. He was getting tired.

I began to daydream, thinking of Dr. Catcher, how she would deal with this situation, when I startled myself with a hazy memory of having to see a school psychoanalyst when I was in second grade. I couldn't remember her name, barely remembered the one hour I spent with her, but I sure as shit remembered what I had done to merit the visit. I hadn't thought about that for years, not even when I had to see Catcher.

"Hey Anthony? You know something? I just remembered, and I swear on my life I'm not lying, I once had to go see a shrink when I was seven."

No reaction.

"I don't know why you see David, but I had to go because I did something so crazy nobody could believe it."

"What?" He shifted his feet again.

"I'll tell you if you sit down. You can sit looking at the wall if you want, but if you don't sit, I don't tell."

He sat on the floor, facing me. "What."

"I was in the second grade? Third grade, maybe. My class went on a trip to a TV station in New York City. They had this special camera set up where you could stand in front of it and the class could see you on a TV screen. And they let anybody who wanted get up for two minutes in front of the camera and tell jokes or sing, right? I was the class clown, so I wanted to get up and tell jokes, but when it was my turn, you know what I did? I sang a song. And I can't sing but I liked this one song on the radio and I really got into it and it came out pretty good."

"Huh." He picked his nose, squinting at me like he was near-sighted.

"Anyways, everybody in the class started applauding and cheering. And that's when I went crazy. I was so used to the kids *laughing* at me that I couldn't deal with them *cheering* for me . . . you know what I did?"

"What?" He was mine.

"I took out my dick. Right on the television. Everybody saw it."

"The girls too?" He seemed worried.

"Everybody . . . and they sent me to the school shrink."

"Well I don't see David because I'm bad."

"I wasn't bad." I sounded defensive.

"What did the doctor do to you?"

"Just talked. I don't remember too well. The only thing I remember is she showed me all these pictures of people and things with one piece missing and I had to tell her what was missing."

"Like what?"

What. The table. "She had this picture of a three-legged table. What's missing?"

"The chairs." He smirked.

I was so amazed by his answer that I just gawked at him.

"Anthony . . ." I leaned forward and touched his knee. "I swear to God, you know what I said? 'The tablecloth.' I'm not kidding. She kept trying to get me to say 'another leg' and I wouldn't. I kept saying things like dishes, food, people, a bowl of flowers."

"Why didn't you say 'leg'?"

"Why didn't *you?*" My turn to smirk.

"What song did you sing?"

My God . . . "This rock and roll song . . . 'Speedo.' "

———

I drove him over to Zybysko's. It was a relatively stupid idea. Roy Zybysko was down in Florida for the week. Otherwise I'm sure he would have kicked us out. It was only eleven o'clock and there were five lifters spread over two rooms.

"This is where the dinosaurs come."

He didn't respond. His eyes were fixed on one sweaty behemoth who was squatting, his shoulders supporting two horizontally extended wooden boards facing a pulley-connected five-foot stack of plates. He groaned as he straightened up, lifting the boards with his towel-buffered shoulders. He went up on tiptoes and started bouncing on the balls of his feet. Just your basic calf-raise apparatus.

Some guy roared behind us and Anthony wheeled nose first into my leg. A guy with a shaved head and a tattoo of a stalking clawing panther climbing up his arm was grimacing at himself in the mirror while doing dumbbell curls.

Anthony stared at these guys with a hypnotic open-mouthed concentration. He had slipped his hand in mine and the dry rustling of his small fingers shot through me like electricity. I was afraid to move because I was sure that the minute he realized what he had done he would have whipped his hand away as if it was touching something with teeth.

I grabbed some three-pound dumbbells off the end of the rack and ushered him into the other room, which was deserted.

He faced the mirror and imitated the bald guy's grimaces and growls as he alternately curled the right and the left bells. He even had the jerking straight-spined lurch down. I went into the other room, came back with two thirty-pounders for myself, and we stood side by side working out. I flashed on a famous photo of a proud Pappy Klansman kneeling by his tyke dressed in a cute little Klan rig, but I didn't really give a shit. After we did the curls I sat down on a prone bench, brought him standing between my knees, rolled up his T-shirt sleeve and drew a tattoo high on his arm with a felt tip pen. I drew a skull and crossbones—like the snapping bag, my specialty. He frowned at it and took the pen from me. I thought he was going to correct it or cross it out but instead he rolled up *my* T-shirt sleeve and drew a crude panther which revealed no artistic talent on his part whatsoever. He grasped my bicep for steadiness. His breath on my shoulder smelled slightly of sweet cereal.

"What's that?" He tilted his chin at the bench press apparatus.

"That's off limits."

He walked over and ran his hand along the bar, his finger tracing the circumference of a fifty-pound plate that hung past the frame from the last workout.

I removed all the plates and showed him how to lie on the decline bench. I stood over his head, disengaged the hooks and let the bar slide down to his raised arms.

"I can see your balls." He smiled upside down at me.

I raised and lowered the ten-pound bar with him ten times and hooked it back on the pegs. He struggled to sitting-up position and feigned goofy dizziness.

"Now you."

I slid down the bench after lifting him off. "You're gonna spot for me, right?"

"Put the wheels back on."

"No, I can't lift them again . . . they're too heavy."

"My *father* can," he said neutrally. "My father can beat up everybody in this place."

I got up, stacked one hundred and twenty pounds on the bar for myself and told him to stand the hell back.

Part Three

BIG TIME

FRIDAY MORNING'S SKY WAS DARK GRAY, tense and bulging.

I had Fonseca pick me up in the Mall. In my half-assed state I didn't want to give him my address, because then he would know where I lived.

He shot into the parking lot in his orange Mustang, which screamed to a rocking stop in front of me.

"Get me from this scene im-*me*diately!" Fonseca howled, and as soon as I slammed the door he floored it and I wound up rubbing the bone ridge around my temples with a sheltering hand to casually hide the fact that my eyes were shut in terror although my right leg was frozen rigid on an invisible brake in front of me.

As Fonseca barreled out of town onto the Quickway, the windshield got hit with the first fat splats of rain and in seconds it was coming down so heavily it felt as if someone was tracking the car with a fire hose.

"Cock-fucking sucker," Fonseca hissed, but he was in a great buoyant mood, driving with his kneecaps, grinding in his seat, snapping and clapping along with the white bread coming over the radio.

The rain jackhammered the roof of the Mustang, making me feel trapped in a two-man bathysphere, but every time I opened my window a crack, raindrops leapt into my eyes. Maybe I'd be able to vanish the minute we got to New York. I had Crown's address with me. I wanted to see him. He didn't have a phone listing but I figured I could find him through the theater where he was working.

The station played "The Theme from Exodus" and Fonseca basso-profundoed along with the regal sledgelike piano notes.

"That's us. Exodus." He grimaced.

"Yep."

"Check this out." Eyes on the road, Fonseca reached under his seat, grabbed a manila envelope and shook out a large cardboard-matted black and white class photo. The edges of the matte were frayed and furry and there was a squadron of prehistoric coffee spatters starring across the picture like a constellation. Two shrimps squatting cross-legged in the front row held a black velvet pegboard between them that announced the class as 6–3, and Mrs. Weinstein's.

"Can you find me?" Fonseca had one eye on the road and one on the picture. His tongue tip diddled the corner of his mouth in amusement.

There he was, in the back row on the end, with the big goony tomahawk-faced teacher's hand on his shoulder. He was a big kid in a white shirt and a grotesque multicolored wide tie. I couldn't miss that expression in a million: eyes narrowed and smirky, head slightly tilted back and to the side, mouth twisted into the first syllable of a wisecrack. The only thing that looked different was his hair, which was combed back off his face into a lopsided pompadour revealing a hairline that almost came down to his eyebrows.

"Smart ass . . ."

Fonseca cackled, "You see that kid on the bottom right holding the sign?"

I checked out one of the front-row gnomes, squatting on the floor in a no-neck hunch, three inches of argyle sock and shin showing on each crossed leg. His eyes were bulging and his lips were drawn back from clenched teeth like an astronaut going through G-force.

"Yeah?"

"That's Richard Robert Lisi."

"Who is . . ."

"Nnnicky."

"Who?"

"Nnicky."

"And the Naks?"

"And the Nnnacks."

"Why's his name Nicky?"

"Sounds better, I guess. I dunno."

"Why does he look like that?"

"Because look at the guy behind him."

The kid seated directly behind Nicky was squinting in strain, his face twisted to the side. "That guy just kicked Nicky in the spine. That's why they both look like that. Right after the picture they got into a fist fight. Everybody used to fight with Nicky, man, everybody . . . I think *I* even beat him up once or twice . . . it was the thing to do. Anyway, I always liked him, not really *liked* him, I always felt sorry for him because he was such an *ang*ry little kid . . . he always had that voice though, he always had them pipes . . ."

I scanned all the faces in the photo. To me, every kid in the picture looked like an angry little kid. Every face had its own brand of pain. So what else is new.

"Anyway, I don't think he remembers me at all . . . I'm almost sure he doesn't—but I was thinking . . . tonight, when we get to this supper club? I'm gonna show him this picture. I think he'll get a kick out of it. I don't imagine he'll remember me, but maybe from the picture."

"Well look, Tony, maybe you won't get a chance, there might be a lot of people."

"Nah." He screwed up his face. "It's a supper club. It's a small joint. He's nobody now. This book is gonna mean more to him than to me . . . Richard Robert Lisi . . ." He paused, chewing memories. "I'll probably be the only guy there who knows his middle name . . ."

Fonseca tapped the brake lightly as we passed a speed trap. "Fuckin' bastards." He turned his head completely around glaring at the patrol car. "They should be out arresting Communists and fellow travelers, not Joe Citizens like me. Anyway, Nicky, there's a pattern and a poetry to his whole life story, man, becoming a rock and roll star, a destructo junkie . . . the whole show . . . because he was famous when he was seven, he was in the newspapers and everything and this wasn't for being a child star either. When he was seven he was a *saint*, man—not a saint, a visionary, a, a, *vision* recipient. He woke up one morning and there was the reflection of a cross glowing over his bed. Nobody could figure out where it came from. His parents went apeshit. They had cops up there, priests up there. Soon word got out in the neighborhood that this miracle happened. People were lined up for blocks to see it. It took Lisi's parents about an hour to get over their religious awe, then his father called up his brothers, Nicky's uncles. And they got everything organized and started charging people a dollar to see the cross. It was in the papers. The cross was up there on the wall for three days before it went away, and Lisi's family must've cleared at least two grand. Then they sold all of his furniture; his bed, his dresser, even his clothes, everything in the room, like reliquaries. *The Daily Mirror* called him the Bernadette of the Bronx. The thing was, he was just a little goon like anybody else, but the whole thing bent his brain back. His parents started renting him out for visits, you know, if you were sick or dying. . . . He became a freaky little object of adoration. The thing was, the kids in his school went crazy . . . they hated him. He was going to a parochial school, Perpetual, and that whole Catholic terror-soup came down on his head. He used to get beat up every day, just as a martyr should. It got so bad they had to take him out of Perpetual and put him in the public school with us. The whole thing died down in about a year, but that was some goddamn year. He's been nuts ever since. I mean, he was probably nuts all along, but nobody noticed."

"So he was really twisted, hah?" I asked redundantly.

"Aw man, the kid was a mess . . . he used to vandalize stuff, books, desks, property. You never knew when he was going to blow. He never played with us.

"See, that was back then. Now he'd see a shrink, they'd deal with things, but then, it was the John Wayne school of child psychology. There ain't nothing wrong with *my* fucking kid. The kid needs a doctor? We'll meet Doctor Backhand. A kid was like a TV or a radio. It don't work, right? Give it a boot. Now, they'd say he was mildly autistic or whatever, it's not my field, but man, I'm telling you, poor Nicky was like violent furniture. But it's interesting that he would become a teen idol, you know, rev up that adoration thing again, and then *zoom*, after that's over—junkiehood, which I guess was common enough in the wonderful world of musical burnouts. But you see that whole pattern in there of elevation, mortification, elevation, mortification? There's something there . . . it's very interesting. Degradation, resurrection, the things get more resonance, you know, in terms of symbolism, myth; it's got more echoes than the Grand Canyon . . . somebody should write a book . . ."

I was totally gone, thinking about Anthony and his shrink. About Crown. Suddenly Fonseca backhanded me in the chest and I jumped like a squeeze toy.

"I said we're staying at the Venus De Milo Arms."

I frantically looked out the windows. I couldn't clear my head and I thought Fonseca meant I just missed something that he was pointing to on the side of the road. "Whatta you, on depressants? Venus De Milo Arms . . ."

"Do you know Crown?"

"Who?"

"Crown."

"Bill Crown?"

"Yeah."

"What about him?"

"He left school and started acting again."

"Yeah, I heard something like that."

"Isn't that amazing, man? Talk about wanting it."

"I guess." He shrugged as if unimpressed.

I wanted to drum up some kind of pep talk rap about the Big Time, the Curved Road, and I was surprised and disappointed that Fonseca sounded so flat about Crown.

"He just goddamn dropped out . . . he was in his forties too."

"Crown's always been a little bent." Fonseca sucked his teeth.

"But you *gotta* be a little bent, right?" C'mon, Tony, help me out here.

Fonseca gave it another shrug. For an instant he reminded me of my father, flat, dismissive, apathetic, nowhere. In that moment I felt very strongly that Fonseca would never pull any of his irons out of the fire, that this would be a disastrous trip for him, he was faking it, to me and to himself. I decided not to tell him that I was going to track down Crown this weekend. He'd probably try to talk me out of it. He'd be jealous and threatened. I felt a little cold and superior.

"Hey, Tony? You remember that story I gave you about my father and the Messerschmitt? Do you remember what you wrote on it?"

He shook his head, eyes on the road.

"You wrote 'very sweet.' What was that, was that sarcastic?" I tried to look innocent.

"Very sweet," he said to himself. "Very sweet. I dunno, it was probably very sweet." He shrugged. "I'm a sucker for father stories. I probably liked it."

"Huh . . . you know when you were telling me about you and your old man? About how you wound up writing him all that poetry after you whacked him out? I do the same thing. Any time I want to kill him dead I cover by buying him gifts. When he got remarried I bought him a honeymoon weekend in the mountains."

"Gifts," he mused grimly, shaking his head. "Gifts are fucked,

my man. Somebody gives me a present, it's not my birthday, not
Christmas, I go get my gun. People give you presents, it means
they're either scared of you or they're guilty about something they
did to you. Either way it means they hate you . . . I'm serious, go
ask your girlfriend Kimberly there . . . she knows." He winked at the
road.

I couldn't tell if there was any antagonism in his voice. I felt like
saying "She's your girlfriend *too*, Tony," but it would have come out
like a gift.

"So how come you got me those sunglasses?" I was afraid of
my own question. "You scared of me or guilty about something?"

"I dunno . . . we'll find out, I guess." He turned to me and lightly
pinched my knee. "Stay tuned, right?"

———

After a few hours, despite the unrelenting rain, the radio signals
started getting stronger. We were closing in on New York. I jiggled
the tuner and got the WABC theme jingle. The minute we got off the
Quickway and hit the Thruway forty miles from the city, the rain quit
and the road and the greenery shone slick and luminous. The entire
world seemed to dance with an insane trembly brightness.

———

We got down to the Village around four and sat in a traffic jam in
Sheridan Square. Fonseca drummed a nervous paradiddle on the roof
with his fingers. I felt like jumping out of the car. Everything still had
that post-rain placental shimmer to it, enhanced by the deepening
slant of the late afternoon sun. People walked at a self-contained ru-
minative pace. They lived there. They were going home, to bars, to
wherever. There were droves of throngs. Throngs of droves. Even
though no one was scampering or scurrying, my head was filled with
that frantic riddling diddling piano run punctuated by da-DA-da-
DAT taxi trumpet notes that they always used in movies as a bustly
Manhattan theme song.

"C'mon, sweetheart, it ain't gonna get any greener," Fonseca
yawped out his window.

"Where the fuck is the park, the hotel's on the park," Fonseca
snarled.

"I'll ask." I jumped out of the car, ran across the traffic jam into Village Cigars. I felt acrobatic with excitement. The cashier gave me directions and as I zoomed back into the sunlight I saw across the street, over an A&P, six long second-story windows filled with lounging balloon-chested weight lifters, elbows on the sills, checking out the action. Like a shmuck I waved, slightly tensing my arm to show that I was into lifting too, which, if anybody cared, might have been an understandable gesture if I hadn't been wearing a ski jacket.

"What the fuck are you doing, working the base at San Diego?" Fonseca ragged me when I dove back into the car. He tilted his chin at the upstairs windows. "That's a fucking meat rack up there. Where's the park?"

"Two blocks left. What do you mean, a meat rack?"

"What do you mean, a meat rack," he mumbled. "Look at this . . . we drove right into the tunnel traffic."

"Just make a left."

"It's one fucking way, asshole!"

"Whatta you getting so snappy for?"

"I'm sorry, I'm sorry." He winced in annoyance at his own half-hearted apology.

Suddenly I lost my self-consciousness around Fonseca. We were in New York bubba, it was too big and he was too small. I didn't know why he was on the rag but that was his problem. We were in my house now, even though the last time I'd been in the Village was when I was nine and my father took me to Albert's Real French Restaurant, because it was an all-you-could-eat deal; even though I half expected to see everybody in berets and leotards carrying City Lights paperbacks; even though I was a stone yutz yokel as far as this place was concerned. I kept squinting and studying the heart of every gaggle of people because any second I was sure I was going to run into a friend, a relative, a something. Not a relative.

———

In order to get to the hotel we had to follow a maze of narrow one-way streets lined with low mansard-topped old houses. It was a chewy mishmash of New England, Spanish and Fairy Tale, house after house like a loony architectural chorus line; even with traffic slower than creeping Jesus, we were going too fast for me.

"It looks like the Belgian Waffle Village at the World's Fair," Fonseca muttered.

"God, I'm dying to go to Europe someday," I bubbled, squinting at the window of a leather craft shop that was filled with burgundy bowl-shaped leather hats with flat circular rims like what a plump monk riding a donkey would wear.

"Yo, Don Pedro." I laughed at Fonseca, envisioning him in a burlap cassock riding up a mountain pass. I was out of my mind with nonsequiturious happiness.

————

We checked into the Courtney Hotel, which was about two blocks from the Washington Square arch. The place was old and gray with two sets of newly installed glass double doors, locked and bordered in metal; very homey. The vestibule in between the doors housed a bald sixtyish desk clerk wearing thick glasses and standing inside a bulletproof glass cage plastered with more homemade stenciled warnings and rules than a federal prison. As Fonseca proceeded to get into an argument with him over everything from checkout time to the weather, I had my nose pressed up against the second set of glass doors that guarded the lobby.

Fonseca finally laid down the cash and we were buzzed in. The lobby had recessed fluorescent lighting, cheap blond wood paneling, a tight nubby gray industrial carpet and for some bizarre reason a six-foot high, five-foot wide aquarium filled with water and hundreds of Ping-Pong balls; no fish, no little plastic Diver Dans, just Ping-Pong balls frantically circulating in the filtration current like a berserk traffic jam of asteroids.

I stood there in the mole-light, gawking in astonishment at the fish tank as Fonseca impatiently punished the elevator button as if he was trying to wring a confession out of it.

Our room was surprisingly neat and spacious, in a seedy sort of way. It had two swaybacked single beds, made; two big squat white plaster Woolworth-looking lamps with Saran-Wrapped shades, two dressers and a clean bathroom. On the minus side, the window looked out on an air shaft, which was to be expected; there was no TV, no phone, the walls were despair-colored—an impersonal light gray, as if to complement steel filing cabinets—and hanging on the wall between the beds was a bucolic autumnal scene heavy on the reds and oranges depicting a Huck Finn type napping on a leafy river bank, chewing a sprig of wheat, hands behind his head, a fishing string tied to his big toe—so much like my own childhood.

Fonseca headed immediately for the John, massaging his gut.

Through the wall behind the bed I heard a black male voice dressing someone down, barking about "attitude." Whoever he was yelling at was taking it on the chin, probably an NYU coed whose parents didn't understand her. As I was fleshing out the scenario Fonseca's foot came crashing through the center of the bathroom door, a startling way to show off your Thorn Mc Ans. He started screaming about fucking roaches. Trapped in the bathroom, his disembodied voice sounded as if it emanated from his furiously wriggling shoe like some kind of bizarre puppet.

I stared at that Pepperidge Farms picture again. The peaceful horseshitty quality of it started working on my nerves. The Ping-Pong tank was more my speed, and with Fonseca cursing God and checking his Achilles' tendon for splinters, I split for outside to catch some fast sights.

I bypassed the leafless barren field of Washington Square Park, later for nature, and wandered up and down the Cabinet of Dr. Caligari streets wishing I was everybody I saw.

I had run out of the hotel wearing only a sweater and as the city crept toward sundown I started shivering, so I proceeded to hightail it back to the room, but I kept getting sidetracked by show-stoppers. At first it was just touristy show-stoppers like a window of an oldies record shop that was plastered with outrageously overpriced forty-fives. And of course I had to stop in every record and book store and flip through the stock, even though there was nothing there—except a small-press book on gay isometrics—that I couldn't have picked up in the Plunkett Mall. And of course I had to gawk at every whack-a-doo sitting on a stoop debating the Taft-Hartley Act with his bottle of Champale, but then the shit started getting bizarre. A Frisbee zipped over my head and turned a corner; I saw a greeting card store window completely covered with a grid of forty-eight stark black-and-white Pierrot the Clown masks, crucifixes of makeup crossing over the narrow eyes, the mouth-slits tittering in tight amusement; six stiletto-heeled business-skirted Italian or

Puerto Rican chicks came strutting taut-calfed up the block, all wearing 1940s Lucille Ball-Rosie the Riveter hairdos and big plastic clip-on earrings—a street gang of class ass with seamed stockings and skid-chain-slick lipstick. As soon as they passed I tried to leapfrog a parking meter and wound up crunching my nuts on the stickleback bridge of my clasped knuckles. I almost came down on my ass and a passing boing-boing with a camera around his neck wailed "Wo Cap'm: How's yer kidneys!"

"Good, good." And that was no lie.

I sat in the lobby by the Ping-Pong tank and skimmed through the *Post*. I didn't feel like seeing Fonseca just yet. A big naked white-faced clock in the manager's cage read 5:30.

The *Post*. We got the *New York Post* every day of my life when I was a kid in the Bronx, in Yonkers, but now that I was in Manhattan it seemed as exotic and alien as the *Paris-Match*. In back of the movie listings was an eighth of a page ad for Nicky and the Naks. They were playing at a supper club out in Long Island City called D'Alessio's. The ad was composed of five grainy gray stars. At the center of each was the disembodied head of Nicky and the four Naks. The heads were all tilted at different angles—I guess to communicate liveliness. Nicky looked slightly chubby, smiling with capped teeth, his hair in a manicured shag cut that made me think he was going bald. Fonseca had described him as having gaunt cheekbones and a curly waterfall like Frank Sinatra. Well, Sinatra didn't look that way anymore either. The four decapitated Naks appeared maybe ten to fifteen years younger than Nicky. They had hippie long hair and they weren't smiling. The tag line was, "He's back! And we got him! One night only!" The ad said to call for a reservation. I didn't know if Fonseca had done that or not, so I hit one of the lobby pay phones and got us a table for two for the eight o'clock show. As I hung up I debated calling Kim. Being with Fonseca made the prospect nerve-wracking. I halfheartedly dug into my pocket to see how much change I had.

A Chinaman with drumsticks in his back pocket came up and made a call on the adjoining phone. He started How Dow Cow

Yowing into the receiver so loudly that I backed off from my own call. Didn't have enough change anyhow.

I figured it was time to go back upstairs, but as I stepped up to the elevator the door groaned open and Fonseca walked out, spiffed up and slicked back, laying down a cologne track strong enough to pull your face off. It looked as if he had oiled his leather car coat, and he had a sports jacket folded over his arm like a serving napkin.

"I left a note for you." He tilted back his chin to connote the room.

"I'm goin' over to MacCarthy's on Grove Street. You know Mac-Carthy's?" Fonseca had his manila envelope smack up his armpit.

"It's early yet." I frowned at the folder.

"I wanna check this place out first. It's over on Grove about four blocks down . . . meet me there, okay? I used to hang out . . . I dunno, meet me there." He did an impatient shuffle and I stepped into the elevator.

Up in the room, the bathroom door had a softball-sized hole about a foot up from the floor bordered by a shattery corolla of whitish splinters. The note was folded on the dresser.

As I was changing into evening wear, Fonseca came bursting in.

"Forgot my wallet. Let me see, you . . . you brought a jacket, right?"

"I didn't bring a jacket. You didn't tell me to bring a jacket."

"Aw *shit*, man! What if this place has a dress code?"

"They probably have extra jackets in that case, right?"

"But what if . . . aw fuck it . . . relax . . . relax . . ."

"I'll try."

"Anyway, let me see you."

I was standing there in a white shirt, a blue crewneck, socks and underwear.

Fonseca gave me a firm-faced head-to-toe, then squinted, nodding toward my open suitcase. "What kind of pants you wearing?"

I was blushing, feeling a mixture of embarrassment and affection. No guy ever wanted to check out my clothes before. I didn't know if it made us like father and son or two sisters.

I held up a pair of tan bells and Fonseca nodded distracted approval.

As I continued to dress, Fonseca took a horse piss, washed his hands and called me into the bathroom.

"C'mere." He poured a small puddle of cologne into his palms, rubbed his hands together as if he was trying to raise a lather, and briskly peppered my cheeks with his palms. I closed my eyes in startled embarrassment and alcohol smarts and suppressed a laugh. I was so jarred and nonplussed that seconds after he finished my eyes were still closed, I was still feeling the sensation of his broad fingers on my cheekbones and hadn't realized that he was already out of the bathroom, out of the hotel, and halfway to the bar.

MacCarthy's was shadowy with a white octagon-tiled floor and dark glossy scarred wood walls and tables. Even the mirror looked wood-stained. There was only one guy drinking at the bar, middle-aged, ex-handsome, with high cheekbones, piercing eyes and a high thinning pompadour, with everything else pouchy and dropped down from drinking. The bartender was heavyset in an immaculate white shirt, the sleeves rolled back to reveal bellows-like forearms. He was just about bald, and his features were both slanty and flattened as though he was used to wearing hosiery over his face.

Fonseca sat at a rickety table in the back room, thick and impassive, a fist on his hip, kneecaps spread wide, a dark beer in front of his chest. He looked like a rugby player waiting to be cued to do a lager testimonial.

I took a seat on his left as two other guys came in and bellied up to the bar.

"See that bartender? When I was going to NYU I used to come in here. He looked just the same. I know that guy too. He used to write for the *Voice*. I think he did a book. The other guy I think used to be a middleweight. I think he wrote a book too. I used to go here all the time." Fonseca heaved himself sideways in his chair, crossing his legs and making a motion with his hand as if distractedly brushing a fly from his face. "All the time."

"Do they know you?"

He shrugged. "Who cares?"

A waitress in dungarees came and took our order. Two more dark beers, what else.

"Did you see these?" Fonseca twisted a finger in front of his nose. I looked at him in confusion. "See what?"

"The pictures," Fonseca said low out of the side of his mouth.

Ever since I'd walked in he seemed to be whispering and all his gestures were abbreviated as if he didn't want to draw attention to himself.

The pictures. Out of the shadowy walls emerged a gallery of framed photos. I pushed my chair back—the hollow scraping made Fonseca wince—and got up to take a closer look. All the pictures were portraits of customers bellied up to the bar; some looked startled, some were winking and holding up mugs, some looked irritated. By the clothes and the haircuts it seemed most of the pictures were taken in the late forties to midfifties. I recognized three or four writers and a boxer. The others could have been famous or just regulars. There was a tabloid quality to the shots and a sadness to the time-gone-byness.

The faces that I recognized, even the fat and ugly ones, had an automatic handsomeness, mainly because I associated them with an older more corrupted appearance. Everybody seemed to be saying, "This was then, I'm dead now."

When I got back to the table the beers were down. Fonseca sat supporting his head with a thumb and index finger pressed into his temples.

"It's like a fuckin' who's who, right? Okay, now go back, check out the third picture from the right, top row back wall, check it out carefully." He said that all to his beer as if we were being tailed.

I got up again. The picture was of a popeyed puffy-faced tight-lipped bloke with a head of short curls in a V formation retreating from his middle-aged hairline. He looked like one of those Irish jailbird playwright-poet drunkards, but he also might have been Jewish. I felt I had to come up with the correct name, that Fonseca would spot-quiz me. I didn't know, maybe it was Brendan Behan, Dylan Thomas, Delmore Schwartz, or maybe it was a famous Socialist journalist war correspondent or maybe it was a younger Jackie Gleason. What the hell did he want from me?

But then I saw what I was really supposed to see. Over his right shoulder, slightly out of focus, way in the background, stood Fonseca, squinting and raising a brew to the camera. He must have been nineteen, tops, and his dark features had that honeyed softness of "but that was then." His expression was half mugging, half confident, narrowing an eye, biting the corner of his lip, a just-you-wait face with no bitterness.

"Is it still up there?" Fonseca murmured, crystal-balling his glass.

"Yeah."

He snorted, then took a tentative suck at his beer, hunched over as if he had a blanket over his shoulders and the mug was filled with hot tea. I debated putting a hand on his shoulder, then vetoed it.

"You know this guy might not remember you, man," I was saying. We were driving over the Queensboro Bridge into Long Island City.

Behind us lay a rolling-hilled necropolis of mix-and-match tombstones which from our present position looked as though they were sprouting from the feet of the hot shit Manhattan skyline like some kind of ironic statement about mortality.

"Well, yeah, no, oh yeah, I don't imagine he will, but the picture will knock him out, no? Unless his fucking *brain* is fried, in which case fuck 'im, right?" Fonseca tapped the manila folder which was wedged over the dash.

"Yeah, well, I'm just sayin' don't be disappointed if things don't work out . . . you might not even get a chance to lay it on him."

"Look . . . the guy is a nobody. He lives in a goddamn housing project, or he did at any rate, and I'm saying, hey, I wanna model a book on your life, a great American whatever, a Rise and Fall and Rise, man, heavy on the Rise part."

I made awkward silent gestures of concession, more out of a desire to change the subject than because of Fonseca's impeccable reasoning.

———

D'Alessio's had valet parking. There were a few couples at the entrance to the club milling about.

"Oh shit, is this a line?" Fonseca moaned, then realized the couples were just standing and talking. Six kids, all about ten years old, ran out of the door, the girls in dresses, the boys in dark suits. "What're *kids* doin' here?"

We walked into a dimly lit red carpeted wood paneled square entrance room that had corridors running off in two directions.

A woman, fortyish, wearing a bottle-green dress and beige

strapped shoes, came out from behind a coat room dutch door. "Hi! Are you here for the LoQuesto wedding?"

"The *what?* I thought Nicky and the Naks were playing here tonight!" Fonseca looked as if he was starting to hyperventilate.

"He sure is . . . there's a wedding reception in the other room." Her silver hair was frosted and swirled on top of her head like a wrapped towel.

Two couples came in behind us.

"Anybody here for the LoQuesto wedding?"

"Yes, ma'am."

"Okay . . ." She turned to us, raised a finger for time out, stepped to the side. "It's right in there." She pointed off to one of the corridors, then grabbed three gigantic gold-tasseled red menus and stepped behind a lectern with a huge ledger book open to a drawing of a seating plan. "What name is the reservation under?"

"*What* reservation! I didn't know anything about a reservation," Fonseca squawked.

"Keller." I stepped forward. "Party of two?"

She found the name in a circle on the floor plan, checked it off.

"Jesus Christ, she scared me to death!" Fonseca touched his heart, fanning himself with the photo.

"Easy, big boy," I murmured out of the side of my mouth. I felt a belly glow at having come to the rescue.

She looked up at us a second time, "Excuse me?" She squinted as if lost in thought. I didn't know who she was talking to. "Excuse me, do you have a jacket?"

Shit! "I left it home."

"Aw, Keller!" Fonseca whined, dropping into a crouch of despair.

She gave me a guest-rack jacket, a plaid Pinky Lee special that was so tight that every time I raised my elbows the sides shot back like waterwings.

"No sweat, no sweat." Fonseca the umpire motioned safe and jutted his chin at her to lead on.

Carrying the menus like biblical tablets, she weaved us a path through a wood-paneled room with tables three-deep arranged in a horseshoe pattern that enveloped a thrusting runway stage lined with large black speakers as big as jukeboxes. Most of the tables were occupied, some with young kids who couldn't have remembered Nicky, but mainly with couples and groups somewhere between Tony's and my age. She led us to a table right at the side of the runway and dealt out the menus.

"These are great seats, hah?" Fonseca jerked his head around. The tablecloths were a heavily starched deep gold, the napkins, blood red. The silverware was broad and heavy, gleaming dully in the illumination of yellow bulbs suspended from wagon-wheel chandeliers. Four or five waitresses in ruffled outfits and with what looked like huge upside-down disposable pleated paper cups pinned on their heads moved through the room. The ones with enormous trays laid out with dinners were smiling grimaces of strain, hunch-walking swiftly like Groucho Marx, propelling themselves from the kitchen to the collapsible tray stands. Behind us sat three couples in a haze of cigarette smoke, late thirtyish, loud. One woman was wearing a blond fall and a maxi-dress; her man, a chocolate brown doubleknit suit with a tie that matched the tablecloth. The two other ladies were twins, gaunt and hyper, wearing matching simple sleeveless dresses over pale purple blouses. They had short hair, swept back in a frozen straight line from their foreheads and stopping dead at the neckline like crash helmets. Both of them puffed like demons. Before them sat glass goblets with the remains of fruit cocktail stuck to the sides.

Fonseca cocked his head and opened the menu. "Look, this whole thing is in bar mitzvah French . . . Roast beef *au jus avec* French Fries."

"I'll just have a Macedonian Fruit Cup."

Suddenly the house lights dimmed to sporadic applause. One of the twins jumped up, screamed, clapped her hands and then collapsed, curling into her sister, hands over her face, giggling in embarrassment. People laughed in sympathy. Fonseca muttered "Jerk," his stomach hanging ten. Three guys moved in the darkness on stage, turned on the amps. A sax player blew a warm-up riff, a guitar was tuned, a short drum roll. The crowd was holding their breath; there was a sporadic clinking of dinnerware; the waitresses stood against the kitchen entrance wall, their trays perpendicular to their hips.

From a PA system came a brief electronic hum, then a low male voice. "Ladies and Gentlemen. D'Alessio's is proud to present . . . the one and only . . . the incomprable . . . the unbeatable . . . the original 'street hitter' . . ." Three women screamed. ". . . the one and only . . . Nicky Lisi!"

People cheered. The stage runway lit up. The band played some cocky bluesy instrumental and Fonseca slapped my bicep with the back of his hand. "That's 'Street Hitter.'" Suddenly a spotlight hit the room entrance and everybody turned, screaming, hands flapping clapping waving, fists punching the air.

"Look at him, look at him," Fonseca murmured, a hand over his mouth.

Nicky stood in the center of the doorway, ankles touching, hands raised over his head like a triumphant wrestler, grinning, then breaking into a jog toward the stage as his theme song played, waving, slapping outstretched palms, a gauntlet of writhing fingers. He gave a sprightly little leap onto the runway, whirled around to face the audience, smiling, all his teeth showing, raising one hand in a clenched fist, winking at his backup boys, all with girl-long straight hair, boat-necked striped shirts over humpy thin frames. He blew a kiss out to the audience and women screamed, the twins standing red-faced, hugging each other, pounding their husbands on the back. "Nicky! Nicky! Nicky! Oh shit, oh man, Nicky! Nicky!"

Fonseca was totally unreadable. He was slouched back in his chair as if he had already eaten, his hand still covering his mouth and his narrowed eyes the only thing in motion, following Nicky's every gesture.

Nicky was laughing, waving, dressed in tinted glasses, black leather pants and a black leather pullover open to his flat stomach with loose crisscrossed leather laces over his chest. A black leather motorcycle cap on his head looked slightly like a yachting cap, and instead of engineering stomper boots he wore black-lacquered laced shoes with three-inch elevator heels.

Nicky held a mike to his mouth and swung his head to both sides of the stage. "Hey-y people! Long time no see! You remember me!" He coyly touched his fingertips to his chest in between the leather lacing.

Everybody went batshit. Even the men were screaming out his name.

"He looks fucking great!" some guy behind us hissed.

"Hey! I love you ladies!"

"We love *you!*" one twin shouted.

"An' where mah *boys!*" He punched the air. Half the guys roared, shaking clenched fists, bellies peeking out under ties.

It seemed that ours was the only table not going through epilepsy. I felt totally uninvolved with the show, totally focused on Fonseca.

"Awright! Do we have people from the *Bronx* here!" The entire table of twelve to our right suddenly raised a banner as if they were in the bleachers:

EDENWALD PROJECT'S MAIN MAN
NICKY LISI

Nicky craned forward, smiling, touched his glasses, read the sign. "Awright! Edenwald Projects!" He laughed.

"Hey Nicky! Hoffman Street!"

"Tremont Avenue!"

"1711 Southern Boulevard!"

"Mace Avenue!"

"James Monroe!"

"Immaculate Conception!"

"Mother Cabrini!"

"Junior High School 113!"

Everybody was flipping out, yelling up bids on his history, his hangouts.

"Bronx River Boulevard!"

"Mister Skuthan's shop class!"

"Hey! Hey! Okay, okay! I love you all!"

"Poe Park!"

I nudged Fonseca. "Hey, why don't you yell out that school?" I was semi-joking, but Fonseca shifted his eyes from Nicky to me, and his gaze was as blank-eyed as a shark's, and he held it on me long enough to make my stomach and chest feel as though they had just switched positions.

"Bathgate Avenue!"

"Finelli's Dry Cleaners!"
Nicky waved, nodded to his band.

> "Ev-ah-ry bah-dy
> needs some bah-ah-dy
> to luh-uv
> someone to luh-uv
> and I need you! you! you!
> and I need you! you! you!"

"Mr. Garafolo's gym class, Nicky!"
On every "you!" Nicky pointed to another person at ringside, touched an extended hand or two.

When he came to us, Fonseca stared down at his empty place setting, immobile and looking lost in thought. Out of reflex politeness I reached up to shake Nicky's hand, feeling a mixture of embarrassment and excitement as I felt the blinding spotlight on the side of my face. I think I even said, "Howareya" or nodded it.

People were still flipping, screaming out proper nouns. The song sucked, was very third-rate Vegas, but nobody cared.

At the final flourish of the band, Nicky straightened up with "Hey!" waving, blowing kisses.

"P.S. 41, Nicky!"

"Juvenile Court!"

"Awright, okay, awright! Enough already with the names. Ooh yeah! Memory Lane! I love 'em all. I love *you* all!"

I didn't know if Fonseca was mad at me or not, and I adopted his posture of sullen repose, staring off, focusing on the shoelaces that peeked beneath Nicky's black leather bellbottoms.

In my head I kept saying, "Howareya."

"I bet I know what you people want to hear," Nicky said slyly, winking at the room.

"Street Hitter!" roared a short bulky gravel-throated guy about Fonseca's age, red-faced, mustachioed, eyes blazing with urgency, beefy hands cupped around his mouth. The suddenness, the loudness, caught everybody off-guard. The room turned to him, some people laughing. Embarrassed, he quickly sat down.

"Hey!" Nicky laughed. "You want to hear 'Street Hitter'?" he said directly to the guy, so that no one else shouted out "yeah."

"Yes I do," he harumphed, his eyes averted.

"Well, why don't you come on up here and help out with it, okay?" The guy leaned back in his chair, waved no.

"Ah, c'mon!"

People started shouting encouragement. The guy's date nudged him in the ribs. He let his head hang to one side, smiling, considering, then hoisted himself to his feet. People applauded. Nicky, mike in hand, joined the applause. The guy scraped his chair back, came around his table and began the long walk up to the stage. He was a short chunky bruiser, no more than 5'6". He shot his cuffs, straightened his tie, and walked with a side-to-side jerky self-important swagger. His hands kept moving from his cufflinks to his tie knot, his face serious, puffy. He pulled his trouser material up his thigh before stepping up on stage, shook Nicky's hand, waved back to his table.

"You gonna help me sing 'Street Hitter'?"

"Yes, I am." His voice was tough and hoarse.

"You ever sing before?"

"Ah used to sing with mah boys on the *street!*"

"Awright! Me too!" Nicky smiled. "What street are we talking about?"

"Matthews Avenue, between Burke and Allerton in the *Bronx!*" He gave a short jerked fist-shake. Some cheers.

"That where you live now?"

"Now I'm right here in Queens . . . Nicky, I just wanna say I think you are the greatest."

Some applause.

"What's your name, mah man?"

"Louie Fisher." He wiped sweat from his mustache, planted his legs and shot his cuffs again.

"You *work* in Queens, Louie?"

"Yes, I do. I am assistant sales manager for Two Guys."

"And one last question before we do 'Street Hitter,' Louie . . ." He put his arm around Louie's shoulder and whispered into the mike. "Who is that sly fox out at that table you got up from?"

Louie barked and waved. "That's my beautiful wife, Sonia."

"Awright, Sonia!" Nicky turned to the band. "You ready, boys?"

"Ah got a son, too," Louie said, but only the tables by ringside heard him, because Nicky had swung the mike around.

Fonseca closed his eyes and let out a short "phew" of sadness.

The sax did a lead-in that got people screaming again, everybody rising, standing over their dinners.

"Ready, Louie?"

"Yes, I am." He pulled his tie down.

The waitress came with the food for our table. Fonseca, with a minimum of movement, slid the manila folder out of the way. "Tony, you okay?" I leaned toward him.

He put a hand up, palm to me. I couldn't tell if it signified that I should back off, or if it meant he was okay. I think it meant back off.

> "We're street hitters, no quitters,
>   well we'll fight all night and we'll come out on top
>   you know it's be all right because no one can stop
>   the street hitters,
>   the street hitters."

People stood up all around, grim-faced and tight, clapping hands, some singing alone, neck cords straining.

I hunched over my dinner, eyes down. Fonseca seemed to be entranced by the glittering tributaries of fat in his prime rib. He made no movement to eat.

Louie Fisher was flat, off key, but serious as hell, punctuating every other word with a short punch. The whole room was stomping and singing like a cabal of old Nazis five years after Hitler's death doing *"Deutschland Uber Alles"* in a secret beer hall.

"Street hitters, no quitters . . ."

The twins behind us were rocking from side to side, swirling their hands between beats in a hand jive.

"Because no one can *stop!*" Nicky raised his hand. The band cut it dead.

"The street hitters!" Louie sang a cappella into the mike, realized he sang it alone and flushed red.

"Yeah!" Nicky applauded Louie and himself, and everyone roared approval.

Louie and Nicky slapped palms, then Louie grabbed Nicky's hand in his own two, looked up at him, talking intensely, words inaudible in the cheering, eyes narrowed, shaking that hand, finally letting go, waving to the crowd, strutting back to his table, glowing and shaking a raised fist to the room.

"Awright, mah man Louie!"

Louie leaned back expansively in his chair, face glistening, nodded and gave the "V" sign, his head rearing back from his fingers. He had his other arm around Sonia.

"What a fucking moron," I muttered to Fonseca.

No reaction.

"But that takes balls, what he did, though. I would die if that was me."

No reaction.

The whole show was a lounge act, not good not bad. He did a nice version of Jay and the Americans' "Only in America" and a totally embarrassing version of "Soul Man." He threw in a few lame jokes about the old neighborhood and then he got serious. "You know people"—adjusting his glasses—"I guess I can talk to you frankly 'cause you're like family to me and tonight, I dunno, tonight is magic." He looked at his shoes. ". . . real magic for me. The last ten years, the last . . . aw, I'm not gonna bullshit you. The last ten years were hell . . . man, when I hit the skids I landed hard. I was a, I was a *smack* freak, a *pill* freak, *booze*, my *wife* walked out on me, whom I *still* love," he sighed. "I lost my *voice*, my *friends*, I lost everything. But mostly I lost myself. I lost Nicky Lisi . . ."

The place was a church. Louie Fisher frowned knowingly. I thought it bizarre that in his Hour of Truth he would refer to himself as Nicky. Fonseca had said his name was Richard.

"Then one day I was in some flea-bag hotel in Lost Angeles lying in some bed, swimming my way to the bottom of a bottle of Scotch and . . . I still don't know what happened . . . I heard a voice . . . it said Get up! I guess it was the DTs, but it sounded like my old man, God rest his soul. Get up! it said. So shit, I got up. Then the voice said, Look at yourself in that mirror! So I shambled over in my funky unshaven state to this cracked mirror and the voice said, Take a good look! And I did. And what I saw scared the *hell* out of me, people. I was twenty-seven and I looked fifty. Eyes all red and baggy, my skin was yellow, cheeks sunk . . . but the eyes . . . the eyes were the worst. They were eyes of a man who got kicked in the ass by life and slunk away like a dog with its tail between its legs . . . they were the eyes of a weakling, a *coward*. And then I heard the voice say, Nicky, you can leave this room one of two ways: you can straighten up and go out the door, or you can go out the window! And I tell you, I stood over that open window a good long time, but I guess you people know which exit I finally took and . . . and there's been a lot of times since then I felt like I shoulda taken that damn window but . . . I think of nights like tonight and nights to come, and all I can say . . ." He choked and gulped.

Sporadic sniffs came out of the darkness. The twins were weeping.

"All I can say is . . . I love you, people. I love you . . . you're family, people, and if . . . if you weren't here . . . *I* wouldn't be here."

"We love *you*, Nicky!" the woman in the blond fall blared out, clapping her hands, squinting, a cigarette between her lips.

"Yeah," murmured through the room.

"You're the *best*, Nicky!"

"I'd like to finish with a song, that's *not* mine, a song you all know, a song which has had very special meaning for me these days . . ."

Without a cue the band started up.

> "That's life . . .
>   that's what the people say,
>   you're ridin' high in April,
>   shot down in May,

c'mon everybody!"

People joined in. Guys were sniffing, women wiping their noses. The twelve-person table held up their "Edenwald Project's Main Man Nicky Lisi" sign, moving it back and forth in time.

> "I been a puppet, a pauper,
>   a pirate, a poet . . ."

"Hey Tony? You should take notes, man." C'mon Big Boy, gimme a sign.

Fonseca's hand was still covering his mouth, his eyes in a neutral squint. Suddenly he dropped his hand, exposing a killer smirk, reached for his heavy fork and started to bang it loudly against his plate in time to the music. The sound made me flinch. I did a quick scan for bouncers or pissed-off customers. Somebody else started in with his silverware, then somebody else and pretty soon there was a fork chorus in time to "That's Life."

Fonseca snorted, grabbed his steak knife and started waving it in the air like a baton, all the time staring down at his untouched dinner.

Nicky took it in stride. He started imitating Fonseca's sing-along gesture, batoning the crowd with both hands.

My stomach started ejaculating adrenaline. I got up and duck-walked toward the door as if I would be blocking a movie projector light.

From out in the vestibule the clinking and clanging sounded more like a prison mess hall protest than a Sinatra bang-along, but over it all Nicky's voice came through loud and clear:

> "Each time I find myself,
> flat on my *face*
> I *pick* myself *up*,
> and get *back* in the *race*!"

The vestibule was deserted. Behind the closed door where the LoQuesto wedding was going on I heard some guy over a mike singing "Up Up and Away," backed up by an accordion.

It was like fucking Collegetown-mall-land all over again. I didn't know what to do with myself. I wandered down a long narrow red-carpeted lane looking for a bathroom. About halfway down a guy stood leaning against the wall, picking his teeth with a photograph. Past him at the end of the lane was a door.

"Excuse me, is that the john?"

"Uh-uh, no."

"Do you know where it is?"

He shrugged, more lost in thought than rude, and, ignoring me, slid down the wall into a squat, the photo balanced on his kneecaps. He was tapping his thumb knuckle against his forehead. From back in the room I heard Nicky finishing up. "I tried to quit . . . but my heart—and my fans—wouldn't buy it."

There was an ending flourish, declarations of love. The guy against the wall gave out with a shuddery nasal exhalation, stood up straight, held the photo chest height like a help-me-I'm-blind sign, tucked it under his arm, put it between his knees, smoothed back his hair, squatted on his haunches, stood up.

I heard a soft tromping coming from the room and saw a shadow growing from around the bend, heard dozens of people shouting "Hey Nicky! Nicky!" and just as I got up to the guy against the wall, I saw Nicky wheeling into the lane, leading what looked like the entire audience, shouting in his ear, waving photos, yearbooks, various mementos.

I felt a palm on my chest and I was thrust against the opposite wall by the guy with the photo. He didn't do it to save me from being stampeded, he did it to get me out of his way. I stood flattened as the flood came closer, Nicky chanting, "Yeah, hey great," moving fast, almost running, smiling nonstop.

"Nicky, you remember my Aunt Felice? She fainted at a concert a yours in Wildwood, You remember that?"

"Yeah, great!"

Louie Fisher had his hand on Nicky's shoulder, thumping along, his head turned to the following pack. "Hey, lay off him, hah?" Protecting Nicky's face, serious, important, Nicky trying to move out from under the sweaty sport-jacketed arm without losing his smile. Suddenly the four long-haired band members broke through the crowd, racing ahead, brushing past me and the photo guy to get the door.

As Nicky came abreast of us, the photo guy flashed his picture, an ancient color print, tinted yellow, of two kids on a camel. I sucked in my gut and leaned my cheek against the wall, my hands protecting my ribs as the crowd surged past. Nicky may or may not have said "Howareya" to me. Someone stepped on my foot.

Nicky lunged for the dressing room door held open by a band member.

"Nicky! I dated your cousin!"

Louie Fisher let go of Nicky's shoulder and wheeled to face the crowd. "Lay off the man, hah?" Then he turned to Nicky. "You mind if I come . . ." The dressing room door slammed in his face.

Louie, looking gutshot, turned to the crowd, which was still yelling out Nicky's name: "Okay, he's tired, let him rest, let him rest." His voice was gravel hoarse and he stood there white-faced, pulling on his cuffs, planting and replanting his legs, standing up against the closed door.

People were pissed. "What's he doin' in there! Hey Nicky! What kinda shit is this!" Then slowly, in groups of threes and fours, they started shuffling back toward the lobby, until it was just me, the photo guy and Louie Fisher. I was still flat against the wall, my hands and arms still protecting my body. In the new breathy silence I could hear my heart beat hammering away in my temples.

Eventually, the photo guy casually lurched himself off the wall and, ignoring Louie Fisher, walked up and kicked the dressing room door before trudging off without looking back. I stood up straight and smoothed back my hair with trembly fingers. I thought I had a broken toe. Louie Fisher just stood there guard-dogging, constantly lifting his feet as if he was standing in muck, rolling his neck, and staring wild-eyed down the corridor, not even seeing me.

From behind the dressing room door came the smell of grass. Someone yelled for a Pepsi.

I limped back into the room. Fonseca was still slouched at the table, thrusting his tongue against the inside of his cheek, making him look like he had a case of rolling mumps, his head cocked so that his ear was almost touching his shoulder. He was absently playing with his spotless manila folder, standing it on its edges and running his fingers down the borders.

"C'mon let's blow," I warbled, nodding toward a vague outside.

Fonseca got to his feet without the slightest hiss or sigh. His face was so chillingly composed that I was afraid he'd head straight for the dressing room, bull through the door and calmly strangle Nicky Lisi.

Halfway across the room I looked back at our table and saw the manila folder still lying there.

"Hey Tony?" I touched his arm and he turned to me with that murderously even expression. If I wanted to die, all I had to do was tell him he forgot his picture.

"We paid, right?" I grinned.

Out in the vestibule, Fonseca paused at the head of the lane to the dressing room. Louie Fisher, down by the locker door, waved him away. "He can't see anybody now, he's resting."

As we walked out, Louie's wife, Sonia, was standing near the reservations podium. She wore a turquoise dress and had her hair pulled to one side, draped over her breast in a lone snakey tress. She smoked a Virginia Slim. Four lipstick-smudged Virginia Slim filters stood upright like milestones in a sand-filled urn at her side.

Fonseca lay belly down on his swaybacked bed in the hotel room. I stood there, frowning down at his corpse, asking monotonous and moronic "Y'awright? Y'okay?" type questions. He hadn't said word one since we left D'Alessio's.

The overhead was making me freak. I wanted to turn on a more indirect light or shoot Fonseca.

"Y'okay?" I asked again, shifting my weight so that I stood with one hip high, my thumbs hooked into the corners of my front pockets. Fonseca's face was sunk into the pillow.

I wanted out of that room. All Nicky Lisi had sung that night was "Tony's Swan Song" and now I knew Tony was lying there thinking nothing meant anything anymore, and I was afraid to see what he would do with that notion once the sulks wore off, given the fact that he still had his health.

"Listen, I'm gonna go down now, okay?" I said, staring at Fonseca's lifeless upturned palm. "Okay? Do you want anything from downstairs? You want me to bring you up something?" I had the image of an old-fashioned cardboard pint container of Breyer's Vanilla with a dainty little wire handle. "Okay, so I'll see you later . . . take care."

When I got downstairs the Village nighttime street scene was in full wail. It reminded me of a post-dinner-pre-taps armed camp. Lots of blazing lights, hovering clusters and scattered music. From where I was standing I could see the herky-jerky elevated torso of a unicyclist, his wheel blocked from my view by the shoulders of his crowd; a handwriting analyst who was holding court on a card table in front of a supermarket; two arroyo-faced old cowboys playing

Hawaiian guitars in front of a cash machine and four purple-faced derelicts nodding out over each other in a half-assed bleary huddle trying to get it together to harmonize a cappella on "Johnny B. Goode."

I walked the few blocks to Sheridan Square, a triangular island with a subway entrance and a newsstand. The unicyclist whooshed down below the shoulders of his audience. There was applause and although I couldn't see him, his unicycle was being held aloft in triumph. The brown-bag quartet moved on from "Johnny B. Goode": three of them doing "Maybelline" and the bass man trying a cross between "Nadine" and "Roll Over Beethoven."

Behind me two chicks in watch caps and peacoats, arm in arm, leaned against the wall of a dyke bar, smiling in patient amusement as a drunk black guy struggling to keep his eyes open frowned grumpily and gestured with his hand over his head, wrist curled, finger pointing downward like a question mark. "Now . . . I wan' you chicks to es-*plain* to me." He shot his finger toward his shoes. "Is a damn *shame*, you's *pretty* wimmin!" He crumpled into a crouch on "pretty."

One of the chicks laughed, pumped a cigarette out of a pack, brought it to her lips, gave the pack another shake to shoot some butts past the foil, and extended it to the black guy.

"Thank you," he said in a sad mollified voice, taking half a dozen cigarettes in one whooshing motion of four long fingers.

I was standing across from Village Cigars, pretty much where we had got stuck in traffic earlier. There was no jam now, but the traffic around the square bled into Seventh Avenue at six different points and the nonstop bullet-fast fuck-you maneuvering, the near misses, the synchronized swervings, were making me swoon. Standing on the traffic island at night watching this gleaming horsepowered death ballet was ten times freakier than anything on two feet, including the guy standing next to me yelling "Read all about it! Read all about it!" He didn't have any newspapers.

I felt hypnotized with that same smiley shock that people experience the first time they snorkel over a coral reef, that first head-dip into another world, another medium. I felt a dreamy surrender to gliding things that could either put on a show or eat me and all I was able to do was watch, drift and remember to breathe.

Across from me the winos were wallowing their way through "Good Golly Miss Molly." A well-dressed gray hair in a turtleneck and a camel coat hand in hand with a piece of ass thirty years his junior glared at them and gnashed his teeth. "I *love* this! I *love* this! *This* is life! You won't find this in L.A." He sneered, shaking his head ferociously. "This is New *York!* . . . I'll show you things here, I'll show you . . . Oh Chr*rist!* It's a life *soup* here!" He squeezed her cheeks with his fingertips so that her gums showed, top and bottom, kissed her, "Mm*ma!*" and thrust a dollar like a subpoena at one of the singers before moving on down the line. The dude pocketed the bill and stepped forward; "And now, a tribute to Danny and the Juniors . . . the early years."

I stood on the island from ten-thirty to eleven-thirty. I didn't have any thoughts worth recollecting, but I didn't miss a trick. My eyes were narrowed and my head was cocked to the side as if I was about to say "listen." The real newsdealer on the traffic island, an old guy with a kind voice standing under the green canvas flap of his stand, kept saying, "Thanks pal" to everybody who bought a paper. He sounded out of his mind with sincerity, hundreds of deep "thanks pals," and I heard every one.

There was so much to scope out it felt dangerous to move, because to shift a fraction of an inch changed the angle of vision, made everything different. I wasn't a street whack, I was just getting oriented. When I was fifteen I had held on to my first tit without moving a finger for three and a half hours. When I was sixteen I put "James Brown Live at the Apollo" on my record player, sat on the edge of my bed one afternoon, and when I next raised my head I saw it was eight-thirty. At first I thought someone had fucked with the clock until I looked out the window.

So now I was standing in the middle of Sheridan Square, ignoring two screw-bolt spasms of cold boring into my shoulder blades, flat-footed, gaping, thinking great blank thoughts, feeling as if someone had just plunged his thumbs in the plumb of my substance, his fingernails on my outlines, then deftly flipped his hands so that everything went inside-out like a photo negative, an X-ray, a James Brown shriek.

I felt a grinding in my stomach, my jaws, my fingertips, that made me want to growl. I wanted to eat the street.

I started roaming the streets, walking all the way from the Square to the Hudson River and back. At some point I found myself cruising down a short landmark-looking block of eighteenth-century pastel three-story darlings and I got caught up short by the sound of group singing emanating from the doorway of a bar called Attar.

The place was below street level and I had to walk down six steps to get to the floor, but that was as far as I could go. The room was packed to capacity.

The walls were lined with autograph-littered theater posters and round frosted vanity lights. In the far corner were a spotlit piano, piano player and a singer on a bar stool. The singer was leading everybody in a rousing chorus of "Oklahoma!," the whole joint going "Ohhh-hh-kla-homa, where the wind comes . . ." right on cue and in perfect pitch, a hundred youngish, attractive faces tensed, arched and heartily furrowed with dramatic gusto. They sang all the words, everybody. Lyrics I never knew existed. And everybody was good. I felt as if I had walked into the set of a musical. Next came "Bali Hai," the whole place singing and swaying gently like palm fronds in the trade winds. Once again, everybody was totally in tune. I sat down on the top interior whitewashed step and watched the show. I wondered if you had to pass an audition to get a drink. It had to be the world's most talented bar crowd. The singer got up from the stool, waving coyly to the applause, and weaved his way through the tables to his clique. People descended into a chattery hubbub. The piano player, thin, tortoise-shelled, casually spiffy in a cashmere sweater and no shirt, craned his head over the top of his piano.

"Is Emmett here?"

"Yes!" One of the waiters stopped with his tray. "He's in the john . . . Emmett!" he yodeled.

People picked up the call and, on cue, Emmett came banging out of the bathroom to a roomful of hah-hahs, and plopped down on the stool passing the heel of his hand carefully across his forehead.

"Christ, you made me pee all over myself!" He was a chubby toothy guy, prepped out in chinos and a Lacoste shirt. He reminded me of James Madison. He had that same pink boiled skin and impeccable short shiny hair. James Madison. I clapped my hands and laughed out loud. All those fantasies I used to have at A.C. of where

everybody went afterwards. They must have come here. Or someplace like here. The whole joint looked as if they were packing
photo resumés. From my elevated seat I had to squat down, my
chest almost touching my kneecaps, in order to get a clear pan of
the low-ceilinged room. I didn't imagine I'd actually see anybody
from A.C. and I didn't.

Emmett and the piano player exchanged nods and this chubby
little pink ball of talent began to sing, "Be-ess, you is mah womann
naowww." The song was so wrong I thought he was doing it as self
-parody. His voice was clean and rich, his head tilted toward the
audience, eyebrows arched in expressive sincerity, but you have to
be fucking kidding.

Next he did, "Ohh, I got plen-ty o' nuffin' an' nuffin's plenty fo'
meee." It was like Margaret Dumont doing Big Mama Thornton or
Wally Cox doing a medley of chain-gang work chants.

But people dug him, some singing along, responding more to
his good clear voice, his earnest face, than anything else.

He finished up with "The Impossible Dream," which was a little
more appropriate. That song must have been a house special because everybody joined in, audience, bartender, waiter, piano man,
everybody throwing back their heads and doing the do, raising the
roof in Youngbloods harmony.

Next up was another rotund fag, this one though was not so pink
and Lacostey; he wore bib overalls over a silk shirt with bloused-
out sleeves. He had shoulder-length bleached hair and a touch of eye
makeup. People started laughing before he even got comfortable on
his stool, and he gazed out over the room with mock innocent be-
wilderment, one eyebrow raised in droll dismay. He held a cigarette
Bette Davis style, the V line of shoulder, elbow and wrist ending in
an upturned palm as sharp and angular as a hieroglyph.

He made no move to speak, just Jack Bennyed the joint, seeing
how long he could keep the laughter rolling. After two effortless
minutes, he put everybody back on the ground with a weary sigh.
"Okay." He grabbed the mike. "Listen . . ." He paused. People sat,
their mouths slightly ajar, eyes glistening as if to get a jump on the
next guffaw. "I *really* don't feel like singing tonight. I'm feeling kind
of . . ." He squinted off into the posters. "Oh, I dunno, *mono*loguey.

I dunno, I want to re*cite* something, okay?" He cleared his throat, fingers on his breastbone. Blurty ripples of expectant laughter gusted lightly through the room.

I wished that was me up there, a house favorite, a powerhouse of irony and timing, cool and supple on stage, kicking ass with my presence.

"Okay, this is one of the great speeches by a great actress in a great movie . . . here goes."

I was expecting one of the great hawky bitches of years gone by, but when he started in I found myself laughing so hard and so fast that my face felt twisted; my mouth shaped for yoks and my eyes and forehead wrinkled in dismay at losing my self-control so easily.

"No, no, it was *you* Chah-lee. It was *you*. You was my brother. You shoulda taken better care of me."

He did it straight-faced, his natural slightly breathy effeminate voice made no effort to sound like Marlon Brando, but he looked serious, no winking, leering.

"He got a shot at the title . . . and all I got was a one-way ticket to Palookaville." He stopped, looking incensed and baffled by the hysteria.

People were buckled over as if someone had just sprayed the room with stomach-cramp mist. He sat up there looking slightly pissed, patiently smoking, unsmiling, until the laughter died down enough for him to continue. "It was my *night*, Chah-lee."

Everybody fell apart again, braying and bawling. By the time he finished up, people were sprawled back cooing and sighing from exhaustion, myself included. I was laid out on the white steps as if I had been trampled by a fire-panicked mob. But I kept trying to fight it.

Nobody had the balls to go up after that, and the piano player had to play with himself, diddling around with familiar show tunes. Occasionally someone would sing along solo from a seat in the midst of the tables or from the bar, but after that monologue the spotlit stool was glowing with Excalibur-like challenge.

People at the bar milled around the fat fag, pawing him, imitating him to himself and each other. He was still playing his bewildered act, whining "I don't under-stannd!" but he was bubble-bathing in the adoration.

I stared at that stool like a crazed housewife would stare at a curtain on a game show. I couldn't do what he did, but I could do something else. I could do that, get up there, get up there . . . But with what? I felt empty-handed, empty-headed. What. What. I felt like marching up there, sitting down and screaming, "I want! I want! I want! I want!" until everybody applauded my Richter scale.

I started chuckling out loud, briskly scratching the back of my hand. I felt terribly lonely, un-egged on. I shrugged with animation once. I stood up and nudged the first guy I saw who wasn't in a conversation, a quiet long-necked tight-lipped customer with a triangular Adam's apple.

"That guy was a scream."

He nodded in agreement, his head bobbing slowly like a float in syrup.

"It must be a bitch to get up there like that."

The same gluey head nod.

Feeling encouraged, I wandered through the room, casually squeezing my way through the crowd, both hands jammed into my back pockets. I managed to make it up to the front near the piano. The stool seemed slightly out of proportion, slightly larger than a stool should be. As the piano player worked his way through "Maple Leaf Rag," I took a casual swipe at the edge of the seat as if to free some shred of fabric caught in a splinter, then retreated, bulling my way to the bar. I wound up sitting next to two women who were in a vigorously pleasant conversation, puffing and laughing away. What. What. What. Power Plower. Mom at the monster movies. Get fucking real, this is show-time, not psychoanalysis.

The two women sitting next to me were an odd couple; one was middle-aged with choppy ash-blond hair, an expensive-looking plum wool pants suit, a silk scarf around her tendony throat, and matching lizard shoes and bag.

Her friend was black, my age, with a short parted Afro forming a slanted triangle shooting off the side of her head like a jaunty Nehru cap. Her facial features were all coarse and outsized; a big gap between her huge front teeth, lips as thick and grainy as thumb-knuckles, bulbous apple cheeks and blotchy skin. But her eyes and voice crackled with dream energy, a crazy rough-edged power. I had a feeling that if she decided to take a shot at a song she'd hit some notes that would make the frosted bulbs around the posters pop like carnival-booth targets. Unlike her fashion-plate pal, she wore an unflattering pair of striped bellbottoms, sandals over socks, and a linty blue pullover.

The two of them sat cross-legged on their stools, smoking and yakking like sisters. The older woman, who was sitting closest to me, kept rubbing the bottom of the shoe of her crossed leg against my knee. Every time she jerked with laughter or a cigarette cough she would leave a little dirt track along the side of my lower thigh. I didn't say anything because it was unexpected contact. I stared down at the upturned ankle that showed above the smart grayish pump. She was wearing hosiery and one corner of the reinforced heel peeked out in a dark triangle above the edge of the shoe. I had a desire to straighten her stocking so it didn't show. Just beneath her ankle was a tangled ganglion of fine blue veins.

Suddenly they both exploded in a big yok, leaving a stripe up my leg from kneecap to hip.

"Oh dear," the white woman singsonged, a four-finger prong on her breastbone. "I *love* to laugh." She stubbed out her cigarette and split for the bathroom. The black woman chuckled, her yellowy slanted eyes watching the other one's progress, then she turned her attention to gently sculpting the ash end of her cigarette on the rim of the ashtray. She wasn't smiling anymore, in fact she was frowning, almost scowling. At first I thought the change-up was because she was concentrating on the ash-work, but suddenly her face completely caved in and she started crying. It was a turnaround of such abrupt violence that I was convinced in a second that she was totally, hospitalizably, nuts. She stood up, face down-curled and soured with misery like a Greek tragedy mask and stuffed all her shit in her bag, pausing for a split second to wipe tears from her bulbous cheeks with the heel of her palm.

"Get *out* of here, Deirdre!" she scolded herself with theatrical clarity. By the time the bathroom door swung open, she was halfway up the six steps to the street.

"Ahh," the white lady sighed as she returned refreshed to her stool, ready for another round of laughs. She took in the vacated seat with startled bird's eyes.

"Did you see where my friend went?" She cocked her head at me. The knot of her scarf was on the other side of her ropey neck since leaving the bar.

"She split." I shrugged.

"Awwww," she pouted, with that same theatrical clarity. "Did she say anything?"

"No." I had the weird heady sensation that I was talking to the richest person I had ever met in my life. It wasn't so much the taste-ful expensive clothes, the gold lighter, the understated jewelry, the trained thrum of her voice, as much as it was a smell coming off her on this chilly mid-November night that jarred me into thinking of suntan oil and beaches.

"Hmpf!" Hand on hip she frowned, furrowing her brow with hambony perplexity. Finally, she sighed, her shoulders shooting up to her ears, and lit another cigarette.

She sat back down, propped up her foot and got back into the dirt track on my leg, but this time she saw what she did and her face turned all Os with horror, and she immediately started rubbing a cocktail napkin along the outside of my leg.

"Hey no, that's okay," I blurted, making no move to stop her.

My price for this defilement of my person was conversation, which was A-okay with her.

"This place is great." I panned the room.

"Oh!" She threw back her head. "It's wonderful! And *I* discov-ered it! Can you believe that? Deirdre has lived in New York all her life, and I've been here a grand total of four months in the last thirty years, and she didn't even know this place ex*i*sted! I said to her, 'You have *got* to come down with me and see it to believe it . . . *won*derful, *tal*ented, *beau*tiful kids, you'll fit right in, you'll never leave . . .' Is she coming right back? She didn't say anything?"

"She looked like she was leaving for good." I tried to guess the lady's age; it was hard to tell except that I imagined she was older than she looked. Her face had that buffed, translucent skin-clinic glow.

"She's a strange one, Deirdre, but she's got it." She winked like a shrewd gypsy. "She's got it. I see people in our class, I don't know if *I've* got it, but I can always tell if somebody else's got it, and she's got it. I'm the oldest one in there by a good twenty-five, thirty years,

I've got a good twenty years on the teacher even, and let me tell you something, I can see things . . . people's character, their carriage, I can tell just how far people are going to go . . ."

"Go where?" I felt slightly troubled.

"Yup. That poor kid has definitely got it."

"Got what?"

"I'll tell you honestly . . . my only fear is that when success finds her, and it will, it will, I know these things, when success finds her, I hope she can handle it and I hope it doesn't destroy her, but as soon as I saw her in class I said Natalie, make that gal a friend of yours. I've been on this campaign since I came to New York . . . new life, new friends, and that girl is gonna be friend number one, because she's hungry, she's a doer. I've had thirty years of fat-ass suburban friends and now my kids are grown, my husband wants out. I'm goin' to New York and pick up where I left off in 1951. So I checked into the same hotel I lived in before I got married, I take class at the same Playhouse, and I'm gonna have girlfriends like I used to have. The thing with Deirdre is that she's kind of shy. I think it might be a racial thing too, but I have been dogging her to be friends for months. I've offered her clothes. I've offered her dinner. I've offered her my experience. I've been hounding her like a suitor." She suddenly stopped and popped a hand over her mouth. "Oh, my God," she drawled. "Maybe she thinks . . . maybe she thinks I'm a lesbian . . . I'll be damned . . . can you imagine that?"

"I'm gonna be in an acting class too," I said more to myself.

She rested three papery fingers on my wrist. "She's young enough to be my daughter . . . oh, my God, I'll bet that's it. . . . I even said to her one of the nice things about this place is that it's probably the only bar in town where a single woman can go without being hassled by men . . . that *is* funny . . . I wonder if I should confront her on that. I've spent thirty years keeping my mouth shut and it gets you nowhere . . . unh!" She closed her eyes and shook her head like a heavy bell. "What I have learned in the last thirty years, what I know now, I'm like a Geiger counter of truth . . . I'm telling you I look into those kids' faces . . . you, you and you, everybody else, you might as well save your money for law school."

I had been listening to her babble-ogue with a mixture of sadness, awe and a pinch of lust. I couldn't tell if she was hitting on me, but something about her last statement caught me up short; I totally believed she could tell who was going to make it. Maybe it was hitting home with the law school rap, but all of a sudden I felt my stomach whitecap with anxiety as if I was in the presence of someone who had the test results, the letters of acceptance. She became as old and powerful as a kindergarten teacher.

"How can you tell who's gonna make it?" My voice came out weak and far away.

Before she could answer someone harrumphed into the mike, and we both wheeled to the piano. Sitting on the stool was some Sad Sack with coat hanger posture and a big long nose like an inverted question mark. He started reciting Lenny Brace's "Lima Ohio" routine about playing a small midwestern club and being invited to dinner by the only Jews in town.

"So then they show me the closet. It's nice, it's nice . . . I like the way you put the towels on top like that. Some people do it the other way. The piano, which nobody can play; the whole purpose of the piano is to hold up that eight-by-ten photo of that shlub in the army suit . . . that's Morty. See, the whole purpose of showing you the house is to point out how dirty the earlier tenants were. 'We cleaned and cleaned . . .' "

People were laughing mainly, I assume, because they'd never heard the routine before. But I knew the guy was fucking it up, saying lines out of sequence, making up stuff, he didn't even have it memorized properly. And his pacing was off, too fast and punchliney. He didn't have the right inflection. It was all fucked up. Natalie was laughing too, a strange titter like Margaret Dumont getting hit on by Groucho Marx. She had to be kidding.

I sat there on my stool scratching my arms, mouthing corrections. This guy gave me the anxiety sweats about ten times worse than the fag, because I knew I could do better than this guy and that there was no excuse for me not to get up there if *he* could. I went into the bathroom and whispered Lenny Bruce to the blurry mirror.

". . . and I could see that he had this searching look in his eyes. . . . Are you Jewish? I said yeah, what's the big deal, are we hiding out from the Bund?"

I couldn't remember it either.

"I was staying in the show business hotel. One guy staying there ran the projector at the movie house and another was the Capezio shoe salesman."

The hell with it. My face kept going from Lenny Bruce's shruggy heavy-lidded expressions to one of bug-eyed frustration.

Fuck it. I don't want to do tributes, man, I want to do my own, my own stuff.

When I came out again, the guy was going on about the chick that the Scheckners invited over for Lenny Bruce to look at, who looked like a hockey stick with hair.

"Can you imagine anyone who looks bad in a *knit dress?*"

Laughter. That line comes first, putz.

In the middle of his applause, I touched Natalie on the arm: "How can you tell who's gonna make it?"

She gave me a weary-wise expression, but no words. I was getting pissed. Before I could push it, the place abruptly broke out in cheers of encouragement as three "kids" took the stage. There was a chubby buoyant girl in mannish clothes and a big floppy Spanky hat. She was flanked by two sylphlike fay males. As the piano started with simple rhythmic repetitive tink-tonk notes, the three of them started bobbing up and down out of synch with each other like playful pistons and singing some song inviting me to take a ride in their Model T. It was a bouncy googley piece of shit, and their asexual cheerfulness came across to me as kiddy-show false as that Huck Finn picture in the hotel room. Natalie's hands were clasped over her crossed knees, and she tick-tocked her head from shoulder to shoulder in time to the piano, her face spray-painted with delight. As I watched her responding so dutifully to the Model T song I had the depressing thought that not only was she full of shit about her power to read futures but that she probably hated and envied everybody in the room.

After the number was finished she turned back to the bar and sighed a loud "Ahh!" as if the air was flushed with mint.

"So what do *you* do?" She lit her cigarette with two hands, the fingers of one forking the filter against her lips, the other holding the gold lighter. Head bowed, she peered at me, her eyes on either side of the blue flame. For a suspended instant I lived inside her and had a flash of bright white molten pain inside my forehead.

"Me?" I gave it a full ten count. "I'm in an acting class too . . .

but also I'm a comic . . . a comedian." I smiled, trying to fight down a nervous blurty laugh at the sheer ballsyness of what I had just said. For a few seconds my vision went double on me.

"Ah . . . ah-ha," she said neutrally. She looked away as if lost in thought, half-smiling, gazing at the ceiling. The lights gleamed around the scrubbed alabaster bumps and boulders of her scoured and lubricated face.

"A comedian," she said lightly, refocusing her eyes on me.

"That's what the man said . . ." I felt calm. We sat facing the piano without speaking. I kept running that line, "That's what the man said," through my head.

Suddenly she stood up and shrugged a fur over her shoulders. "Time for my beauty sleep."

"I'm not a one-liner type comic." I sought out her eyes. "I'm more like a storyteller comic . . . I do narrative stuff."

She smiled at me as if that explained everything she wondered about in terms of the cosmos.

I stood there slightly hunched over, absently popping my knuckles. "I do a lot of autobiographical stuff."

I left fifteen minutes after she did, right in the middle of "I'm Gonna Wash That Man Right Out of My Hair," sung by a young emaciated guy with heavy black horn rims and a blond crop, center parted and pomaded down as flat as paint. He punctuated each line with Rockette high kicks.

It was three in the morning, and I paced the streets frowning, still popping my knuckles, thinking out loud. What to do. My class. Me and Mom at the monster movies. I could do . . . I could do . . .

At four-thirty in the morning, just as the street was settling down, it hit me. I should do Power Plower. Half that place knew what that scene was. I could do a Power Plower riff just like I did for Madison.

I proceeded to walk up and down the streets with my fist to my ear as if I was holding a receiver, squinting and mumbling, trying to remember how that rap went.

I semi-knew what I looked like, but nobody gave a shit. I went into an all-night disgusto overhead-fluorescent grocery to buy a pen and a notebook. It was five-thirty. There were two Indians behind the counter, boy and girl, wearing light blue barbershop tricot tunics

with name tags; Riaz and Bahartee. A noddy spade was buying
cupcakes and a strawberry soda, and some balding hippie was
standing behind him clutching cat food. The place seemed to be
heavy on the emergency stuff: cat food, Tampax, bags of ice, anti-
histamines, lots of sweets for the noddies, maybe I could do a thing
on all-night groceries.

When I came out on the street the sky had the slightest rising
blush to it, the moon was hanging lower but still strong and yellow.

Five-thirty. I was pulling an all-nighter, getting on intimate
terms with the streets. I wasn't even tired, but just to play it safe I
went back into the grocery and got some black coffee. Then pen and
pad in one hand, coffee in the other, I walked over to Washington
Square Park, sat on a bench in the shadow of the arch, inhaled some
coffee mist and stared at page one of the memo pad. I felt jammed,
afraid to commit the spiel to words on paper, afraid that it wasn't
funny after all. After ten minutes I got as far as writing down the
word "Hi," when my attention was diverted by a slowly cruising
Cadillac trolling the northern border of the park. It was a huge blue
steel deal and in the front seat sat an elderly couple, sober and slit-
faced. He wore a homburg and she, in the shotgun seat, wore a mink
coat. She must have slammed the car door on the hem because as
they purred by me, a large wedge of mink flapped lewdly over the
gutter directly beneath her oblivious stony profile like a huge dis-
gustingly hairy tongue. I snorted in amused amazement and felt a
surge of confidence. I stared at the blank page, took a sip of coffee
and immediately fell asleep. When I woke up, slowly raising my
chin from my chest, I was slouched over on the wood slat bench like
some junkie.

I couldn't have slept that long, because it wasn't full daylight
yet. The park seemed to be covered by a tawny mucus-colored mist
out of which the Washington Square Arch rose like a monstrous
hallucination. I licked my gummy lips and reached for my coffee.
Not only was it empty but there was lipstick on the rim.

I got up, creak-boned, and walked around until I found an open
breakfast place. It was a Greek diner on Eighth Street, and I took a
booth under the blue mural. Two bites of a feta cheese omelet was
all I could handle, and I settled for coffee. Behind me sat four tanky
guys. One of them seemed to be delivering a lecture on looking out

for yourself. He was back-to-back with me, and when I twisted my head around all I could see was a twenty-inch neck, a starched four-inch wide disco collar laid over a sports jacket and tiny cup-like ears smothered in garish corkscrew sideburns. I arched myself up so I could see over his shoulder. He held a stack of pink invoices or receipts in an ID-braceleted multi-ringed fist. "Now look." He dealt a pink sheet to his opposite fist. "That's *his* problem." He dealt another. "That's *his* problem." Another. "That's *his* problem." On each "that's his problem," he snapped his fingers on a new pink slip, making a sharp popping sound similar to the bag trick I did for Anthony. Anthony. Fonseca. Kim. Suddenly I felt in Big Trouble. My stomach whee'ed. Why did I lie to her? I was afraid to go back to the hotel room. I was scared to death. The Terror came from all directions at once, and I huddled over my coffee, feeling like a killer on the run.

"And it's money in *your* pocket . . . you understand?" They all nodded slowly. I think I nodded too.

Maybe it was just the caffeine.

I had to go back to the hotel. I zeroed in on Fonseca and got that nervous gut rush again. Maybe fear of that room had as much to do with staying out all night as did enchantment with the midnight hour. I felt I had stayed out way past my curfew and there would be hell to pay.

When I got back to the room it was nine A.M.

Fonseca's rumpled bed was empty, mine untouched. Fonseca was in the bathroom.

I slipped into my bed and practiced sprightly clever one-liners about staying out all night that I could lay on him when he came out. He wasn't a bad guy.

———

The door slammed and I shot up in bed. Fonseca, fully dressed, was looking down at me. I blinked wildly.

"Hey Tony! How you doing? You feeling all right?" My eyelids were gluey. I didn't know what time it was. I thought I was still waiting for him to emerge from the bathroom.

"You okay, Tony?" My voice sounded smooth and alert despite my panicky crud-head.

He was chewing gum, regarding me with semi-amusement, his hands in his pants pockets, sweeping back his car coat.

"So how you feeling?" I repeated, instantly hating the fear behind the words.

"You have breakfast yet? I'll be ready in a second." I started to bolt from bed then froze, checking to see that I had underwear on, before I threw back the covers.

"I just came back from lunch," he said. "It's one-thirty."

"Oh no!" I slapped myself; why, I wasn't exactly sure.

Fonseca handed me a bag from the dresser. "Watch, it's hot."

He had gotten me a coffee to go. I felt my heart bleat with relief. What a great guy. I started speed-rapping about the night before, how sorry I was that Lisi was such a dick, and how I went to sixty-eleven bars last night, but I really didn't enjoy myself, what'd *you* do?

Fonseca stood at the foot of the bed absently kicking one of the legs, then went into the bathroom.

I couldn't believe he was still so calm. I wanted him to flip. It *had* to be coming, and the longer it took, the bigger the blow.

Over the sound of running water, Fonseca began to sing "Choosy Beggar" in a sweet high Smokey Robinson tenor. My blood was burbling with a mixture of sleep, no sleep, caffeine, anxiety, disorientation and that persistent nagging sensation that I was in Deep Trouble.

I wanted to see Crown that afternoon.

Fonseca emerged from the john. "So what's the story for tonight?"

I told him about the piano bar and how I wanted to try it out.

"You're gonna *what?*" his face twisted in amusement.

"I'm gonna try it. I'm gonna think up a routine and work on it this afternoon and just do it. What could be?" I shrugged. "It's just for laughs." Hah hah.

Fonseca stared at me evenly, then snorted.

"What . . ." I winced.

"Nothin'," he said mildly. "Go to it."

————

By two-thirty I was out on the street again working on the Power Plower routine, blind to the sights and sounds this time, staring at my advancing shoes, trying out lines, offers, reactions, personas. Fonseca had gone off to parts unknown. I couldn't sit in the room and work on it. I had to walk it and talk it. I stopped at a pay phone, held my hand down on the tongue to kill the dial tone and tried a Power Plower pitch, talking in a normal tone of voice, practicing pausing, as if someone were talking back to me, repeating what they'd supposedly said, improvising wild guarantees. I put the receiver back and continued walking a few blocks before I grabbed another phone and tried it again. By the time I had something I liked, I'd covered maybe thirty blocks, picking up a half-dozen pay phones and throwing various Power Plower pitches into dead mouthpieces.

Occasionally when I picked up the receiver I imagined calling Kim and checking in, telling her how much I loved her, but when I reached for the change, my shaking fingers made it sound as if I had a tambourine in my pocket. For the first time since we'd met, I felt real dread in the prospect of dealing with her.

Crown lived in the West Fifties, two blocks away from Carnegie Hall. It was a narrow, pretty street of three-story buildings, housing antique poster shops, music stores and small expensive restaurants.

He buzzed me in without screening me through the intercom and as I made my way up a steep flight of stairs I heard rapid rhythmic tromping as if someone was hammering a nail into felt.

His buzzer had a harsh nasty tone like a game show timer and when he swung open the door we both jumped back in surprise. Crown stood there, bald as an egg again, shirtless, wearing butter yellow drawstringed sweat pants and black Kung Fu slippers. His face, chest and shoulders were covered with a fine frost of sweat beads. His torso was lean and youthful, the only sign of middle age some pectoral crow's feet around his slightly sagging but well-defined chest muscles.

"What the hell are *you* doing here?" He furrowed his brow, smiling though, and wiped the sweat off his face with his hand. He was panting.

"I was in the neighborhood. My father's thinking of buying Carnegie Hall and I said I'd check it out for him."

"You look like shit, c'mon in." He stepped back and extended a hand to show the way.

Given the neighborhood I fully expected to see elegant and tasteful digs, something with a drawing room perhaps, whatever the hell a drawing room might be, but Crown was living in a one-room dump that looked as if it had been decorated by a stoned high school senior. The walls were painted the color of dried blood which shrunk the place even more: the decor consisted of a thickly built, heavily scarred, sloppily wood-stained loft bed, the mattress too close to the ceiling; two Woolworth's-quality imitation Turkish throw rugs; and two dirty white bean bag chairs that looked like overblown pin-cushions. An airplane-bathroom–sized kitchenette off the side featured a potless sky-blue pegboard over a sink that was piled high with dirty plastic dishes.

"The place is a little too big for me, but I'm adjusting." He stood next to me, surveying the damage, hands on hips, still huffing. "I sublet it from an old student of mine. She's dancing her way across Poland or somewhere right now. It's very cheap. So what are you doing here, really?" He ran a thumb back across his forehead and breathed through his bared teeth.

"I just came in for the weekend with Tony Fonseca."

"What are you doing with *that* lunatic? . . . Excuse me . . ." He centered himself at attention on one of the throw rugs and abruptly began running in place, throwing himself down into a fit of push-ups every thirty seconds, springing back and pumping his knees again. "Aerobics," he shuddered. "S-so what are y-you doing w-with Ffonzzeca?"

"It's complicated." I sank into a bean bag.

"T-Two minutes."

I watched him accelerate into a final violent set of push-ups and a final flurry of running, his knee caps almost kissing his chest. "Ah!" He finished, reached up and pulled down a towel hanging over the edge of the mattress.

"I feel like a vampire up there." He glanced up to the bed. "You need a place to stay?" He wiped his face and chest. "These two chairs together are more comfortable than you think. They're very form fitting." He draped his towel over the empty bean bag and eased himself down.

"Nah, thanks."

"You want tea?"

"Nah, it's okay . . . so how's it going?"

"Not great," he said in a tone of voice so firm and lively that it took the negative information a minute to sink in. "The play's closing next week."

"And then what?"

"And then what . . ." He raised and dropped a limp hand.

"What happened to the toupee?" I tapped my skull.

"I hocked it."

"What?"

He laughed. "Nah, I don't wear it anymore. I do the part bald . . . maybe I can do *The King and I* afterwards."

He seemed too up for me to feel sorry for him.

"Tell me something good, Peter." He yawned and stretched his arms as high as they would go.

"I'm doing a stage thing tonight," I said, feeling excitement and danger.

"What?" He frowned. "Where?"

Suddenly I felt like an interloper, a dilettante. I had no right . . .

"It's just a place in the Village, a piano bar. Anybody can get up for a minute and do something. It's no big deal."

"Oh what . . . that place. I know, it's one of those euphoric I-love-New-York sissy bars where you walk in and everybody's singing 'The Impossible Dream'? What, Attar?"

"Fuck you."

He stared at me for a few seconds then shrugged. "I'm sorry. I'm feeling pissed . . . break a leg, kiddo . . . break two."

I didn't like him. I expected him to be more excited and supportive. But maybe he was having a rough time.

"I'd come and watch tonight, but I have to work."

"Are you doing auditions for stuff?"

"Yeah, a few . . . taking classes, you know . . ."

"What kind of classes?"

"I take an acting class with this guy who's a freelancer from the Neighborhood Playhouse. He knows his stuff, it's good."

"Do you know Doobie at the school?"

"Doobie's a dick."

"How much does it cost?"

"Fifteen a class."

"Can anybody take it or do you have to pass an audition?"

"Audition."

"What's the guy's name? Can anybody audition?"

"Sure." He looked at me tentatively. "Stanley Hartnett."

"Stanley Hartnett . . . when's the next audition?"

"Couple of months I guess. What, do you want to take acting?" He jerked back.

"I dunno, yeah, why not, I gotta do *some*thing next term."

"Why don't you stay up there?"

"Why don't you?" I shot back, pissed off.

"Maybe I should have." He let his head hang back and covered his eyes with his palms. He looked like an entirely different person than in my memory of him, older but younger, a bald teenager who needed a good night's sleep. "I tell you, Peter, when I decided to do this, I really didn't think it was all going to be that hard. I don't know *why* I didn't, but I didn't." He dropped his hands on his thighs and gave me a smiley shrug.

"You can always go back to Buchanon, right?"

His face twisted into an expression of disdainful incredulity as if I'd just said "Isn't it great that we live in the land of the free and the home of the brave?" That look was all the pep talk I needed, and minutes later I left feeling totally bolstered and unstoppable.

I got back to the hotel room around five. My eyes felt sandy from no sleep and my bones felt as though they were contracting on me. I got in bed and tried to nap, but I couldn't turn off my head. I tried whacking off, but my mind kept wandering back to the routine. I wondered if I should try to clip some phone receiver for realism or just use my fist. I was lousy at pantomime. I couldn't remember who was the famous phone comic, Bob Newhart or Shelley Berman, and if he used a real phone or not. I lined up those six high-heeled women I passed in the street the day before and gave it to them from behind one after the other in size order, their panties pulled down to the backs of their knees, watch them high heels.

"Are you whacking off?" Fonseca caught me with my hand under the blanket. I was so preoccupied I didn't even hear him come in, didn't even get flustered when he caught me.

"I'll be out in the hallway, give a yell when you're finished." He headed out the door.

"Get back here, asshole." I threw off the covers and sat up in bed. "I'm gonna do it, Tony."

The air in the dusky room was the color of cigarette ash, of television snow.

Facing me, he sat on his bed, pulled out some dental floss and worked on his teeth, absently tilting his head from shoulder to shoulder.

"So how was your day?" I said mechanically, then put a hand over my eyes and grunted with nervous exhaustion.

"So what time we have to be there?" he murmured, frowning at his used floss.

"Be where?"

"The club, the place, wherever you're gonna do your stuff."

"We?"

It never entered my head that I could have a friend in the audience, an ally. The idea seemed so excellent, so obvious, that I smiled at him as if he'd just invented the wheel. I remembered how alone I'd felt the night before, laughing at that campy swish, walking the streets, talking to dead phones.

"So what time?" Fonseca was reduced to a luminescent outline as the room descended into a more purple darkness.

It struck me that maybe Fonseca wasn't going to blow after all. Maybe last night had been a hard lesson in acceptance. Maybe I wasn't giving him enough credit. Nonetheless, I wasn't going to bring it up until he did.

"Tony, you're a great guy," I said almost apologetically.

"Good for me," he shrugged and continued sawing through his teeth.

I sat on a bar stool looking across at Fonseca, who sat at a small table by the piano. Over his head was an autographed *Fantasticks* poster. He looked out of place and uncomfortable, squinting at the growing throng of chatties and laughies, the darling heads and divas. I started out sitting with him but as the place began to fill up, I moved over to the bar, where I felt I had more freedom. We had been the first ones there, and had sat in silence for an hour drinking and watching the bartender funnel together half-full bottles of grenadine, crème de cacao and other booze candies. Then it was another hour until more than a handful of customers made the scene and then in what seemed like an instant, the place filled to capacity, which was when I bolted for the elbow room of the bar.

Usually I'd be apologizing all over the place for the two-and-a-half hour hurry-up-and-wait, but it was Diaper Time for me, and I had other things on my mind. The sound and smell of the place seemed entirely different tonight, less generous, more battle-scarred. From my damp hunch I imagined everybody was checking me out, everybody knew that I was going for the Dreaded Stool. Even though the place had become jammed, the piano player was bantering at the bar, sipping a White Russian, torturing me like a civil servant. When he finally got his ass over to the bench he spent a good ten minutes chatting with the couple whose table was flush up against the back of the piano. Finally he allowed his fingers to float down to the keys and still talking and laughing, he absently fingered his way across whatever the song was from *West Side Story* where the Puerto Ricans were arguing the relative merits and demerits of Puerto Rico versus America. Halfway through his instrumental the girl sitting at the table next to Fonseca's decided she was Rita Moreno and belted out a few lyrics and a hand-clapping Latino tongue trill. Startled, Fonseca spilled some beer on himself, then looked across the room to catch my eye and ham up some low-key face fear. Despite my own wet-ass status I started laughing, more than half-wishing I was sitting back at the table goofing on the hambony bravura of the place instead of making my pitch for world fame.

I saw Fonseca smirk as the fat blond guy who did Marlon Brando impressions made his entrance. I tried to catch his eye and exchange knowing glances but he wasn't looking my way.

The piano player shifted into "Maria" and about a third of the crowd joined in.

Next came *Camelot*. Fonseca caught my eye and slightly bowing he gestured toward the Stool with an upturned palm like an ironic butler. I nodded "Not yet."

A thin frizzy-haired albino girl rose from a table and weaved her way to the spotlight. My gut scrunched with anxiety. She took the stool, the place clammed up, half expectation, half curiosity at her bizarre appearance. Her skin was a pale clammy yellow, her L'il

Orphan Annie-like hair a bleached gold, her nose and lips were flat and thick and her albino eyes were blazingly iridescent. She was young and skinny—both her thighs fit on the stool.

She sang "A Taste of Honey" in a voice that was as thin and weak as herself. The room was embarrassed. If she had not been an albino, if she had been heftier, I had the feeling that they would have ignored her, gone back to their conversations, but all they could do was squint at their drinks or at her, and hope she wasn't going to do another song. I checked out the table she came from; a middle-aged black couple, probably her parents. They sat there, eyes drilling into her, entranced, unconsciously nodding encouragement. The mother was damp-eyed and smiling. She was light-skinned, her face splashed with a saddle of dark brown freckles. The father, iron-haired, was wearing a business suit and tie. He was tense. He kept rubbing his thumb against his fist. Suddenly I started crying, a three-second burst, a loud gulpy hoot, my head lurching forward like a snapping turtle before I got it under control. I felt startled and embarrassed, it was as involuntary as stomach gurgling. I puttered around my face, blowing my nose, clearing my throat, frowning and twisting my neck, putting on a whole preoccupied show to disguise my outburst.

When she finished the song there was enough applause to save face. Both her parents sat spine straight, violently beating their palms like flamenco dancers.

The girl made her way back to their table, blushing and smiling. The mother reached up and kissed her. The father reared back, still neck-brace erect, shifted his chair to face his wife and daughter, and continued applauding.

I let out with another hoot.

Out of sheer relief the crowd got into a singalong with a young guy on "If Ever I Would Leave You."

Then the fuckhead who mangled Lenny Bruce got up and did the same botched "Lima Ohio" routine. And he got the same laughs, which made me think I was the only regular in the joint.

The piano player led the place in your basic rousing chorus of "Jubilation T. Cornpone," after which I saw the blond impersonator go for the stool, and I was instantly on the move to cut him off. It would be Goodnight Irene for anybody trying to do comedy up there after him, and the next thing I knew I was sitting high, squinting into

the spotlight, and the piano player was leaning toward me waiting
for his cue. I had my heels locked behind me on the lowest foot rung,
and had no idea how to get off the stool without falling on my face. I
was aware of the bartender busily lunging and lurching behind the
bar. I couldn't see faces, just rotund balloon slices of heads. There
was a brandy snifter on the top of the piano, with a single stiff dollar
bill lying like a slant board in the glass. The piano player said something to me, but it didn't register. I was staring out at the shadowy
crowd waiting for a sign that they liked me so far. The piano player
said something to me again. The crowd started talking among
themselves—not about me. Out of the corner of my eye I saw the fat
blond guy shift impatiently by the bar waiting for me to shit or get off
the pot. Two seats down from him I saw Natalie, the rich lady from
the night before. I couldn't see her face, only the silhouette of her
hair and the knot of her scarf.

"This is my first time up here . . ."

Most people clammed up, which jarred me.

"This is my first time up here, or anywhere. How'm I doin' so
far?"

Somebody laughed by accident, but it was enough for the likes
of me, and I started to roll.

"This is nonsense man, I work as a phone solicitor in midtown
at this place called National Communicators?"

A few knowing groans.

I saw two people kissing and one yawning. I had to keep my
eyes away from the audience. I had a fear of getting yelled at. I focused on the rigor mortis-like dollar bill in the snifter.

"There's a couple of hundred people there. Everybody's a something else, dancers, actors, you know the scene, Broadway heads,
so me too . . ." I cleared my throat.

"Anyways." I shrugged at my kneecaps. "It's a wild gig, you sell a
lot of bizarre stuff to all kinds of people, magazine subscriptions, po-
litical candidates, Fruit of the Month Club . . . ruby red grapefruits!
You know, the picture of the guy in the back of *The New Yorker* with
the Bud Abbott mustache and the plaid shirt holding up the grapefruits. 'These babies are Ruby Reds, and they can only be grown on
my goddamn farm along the banks of the Tex-Mex River.' . . . and
you get the crate of them in the mail . . . squashed, frozen . . . Febru-

ary is kiwis, March, Northern Spy apples, April's Daniel Moynihan Irish walking hats, May's the sidearm elevator for people who can't walk up and down stairs, you know, that photo in the back of *The New Yorker* of the blue haired lady with the pearls riding up the stairs of her mansion, 'Reeeee' in that ski lift . . . May, you get the elevator, June you get the old lady." I had no idea what the hell I was talking about. None of this was on my program.

"So that's June. July, we send you Hummel figurines of small birds, which has got to be the most goddamn boring thing you could ever want to see in someone's house . . . it's like my grandmother had that type of crap. It fit right in there with the linoleum on the living room floor and the candy dish with the individually wrapped sour balls that were untouched for years. . . . Anybody who's into figurines probably believes in UFOs or likes to watch daytime TV or something, I mean really . . ."

Don't say "I mean really." Nobody was laughing except one lady who was hysterical and kept gasping, "Yes! Yes! Yes!" I wasn't going over so hot, but I'd broken the ice with myself and I was winging it. I couldn't believe my own balls. I was totally making up stuff on the spot and I felt totally relaxed as long as I kept looking at the brandy snifter or my kneecaps.

". . . But seriously, folks, the weirdest, the weirdest thing I ever had to sell . . . the weirdest thing . . . was called . . . Power . . . Power . . ." Power Pleaghh. I didn't want to do Power Plower. I didn't know if it was stage fright or what.

The room was mine, but they were waiting. It couldn't have been stage fright because I felt too calm. I wanted to talk—tell them about myself. I wanted everybody to hop in the sack with me and hear a bedtime story.

"Jesus Christ, I'll never forget the last time I was in Atlantic City . . ." me talking, "I got mo*les*ted." That was a bit of a showstopper, and before I knew it I was off and running. "It was incredible. I was twelve and my old man took me and him for a weekend vacation at this place called the Ritz-Carlton? This place the Ritz had a pool on the roof and it was pretty wild because it was snowing and all, outside of course, so we went up there to take a dip, but there was a problem because they didn't have changing rooms and I had to put on my swimming trunks in the public bathroom. Anyways, that was probably the only time I was excited about putting on swimming trunks in my life because my father just bought me my first jock-strap. I guess it was a training jock . . ." Laughs. I felt as if I was gliding. There was a warm dreamy ease in my voice. "Anyways, I go into the bathroom to change, and it's really small, very cramped and there's already a guy in there washing up, so I just stand around, feeling a little self-conscious, you know, finally he finishes, smiles at me and splits. The weird thing about the guy was that I *knew* he was a scientist because there was a biologists' convention at the hotel and he had a name tag on his jacket. I don't remember his name but I remember the tag said he represented Northwestern University. So, he leaves, and I take off my pants. All of a sudden, the door swings open again just as I got my pants down by my sneakers, and it's Mr. Science again. He smiles at me and says, 'Excuse me, did you see some room keys in here?' I said no and I pulled up my pants." Stop for laughs. A gift exchange. "I was not crazy about this guy. He was pretty beefy and he had a big white face with a blond crew cut and rimless glasses. He looked like a fat Bill Cullen, so I pull up my pants, he leaves again, and I pull down my pants again. Two seconds later, bing-bong Avon calling, he comes in again. 'Are you *sure* you didn't see a wallet?' I pull up my pants again. In the back of my head I could have sworn he was looking for room keys, but I don't think anything of it and meanwhile I'm starting to feel like a jerk with my pants up and down, up and down, every time he walks in, so I just ignore him and did the whole thing, undressing, while he's making this big deal of searching for his keys or his wallet or whatever. But what happened was, as soon as I was nude from the waist down, all of a sudden he stands up straight and he starts smiling at me . . . not *me* exactly . . . he's staring at my wanger . . ." I had the marginal thought that I might be offending the gays, of teasing them with the image of my adolescent sexuality. Nah. "Now . . . I was like twelve, closer to thirteen and I had been whacking it for about six months, but on the sly, my father wasn't real big on the facts of life and the thing was I didn't know what the hell I was doing, what that stuff was . . ."

I stopped, suddenly embarrassed. I checked faces to see if I was grossing anybody out. Fonseca was listening with his head tilted back, slightly frowning with interest. He looked like a nearsighted man examining a newspaper. Go. Go. "All I knew was I was doin' something that felt really good but it caused this—you know—to come out, so obviously I had cancer, and for six months before we went to Atlantic City I had been walking under this doom cloud of cancer and I decided that every time I did it I was bringing myself closer to death . . . not that that was enough to stop me, and not that I probably *really* thought I had cancer, but that craziness of touching yourself and whoops, what's *this* stuff . . . you know. So anyways, there I was in this bathroom with my cancerous carrot hanging out, which of course only *I* knew was cancerous, and there's this hulky fucking boing-boing smiling at me, reaching out, *fondling* me and I don't think, 'Yikes, a pervert.' All I see is this guy is a *scientist*, it says so right on his sports jacket, and so as far as I'm concerned all he's doing is reaching out with this . . . instinctive scientific curiosity, you know, 'Ah-ha! a diseased dork!' and all my worst fantasies are being here and now validated. So instead of yelling for help I'm screaming at this guy who's tickling and pulling on my yutz, I'm screaming at him, 'What's *wrong!* What's *wrong!*' and he's just smiling and fondling me saying, 'Nothing, nothing,' and I'm scream- ing, 'You can *tell* me! You can *tell* me!'"

Laughs and a low chorus of "Aww"'s that made me think of Randye. Fonseca was still squinting at me like small print.

"Anyways, he only touched me for a few seconds. I think I started freaking *him* out, you know, 'Hey kid, lighten up, I'm only a child molester. . . .' So he leaves the bathroom and I'm standing there with my new jockstrap in my hand and I'm shaking like a leaf . . . I am absolutely terrified . . . no more bullshit, the test results are *in* and cancer it *is*. So I force myself to put on my trunks and I drag my ass out to the swimming pool where my father is and I figure fuck it, he's got to be told . . . and he's sitting there reading a magazine in a chaise lounge, you know, and in the background there's a funeral dirge and I go up to him and I say, 'Dad, I have to talk to you,' and he doesn't even look up, he just . . . 'Yeah, buddy?' and I say, 'Dad, I got cancer of the penis.'" Laugh break. "'Yeah? How do you know?' he's still checking out the magazine, and I say, 'Well, I thought I'had it for a while but I wasn't sure . . . but this scientist just examined me in the bathroom and I think it's definite . . .'"

People laughed so hard and real, there was such a rush of

warmth coming at me that I immediately wanted to be James Brown-Mick Jagger and flood the room with my grace and fire.

I felt like shooting my arms straight up to the ceiling and soaring around the room.

"So anyways!" I was almost shouting. ". . . anyways! there was about a ten- to twenty-second delayed reaction before my father did a double take . . . *'Wha-at!'* "

" 'Yeah . . . this scientist . . .' "

" 'Don't ever! ever! ever! go into a bathroom with a strange man! . . . Don't ever follow anybody into a building . . .' he went on like that for fifteen minutes, reminding me of small children killed in hallways by strangers with candy. I thought he was missing the point of my anxiety, you know? But I was feeling too doomed to pursue it." I paused and basked, sweating with happiness. "I didn't find out what masturbation was until six months later. I was reading this book about vampires and it had a description of nocturnal emission . . . then I was home free." I waved my hand dismissively. Say goodnight, Grace.

People started to applaud. I applauded with them. I had totally checked out and imagined that there was someone else on the stool and I was in the audience, and even though I missed the content of that person's act it would be rude not to applaud. Then I saw Natalie's silhouetted head and I had this fantasy of her watching me riff in front of an audience, which was, of course, what she'd just done. As I got off the stool and moved toward the bar, people slightly parted for me, and I walked down a lane of pleasantries, smiles, a low velvety croon, "Verrry funny, verry funny." I felt a tiny charge as if miniature jumper cables were hooked up to my big toes.

The bartender wouldn't take my money.

"I'm only a molester . . ." he chuckled.

I ordered a melon-flavored liqueur, bright green, syrupy and reminiscent of allergy medicine. I found Natalie and started hitting on her, babbling I-can't-believe-its, and I-was-so-nervouses. She freaked slightly that I would seek her out, sitting up straight, touching her throat, smiling that spray-paint smile. She looked pained and awkward. She wanted me to go away.

"You smell so incredibly good." I bit my lip and narrowed my eyes in sincerity.

"Oh look!" She leaned to look past me to the spotlight where the Playful Piston triplets were doing their Model T song. Where'd the blond fag go?

I felt a hand on my shoulder. Fonseca stood behind me, squinting at the stage.

"I probably grossed everybody out," I blurted.

He shrugged. "You were all right," then rapped me in the chest with his knuckles. "Let's get the fuck out of here."

I wanted to hang on and have everybody purr "verrry funny" on me for a few hours, but I followed him out, wading through more verbal caresses, amused curious faces. When we got to the top of the steps I stopped. "Let me just go to the john." I backtracked slowly into the room so that people could stroke me one more time. I scored two "verrry funnies," one "Atlantic City," one "cancer of the penis," and a lot of smiles. I stopped at the bar to ask the bartender what time it was. He turned around to read the gigantic clock that was staring me in the face.

"Is that the real time or is it bar clock time?" I asked, as though I was trying to get the lowdown on the Bermuda Triangle.

"It's five minutes fast." He smiled, patiently and attentively.

"Well, I have to split. . . . That was my first time on stage. I was really nervous."

He got flagged to the other end of the bar. I could see Fonseca leaning on a car outside.

When the bartender gravitated back I sighed, "Well, I have to go."

"Come back next weekend." He started making a Golden Cadillac.

"You mean go on stage?"

"Sure." He shrugged, frowning with concentration at his silver shaker. "Only a child molester," he chortled, upending a golden megaphone of Galliano.

"Next week, hah?" I squinted and pouted at the ceiling as if trying to envision what was in my datebook. I might not ever make it.

On the way out, some guy clutched my bicep. I could smell the vodka on his breath before I turned around. He was dressed completely in leather; pants, T-shirt, motorcycle jacket and *Wild Ones* cap. Even with the heavy stiffness of the costume I could tell he was a lifter. He couldn't have been more than eighteen. I stood there patiently waiting for him to get it together. He moved his lips but the alcohol was choking his thoughts. He looked so pained and frustrated I didn't have the heart to walk away. Such is the price of stardom.

"Listen . . ." he finally said, shaking my arm, "listen . . . that . . . your father?"

"Yeah?"

"I just want . . . that story, man . . ."

I felt touched by how moved he seemed. If he hadn't been already on his ass I would have bought him a drink.

"Your father? . . ."

Let's go. Let's go.

"What the fuck is *wrong* with him, man?" He gave my arm a downward tug.

"What?" Trouble.

"What the fuck is *wrong* with the dude? . . . I'm drunk . . ." He worked his lips for moisture. "I'm drunk right? But, okay, just, how come your father didn't go *after* that fuck? Right?"

I felt sucker-punched, stunned. He gripped me harder.

"Look, I don't have a kid, right? Obviously. But . . . but if I did? You know what *I'd* have done? . . ."

I twisted my arm free and ran up to the street. He was right. But not tonight.

———

"Let's fuckin' eat." Fonseca made an Alka Seltzer face and touched his gut. He studied the heavy taxi traffic shooting down toward the World Trade Center towers.

I was afraid to fish for compliments so I just walked behind him.

Fonseca steered us to a soul place on Hudson Street called Baby Blue. It was a bona fide greasy spoon, nine ratty Formica tables, harsh fluorescent overheads, a juke box, hi-gloss baby blue painted walls, and some kind of fucked-up ventilation system which managed to draw off the oxygen into the street and keep the griddle smoke in the room. The air was so tangible and heavy I felt I could step up and walk on it.

"Try the ribs." Fonseca took a table. "They got the only good ribs north of Washington in here."

I pulled up a stuffed vinyl dinette chair. Scotch-taped over our heads were fifteen-year-old black and white glossies of Smokey Robinson, John Glenn, Brook Benton and a Tamla publicity still of a black chick, chin on fist, wearing a sixties Supremes wig and a ton of eye makeup. The picture was signed, "To the Baby Blue, always, Mavis Truax."

"There's the ribs." Fonseca nodded two tables down, where some skinny black kid in dime shades, a Cuffney cap and an ascot sat over a plate of what looked like your basic spareribs with a stack of white bread on a separate plate. I was more interested in the guy than the food. He was there with a coed-looking blond and he kept calling the middle-aged black waitress "Mama." As in "how you be, Mama" and "Mama, can you be gittin' us some coffee?" "Thank you, Mama." And making this big jive play at being a soul regular for his little blond girlfriend. The waitress seemed to be tolerating his act, letting him hold her hand for a second, but the tight wry look on her face was the story with him.

The girl took out a cigarette and in the middle of gnawing on a rib her Afro-American date stopped and gave her a light.

"That guy is a plate-glass asshole," I mused, not really caring.

"Don't *you* be an asshole," Fonseca snapped. "Look at him. He's in fucking pain, man. I know those guys, when he's not doin' five on the Black Hand side he's in his dorm room reading Camus. He's probably got a three-point-eight index. He's a fucking kid, and he's got more change-ups coming than a catcher in a bullpen. Where's your compassion?"

There seemed to be wild scenes at all the tables. Behind us a high-Afroed husky Jew was leaning across the table arguing with his date, who could have been Chinese or Puerto Rican, a slightly chunky flat-faced high-cheekboned girl, wearing tinted aviator glasses, her chest and shoulders covered with a fine shower of shimmery straight blue-black hair. Diagonally across from us sat three screamers, lowlife semi-transvestites with pancake makeup, mascara and five o'clock shadow. They seemed to go with the air in the place. And directly across from us sat a lone black guy wearing a delivery man's brown "Good Health Seltzer" jacket and slacks. He was drunk, sucking soup and looking as if the control spring in his eyelids was broken. His table was flush up against the glass cake-display counter, which separated the heart-attack factory from the dining area. Instead of holding cakes, the counter was a reliquary, a mini-museum of Kennedy and King mementos, John, Bobby, and Martin Luther each having his own shelf of commemorative plates, plaster busts, photos; and centered one, two, three in a vertical line, were small framed form letters thanking Louise Howard and the employees of Baby Blue for their kind letters of condolence signed by Jackie, Ethel and Coretta.

"We'll have two orders of ribs, some Pepsis and you still make those biscuits?" Fonseca winked at the fat black waitress.

"Yeah, but we're out, we got white, rye or whole wheat."

"We'll have white." Fonseca winked again.

We sat in silence. I was pissed. Fonseca was making me afraid to be feeling good, afraid to be speed-rapping about my night. *My* goddamn night! Speedo!

"Well, fuck you!" the Jewish guy snapped at his Chino-Rican date, and it seemed like such a natural extension of my own combat head that for a second I thought *I* said it.

Fonseca made a big show of slowly turning around to register his irritation at their argument.

When he turned back again, I jumped right on him. "I was good tonight, right?"

"You should look directly at people," he answered soberly, rubbing his chin. "Otherwise, it looks as if you're afraid of them. You've got to meet people with your eyes." He raised his hand palm up.

"But I was good, right?"

"Oh yeah, no." He shrugged, wrinkling his face and standing up. "I can't believe nobody's playing the juke box. This place's got the greatest soul box north of Washington." He sauntered away from the table, poking through a palmful of silver.

I sat there fuming until he came back.

"Well *I* thought I was *good*."

"Well, hey, yeah, don't get me wrong, but one thing you gotta realize, that place was kind of like a protected environment, right?"

"What?"

"I mean, everybody was on your side."

Except you, you cocksucker.

"I mean you got to go to the killing floor to see what you're made of, you know? Like one of the joints where they come to see you fall on your face."

"Yeah? Next week I will."

I got up and headed for the john. There were those cherry-scented camphor cakes in the urinal that made me feel as though I was taking a leak in a Pez factory. I stood in front of the speck-flecked mirror and redid my routine. Killing floor.

When I came out, the ribs and bread were spread and Fonseca was hunched down and eating. Jackie Wilson was wailing away on "Lonely Teardrops" from the jukebox.

"Yee-ah." The drunk Good Health Seltzer delivery man lifted a half-chewed chicken wing at Fonseca. "Thas Jackie!"

Fonseca nodded once and got back into his ribs.

"Yee-ah! Thas Jackie. He's *dead* now; he got shot by a wax."

"A what?" Fonseca tilted his head.

"A wax! See, he was a fruitcake, and she didn't like that shit, so the bitch shot him."

"What the fuck's a wax?" Fonseca asked me.

I shrugged, ignoring him.

"A *ar*my wax," the black guy said. "See, he was a fruitcake, I know, because he's mah cousin, mah name's Wilson, his name's Wilson, so I know he was a fruitcake and she shot him."

"No man," Fonseca said calmly, sucking his rib and popping the tab on his Pepsi. "He had a stroke . . . you're thinking of Sam Cooke."

"Naw." Wilson rattled his head. "It were a wax."

"Sam Cooke got shot, King Curtis, not Jackie Wilson. He had a stroke."

"Yeah, well maybe he had a stroke, but he were a fruitcake and that army wax shot him, maybe she shot all them others too." He pushed around the collard greens and yams on his plate with a piece of white bread. "Yeahp, maybe that were the busiest wax in the army," Wilson said to his plate.

Fonseca laughed.

Wilson looked up. His eyes were almond-shaped blisters. They locked glances. Wilson nodded. He looked as though he was studying Fonseca. "You a *young* man still . . ." he said. "You gonna have it *all*."

Fonseca's face got tight and for a second I thought he might take a swing at Wilson, but suddenly the tension left his eyes and mouth and he relaxed into a small sad smile of surrender. Gazing at the floor, Fonseca jerked his head back in an almost imperceptible dry snort.

"Are you drivin' tonight, Pop?" Fonseca asked softly, still looking down.

"Nawp . . . nawp." With a great effort Wilson lifted a sly eyebrow. "I'm flyin'."

"Where you flyin'?"

"Stratosphere. . . ." He took a bite of chicken. "At-mo-sphere." He slapped his hand against his leg and his ring clinked glass.

Fonseca tilted his chin at the bulge on the outside of Wilson's thigh. "Rocket fuel?"

"Uh-huh." Wilson squinted and crooked a finger at Fonseca's Pepsi can. Fonseca thrust the soda toward Wilson's table as Wilson leaned back to pull out his pint.

"Wilson!" one of the waitresses barked in a paddle-crack voice from behind the assassination display.

"Uh-oh!" Wilson hunched over his meal and gave our table a schoolboy grin. He started eating fast.

"Wilson, you drinking?" Only her head was visible.

"I ain't never been in jail, Wilson, and I ain't goin' now over someone's weakness!"

The whole restaurant was laughing, but low key because she was really pissed.

"Naw, naw, Miss Howard, nobody's drinkin'." Wilson ate faster. "False alarm, false alarm."

"Raymon'!" the waitress shouted.

A sullen dull-eyed black kid came out of the supply room. He was dressed in baggy kitchen whites, and he headed right for Wilson's table, picked up Wilson's coffee cup and passed it under his nose.

"See, I told you." Wilson smiled, but he hunched forward.

Raymond then turned and grabbed Fonseca's Pepsi can and whiffed it for booze.

"What the hell you think you're doin'?" Fonseca reared back, but the kid ignored him, and instead of dancing with Fonseca he grabbed and sniffed my can. His naked forearms were fat-veined and slabbed with muscle. He might have been a lifter, but it was hard to tell because of the bagginess of his whites.

Wilson kept singsonging. "It's my fault, it's my fault," but everybody ignored him.

Fonseca looked out of his mind. His face was twisted up to catch Raymond's eye, and he was grinning for the first time tonight, a wet-eyed toothy rictus grin, and as soon as Raymond put down the cans, he backhanded one of them onto the floor, but it was light aluminum and almost empty. Without breaking stride, Raymond vanished into the supply room, his job done.

Fonseca was breathing heavily. Suddenly I felt this horrible sensation of being assaulted, almost raped, an inflamed rasping sensation in my chest.

Wilson was still droning on. "My fault, my fault."

"Let's get the bill," I said.

The waitress was glaring at us over the display counter.

Fonseca turned his head back toward the kitchen. "Fucking creep," he said, then he turned forward to check his wallet.

"Hey." The husky Jewish guy sitting behind Fonseca tapped him on the shoulder. "What did you just say?"

"What?" Fonseca asked mildly.

"I said, what did you just say?" His face mottled with anger.

"What did I just say about *what?*" Fonseca was genuinely confused.

"Did you just say 'fucking Cree'?" His eyes were bugging.

"Cree?" Fonseca's head went into his shoulders.

"Yeah, *Cree!* Because there's a fucking *Cree* . . ." He shot a finger at the Chino-Rican looking girl sitting across the table from him. "There's a fucking *Cree* sitting right here!"

His Cree girlfriend held her head in her hands. She was totally mortified by her rage-ball boyfriend.

Fonseca was so stunned at the bizarreness of the accusation, his voice was almost tender. "No, I didn't say Cree, I said *creep*, with a p . . . fucking *creep*."

"Harry . . ." The Indian girl leaned across the table. "I'm gonna leave . . ."

"Creep," Fonseca repeated.

They tried to stare each other down. Harry was breathing through his nose. He didn't know what to say. He didn't want to let it go.

His Cree girlfriend called his name again, her voice getting final. Without apologizing, he slowly turned himself away from our table and faced her.

We sat in silence, waiting for the bill. That rape-inflamed sensation was working its way up to my head. I stared at my hands. I was having a hard time breathing. So was Fonseca, judging by the heaving of his shoulders. So was Harry, his head so close to his chest that from the rear he almost looked decapitated.

How come he didn't go after that fuck? Come to Atlantic City.

Wilson started in again. "It's my fault, it's my fault, it's my fault."

Suddenly, as if by some bizarre mental telepathy, all three of us leapt up at once; me, Fonseca and Harry, straight up, Fonseca and Harry immediately swinging away at each other. Once I popped up like that, I felt that I had made my statement and didn't particularly need to lock assholes with anybody, but Fonseca had the guy by the throat and by reflex I semi-dove in to break it up. But as I moved forward Fonseca was cocking his fist, and I wound up thrusting myself face-first into a Fonseca backhand. I felt a splat of pain bloom from somewhere below my eyes, and the next thing I knew I was staring at the grimy pressed-tin ceiling. Someone shouted, "Easy up!" Fonseca shoved the defender of the Cree nation against the wall with a forearm pressed to his Adam's apple and a kneecap against his groin. Fonseca kept punching him in the face, swinging with hectic speed, lifting himself up on his toes with each blow as if he was hefting a sledgehammer.

No one was moving to break it up, even though half the restaurant was standing. Going on automatic pilot, I jumped up and tried to bear-hug Fonseca, pressed my face into his chest to keep everybody apart. I felt terrified by the abrupt jerky power of Fonseca's movements. Even though he was ten times stronger than me I just locked my wrists behind his back and held on, too afraid to let go. Raymond came charging out of the kitchen. The next thing I knew Harry was pounding on my back trying to get to Fonseca. Fonseca was batting my head with the inside of his shoulders trying to get at Harry. Every time Harry hit my back I yelled "ow!" I should have slipped to the floor, but I squeezed Fonseca harder, my arms right under his armpits. My mouth was filled with blood, but I couldn't tell if it was from my nose or my lips. Out of one shocked-glazed eye I saw the young black guy who was with the blonde standing flush against the wall, his arms raised high as if he was being held up. I saw the three scuzzed-out drag queens sitting calmly, holding coffee cups up to their lips with both hands, elbows on the table. I realized I was calm, still shouting "ow!" every time I got hit in the back, but my "ows" sounded conversational. Suddenly Harry was peeled off my back. I saw Raymond grab him by the shirt front with one hand, clutch the side of his neck with the other, his thumb dug into the soft flesh under his chin so that he was frozen in pain and couldn't move his neck or head, and slowly tango him out of the restaurant. Harry chanted, "Let me get my date! Let me get my date!" Once they were outside on the sidewalk, Raymond, his thumb still drilled into the guy's gullet, whispered like a lover into Harry's ear, then looked up at the stars. Wincing in pain, and with some slight urging, Harry followed Raymond's gaze. Then Raymond whispered something else, released his grip and Harry quickly walked away.

I watched all this with my cheek against Fonseca's chest. He had stopped struggling now, and we must have looked like last-leg Marathon dancers. I couldn't figure out how to unclasp my hands. "Get off me," Fonseca spat suddenly, and flicked me away. I was so wiped, I just fell to the floor in a sitting position. I slowly moved a stiff arm to touch the pulpy feeling in the back of my head. I looked up at Fonseca for sympathy, a thanks, a hand up, but all I got was a ground-to-ceiling shot of his face: eyes placid, lips curled into a cool roller coaster of hatred.

"Help me up?" In my shock I sounded lighthearted.

"Fuck you." I thought he was going to kick me in the ribs and I dropped my arm to protect my side.

The Indian girl briskly strode past me, crying with anger. She almost stepped on my hand.

I was roughly hoisted upright from behind, Raymond hooking me under the armpits. He mumbled, "Pay ya bill," and flicked a finger at our cockeyed table on his way back to the rear of the restaurant.

Stony-faced, Fonseca dug into his wallet, dropped a ten and bulled past, knocking me lightly with his shoulder. His shirt front was dappled with my blood.

Wilson, through a mouthful of food, started up again, "It's my fault, it's my fault."

My blood. *My* blood. Why didn't he go after the fuck? I ran out into the street and stood spread-legged in front of the restaurant. Fonseca was a block away.

"Hey Tony!" I shouted. "Tony! C'mon man! Let's go into New York! Let's go see Nicky!"

Fonseca stopped, but didn't turn.

"Don't you fucking run," I said out loud to myself, totally high on fear.

Fonseca never turned around. He arched his back, his face to the sky and raised his fists over his head in a gesture of victory. Then he was gone.

I went back into the restaurant to pay my tab but Fonseca had covered the whole thing.

———

Out on the street I walked at a brisk yet spaced-out pace. I held a fistful of napkin to my leaky tender face. I had no idea where I was going. I had no idea where Fonseca had gone. Every time I stopped in front of a darkened store window to peer at the damage, my kneecaps started trembling. I had to get to some water and a mirror. As far as I could tell, the right corner of my mouth was cut, my right nostril was bleeding, and the rosy beginnings of a huge bruise were taking over my right cheekbone. I felt a long pigtail of bruises from the top of my head to the base of my spine. I wasn't going back to the hotel room. But I couldn't walk around all night again.

I couldn't go back to the hotel room. Why not? Because it's Fonseca territory. But it's Keller territory too. You paid for half. At least go back and get your shit. No. Go. No. Go.

I made myself run to the Courtney so I would have less time to think.

I stood outside the door to our room and listened for life. Nothing.

Once inside, I felt so tense I forgot what I had come back for. I started to make my bed. I found some stationery and wrote a note.

> Tony.
>   I came to New York to help you out. I really
> tried. Now I don't want to see you again. That's my
> blood on your shirt.
>   Good luck,
>   Peter

I laid the note on his pillow and left. Down in the street I realized I forgot to get my stuff. I didn't even wash my face, which was still sticky with blood. Fuck it. I wasn't going back up there.

I was free from Fonseca. Paid for my freedom in blood.

I started walking west toward Sheridan Square. I felt light and alert. Happy, Real happy. I still had to wash the blood off my face. Where to.

I thought of the gym over Sheridan Square. Maybe I could run up and use their john. I headed in that direction, damming up my nose, and for the first time since Friday thought of Kim without that naggy sense of dread. I was not just thinking of her, but missing her, wishing she could have watched me do my stuff. Wishing that tonight I could end up in bed with her, spooning, my nose in the nape of her neck, my arm between her breasts. I walked down the street imagining being inside her, my palm under her ass and I almost hailed a cab for the Port Authority, but I didn't.

I didn't make it to the gym either. I passed Attar first, and on hearing the endless sing-along I felt a comforting pang and descended inside. It was around midnight, and the place was disaster-level mobbed like the night before. Ducking my head and holding a hand up to the side of my face to hide my blood crust, I sidled my way back to the john.

I was amazed at how tiny the cuts were on my lip. In my imagination my face looked as though I had tried to brush my teeth with a blender but, outside of the rising bruise on my cheek, I looked only slightly mottled. I took off my shirt and checked my back.

Same thing, except I could tell I was going to wake up the next day feeling like pounded veal.

When I emerged, face washed, hair combed, into a two-hundred-person all-city chorus of "There But for You Go I," I got caught up in the joyous barrage of it all and within seconds I had Kim on the pay phone. Bypassing the formalities, I opened up with a medley of growling and purring I miss yous and I can't wait to see yous.

"Where are you, in church?" She yawned.

"Nah, I'm in this club in historic Greenwich Village, Kim it's fuckin' wild . . . I'm telling you Kim, me and you . . ."

"Who do they have singing there, the Mormon Tabernacle Choir?"

"Nah, it's mainly closet Nazis, it's a fund drive. Kim, I can't wait to get in bed with you, don't you miss me? Don't you want to kiss me?" I felt this squeezy huggy-bear rapture, this freedom. It was as if I had been courting both Fonseca and Kim, and I had just dropped one for the other and whoosh, all that split juice was now channeled into one pipe.

"Don't you miss me?"

"Ye-es!" she said with mock anguish.

"And what's my name?" I grilled her.

"Pie."

"Right. Ohh Kim . . . ohh tomorrow night."

Despite my euphoria, tomorrow night, upstate and that whole world and its cast seemed incredibly far away to reach in just twenty-four hours. I felt a little guilty about going from no thoughts to my love my love, but I had a roll going here that felt sincere.

"And you can't wait to see me, right?"

"Ye-es!" she wailed.

"Ohh . . ." I growled and made involuntary chewing motions with my jaw. "I love you, you little face, you face, you. Oh sweetie, I got so much to tell you . . . things are falling into place. You're such a little face."

Kim giggled unsteadily. I wasn't usually such a kissy fuckhead when it came to words of love. I just felt so goddamn good.

"Pie?" She said the word tentatively, trying it out to match my boodly-acky-sacky love riffs. "How's your parents?"

"They're great, they're great."

I decided right there that I would tell her the truth, everything that went down this weekend. I envisioned the two of us, the three of us, living in the Village. The New Deal. "Kimberly, I'm so insane in love with you . . ."

She laughed that shaky dopey laugh of someone who was a little scared but psyched nonetheless. I was hitting her with a midnight attack, a buoyant floodrush. She still hadn't ever said I love you, but she was toppling.

"And don't forget Monday . . ." she ding-donged.

"What?"

"Payne House!" she whined, how quickly we forget.

"Oh yes! Garters! And bodies and coziness! Oh right, oh right, I'm gonna have a seizure. I have to get off the phone before I bite through a knuckle. I love you, my face, I'll see you tomorrow."

I side-skipped out to the bar and had a Scotch straight up, which went right to the top of my head.

I was feeling very very good. I felt like letting loose with a James Brown "AAOW!" clapping my hands and segueing into some Soul Train-caliber whirligigs.

The singer on the stool was belting out "It Ain't Necessarily So." Yes it is, my dear.

I wound up spending the night, or what little was left of it, in a chair at the Port Authority Bus Terminal. I thought of staying with Crown but I was afraid of ringing his doorbell at four in the morning. I might also have been afraid of any small traces of Fonseca-hood that Crown himself might harbor.

At seven in the morning I took the Greyhound back upstate. The ride was horrendous; I was hung over and strung out. I kept feeling I wanted to apologize to Fonseca, but anytime that pangy feeling came up I just wrote it off as exhaustion. That shit was over. I was coming into my own. Respect yourself and all that.

But one thing I knew both Crown and Fonseca had been dead on about was that the Attar was no acid test. It was too kind, too easy, and I had to try somewhere harder next time, some place that didn't peddle euphoria. But, whatever. At least I'd finally made a move. I'd broken the ice. I still had no idea if I wanted to be a comedian, or what, but at least I found out I could think under fire, that I wasn't quick only in the comfort of my own living room. And that was major news. That was enough to start with. Now more than ever I had to, had to, had to, break away. When I suggested to Crown that he could always go back to Collegetown if things didn't break for him in the city, he had looked at me as though I was both nuts and foul-minded. And he was right.

All I had to do was convince Kim to come with me. I had to.

When I finally got into the gentle rhythm of massaging Kim's clit so that she wasn't wincing or slightly steering my hand to a less sensitive spot, I grew glassy-eyed staring at the two swollen strawberries resting in tall thin champagne glasses on the night table. Air bubbles would slipstream around the fat fruit and shoot straight for the surface to pop or cluster against the glass. I'd never been able to bring her off like this—either she or I would get too frustrated and we'd just wind up fucking before we had a nervous breakdown, but tonight I was hanging in, tonight I would find out. I would be a safecracker, a diamond cutter, a miniaturist, because tonight we were celebrating, tonight we were in Payne House, sprawled on a huge two-hundred-year-old four-poster in a room that was maybe two square feet larger than the bedframe. The room had a terrace overlooking a river, and antique furniture whose collective age predated the discovery of America. A standing silver ice bucket hosted what remained of the forty-dollar-a-pop bottle of champagne and the pint of strawberries.

Kim, nude except for a bone-colored garter belt hooked up to taupe stockings, lay unresisting on a patchwork quilt, her sandy hair splayed out in a fan behind her shoulders, her hands palms up, resting on the bed in a don't-shoot attitude. Her heavy breasts were settled into her chest. I could see her eyeballs moving under lightly shut lids, and she absently smacked her lips as if her mouth was dry and she was asleep.

As I gently rolled her mound, I looked at the delicate glasses again, at the crystal-knobbed marble-topped dresser, the large framed water-stained lithograph of the Piazza del Popolo, the pale blue porcelain bowl and basin, the river racing under the moon outside our glass-doored terrace.

I had been slowly stroking her for fifteen minutes, periodically stopping to moisten my finger with saliva, my eyes and mind going in and out of focus when suddenly she tremored and eyes still closed, bunched her neck and shot out her chin. It passed, though, and all went back to silence, except that I realized that I was massaging her clit harder than I ever had and that it wasn't hurting her, that I had found the right chord, and that we were taking it home. A minute later she jerked her chin up again, and her stomach bunched. Eyes closed, she started rolling her jaw in concentration. I took a chance and massaged her faster. She shot out a hand that hovered over mine, and I slowed down slightly. Her body jerked again as if she was trying to sit up but was strapped to the bed. I thought her jaw was going to dislocate. The jerkings came faster, then suddenly like a submarine rising from the sea, from her pubic hair to the undercurves of her breasts, rose a huge breadloaf of muscle, a long powerful knot of sex, that made the frilly bow of her garter belt look absurd, a rock of tension that she held against my quivering finger for a long minute, until suddenly the whole thing began to flatten in shuddering graduations, releasing against my hand at one end and through an endless warbling soprano groan at the other. She trapped my wrist with her thighs, curled toward me, reached for me and continued groaning, breaking into a nervous laugh when I couldn't get my hand out and I was pressing her clit past the pleasure point, but I couldn't move my fingers and she couldn't unhook her thighs.

––––––

"Listen, would you be offended if I took off this garter belt? It's cutting me to ribbons." Kim winced, hands poised at the hip clasp.

"Yeah, do." I felt embarrassed that she had to ask me like that. She got up off the bed and worked the stockings off her legs.

"Kim . . ." my heart now-or-nevered. "I have to tell you something."

She ceremoniously held the two stockings up in front of her and dropped them to the floor. She didn't have to act so relieved about taking them off.

"Kim, I wanna tell you something, but you have to promise not to flip out on me or anything until I'm through, okay? I lied to you about this weekend. I didn't go in to talk to my parents."

"Did you go in and see some other girl?"

She said it lightly, but too fast for me to believe it wouldn't be a big scene if I had. "No, nothing like that." I made a face like, "Hey, you're talking A-bomb, we're talking BBs." "No, I went in with Fonseca." It sounded weird. Her name was Fonseca too. "Tony. . . . I went in with Tony, but hey it's over, I swear to you I had to work stuff out and it's worked out and I swear to Christ on my dead mother's . . ." I couldn't think of a body part sacred enough, "chest . . ." That was wrong. It sounded like a sea chantey. ". . . on my dead mother's heart, Kimberly, I'll never see him again, but he was my friend. I liked him. I liked you, I liked him. You liked him. That's why we're compatible—we have the same taste in people. We make the same mistakes. But I swear it's over. We're not even on speaking terms."

I was talking fast so she couldn't get a word in. She stood there naked, a pile of sex fetishes at her feet, her face going through changes of color and musculature. Keep talking, keep talking.

"But listen, it's over, it's not so easy breaking off a friend. You had to give me time, I know it freaked you out I was with him but I'm telling you this now because there is no reason to flip anymore, it's over. Jesus Christ, I feel like I'm talking about another girl, but hey look, everybody, Sing Along with Pete, It . . . is . . . over." I pinched my thumb and forefingers Mitch Miller style.

"Don't humor me, Peter." She narrowed her eyes.

"I'm sorry. Just tell me how to tell you this without your flipping out on me."

"Well, for starters stop telling me not to flip out!"

I snapped my fingers and pointed at her. "You got it."

She sat down on the edge of the bed, her hands collapsed in between her thighs. "Did he do that?" She jutted her chin at my now violet cheekbone.

"Yeah, but it was an accident, it wasn't, it was the opposite. Look, that's not even what I wanted to talk to you about . . . that's all out with the bad air. I wanna talk about in with the good." I refilled our champagne glasses, handed her one, which she took, thank you, thank you, and I sat up and hunched over, getting as close to her on the edge of the bed as possible.

"Kim, listen to me, listen, I pulled off some stuff this weekend that I can't believe myself. I found out about this acting guy, Stanley Hartmann, who I can audition for, he's got a class. I got up on a stage, and I did riffs, stories, a routine. I can't even remember, but I did it. I got up there and blew people away, not really blew them away, but I held my own—they were laughin', they weren't laughing, at one point I had them fucking enraptured, just for a minute, it was a stand-up place in the Village, that place I called you from, they wanted me back for this weekend, Kim, it's showtime for Peter . . . annnd, this coming weekend, me"—I pushed a finger into the quilt—"and you"—I pushed a finger down again closer to her thigh—"we're goin' into New York and we're going to get a taste, and you're gonna see me do my stuff, just me and you, because Kim"—I started stabbing the quilt again with my longest finger—"Kim, I can't tell you, all my life, all my life . . . I don't know . . . I can't be the home-head good little teacher, I'll go crazy up here, this'll kill me, it's bad for my posture, I swear I'm starting to hum the Muzak, so come January hell or high water I'm out but ah . . . I have this fantasy of having my cake and eating it too, Kim, of you, me and the demon seed moving to New York. I mean, you're a writer, you can write anywhere, a school's a school for Anthony and I can do anything. I can earn a living any-where, but I felt so hot last weekend it's not to be denied, we wouldn't starve and I love you, Kimberly." I started to get hot eyes and golf ball throat. "But there's nothing up here for me, and I refuse to be a burnout-in-residence like Tony."

"Don't you come down on Tony," she snapped.

I felt my face go white. That word "you"—all of a sudden every-thing changed and they were back together again.

"You're still seeing him?" I nodded yes to my own question. My heart was a frog.

"No," flat out.

"You still love him." I nodded yes.

"No." She hid her face under a trembly palm.

"Kimberly . . ." I pressed my palms together. "I love you . . . I love you . . . I love you . . ." I closed my eyes, both hands pressed in front of my chest. "I don't want to lose you."

I was shocked by my own ardor. I knew the violence of it came from her defense of Fonseca. She knew it too. I saw her studying my face.

"I don't want to lose *you*," she mumbled, still staring curiously at me.

"Good." I sighed, still feeling shaky. "Look, forget about January, let's go into New York this weekend, let me get up there in that place with you in the front row, let's just walk around, let's just take it a week at a time."

"I can't."

"Why!" Easy, easy.

"I have to go see my parents, remember?"

"Aw fuck!" I felt totally flushed with disgust.

"And you said you'd come with me," she added timidly.

I slid myself back against the headboard and stared at the Piazza del Popolo. Rome. The World. She didn't want to go to New York. Next weekend or ever. She sidled up next to me, but I wouldn't look at her. She rubbed her fingers on the back of my hand for a moment, but when I wouldn't turn my hand to her, she stopped, got up, put on a bathrobe, and walked out on the tiny terrace.

"I'm goin' in, Kim." I frowned at my stomach hair and raised my voice to carry outside. "I'm not going crazy up here."

She was out there in the November cold for a good ten minutes, and when she came in and sat back on the bed her body was jerking with chills.

"Do you know I'm registered at the hospital as a battered wife?" Her voice was sprightly and chipper as if she was announcing her membership in a sorority. "Tony used to beat the shit out of me like clockwork."

I flashed an old Sid Caesar routine where he and his crew played figurines on a huge Swiss weather clock. They came out of the clock-face every hour on the hour, and with stiff wind-up movements proceeded to whack out each other with mallets and gongs to announce the time.

"I'm talking to you about something, Kim." Everything inside me was shouting and running in different directions. "I'm talking to you about something."

"I'm talking to *you* about something." She stared at me with those eyes. She was biting her thumbnail, absently flicking and chipping it off with the bottom of her huge front teeth. Spasming with cold, she jerked abruptly as if someone had poked her in the ribs, but her eyes never left my face. "I'm going to tell you the whole story with me and him . . ." She shook her head No and passed a hand between us in a wide sweep, palm to me. ". . . because I think you should know."

"I know what you're doing, Kim, don't do it. I'm going to New York. I'll go right this second, I swear." I lay glued to the bed. "I swear."

"You should know." She ignored me. "You should know about me and your pal Tony."

"Don't start with me . . ." My voice was weak and I raised and dropped my hand on the bed.

"I told you about Tramp and Otis Redding and meeting at the bar with Whoosh and all, right?" She shrugged and started picking at the patchwork. "Kindred spirits and taking each other home that night and all . . . anyway, the minute we get in his car he turns to me and says,

" 'Whatta you hangin' out with those niggers for?' I couldn't figure it out. I thought he'd be impressed that I was in there. But anyway we started going out, not there though, after that night. He asked me not to hang around there anymore. I didn't really care because I thought I was in love with him, and I even felt flattered, like he was worried about my welfare . . . but *he* still hung out there. I had the key to his place, and I'd wait for him to come back because living with the teacher was even heavier than hanging out in S and L's, and he'd come in late and at first he'd say, 'Did you ever date Whoosh?' I never dated *any* of those guys. I'd already told him that. I'd say no, and he'd drop it, but he must've asked me about every guy in that bar at one time or another those first few months . . ."

"Kim, I don't wanna hear it," I begged.

She ignored me again, talking fast, conversationally, tracing a reed of blue through the patchwork, her eyebrows doing jumping jacks, even though she never looked at my face. "But as I said, I was pretty happy, because I didn't like school. All I wanted to do was be a writer, and here I was living with Mr. Official Writer himself. And I was a good writer too . . . he told me so, and I would have known if he was just flattering me—besides I *knew* I was good. I guess I moved in with him after about a month, everybody knew, everybody in school hated me, but I didn't care, I just wanted to be with him. He used to read to me, he gave me books, he'd read my stuff, he'd read me *his* stuff. Really, I could care less what anybody thought. I was in heaven with him.

"Then in December I got pregnant with Anthony, and at first I was just going to get an abortion, but he wanted me to have the baby. He wanted to get married . . . he was about thirty then . . . so I thought about living my life married to a great writer, having his child, maybe becoming a great writer myself. I was only eighteen . . . I thought, what more could a young girl want?" She shrugged at the champagne stand, then looked down at the quilt again, tracing a vein of red thread. "We got married in January, it was at my parents' house outside Albany. My father's pretty well off and we had a nice ceremony. At first my parents were furious because I was pregnant, and when they found out the guy's name was Fonseca they got double-pissed because they thought he was Puerto Rican and then when I straightened them out on *that* score that he was *Jewish* they got triple-pissed."

"What!" I squawked. "Fonseca's *Jew*ish?" Despite myself I started laughing with amazement.

"Oh yeah, he's that Mediterranean brand of Jew, I always want to say Seraphic . . ."

"Se*phar*dic?"

"Right."

"Tony's Se*phar*dic? . . . oh man . . ." For a second he was my pal again. I still had that knee-jerk reflex of dividing the world into teams, us and them. "He told me he had a Christmas tree."

"We did."

That "we" brought things back into focus.

"No, I meant when he was a kid," I said sullenly.

"Who knows. Anyway, as I said, at first they were fit to be tied, but when my father met Tony that all changed, Tony can charm the eyes out of your head if he wants to." She gave a little snort and a reminiscent smile. "Anyway, right after we got married the trouble started. I dropped out of school the second term . . . I planned to just write and read and have my baby. But Tony was getting jammed up with his writing. I think he was feeling the pressure of being a potentially important writer, getting some bigger project done . . . you know, and I had such admiration for him I was always bragging and gushing about how important he was about to become, and at first he'd laugh, nicely trying to tell me to cool it, then he'd say he couldn't look at my work too much, he said it was too distracting, then he wouldn't want to talk anymore about what I was reading, or what he was working on. Before this he used to read his stuff to me all the time . . . no more. I picked up pretty fast to keep my work to myself. When the baby came he couldn't deal with it . . . the baby was keeping him awake, it was taking all his time, he was under the gun with money, he was too wiped out, he couldn't write, he couldn't write, he couldn't write. Well, how about me? I couldn't write either."

"Yeah!" I shrugged angrily.

"He started bitching about the school . . . they're killing him with work, they envied his youth and talent, they have him over a barrel. I mean, he never liked the school to begin with, and he always used to get off on his angry young man thing, but now *everybody* was a vampire. Everybody wanted to load him up with bullshit work so he could never write, so he could never get away, so he'd be a slave to the English Department. He used to rant and rave about everybody but Jack, he loved Jack, Jack was on *his* side, he always was kind to Tony, told him to have patience with himself. Jack could talk to him. Jack was his friend. He didn't *know* how much Jack was his friend—have you ever heard of somebody almost thirteen years on the job with no tenure? They were dying to get rid of him, they couldn't stand him, Jack kept fighting to keep him on, contract after contract. So while Tony's stomping around complaining about how they don't want him to write so they'll have him forever, Jack is fighting them tooth and nail not to fire him. I think Jack really thought Tony was gifted and if he could only find some peace within himself he really could be great. I used to think that too, but now he's pretty much past it . . . well, who can say. I hear he's writing again, but outside of Jack, forget it, he cut off all our friends. I didn't really care that much, I was always a loner anyhow. I had my kid, my writing, and I had Tony on good days. See, he'd only be flipping out in front of me; as far as anybody else saw, he was still Tony, he was always Tony, and nobody ever took his anger as anything more than part of his act. But he was cracking up, Peter . . ." She grimaced and shook her head at her hands. "He was really losing it fast. When Anthony was a year old, Tony got it into his head that I was running around behind his back with the S and

L crowd. I had not stepped into that place for almost two years, but he said they were laughing at him behind his back, and that was bullshit because they'd *always* laughed at him behind his back because of his act. But one night, right after I put Anthony to bed, Tony comes marching in the house and he's got four of those guys in tow—Whoosh, David, Brandon and this guy Willis. 'Hey honey! Break out the beer, the bourbon . . .' He had those poor guys sit on our couch, and me and him face them on the other couch, holding hands, rubbing knees, his arm around my shoulder, smiling like a Kodak picture, showing them how happy and tight we were. He was watching them like a hawk—watching eyes, eye contact, eyebrow raising—I was never so embarrassed in my life. I still remember poor David, Big David sitting on our couch with his knees higher than the coffee table. All those guys were so uncomfortable, I don't know if they knew what was going on . . . Whoosh probably did . . ."

I started to relax. I was even beginning to enjoy the tale. Fonseca was such an asshole.

"But I always took care of Anthony. I always took care of him. As soon as he was old enough I had him in nursery school . . . I always made sure he had other kids around. I always tried to keep him away from Tony. The thing is, Tony never zeroed in on Anthony. He never yelled at him, he never *anything*'d him. The kid was mine, my problem, his bill. Tony's definition of a child was a living thing that kept you from writing."

"Anthony's so great!" I sounded indignant and strong. She didn't respond.

"So everybody's a scumbag, everybody's keeping him from writing, the school is killing him, I'm running with niggers, his students are morons, his kid eats money," she ticked off in a tired sing-song.

"So why don't you leave him?" I snapped with that same hard-ass indignation.

Kim dropped her head. "That's a very good question."

"You get a fucking job, leave him to his goddamn writing, you take the kid and split!" I rapped my palm with the back of my knuckles.

She frowned down at two clacking nails. "Don't get *angry* at me."

"Who the fuck is angry? You tell me all this shit, and I just don't understand why you put up with it. Why the hell didn't you leave him? You're damn right it's a good question." Slow it down, slow it down.

"Well," she shrugged again, "he wasn't always *like* that, you know? When he was feeling good, when he felt hopeful about his work, he was fantastic. He used to sing to me old songs his grandfather taught him. He used to tell me stories about growing up in New York. He used to read to me, not any of *his* stuff, not any contemporary stuff, but he'd read me Dickens, he'd read me poetry . . . can you believe that? Meatball Tony used to read me nineteenth-century poetry . . . and I wasn't ever hot for gifts . . . I don't believe in gifts, but he would *make* me things, he drew me pictures, he wrote me rhyming poems, he made me a necklace once, a horrible thing with seashells, but he *did* it . . ."

Gifts. Go ask your girlfriend there.

"Did he ever dance for you?"

"Dance for me?"

"Yeah, *dance* for you . . . you know, like *dance!*" I spread my legs on the quilt and did the Monkey quickly, jerking my fist up and my shoulder down. I felt like a fool.

Kim shrugged in confusion. "I don't think he ever *dan*ced for me, but you've got to understand, when you're used to someone stomping around all the time, if he stops, if he lightens up, it's like the sun breaking through and you're twice as happy as you should be. You know, they say you can't know what pain is unless you know what pleasure is. That's bullshit. If someone's knocking on your head, you don't need a scalp massage to know pleasure. All you need is for him to *stop* knocking on your head and you think you're in heaven. So when Tony was feeling good I was on Cloud Nine."

"You sound like a dog."

She stopped. "Why are you being so mean to me?"

In that moment I despised her weakness, despised the "sweet mysteries." In that moment my motto became "the shortest distance between two points is a straight line."

"I'm sorry," I mumbled.

"I'll tell you another reason why I hung in, those first few years. I'm a great believer in paying dues, I'm a great believer in justice. I really believed that Tony was in the middle of going through changes in his work and his life that were driving him crazy, but would eventually make him a better writer. I really felt that this pain would end up in reward and that he would come out of it like a phoenix and that that's the way these things happened, and he had to have patience. I just could *not* believe that anybody could go through that amount of torture and not come out rewarded in the end. And when it did, when *he* did, the marriage would be back on the track. See, I thought a few bad years was nothing in a marriage, you had to have faith and you had to have vision . . . I felt that was my job . . . the keeper of the faith . . . to hold everything together. Besides, he used to say I was the only one he could count on, the only one who wanted him to *be* anything . . . he used to say he lived for me, and even though I know it was fucked up, that used to knock me out, that always used to get to me.

"Then five years ago he had a sabbatical coming up and he got a job offer to teach at NYU as a visiting writer and I begged him to take it, stop talking about New York, let's just go . . . get away from here . . . see what New York can do. So we did, and it was a total disaster. He couldn't write. He said he was under too much time pressure, a year, what's a year, you need a year just to get comfortable. So at the end of the year we wound up back here with nothing to show for it and then he totally . . . totally flipped out because the trip to New York had been his out . . . but now it was over, now it was blown and he had nothing, no changes coming, this was it . . . square one forever. So, I've been to New York, Peter. I lived there. It's a very exciting place." She sounded tired.

"But you've never been there with me."

"I know, but . . ."

"But nothing, me and him are two different experiences."

"I'm sure."

"I've been to *his* New York, it's like not going."

I lightly touched her hand with my fingertips. "My father used to say he had no desire to go to Europe because he'd seen it already during World War II . . . and don't get patient and conceding with me . . . you've never been to New York." I tried to give her an alluringly wise wink.

"Could we put this on hold?" She looked as if she needed an aspirin as big as a pie-tin. "Anyway, we come back up here, his classes were hell, his thing around the faculty intensified so badly that he even stopped talking to Jack, and then he started in on *me!* Before, outside of that crazy jealousy with S and L's he never came down on me as an individual exactly, it was more like he came down *around* me, bitching about marriage and money obligations and mouths to feed, but now it was why did I marry him—because I thought I could suck off his energy? his talent? so I could have a private full-time writing coach? Why did I get pregnant, so I could cement him in? Never laid a hand on me, just verbal abuse, but he would also get crazy that I was writing when he couldn't, like we were on this energy seesaw, like there were two showers but only one hot-water pipe, and so he forbade me to write. I couldn't write, and I just felt like hold on, hold on, hold on to the vision, do not take your eye off the horizon. I actually convinced myself that this was a good sign for us, this was the big blowout coming up, and to walk away now would be to snatch defeat from the jaws of victory. Meanwhile, at the same time the other extreme was intensifying, the gifts, the, the Only yous, You're the only one who wants me to live, the I'd die without yous, the How could I yell at you you're my babys. He'd grab his head, he'd grab his chest, he'd write me this crazy poetry, he'd cry . . . he'd put his hand over his mouth and look at me and cry . . . and then *I'd* cry and we'd wind up swearing to help each other. See, you also have to understand we had no friends, no one coming into the house, Tony was never like this outside, he used to walk around all day holding it in until he got home. He never had friends, just followers, he only hung out with students, kids he could dominate, who were in awe of him, and even with them he always had that Guys and Dolls nonstop act, and if they got too close he would scare them away by getting real physical, not hitting anybody, but he'd give them a bear hug or something that would freak them out . . ."

That stung. The fact that Fonseca was totally in control the night he almost cracked my back outside Fitzie's made me feel betrayed.

"Anyway, pretty soon after New York he decided that he didn't want me to go out of the house unless he knew where I was going . . . like to pick up Anthony at school. He started doing all the shopping, he never gave me money, one time we got a phone bill five dollars over the usual and he flipped out . . . who was I calling, he wanted me to write down all my calls, and the times, and he would check them against the incoming bills . . . and I went along with everything . . . I never disagreed. He would lay some bombshell on me, some new martial law, and then start crying and begging me to understand. One time he flipped out because he found a fifty-dollar bill I had stashed in my underwear drawer—it was a birthday present from his parents. Next thing I knew, he was on his knees begging me not to leave him. . . . See, but he didn't even have to go through all that. He could have told me anything, laid down any law for me . . . I was losing my grasp on the horizon, that keeper-of-the-faith role I had . . . I don't know at what point things snapped for me, but gradually over that year with *no* outside stimulus, *no* internal stimulus, I really started losing it altogether. I mean, he still felt he had to con and justify his act to me, but it was becoming more and more the case that he was dealing with an anchorless person with no stimulus in the world except the sound of his voice and the physical presence of his being. I had Anthony put in boarding school, got him out of the house, the way someone going under holds her kid over the waterline so someone in a boat can grab him . . . and I felt it too. I felt it happening—me going under—and sometimes I fought it. I wrote behind his back . . . I don't even know what I wrote. I should have kept that stuff . . . I'm sure some shrink could have had a field day. I burned everything as soon as I left him. But usually I never disobeyed him, and that's what it came down to . . . obey and disobey . . . when he yelled I usually cringed . . . when he scratched me behind the ear I rolled over on my back. Yeah, you're right. I *was* like a dog."

"Sorry,"

"But there was this one day about three years ago when he came in the house and I didn't hear him and I was writing something. It might even have been a letter to Anthony, and . . . he picked me up, wheeled me around and slapped me once, twice, forehand, backhand, and I believe it was at that moment, that moment—no one had ever struck me in my life . . . my father, nobody—and I believe whatever I *did* have . . . boom. I just lost it. I didn't cry. I didn't even lose my balance, but, you know how people sometimes say they can actually *see* the spirit leaving the mouth of a dying relative? And I saw in that moment *he* lost it too . . . he looked at me like he couldn't believe what he did, and he kind of *slumped*, and that was that. In a funny way this was the payoff. This was the phoenix rising, this was the big payoff from all the bullshit of those first five years, and we came out of all that crap into this weird kind of ballet, this trancy kind of dance. . . . We just got into this slap-caress thing. And I just submitted. I just surrendered to it. He did too. He never really tried to write after that. He'd go teach his class, go out maybe, come home whenever, sometimes he'd be drunk, not drunk. He never got really drunk, but he'd have liquor on his breath. Like you said, he rarely gets drunk, he just drinks as an excuse for things. . . ."

"Except at that artists' colony," I said without thinking.

Kim's eyes got wide. "Who told you about that?" She sounded borderline enraged.

"Jack. Tony was telling us about it and Jack filled me in on the real story."

"What else did he tell you?" Her lips vanished.

"Nothing. I swear. Nothing."

Kim took a deep breath and let it out slowly through her nostrils.

"He didn't tell me anything else, Kim, I swear."

She dropped it. "So he'd come home, find some reason to punish me, slap me, punch me, blacken my eye, then he would freak out and put me to bed and kiss me and caress me and read to me and *feed* me even sometimes, and then two days later it would start again. He'd make me sick, then make me better . . . sometimes I'd provoke him to do it. I could always tell when it was coming by the look on his face . . . the minute he walked in the door . . . sometimes it was right away, sometimes it took hours for him to lose control, but sometimes I pushed him on purpose. I would write in front of him like a kid teasing an adult. I'd do it sometimes just to get it over with, I'd do it sometimes just so we could get to the loving part where he would take care of me. I'd do it sometimes so I could feel as though I had some power, even if it was the power to provoke a beating for myself. I can't tell you enough . . . I knew no other people, I had no other reality . . . I had no other world . . . my whole world was Tony. I just turned myself over to him. I just surrendered. *He* just surrendered . . . we just drifted into this together. It was like dream drugs . . . pretty sick, right?" She nodded encouragingly to me.

I shrugged. "What do you want me to say?" I had to keep it tight and close to the vest because suddenly what I felt, more than horror, anger, outrage, more than any Huns Rape Nuns reaction, was jealousy, a panicky sexual craziness. And although I couldn't swear to it, I had a suspicion that that was what I was supposed to feel. She'd seen me freak when she defended Tony earlier, and now she was giving me both barrels. I believed every word she said, but I could swear the whole thing was a siren song, and it was working too. With every detail I felt something crack and cream inside me. I wanted this motherfucker to end.

"So how'd you break it off?" I said through tight lips. In my effort to control myself I probably sounded bored.

"Do you know that I didn't want to leave him? It took three tries to make me *want* to leave . . . I'm not talking about him *letting* me leave. The first time I tried was when Jack stopped by the house in the middle of the day with some stuff for Tony. I hadn't seen Jack in a year, and I came to the door looking like a raccoon with two black eyes . . . he totally freaked out . . . he was going to kill Tony, but I begged him to sit down, I hadn't had anyone in the house for so long I felt scared. I think he saw how crazy I was . . . he promised me he wouldn't interfere only on the condition I went with him to the Family Court and filed a complaint against Tony. He said I could stay in his house if I was afraid . . . I don't even remember details. I just remember clerks and questions, clerks and questions and Jack's hand on my arm. Then I was home with this piece of paper from the Family Court. And when Tony came in I was standing in the middle of the living room shaking like a leaf holding out that paper in front of me. He couldn't even tell what it was, so he came closer to read it and then he laughed and he said, 'Like the Jewish vampire said to the lady holding the crucifix,' and then he rattled off some line of Yiddish which meant It ain't gonna help ya. I was so relieved he wasn't mad at me I just collapsed in this laughy kind of sobbing, and he put an arm around me, and he said 'C'mon, let's go get some ice cream,' and we walked out of the house. I saw Jack sitting in his car across the street and I winked at him. The next day he knocked me around about something else, but I can't even remember what. Even though it looked like I blew it then, there was something about that day that changed things in a way that eventually got me out of there, and it wasn't getting the restraining order, it wasn't Tony balking at hitting me and turning nice for the night . . . it was Jack . . . Jack listening to me . . . Jack's hand on my arm for two hours and Jack sitting outside the house in his car. And it wasn't Jack the romantic hero coming to rescue me, it was Jack the third person, the human being breaking the trance for a few hours, trying to wake me up from my daily sleeping-pill overdose."

"Yeah, so then the next time?"

"The next time I left him, I *tried* to leave him, I went down to the police station with two more black eyes . . . this was about six months later. I went right to the police. They didn't give a shit; the duty sergeant told me to file for a temporary order of protection. I said I'd already done that, that was that paper I got, and he asked me if I had it with me and did I want him arrested. I said that I'd filed for it six months ago. He asked me if I ever made my court appearance to get a Permanent Order, or was I a no-show like three-quarters of the women in the county filing a complaint against their husbands . . . I ran out of there crying. I called my parents, they didn't want to know from nothing, they have this way of ignoring anything that agitates them, they just don't hear it . . . especially my father. They never forgave me for getting pregnant to begin with, and they never forgave me for sending Anthony to boarding school, which, incidentally, *they* were paying for, and they just didn't want to hear about Tony beating me up . . . my father's involved with this evange-list television show? and I had never been anything but trouble and an embarrassment to him—hanging out with blacks—so I got no help there. And I was too afraid to call Jack . . . probably because Jack would actually have done something effective to get me out of there, and maybe I just wanted to complain . . . maybe I couldn't conceive of life without Tony yet . . . but I was getting close . . . I was getting ready . . . it's almost impossible to do it on your own. Do you know why I finally left him? Last September he brought his freshman writing class over to the house. He was real mad about something I did the day before, and he made me sit with the class on the floor in the living room. I was surrounded by fifteen freshmen and he introduced me as his new wife, Briget, and he proceeded to tell the class about how his first wife, Kimberly, committed suicide the year before, and how he didn't think he could go on until he met

Briget here . . . and he talked about how tormented his marriage to Kim was, and how it was almost inevitable that one of them would have to die so the other could live.

"Those poor little kids were totally freaked out by this rap . . . they didn't want to hear about it. All through the class he kept calling me Briget . . . What do *you* think of this story *Briget? Briget*, can we get some soda? And for the next two days he called me Briget until I was half-convinced my name really was Briget and this Kimberly person was dead. It was the closest he came to killing me, closer than any beating. I got so terrified I wrote a letter describing the last five years of our marriage, and I left it on the kitchen table with a note saying that I had four copies of this letter in envelopes addressed to Jack, the town paper, the student paper and Tony's father, and that all these envelopes were with a friend, and if he ever came near me again, if he ever came near Anthony or if anything ever happened to me this friend was to mail the letters. I was lying, I didn't make copies, Jack already knew what the story was anyhow. He didn't want to go after me . . . he was giving me the message to leave him . . . he was dying too, with me . . . but, anyway, I lived with Jack and his wife for a few weeks. Jack got me that office job in Geology. Christ, I couldn't even type. Do you know how awful it is to hunt and peck on a fifteen-hundred-dollar IBM typewriter? Well, I learned soon enough, and I got my apartment, I pulled Anthony out of boarding school, and here I am. But I'll tell you something, and maybe I should be ashamed to say this, but I miss him . . . I miss Tony. He used to jump out of bed in the middle of the night and hunch over and walk fast into the living room like he had somewhere to go or something to do and he would always wake up bewildered, not knowing where he was or what he was going after, and I had to put him back to bed and calm him down, and in his sleep he used to tell me he loved me. When he stopped writing he stopped jumping out of bed and sleepwalking like that, and that made me sadder than anything, because I knew that gone with whatever the hell it was that drove him into the next room in his sleep every night was the hope that he would make it big. He slept like the dead after that . . . and that's fucking sad, don't you think? I left that house just as much for him as for me, and I knew it was sick, after all I just said, but I still care about him, and that's the fucking truth." She started crying, wiping her cheeks like a kid with the heel of her palm. "I can't go back to him."

I felt everything slipping through my hands. She was telling me all this because she was afraid she was losing me, and now I was afraid *I* was losing *her*.

"So how many times have you seen him since?" I asked flatly. I felt beat. Beaten out.

"Twice. I told you that a hundred times already." She started snapping, but pulled out of it. "But both before meeting you." She crept closer to me on the bed.

"Did you get beat up?" I asked calmly.

"Once."

"Why!" I screamed, holding down my own impulse to smash her face.

"I was lonely! You know lonely? That night I met you I was going back to see him again. But now I've got you. You saved me, okay?"

"Hold it! Hold it! What do you mean you were going back to *see* him? What the hell were you doing at Chee Lok? You told me you were waiting for your friend."

"I lied." She shrugged.

"About *what?* . . ." I felt totally turned around.

"About waiting for my friend."

"I still don't understand . . . were you supposed to meet Tony there?"

"Nope. I was trying to find something to keep me from going to Tony's."

"Some *thing?*"

"Some *one* . . . excuse me."

"But why'd you *lie* to me, Kim?" I hunched my shoulders and touched my chest.

"What the hell was I supposed to say . . . I'm looking for a pickup so I don't have to go to my husband's place and get my ass kicked?"

"Kim, I don't know . . . of all the fucking places to go for a pickup . . . Jesus Christ . . . that joint's a total shit hole."

I tried to envision Kim going home with any of the guys who had been doing the cha-cha the night we met. It was such an absurd vision I couldn't even get a jealousy roll going. "Chee fucking

Lok . . . Kim, if you were serious about scoring you'd probably do better going to McDonald's."

"You bet," she said with no apology.

"Well, that's just great . . . I'm sorry I fucked things up. I really didn't mean to interfere with your beatings."

She looked at me popeyed as though I just punched her in the stomach. I couldn't believe that after hearing all these horror stories I was being such a shitass. I felt like it was out of my control.

"Kim, you tell me this stuff about Chee Lok, you make me feel like an accident—a 'something.' " I wanted to slap my own face.

"Jesus *Christ*, Peter!" She punched her own soft thigh, hot eyed and choking. "You were supposed to be some goddamn fast fuck and we're still together. You're my boyfriend now! Doesn't that say something?"

The word boyfriend broke me up. It was so gentle. But I still felt that crazed weepy anger.

She inched toward me but didn't touch me, as if she could read my mind. I sat rigid against the headboard. Relax.

"How come Anthony's so angry at you all the time? Is he mad about boarding school, the shuffling and all?" I tried to sound conversational and peacemaking.

"Maybe." She shrugged at her knuckles. "Anthony sees this psychoanalyst, Dr. Lane. Lane told me sometimes kids take the father's side because they believe in justice."

"What justice?" I refrained from saying I knew about the shrink.

"Well, if you're good you get rewarded; if you're bad you get hit. If Mommy's getting hit she must be bad. If Daddy's beating Mommy and Mommy's *not* bad, what's to keep Daddy from hitting Anthony? Therefore, Mommy must be bad. Otherwise, Anthony is in deep shit, and the world is in chaos. So Mommy's bad . . ." She shrugged again, almost laughed. "Bad Mommy, that's me. My parents paid for the shrink." She crawled on all fours to lie beside me. I wasn't ready for that. She reached to hug me, her arm across my chest, but I wasn't ready yet.

Sensing I wasn't coming across, she collapsed into herself with exasperation. She was lying flat out with only her head up at a neck-breaking angle against the base of the headboard. She looked as miserable as she did uncomfortable. I wasn't ready to go all huggies yet.

"Why me, Kimberly? What do you see in me? Because I'm not *like* him. I'm not gonna wind up like him."

"I know!" she whined, raising and dropping a hand. "I don't *want* him anymore. I'm *try*ing! I want *you!*"

"Oh yeah?" I got up to leave, naked, totally full of shit. "Then you better come to New York."

"I'll go back to him," she said, like "I'll jump." She looked scared to death, still in that uncomfortable corpse-like position.

"That's your choice, Kim." I stood by the lithograph over the dresser.

"I know it." She shrugged, then burst out crying, raised her arms for me to come to her, and I felt myself jackknife in sadness, knowing full well that's exactly what she would do.

———

For the next week I went insane, swinging back and forth from rage at Fonseca to rage at Kim. I felt self-loathing, fear, a panicked kind of love, sexual overdrive. I yearned to have a physical fight—with Fonseca mainly, but also with Kim. I started having the queasy horrifying thought that Kim *wanted* me to take a swing at her, that maybe if I started punching her out she'd *really* fall in love with me. And maybe if I started acting like that, then ten years from now she'd be sitting there with some other young shithead telling *him* how horribly *I* treated her but she couldn't deny it, she still loved me, she still missed me—isn't that sad? And then the tears would flow. She'd tell him if he didn't stay with her then she'd come back to *me*. *Me!* Speedo burn-out shithead panic face. I had no idea what to make of that tale. I didn't have the tools to handle it. Didn't have the experience, and overriding all the horror was my feeling jealous of Fonseca, of his hold on her. On me too. I had felt the same way toward him too—scared to death but grateful for his kindnesses, for his good moods. And my thing had ended in a beating too. I started to think about my mother a lot. I missed her more strongly than I ever had since I was a kid. One night I even started crying for her. I was going berserk and I had to have it out of me. I had to call Fonseca out, and I was scared to death of him all over again.

———

"Hey Pete, how was New York?"

"It was great . . . it was very good. . . ." I didn't feel like getting into it. "Jack, talk to me. Tell me about Fonseca." I sat on Jack's desk. He leaned back in his chair, squinting at me warily. "What do you mean? What happened?"

"Nothing. Kim told me the whole story with the marriage and I'm going crazy. I don't know what the moral of the story is."

"What story? Pete, you look horrible . . . you getting any sleep?"

"Okay." I held up my hands in submission. "Tell me premarriage. Tell me about early Fonseca. You hired him, right?"

"I didn't hire him," Jack said, like it wasn't his fault. "Becker hired him."

"Who was Becker?"

"He's dead now. He used to be chairman. He hired me too."

"So you were here before him? Fonseca? Before Fonseca?" I tried to catch my breath and slow down.

"No, I was here about five years before Fonseca. Becker hired Tony when Tony was maybe twenty-seven, twenty-eight, what's he now, forty?"

"Almost thirty-nine."

"So maybe he was younger."

"Anyway . . ."

"Anyway what? What's the matter with you?"

"I'm just trying to figure something out here, Jack."

"Okay," he said faintly. "What do you want to know?"

"What was he like when he started?"

"Tony?" Jack swung around so he was facing his bookshelves. "He was crazy," he said mildly. "Like he is now, but not so bad. He was nuts, though. He had just come off a lot of attention for his short stories and he was very excited. He was a great teacher, but he was very manic, very full of himself. He must have screwed half the school in those first few years . . . women teachers, graduate students . . . not undergraduate kids though, except Kim . . ." Jack flinched but I shrugged it off. "He had a lot of blood in his veins, a lot of talent, teaching, writing talent, very charming . . . he was great here. For a while he really was a bit of a sensation, even though the fucking-around part wasn't so hot—not that *I* gave a shit, for one—

but when he got jammed up with his writing he cut back on that, he stopped trying to be such a lady killer. By the time he got involved with Kim, he was almost like a monk . . ." Jack swung around to face me, shrugged as if that was all there was.

"Okay, let me ask you something. If he was . . . *is* . . . such a maniac, if he couldn't write anymore, for *his* sake, for the *school's* sake, how come you fought so hard to keep him on? What are you, a sadist?"

"Nah, Pete . . . let me tell you. First of all, he was, and *is*, a terrific teacher. Second of all, the writing block thing is bullshit . . . if he really wanted to write he'd write. And if he were to leave, where would he go? What would he do for money? You know what he'd do? He'd get another teaching job. What do you think, he'd work with his hands? He'd become a steelworker? The fucking guy's almost forty years old, right? Not only that, but he'd have to wind up teaching in some small tank-town college somewhere because nobody'd hire him—he doesn't have a doctorate, he hasn't published anywhere in ten years, and he has no friends teaching anywhere else who could lobby for him. But I'll tell you the main reason I always fought to keep him on . . ." Jack hunched forward to me and lowered his voice to a whisper. "Tony . . . is . . . crazy! And I don't think he could survive anywhere else. He's in fucking protective custody here . . . he's an inmate of the asylum and he ain't ready for the outside world. There are certain people here, and I won't mention names—drunks, hermits, eccentrics—they'd *die* without a campus . . . and Tony's one of them." He leaned back. "I'm serious, Pete, I'm not being cynical."

I snorted. "How about you? . . ." I felt calmer. "Are you an inmate?"

"Me?" Jack belched into his fist. "I'm a guard. They throw me out, I take off on *The Thin Man*, go down to the Keys and open a restaurant. I'm a guard." He broke out into one of his belly laughs.

"Is Fonseca going out with anybody now?"

"I don't know, Pete, the guy's pretty private. I think he was going out with some black lady from town for a while a few years ago, but he's pretty much of a loner . . . he doesn't ever really say anything to anybody . . . I don't hang out with him or anything. I think he was

seeing that woman for a while, though . . . maybe he's seeing somebody. If he is though, it's nobody from around here. I really don't
know . . ."

"Kim says you took her to the cops when he beat her up."

Jack abruptly stopped laughing. His face got mean and hard; it
was a face I'd never seen before. His jowls seemed to turn to concrete, his eyes were sunken and dull with anger.

"I swear to you Pete . . . when I opened that door and saw that
poor kid's face I wanted to *kill* that fucking bastard . . ." His voice
came out in spits and hisses, an icy growl of pure fury and righteous instinct devoid of all my pathetic wing-flapping and Hamlet-
like hesitancy.

"Kim stopped you?"

"Yeah," he grunted, running both hands through his hair and
scratching the back of his scalp.

"She stopped me too," I muttered, lying, feeling totally disgusted with myself, feeling totally over my head, lost and ashamed
for my anger at Kim. Jack didn't seem to hear me, which was just
as well.

"It all seemed to work out in the end," he said in a milder, lighter
voice as if shrugging the whole thing off. "It's over."

––––––

My cock died in Kim's fist. She looked up at me from her hunched
shoulders and passed the back of her free hand across her lips. With
a casual expression of concern, her eyes trained on my face, she
absently lapped the head one more time. Nada.

"What's up?" she asked calmly.

I closed my eyes. "I dunno . . . it's okay." I couldn't bring myself
to say I couldn't get it up because I was thinking of Fonseca.

Kim crawled up my body and rested her head on my arm. My
cock felt cool from her mouth.

"It's okay," she murmured.

"I know it's okay. I already said that."

Jack was a *real* man.

"You like to dance?" she asked in a small teasing voice. "Maybe
we should go dancing."

I thought of Fonseca dancing in the gorilla cage.

"What, the Latin Hustle in the Mall?"

"Noo. . . ." She slapped my chest. "Real dancing."

"Yeah? What do they do up here, hoe-downs?" I thought of her and Fonseca grinding at the S and L that first night ten years ago.

"Don't be such a smart-ass." She gently took the head of my cock and made it jounce like a marionette.

"Cut it out," but it was getting hard.

"El-lo! What's this?"

Before I could stop her, she curled down my body and was sucking me off again. Her ass was raised toward me, and lifting her by the hip bones—I was getting pretty strong from bench presses—I gently lowered her on my mouth, draping my hands around the small of her back. There was a faint bitter smell of pee, but I pushed my tongue straight up inside her until my gullet muscles ached.

Jack was a *real* man. Kim clucked in frustration as my cock died again.

"Well, if you're not going to fuck me, then dance for me." Her head was back on my arm, and she was poutily pulling out my chest hairs one by one.

"I'll dance for you," I muttered.

"Dance for me," she whined. "You just said you danced for strangers—what am I, Swiss cheese?"

"If you don't shut up, I'll dance *on* you."

She shrugged. "Dance *on* me, then."

"Don't talk like that." I thought of her with blackened eyes and suddenly I was up, nude, crouching by her anemic record collection. I flipped to an old scratchy Stax Volt anthology called Memphis Gold, and as a mournful cat wail back-up group played off a slow falsetto, I started hopping to it. I worked against the music, doing all these non-sequiturious moves as if I were deaf. Not real dancing, but doing all these numbers, walking across the room like a hieroglyph, my spine rigid, my arms bent like a swastika, my neck and head jerking like a cobra. Then leaping Duncan-dance Grecian-urn moves, twirling into back-of-hand-on-forehead anguish postures, dying Gauls, the archer, the lovesick swain, all to that Memphis grind, all with hambony faces to hide my panic. Kim giggled, and when I stopped she clapped her hands and yelled, "Dance more!" So I did. I always kept a mocking theatrical look on my face so I wouldn't feel embarrassed. The next cut was a Green-Onions-type instrumental and I found myself doing a twitchy-assed pixie mince across the room followed by a Frug, a Twist, a Jerk, and finally The Monkey. Somewhere in the middle of this early-sixties dance medley I got lost in Fonseca again, and without realizing it I started dancing in earnest, straight-faced, keeping time. Kim was laughing and applauding from the bed. She yelled, "More! More!" just as I was in the midst of a Kung Fu fight to the death with Fonseca in my head. Her command snapped me out of it, and totally embarrassed, I went back to broad Duncan moves, The Cleopatra, The Popeye, the Hitchhike, all with a frantically self-mocking leering face, but it was too late. Kim could say, with total honesty, that I had got up and danced naked for her. I would have to kill him. Bees in my head.

I sat in the back of the auditorium watching Fonseca in the lecture pit go through his paces, wisecracking his way through a half-dozen contemporary American authors, none of whom seemed to be getting glowing retrospectives.

It was the first time I'd laid eyes on him since the night of that fight in the Baby Blue. I had been purposely avoiding him, and I assumed he had been avoiding me, but that morning I found the suitcase that I had left in New York standing in my office like Exhibit A, and propelled by blind alarm I rushed out of my room to challenge him in some way, but I had no real idea of what I was up to. I felt like an asshole, just sitting there listening to his lecture. Halfway through the class I caught myself taking notes. Stifling a groan, I just slumped down in my seat and covered my eyes.

I didn't raise my head until I heard, "This is Associate Professor Anthony T. Fonseca, signing off."

He was immediately swamped by a dozen students jumping all over him with How can you says and What about the importance ofs. Taller than all of them, he twisted his neck right and left, making faces as if he was being attacked by Marabunta ants. He broke loose, physically parting them with a courtly breast stroke, and lurched for the auditorium door. Suddenly he turned, walking backwards, and raised a hand: "Look, you disagree with me? Fine. You got term papers coming up, take me on with a term paper, okay? This is the free marketplace of ideas." He wheeled again, rolling his eyes heavenward.

As his hand touched the swinging door he saw me sitting alone in the sea of emptying chairs. He stopped. I tried to give him a hard-ass glare, but I was frozen in my seat with fear.

Regarding me, he raised his chin and passed his curled fingers under his jaw. I didn't know if it was an absent-minded gesture, an Italian fuck-you, or, like some horrifying intimation of my old nightmare about him, an invitation, a dare, to take a swing at him.

The whole thing lasted a second or two before he was swept out the door by a wave of undergraduates.

———

"Pie?" Kim had her arm across my throbbing chest. "Are you going to come with me over the weekend or you going to New York?"

I felt defeated. Her giving me a choice like that sealed it more than if she had held a gun to my head.

"Yeah, I'll go with you." I ran a thumbnail across my forehead. It came away heavy with greasy sweat.

"Oh, I can't believe I forgot to tell you." She kissed my temple. "I sold another story."

"That's great." I fought down an impulse to say "Yeah, to me."

"Pie?"

"Yeah?"

"Let's do what you said."

"What?"

"Let's take it a week at a time."

"I'm telling you, Kim, next weekend after that I'm going to New York."

"I know." She burrowed her head under my armpit and up onto my chest. My nose filled with that coconut fragrance. I don't even think it was her hair. It was her actual *head* that smelled like that.

"Pie?"

"What . . ."

"I love you."

———

As compensation for holding off on New York another week, I decided to put an iron in the fire via the telephone.

"Hi, is Stanley Hartnett there?" I was holding the mouthpiece with both hands.

"Speaking . . ." He had a young strong voice. For some reason I was assuming he'd be an elderly statesman like Lee Strasberg.

"Yes . . . this is Peter Keller. I'm a friend of Bill Crown's? Your student?" It felt strange referring to my teacher as a student.

"Yes?"

"Yes. My name is Peter Keller, and Bill told me you were having auditions for your class, acting class, in a few months and I was wondering how I could go about applying . . ."

"Well, what's your background?"

"Jewish lower middle class."

He laughed and it took me a minute to figure out why. Good sign that he laughed, though.

"Oh, my *acting* background!" That *was* pretty funny.

"Well, I'm teaching English now at Simon Straight College. But I've taken classes with Jim Doobie . . ." Please don't say Doobie's a dick.

"And I've done some work here at the Tushkin Playhouse. I played an executioner in *The Good Woman of Setzuan*." I froze, thinking maybe I fucked up. All European-authored plays taking place in the Orient seemed to have an executioner in them. Christ, at least *The Mikado* did. But if *Good Woman* lacked an executioner, Hartnett didn't let on. Just to play it safe, I threw in an obvious goofball. "And I played a hernia belt in *She Stoops to Conquer*."

"Very impressive," he chuckled, "Actually Bill Crown told me about you."

"He *did!*" What a great, truly great, guy.

"The problem is that the class I have now is full up and I don't think there'll be any openings. I'm starting a second class in the spring but that'll be a beginner's class."

"So? That's perfect!"

"It sounds as though you may be pretty advanced for that."

"Oh c'mon, please don't break my chops. The hernia belt was only a supporting role."

He started whooping with laughter. I didn't think it was *that* funny, but once again I didn't get my own joke for a few minutes.

"Okay, okay. Look, the class won't start until April," he laughed lightly, cleared his throat. "When are you coming into New York?"

"January!" I bit my knuckle.

"Okay, call me when you come in and we'll talk."

"Bless you."

The minute I hung up I got up and did a joyous aerobic dance of push-ups and running in place, but then I thought of Kim putting up a fight about going, and that led to thinking about Man Mountain Fonseca and it was all I could do not to take off from my stationary sprint and hurl myself into the wall of my office. Come with me. Let me go.

———

It was ten-thirty the following New York–less Saturday morning. Kim and I were sitting in her living room waiting to be picked up. The party was in honor of her grandparents' sixtieth wedding anniversary. We were all dressed up and sitting quietly and tensely as though we were in a doctor's office instead of the room where we watched TV, ate food and sometimes, late at night, fucked. November sunlight streamed in through the Venetian blinds, making the portable TV glow as if its molecules were going to disassemble and then reassemble in a hovering spaceship.

Kim was wearing panty hose and a skirt the color of tree bark. Her strapped pumps swished back and forth under her crossed ankles. She looked like a cover model on a Simplicity Patterns catalogue. She smiled at me and started thumbing through a coloring book. I touched my tie knot. I didn't feel as stiff and nervous as I was acting. It was more a sympathetic gesture. Kim's anxiety was like a gas in the air. Anthony came running in the room, the knot of his blue tie wrenched to the side and the waist of his white shirt wrinkled and billowed out of his blue pants. He looked like a Catholic-school kid during recess.

"Anthony!" Kim's eyes widened and she gently yanked him back and forth as she straightened out his costume. He sucked air noisily through his nostrils.

"When are we goin' to Poppy's?"

"As soon as Aunt Emma Sweet comes to pick us up."

"Do you know Poppy?" Anthony twisted the top half of his body to me.

"Anthony, please sit down."

"Do you know Poppy?"

"Pink eye?"

"Poppy!"

"I know Popeye." I shrugged.

The doorbell rang and Kim jerked as if it were wired to her insides.

"Anthony, put your jacket on, please."

I stood up and faced the door.

Kim opened to a small taut mannish woman with a Joan of Arc hairdo and aggressive eyes behind large glasses.

"Hello dear, are you ready?" They both stooped forward from the waist to brush cheeks like partners in a Bavarian knee-slapping dance.

"Aunt Emma Sweet? This is a good friend of mine, Peter Keller." Kim smiled at me as though she had just met me five minutes ago. "Peter teaches at the College," she said in a slight singsong.

Aunt Emma Sweet leaned into the room as though there was a puddle between us, and shook my hand.

"Anthony?" Kim called out. "Do you have your jacket?"

Anthony came charging in, ignoring his aunt.

"Don't you say hello?" Kim bing-bonged.

"Hello" he monotoned, still not looking at her.

Kim shot me another eyeless smile.

"Would you like some apple juice or something?" she asked her aunt.

"No, we better get going . . ."

As Kim reached for a winter jacket off a coat tree, Aunt Emma Sweet pointed a finger at her like Moses warning the Pharaoh. "It's hot outside."

Kim backed off from the coat tree as if it had just burst into flames.

It felt more like April than November. As we followed Aunt

Emma Sweet to her car, Kim walked with a hand lightly on Anthony's shoulder.

Halfway down the block she stepped on the heel of his shoe and his foot came free.

"Oop, excuse me." She laughed lightly.

Anthony fixed his own shoe as Kim stood over him smiling amiably, giving me a totally repulsive false wink.

We piled into the back seat of a large Pontiac. Sitting next to Aunt Emma Sweet were two kids about seven years old. One was white, one was Asian.

"Peter, this is Harlan and this is Cam Dong," Aunt Emma Sweet said as she grimaced through the driver's side window at oncoming traffic. The Asian kid turned and peered at me. I looked at Kim.

"Aunt Emma Sweet and her husband Ralph adopted Cam Dong," Kim explained in her new kindergarten-teacher lilt.

"Our family, our larger family, not Ralph and I, have adopted seven Cambodian and Vietnamese orphans." Aunt Emma Sweet looked at me in the rearview mirror.

"That's terrific." I smiled.

Kim nodded in agreement.

———

"Yesterday, I got Daddy a birthday present from the three of us," Aunt Emma Sweet said to her two kids, thirty minutes into the ride.

"Whadja get him?" Harlan asked.

"No, I don't think I should tell you because you kids have big mouths and he'll know what it is three full days before his birthday."

"Tell us, Ma!" Harlan whined.

"Tell us . . ." Cam Dong monotoned mindlessly, twisting his head to check out the back-seat passengers again.

"No, I don't think I will . . . this year I want it to be a surprise."

"Ma-aa, tell-luss!" Harlan writhed.

"If I tell you . . ." she paused, ". . . and if I find out in any way shape or form that anybody in this car has blabbed to him beforehand, that person will go to bed at seven o'clock for six days in a row. Do I make myself clear?"

Harlan, Cam Dong, Anthony and Kim chorused a solemn "Yesss."

I snapped my head up and glared at Kim. Her eyes caught mine for the first time all day and she blushed, curling into the corner of the rear seat, her head against the glass, hiding her crumpled face under the canopy of her hand. Jesus Christ. I was chilled with revulsion. I decided to boycott everybody in the car. Especially Kim. I could have been in New York now, *she* could have been in New York.

The car hummed along the highway. I stared at the argyle pattern on Anthony's socks. Who the fuck was I kidding? Who the fuck did I think I was? I put my hand in Kim's lap, and the hand that gripped mine was trembly and damp, squeezing me so hard that I thought my knuckles would pop.

It was two hours to the suburbs of Albany. Anthony picked his nose and swung his crossed ankles the whole way. Kim was pulled into her family-terror head, and I had plenty of time to do calliope swirls of agony over her, me, New York, Stanley Hartnett, Fonseca, my own family. A pleasant drive.

When we finally parked on the Professionalsville-type suburban street, Aunt Emma Sweet and her kids vanished ahead into the house without looking back. The three of us walked holding hands as stiff as a family symbol in a UNESCO demography chart.

Surprisingly, the house was almost empty. The vestibule fronted a deserted sunken den on the left and a kitchen up five steep steps. I heard outdoor voices coming from beyond the kitchen though, and through an open rear door I glimpsed laughing faces and a small square of a huge green and white striped tent. Aunt Emma Sweet and her kids had already cleared the vestibule, marched up the stairs, walked through the kitchen past college-age girls in skirts and polo shirts scurrying in and out with broad platters, and disappeared into the yard, the impact of their entrance coming back to the three of us in cooing ahhing waves of Hellos and There they ares.

———

"Hi, Mom." Kim touched her mother on the shoulder. We were standing on the shadow line of the open party tent. Kim's mother was a small wiry bat with a slight hunchback, no lips, a high gray shellacked hairdo and sun-cracked caramel skin. Despite the hump, she had the ginger moves of an old she-jock, riding, tennis, cow-punching, maybe. She seemed totally uncomfortable and absurd in her dress and string of jaw-breaker-sized simulated pearls. I was sure she had denim underwear on. She narrowed her eyes at me and pursed her almost lips. I tightened up my pecs and looked severe.

"Mom, this is Peter Keller."

"Peter?" She had a raw bark like George C. Scott.

We shook hands.

She made no move to kiss Kim, nor Kim her. It was amazing to me that this old Marjorie Main prison matron produced a daughter as moist as Kim. I could see her and her sister Aunt Emma Sweet both heads-down, pummeling Kim in the stomach with their fists.

Scanning the crowd, I saw that more than a few of the women there had that small tight leatherneck look to them. No wonder Kim was freaked. She was probably the biggest pussy in the clan.

Kim's mom turned to the huge lawn tent. "Poppy heard it was gonna be sixty today, so we decided to have it outside. He called Petersen last night. I watched 'em put it up this morning. It took seven men. Ohh, you should see the cake we got . . ." She brushed Kim's arm, her eyebrows arched in pleasure. ". . . it's huge, it took two men to carry it, I doubt if thirty men could finish it off. Oh! Kimberly!" She bowed her head and snapped her fingers. "Do you remember Mrs. Cavett? She's a friend of Mother Carmichael's." She offered Kim a staggeringly old lady who had been steadily inching toward the three of us since we started talking. It was as if Kim's mother saw her from ten feet off, had calculated her pace and knew she had time for a conversation before the old bird came within earshot. Mrs. Cavett had blue hair, which peeked out of a baseball cap. She wore a blue suit, real pearls and tennis sneakers. Her swollen lower legs were the size of stovepipes. Mrs. Cavett's entire broken face painfully lifted into her smiling eyes. Kim's mother checked me out as Mrs. Cavett hoisted a twisted amber smooth finger to Kim's chest.

"I ri-member you when you waz nakid." She jerked up and down in silent laughter, then slowly turned her head to Kim's mother. The finger swayed toward me. "Watch 'em . . . he's a Cor*nell* man."

"I'm sure he is . . ." She smiled at me. "Kim, you should find Poppy and tell him you're here. I think your grandparents are over by the bar."

"Wait, talk to me before we meet anybody. What's the story here, who's who?"

Kim and I meandered around the perimeter of the tent.

"Well, my family are the Carmichaels. Just about everybody here is a Carmichael or a Sweet, that's my mother's family."

"Who's Father Carmichael, is he a priest?"

"No, he's my grandfather. Mom's always called them Mother and Father Carmichael."

"How come you call that cunt who drove us over Aunt Emma Sweet?"

"Because I have an Aunt Emma Carmichael too."

"Okay, so what does your father do again? He's a religious singer?"

"No, he's a songwriter, he's an Evangelist songwriter . . . he writes inspirational songs for Reverend Howie."

"Howie . . . is *he* here today?"

"Howie's in Gabon."

"Does your old man have any big hits?"

"In fact, yeah, he wrote this thing about two years ago called 'Christian's My Way.' He gutted all of Paul Anka's lyrics about how the guy is reflecting on his life, you know, win lose or draw at least he did it his way, and he replaced them with all these lyrics about how wretched and empty life has been because he did it his way but then he met Christ and Christ showed him salvation and now he does it *'His'* way, if you know what I mean."

"This is the motherfucker who wouldn't help you out when Tony was doing his number, right?"

"Yeah. *Please* don't start . . . don't say anything smart to him . . . it's hard enough with him as is—you saw me coming over here—let's say just hello to everybody, eat and go home, okay?" She steered me under the tent toward four generations of Sweets and Carmichaels with a light garnish of Asian orphan.

I was introduced to the party couple, Mother and Father Carmichael. Mother was small and self-consciously spry. She stood guard over Father, who sat vulture-necked and glum in a high wooden-framed wheelchair with a woven cane seat and back. He had blue skin, speaker-sized ears, liver spots on his temples and a thick yellow-white mustache.

". . . and this is my friend Peter." Kim spoke in that universal singsong used on oldies and infants.

"How are you?" I shook hands with Mother Carmichael. Her skin felt wax smooth and cool.

"How am I? I'm eighty-five years old, and thanks to Christ I feel like a teen-ager."

Father Carmichael raised disgusted eyes to me and Kim. His mustache twitched on one side as if he was sucking his teeth.

I was introduced to a battery of relatives as we zigzagged from the food end to the liquor end. Everybody looked comfortable and inoffensively plain, although there was a lot of booze being thrown back.

At one point Kim got cornered by a cousin and I sauntered off by myself.

Anthony flew by me, his shirt flapping out of the back of his pants. Two little giggling Asian girls came running after him. He hid behind some fat guy in a beige silk suit holding a plastic glass of bourbon neat.

"Peter! Help me!"

The little girls ran into the fat guy's thighs and the three of them started running around him in circles. The guy whooped and whirled his head to see what was happening.

"Peter! Help me! They want to kiss me!" Anthony shouted, making flamboyantly athletic fakes and dodges.

One of the girls absently rested her hand on the fat man's crotch, and he jerked back, splashing his drink on his jacket and tie.

Anthony zoomed away, the girls in pursuit.

Kim grabbed my arm. "Here we go."

She headed for a heavyset fiftyish crew-cut guy with narrow but warmly beaming eyes and a facial cast that suggested that any expression other than smiling was a concerted effort. His head was figure-eight shaped, bulging out along the jawline and above the deeply indented temples. He was standing with a young couple who held hands. He briefly glanced at Kim, flashed her a fast eye-smile and turned his head back to the twosome, his face drawn into a serious listening expression. As he nodded intently, he blindly extended a hand out to receive number one daughter, and Kim stepped forward as if to a podium.

"Ex*cuse* me, Greg . . . hello baby . . ." He tapped cheeks with Kim while eying me over her shoulder.

"Pop-peee." Anthony came running, and Kim's father crouched like a catcher, arms extended to scoop him up.

"Tony Baloney! Ha-haa!" He swept Anthony up in the air. "*There's* my boy!"

Kim stood and smiled, her hands clasped in front of her crotch.

"Greg, Linda? Do you know Tony Baloney here?" He had Anthony up to his chest, perched on his forearm. Both Kim and Fonseca were healthy-sized people. I never realized how runty Anthony was. Anthony peered down at them from under his lined eyelids like an aged monkey or an old Martian.

"This is my daughter . . . Kimberly . . ."

She smiled, cocking her head to the side.

"And you are . . ." He smiled encouragingly, as if he assumed I was afraid of him.

"Peter Keller."

"Evan Carmichael." He nodded, extending his hand.

"Reverend . . ." I nodded.

"No . . . no, not *Rever*end . . . *Ev*an." He laughed to Kim.

"Sorry . . . I was swimming this morning and I still have water in my ear."

Kim glared at me.

I wandered under the tent as Kim talked with her father. Two long collapsible tables were covered with food sculptures. The most startling creation was a peacock, the body, head and base of its broad fantail molded out of pale yellow paraffin. The tail was covered with dazzling rows of asparagus stalks, sporadically dotted with sun-centered slices of hard-boiled egg.

Mother Carmichael was hunched over the table, a dark blue plastic-coated plate in her papery hands. She looked agitated and grabbed the arm of the serving girl.

"Excuse me, dear, is there any jello or creamed chicken? I'm trying to make up a lunch for him . . . he can't eat any of this."

We locked eyes and I nodded.

"How you doin'?"

Her face went up in spryness again. "How am I? I'm eighty-five years old and thanks to Christ I still feel like a teen-ager."

"No, there isn't." The girl smiled apologetically.

"There's some tuna salad at the far end," I offered, extending my hand to take the plate from her and pointing my chin to a creamy mosaic pyramid.

"Oh, maybe that." She ignored my outstretched hand and walked toward the tuna.

———

"So, Peter?"

I found myself looking down at Kim's mother, who squinted up at me, her speculating mouth bordered by a corolla of whistle marks. "What is it you teach?" Those eyes had checked out Fonseca once and were now doing comparisons.

"Phys. ed." I shrugged. She nodded neutrally. "Actually, I'm a comedian, a nightclub comedian in New York."

She made some kind of short humming noise that was hard to interpret. She looked up into the sun and grimaced. Although her skin had no emollients or moisture to make her face gleam like that lady Natalie in the piano bar, her features took on that same pained expression that Natalie's had when I laid that line on her. I wished to Christ I knew what the hell it meant, it scared me.

"Yeah, I'm a comic." I nodded. "But I also teach gym . . ." I shrugged. ". . . Lift weights." What the fuck was I saying? I had the mature thought that my three-hundred-pound mother, if she were alive, could probably mop the floor with Kim's old lady, Aunt Emma Sweet, and all the other Sweets and Semi-Sweets under the tent.

"This is a beautiful house." I raised my glass at the roof. "How long have you lived here?"

"Ohh . . ." The whistle marks deepened. ". . . twenty years, but the Sweets have been in the area for close to two centuries now."

"Wow." Also, wait a fucking second. Why was I anxious about coming on favorably compared to Fonseca? Fonseca was a no-good scumbag burnout who used to punch out this lady's daughter like a time clock.

"Yes, in fact the Sweets built and owned half of the county. There's a Sweet Building in four different towns around here, all built by my grandfather—he had one hundred fifty men under him. My great-uncle sold his farmland to the state, turned contractor and built the highway that passed over his own property. He had, I believe, seventy-two men under him, and my father owned a shoe factory before the Depression, he had three hundred and six men under him. The Italians used to come off the boats down in New York, shoemakers, they only knew one sentence, 'Swit, which way Swit?' My father owned buses to pick them up at Ellis Island—and shot them right up here. They called him Papa Swit. The factory closed in thirty-four but there's still an Italian town around here because of my father. Half the high school football team's grampas worked for my father . . . 'Swit, which way Swit?' " She laughed.

She squinted at the sun again, but the grimace was no longer there, which meant the grimace that she'd made when I said I was a comedian was voluntary. Fuck her. At least I didn't beat the shit out of her daughter. Where the hell were the two centuries of leatherneck Sweets when their youngest daughter was getting whacked?

"Movers and shakers." I smiled.

"You could say that." She arched her eyebrows and closed her eyes.

"Yeah, well, my family wasn't as heavyweight as all that, but you see that fourth building up there?" I hunched down and pointed at the ghostly distant skyline of downtown Albany over the hills. "The fourth building? That's Albany Memorial Hospital." I could tell she couldn't see what I was pointing to. No matter. "Now the top two floors? That's the V.D. ward. My father's very big there."

"He's a doctor?"

"Uhn-uhn, East Coast distributor, he had about three hundred people under him."

She stared at me, totally, totally not getting it. Now what?

"Nah, he was a doctor . . . listen, speaking of doctors, I would love to talk to you more, but my doctor said I have to stay away from Sweets . . ."

I walked off, gritting my teeth. I wished the tent poles would collapse.

We sat in Kim's father's den on a low coffee-colored suede couch. In the corner was a bar with a padded border and padded stools. The deep wood paneling around the bar nook was covered with photos and documents polyurethaned on dark wood plaques. There were seven or eight studio portraits of Anthony, all in color, a large black and white studio head shot of Kim as a bride, her eyes glassily serene and skyward, and a photo of her father shaking hands with various religious leaders while being handed a citation. This too was mounted and laminated onto cherrywood next to the photo. It was from the Christian Musicians' Society of America, naming Evan Carmichael the Alvin De Bakey Inspirational Songwriter of the Year. Kim's father sat on the edge of a piano bench, elbows on knees, smiling at us. We were separated from him by a white piano. Anthony sat next to him and pretended to play on the shuttered keyboard.

"I notice you're checking out my Cy Young Award." He winked at me, shrugging self-deprecatingly.

I hated Regular Joes.

The air of the den was filled with the steely oxygenated gurgle of the filtration system of a huge aquarium. Carmichael's head blocked out half the tank, and if I squinted it looked as if the neon tetras were swimming in and out of his ear.

"You know, the funny thing is, as Kimberly can tell you, Mrs. Carmichael and I aren't really religious at all."

"Oh yeah?"

Anthony got up and went over to the bar. He began rapidly clicking the off/on chain of a novelty lamp, a frosted globe perched atop a lamppost. A plaster drunk in a bedraggled top hat leaned against the light. The strobe effect of Anthony's activity was lost in the afternoon sunlight.

"Anthony, don't play with Poppy's things," Kim warned.

"I'm giving the guy a hangover!"

Carmichael laughed.

Both Kim and I curled like commas inside the deep angular couch. I felt a rustling inside my sports jacket, slipped a hand across my chest and felt the crisp pressed crinkliness of my onionskin resumé. It must have been there the last time I wore the jacket, making the employment agency rounds.

"Of course, we're active in the church, and we're not hypocrites.

We believe in Christ, but . . . I'll tell you, and this should not leave this room . . . I'm more concerned about what good we can do here, *now*, than what's waiting for us over in the next world. Kimberly can vouch for us."

Kim nodded, her hands palms down on the couch.

"You know, Mr. Carmichael, Kimberly here, told me about you, what you strive for in your songs, and, ah, I hope this is not a major imposition, I know this is asking you to work on your day off, but . . . I would *love* to hear 'Christian's My Way.' Do you have a recording anywhere?"

Kim managed to pinch me with one fingernail, breaking skin along my thigh.

"I'll do better than that . . ." Carmichael flipped up the keyboard cover.

He really had a nice easy voice. He never looked at his fingering, just sang to us with an expressive face and gently swaying shoulders, as if he was working two lovers nursing Campari-and-sodas in a piano bar.

My face was jammed with earnestness.

"And so now, it's the time for the final curtain, and he's with me, oh yes with me, of this, oh I am certain . . ."

I winked at Kim.

"I did it . . . Hi-i-s-s . . . ah-way-y-y."

He ended with a little non-sequiturious flourish.

"Whew . . ." I nodded, my eyes narrowed in appreciation. "What are you working on now?"

He returned to the piano playing and singing gently again, as if he was going to break off any second and chat.

"You ain't nothin' but a Hound Dog, sinnin' all the time . . ." He winked at Kim. ". . . but if you turn away from Jesus, you ain't no friend of mine . . ."

Anthony meandered back to our end of the room.

"I'm working on an album now. I'm taking rock and roll songs and, well, 'Christianizing' the lyrics. My main concern as a Christian songwriter is reaching kids. You know, a lot of the old fogies in the church today have kind of given up on kids . . . to say nothing of what they think about kids' music . . . but I say that's the *key*, the very *key* to reachin' them . . . we can *use* rock 'n' roll and *reach* them like never before . . . we can reach right through dope, divorce, broken homes, and *grab* 'em . . ." He leaned forward and swept Anthony to him. "I mean, this is not a new notion. I'm not taking any credit for being any kind of pioneer . . ."

"What else you got on that album?"

He held Anthony and played with one hand.

"He loves me yeah yeah yeah . . . and with a love like that, you know it can't be bad."

"Goddamn! What a great idea! I bet you could improvise a conversion on the spot . . . could you do 'Blue Moon'?"

He tinkled the first few notes tentatively. "I'm ashamed to admit it, but I think I forgot the lyrics."

"Me too . . ." I snapped my fingers. "You could do something, oh please, someone adore him . . . that's no good . . . how about 'Earth Angel'? Can you do 'Earth Angel'?"

He shook his head sadly. "Got me there."

"Doo-doot do do doot, do doot do do doot," I encouraged, then stopped. "I just remember the sound effects myself . . . Okay, how about the Fugs, do you do any Fugs?"

He laughed and shrugged apologetically. Kim coughed so artificially that it sounded like "cough cough."

"No sweat! Let's get back to basics. 'She Loves You!' . . . Oh, you got that already . . . 'Fever' . . . you gotta know 'Fever' . . . hey, could I try it? You know 'Fever'?" I hummed a few bars. He put down the kid and played the melody.

"Okay . . . da da da . . . sun light up the daytime, moon lights the night, my eyes, no my *soul* lights up when . . ." I stopped my off-key singing and straightened up. "What . . . when He calls my name? or I call His name? . . . Is one way profane?"

"It's the spirit that counts." He shrugged.

"Pardon the pun." I flashed teeth.

"Pardon the pun," he conceded with a tentative smile, checking me out a little more carefully.

"God, Kimberly, your father's really into something . . ."

Kim didn't look up at me. Well, as Gamma six twenty-eight would say, "Fuck yah if you can't take a joke."

"Could we do one more?"

I heard Kim exhale through her nose.

"Do you know any Stones? Aw Christ! The easiest . . . Ah can't get no-ho sah-tis-fac-shu-un . . ." I really had a suck-ass voice. His sitting there with hands folded on his knees instead of playing didn't help. "It's a natural . . . we'll make it about a guy who's only into sex, money and status, so he can't get no satisfaction . . . but then!" I started half singing, "I'm dri-vin' in my *car*, a man come on a ray-dee-yo . . . tellin' me more and more 'bout some *Jesus Christ* in-foh-may-tion and all of a sudden I get a re-ve-*lay*-tion . . . I *can!* get some . . . oh yes yes yes! . . . I can get suh-hom, sat-is-faction . . . What do you think? Listen, you can have that one, but anything we do together from now on is halvies, okay? Is it a deal?"

He squinted at me, his hands like crossed empty gloves on his knee.

I stood up. "You know, I never thought about song-writing before? I like it! I really do. Honey? I think your father just hooked another fish. Anthony? C'mon, give Poppy a big kiss . . . we have to get bookin' back to town."

I offered my hand to Kim. She stood up unassisted. Her eyes went every which way but up as if she'd dropped an earring on his orange Rya rug.

He didn't rise, too busy trying to figure out if I had been pulling his chain. My voice and face had come on like the straight poop since we sat down.

"Kimmy? We're having Thanksgiving dinner next week at Uncle Ray's house . . . as always you're welcome to join us . . . and I hope you bring your friend Peter here." His voice was slow and specula-tive, his handshake tentative and faint.

There was an Amtrak station six blocks from the house, and we walked the bird-tweety streets paced by Kim's clipping heels. I walked slightly behind, glaring at her back. She wouldn't even turn to me.

"With mah Kan-zah City baybee, and a bot-tla sac-ra-mental wine . . ."

Kim whirled at me. "Just who do you think you are!"

Anthony danced and whirled, ran and screeched.

"Who am I?" I pulled out my resumé and handed it to her. She actually glanced down at it before flinging it into the street and picking up her pace.

"Ah foun' mah three-yull, do-doot, do-doot, awn Cal-vary Hee-yull . . ." My voice was actually getting better. "He's goin' into the act, babe, Inspirational Songwriter of the Year, Jerry Wiper!"

"Hey, listen!" she hissed.

I took two giant steps forward and grabbed her cheeks, squeezing her lips into the shape of a keyhole. "No, *you* listen!" My pointing finger made her eyes cross. I think I was squeezing too hard. She got scared and touched my hand, which made me blow my whole speech.

I pushed her away and stalked on ahead. I turned, twenty feet up. "You know, *Kimmy*, they made you eat shit with a shovel." I whirled forward and kept moving. Anthony twirled and leapt as if he was oblivious to the two of us.

I covered almost an entire block before Kim cried out. "You know, he loves Anthony." I turned again. She hadn't moved since I squeezed her face.

"What?" I marched back to her.

She flinched.

"He loves Anthony, he loves Anthony, hah?"

I turned and stalked forward, cursing everything and everybody. Big Trouble. Totally lost.

Kim cried out, "It's my family!"

When I didn't turn around she muttered, "It's all I've got."

Instantly I flashed on Fonseca. Her heading to see Fonseca that night she met me because she was lonely. I felt a panic sprout across my chest. I stopped and waited for her to catch up.

"That's all you've *got?*" I squinted in outrage. "That's all you've *got?* What the hell am I!?" I touched my chest and jerked back my head.

"To me? I don't know . . ." She raised her nose with an imperious air. "You tell me . . ."

I waved her off and stalked on ahead again. "That's all you've *got.*" I spat every five feet. "That's all you've *got.*"

I had to save her. Somebody had to save somebody.

I wheeled toward her one more time. "Are you having Thanksgiving dinner with them?"

"Maybe . . ." She pouted.

"Oh yeah? Because next week *I'm* having a fucking dinner. And *you* can come, and *you* can come." I pointed at Anthony. "Or you can go to *Pop*-py's." I made my lips pop on the downstroke. "Anthony? Do you have any friends from broken homes you wanna invite?"

He looked at Kim straight-faced.

"Palmer?" he asked her.

"*Pal*mer!" I exploded. "Aw fuck *Pal*mer! Anybody but *Pal*mer!"

"I *like* Palmer!" Anthony straightened in dismay.

Kim laughed.

"How about you?" I nodded to Kim. "How about your Latin Hustle partner there, your post-divorce bowling-alley friend?"

"Theresa?"

"That's Palmer's mother," Anthony said.

"Good, and then there was five." I turned and started marching in the direction of the train. Kim and Anthony trotted to keep up.

"What's wrong with Palmer?" Anthony pulled on my jacket, but I was gone, lost again in that image of Fonseca lifting his chin to me by the auditorium door. His eyes, I couldn't read his eyes.

"I thought you were going into New York next weekend," Kim said cautiously.

I pulled up short and faded backwards, my knees buckling in despair. Cocksucker. I forced myself to straighten up. "Yeah, well, don't worry about it." I shrugged and tried to think Turkey, a Rockwell Grandpa saying grace, one frosty eyebrow mischievously raised in a sneak peek at the big tom.

The train had huge picture windows. I sat facing Kim and Anthony on high dark-green cracked leather seats as we rolled north up the Hudson.

Kim looked thinky, peering out at the glittering water. Anthony's eyes were glassy as he absently and rhythmically tapped his head against the seat-back while checking out the same vista. The height of the seat-backs made them both look small and waify like brother and sister.

"It was *bound* to happen! I told her it was *bound* to happen!"

A man about forty sat across from us facing his twin daughters. He was furiously brushing drops of grape soda from the leg of his pearl-gray slacks.

"I told her if she continued to play with that straw, something like this would happen . . ." They were the only other people in the car.

The girls were about ten, dark and chubby. The father was short and round with sunglasses perched on his skull. The offending twin slouched in the corner, lackadaisically chewing on her straw, which was still dangerously angled on the inside lip of the soda can.

"Nancy likes to think she's still in diapers," he announced to the other twin.

Nancy shrugged.

As he bent down lower to attend to his cuff the sunglasses on his bowed head peered at the girls as if he had eyes under his hair. Nancy laughed and pointed. Her twin sister smacked her on the arm.

"Daddy, she was laughing at you!" The kid was agitated and hot.

"If Nancy does not finish that soda in thirty seconds sitting up straight and drinking like a young lady, she's in a lot of trouble."

Nancy continued to slouch and chew on the straw. She made a big exaggerated show of shrugging her shoulders again. Her face looked defiant and slightly gut-sick. She was stuck in it.

"She's not doing it! You should punish her, Daddy! Punish her!"

"That's okay . . . I have faith in Nancy . . . she's got twenty-five seconds left."

"Punish her! *Mommy* would!"

Nancy remained silent, swinging her locked ankles and continuing her shruggy show.

"No, no, I don't believe in punishment unless as a last resort. Nancy's basically a good person." His voice was loud and singsongy with theatrical authority. I felt as if all I'd heard all goddamn day was that murderous bing-bong tone.

"No, she's *not* a good person!" the twin snapped, looking anxiously from her sister to her father. "She's not drinking, Daddy, how many seconds does she have left!"

"That's okay. Your sister's a good person, but she's basically immature sometimes and now she's just trying to activate my ulcer. If she does *not* finish that soda right now, when we get home I have a punishment for her."

"You do not! What is it?" the sister challenged.

"Don't you worry. I have a very appropriate punishment for her."
Nancy shrugged again.

"Why don't you leave the kid alone?" I was leaning over into the
aisle, trancy and nervous. My hands were shaking. All three of
them reared back in surprise.

The sunglasses slipped down to the bridge of his nose. He sat up
straight. "Hey, I'll take care of my family, you take care of yours!"
He pointed at Anthony and Kim, and I wanted to break his finger,
but just snapping at him took all my energy.

Kim looked at me startled. Anthony was still knocking his head
against the seat-back and watching the river, his eyebrows rising
and falling in some inner song.

The six of us traveled on in awkward sullen silence for two
more stops.

Suddenly the father leaned over to me, his voice shaking. "Never
criticize a parent in front of a child because the child catches it in
the neck later on, you asshole . . ." He immediately jerked back,
hands up in submission. "I don't want to fight, but I have to say my
piece."

Kim looked at me unemotionally.

I ignored him, and the train ride continued in silence until
twenty minutes later, fifteen miles from the next stop, he suddenly
got up and began hauling down their luggage from the overhead
racks and ushered his twins, unprotesting, into the next car. With
one foot holding the pneumatic door ajar, a floral-patterned bag
under each arm and one in each hand, he leaned back toward me: "I
love my family just as much as you love yours." Then he was gone.

Kim glanced briefly at me, then returned her gaze to the river.
"You know, you really don't have to do this dinner thing next
week." She sounded beat; her head was being gently buffeted from
side to side by the rocking of the train.

I shrugged, frowning at the dead skin around the edges of my
nails. "Yeah, so? I know . . ."

———

When we got home Kim was distant and frowny. I asked her if she
was still pissed at me for goofing on her father. She said no, and I
believed her. She wasn't acting angry, just troubled, but whatever

was bugging her was making her act totally out of character. I followed her around the house trying to hug and murmur and while she didn't push me away, her touch was limp and not really there. She said she was just wiped from the trip, but I didn't buy it, and I turned into an instant nervous wreck. When I told her I was freaking she kissed and patted me. I hated being patted.

That night she passed out immediately, with the light still on.

She lay on her stomach, her face profiling on the pillow, her arms crooked and raised as if she were snorkeling.

My gut doing flip-flops, I lay next to her up on one elbow, gently rubbing her back with the flat of my palm. I passed my hand from her high bony shoulders down the swoop of her spine, barely touching skin, leaving a sprout of goose pimples in my wake; the gesture of a magician saying an incantation, the passage of a hand over a candle.

This is mine, my responsibility. Her welfare is my welfare. To protect is to love . . . I was hysterical.

Kim raised one shoulder, grunted something in her sleep, her face gummy and dazed, and dropped back into the pillow.

The morning saw more of the same: her, cool and pained; me, panic in the streets.

During the day I had a brainstorm; instead of making a dinner at my apartment as I had originally planned, I decided to use "The Country," my parents' summer home down in Putnam County, and make a weekend of it.

It always cracked me up that we owned "property," a beat-up old farmhouse that my parents bought back in the late forties for five hundred dollars. And we always called it "The Country"—we're going to "The Country"—do you wanna go up to "The Country"?— real Land Barons.

We never really went up there that much when I was a kid because my mother had June grass fever, a form of seasonal asthma, and she preferred to spend the summers in that ground-floor apartment in the Bronx. And after she died my father was too freaked to use the house, especially with Vy. It was too much like over my mother's dead body.

The house itself was off Route 6, off a logging road that cut through a bungalow colony then turned into a snaky dirt path with a grassy center hump that went about half a mile through woods and emptied into a two-acre clearing. The interior consisted of a big central room which had kitchen fixtures on one end, a couch on the other, and an eight-foot long oak table in the middle. There were three small bedrooms off at the corners and a huge disgusting cinder-block patio with hip-high walls, looking like some hideous foreign legion fortress, attached to the side of the house and facing a wide grassy clearing and the edge of the woods. That was it.

The next night over dinner Kim said she thought maybe we should cancel our Thanksgiving plans. Both Anthony and I flipped. I was half-expecting that though, and I came on like Mr. Positive Attitude and counterproposed that wonderful weekend in "The Country," a sleep-over with Theresa and Palmer and Mr. Butterball the Turkey. I painted such a wonderful idyllic lavish fun time, in front of Anthony of course, to make it harder for her to say no, that she finally relented, laughed even, and Anthony and I cheered in triumph. We made her call Theresa right then and there. Theresa was booked. I made her call Mary Kay Cicero from the Geology office. Mary Kay was booked. Screw it. I spent the next hour describing the fantasia that was "The Country," all the time with sirens going off in my stomach and a little voice in my head informing me, "This is fucked up." But I couldn't get a handle on what "this" was; it was just a seven-day delay from New York. It was a family holiday anyhow, no time to be doing nightclubs. It would be great, perfect. I had visions of a big bash around the long oak table with me as Patriarch. What a scream. Kim tried to call off the trip twice the next day, and in retaliation, I tried to expand the party again.

———

"Fiona, is Captain in?"

"He's eating lunch, Peter."

"Good, I wanna see the show . . ." I walked in to the interior office. Petty was scarfing down a Dagwood.

"Pete." He wiped his mouth. "Did you eat?" He used his Dagwood to point to a few apples on his desk.

"Nah, I ate."

"What can I do for you, kid?"

"Well, look, I'm sure you got plans but I just wanted to invite you . . . I'm taking Kim and the kid out to this house my family has over the weekend for Thanksgiving . . ."

"Nah, I can't . . . thanks, though . . ." He chewed and winked.

"Yeah, I didn't think so . . . are you having a big thing?"

"I don't know . . . I moved out totally again." He laughed easily.

"Are you kiddin' me? Are you back in that shithole?"

"Nah . . . I moved in with Katherine Mooney."

"Who?"

"That woman in the Anthro Department . . . I've been seeing her for years. But I think she's going to Indiana to spend the weekend with her kids and ex-husband, so I might go home for the dinner . . . it's okay . . . this time it's okay . . . it's getting better."

"*What's* getting better?"

"Ah . . ." He shrugged, picking up a shred of Swiss off his desk. "She knows I'll be back. I know it too."

How sad.

"Does she know Katherine Mooney?"

"Probably . . . we don't get specific." His "we" sounded like a team. Maybe they did have their own customized relationship. Maybe it could be worse.

"Yeah, it doesn't make a hell of a lot of difference. She knows I'll be back."

"Because she's the mother of your children?"

He shrugged again, not reacting to my sarcasm. "Whatever. I need a home base. Everybody needs a home base. Don't you need a home base?" He squinted at me. "Maybe not. You're a kid yet."

"No! I need a home base!" I didn't want to be left out. Did I? Yeah! Kim. But what about New York? Come fly with me.

"How're you and Kim doing?"

"I don't know," I said as if in a reflective trance. "No! I mean it's good . . . it's good." I bobbed my head reassuringly and shook a fist, but I got walloped with another hit of Big Trouble panic and my kneecaps started running.

"So how was New York? You never told me about New York. Everything go okay with you two down there? You came in that last time asking me about Tony, I got worried."

"Everything's . . . everything. It was a good trip. I got some ideas."

"Like what?" Jack finished eating and slowly slapped his hands dry.

"Well, I was thinking maybe about trying to take some acting classes. I talked to this guy. I'd like to just hang around some clubs . . . for bucks I guess I could teach down there, community college or something . . . it doesn't really make a difference." I felt confident.

"What about Kim?"

I felt shaky. "I think she'll come too."

"Yeah?"

"I saw Crown down there," I said quickly to change the subject.

"Oh yeah? How's he doing?"

"It's rough, but he's doin' it. He's in a play."

"Yeah, Crown's got a lot of problems," Jack said dismissively.

"No he don't. He's doing it." Suddenly I felt far away from Jack. How about the jazz trumpet, you fat bastard. At least Crown's still climbing. Jack didn't understand, and it depressed me. He was supposed to be Superman.

We sat there, Jack staring out the window demolishing his apples, me frowning at his desk, trying to shake off the wave of disappointment, wanting to jump in his lap.

"You know something? I don't know if I ever told you this; my mother weighed almost three hundred pounds. But outside of movies I never saw her eat. She ate fruit and drank coffee . . . she used to make sandwiches and cook all the time, but she never ate . . . I mean, whatever she started to eat she finished, but I don't know . . . could that be glands or something?" I talked politely and smoothly as if Jack were black and I had brought up the subject of race.

Jack looked out the window and swallowed. "She ate when no one was around." He said it calmly and with authority, "A lot of fat people are secret eaters. Me, I eat more when people are around . . . people like it when I eat . . ."

I felt mildly reproached, even though I knew Jack wasn't on my case.

I thought about linoleum. Candlelight shining off linoleum and thick glossy white paint layered on ancient molding-bordered tenement walls.

"You know . . . I *do* remember one time when I was about six . . .

I got up in the middle of the night and I walked into the kitchen and she was eating a chicken . . . I remember her sitting there . . . she was eating by candlelight . . . it was one of those memorial candles, a short fat milk glass filled with wax. The light was very wavery and yellow, and she was eating chicken. Maybe I dreamed it. She was wearing a nightgown and eating chicken. She just stopped chewing and stared at me. She had a sliver of white meat right here . . ." I tapped the corner of my mouth, my finger quivering. "I just turned around and went back to sleep . . . she didn't even ask me what I wanted."

My first thought was, what's the big deal about chicken—it's all protein, right? Then I felt a sort of desolation. My mother eating secret meals, having a secret life, as if she was a spy. I thought about my father sleeping or sorting mail while my mother ate.

"I knew a guy once"—Jack tossed the browning apple cores in his garbage pail—"he was four hundred and fifty pounds. Not only did he never eat in front of people, but he only ate in the dark. Myself"—he struggled to his feet—"I personally can't see it . . . no pun intended."

"Wait a minute . . ." I grabbed his hand. "Sit down for a second." I felt desperate and confused.

Jack eased down and hunched forward, elbows on knees. I did the same, and our faces were a foot apart. We looked like opposing linemen. How to say it.

"What . . . I want to ask you . . . I . . . how do you do it, man?"

"Do what?" He grazed his lip with a finger.

I sat up so I could think. What am I saying here?

"You never get freaked. My mother used to be permanently freaked. All the time she'd be freaked. Don't people give you shit? Doesn't it make you crazy?" I winced.

He stayed in his hunch. "Why, because I'm fat? I *am* fat!" He talked in defiance. "Who gives me shit? Do *you* give me shit?"

"No!" I thought back on the thousands of times I had called him Fat Jack.

"*You* don't give me shit. You *love* me, right? Everybody loves Fat Jack," he said in a slightly menacing singsong and I felt crushed.

He laughed mean and low, got up, tousled my hair. "Don't worry about me, Pete . . . I'm on the case." And he left the office.

· That night I found some Greek restaurant with a small bar and I
got drunk by myself, sitting there under framed old caricatures,
thinking about my mother at that table in the kitchen, that yellow
room.

She had slight pop eyes and she used to get this hunted animal
look any time she imagined anybody was staring or she was in the
presence of enemies. She must have been so fucking lonely. She was
so fucking twisted. How did he do it? How the hell did he do it? I
didn't understand him. Where did he stash it? I started getting pissed.
He was holding out on me, too. What did he do with it? In my drunk
head I envisioned him as this huge convex Thanksgiving parade
float, too high to be scaled, the bulges too perilous to be tackled.

———

At one in the morning I stood swaying in a boozy haze in front of a
plum and mustard gingerbread house in Professionalsville, looking
up at two big cartoon window eyes of a second-story bedroom.

"C'mon, Jack," I blared. "Don't give me that shit . . . don't give
me that . . ." The street was as dead as an oil painting. It was cold.
"What's the story . . . I'm on *your* side . . . I'm on *your* side."

I was freezing, hands in pockets, dead leaves charging across my
boot tips. "Let's go, Jack." I clapped my hands. "Talk to me . . .
what's the story?" I was almost down to a complainy conversational
tone. "I'm on *your* side." I scratched my nose and stared at the
pavement.

"Peter, go home." Jack stood in the dark doorway across the small
lawn from me.

I couldn't see him in the shadows. A lamp went on in one of
the eyes throwing down a ladder of light.

Despite the cold, Jack was standing barefoot, wearing only pajama bottoms. Packets of fat festooned his ribs and chest. He stood
solid as a tree trunk up to his hips, then stooped forward, one hand
on the low doorknob, gripping it like the head of a walking stick, as
if his bulk was too much for his spine. His wild hair and hoary eyebrows looked as if they were flecked with driven snow, his eyes
were sagging but patient, his mouth downcurved and tight. Someone moved in the upstairs window behind the curtain.

"Go home, Pete."

I usually had a prissy pride in my take-it-or-leave-it attitude about booze and drugs, but for the next few days I found the only way to deal with the adrenaline terror was to get sloshed every night. I went to different hole-in-the-wall bars in small towns at least ten miles from the campus and got fuckfaced and played the jukebox. I chatted up bartenders and bought drinks for whoever I could get into conversations, but I was a janglebox of nerves around anybody I knew—especially Kim. She hadn't really snapped out of it since the train ride, and it was wearing me down. Instead of getting pissed and impatient, I was getting scared of her. There was something unnerving and spooky in her distance that went beyond rejection.

The night before we were to go to the house for Thanksgiving I called her and said I had to work late on papers and it would be better if I crashed at my own place and picked her up in the morning. I was braced for an explosion, but she just said, "Okay, what time you coming by tomorrow?" and then I freaked because she took it in stride.

I got up at dawn. The birds were going berserk outside my window. I did a ton of sit-ups. Being alert and functional at dawn was totally rejuvenating. Who the hell is ever up at dawn? It feels as if you own the place. It was the big day. Next stop "The Country."

I bought a ton of groceries at a supermarket in town, braced myself and made it over to Kim's place by eight, two hours early.

Kim was tight and distant again. She even got flustered that I showed up early, like I was fucking company or something.

We exchanged strained Hi's. I could see her breasts swaying opaquely through her nightgown and got angry at myself because I was sneaking a peek, I was acting as if I had no right to look.

"Anthony!" she shouted. "Get up!"

"Fucking Nazi hell!" he yelled back.

"Jack called you here about a half hour ago," she said, ducking her head into the refrigerator. "Call him at Katherine Somebody's house. I think he wants to go with us."

"Ree-ly!"

"Really."

"Jack! You comin'?"

"Is it okay, Pete? Nancy's taking the kids to her brother's house for Thanksgiving. I'd die before I'll go there. You *sure* it's okay? I don't want to be in the way."

I was so buzzed and humbled, I had no idea how to reassure him profoundly enough.

We picked up Jack in front of Katherine Mooney's house. He was standing out in front wearing only a tweed sports jacket despite the cold. I felt honored that he was dressed so formally. He was right. I really did love him. He had a small plaid cloth valise in one hand, a frozen turkey and a bottle of Scotch under his arms.

He groaned into the back seat with Kim after we threw the bird in the trunk. "Hey-y sweetie!" He kissed Kim's cheek. "Christ! I haven't seen you in a year! You look terrific!"

Kim gave him a trembly hug and laughed, as Anthony, in the front with me, sang the theme from "Batman" and picked his nose.

"You sure it's okay, Pete? I don't want to get in the way."

"Get serious." I grinned like an idiot and headed on out.

Back in that trunk I had Jack's turkey, my own precooked ten pound Butterball, a half-dozen quart-sized plastic containers chocked with various cold deli salads and pickled vegetables, two rye breads, quarts of beer, Kim's garter belt, a bottle of Mount Gay rum, Jack's Scotch, three quarts of assorted mixers, grape soda, a beach bag filled with fruit, a football, a Frisbee, a half-gallon of milk. The weather was glitteringly stupendous, crisp as an apple, *I* was the Papa Bear, and it would take a highway fatality for me to lose it over the next two days.

It was a six-hour drive, a seven-hour trip with lunch and bathroom stops. Jack's presence loosened Kim up and the three of us got into an extended rap remembering old "Twilight Zones."

Blurty with relief at Kim's comeback, I did a heavy-eyebrow squint, my pinched-face imitation of Rod Serling, biting my words as if it hurt to talk: "Anthony Fonseca, a little man with a big dream, and a bus ticket to the stars . . . but little did he know the ticket was one-way—no deposit, no return—and the bus terminal . . . was in . . . the Twilight Zone." I followed it up with a dramatic burst of climactic shock brass.

"Get lost." Anthony waved me away.

"Aw Jesus." Jack laughed. "I'll never forget this one I saw with my boys—do you remember that one where the guy has the ability to make people vanish and reappear?"

"Uhn-uh."

"This guy is in a diner, and there's this big drippy disgusting bottle of ketchup right by his food, and he's getting repulsed by it, and he says something like 'I wish that bottle would vanish,' and poof, it's gone, and he's fucking amazed, right?" Jack goggled his eyes. "And he's looking to see if anybody noticed and he mumbles, 'I wish that bottle would come back,' and gling! it's back . . . so he goes home and of course he's got this big fat naggy bitch there and she's sitting in this chair and starts in on him, 'You worm, you no good blah blah,' and he says, 'I wish she would vanish,' and poof! she's gone from the chair, and then he says, 'I wish she was back,' and gling!—"

"There's a big bottle of ketchup on the chair," I jumped in.

Kim let out with a cackle, pointed at me, and doubled over with guffaws.

Anthony whirled around in his seat. "Gling!" He flicked his fingers at her. "And there's a big bottle of . . . bananas! Mommy! Ma! Gling! There's a big . . . dog!" He started howling like a mutt. He looked furious.

Jack flinched.

After a few minutes Anthony subsided, still angry though, looking out the window and absently pantomiming gling after gling with his fingertips.

When we rolled into town I started getting in a hysterical tour guide head, pointing out the library and saying, "Oh wow, that's the library . . . oh, and that's the big tree . . ." The closer we came to the house the more ferocious and inane I got. When we rocked and jostled down the narrow bumpy dirt path Kim said, "Oh . . . this must be the dirt path."

It was almost night when we got there. The house, centered in a ring-shaped clearing surrounded by the tall shadowy trees, suddenly seemed the most exciting place in the world. I almost jumped out of the car before putting it in park. I ran around babbling this is this and that is that, as everybody tentatively crawled out, stretched and sniffed, squinting up at the black-on-black skyline of treetops.

The inside of the house was asthmatically damp. Everybody milled around the central room, hands in pockets, or holding luggage as though there was a bus coming through. Kim dropped some groceries on the long oak table that divided the kitchen from the living room. Anthony sat on the moldy couch, whose loose rat-brown slipcover hung limp over the arms and cushions like a bathrobe on a shut-in.

I put up boiling water and started rinsing out coffee cups while continuing my garble of this is the pot and this is the chair I was telling you about.

When I was a kid the only time I liked the house was when I had another kid up there, so I could point with excited possessiveness to all the special family objects, as mundane and dull as they might be: my father's moldy box of *Yank* magazines; my grandfather's Sam Brown belt; a miniature pair of beaded moccasins, souvenirs of my parents' honeymoon in Lake George; a Nazi armband my father had brought back from Europe. I would always be filled with a burbling proprietariness watching some poor friend eating our Corn Flakes, insisting that he take more, and asking if they were good.

"I'll get the heat on in a second, relax!"

They continued to mill uncomfortably like peons in the governor's mansion.

"Oh hey! That's the TV. Why don't you guys turn it on?"

The portable was cater-cornered between the couch and the john. Anthony flipped through twelve varieties of snow before getting a hazy, almost ectoplasmic image of William Buckley, fingers church-steepled under his nostrils, rocking in his chair and throwing a question to a horse-faced man with hair in his ears.

"Oh, William Buckley!" I smiled as if it was Sid Caesar.

"Peter, where's everybody sleeping? . . ." Kim's coat was still buttoned.

"You tired already?"

"Maybe everybody just wants to unpack . . ."

"Oh shit! Sure!" I wrung my hands free of water and ran around turning on the lights in the three small bedrooms. I knew I was acting like a neurotic bozo, but I didn't care.

"Okay." I herded everybody into the first room. "This is my grandparents' room. Me and Kim'll take this . . . they're dead . . ."

I moved them all out and swung them left. "This is my aunt and uncle's room." The room consisted of a maple dresser, a double bed and a tortoise-shell bamboo shade with hopelessly knotted drawstrings covering a small doorless closet. "This is my aunt and uncle's room. Jack, you take this . . . they're living in Florida . . . or maybe you want this." I ushered everybody across the central room to a slightly larger bedroom with a double bed and horrendous yellow and red wallpaper. "Yeah maybe you should take this."

"How about me!" Anthony's voice cracked.

"You can sleep in the bathtub."

He laughed. Kids were pushovers.

"You can take that small room, my aunt's room, or you can sleep in the living room . . . that's a convertible, that couch."

"I wanna sleep in a convertible!" he shouted.

"Well this is just great, Pete . . . I wanna go outside for a minute and smoke this." Jack held up a cigar.

"Oh cut it out, man. Smoke anywheres."

Kim came up behind me, slipped a hand loosely around my bicep, her thumb grazing my armpit.

It was the first time she had voluntarily touched me since her parents' house.

"Ooh man, I'm beat!" I yawned and my whole body rattled.

———

The moonlight coming through our bedroom window turned Kim's face silver.

"You're feeling better, right?" I whispered, half on my side, half hovering over her, my hand resting on top of her crotch.

Kim smiled gamely, eyelids fluttering. But she didn't answer and the hand on the back of my arm was still. The house was filled with sleep.

"That was a riot with the Twilight Zones in the car, wasn't it? Let me just jerk you off," I pleaded.

"Anthony." She winced. We hadn't had sex all week.

"Well bite a pillow then. Just call me Pie. You never call me Pie anymore." I moved my hand in between her thighs.

"Don't." She moaned without pleasure, and then from outside our room, from somewhere in the house came a wheedling mocking high voice, "Oh Pie . . . oh Pie."

I shot up in bed, my heart beating in my face.

"What!" Kim raised herself on an elbow.

I thought I was going to vomit in terror. Anthony? No. Fat Jack? No. Anthony eavesdropping? No. The Bogeyman. I couldn't move.

"Peter! What is it! What's wrong!"

"Did you hear it?"

"Hear what! It's a raccoon!"

I forced myself out of bed.

"Where are you going?"

With my breath coming out in chattering gulps I lunged into the living room. No one. Anthony was on his back, dead asleep. I stood over the convertible and whispered down at him as menacingly as I could, "Who said that?" Nothing. I moved toward the black mouth of Fat Jack's bedroom. He was face down, snoring wetly in a way that was impossible to fake. I stood there, staring down at his naked back. A hand touched my arm, and I whipped around and grabbed Kim by the throat.

"What are you doing!" she squeaked, still trying to whisper.

"Nance?" Jack frumphed and crashed back to sleep.

I lay in bed for an hour, listening to the house.

The next morning we all got up late and played football in the clearing between the cinderblock patio and the edge of the woods. I felt as if I was doing a Pepsi commercial, but it was fun.

Kim played like a girl, holding the football with both hands and tossing it from behind her shoulder. Anthony made a point of falling down whenever he could. Jack, like most intelligent fat people, knew how to play without making any graceless moves. He threw with a windup softball-pitch motion, perfect and true spirals every time, and he never chased a bad throw. He picked up grounders with his foot, soccer-style, flipping them up to his hands.

Kim was laughing again, and I forgot about the noise. The raccoon. The whatever.

During a break, we all sprawled on the cold ground. The air was the electric blue of a Maxfield Parrish painting.

"My mother had a run-in with a horse here." I pointed to the ground.

"What horse?" Anthony asked.

When I didn't answer immediately, he put both hands on my forearm. "What horse?"

"Well, I remember this snowy morning when I was about seven, waking up to 'Yah, yah, get *atta* here, ya bastard!'" I twisted my mouth to the side and made the cries siren-like and distant.

"Get atta here!" Anthony mimicked in a small voice.

"It was the middle of the winter and I got out of my bed, it was like seven in the morning and my window looked out on that huge cinderblock patio and my aunt was standing out there in a bathrobe leaning over the patio wall and she had her knuckles up to her mouth and she was crying down to the clearing, 'Mimi! Leave it alone!' and biting her fist and saying 'Oy gott!' and then I heard again from down below the patio, 'Yah! Yah! Get atta here, ya bastard!'"

"Mimi!" Anthony repeated to himself.

"So I went out on the patio where my aunt was freaking out, and down here, right over there by that rock . . ."—everybody looked— "was this humongous white horse just standing there. And right in front of the horse was my goddamn two-hundred-and-fifty-pound mother in a bathrobe, the snow up to her knees and she had my uncle's rifle and she was shaking it in front of the horse and screaming 'Yah! Yah! Get atta there, ya bastard!' It was the most amazing thing I ever saw in my *life!* This beautiful white horse just standing there looking at my mother with these big bored eyes and my old lady wailin' away. I don't remember how it ended except at one point she fell on her ass in the snow. I think the horse got out of some riding stable outside of town or something. I just remember when we finally got my mother inside she said that the gun wasn't loaded, she was only *bluffing* the horse."

Jack and Kim laughed, but Anthony was freaked.

"Did the horse hurt your mother?"

"Nah . . ." I shrugged.

"Where's the horse now?"

"He's dead."

"Why is he dead?"

"Anthony, stop it . . ." Kim said.

"Why is he dead?"

"He's old, he was old . . . that was a long time ago. I guess he's dead by now . . ." I thought Anthony was afraid of the horse, so I played up the horse's nonexistence, but the kid seemed more freaked at the horse's death.

"When did he die?"

"I don't know . . . maybe he's living in Florida now . . ."

"No, he's not." Anthony hit me, but I could tell he was relieved.

"C'mon." Kim struggled to her feet. "Let's go inside, Anthony. It's time for your beating."

"Yayy, beating time!" He leapt to his feet.

"I'm gonna set the table. We'll eat in about an hour?" she asked us, smoothing down the back of her pants and twisting into an arms-high yawn.

"Sounds good, babe."

"Beating time . . ." Anthony ran ahead of her.

"She's something else," Jack murmured to me, his eyes on Kim's retreating form.

"You think she's happy with me?" I started scraping moss off a semi-buried rock that lay between me and Jack.

I was fishing for compliments and when Jack didn't immediately explode with a "Oh *Christ*, yes!" I got nervous.

"What do you think?"

"I'm sure she's happy with you, Pete . . ." he said, not happy.

"What's the matter?"

"Nah, I was just wondering, are you guys okay with each other?"

"What's wrong!" I was starting to raise my voice.

"How do *I* know what's wrong?" Jack laughed. "I was just wondering if everything's okay. You seem a little on edge."

"Shit, man, what are you, my mother-in-law?" I felt trapped.

"Oh Christ, Pete, I'm sorry . . . I should keep my mouth shut . . . I don't know what I'm talking about. I'm just pissed at Nance. I'm dangerous."

"*I* dunno what the problem is . . . she's got some wild hair up her ass about something," I muttered, trying to dig up the rock.

"Goddammit . . . don't listen to me, Pete," he begged. "Why'd I have to open my mouth, everything's great, I'm sure it is . . ."

It always bugged me to see Jack squirm, to see him in any kind of cringy state, and we started a furious exchange of reassurances. All the while I stared at his shin, which gleamed a bluish white between the cuff of his slacks and the limp elastic of his thin brown sock.

"Well, what was she like when she was with Fonseca?"

"Oh shit, who the hell knew with *those* two . . . they'd vanish for years at a clip . . . you know the story."

"Yeah? Whatever she looks like now at least she don't look punched out." It was a low blow on my part and Jack's face got dark with angry memories just as I wanted.

"Ah takes good cares a mah bitches," I pimp-lisped.

"I'm sure you do, kid, I'm sure she's nuts about you. I don't see how it could possibly be otherwise."

"Me neither . . . you want this rock? Otherwise I'm just gonna throw it away." I got to my feet and flipped it into the woods.

———

Our Thanksgiving dinner was superb, even though the turkey was overcooked. I made a pitcher of rum and pineapple juice that had me, Kim and Jack on our asses. Anthony didn't like turkey and Kim made him a salami sandwich. Everybody sat around the big oak table chewing and grunting.

"Maybe that horse lives in Texas," Anthony said.

"Anthony, it's food-in-mouth time." Kim scraped out the last of the Greek salad from its blue plastic container.

Anthony lunged forward and stuck out his tongue, showing her a half-chewed pile of salami and white bread.

"Pete's mom was almost as big as me . . ." Jack swallowed a belch, his chin pulling into his throat, his eyelids fluttering.

"Yeah, she was a real barge." I poured myself another drink, which I didn't need. "No offense, Jack." I blushed.

"I like that story with the horse and your mother," Kim said.

"Do you miss your mother now?" Anthony.

"Sometimes . . ."

"Do you wish she was here at this table?"

I looked into his big-eyed face, then at Kim who was running her finger around her plate scooping up the last smears of potato salad. Jack was pouring himself a little rum and pineapple juice, smiling, his eyes going from me to his drink. He threw me a wink. He was having a good time. I swear he was.

"Do you, Peter?" Anthony saying my name. "Do you wish she was here now?"

"No . . ." I shrugged, slightly reeling. "No, I do not."

After the meal Anthony began disemboweling my old toy chest in Jack's bedroom. Jack took a little walk down the dirt path.

Through the glass front door I watched him stroll off. He was wearing his sports jacket and his hands were clasped behind his back. His pace was leisurely, almost aimless; he stopped to check out whatever flora and fauna caught his eye. It was the perfect after-dinner pace; a Havana-cigar easy-chair ball-game-on-the-tube pace. I was sprawled on the musty couch, watching Kim wash dishes.

"I hope Jack's having a good time. He's the best, that guy," I said to her back.

She grunted noncommittally. She was pulling out again. It was getting so I could tell by just looking at her back. I yanked myself to my feet, trying to blink away the booze and sauntered over to the sink.

"Are you glad he came up here? He's nuts about you . . ."

"Oh yeah. Jack's great." And then nothing again.

"So how you doing?" My stomach started getting fluttery again.

"Okay." She shrugged, not looking up from the dishes.

Enough. I grabbed her wrist. The glass in her hand broke in the sink.

"What are you doing!"

"Let's take a walk. I wanna show you something."

"Let me finish!"

"C'mon . . . walk with me."

The air outside was cold and tart and cleared my head some-what.

"You know, Kim, I love you. I haven't said that in a long time because you don't love *me*, you twat, but I can't help it, I love you." I said that while walking slightly ahead of her, almost dragging her across the clearing to the woods. I still had her by the wrist, afraid that if I let go she would fling herself back toward the house, back to the dishes. Whatever was going on, we were taking it into the woods, and leaving it there.

"Where are we going?" she complained.

"What the fuck difference does it make? It's the country. When you're in the country you walk. We're walking."

I found a break through the trees, a narrow beaten path that cut through the woods. I smiled. The last time I'd hit that trail was to kill Indians and Japs.

I steered Kim in front of me and moved my hands to her waist. Our feet crackled over twigs and dry leaves. The light leaked down through a canopy of treetops like artificial illumination—aquarium light.

The deeper we got into the woods the slower we walked. I was blind to the landmarks of my summer childhood, lost in what to say, how to say it.

"What's that?" Kim pointed to more stories, a huge snapped-by-lightning tree lying on its side, propped up by thick branches which stuck into the ground like posts.

"That's Noah's Ark. I used to play on that . . ."

I started climbing the trunk, which went up ten feet before it made a right angle and became a bridge. When I got to the point where the tree broke parallel to the ground and shot out twenty feet across the forest floor, I crawled out and sat, straddling the trunk. I extended my hand down to Kim.

"C'mon up . . . let's take it up here."

We sat as if in saddles, facing each other, hovering ten feet above the ground.

"So . . ." I let out a slow lungful. "Tell me something good, Kim."

"Something good?" She peered at me grimly.

"Yeah, are you pregnant? Dying? What." I flipped my hand through the air in front of my chest while looking down at the ground.

"Something good," she muttered, struggling to get a hand in the back pocket of her jeans.

She handed me an ass-curved, folded, torn-open envelope.

I lifted out a long narrow pale-blue check made out to her from

Cro-Magnon Enterprises for five hundred beans. The stub end said, "For 'I Was a Whore at Disneyworld.' "

"Ho!" I barked. "Big time!" I felt totally relieved.

Kim blushed.

"Oh, you face." I stretched my torso across the two feet of trunk and put my hands on her shoulders in a tentative hug. "We're rollin' now. Next time tell 'em to fuck the fee, just send round-trippers to Sweden to pick up the Nobel."

"C'mon, asshole." She fought down a smile and stuck the check back in her rear pocket.

"What's the other story you had taken? Didn't you say you had another story taken?" I sounded blurty. Suddenly I just wanted to talk good-time.

"Yeah, I got twenty-five bucks." She shrugged.

"What, in a quarterly?"

"Yeah. This magazine out in Colorado called *Rocky Mountain Time*."

"What's it about? What's it called?"

Easy, easy.

"It's called 'March of the Tin Soldiers.' It's about this lady who becomes a child molester after her son dies . . . It's good, it's very good." She nodded in that tight-lipped way she had.

"Out . . . standing." I closed my eyes and whirled my head in tribute. "We're both rolling now." Suddenly I had a flash of what the problem was. More than a flash. I knew what the problem was.

"Can we have a celebration weekend?"

"Another one?" She ducked her head into her shoulders and absently slid her hand into the back pocket where the check was.

"Yeah, we can kill two birds with one stone. You can come into New York with me next weekend." My heart was thumping like a fist against the inside of a steel tub. That got the Big Silence that I thought it would. Of course. "I'm going in, Kim."

"I know," she said with irritation and started picking some kind of nature scab off the dead bark. "I don't like New York."

"Kim, we're talking about a weekend."

"No we're not," she muttered.

"See, you associate the town with that fucking rage-king." Anger felt better, got me lucid. Of course of course of course.

"No I don't," she lilted, her eyebrows rising but her eyes never leaving the stripped, now bone-white patch of tree she was working on.

"Okay, I'll stay . . ."

"No . . ." she growled low and lolled her head from side to side. "You should go." She sounded beat.

"What . . . so . . . what . . . you're crazy, Kim. I *love* you, I don't want . . . I don't—I *can't* be down there without you!"

"So stay." She shrugged.

No way. And that "so stay" was so halfhearted, such bullshit, that I knew that she knew it too. No way. And that was the nut of Dread Week right there. I almost said "Ah-ha."

Despite the November chill I sprouted a vest of sweat. "Kim, you *have* to come with me . . . you can't leave me."

The more I realized that I was gone, with or without her, the more insistent I felt, the more eloquent I wanted to become, and the more sputtery I sounded. I was *so* panicked that I felt moisture popping out in a semicircle between my eyebrows and my eyelids. "Don't leave me, Kim."

"Don't leave *you!*" She finally, finally, looked up at me. There was a chinstrap track of tears from the corners of her eyes down to her jaw. She gave a dry "huh!"

I winced and wiped my palms on my chest as if I had smeared away her tears and was drying them off on my shirt.

"You *have* to come with me." I nodded; my throat might have closed off in midsentence.

"Anthony too?" she muttered in that same why-bother tone of voice.

"Of course!" I bellowed, flinging my hands out and puffing up.

She clicked her tongue sullenly and wiped her own goddamn tears.

"Of course!" I made the same peacock's ass gesture.

"Great." She nodded and rocked, went back to stripping bark.

"Of course!" I repeated mindlessly. The chaos and panic of the moment made me feel a raw gush of love for her I hadn't felt since the beginning. I started twitching and grinding. "Don't you love me?" I said in a soft voice. It felt as if my teeth were sweating as I moved down the log so I could enfold her in my arms, my nose up inside her hair, deep in her scent. "Don't you love me?" I was shaking as though I was on amphetamines, a cold empty tremor. I could have easily taken a casual bite out of the side of her neck as if it were the meat of an apple. I could feel her tears splotch my shoulder. "Don't you love me?" I felt her nod yes. My shaking got worse. The terror was right here. Chest to chest, I mindlessly started rocking her.

"What're we gonna do? What're we gonna do?" I whispered in her ear. I began to choke up, felt my eyes get wet. Suddenly Kim broke out with heavy sobs, jerking hard against my stomach. She wailed high into the forest and started hitting my shoulders, not hard, very lightly, her head down, a hair curtain between us. She was sobbing, pushing me back, shoving me and punching me as lightly as an adult would play pattycake with an infant.

"What are you doing? What are you doing?" I found myself inching back. When she had pushed me back far enough, she swung a leg over the log so that she was sitting sidesaddle. At first I thought she was going to jump, but she kept her balance, and with her head still down, with that hair curtain still covering her face, she started tearing at her belt buckle, and kicking off her sneakers.

"Aw Kim," I croaked.

Raising herself one buttock at a time, she worked off her dungarees. Her panties got snagged on her foot. She had trouble kicking them free. They were satiny high waisted bloomers.

I felt a horrible anguish. She ripped open her blouse, popping buttons like a fat man, dropped the blouse behind her to the forest floor, then her bra. Her hair covered her whole face and upper body. Still crying, she carefully lay belly down on the tree trunk in front of me, straddling the roundness with her knees and elbows, opening herself to me from the rear. I stared at her asshole, her cunt, the powdery whiteness of her skin.

"Aw Kim."

She looked back at me in teary desperation, waiting.

I crawled forward, lowered my chest, and dug my fingers into her cunt. When I moved up to kiss the small of her back I slowly slid another finger deep inside her. She started sighing through her crying.

I pulled my fingers out, unzipped myself, worked my pants off like she did, and as I slid myself inside her, my wet fingers in her sweet mouth, I whispered in her ear, more to myself than to her, "This can't end."

———

We lay there like mating salamanders, my belly in the pit of her spine, my crotch glued to her buttocks. Her breasts, belly and the side of her face were pressed against the flaking bark and my hands were outstretched above her shoulders, clutching twin wing-like branches for support. No talking. No talking.

The next thing I knew, Kim violently started and shouted "Oh!" as if she was stabbed. Seams of sweat meandered between our ribs, and she was shivering and trembling like an addict. "Oh! Get off me! Get off!" She tried to toss me and I had to grasp the branches harder, clinch the trunk with my ankles and press down on her back to keep her from throwing me to the ground.

"Whoa! Whoa! Hold it! Hold it!"

"Please! Please! Get off me!"

"Okay! Okay! Easy! Easy! You had a bad dream! Easy!"

"Let's get down, please, let's get down." She was singsongy hysterical, her face pressed flat into the bark, her one visible eye wild with terror. She wrapped her arms and legs around the trunk as if it was a reeling, tottering mast.

"It's okay. It's okay. We just fell asleep. You had a bad dream. You had a bad dream."

Her sweat turned to goosebumps.

"There's no danger . . . let's sit up now." Calmly and soothingly I helped her up and, naked, we slowly made it down the trunk, her face ripped with agitation.

She wouldn't look at me, and as soon as her feet were on solid ground she flung herself at her clothes, gasping in cold and fear. A dead leaf was stuck to her powder-white breast, but she didn't bother to brush it off. She stuffed her underwear in her pockets.

We dressed in terrible silence.

Suddenly she exploded. "I dreamt I *fell!*"

She still wasn't looking at me, and she was crying. I put my arms around her. Violently trembling, she didn't respond to my touch.

"I dreamt I fell!" she repeated in a loud shell-shocked wail.

We walked back to the house, Kim hugging herself, my arm wrapped around her shoulders.

The house was empty. We could hear Anthony shouting and making some kind of rules outside under the kitchen window. Kim walked around the central room unfocused and angry, her bra straps dangling out of her rear pocket like stethoscope tubes. When, in a bid to break the strain, I asked to see the check again, she realized she'd dropped it somewhere in the woods, and she just collapsed in a sobby heap in a corner of the couch.

She wouldn't go back to get it with me, and I found it myself directly under the tree.

———

Kim slumped into a corner of the couch holding the edge of her crumpled check.

Jack came in the door, sighing with pleasure, and immediately picked up on the tension. His eyes went from me to Kim and he had no idea what to do with himself. I felt a combination of gratefulness and embarrassment for his presence.

At one point when I bumped into him by the bathroom door I whispered "Help me!" and he held up his hands and made a whiney pleading noise in the back of his throat.

That night we drove into town to see a movie and Kim sat between Anthony and Jack.

Back at the house, feeling completely dulled out by misery, I fell asleep instantly. She woke me up hours later with her sobbing.

"What's happening, Kim?"

"I don't know!" She sounded choked. "I'm *scared* . . . I don't have any more i*dea*s! . . ." She twisted "ideas" into a high, tortured whine.

"Ideas for what? . . ."

"For stories . . . for stuff . . . I don't have any more stories . . . I can't . . . I don't know what I'm doing. I feel so *lone*ly!"

"I'm here." I hugged her, but it was like we were still in the woods. Her hands were crossed over her chest.

"I can't *do* it!"

"Do what?"

"And I don't love you anymore." She addressed me for the first time since we were on the tree, and as slugged as I felt by her words I also felt grateful that she was finally talking to me, personally, instead of to the walls.

"What do you mean?" I was all politeness and attentiveness. Reasonable.

"I don't *feel* it anymore." The urgency of her words made tact irrelevant. She was crazed with truth.

"I don't *feel* it anymore," she insisted.

"It's the middle of the night." I had no idea what that was supposed to mean. It had been the middle of the night for a week.

Suddenly Anthony started whimpering from the living room, a sleep-laden cranky noise. He called for her, and she flung her half of the cover back over on me to go to him.

I felt dismissed.

———

When I got up the next morning Kim was already packing. I didn't know if she had ever returned to our bed or just slept with Anthony on the convertible.

During the ride back to town, the mood was so tense that at one point, when Anthony let loose with a snappy fart, I almost drove into oncoming traffic.

Kim and I slept together that first night back, but didn't touch. The following morning, she would talk to me a little, but it was all impersonal with no eye contact. She was trying to make it easy for me. I didn't even have to give a speech, just split.

But it boomeranged. I started feeling more achy and grabby. I wouldn't take the out even though I knew what she was doing. I was outraged by her decisiveness. I wanted a fight, so I hung around, not talking either. We slept together in her house the next night but once again not touching. By the following morning I was furious and, despite the illogic of everything, decided to get back at her by not being able to see her the next night, my reasoning being that withdrawal is the best way to get people to love you. I wanted the crazy panic of the sex on the tree. I was still headed for New York come the end of the term, but I wouldn't go without bloodshed.

I kept away Sunday night also, outraged that she hadn't called me to apologize or explain or inquire or complain. By Monday morning's class I was so blackfaced blood-choked angry, and I ripped through three stories so viciously fast and to the point, that we finished twenty minutes early, the class climaxing with my politely suggesting to some fat kid that he might grow as a writer if he were to explore the theme of self-revulsion.

I wanted so badly to have that fight, to split up, make up, stay and leave that I couldn't bear my own silent treatment, and Tuesday afternoon, heart pounding, I let myself into her apartment feeling a total *joy*, an enthusiasm, an involvement in the upcoming fireworks.

I sat in the bloated living room chair and waited. At three o'clock I heard a key in the door and my blood pressure instantly doubled. It was Anthony. He didn't react to my presence, just went about his business as if I weren't there. I didn't know if he was doing this along with Kim or on his own. Every day with him involved some kind of icebreaking for the first half-hour. He almost always acted as if I was a new date of Kim's, then somewhere along the line he would relent and start acting familiar and goofy with me.

He made himself a sandwich and sat down in front of the TV, his back to me. I remembered this configuration when I took care of him for the first time; throwing the crumpled-up bag at his head. It seemed unthinkable to do that now, even to speak first would be like smashing crystal. The power was all his. He turned on cartoons. Endless smoky explosions, dropped boulders on animal heads, dynamite in the mouth, endless recovery, endless anger.

Talk to me, you little fuck. Tell me what's happening.

He turned to a movie. *Captains Courageous.* Early on in the film, Freddie Bartholomew, playing a totally spoiled stinker, fell off a luxury liner after pigging out on ice cream sodas. Anthony growled "Good!" but Freddie got plucked out the ocean by a Portuguese fisherman in his dory—Spencer Tracy a.k.a. Manuel, sounding like Chico Marx. As the luxury liner rolled off into fog, Spencer Tracy dubbed the brat "Leetul Feesh" and took him back to his own mother boat, a commercial three-master out of Gloucester.

The kid was forced to get down and be a member of the crew. No more pampering, no more rank. He started learning about life, love and humility through the benevolent gruffness of primitive but wise Manuel.

Toward the end, Manuel was crushed by a fallen mast. He sat in water up to his waist, lashed to the wood, his legs and lower spine demolished.

He put up a brave front for the kid, but the sailors knew, even though it just looked as if he was sitting out a dance, it was all over for Manuel. Little Fish didn't understand why they weren't helping him out of the water. He cried out Manuel's name in a sobby uncomprehending wail. But Manuel just warned him to be good, told him that he was going to join his father at the bottom of the sea. Half crushed, he was comforting the goddamn kid. I started gulping down sobs. Freddie was baffled, angry, crying. Anthony, hunched over, started punching his crossed knees. "Why can't they *save* him!" His voice was filled with tears. Manuel waved goodbye to Little Fish. I started crying, a dusty pillow up against my face to drown out the noise. If Anthony had turned to me I would have died. I wanted him to turn to me so badly . . . I wanted him to be sitting in my lap asking me teary questions.

At the very end, when surviving family members of the Gloucester sailors lost at sea all throw garlands off the dock into the ocean as the names of these brave men are intoned by the mournful Cape Cod minister, a ghostly image of Manuel is superimposed over the solemn ceremony—Manuel laughing and loving, the sound track an exalted angelic chorus. Both Anthony and I broke into sobs.

Anthony got up, wheeled and bolted. I thought he was charging into my arms, and my guts jumped in panic. But he ran past me and slammed his bedroom door. I sat there numb with the realization that my hands were crossed in front of me to fend him off. I'm sure I would have comforted him in that moment, but the bottom line between me and him was that maybe I really *was* just a Saturday Morning Man, maybe I really wasn't ready to take him on the way I would have to.

This was no fucking game here. I wasn't ready. I left the house before Anthony could emerge from his room, before Kim could get home.

————

I got in my car and drove into Professionalsville to Jack's house. As I pulled into the gravel semicircle I remembered Jack wasn't living there, so I kept driving out the other end and made it to Katherine Mooney's house. It was getting dark as I parked across the street from the plum-and-mustard gingerbread Victorian monstrosity. Someone somewhere was burning leaves and the smell reminded me of that Huck Finn picture in the Greenwich Village hotel room. I realized that right that second I was standing inside a similar picture frame; the leaves, the woodsy turn-of-the-century houses, the plaid overshirt . . . and I also realized that I would have preferred it as a fond memory to a daily reality.

"Hey, Pete, come on in." Jack put the cigar back in his mouth and stepped to the side.

I shrugged a shy thanks and, unnecessarily ducking, took a few loping steps into the living room.

"I was just driving by, I'm not doing anything, are you? I mean, you're not interrupting me . . . you know." I whirled my hands in small circles.

"No, no, come on, kid . . ." Jack led the way. I immediately started sneezing. It was a chokeball museum of nineteenth-century antique-store charm. The walls were covered with brothel-red flocked velvet wallpaper; there were glass-fronted cabinets filled with beer steins, coronation commemorative plates, stuffed fowl. All furniture legs ended in huge oak paws. There were two Tiffany swag lamps hanging over round wooden tables, and behind every easy chair and couch were brass stand-up apothecary lamps with oblong green or amber glass shades. The consistency of everything made me want to gag.

"Take a seat." He offered me a maroon velvet one-armed divan.

Jack sat in a huge brocade-covered easy chair. Facing me on the far wall was a yard-square composite photo of a small upstate fire department, circa 1880; and dozens of oval-framed individual sepia portraits of handlebarred flatheads, their faces unsmilingly serene.

Behind me came a sonorous BONG. Turning around I stared at an enormous Roman-numeraled oak-trimmed railway-station wall clock. Jack watched me check out the house with a look of neutral amusement.

"What's up, kid?"

"Ah, my butter churn broke. I was wondering if I could borrow yours."

He paused, cocked his head, and let out a dry "Hanh."

I flashed on the time I sat down with him in the pre-fab barren-ness of that trail-of-tears garden apartment behind the Plunkett Mall. Have Gun, Will Travel.

"This is all her stuff?"

He answered by closing his eyes.

"Is she here?" I whispered.

"She's still in Indiana with her family. She'll be back tomorrow."

"That's great. I think we broke up." I smiled, hunching forward. I felt embarrassed that I smiled. It was a smile of shame.

Jack winced. "Aw shit, Pete."

"Hey, life's not fair." I raised a hand as though I wouldn't hear of it. When the going gets tough . . .

"You want a drink?"

Why not? I was becoming a total sot anyhow.

"I'll have a Scotch, straight up."

I followed him into the kitchen. More oak. There was an army of milky mint-green translucent glass spice jars, the contents printed in gothic German, more sepia oval portraits of dead-eyed strangers, Gibson-girl calendars. Jack pulled the Scotch out of a top-loading zinc-lined oak ice box; but the oven was a six-burner electric job with a copper ventilation hood and the huge refrigerator was a state-of-the-art affair with a tomato-colored enamel front and a freezer wide and deep enough to keep a family in meat for a year.

Jack made me a Scotch and soda with a lot of ice.

"Is there anything I can do for you, kid?" Jack leaned against the ice box, craned his neck and scratched his jugular.

"I love the color of this refrigerator." I put the flat of my hand on the cool surface.

Jack headed back out into the parlor. I took my seat on the divan again.

"I don't even know. I mean, I'm going to New York in January right? I just want company right now." I raised my drink at him, then scratched my neck like he did. "You know? I don't know how I feel. Bad, I guess. Right? I just want company."

"Yeah, sure." He tilted his head understandingly.

"Hey, listen, I'm sorry about all the tension with me and her that day."

He waved me off.

"Am I taking you away from something?"

"Nah, nah, I'm just waiting for my kids to come over. You know my kids, right? Erland, Donald? My middle guys."

I didn't like the idea of his kids coming over. "Hey, I'll leave." I started to rise, hoping he'd insist that I stay.

"No, no, don't be silly. Stick around!"

"Do you want me to make you a drink?" I offered him.

"I can't drink now. I get wheezy here, so I've been living off Contacs . . . If I drink I fall out . . . I'm very sensitive to dust." He shrugged as if apologizing for his life.

I looked down at my drink. I hadn't even sipped it yet. I gulped down half the glass to catch up with myself, and wound up coughing like a horse.

Jack just sat back and scrutinized me. He probably thought I was a jerk, immature.

"Jack . . ." I breathed deep and kicked out the last dregs of the coughing fit. "You still got that *PDR?* Maybe we could look up some diseases."

He jerked his shoulders again in a silent laugh.

"So what do you read these days? Now that you're the chairman. I mean for pleasure?"

"Peter, you really going to New York?"

"Me? Oh yeah, oh yeah. It's a Boom Town. Boom. Boom." I nodded, my lips tight and my eyes averted just like Kim's. Next thing I knew I started crying, my mouth open, my hand over my eyes. My forehead felt as if it was on fire. Jack got up and sat next to me. He squeezed my neck. I sat there muttering "stupid" over and over.

Jack sighed and squeezed. Under the mantle of my hand I saw his cigar stub held like a cue stick between his fingers as he supported his weight with one elbow locked, arm braced against his kneecap.

"It's too much now, you know? For her too." My chin was vibrating in an effort to smooth up.

It must have sounded as though I was defending myself because Jack reared back, raised his cigar hand and shrugged; declarations of neutrality. But he didn't take his other hand off my neck, for which I was grateful.

When I got to my office the next morning there was a note from Fonseca pinned to my cork board. I felt nothing in terms of High-Noon-type panic. It was over . . . again.

He was sitting in front of a bare desk, hands on either side of his nose, bisecting his face in a praying bridge.

"How ya doin'?" he monotoned as I took a seat, sprawled and shrugged "okay." He seemed embarrassed and sheepish, his eyes averted, a clumsy smile split by his hands.

"What's happening?" he mumbled almost mournfully.

"Nothing much, how about you?" I stared at his bookcase. Maybe he just wanted to apologize, be friends again.

"I'm okay, did you get your suitcase?"

"Yup."

"I brought it back for you."

"Thanks."

"Where'd you go that night?" His voice filled with limp concern.

"I went out."

"Yeah? How was your holiday?"

"Fine, and you?" I started feeling impatient, wanting him to get to the punchline.

"It sucked . . . I went to Thanksgiving dinner at the S and L. You know, one of those all-you-can-eat deals. I'm not gonna hang out there anymore." He screwed up his face like something smelled bad.

"An-nd, ah, I'm working, I'm working." He tilted his head to the side and scratched the back of his neck with a thumb. "I got some ideas. One I like a lot, it's historical. I never did historical stuff before, but I think this might be worth it." He leaned back and threw a spade-shaped cowboy boot up on the desk. So he wanted to talk "stories." He wasn't such a bad guy. I felt a small pang of that old heart-tug sensation of wanting him to feel good. But only a small one—as usual, fueled by fear.

"So what's the idea?" I clasped my fingers across my chest and looked angry and uninterested.

He dropped his boot and leaned forward on his desk staring at his meat-hook hands.

"It's called 'Trachoma.' It's about this doctor who works on Ellis Island. See, when all those immigrants were coming in, they had to have an eye examination to see if they had trachoma. There was a doctor right there, and they'd line up and he'd give them a quick look, and if they had it they—zap—right back where they came from. So you can imagine how terrified these immigrants were of this doctor. So this is my idea . . . I want to do a story about this doctor . . . He's a WASP, he's big, tall, big mustache, big boots, immigration uniform, he lives in the Bronx, say, the year is 1900, so it's a Westchester-type existence. He's fairly well off, old-family American, but his wife is permanently psychosomatically bedridden. He has no kids, he's a drinker, his life is empty. He's like a big square intimidating empty shell. Already the American Dream is a big bust for him, and every day he has to look into thousands of eyes . . . eyes of foreigners filled with hope of a new life . . . terror . . . of him specifically, that moment, but also of what's on the other side of Ellis Island . . . that new life. But the terror is secondary to the hope. And it's torture for him with his deadness and despair to look into all those childlike alien eyes coming from pain into promise . . ." He tilted his head and rubbed the back of his neck again.

"And what . . . how's it end?" I asked more softly than I wanted to. I could feel it; this bastard was sucking me in again. It's fear, pussyface, it's fear.

"I don't know. He goes crazy, I guess . . . or maybe it just ends . . . you know . . . he just goes on. I'll see. It's called 'Trachoma.' " He nodded to himself.

"Sounds good." I wished I had a cyanide pie to put him out of his misery.

"Shhit . . ." He propped up his elbows on his desk and wedged both thumbnails under his front teeth, staring past me. "I think I'm getting back with my wife . . ." His thumbs in his mouth made his words come out in a slightly sputtering lisp, a cartoon speech defect, so I did not react. It did not sound like a serious sentence. "Yeah." He scratched his temple. "I believe I am . . ."

This time the words came clear. I felt a tuning fork go off inside my forehead. I sat there, a sickly frozen look on my face.

His eyes caught mine, and he gave a shy stupid smile. "Sorry." He shrugged.

"My wife." What an expression. It sounded too adult. Too sober, way way over my head, like the word "office" or "business."

"I ran into Kim yesterday over at the mall . . . she's doing good now . . . she's looking for an agent in New York. She's . . . I'm doing better now too. I'm writing again. I'm running . . . so I don't know . . . I thought I should tell you . . . this fucks you up, I guess, right?" He winced. "It wasn't even my idea."

"So what are you gonna do, call her up?" My voice came out as straight and noncommittal as teletype. Even though he seemed to be walking on eggshells, begging my indulgence, he was going to do what the fuck he pleased.

"I mean it"—he touched his chest with ten fingertips—"it wasn't even me who started. She invited me over for dinner for tomorrow night . . . I guess I'll go."

Even though I was seated I felt myself collapse in my chair. Kim. Kim did it.

Fonseca looked unhappy, as though he already knew what was going to happen.

"Look . . ." He leaked air in a squeamish sigh. "I can't—"

"Can't what?" I was glued to my chair, sweaty and buzzing with shock.

"I'm not—" he sputtered.

"Not what?" I snapped.

Anger flashed in his face, and I pulled back. Fuck this apologetic charade; he hated my guts and I was afraid of him.

"Listen to me . . ." He offered his open palms. "I'm no bachelor . . . I'm not making it. I think I need her . . . I don't even know *how* to fuck around . . . it rips me up."

We both sat silent. I looked at my hands. I looked at his. Get a gun.

"You know, my father's been married to my mother forty-five years . . . he cheated on her once. The day he cheated on her he got a heart attack. I was twenty years old. I visited him in the hospital . . . he told me what happened because he was afraid that the same thing would happen to me some day. He said there was a lady who came into the drugstore who he used to flirt with and he finally got up his nerve to ask her out. He rented a room in a hotel. He decided they should eat first, so they go into the hotel restaurant, and my father says he's sitting there with her and he can't talk . . . he was staring at the floor. The place had white tiles and bright lights . . . he says he's staring at the floor and it's too white, it's too white, it's too white, it's hurting his eyes, it's so white, it's too much . . . next thing he knows he's looking up at faces, he's in the hospital. He told me never to tell this to anybody. My mother never knew what he was doing in the hotel, and she was so crazed and worried about him, and he felt like such a shit, that he never told her, and I don't think he ever flirted again . . . I need her . . ." he apologized to me, to himself. "See, I keep thinking of my father and the restaurant."

"Oh yeah?" I struggled to my feet. "You should write about that . . . maybe you'd have a *real* fucking story for a change." I made a low gesture with my fingers as if I was flicking a cigarette butt at his desk and walked out.

In the Geology Office, Kim, sitting backwards, was straddling her swivel chair, arms draped over the top, talking to Mary Kay Cicero.

"Peter!" She sat up.

"Come out." I curled my finger toward myself as I stood in the doorway.

"What's the matter?" She stiffened with dismay.

"Just come out here, please . . ." I stared at my tapping shoe.

We stood in the corridor opposite a display case of minerals. There was a stench of chemicals in the air.

"I want to go to the movies tomorrow night . . . will you come with me?" My hands were on my hips and my head tilted crazily at her.

"Do you want me to?" She looked tentative and confused.

"Do I want you to?" I repeated weakly, collapsing in relief.

She gasped. "Oh, I can't!"

"Aw fuck!" I wrung my hands. "Yeah, I *know* you can't!"

"What . . ." Her voice was small and cornered. She looked like she was in trouble.

She was.

"I *just* talked to Big Bitch Tony!" I paused, my face inches from hers. "What the *fuck* is wrong with you? What's a matter, things going too good? You gotta call out the *riot* squad?"

"Too good." She hefted the words with a tight-mouthed shake of her jaw. "What do you mean, *too good* . . . what's *too good?*"

"You know what I mean, Kim, don't go all bullshit on me." I faltered.

"No, I don't know." Her eyes started reflecting the overheads and her voice started breaking. "No, I don't know . . . you tell me what's so goddamn too good."

"You're doin' this to make me crazy, Kim, you're doing this to make me crazy, and it's working. I feel very crazy." I pointed at my temple. "You're trying to get me hung *up* on you by flirting with him, and you're making me very crazy. This is not necessary. This is playing with fire. It's a real Country and Western move, Kim. It's a very Townie move, and I'm being made to feel very crazy."

"It's just dinner," she pouted.

Suddenly a phrase came back on me that Fonseca used in his office: "It wasn't even me who *started*," like a kid trying to lay the blame for a fight. I felt a sickly sexual pull on my gut and I had to hold back on smacking her myself.

"Just dinner? Just dinner?" My voice was getting higher than smoke.

Kim cringed.

"You stupid cunt! What happened last time, hah?"

A girl, books to her chest, pulled up short halfway down the corridor from us, decided to brave it, dropped her head until her chin touched her book edges and scurried past us.

"What happened last time?" I forced myself to lower my voice.

"It won't happen again," she said more like a question than a statement. She didn't believe it either. She searched my eyes looking for something, help, maybe, and I totally flipped.

I bellowed, "Shit!" and started a freaked-out rain dance in the corridor, cursing and stomping, feeling so scared and up against it that I just wanted to run my head through a glazed brick.

"Peter, don't . . ."

"Oh, fucking Kim, oh, fucking Kim." I started hitting my forehead. "Anthony! How about Anthony!"

"He's gonna be at Mary Kay's . . ." Her voice was shaking and she was dribbling tears.

"Townie, townie, townie, townie, *why!* Why are you getting Anthony out!"

I paced back and forth as if I was in a maternity ward, softly hitting the walls with the side of my fist.

"Peter?" she pleaded. Pleaded. For what? For help. For me to relax. For help. For help.

"Oh Kim, Kim . . ." I walked halfway down the corridor to the exit, wheeled into an entreating crouch, speaking in a simple cracked crazed instructional tone, punctuating my words with rhythmic sing-along gestures of my hands. "You're getting rid of Anthony because you're gonna get beat up. You're gonna get beat up, and *I'm* gonna be there, and *I'm* gonna get beat up."

"Peter, don't come!" She put her knuckles to her lips. "I thought we broke up."

"Yeah . . . I'll take in a fuckin' flick." I turned and charged down the hall.

———

"Okay, okay . . . it's coming down to it, it's coming down to it . . . it's showdown time, she's flirting with death, and I have to be there, break it up, and do the do . . ." I paced Jack's office, speaking in a whack-a-doo singsong.

"What are you talking about?" Jack had three students waiting outside with Fiona.

"Fonseca's going there for dinner, and I have to go there, and blow the show. There's nothing else to do . . ."

"Fonseca's going . . . aw *Christ*, Peter." He winced and dropped his cigar butt in the garbage. "They're going back?"

"No! No they are not . . . I'm stepping in. They are gonna have dinner, he'll beat her up, and I'll kill him."

He sighed heavily and looked out his window.

"That's what I have to do . . . there is nothing else for me to do . . . I *have* to go, right?"

"No you don't . . ." he muttered tiredly.

"Oh good!" I exploded, then blushed.

"I'll call Fonseca and talk to him."

"No! What're you, crazy? It's gonna sound like my father. It's gonna sound like I *told* on him. Maybe you should call Kim? . . . No! No! What am I saying! It's my fight. It's my fight."

"It's *not* your fight, Pete . . ." He wheeled to me. "It's nobody's fight. She can do whatever she wants, I guess."

"Yeah, but don't you *see?*" My voice climbed to the ceiling. "She's only doing it to hang me up. She knows I'm crazy around Fonseca and she's doing it so I won't leave. It's so fucking obvious . . . it's killer chess, man, it's so obvious."

"So what can you do? She doesn't want you to go. She loves you. Welcome to the real world. I'll talk to him if you want. I'll talk to *her* if that's better."

"Shit, no, no, no . . . you can't."

"Then you just have to bite the bullet."

"I'll bite his fucking throat."

"Pete . . . please . . . you can't do anything. There's nothing to do. Promise me you won't go over. You want me to butt in, I'll butt in, if you don't want me to butt in I won't, but don't you, either. She's not stupid. Promise me."

"No."

"Promise me, Peter."

"Okay, I promise."

———

Moon's was out of town about six miles on the road of a two-lane highway. It looked like a huge corrugated barrel cut vertically down the middle and laid on its side. The inside was a mirrored bar, a dance floor and some gold-flecked Formica tables. The walls were a deep nighttime blue on which someone had painted a desert scene from floor to ceiling; a coyote on a rise in the desert, baying up at small white stars and a large yellow slice of moon, all against that deep blue backdrop which gave the painting an endless depth. I stood up at the bar looking at prospects. There were six or seven guys and one woman. Everybody was watching Bob Hope on the overhead TV. The bartender was grizzly-bear large, had a beard and smile lines around the corners of his eyes. I had thrown back five beers, but felt only bloated. Everybody looked disappointingly average in appearance and temperament, except the smallest guy there, who was the guy with the woman. His skin was a leathery apricot color, his head lizard-small, eyes a startled light brown and stupid. His wet sandy hair was swept high in an Elvis pompadour. His blond and frizzy-haired girlfriend was skinny and was wearing a sleeveless black jersey over no-account breasts. She was a chain smoker. The guy was the only one to meet my challenging gaze. As soon as he read me, he picked up on it, and I lost my nerve and pretended to watch TV. Bob Hope was doing a skit with Joe Namath. Namath flubbed a line and turned it into an outrageous double entendre and the bar cracked up, all except the outraged jockey and me.

He continued to stare at me, the square edges of his teeth glinting behind his lasso-slack mouth and I realized I'd totally bought it, like it or not.

After another five minutes he nudged his girl, tilting his head to her without taking his shellshocked eyes from my face. "What's that, a boy or a girl?"

Not only was that the tiredest line to use, but the moron must have been totally dead dick drunk because my hair was at least three inches shorter than his. I didn't even have sideburns. He repeated himself. "Is that a boy or a girl, do you think?"

His fists were the size of muffins.

I took a deep breath. "How would you like to suck my dick and find out?"

We got off our stools at the same time. He was only about five-five. He had a round steel tape measure clipped to his belt and wore imitation Clark desert boots.

The fight lasted all of ten seconds. I squared off nice and gracefully. Next thing I knew my head was ringing and my ear felt as if it was on fire. When my vision cleared, which is to say when my eyes went from my thoughts back to the physical world before me, I was still standing in my boxing pose and the bearded bartender was calmly leaning across the bar and holding the short guy in place by grabbing the entire front of his shirt in one hand. "That's enough, Arnold."

Nobody had even turned from Bob Hope, including Arnold's girlfriend.

———

I'd never realized how much I had come to hate my place; there was nothing that I could draw solace or strength from. I just as soon would have lived in a car. I had to drink a half a bottle of cough syrup to get to sleep that night.

———

On D-Day, I got to the gym at three. There weren't many guys. Most were into solitary workouts, straining and staring thoughtfully at their bodies in the mirrors. Everybody was bigger than me. I wished I could show up with my head on one of those bodies. No. One of those heads, in case of brain damage, broken nose, concussion.

The prone bench was under the barbell. I pulled it away and slid the decline bench in its place. I stacked my plates, slid down under the bar and slowly worked it without a spotter. Stand up for her. Stand up for yourself. What the hell was I doing? What the hell had I been flirting with? Sunglasses, bar-hopping, going to New York. We had both been courting it . . . two cunts in search of a beating. No wonder Fonseca looked so fucking miserable, hooked into that dance. Well, fuck him too. Fuck his pain. You don't hit people. You don't hurt people. I wished I'd been descended from hillbillies, or townies; I would have been a half-crazed dog right then. What the hell did I have? I thought of my father yelling at *me* in Atlantic City, just like I'd yelled at Kim when she told me her saga. How dare you put my weakness on the line? How dare you force me out of myself? I thought of my walking around in front of relatives. "Whadya want from *me?*" So what did I have? What ancestors could I call down from Valhalla? The only time I remember anybody putting his body on the line was when I was little. I was getting on a bus and some big bastard knocked me down getting off. My mother grabbed him by the shirt and started broadswiping his head with those flab-bunting arms, her pop-eyes wild, a high keening song in the back of her throat. The guy was so freaked he just froze, letting her swing away until the bus driver pulled her off. Not much. Not much to go on. I finished four sets, clamped the bar in place and struggled to a seated position.

I studied my face in the wall-length mirror. To my amazement I was smiling; not a winning smile to be sure, but the goony twisted smile a kid hides after he does something dumb-ass and an adult says "I'll bet you're *real* proud of yourself, aren't you?" And, in fact, the kid is, somewhat.

The whole thing was making me shit pickles, but somewhere, somewhere, I was up for it. It would really sweep out the attic. Besides, even though I felt set up, it showed Kim still cared. I think. Cared enough to kill me.

I stood in front of the mirror and examined myself. I looked real nice. Slim still, but outside of identifiable scars I lived in a new body. I touched myself, feeling the various fresh ridges, new surface veins.

Over my head was a photo of gimp ass Roy Z. happily ripping a phone book. What a yutz. Physique didn't mean shit in a fight. Moon's. I did look nice though. Too bad upstairs it was still shit-for-brains. I thought about Red psyching up for a set, stomping and pacing, his face flushed, his chest heaving, finally attacking the bar with everything but his teeth. Not my style. I felt cool. Reasonable. It was very simple. I had to step in and break away from myself. I had to help her break away from herself. Blah blah.

I did a short two-take pose-down; curled biceps, then expanded chest. I held the chest pose. I held it until blue veins sprouted on my blood-thickened neck. I held it until my eyes turned shimmery. I looked like a wired beast, but I wished to Christ that somewhere along the line Kim had joined a women's group.

———

I went over to the diner for my traditional post-workout bulk-up, but I was too tense to eat, so I had a coffee instead, which I needed like a hole in the head.

I kept High Nooning the clock over the grill. It was five-thirty. What time would dinner be, six, seven, eight? Seven-thirty.

———

"How ya doin'?" My eyes were focused on a milky smear on the clear plastic partition of the diner pay phone.

"Oh hiya, buddy." There was heavy long-distance static on the line that sounded like popping corn or an armed skirmish in the background. My father's "oh hiya, buddy" was supposed to come off casual, but it was so light and gentle it sounded as though he was about to faint away.

"What's been doin'?" I mumbled. The smear on the clear plastic was a paint stroke, dried semen, spit. People walked past me to use the bathrooms. I kept my head down.

"Oh, nothin' much," he sighed. "Same ol' thing. Vy's *niece* is gettin' married . . ." He came down heavy, on the word "niece" like there was something exhausting about the woman. "So what's doin' with you?"

"Uh," I winced. "Nothin' . . . listen, I had a bet with a friend . . . you could help me out . . ." I had no idea what I was saying.

"Sh-sure," he said, nice and easy.

"The bet was . . . uh . . . in Europe? During the war? . . . This guy, he's black, he said that they didn't allow any blacks in combat units . . . is that true?"

"You know something . . ." he chuckled. "I swear, what was I there, three years? I don't even know. We had a black guy in the maintenance division . . . give me a second, I'll tell you his name . . ."

"I miss you," I said with a faint offhand cockiness, throwing my head to the side and raising an eyebrow. I licked my thumb and tried to clean off the smear, but it was inside the plastic.

"Robinson . . . Ernie Robinson."

"Did you hear what I just said?"

A long long pause. "So when are we gonna see you, buddy?"

"Ayye," I sighed. I flashed on Fonseca and experienced a swift updraft in my belly. I had to get off the phone. "Soon. And no more bullshit, okay? We gotta sit down and talk." I was breathless with anxiety, each word came out in a gulp of air. I was totally convinced I would be killed in the next few hours. "I'm *serious*, Dad, time is like a clock." I slowly blew air out my mouth to calm myself down. "I'm sorry I called you a stupid man, back then."

There was another long heavy silence on his end. "We'll talk," the words rich and sober. A real promise.

"Okay, Dad, I got to go . . . give my love to Vy." I hung up, but held onto the receiver. Despite myself I was smiling that stupid smile. Time is like a clock. Give me a fucking break.

———

I sat in my car across from Kim's place. It was seven-thirty. Fonseca's Mustang pulled in down the street. I rested my pulsing head against the steering wheel.

Fonseca got out, slammed his door and just leaned against the fender, staring at the boarding house across the street for a few minutes before heading over. Amazingly, he was wearing a tweed sports jacket and a turtle-neck, and was carrying a Whitman sampler, the embossed gold candy box shimmering like a mirror in the desert. He looked grimly unhappy.

I was wearing a bomber jacket over a gray T-shirt, tight dungarees and basketball sneakers—the clothes I felt most springy and comfortable in.

I couldn't get out of the car. There were sweat seams along my thighs and the backs of my knees. Get *out* of the car. No. What if I beat him up so badly that I violated my parole? Jokes helped. I got out and leaned against the passenger's door, as Fonseca had done, my arms folded over my chest, my legs casually crossed like a model in an ad for cars. I was so scared I was sighing. I couldn't turn my head to look directly at the building.

I stood in the dark and oily lobby. The television and the baby squalls sounded as though they were coming through amps. The smell of frying cabbage was making my throat catch. I heard a woman shout, and I knotted up. It wasn't Kim's voice. I collapsed onto the snake head on the ground floor banister.

I stepped back and did a final pose-down, biceps, pecs, lats, delts, abdomen. The main door opened behind me and I jumped. It was the jogging graduate student. He looked at me without interest, his perspiration-drenched gray sweat suit adding B.O. to the aroma of the fried vegetables. He walked past me and started up the stairs, and I motioned for myself to follow in his updraft. We climbed past two flights of window hangings. He dropped off on the third floor, swiftly closing his computer-strip-plastered door behind him.

I looked up the spine of the fourth snake to Kim's door. I couldn't go up the stairs. I fantasized standing in front of that door and plummeting backwards down the vortex of the four climbing snakes and crashing like a dot, flat on my broken back, in the foyer.

The computer door opened. The graduate student frowned at me. "Are you looking for someone?" I saw the iron claw of a hammer peeking out behind his back.

"No, I was just resting." My nervous breath made me sound winded anyhow. While he stood there watching me I bent down, took a chattering gulp of air and continued to climb. I stood in front of the wild-eyed screaming *Guernica* horse. I reached for the hidden key. I heard Fonseca's loud voice. "Kim? I swear on my child's eyes!" Each distinct and separate word punctuated by the slow firm slap of a palm on wood. "On . . . my . . . child's . . . *eyes*, Kimberly."

I put the key back in its place. The graduate student was standing on the third landing, peering upwards, waiting for me to do something to convince him that I was legitimate. He made no effort to conceal the hammer now. This one's for you, Mom. I rapped on the glass of the door.

The apartment got quiet. I heard the graduate student breathing through his nose, Kim's padded footsteps. She opened the door, and her round eyes looked starry with shock. She was barefoot, and seeing her naked toes I experienced a horrible yank of sexual vulnerability. Submission. My chest ballooned with that horny terror.

Behind her, Tony was standing hunched forward over the dining table, resting on his palms like an embattled lawyer driving home a point. In between his big hands was an orange plastic plate covered with fish sticks and green beans.

"Hi, Tony!" I actually smiled and waved. I heard the computer-strip door close on the third floor.

Kim was blocking my entrance, and I was standing on tiptoe and smiling down my nose at him as if she were six inches taller than me.

He did not look startled or angry to see me. He also did not look happy. "Come in." He arched an eyebrow and bobbed his head in a tight-lipped mock courtly gesture.

As I brushed past Kim, who was still facing the hallway, I murmured to her through my closed mouth, "Put on shoes."

"Have some dinner." He spoke in an ironic singsong as he gestured toward an empty patch of tablecloth.

Even though everything he was saying and doing was dripping with sarcastic menace, my first reaction was, What a nice guy. And then I revved up, thinking it wasn't his house or food. He didn't even have the right to invite me in, charade or not.

"Kim?" The singsong again. "Get him some dinner."

As quiet as a scent Kim wafted into the kitchen, nothing moving from the hips up. The gold box of candy stood on its side, unopened, on a cabinet behind Kim's seat.

———

The three of us sat over plates. My four fish sticks formed a "W." Nobody was talking.

Kim sat there glassy-eyed, chewing mechanically. She had totally checked out. I was in an introspective coma myself, and Tony moodily ate, holding each fish stick like a chicken leg, peering down at it after each bite.

In the center of the table was a typed manuscript, the pages slightly spread like a hand of cards.

Tony tilted his chin at the work. "She's sold two stories, and she's running around looking for agents." He shook his head slowly and sadly. "Where you runnin'? Where you runnin'?" He shrugged at me.

Go.

"Well, listen, why don't you just slap the shit out of her?"

He sat up straight. "What?"

Kim bowed her head, her fingers crabbed in her hair.

I leaned toward him, my shirt buttons in my food, and pointed a finger at her. "We know . . ." I paused for emphasis, ". . . that she is officially . . . registered . . . as a battered wife with the hospital and county." I sounded like a senate investigating committee.

"What?" His face twisted high on the left side.

"You heard me." I resumed erect posture, my face eagle serious, but I could only keep it up as long as I could hold my breath, as long as I could keep my head free of images and thoughts, and I suddenly deflated with a long wracking sigh.

"Oh Tony, I'm so fucking scared of you right now I'll kill you." I curled my hands around my plate. But he was totally ignoring me. He was staring at Kim, who was staring at her food. Her fingers twitched in her hair.

Tony's face got dark. Still staring at Kim's bowed head, he snorted in humorless amazement and slowly rose, disgustedly flipping over his plate with a quick flick of his middle finger. A fish stick hit the wall and some of his peas came to rest against the back of my curved hand. Shaking his head, he waved us away and stalked out the door, knocking into the corner of my chair so brusquely that suddenly I was facing the living room. By the time I put up my fists all that was left of him was descending footsteps.

After a while I slowly turned my head from the living room to Kim, who was still looking down at her plate.

"You don't understand," she mumbled wearily. It was hard to hear her because her chin was pressed into her chest.

"Don't understand what?" I asked in a delicate tone of voice.

Her whole body jerked with silent sobs. I was paralyzed with indecision about embracing her.

I got up and left the apartment, walked two blocks to a liquor store, bought the most expensive Scotch they had and headed back to Kim's place. As I put my hand on the front doorknob, someone called out my name from the shadows. My heart twisting, I stepped down the sidewalk, squinting and holding the Scotch by its neck. Jack emerged into the street light. He also had a sports jacket on. It was an out-of-season crinkly pinstriped seersucker, white and yellow. He removed his cigar butt from his face, looked down at his shoes, which were new, and brushed a fleck of tobacco from the crease of his slacks. I had never seen him so dressed up.

"I don't think you should go up there, kid." He smoothed back his long lanolin-slick hair. "Or let me go with you . . ."

"It's over, Jack." I was grinning.

"*What's* over?" he squinted at me as if unconvinced.

"Fonseca came, then me, we had an argument, and he left. That's what's over."

"Yeah?" Jack sounded distant and distracted. He dropped his cigar butt on the ground and took a long time grinding it down to scattered flakes. "How's Kim?" he said faintly, looking off over my shoulder.

"She's freaked . . . she'll be okay. You wanna come up?" I tried to sound flip and casual as if we were having a few people over for drinks.

He put his hands in his pants pockets and shrugged. "Ah . . .
nah . . . you go up . . . I should go home."

He walked off without saying goodbye.

———

Kim and I sat at the table with downcast heads as if we were trying
to levitate the dirty dishes.

Kim hadn't said one word since "You don't understand."

Despite the wretchedness of the tableau, I wasn't feeling all that
bad; it took a lot of balls on my part to do what I had done. I was
proud of myself.

"Kim," I tried to laugh. "I can't tell you how fuckin' scared I
was coming over here tonight."

"My hero . . ." she muttered, and got up and stalked out of the
room. A second later, the bedroom door slammed shut with a pneumatic whomp.

"That's *right* . . ." I said to her empty chair. "Your goddamn
hero." I left the apartment and headed home.

———

As I drove down to the end of Kim's street, I passed a parked station wagon with someone sitting in the driver's seat. It had to be
Jack. I slammed on the brakes and put the car in reverse.

When I was parallel to the wagon I leaned over to my passenger's window, stuck my head out and barked "Jack!"

It wasn't Jack. It was some teen-ager sprawled back, eyes closed,
mouth open as if in a deep sleep.

I scared him so bad he almost put his head through the roof.

"Shit, I'm really sorry," I murmured. Sorry it wasn't Jack.

He didn't even look at me, just went into a wild-eyed frenzy trying simultaneously to start his car and roll up his window.

"Hey listen . . ." I tried to calm him down.

"What happened?" The voice was female and from somewhere
below window level, like the kid's crotch.

I drove off before she raised her head and we had to gawk at
each other.

———

At four A.M. my phone shrieked. I shot up straight, said "Yes!" and then picked up the receiver.

"Who the *fuck* do you think you are! You stay the fuck away from *her*, you stay the fuck away from *me!*" A list.

I would be lying if I said I wasn't expecting the call or something like it. I was about to say, or at least I was thinking, "That's okay, Tony, I'm going to New York anyhow," when from Fonseca's end I heard Kim shouting in the background for him to leave me alone.

I was dressed as fast as a fireman. How fast could I get over there? It had to be faster than thought, because unformed in the back of my head was the notion that I was rushing to embrace a beating, to pay a toll fee for New York. Which was probably why I didn't call Jack. On my way out the door I grabbed a steak knife from the kitchen, looked at it, freaked, put it back and grabbed a small pair of pliers instead. Maybe I'd pull his teeth.

I ran downstairs, ran red lights and ran up the spiral staircase.

I ran right in; the door was unlocked as I expected. All I saw was Kim, teary, flushed but unmarked. On seeing me she slapped her forehead and wailed, "Oh no!" in a cranky sob.

"Kim? Put your shoes on." They were on.

I didn't see Fonseca. I saw on the kitchen table a bottle of house brand vodka and a half-filled quart bottle of Tropicana apple/cran-berry juice, the lewd little pot-bellied Hawaiian girl on the decal winking suggestively at me under her Carmen Miranda hat.

I turned slightly in the opposite direction and yelped. Fonseca was slunk down on the couch, not moving, his eyes blazing sullenly at me.

I felt humiliated at yelping like that. I took the pliers out of my back pocket and pointed at him. "Tony, get out of here. I'm serious." He squinted in confusion at the pliers. The handles were insulated with cracked bright blue rubber. "Get *out* Tony!"

He got up slowly, absently groaning as if he was stiff. I thought, "Hey, that was easy." Next thing I knew I was flying backwards into the dinette set, landing on my ass and feeling a sharp bruisy pain in the middle of my back from the edge of the table.

All he had done was shove me. My shirt front was still molded into his grip. Kim was shouting his name angrily and tugging inef-fectually at his arm.

I said "Ouch." And as he towered over me I added, "Don't make me mad, Fonseca."

"Out," he said, lightly kicking one of my splayed out legs, not hurting me, just brushing me like a pile of leaves.

"No." I spoke to his foot, "*You* get out."

"Out," he repeated, bending down and hoisting me up by the armpits. Everybody grabbed me by the fucking armpits.

"No," I insisted, backing up nonetheless.

Kim wailed and paced behind him.

"Out." He placed a palm on my chest and calmly backed me to the door. It was a gauzy nightmare of humiliation and powerlessness.

"What you call me *up* for!" I barked like it was a debate, like I could win on points. Asshole. Asshole.

"Out." He continued to gently shove, not even looking at me.

"Where's my pliers!" I complained. I knew if I left via his hand, ass to the door, I'd never let myself go to New York, I'd hover around the town for years mumbling "oh *yeah?*" to myself.

"Out."

Suddenly his hand on my chest became a major violation of human rights, an outrage against liberty, and the next thing I knew my knuckles were throbbing, my shoulder felt totally pulled and the crossover momentum had my chin turned until it was directly over my right shoulder.

I had popped Fonseca on the jaw and the punch turned him around 180 degrees so that now his back was to me. He stood there, head down, hands on hips, as if he was lost in sad thought. He wasn't even probing his jaw.

"Oh shit, oh, Tony, oh, you made me do that." I hopped and bounced in place as if I had to pee. I was in a total dream. Behind him Kim's face was frozen in such a wide hissy grimace of disbelief that I could see her lower gums. Fonseca was as high as a volleyball net between us.

"You know, I can't remember the last time I threw a punch before, Tony!" I said in a sprightly conversational tone to his back.

"If I turn around and see you I'll kill you," he said dully.

"Okay . . . okay . . . wait a second, wait a second." Still in that dream-head, I moved almost tippy-toe to the dinette table, grabbed the glass bottle of apple/cranberry juice by the mouth and swung it at his head.

I missed and it smashed against his left collarbone. He roared and sank to his knees, reaching up to his neck in pain. The bottle didn't break, but the plastic top popped off and his back and shoulders were splashed with a mantle of purple, as were my pants from the knees down.

"Oh shit, I'm sorry, I'm sorry." I danced in place, my hands trembling up against my chest in cringing disgust. He was still faced away from me.

"It's broken," he declared flatly. On his knees like that he looked as if he was awaiting a Japanese beheading.

"No, the top just came off. . . . Eeesh." I winced. "I'm sorry, man." I gingerly reached over him, grabbed Kim by the hand and literally yanked her into the air to the door side of Fonseca. Dragging her as she gawked at his back, and then up at the shrinking door, we clambered and clattered down the stairs.

———

"Where does Mary Kay live?" I was driving in endless square-dance patterns through the deserted streets of Lesser Linoleumsville.

"I'm not staying at Mary Kay's," she said in a weary sulky singsong. It was the first exchange between us.

"Yeah, I know you're not. We're picking up Anthony and going to New York. Now. I can't believe I did that."

"I'm not going."

"Yeah, you are."

Kim called Mary Kay from a pay phone that was centered in a cone of street-lamp light on the otherwise coal-black street. I sat in the car, which I left in drive, my foot on the brake, my hands on the wheel, elbows locked, like a snapshot of a motorist a second before a head-on.

She came down the stairs with Anthony in his pajamas and shoes, his face puffed, his steps small and stumbly with sleep.

He immediately fell out again on the back seat.

"This is stupid," Kim muttered as we shot out onto the desolate

Quickway like a comet plummeting through starless space. There were no other cars, nothing, a total humming silence, inside and out.

After fifteen speeding minutes, a single light approached us from the horizon. I couldn't tell if it was a motorcycle or a one-eyed car. And if it was a one-eyed car, I couldn't tell which side the headlight was on. As we got closer, both of us doing at least seventy, I had this fantasy of plowing into the invisible side of his grill, which I was convinced was closest to me. I physically experienced the crash over and over, flinching and hissing until we finally passed each other a good twenty feet apart.

Sweating and chilly, I pulled into an overlook rest stop, my arms vibrating.

"I thought we were gonna crash," I said lightly.

"Turn us around."

"What are you, crazy?" I said without conviction.

"I'm not going to New York, I'm not." She raised her eyebrows and shook her head in a "that's that" gesture.

"Well, I'm not goin' back. He'll kill us. I'm sorry I missed his head." I lied. "We go back, he'll kill us."

"No he won't." She sounded bored.

Anthony frumphed through his nose and turned over on his stomach.

We sat in the car at that rest stop for ten minutes, listening to Anthony sleeping, the ticking of the dashboard clock, my fingernail tapping against the cold plastic of the steering wheel.

"Hey Kim? I hope you're not gonna go back with him now." There was something in the tone of my voice, a calm truce tone, that signified to both of us that it was over with us.

Her face got puffy and bitter for a second. She looked ancient and ass-kicked and I felt a horrible pang of Major Mistake, but before I could act on it, her face cleared and she looked at me straight on and strong.

"I'll play it by ear."

I made a slow U, my headlights sweeping the void-like darkness and I started driving back to town at about half the speed that I made leaving.

"So it backfired," I said mildly.

"What did?" She leaned over the seatback and brushed Anthony's hair out of his sleeping face.

"You go out with him to pull me back in. This happens and now I *have* to leave." There was something artificial, forcibly jocular in my voice. I wasn't sure if what I said was arrogant horseshit or truth.

"You don't have to leave," she said in that weary singsong. How about the first part.

I snorted with gurgly nervousness. "I guess I would like to think so, though."

"I know," she said.

She absently scratched her kneecap, pulling her skirt slightly up toward her crotch. Watching her exposed thigh out of the corner of my eye I was filled with a ferocious melting sensation. I flashed on being driven to her house that first night after Chee Lok. I remembered everything she wore. I remembered the sensation of her caressing my thumb in the car, the smell of necking with her in the deserted root-beer stand. I got another assault of Major Mistake followed by a stronger terror that I would never leave this town and what was worse, it would be just as well that I didn't because I was going to New York with a thumb up my ass, like a human popsicle. I was throwing "all this" away, just to get eaten alive.

"Hey Kim?" My voice was light, tentative and fluttery.

She must have read my mind, because as she turned to me she slipped her arm between her legs, raising her skirt even higher, and I sighed with sad desire.

"Kim. I'm gone. Now. Tonight. I'm not going back into town. I'm not going to my place or anywhere. You want to go back, we'll go to the airport. Drop me off. You take the car back. Keep it, sell it, drive it into New York sometime if you change your mind, but I'm gone. Tonight."

She didn't say anything until I came to the airport exit.

"You're gonna miss Christmas."

I flashed on the Santas in the mall. Exterior Street strung with silver stars and green plastic fir. For some reason I thought of televisions with bad reception in small living rooms. It made me feel achy. She was right.

"They have Christmas in New York," I said irrelevantly. "It's not exactly California, you know."

A car sped by from behind us, firing into the oncoming lane, then sweeping easily back ahead of us. The entire sound-and-light show of his existence crescendoing, climaxing and diminishing in seconds.

"You ever take physics?" I asked with false playfulness.

She grunted and frowned at her knuckles.

"Kim? Would you please come with me?"

For a long moment I thought she would say yes.

———

The airport terminal was the size of a middling department store. It was on a hilltop shouldered on two sides by grilled parking lots, which at five-fifteen in the morning were populated by a few lonely Hertz and Avis cars in their assigned slots.

I shot into the curve of the Arrivals driveway and was filled with the giddy novelty of being in such a strange empty place at such a strange empty time.

Kim recited a dull catechism of "I promises": to staying at Mary Kay's that night, what was left of it; to calling Jack and letting him know what happened, and to visiting me in the city. She also promised me that Fonseca was no problem. I had totally forgotten about him in the last half-hour. Of all the promises, strangely enough that one was the one I believed the most.

I leaned over the seat-back and kissed Anthony's cheek. He was still asleep. As far as I could remember it was the first time I had ever kissed a child. I got out and Kim slid over to the driver's side. Frowning with concentration, she adjusted the seat so it slid closer to the steering wheel. I felt comforted that she was taking the car. It meant to me that it wasn't totally over. I hunched down and leaned my elbows on her window.

I had no idea how to say goodbye, how to kiss; cheeks, lips, tongues, lingering, a peck, nothing at all.

"It's not over," I said softly.

"Oh yeah? That's great." She had both hands on the wheel and was looking straight ahead.

I cupped her cheek with my palm and tried to kiss her, but she wouldn't turn her head. What did I expect? Maybe we could have a last hump over the hood while we were at it.

I straightened up and Kim took off.

Even though there were no other cars around the airport she used the turn signal for every pissy left turn, but not for the rights.

When she finally got out to the main road, I watched the car smoothly shrink into a speeding dot of light until it veered out of my line of vision. Maybe the right signal blinker was out. I'd call her when I got to the city and warn her.

I felt the windless cold weigh down on me in bales. My legs in particular were freezing and leaden because my pants were still soaked from the apple/cranberry juice. I couldn't believe I did that. Why didn't he turn around? He *let* me do that.

Shivering, I turned to the pneumatic doors. They were locked. The fucking airport was closed.

With my hands in my pockets I lumbered in place like an old Indian dancing for tourists. After a half-hour I finally saw headlights creeping up the hill and onto the grounds.

It was the terminal cook. I sauntered over to the parking lot and greeted him with an apologetic shrug. "Early bird gets the worm!"

He let me in through the service entrance of the cafeteria and made me a cup of coffee. I was babbling and cheerful. I sipped the coffee, leaning against a deep stainless steel sink in the glazed tile gloominess and watched him prep for breakfast. The kitchen reeked of Comet or Bab-O and it started making me sick.

He said I could sit out at the counter if I wanted, so I pushed through the swinging doors and took a stool at the Formica horseshoe. Through the glass observation wall I watched the sun inch up over the mountains like a distant orchestra tune-up. Colors began to dribble and spill over the countryside and I found myself chortling and muttering "Wow, neat."

At six-thirty the overhead lights in the terminal clicked on, but when I ventured into the hallway the place was still deserted except for some janitor type with a floor buffing machine.

In the waiting area I slouched into one of the hard plastic lounge chairs and watched the place grudgingly come to life; waitresses, candy-stand operators, bland-ass ticket agents. I was totally buzzed out and disoriented; amazed at everyone and everything I saw. I had been the first one there and I thought there was something athletic about that. When any of the terminal personnel stared at me, obviously not used to seeing customers there an hour and a half before the first flight of the day, I would wink and call out, "Early bird catches the *worm!*" By seven, civilians, mainly businessmen, started showing up and in the next half-hour the terminal became packed. The sunlight hurt my sleepless eyes, and the novelty of my situation began to wear off as the place began to resemble your basic terminal.

I dreamt that I was in the cargo hold of the airplane in between a caged otter and a plaid suitcase. I was amazed that it wasn't cold, although the drone of the engines was splitting my eardrums and making me drool.

I slowly raised my head and wiped some dried saliva from the side of my chin. I had fallen asleep in my chair in the airport directly across from a bank of ticket counters. A three-year-old kid was standing in front of me staring and rocking. As soon as I trained my lizard eyes on him he began to wail. I bared my teeth and growled and he took off. Fuck. I knew the first plane out was 8 A.M. The PA crackled and some cowgirl announced that the 12:30 Eastern flight to Buffalo was now boarding, wheelchairs and infants first.

The wall clock read 12:20 and I jumped up, my head pulsing with a hangover-like throb, which put me right back in my seat. Think fast. Afternoon flights. Don't panic. Brush your teeth. I got up, more slowly this time, toddled off to the newspaper-concession stand, and bought a tin of aspirin, some toothpaste and a collapsible toothbrush.

In the wall-length mirror over the bathroom sinks I saw purple-face Mossi emerge from a stall. Still feeling crusty with sleep I froze over the sink, my mouth filled with sweet toothpaste foam. He was the teacher and I was playing hookey. Holy shit, my class.

"Jack . . ." Whoever used the phone before me had been wearing too much perfume and my eyes began to tear.

"Oh hi, Pete." He sounded cool and distant. "Are you in New York?"

"New York . . . how'd you know? No, I'm still at the airport. Did Kim tell you?"

"Yeah," he said as if faintly bored. He was mad at me. Goddammit.

"Jack, I missed my class."

"Yeah, I covered for you."

"*You* did?" Eeek.

"Yeah, I took it over." Too, too flat.

"Listen, um, I'm not into making it back up there, Jack. I mean my class. I'm sorry. I know I'm fucking you over. It's mid-term, but I can't. I'm fucking you over, I know."

"We'll manage."

"I feel terrible." I did.

"Well, look, Pete, you have to do what you have to do . . . I guess."

"You're making me feel guilty."

"Nah, don't feel guilty."

"Say it like you mean it."

"You know Fonseca's in the hospital . . ."

"How come?" Appendicitis.

"He's got a broken collarbone."

"*Col*larbone!" The apple/cranberry juice.

"He'll live."

"Where's Kim?"

"At work, I guess."

"His *col*larbone? Because of me?"

Jack sighed.

"Why don't you get some graduate student to take over my class? Don't *you* do it . . ." I winced.

"We'll see."

"Yeah, well look, whoever takes over, tell them to watch out for that kid with the crew cut, Ramsey. All his stories are first person from the point of view of appliances . . . you know . . . Uh-oh, here comes Johnny. I hope he doesn't forget to turn me off before he pulls my plug. I almost started a fire last time!" I made my voice come out like Smokey the Bear. "The kid sounds like a safety film. He once did a story from the point of view of a clam knife. I almost ruined my socks. You gotta drain your bladder before you take over in there. Always drain your bladder. You're mad at me, right?"

"Nope," he said in a shruggy lilt. "I'm not *mad* at you Pete. I'm kind of disappointed, if you want to know the truth. New York'll be there in January . . . I mean you're kind of walking out on us."

Us. Him. Kim. My class. Shit. I started to crumple. Shit. "You're a real velvet hammer, you know?"

"I'm just telling you, Pete . . ."

"You know it was supposed to be *your* class anyhow, Jack. Fiona told me that."

"I guess so." Unmoved. Big fat bastard. God, goddammit.

"Okay, I'm coming back. I'm coming back."

"It's your life, Pete."

Bullshit. Suddenly filled with a wild mindless hope that Jack might say something to let me go after all, I kept my mouth shut; waiting, hoping to force his hand.

———

"Pete?"

I blinked. I had no idea how much time had passed since I decided to psych him out; couldn't have been more than a few seconds but I'd fallen asleep with the phone to my ear.

"I'm here," I said dully. "So at least tell me you're glad I'm coming back."

"You're my buddy, Pete, you know that. . . . I'm telling you kid, New York'll be there in January."

———

Wobbling into the afternoon sunlight, I left the terminal building and headed for the line of cabs. Why I told the driver to take me to Misericordia Hospital instead of my apartment, I can only guess. The best explanation I have been able to come up with was that I was so pissed off at Jack for making me "do the right thing" that I decided to "do the right thing" with a vengeance.

———

The astringent reek of medicinal alcohol has always filled me with an infantile dread. To smell that pungency in a hospital patrolled by nuns and housing Fonseca was plain paralyzing.

I headed down the corridor that led to his room. Sisters of Mercy, looking like Black Cross volunteers, glided past plaster Virgin Marys stationed in wall niches every twenty yards. Overhead the PA bonged like a department store elevator and droned out an endless roll call of doctors.

Every room I passed seemed to have the ceiling-bolted television set turned to game shows. The contrast between the gloomy immobility of the patients and the manic gurgling of the various masters of ceremonies was enough to make me want to flee the country—if they'd only let me.

Occasionally I'd pass a room in which the patients, young and old, were gingerly hobbling around in their pajamas or gowns and I'd feel overwhelmed with a cringing disgust for whatever was making them walk like that.

What the hell was I supposed to say? Sorry, I'll never do it again, cross my heart and hope to spend the rest of my life in Buchanon?

Fonseca's window-side bed was concealed behind a green curtain. He was sharing a room with a dying man; gaunt and old, already the color of paraffin. Lying there hot-eyed and motionless, blanket cutting across the knot of his Adam's apple, the man looked as though he was already on an autopsy slab.

His toothless stubby face was chin-up toward the ceiling, his thin-lipped mouth frozen in a curved gape like a black apple slice. The only signs of life were in his sightless pain-smitten shining eyes. He moaned non-stop, a mindless mooing that was so constant in pitch and repetition that I blocked it out almost immediately.

I walked across the room to see the prize behind the curtain. Fonseca had no choice but to sit perfectly upright. He was in a cast from his shoulder to his wrist, his upper arm parallel to his shoulder, elbow bent at a right angle, fingers high over his head. The entire agonizing sculpture was chained to a hoist. The chains made it seem like a punishment from hell. I could not believe that there was no substitute, synthetic or otherwise, for chains. I could not believe that the medical world, let alone the Sisters of Mercy, were so insensitive to the devastating image.

Fonseca ignored me and gazed out his window which over-looked the doctors' parking lot. The half-raised Venetian blinds threw shadowy bars across his chin and chest. His face was set in that same chillingly placid expression I saw on the night of the Nicky Lisi catastrophe.

I didn't want to say I was sorry.

I didn't want to say that I didn't know what to say.

"You know what's the most galling thing about teaching up here for me?" He continued to look out at the parking lot, but he narrowed his eyes into a reflective squint. I'd never heard his voice so calm and free of affectation.

"No, Tony, what's the most galling thing? . . ." It sounded as if I was humoring him. I was bushed.

"Every fucking day, year after year, I have to go in and stand in front of an entire roomful of people who have no *idea* that some day each and every one of them is going to die."

"Huh."

He tightened his mouth and shook his head sadly as if he was witnessing some act of wastefulness or human folly out in the lot below. "If you do not understand that, then you are incapable of understanding anything. I mean *really* understanding anything . . . and I'm in there as the teacher . . . so what can I teach them?"

"Huh." The point, the point, Fonseca.

He slowly turned his head and grinned at me. "You don't think you're going to die, do you Pete?"

"No," I mumbled, transfixed by the slow blind flex of his reddened fingers over the chalky lip of his cast. I thought of them as baby birds waiting to be fed. There was an icy mouth sucking air from my lungs. Kiss of death.

"Kim knows." He winked at me. "That's why I married her. She was very advanced for her age."

I wasn't falling for that shit anymore. "I'd rather have half a brain than a flat ass," I drawled.

Fonseca didn't push it. "But, see, it's like damned if you do, damned if you don't, because once you *do* know, once you really and truly understand that you're going to die . . . there are times . . . sometimes . . . you just can't *wait*, man, you just . . . you get . . . just *think*ing about it makes you hard . . ." His voice had dropped to a hot hiss.

". . . Makes *you* hard." I couldn't take my eyes from the nest of writhing baby birds at the end of his cast. Feed the birds. No.

"It makes you hard." He smiled in pregnant triumph, tilting his head to catch my eye. "That's what I said."

"Tony, this is a fucking gift, right?" My voice came out flat and distant. I was going under.

"You're a very brave boy, Peter," he crooned. "You came back to town to face the music, you put history on hold and everything. You even came up to confront big bad Tony . . . don't you think you're brave?" He returned his gaze to the parking lot. "Another milestone in the emerging manhood of Peter Keller."

"You don't know my name . . ." I murmured.

"Yeah?"

"Yeah."

"Nah, you did the right thing, you came back. Good, good for you. Fuck it. New York'll always be there, plenty of time . . . all the time in the world . . . you can go home now, honey . . . mission accomplished."

I couldn't move. I had to throw it back in his face. I was never going to die.

Sputtering with desperation I suddenly dropped down into an ape-like crouch at the foot of his bed and started singing in a moronically crude bass, "When I was *sev*-en-teen, it was a *verry* good yeeerr . . . it was a *verry* good yeeerr . . ." It was all the words I knew.

The corpse on the other side of the curtain started howling like a dog.

Fonseca snorted in amusement and closed his eyes. I strode out of the room.

———

"I thought you went to New York." Kim came up behind me as I sat lost in thought on a couch in the center of the ground-floor lobby of the hospital. The room was on fire with sunlight.

"I'm going to stay until the end of the term. New York'll be there in January."

She grunted in disappointment. There was a stack of weathered paperbacks under her arm. They had to be for Fonseca. I felt nothing either way about that.

"What are you doing here?" I tried to sound stern.

"Visiting." She shrugged and looked at her feet.

"So are you two an item again?"

"I'm just visiting," she muttered.

"So is that it for me and you?" I said mechanically.

She gave a ragged-out dry laugh. "You tell me."

"I think the right rear blinker's out on my car. You should get it fixed soon, it's dangerous . . . and I don't want that sonovabitch driving my car. I'm serious." I didn't even know what the fuck I was talking about.

"You don't want your car back?" Her voice climbed with small squeaky sobs and one big fat murderous tear dripped down her cheek. "How are you gonna get *around* for two months!" Her voice was high, like the voice of a cartoon mouse. She sounded heartbroken. "It's two whole months!"

A nun swished between us, all rimless glasses and black robes, laying down, I swear to God, a track of Patchouli. It felt like a reprieve.

"Did you smell that?" I smiled with astonishment at Kim.

"Smell what?" Her eyes were prisms of tears and I grabbed her in a trembly bone-cracking hug.

"Jesus, Peter, that's two months without a car!" She breathed into my ear, her chin drilling into my unbroken collarbone.

"Okay, so I'll stay with you and borrow it. You got two cars."

When we broke the clinch, I held her at arm's length and in the euphoria of the moment I said, "Aw shit, Kim, I can stay up here and teach to June" but as the words left my mouth I felt that icy sucked-out sensation in my lungs again. January was truly it. The End. Kim knows.

"Great." She smirked. "And then what?"

"You should go." I pointed to the ceiling. Fonseca's room was on the second floor. "Go make your sick call. I'll meet you back at the house."

"And then what . . . what happens in June?" She drilled me.

"January, I meant."

"January." I'd just cut six months off my offer but she didn't even blink. "What happens in January?"

"Everybody goes to law school."

"Bull*shit*." She almost laughed.

"You bet." At least we agreed on that. "Go see him. I'll meet you home."

———

Outside the hospital I disregarded the taxi drivers lounging on the hoods of their cars. It was only a three-mile walk to Kim's apartment. Keep in shape.

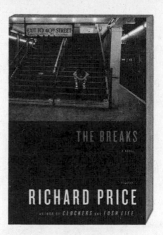

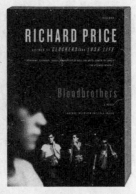